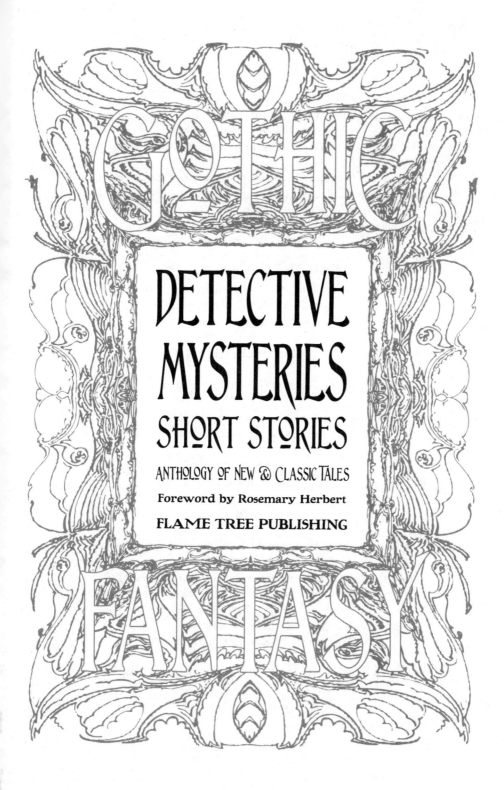

GOTHIC

DETECTIVE MYSTERIES

SHORT STORIES

ANTHOLOGY OF NEW & CLASSIC TALES

Foreword by Rosemary Herbert

FLAME TREE PUBLISHING

FANTASY

This is a FLAME TREE Book

Publisher & Creative Director: Nick Wells
Project Editor: Gillian Whitaker
Editorial Board: Josie Karani, Taylor Bentley, Catherine Taylor

Publisher's Note: Due to the historical nature of the classic text,
we're aware that there may be some language used which has the
potential to cause offence to the modern reader. However, wishing
overall to preserve the integrity of the text, rather than imposing
contemporary sensibilities, we have left it unaltered.

FLAME TREE PUBLISHING
6 Melbray Mews, Fulham,
London SW6 3NS, United Kingdom
www.flametreepublishing.com

First published 2019

ISBN: 978-1-78755-694-2

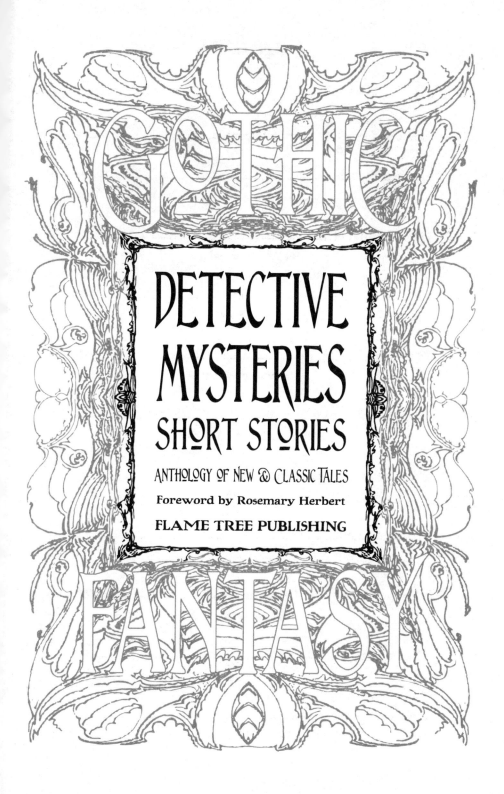

GOTHIC

DETECTIVE
MYSTERIES
SHORT STORIES

ANTHOLOGY OF NEW & CLASSIC TALES

Foreword by Rosemary Herbert

FLAME TREE PUBLISHING

FANTASY

Contents

Foreword: Detective Mysteries Short Stories

IF EVER there was proof positive of the enduring appeal of the mystery short story, we have it here, in a volume that brings together work from the early days of the genre through a lively sampling of contemporary writing. For the reader, this book provides an experience that includes imaginatively entering a wide variety of fictional crime scenes, some as privileged as the classic stately home and others as plain as an isolated Iowa farmhouse. In many, atmosphere is everything, as in the cases that occur on the fog-enshrouded London docks, on a high crag in the Yorkshire moors, in the steamy interior of a Turkish bath, or inside a darkened train compartment. These scenes of the crimes and many more may be enlivened by amusing dialogue, disappearing acts, high jinks galore, and of course some bumps in the night. And finally, the solution of the crimes that occur in such places are ultimately explained by male and female sleuths who are as memorable as they are clever, including omniscient and often eccentric amateurs as well as members of official police forces.

The joy of this collection lies first of all in the reading pleasure afforded by the sheer variety of settings, puzzles, and ingenuity displayed. But it is instructive, too, to recognize how the stories gathered here exemplify elements of the literary history of a genre that has now flourished for nearly one hundred and eighty years. Precursors of the genre include police memoirs and accounts of sensational crimes, but scholars agree that this popular literature's origin dates from the 1840s, when Edgar Allan Poe's three stories – 'The Murders in the Rue Morgue', 'The Mystery of Marie Roget', and 'The Purloined Letter' – established a remarkable number of conventions of the genre, including the ingenious and eccentric sleuth, the armchair detective, the 'impossible crime' (also known as the locked-room mystery), and the sidekick narrator.

In this volume, we see how Poe's successors employed their own considerable cleverness to build on these conventions. A particularly memorable example is found in the 1925 story 'The Tea Leaf' by Edgar Jepson and Robert Eustace. Here, after one of two 'bad-tempered men' who have been heard arguing in a Turkish bath in London is found dead in that steamy chamber, it looks like the other must be responsible. With an unfindable weapon, it takes extraordinary ingenuity to discover how the death occurred. Another 'impossible crime' – this time in a sound-proofed locked room – is presented and solved in Hugh C. Weir's 1914 piece, 'The Man with Nine Lives', a story that is also notable for its reliance on an early female sleuth, Miss Madelyn Mack. These stories fall within a period known as the Golden Age of the detective short story, dating from the creation of Sherlock Holmes in 1887 through the end of World War II.

Other early female sleuths who appear in these pages include Anna Katharine Green's Violet Strange and Catherine Louisa Pirkis' Loveday Brooke. Two Iowa farm women also scrutinize their neighbor's kitchen to chilling effect in Susan Glaspell's 'A Jury of Her Peers' (1917), a story that also exemplifies three more developments of the genre: the use of the average person as sleuth, aspects of a distinctly drawn regional scene literally becoming essential to the crime and its solution, and the tale of detection as a statement of social commentary.

But let us not forget Great Detectives – those paragons of ratiocination who delight to this day. Look within this volume for Sir Arthur Conan Doyle's Sherlock Holmes and Jacques Futrelle's The Thinking Machine. More sleuth types found here include Margery Allingham's aristocratic sleuth, Albert Campion; G.K. Chesterton's clerical detective, Father Brown; Baroness Orczy's knot-tying armchair detective, the Old Man in the Corner; and R. Austin Freeman's medical-legal wiz Dr. John Thorndyke.

Finally, listen as you read to the many voices that sound here. They speak in tones that range from gentlemanly banter to hardboiled wisecracks, with regional accents especially enriching contemporary work. Prepare, too, to be startled by shrieks of horror and perplexed by some significant silence in the night-time.

In short, bring to this volume great expectations of a reading experience that will stir you on many levels. You won't be disappointed.

Rosemary Herbert

Publisher's Note

What better way to exercise the 'little grey cells' than with a set of mysteries putting some of the best minds of detective fiction to the test? In this anthology, we have aimed to include representative examples from a fascinating genre that has spanned the last two centuries. Trailblazing figures from the field crack cases that are as thrillingly varied as they are puzzling, with notable early stories like William E. Burton's 'The Secret Cell', and characters including Sherlock Holmes; Dr. John Thorndyke and his 'collecting-box' of forensic evidence; Miss Madelyn Mack; Paul Campenhaye ('the famous specialist in criminology'); the clerical sleuth Father Brown; Hamilton Cleek ('the man of forty faces'); The Thinking Machine; Mr. J.G. Reeder (the police officer with 'the mind of a criminal'); Albert Campion; the first supernatural detective Flaxman Low; and the archetypal PI Race Williams.

Alongside these and more, we have selected a range of stories by modern authors, some published here for the first time. It's always an incredibly difficult process to choose the new fiction, but immensely rewarding to include tales that complement the classic works and show how the genre has developed for a new age. Demonstrations of logic, deduction and keen intuition still shine out, but adapted for different times, different settings and different attitudes. Here, we have locked-room murders, codebreaking, and gripping hunts for missing children, as well as stories which extend the boundaries of the form further – whether that be tracking down the mythical divine horse Pegasos, investigating a murder set on the moon, or following the adventures of a feline protagonist in a pastiche of the hardboiled PI tradition. UK/US spellings have been retained as appropriate for each story, in attempt to preserve authenticity of author voice in classic and modern stories alike. In all, we hope that celebration of this enduring genre can be found through these stories as they weave a trail of intrigue that's hard to resist.

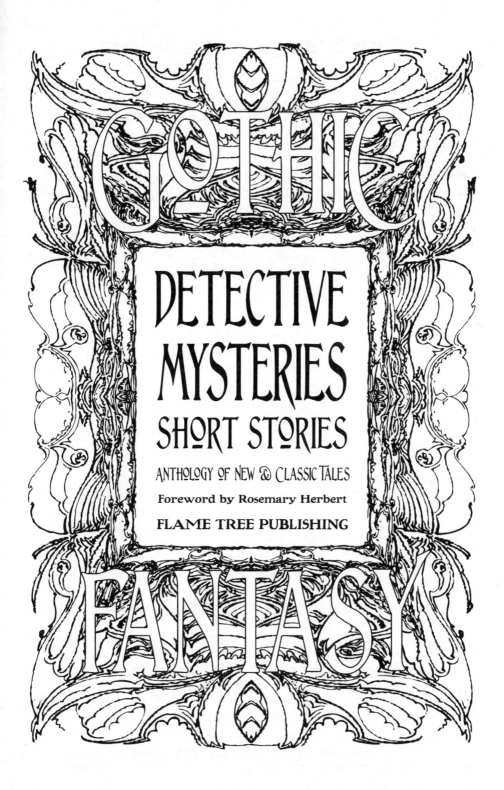

GOTHIC

DETECTIVE
MYSTERIES
SHORT STORIES

ANTHOLOGY OF NEW & CLASSIC TALES

Foreword by Rosemary Herbert

FLAME TREE PUBLISHING

FANTASY

The Meaning of the Act

Margery Allingham

"TRIVIAL, VULGAR, pettifogging, puerile, footling. At times even dirty," said Lance Feering, taking up his glass. "I don't want to be hypercritical, old boy, but that's how I see this life of yours. It repels me. My stomach turns at it. I gag... You see what I mean?"

"The light is filtering through," agreed Mr. Albert Campion affably, as he flattened himself against the ornate tiles behind him. "Criminology does not appeal to you tonight."

They were in the famous bar of the Pantheon Hall of Varieties, more affectionately known as the Old Sobriety, in Rupert Street. It was almost the last of the great music halls and, as usual, the small circular room with its wide window giving on to the auditorium was crowded. Lance was in form. He was demanding a considerable favour from his old friend and, since such was his temperament, the experience was making him truculent.

"Of course you batten on it, I know," he continued vigorously. "It's a mania with you. It's got into your blood like a bacillus. That's why I asked you to come along tonight to this ungodly hole." He paused. "I thought you'd like it," he added, glancing anxiously under his thick brows at the tall thin figure beside him.

"Quite," murmured Mr. Campion, bending forward to look through the window across the dark stalls to the boxes beyond. "He's still sitting up there."

"So I should hope. There's still a turn to go before the lady comes on, isn't there?" Lance set down his glass hastily and took a look himself. "Good Lord, we don't want to lose him. Shall we go back?"

"No, I don't think so." His companion surveyed the small bent figure in the second tier box. "He's all right. He seems to be enjoying himself."

"That's what I mean. That's why the whole thing is so repellent," Lance sounded querulous. "Why shouldn't he have a night or two on the tiles if he wants to? I shouldn't have dreamed of stalking the poor old badger if Marguerite hadn't been so insistent and so frightened. You haven't met Marguerite, have you?"

"His daughter?"

"Yes." Lance was unusually laconic. He signed. "A beautiful woman frightened out of her wits can be very demoralising. She's got bone, Campion, exquisite bone."

"I thought you designed stage sets?" remarked Mr. Campion unsympathetically. "Still, we won't go into that. Why is this poor bony female afraid?"

"Well, he's a distinguished bird, you know. He's a recluse, a famous man, an Egyptologist of world renown, he's lived like a bishop all his life, and now he's started sneaking out of the house like an adolescent and trotting off to music halls alone, all up and down the country, performance after performance. She thinks he's either up to something or nuts. And I said 'bone', not 'bony'. It's a question of design."

"Dr. Clement Tiffin," murmured Campion. "He's everything you say, and yet why should that name make me think of crossword puzzles?"

"It shouldn't." Lance was irritated. "It should make you think of pyramids, incredibly decent and decaying clubs, and the pavilion at Lord's. Anyway, don't go deducing *who* he is; we know that. I've got you along here to help me find out what he's up to. I mean, does the poor girl call in an alienist, or resign herself to the fact that the poor old boy at the age of seventy-seven has fallen for a beautiful Egyptian hip-waggler?"

Mr. Campion eyed him over the rim of his glasses.

"Is that your only problem?" he said. "Because believe me, if you've had the impudence to get me out here simply for that…"

"Well, not quite," Lance admitted hastily. "Marguerite certainly isn't a fool, and she's got something pretty serious on her mind. I couldn't get much out of her, but she seems to think that the old man is in some sort of danger."

"Spiritual or bang-on-the-head?"

"Oh, physical. No dream stuff. I told you Marguerite's got brains."

"Brains and bone," said Campion. "Dear me, and a very fine seat on a horse, too, I shouldn't be surprised."

"I rather resent that, old boy." Lance was not smiling, and Campion, who knew him so well that his mercurial temperament was not the mystery it might well have been, suddenly perceived the situation. Lance was indulging in a phase of 'utter decency' and, since he invariably took colour from the people who happened to be interesting him at the moment, it followed as the night the day, that the Tiffins were of a very definite class and type.

"Marguerite is not the sort of girl who'd come roaring round after Papa herself?" he suggested.

"Good heavens, no!" said Lance, scandalised.

"Ah," murmured Campion.

Lance was silent for a moment or so and finally decided to unbend.

"If you only knew old Tiffin, you'd see how remarkable it all is," he said. "He's so very much the – er – the top drawer, if you'll forgive the phrase. He's got a great brain, too. The idea of him sneaking out to see this blessed woman dance time after time in the most revolting little halls all over the place is incredible. He's not that sort of chap."

He looked round the pleasant dirty little bar as if he had never seen it before, and Campion watched him with his eyes dancing behind his spectacles.

"'Ullo, Bert."

The salutation rang out across the room, and, as soon as he heard the familiar cracked Cockney, Campion became aware of an impending social crisis.

"Cassy," he said.

"Wot O! Cor, this is a bit of all right. 'Ow are yer, chum?"

The crowd heaved and billowed, and a figure emerged from it. He landed squarely before them, his small rodent's face alight with bonhomie and gin. He was a little man, narrow-chested and narrow-faced, with slit eyes and a long slender nose with a twitch to it. Sartorially he was quite remarkable, for he wore a vivid blue suit. His mind seemed to be running on clothes also, for he flicked Campion's shirt front with a grubby thumbnail.

"Washington's come 'ome, I see," he said. "Come and 'ave one. 'Oo's yer pal?"

Campion performed the introduction with misgiving.

"Lance, this is Mr. Cassy Wild, a very old friend of mine," he said. "Cassy, this is Mr. Lancelot Feering, a celebrity."

If the final description was intended as a warning, Cassy was in no mood to take it.

"Sir Lancelot. 'Strewth, that's a moniker to go to bed with," he said cheerfully. "Named after an 'orse, mate? No offence meant and none took, I 'ope. What is 'e, Bert? A dick?"

Lance was eyeing him coldly. "I'm afraid I don't follow you," he said with the half apologetic smile which contains the deadliest insult.

"And that is lucky," cut in Campion, with haste and emphasis, as he trod delicately on one of Mr. Wild's long narrow shoes.

"Oh, I see." The newcomer cocked an intelligent eye at his friend and a long and meaning look was exchanged between them.

"How's business?" inquired Campion.

A row of abominable teeth appeared for an instant across the pallid waste of Mr. Wild's ignoble face.

"Not so bad," he said. "I caught a shice and did a carpet in the spring. Had to come to town without a coal. But a denar here and a denar there soon mounts up, you know, and I'm in clover. By the way, this is my monkery, so who's your party?"

"Myself, my friend, and our punter is an elderly and distinguished finger in Box B," replied Campion without hesitation.

"Okay, Bert." Mr. Wild shook hands effusively. "See you some other time. So long. It's a nice show. The palone in the Didikye turn is a knockout. Wot 'o."

Lance conducted Campion back to their seats in silence.

"That was rather an extraordinary thing to do, wasn't it?" he muttered as they sat down. "Surely there was no need to mention Dr. Tiffin to your repulsive friend, was there?"

"Didn't you take to Cassy?" Campion seemed surprised.

"He's a dear chap. As a matter of fact, that was most considerate of him. This is his district, as he told us, and he did not want to embarrass any friend of mine with his professional attentions. Very thoughtful. Cassy has gentlemanly instincts, if they are not sartorially expressed."

"Professional...?" Lance twisted round in his seat. "D'you mean to say that fellow was a thief?"

"A whizz-boy," said Campion modestly, "i.e., pickpocket. The most skilful practitioner in the country. Don't raise your voice, old man. Listen to the pretty accordion player."

"Yes, but I say, Campion..." Lance was positively blushing. "You do know some most amazing people. Good Lord!"

"Marguerite wouldn't like him?" suggested Campion, and Lance did not deign to reply. He sat glowering, ill at ease and apprehensive, while every now and again he glanced up at the dark box above them where the bent figure of a little old man sat alone, watching the glittering stage with idle introspective eyes.

Campion lit a match to look at his programme.

"Charmian, Exotic Dancer of the Desert," he read softly. "She's due any minute now. Cassy said she was a knock-out, although he thought she was a gypsy. Still, he's no connoisseur. I wonder... Why *does* that name Tiffin remind me of crosswords?"

"It doesn't. Don't keep saying that. You're getting on my nerves." Lance stirred uneasily in his chair. "Thank heaven this chap's finishing. Here we are; number eight at last."

The dusty red curtain had descended with a sweep of tarnished tassel and fringe, and the accordion player was taking his call. The old man in the box drew back a little and raised his white head expectantly. The orchestra played a fanfare and the curtain rose again, disclosing a semi-darkened stage.

Gradually the light grew stronger, and Campion, who had expected the usual pseudo-Eastern eurythmics, sat up. The dancer was standing in the centre of the stage, her arms at her sides. She was dressed in a long white tunic and an Egyptian headdress and collar. She was not particularly beautiful, and the profile, outlined against the dark hangings behind her, was strong rather than lovely. He glanced up at the box.

Dr. Tiffin had moved forward and the light from the stage caught his face. There was something unexpected in his expression, a sternness, almost a dislike, and Campion, seeing it, suddenly remembered why his name had reminded him so strongly of crossword puzzles. His eyebrows rose and his lips pursed to a soundless whistle as he turned back to the stage.

The girl who was billed as 'Charmain' was no ordinary dancer. There was even something of the old-fashioned contortionist in her performance, yet she contrived to make her slow, unnatural movements peculiarly graceful, and, what was far more extraordinary, peculiarly Egyptian, or, more specifically, ancient Egyptian.

Campion sat with his eyes fixed upon her, and again and again the rows of painted figures on the mummy cases in the British Museum leapt to his mind. The dance continued to slow music, and Charmain held her audience. The strange thing about her was her lack of facial movement. Throughout her turn she might have been wearing a mask, yet her powers of expression were amazing. She danced with an urgency of meaning which was unmistakable, and it seemed to be this dumb striving towards communication which reached out over the footlights and forced attention.

The clientele of the Old Sobriety was an exacting audience, and it could scarcely be called highbrow, yet it sat up and watched, fascinated.

Lance appeared to be spellbound. He did not stir throughout the turn, but remained rigid, his dark eyes round and surprised.

"Good Lord," he said, when at length the curtain descended upon her. "Good Lord, how incredible! She's like a blessed papyrus. Hallo, what's the matter with you?"

Campion said nothing, but there was a startled expression on his face, and his eyes were raised to Box B. Lance followed his glance and an exclamation escaped him.

"Gone," he said disgustedly. "Slipped round the back, I suppose, while we were gaping at his girlfriend. Well, I don't altogether blame him for his enthusiasm. She's an experience to watch."

"Be quiet." Campion was on his feet. "Come on," he murmured, and there was so much anxiety in his voice that the painter rose and followed him without a word.

Lance did not catch up with him as he hurried through the auditorium, and only reached his side as he sprinted down the dusty corridor behind the circle.

"I say, you can't butt in on him," he protested in a flurry. "He's not that kind of old boy. We can't, Campion. Marguerite would never forgive me."

Campion flung off his restraining hand and opened the door of the box.

Dr. Tiffin lay on the floor beside the chair from which he had fallen. He had crumpled up and slipped forward, and there was a thin dark streak among his white hairs.

They got him out of the theatre and into a taxi. It was not altogether a simple matter, for the old man was still unconscious, but Lance was convinced that the absence of any scandal was of paramount importance, and Campion, for entirely different reasons, was disposed to agree.

"We'll get him home first and then find his own doctor," he said. "He's all right. I think. His heart is sound, and there's no fracture. He'll be all right in a day or so."

"I don't understand it." Lance was white with apprehension. "When Marguerite said 'danger' I thought she was exaggerating. This is fantastic. He's only a fan of the dancer's, as far as I know. No one can mind him looking at her, surely, however attentive he is?"

Campion glanced up from his patient, whom he was supporting in the back of the cab.

"That rather depends," he said slowly. "Look here, Lance, I fancy we're on a dangerous ground. I think you may just have to wipe this incident clean out of your mind. Forget it. Pretend it didn't happen."

"What do you mean?"

Campion did not reply. Dr. Tiffin had begun to stir, and his voice, thick and slurred, startled them both. At first the muttered words were indistinguishable, but as they leaned forward anxiously a single phrase came out clearly in the darkness.

"Thine uncle bears thee gifts," said the Egyptologist distinctly. He repeated it again, and the extraordinary words ceased to be ludicrous in that thin pedantic voice. *"Thine uncle bears thee gifts."*

"What?" Lance was shocked into the question. "What did you say, sir? What gifts?"

The old man did not answer. His head had fallen forward and he went off into incoherent mutterings once more.

"Did you hear that, Campion?" Lance's own voice rose to squeak. "It's turned his brain. What an extraordinary thing to say. 'Thine uncle...'"

"Hush," said Campion gently. "Hush, old boy. Forget it. Here we are. Help me get him into the house."

Miss Marguerite Tiffin turned out to be a pleasant surprise to Campion. Lance's reactions had led him to expect, if not the worst, something very near it, but he found, instead of the academic snob he had envisaged, a very sensible and charming young woman with a snub nose and a quick, shy smile. Moreover, for a girl who was not used to having her Papa brought home on a shutter, she was remarkably cool and quick on the uptake. It was only when the old man was safely in bed with his doctor in attendance that she betrayed any sign of strain.

"I'm tremendously grateful to you, Lance," she said, "but you do see now that I was right to interfere?"

"Good Lord, yes." Lance was holding her hand far too long, and Campion was inclined to sympathise with him.

"All the same I'm still in the dark. The whole thing bewilders me. It seems to me to be an entirely meaningless attack on an inoffensive old gentleman who wasn't doing anyone any harm."

Marguerite hesitated. She had round grey eyes, and at the moment they were intensely serious.

"Lance," she said slowly, "do you think you could go on thinking that, and then – then forget the whole thing utterly? Never mention it to daddy or to anyone else. I can rely on you to do that, can't I, Mr. Campion?"

"Yes," said Campion gravely. "Yes, I think you can."

Lance came away unwillingly after lengthy farewells.

"I do wish you wouldn't be so darned mysterious," he grumbled, as they walked out of Bedford Square together. "I'll do anything Marguerite asks me within reason, of course, but why the hush-hush? What's the matter with the old man? Has he got some well-known form of bats-in-the-belfry which I've not heard about? What was all that about his uncle? Damn it, are you or am I?"

Campion hailed a cab, but Lance drew back.

"Now where are we going?" he asked.

"Back to my flat."

"What for?"

"Drink," said Campion. "If you must know, drinks, ginger biscuits, and I should rather think a visitor."

By midnight Lance was beside himself with irritation.

"An impossible evening," he declared. "What infuriates me is your blessed calm. Hang it, I invited you to help me follow old Tiffin, and what happens? First you introduce me to a little sneak-thief who seems to regard you as some sort of favourite relative, then we find Tiffin biffed over the head and we take him home, where Marguerite behaves as though she was taking in the laundry and you back her up in treating the entire thing as nothing to write home about. Finally, we sit up here waiting for a caller. Whom do you expect?"

Campion pushed the decanter towards him.

"I haven't the faintest idea," he said truthfully.

"You're potty." The childish accusation seemed to relieve the artist and he refilled his glass. "You haven't invited anyone and you don't know who is coming, but you've just got a psychic feeling that a visitor is imminent. Well, if I've got to sit up all night I may as well make something out of it. I'll lay you a hundred to one in shillings…"

He broke off abruptly. Out in the hall the electric bell had begun to ring authoritatively. An instant later Campion's man admitted without ceremony Superintendent Stanislaus Oates and a companion, and closed the door after them.

The two men stood on the threshold looking tall and official in the brightly lit room, and Campion rose to greet his old friend. The superintendent was cool. He was not hostile, but there was a formality in his manner which was not customary. After his first greeting he introduced the stranger with warning deference.

"This is Captain Smith, Mr. Campion," he said severely. "He'd like a few words with you and Mr. Feering about your activities tonight, if you don't mind. No, thank you, we won't drink."

The little company sat down stiffly. Captain Smith was a restraining influence. He was a lean, brown man with a dry precision of manner which enhanced the natural austerity of his personality. The one obvious fact about him was that his name was not Smith and that his rank was understated. Lance, who fancied himself as a student of faces, was startled by the impersonal penetration of his blue eyes. He glanced at Campion and was relieved to see that, although grave, he did not seem surprised.

"I rather expected a visit from the police," Campion remarked to Oates. "You've seen Dr. Tiffin, I suppose?"

"Yes." Captain Smith answered quietly, before the superintendent could speak. "Will you explain exactly why you went to the Pantheon Music Hall tonight, and why you were so peculiarly fortunate as to have been on the spot to render assistance as soon as it was needed?"

"Mr. Feering can explain that better than I can," Campion was beginning, when a second ring at the bell outside jolted everybody. No one spoke, and the two visitors turned slowly in their chairs to watch the door.

The manservant was some time in coming, and when at last he did appear he spoke dubiously.

"Mr. Cassy Wild to see you, sir," he said.

Lance stiffened. As an addition to this already somewhat sticky party the ebullient Cassy did not appeal to him. The same notion appeared to have occurred to Campion, he was relieved to see.

"Oh, ask him to wait," he said hastily. "Put him in the study."

"Very good, sir." As the man withdrew, Captain Smith swung round on Campion.

"A friend?"

"Yes. A very old one."

"That's all right, sir." The superintendent spoke deferentially. His grey face was impassive, but there was the hint of a twitch at the corners of his mouth. "I know him."

"I see. Then we'll go on. You were on the point of giving me an explanation, Mr. Feering."

Lance told his story frankly. He was a friend of Marguerite's, and she had confided to him that she was alarmed by her father's new habit of going off by himself after a lifetime of regular and studious habits. She had discovered that he had made a habit of watching every performance given by the dancer, Charmian, and that in order to do this he followed her all round the country, sometimes to the most disreputable little halls. To satisfy Marguerite, Lance had gone to the Pantheon to see the dancer for himself and to watch the old man's reaction to her. Since he did not feel like going alone, he asked his friend Mr. Campion to accompany him.

Captain Smith listened to the recital with a perfectly impassive face, and when it was over he turned to Campion.

"Perhaps you would describe the incident as you saw it? Please don't omit anything."

Campion told the story of finding the old man half unconscious in the box, and Lance corroborated it.

"After the turn we looked up and could not see him in the box, so we went to investigate. We found he was hurt and did what we could," he repeated.

"You saw no one else in or near the box?"

"No."

"You're quite sure of that? No one at all?"

"No one," said Campion. "Nor," he continued firmly, "did I see him speak to anyone at all during the whole time that I was in the hall. He was entirely alone throughout the performance. Whoever attacked him must have opened the door of the box during Charmain's act, delivered the blow and left immediately. Nothing was touched. His pockets were not rifled. It was a personal attack. Someone meant to push him out and no one but him."

Captain Smith's heavy-lidded eyes flickered and he looked at Campion steadily.

"An attendant?" he suggested.

"No," said Campion decisively. "No, I don't think so. He was sitting up there in the box throughout the entire show, you see. Anyone could have noticed him. I don't see that it need have been an attendant. Anyone was at liberty to walk down that corridor. It might have been anyone in the entire audience."

"That's the devil of it," murmured Captain Smith, and for the first time a smile appeared upon his face. "Well, thank you very much for putting up with this intrusion. I shan't bother you either any more tonight, Superintendent."

"Very well, sir."

Oates took the dismissal respectfully and rose as the younger man took his leave.

After he had gone the atmosphere seemed a little easier, and Campion had just persuaded Oates to take a nightcap when the manservant reappeared.

"It's that Mr. Wild, sir," he was beginning, but broke off abruptly when he saw Oates. "I beg your pardon, sir. I heard the door and I thought both the gentlemen had gone."

"In a moment," said the superintendent, who was thawing visibly. "I'll be gone in a moment. Let him cool his heels. I'm fond of you, Campion," he continued as the man went out, "and there's a lot I'd do for you, but some of your pals are beyond me. I just couldn't bring myself to take a drink with Cassy Wild."

Campion shook his head. "You don't appreciate him," he said regretfully. "You're too conservative. You expect everyone to have the same virtues. Cassy has *unusual* virtues. They are quite as numerous, if not more so, than most people's, but they're different."

"Very likely," Oates observed without enthusiasm, "but I'd want my pockets sewed up and my shirt padlocked to my collar before I went for a walk with him. Still, I didn't come up here to talk about Cassy. It was a pity you couldn't give the captain what he was after. You might have made yourself really useful for once. However, if you saw no one you saw no one; that's all there is to it."

Lance frowned. "I seem to be out of this altogether," he said bitterly. "The entire business is getting more and more bewildering. Who was that chap Smith, anyway?"

The superintendent coughed. "He's a very important officer, sir. I don't think we'll discuss him, if you don't mind. Just keep the whole matter under your hat, if you will. It was a chance in a thousand and it got missed. That's the long and the short of it. It can't be helped."

He paused and glanced at Campion with a sly smile. No one spoke, and the superintendent's grin widened in spite of himself.

"I ought not to laugh," he said, "but I can't help it. It's not often Mr. Smarty gets himself into something that he doesn't understand. Right under his nose, it was, and he couldn't see it for looking."

Campion did not smile. He lay back in his chair, his eyes half closed behind his spectacles.

"Smith's a newcomer in the Special Branch, isn't he?" he said.

Oates choked, and his thin face grew a dusky red.

"Who said anything about the Special Branch?" he protested. "I don't know what you're talking about. I don't understand you at all. It's time I went home. It must be one in the morning."

Campion let him rise without demur, but spoke again before he had reached his greatcoat.

"When I first heard Dr. Tiffin's name tonight it reminded me of crossword puzzles," he remarked. "I could not think of the connection until I happened to see his expression as he sat looking at that dancer. Then it came back to me. He was in Room 40 OB during the war, wasn't he?"

"What if he was?" Oates was flurried. "Campion, for goodness sake stay out of this. It's not your cup of tea. It's not mine either. As it happened, you couldn't help. Let it rest like that. I can't discuss it with you. I daren't. It's not our show."

"Quite so. All the same I find it interesting, and if I'm right I think I might be useful." Lance had never heard Campion so gently obstinate. "Sit down and listen to me. I'll tell you how my mind is working. I may be shinning up a gum-tree, and if I am you can tell me so, politely and in official language. Now look here, this is how I see it. Dr. Tiffin happens to be a distinguished Egyptologist. His books on cuneiform and even earlier writings are famous. Also he was in Room 40 OB, the cipher decoding office, during the war. Those are two facts. Here are two more. Tonight I heard that he has suddenly started to visit every performance given by a certain dancer and during her turn this evening he was knocked out, presumably by someone who did not want him to see the whole of that dance. That gives me furiously to think."

"Don't." Oates' advice was brief but heartfelt. "Forget it." Campion sat up.

"I think I would," he said earnestly, "but I saw that girl dance, and I think Lance here said the most enlightening thing about her show. When it was over he turned to me and said, 'She's like a papyrus.' She wasn't, of course, but I saw what he meant. She *was* like some of that picture-writing on the mummy cases. Now do you see what I'm getting at? Suppose that long, slow procession of poses of hers was like writing, Oates? Suppose she danced some sort of limited message? It would have to be limited, of course, because it would be in a sign language, and sign languages are limited."

Oates was staring at him. Presently he swore softly.

"You're too bright," he said. "You'll blind yourself one of these days."

Campion laughed. "I thought so," he murmured. "It's fantastic, but not so fantastic that it couldn't be true… 'Thine uncle bears thee gifts.'"

The final words, uttered casually, had an astonishing effect on the superintendent. The blood receded from his face and his jaw dropped.

"Where the devil did you get hold of that?" he demanded.

"Overheard it. Nothing clever about that," Campion admitted modestly. "Dr. Tiffin was muttering it when we carried him home. That was the message, I suppose, or part of it. He must have been rather quicker on the uptake than his assailant expected. Quite an easy message, I should think. Most of the tombs have something of the sort among their lists of funeral offerings. The burning question, I take it, Oates, is…*whose* uncle?"

The superintendent did not reply. He seemed to be hovering on the verge of a confidence, and the soft knock on the door came as an unwelcome interruption. Campion sighed with exasperation.

"Oh, come in," he shouted.

The manservant entered with a dilapidated newspaper parcel on a silver tray.

"Mr. Wild has had to leave and wished me to give you this, sir," he said gravely. "I was to tell you he didn't mind waiting, but he took exception to the company you keep. I happened to let fall that the superintendent was here, sir."

"Blast his impudence!" said Oates, laughing. "What's he sent you? The fried fish supper you were going to share?"

Campion took the parcel and laid it on the arm of his chair unopened.

"Isn't that the question?" he persisted, as the door closed. "Whose uncle?"

Oates shrugged his shoulders. "You know too much," he said. "You'll get yourself in the Tower. It's all right to muscle in on my job, but you get your fingers into the espionage machine and you'll get 'em bitten off."

"Espionage?" muttered Lance under his breath. "Spy hunting, by George!"

"Put it out of your mind, sir." Oates made the admonition firmly. "You can see exactly what's happened. That dancer has been under observation by our people for months. No one at all suspicious seemed to have access to her, and they could never get the link between her and an espionage system which must exist. Then it occurred to someone at Headquarters that she was transmitting instructions in this peculiar way through her dancing. Dr. Tiffin tried to decode the messages and I think he had been very successful, but the thing he couldn't tell, of course, was who else besides himself in each audience understood what she was saying, and that was the vital thing. That was what our people needed to know. Tonight there might have been a chance of finding out. No one thought the old gentleman might be attached, although his interest in the lady must have looked highly suspicious to anybody in the know. If such a thing had been foreseen, he'd have been watched and we'd have found out something. Whoever attacked Dr. Tiffin is the key man, you see. He's probably living quietly over here under his own name like a respectable citizen."

"I still don't quite follow," said Lance frankly. "What would they do if they found him? Arrest him?"

"Arrest him?" Oates seemed scandalised. "Oh, no sir, foreign agents are never arrested. They're watched. They're even supplied with certain fancy information if they're mugs enough to take it. No, no, he'd have been followed. He would lead us to this 'uncle' who has the gifts, or the doings, whatever it is, and then *he* would be watched in his turn. Like that we'd uncover the entire network, you see. As I said, it was a chance in a thousand, but now it's gone. We'll never know who in all that audience was the other man who knew."

Campion nodded gloomily. "Yes," he said. "My hat, I wish I'd cottoned on to it a bit sooner." As he spoke he took up the newspaper packet and unwrapped it idly. An old brown leather wallet flopped on to his knees, and Oates laughed.

"Lumme," he said, "Cassy's brought you a bone! I'll have to pull you in one of these days, Campion. You'll get into trouble, mixing with scum like that. What *is* the explanation of that, may I ask? It looks darned fishy to me, I don't mind telling you."

"I haven't the faintest idea." Campion seemed surprised himself, and he bent down to retrieve a sheet of his own notepaper from the library desk which had fallen to the ground with the wrapping.

"Cassy's a dear chap, but he can't write," he observed as he glanced at the dreadful hieroglyphics spread out before him. "'Strewth!"

The final word was forced from him and he sprang up, the wallet clasped in his hand.

"Oates," he said unsteadily, "read that."

Lance and the superintendent read the message together. Some of the slang was beyond the artist, but the general meaning was clear.

"Dear old sport," it ran. "hoping this finds you as it leaves me, dry as bone. I kept an eye on your punter in Box B partly because I wondered what you was up to I admit that. Well, I took sights of the finger who sloshed him. I did not interfere because I did not want to be mixt up in anything thank you, specially there, but I thought you'd like a memento of him so I took his number which I give you gratis. I have not took above ten bob from it, may I die if I lie, but the rest will give you the dope on him and where to find him. I wouldn't do this for anyone but an old pal, Bert, as you know, but you've always bin one to me. Give old Oates a wish on the kisser from me. Ta ta. You know who. C. Wild."

Oates read the note through twice without speaking. Words seemed to have failed him. Finally he took the wallet which Campion held out to him, and his hand shook a little as he opened it and spread out its contents upon the coffee table. Some minutes later he looked up, and his expression was wondering.

"His name and address on two envelopes, a prescription from his doctor, and his driving license," he said. "Cassy's word might not jail a man, but it'll get this one watched. He's in the bag. Campion, you frighten me. Something looks after you."

Campion took up Mr. Wild's note and put it carefully in his pocket.

"Care for my secret, Superintendent?" he inquired.

"I'd like your luck," said Oates. "Well, what is it? I'll buy it."

"Take a drink with anyone," said Mr. Campion, "and pick your pals where you find 'em."

Lord Chizelrigg's Missing Fortune

Robert Barr

THE NAME of the late Lord Chizelrigg never comes to my mind without instantly suggesting that of Mr. T.A. Edison. I never saw the late Lord Chizelrigg, and I have met Mr. Edison only twice in my life, yet the two men are linked in my memory, and it was a remark the latter once made that in great measure enabled me to solve the mystery which the former had wrapped round his actions.

There is no memorandum at hand to tell me the year in which those two meetings with Edison took place. I received a note from the Italian Ambassador in Paris requesting me to wait upon him at the Embassy. I learned that on the next day a deputation was to set out from the Embassy to one of the chief hotels, there to make a call in state upon the great American inventor, and formally present to him various insignia accompanying certain honours which the King of Italy had conferred upon him. As many Italian nobles of high rank had been invited, and as these dignitaries would not only be robed in the costumes pertaining to their orders, but in many cases would wear jewels of almost inestimable value, my presence was desired in the belief that I might perhaps be able to ward off any attempt on the part of the deft-handed gentry who might possibly make an effort to gain these treasures, and I may add, with perhaps some little self-gratification, no *contretemps* occurred.

Mr. Edison, of course, had long before received notification of the hour at which the deputation would wait upon him, but when we entered the large parlour assigned to the inventor, it was evident to me at a glance that the celebrated man had forgotten all about the function. He stood by a bare table, from which the cloth had been jerked and flung into a corner, and upon that table were placed several bits of black and greasy machinery – cog wheels, pulleys, bolts, etc. These seemingly belonged to a French workman who stood on the other side of the table, with one of the parts in his grimy hand. Edison's own hands were not too clean, for he had palpably been examining the material, and conversing with the workman, who wore the ordinary long blouse of an iron craftsman in a small way. I judged him to be a man with a little shop of his own in some back street, who did odd jobs of engineering, assisted perhaps by a skilled helper or two, and a few apprentices. Edison looked sternly towards the door as the solemn procession filed in, and there was a trace of annoyance on his face at the interruption, mixed with a shade of perplexity as to what this gorgeous display all meant. The Italian is as ceremonious as the Spaniard where a function is concerned, and the official who held the ornate box which contained the jewellery resting on a velvet cushion, stepped slowly forward, and came to a stand in front of the bewildered American. Then the Ambassador, in sonorous voice, spoke some gracious words regarding the friendship existing between the United States and Italy, expressed a wish that their rivalry should ever take the form of benefits conferred upon the human race, and instanced the honoured recipient as the most notable example the world had yet produced of a man bestowing blessings upon all nations in the arts of peace. The eloquent Ambassador concluded by saying that, at the command of his Royal master, it was both his duty and his pleasure to present, and so forth and so forth.

Mr. Edison, visibly ill at ease, nevertheless made a suitable reply in the fewest possible words, and the *étalage* being thus at an end, the noblemen, headed by their Ambassador, slowly retired, myself forming the tail of the procession. Inwardly I deeply sympathised with the French workman who thus unexpectedly found himself confronted by so much magnificence. He cast one wild look about him, but saw that his retreat was cut off unless he displaced some of these gorgeous grandees. He tried then to shrink into himself, and finally stood helpless like one paralysed. In spite of Republican institutions, there is deep down in every Frenchman's heart a respect and awe for official pageants, sumptuously staged and costumed as this one was. But he likes to view it from afar, and supported by his fellows, not thrust incongruously into the midst of things, as was the case with this panic-stricken engineer. As I passed out, I cast a glance over my shoulder at the humble artisan content with a profit of a few francs a day, and at the millionaire inventor opposite him, Edison's face, which during the address had been cold and impassive, reminding me vividly of a bust of Napoleon, was now all aglow with enthusiasm as he turned to his humble visitor. He cried joyfully to the workman:

"A minute's demonstration is worth an hour's explanation. I'll call round tomorrow at your shop, about ten o'clock, and show you how to make the thing work."

I lingered in the hall until the Frenchman came out, then, introducing myself to him, asked the privilege of visiting his shop next day at ten. This was accorded with that courtesy which you will always find among the industrial classes of France, and next day I had the pleasure of meeting Mr. Edison. During our conversation I complimented him on his invention of the incandescent electric light, and this was the reply that has ever remained in my memory:

"It was not an invention, but a discovery. We knew what we wanted; a carbonised tissue, which would withstand the electric current in a vacuum for, say, a thousand hours. If no such tissue existed, then the incandescent light, as we know it, was not possible. My assistants started out to find this tissue, and we simply carbonised everything we could lay our hands on, and ran the current through it in a vacuum. At last we struck the right thing, as we were bound to do if we kept on long enough, and if the thing existed. Patience and hard work will overcome any obstacle."

This belief has been of great assistance to me in my profession. I know the idea is prevalent that a detective arrives at his solutions in a dramatic way through following clues invisible to the ordinary man. This doubtless frequently happens, but, as a general thing, the patience and hard work which Mr. Edison commends is a much safer guide. Very often the following of excellent clues had led me to disaster, as was the case with my unfortunate attempt to solve the mystery of the five hundred diamonds.

As I was saying, I never think of the late Lord Chizelrigg without remembering Mr. Edison at the same time, and yet the two were very dissimilar. I suppose Lord Chizelrigg was the most useless man that ever lived, while Edison is the opposite.

One day my servant brought in to me a card on which was engraved 'Lord Chizelrigg'.

"Show his lordship in," I said, and there appeared a young man of perhaps twenty-four or twenty-five, well dressed, and of most charming manners, who, nevertheless, began his interview by asking a question such as had never before been addressed to me, and which, if put to a solicitor, or other professional man, would have been answered with some indignation. Indeed, I believe it is a written or unwritten law of the legal profession that the acceptance of such a proposal as Lord Chizelrigg made to me, would, if proved, result in the disgrace and ruin of the lawyer.

"Monsieur Valmont," began Lord Chizelrigg, "do you ever take up cases on speculation?"

"On speculation, sir? I do not think I understand you."

His lordship blushed like a girl, and stammered slightly as he attempted an explanation.

"What I mean is, do you accept a case on a contingent fee? That is to say, monsieur – er – well, not to put too fine a point upon it, no results, no pay."

I replied somewhat severely:

"Such an offer has never been made to me, and I may say at once that I should be compelled to decline it were I favoured with the opportunity. In the cases submitted to me, I devote my time and attention to their solution. I try to deserve success, but I cannot command it, and as in the interim I must live, I am reluctantly compelled to make a charge for my time, at least. I believe the doctor sends in his bill, though the patient dies."

The young man laughed uneasily, and seemed almost too embarrassed to proceed, but finally he said:

"Your illustration strikes home with greater accuracy than probably you imagined when you uttered it. I have just paid my last penny to the physician who attended my late uncle, Lord Chizelrigg, who died six months ago. I am fully aware that the suggestion I made may seem like a reflection upon your skill, or rather, as implying a doubt regarding it. But I should be grieved, monsieur, if you fell into such an error. I could have come here and commissioned you to undertake some elucidation of the strange situation in which I find myself, and I make no doubt you would have accepted the task if your numerous engagements had permitted. Then, if you failed, I should have been unable to pay you, for I am practically bankrupt. My whole desire, therefore, was to make an honest beginning, and to let you know exactly how I stand. If you succeed, I shall be a rich man; if you do not succeed, I shall be what I am now, penniless. Have I made it plain now why I began with a question which you had every right to resent?"

"Perfectly plain, my lord, and your candour does you credit."

I was very much taken with the unassuming manners of the young man, and his evident desire to accept no service under false pretences. When I had finished my sentence the pauper nobleman rose to his feet, and bowed.

"I am very much your debtor, monsieur, for your courtesy in receiving me, and can only beg pardon for occupying your time on a futile quest. I wish you good morning, monsieur."

"One moment, my lord," I rejoined, waving him to his chair again. "Although I am unprepared to accept a commission on the terms you suggest, I may, nevertheless, be able to offer a hint or two that will prove of service to you. I think I remember the announcement of Lord Chizelrigg's death. He was somewhat eccentric, was he not?"

"Eccentric?" said the young man, with a slight laugh, seating himself again – "well, *rather*!"

"I vaguely remember that he was accredited with the possession of something like twenty thousand acres of land?"

"Twenty-seven thousand, as a matter of fact," replied my visitor.

"Have you fallen heir to the lands as well as to the title?"

"Oh, yes; the estate was entailed. The old gentleman could not divert it from me if he would, and I rather suspect that fact must have been the cause of some worry to him."

"But surely, my lord, a man who owns, as one might say, a principality in this wealthy realm of England, cannot be penniless?"

Again the young man laughed.

"Well, no," he replied, thrusting his hand in his pocket and bringing to light a few brown coppers, and a white silver piece. "I possess enough money to buy some food tonight, but not enough to dine at the Hotel Cecil. You see, it is like this. I belong to a somewhat ancient family, various members of whom went the pace, and mortgaged their acres up to the hilt. I could not raise a further penny on my estates were I to try my hardest, because at the time the money was lent, land was much more valuable than it is today. Agricultural depression, and all that sort of thing, have, if I may put it so, left me a good many thousands worse off than if I had no land at all. Besides this, during my late uncle's life, Parliament, on his behalf, intervened once or twice, allowing him in the first place to cut valuable timber, and in the second place to sell the pictures of Chizelrigg Chase at Christie's for figures which make one's mouth water."

"And what became of the money?" I asked, whereupon once more this genial nobleman laughed. "That is exactly what I came up in the lift to learn if Monsieur Valmont could discover."

"My lord, you interest me," I said, quite truly, with an uneasy apprehension that I should take up his case after all, for I liked the young man already. His lack of pretence appealed to me, and that sympathy which is so universal among my countrymen enveloped him, as I may say, quite independent of my own will.

"My uncle," went on Lord Chizelrigg, "was somewhat of an anomaly in our family. He must have been a reversal to a very, very ancient type; a type of which we have no record. He was as miserly as his forefathers were prodigal. When he came into the title and estate some twenty years ago, he dismissed the whole retinue of servants, and, indeed, was defendant in several cases at law where retainers of our family brought suit against him for wrongful dismissal, or dismissal without a penny compensation in lieu of notice. I am pleased to say he lost all his cases, and when he pleaded poverty, got permission to sell a certain number of heirlooms, enabling him to make compensation, and giving him something on which to live. These heirlooms at auction sold so unexpectedly well, that my uncle acquired a taste, as it were, of what might be done. He could always prove that the rents went to the mortgagees, and that he had nothing on which to exist, so on several occasions he obtained permission from the courts to cut timber and sell pictures, until he denuded the estate and made an empty barn of the old manor house. He lived like any labourer, occupying himself sometimes as a carpenter, sometimes as a blacksmith; indeed, he made a blacksmith's shop of the library, one of the most noble rooms in Britain, containing thousands of valuable books which again and again he applied for permission to sell, but this privilege was never granted to him. I find on coming into the property that my uncle quite persistently evaded the law, and depleted this superb collection, book by book, surreptitiously through dealers in London. This, of course, would have got him into deep trouble if it had been discovered before his death, but now the valuable volumes are gone, and there is no redress. Many of them are doubtless in America, or in museums and collections of Europe."

"You wish me to trace them, perhaps?" I interpolated.

"Oh, no; they are past praying for. The old man made tens of thousands by the sale of the timber, and other thousands by disposing of the pictures. The house is denuded of its fine old furniture, which was immensely valuable, and then the books, as I have said, must have brought in the revenue of a prince, if he got anything like their value, and you may be sure he was shrewd enough to know their worth. Since the last refusal of the courts to allow him further relief, as he termed it, which was some seven years ago, he had quite evidently been disposing of books and furniture by a private sale, in defiance of the law. At that time I was under age, but my guardians opposed his application to the courts, and demanded an account of the moneys already in his hands. The judges upheld the opposition of my guardians, and refused to allow a further spoliation of the estate, but they did not grant the accounting my guardians asked, because the proceeds of the former sales were entirely at the disposal of my uncle, and were sanctioned by the law to permit him to live as befitted his station. If he lived meagrely instead of lavishly, as my guardians contended, that, the judges said, was his affair, and there the matter ended.

"My uncle took a violent dislike to me on account of this opposition to his last application, although, of course, I had nothing whatever to do with the matter. He lived like a hermit, mostly in the library, and was waited upon by an old man and his wife, and these three were the only inhabitants of a mansion that could comfortably house a hundred. He visited nobody, and would allow no one to approach Chizelrigg Chase. In order that all who had the misfortune to have dealing with him should continue to endure trouble after his death, he left what might be called a will, but which rather may be termed a letter to me. Here is a copy of it.

> My Dear Tom, –
> You will find your fortune between a couple of sheets of paper in the library.
> Your affectionate uncle,
> Reginald Moran, Earl of Chizelrigg.

"I should doubt if that were a legal will," said I.

"It doesn't need to be," replied the young man with a smile. "I am next-of-kin, and heir to everything he possessed, although, of course, he might have given his money elsewhere if he had chosen to do so. Why he did not bequeath it to some institution, I do not know. He knew no man personally except his own servants, whom he misused and starved, but, as he told them, he misused and starved himself, so they had no cause to grumble. He said he was treating them like one of the family. I suppose he thought it would cause me more worry and anxiety if he concealed the money, and put me on the wrong scent, which I am convinced he has done, than to leave it openly to any person or charity."

"I need not ask if you have searched the library?"

"Searched it? Why, there never was such a search since the world began!"

"Possibly you put the task into incompetent hands?"

"You are hinting, Monsieur Valmont, that I engaged others until my money was gone, then came to you with a speculative proposal. Let me assure you such is not the case. Incompetent hands, I grant you, but the hands were my own. For the past six months I have lived practically as my uncle lived. I have rummaged that library from floor to ceiling. It was left in a frightful state, littered with old newspapers, accounts, and what-not. Then, of course, there were the books remaining in the library, still a formidable collection."

"Was your uncle a religious man?"

"I could not say. I surmise not. You see, I was unacquainted with him, and never saw him until after his death. I fancy he was not religious, otherwise he could not have acted as he did. Still, he proved himself a man of such twisted mentality that anything is possible."

"I knew a case once where an heir who expected a large sum of money was bequeathed a family Bible, which he threw into the fire, learning afterwards, to his dismay, that it contained many thousands of pounds in Bank of England notes, the object of the devisor being to induce the legatee to read the good Book or suffer through the neglect of it."

"I have searched the Scriptures," said the youthful Earl with a laugh, "but the benefit has been moral rather than material."

"Is there any chance that your uncle has deposited his wealth in a bank, and has written a cheque for the amount, leaving it between two leaves of a book?"

"Anything is possible, monsieur, but I think that highly improbable. I have gone through every tome, page by page, and I suspect very few of the volumes have been opened for the last twenty years."

"How much money do you estimate he accumulated?"

"He must have cleared more than a hundred thousand pounds, but speaking of banking it, I would like to say that my uncle evinced a deep distrust of banks, and never drew a cheque in his life so far as I am aware. All accounts were paid in gold by this old steward, who first brought the receipted bill in to my uncle, and then received the exact amount, after having left the room, and waited until he was rung for, so that he might not learn the repository from which my uncle drew his store. I believe if the money is ever found it will be in gold, and I am very sure that this will was written, if we may call it a will, to put us on the wrong scent."

"Have you had the library cleared out?"

"Oh, no, it is practically as my uncle left it. I realised that if I were to call in help, it would be well that the newcomer found it undisturbed."

"You were quite right, my lord. You say you examined all the papers?"

"Yes; so far as that is concerned, the room has been very fairly gone over, but nothing that was in it the day my uncle died has been removed, not even his anvil."

"His anvil?"

"Yes; I told you he made a blacksmith's shop, as well as bedroom, of the library. It is a huge room, with a great fireplace at one end which formed an excellent forge. He and the steward built the forge in the eastern fireplace of brick and clay, with their own hands, and erected there a second-hand blacksmith's bellows."

"What work did he do at his forge?"

"Oh, anything that was required about the place. He seems to have been a very expert ironworker. He would never buy a new implement for the garden or the house so long as he could get one second-hand, and he never bought anything second-hand while at his forge he might repair what was already in use. He kept an old cob, on which he used to ride through the park, and he always put the shoes on this cob himself, the steward informs me, so he must have understood the use of blacksmith's tools. He made a carpenter's shop of the chief drawing room and erected a bench there. I think a very useful mechanic was spoiled when my uncle became an earl."

"You have been living at the Chase since your uncle died?"

"If you call it living, yes. The old steward and his wife have been looking after me, as they looked after my uncle, and, seeing me day after day, coatless, and covered with dust, I imagine they think me a second edition of the old man."

"Does the steward know the money is missing?"

"No; no one knows it but myself. This will was left on the anvil, in an envelope addressed to me."

"Your statement is exceedingly clear, Lord Chizelrigg, but I confess I don't see much daylight through it. Is there a pleasant country around Chizelrigg Chase?"

"Very; especially at this season of the year. In autumn and winter the house is a little draughty. It needs several thousand pounds to put it in repair."

"Draughts do not matter in the summer. I have been long enough in England not to share the fear of my countrymen for a *courant d'air*. Is there a spare bed in the manor house, or shall I take down a cot with me, or let us say a hammock?"

"Really," stammered the earl, blushing again, "you must not think I detailed all these circumstances in order to influence you to take up what may be a hopeless case. I, of course, am deeply interested, and, therefore, somewhat prone to be carried away when I begin a recital of my uncle's eccentricities. If I receive your permission, I will call on you again in a month or two. To tell you the truth, I borrowed a little money from the old steward, and visited London to see my legal advisers, hoping that in the circumstances I may get permission to sell something that will keep me from starvation. When I spoke of the house being denuded, I meant relatively, of course. There are still a good many antiquities which would doubtless bring me in a comfortable sum of money. I have been borne up by the belief that I should find my uncle's gold. Lately, I have been beset by a suspicion that the old gentleman thought the library the only valuable asset left, and for this reason wrote his note, thinking I would be afraid to sell anything from that room. The old rascal must have made a pot of money out of those shelves. The catalogue shows that there was a copy of the first book printed in England by Caxton, and several priceless Shakespeares, as well as many other volumes that a collector would give a small fortune for. All these are gone. I think when I show this to be the case, the authorities cannot refuse me the right to sell something, and, if I get this permission, I shall at once call upon you."

"Nonsense, Lord Chizelrigg. Put your application in motion, if you like. Meanwhile I beg of you to look upon me as a more substantial banker than your old steward. Let us enjoy a good dinner together at the Cecil tonight, if you will do me the honour to be my guest. Tomorrow we can leave for Chizelrigg Chase. How far is it?"

"About three hours," replied the young man, becoming as red as a new Queen Anne villa. "Really, Monsieur Valmont, you overwhelm me with your kindness, but nevertheless I accept your generous offer."

"Then that's settled. What's the name of the old steward?"

"Higgins."

"You are certain he has no knowledge of the hiding place of this treasure?"

"Oh, quite sure. My uncle was not a man to make a confidant of anyone, least of all an old babbler like Higgins."

"Well, I should like to be introduced to Higgins as a benighted foreigner. That will make him despise me and treat me like a child."

"Oh, I say," protested the earl, "I should have thought you'd lived long enough in England to have got out of the notion that we do not appreciate the foreigner. Indeed, we are the only nation in the world that extends a cordial welcome to him, rich or poor."

"*Certainement*, my lord, I should be deeply disappointed did you not take me at my proper valuation, but I cherish no delusions regarding the contempt with which Higgins will regard me. He will look upon me as a sort of simpleton to whom the Lord had been unkind by not making England my native land. Now, Higgins must be led to believe that I am in his own class; that is, a servant of yours. Higgins and I will gossip over the fire together, should these spring evenings prove chilly, and before two or three weeks are past I shall have learned a great deal about your uncle that you never dreamed of. Higgins will talk more freely with a fellow-servant than with his master, however much he may respect that master, and then, as I am a foreigner, he will babble down to my comprehension, and I shall get details that he never would think of giving to a fellow-countryman."

* * *

The young earl's modesty in such description of his home as he had given me, left me totally unprepared for the grandeur of the mansion, one corner of which he inhabited. It is such a place as you read of in romances of the Middle Ages; not a pinnacled or turreted French château of that period, but a beautiful and substantial stone manor house of a ruddy colour, whose warm hue seemed to add a softness to the severity of its architecture. It is built round an outer and an inner courtyard and could house a thousand, rather than the hundred with which its owner had accredited it. There are many stone-mullioned windows, and one at the end of the library might well have graced a cathedral. This superb residence occupies the centre of a heavily timbered park, and from the lodge at the gates we drove at least a mile and a half under the grandest avenue of old oaks I have ever seen. It seemed incredible that the owner of all this should actually lack the ready money to pay his fare to town!

Old Higgins met us at the station with a somewhat rickety cart, to which was attached the ancient cob that the late earl used to shoe. We entered a noble hall, which probably looked the larger because of the entire absence of any kind of furniture, unless two complete suits of venerable armour which stood on either hand might be considered as furnishing. I laughed aloud when the door was shut, and the sound echoed like the merriment of ghosts from the dim timbered roof above me.

"What are you laughing at?" asked the earl.

"I am laughing to see you put your modern tall hat on that mediaeval helmet."

"Oh, that's it! Well, put yours on the other. I mean no disrespect to the ancestor who wore this suit, but we are short of the harmless, necessary hat-rack, so I put my topper on the antique helmet, and thrust the umbrella (if I have one) in behind here, and down one of his legs. Since I came in possession, a very crafty-looking dealer from London visited me, and attempted to sound me regarding the sale of these suits of armour. I gathered he would give enough money to keep me in new suits, London-made, for the rest of my life, but when I endeavoured to find out if he had had commercial dealings with my prophetic uncle, he became frightened and bolted. I imagine that if I had possessed presence of mind enough to have lured him into one of our most uncomfortable dungeons, I might have learned where some of the family treasures went to. Come up these stairs, Monsieur Valmont, and I will show you your room."

We had lunched on the train coming down, so after a wash in my own room I proceeded at once to inspect the library. It proved, indeed, a most noble apartment, and it had been scandalously used by the old reprobate, its late tenant. There were two huge fireplaces, one in the middle of the north wall and the other at the eastern end. In the latter had been erected a rude brick forge, and beside the forge hung a great black bellows, smoky with usage. On a wooden block lay the anvil, and around it rested and rusted several hammers, large and small. At the western end was a glorious window filled with ancient stained glass, which, as I have said, might have adorned a cathedral. Extensive as the collection of books was, the great size of this chamber made it necessary that only the outside wall should be covered with book cases, and even these were divided by tall windows. The opposite wall was blank, with the exception of a picture here and there, and these pictures offered a further insult to the room, for they were cheap prints, mostly coloured lithographs that had appeared in Christmas numbers of London weekly journals, encased in poverty-stricken frames, hanging from nails ruthlessly driven in above them. The floor was covered with a litter of papers, in some places knee-deep, and in the corner farthest from the forge still stood the bed on which the ancient miser had died.

"Looks like a stable, doesn't it?" commented the earl, when I had finished my inspection. "I am sure the old boy simply filled it up with this rubbish to give me the trouble of examining it. Higgins tells me that up to within a month before he died the room was reasonably clear of all this muck. Of course it had to be, or the place would have caught fire from the sparks of the forge. The old man made Higgins gather all the papers he could find anywhere about the place, ancient accounts, newspapers, and what not, even to the brown wrapping paper you see, in which parcels came, and commanded him to strew the floor with this litter, because, as he complained, Higgins's boots on the boards made too much noise, and Higgins, who is not in the least of an inquiring mind, accepted this explanation as entirely meeting the case."

Higgins proved to be a garrulous old fellow, who needed no urging to talk about the late earl; indeed, it was almost impossible to deflect his conversation into any other channel. Twenty years' intimacy with the eccentric nobleman had largely obliterated that sense of deference with which an English servant usually approaches his master. An English underling's idea of nobility is the man who never by any possibility works with his hands. The fact that Lord Chizelrigg had toiled at the carpenter's bench; had mixed cement in the drawing room; had caused the anvil to ring out till midnight, aroused no admiration in Higgins's mind. In addition to this, the ancient nobleman had been penuriously strict in his examination of accounts, exacting the uttermost farthing, so the humble servitor regarded his memory with supreme contempt. I realised before the drive was finished from the station to Chizelrigg Chase that there was little use of introducing me to Higgins as a foreigner and a fellow-servant. I found myself completely unable to understand what the old fellow said. His dialect, was as unknown to me as the Choctaw language would have been, and the young earl was compelled to act as interpreter on the occasions when we set this garrulous talking-machine going.

The new Earl of Chizelrigg, with the enthusiasm of a boy, proclaimed himself my pupil and assistant, and said he would do whatever he was told. His thorough and fruitless search of the library had convinced him that the old man was merely chaffing him, as he put it, by leaving such a letter as he had written. His lordship was certain that the money had been hidden somewhere else; probably buried under one of the trees in the park. Of course this was possible, and represented the usual method by which a stupid person conceals treasure, yet I did not think it probable. All conversations with Higgins showed the earl to have been an extremely suspicious man; suspicious of banks, suspicious even of Bank of England notes, suspicious of every person on earth, not omitting Higgins himself. Therefore, as I told his nephew, the miser would never allow the fortune out of his sight and immediate reach.

From the first the oddity of the forge and anvil being placed in his bedroom struck me as peculiar, and I said to the young man, –

"I'll stake my reputation that forge or anvil, or both, contain the secret. You see, the old gentleman worked sometimes till midnight, for Higgins could hear his hammering. If he used hard coal on the forge the fire would last through the night, and being in continual terror of thieves, as Higgins says, barricading the castle every evening before dark as if it were a fortress, he was bound to place the treasure in the most unlikely spot for a thief to get at it. Now, the coal fire smouldered all night long, and if the gold was in the forge underneath the embers, it would be extremely difficult to get at. A robber rummaging in the dark would burn his fingers in more senses than one. Then, as his lordship kept no less than four loaded revolvers under his pillow, all he had to do, if a thief entered his room was to allow the search to go on until the thief started at the forge, then doubtless, as he had the range with reasonable accuracy night or day, he might sit up in bed and blaze away with revolver after revolver. There were twenty-eight shots that could be fired in about double as many seconds, so you see the robber stood little chance in the face of such a fusillade. I propose that we dismantle the forge."

Lord Chizelrigg was much taken by my reasoning, and one morning early we cut down the big bellows, tore it open, found it empty, then took brick after brick from the forge with a crowbar, for the old man had builded better than he knew with Portland cement. In fact, when we cleared away the rubbish between the bricks and the core of the furnace we came upon one cube of cement which was as hard as granite. With the aid of Higgins, and a set of rollers and levers, we managed to get this block out into the park, and attempted to crush it with the sledge-hammers belonging to the forge, in which we were entirely unsuccessful. The more it resisted our efforts, the more certain we became that the coins would be found within it. As this would not be treasure-trove in the sense that the Government might make a claim upon it, there was no particular necessity for secrecy, so we had up a man from the mines near by with drills and dynamite, who speedily shattered the block into a million pieces, more or less. Alas! There was no trace in its debris of 'pay dirt', as the western miner puts it. While the dynamite expert was on the spot, we induced him to shatter the anvil as well as the block of cement, and then the workman, doubtless thinking the new earl was as insane as the old one had been, shouldered his tools, and went back to his mine.

The earl reverted to his former opinion that the gold was concealed in the park, while I held even more firmly to my own belief that the fortune rested in the library.

"It is obvious," I said to him, "that if the treasure is buried outside, someone must have dug the hole. A man so timorous and so reticent as your uncle would allow no one to do this but himself. Higgins maintained the other evening that all picks and spades were safely locked up by himself each night in the tool-house. The mansion itself was barricaded with such exceeding care that it would have been difficult for your uncle to get outside even if he wished to do so. Then such a man as your uncle is described to have been would continually desire ocular demonstration that his savings were intact, which would be practically impossible if the gold had found a grave in the park. I propose now that we abandon violence and dynamite, and proceed to an intellectual search of the library."

"Very well," replied the young earl, "but as I have already searched the library very thoroughly, your use of the word 'intellectual', Monsieur Valmont, is not in accord with your customary politeness. However, I am with you. 'Tis for you to command, and me to obey."

"Pardon me, my lord," I said, "I used the word 'intellectual' in contradistinction to the word 'dynamite'. It had no reference to your former search. I merely propose that we now abandon the use of chemical reaction, and employ the much greater force of mental activity. Did you notice any writing on the margins of the newspapers you examined?"

"No, I did not."

"Is it possible that there may have been some communication on the white border of a newspaper?"

"It is, of course, possible."

"Then will you set yourself to the task of glancing over the margin of every newspaper, piling them away in another room when your scrutiny of each is complete? Do not destroy anything, but we must clear out the library completely. I am interested in the accounts, and will examine them."

It was exasperatingly tedious work, but after several days my assistant reported every margin scanned without result, while I had collected each bill and memorandum, classifying them according to date. I could not get rid of a suspicion that the contrary old beast had written instructions for the finding of the treasure on the back of some account, or on the fly-leaf of a book, and as I looked at the thousands of volumes still left in the library, the prospect of such a patient and minute search appalled me. But I remembered Edison's words to the effect that if a thing exist, search, exhaustive enough, will find it. From the mass of accounts I selected several; the rest I placed in another room, alongside the heap of the earl's newspapers.

"Now," said I to my helper, "if it please you, we will have Higgins in, as I wish some explanation of these accounts."

"Perhaps I can assist you," suggested his lordship drawing up a chair opposite the table on which I had spread the statements. "I have lived here for six months, and know as much about things as Higgins does. He is so difficult to stop when once he begins to talk. What is the first account you wish further light upon?"

"To go back thirteen years I find that your uncle bought a second-hand safe in Sheffield. Here is the bill. I consider it necessary to find that safe."

"Pray forgive me, Monsieur Valmont," cried the young man, springing to his feet and laughing; "so heavy an article as a safe should not slip readily from a man's memory, but it did from mine. The safe is empty, and I gave no more thought to it."

Saying this the earl went to one of the bookcases that stood against the wall, pulled it round as if it were a door, books and all, and displayed the front of an iron safe, the door of which he also drew open, exhibiting the usual empty interior of such a receptacle.

"I came on this," he said, "when I took down all these volumes. It appears that there was once a secret door leading from the library into an outside room, which has long since disappeared; the walls are very thick. My uncle doubtless caused this door to be taken off its hinges, and the safe placed in the aperture, the rest of which he then bricked up."

"Quite so," said I, endeavouring to conceal my disappointment. "As this strong box was bought second-hand and not made to order, I suppose there can be no secret crannies in it?"

"It looks like a common or garden safe," reported my assistant, "but we'll have it out if you say so."

"Not just now," I replied; "we've had enough of dynamiting to make us feel like housebreakers already."

"I agree with you. What's the next item on the programme?"

"Your uncle's mania for buying things second-hand was broken in three instances so far as I have been able to learn from a scrutiny of these accounts. About four years ago he purchased a new book from Denny and Co., the well-known booksellers of the Strand. Denny and Co. deal only in new books. Is there any comparatively new volume in the library?"

"Not one."

"Are you sure of that?"

"Oh, quite; I searched all the literature in the house. What is the name of the volume he bought?"

"That I cannot decipher. The initial letter looks like 'M', but the rest is a mere wavy line. I see, however, that it cost twelve-and-sixpence, while the cost of carriage by parcel post was sixpence, which shows it weighed something under four pounds. This, with the price of the book, induces me to think that it was a scientific work, printed on heavy paper and illustrated."

"I know nothing of it," said the earl.

"The third account is for wallpaper; twenty-seven rolls of an expensive wallpaper, and twenty-seven rolls of a cheap paper, the latter being just half the price of the former. This wallpaper seems to have been supplied by a tradesman in the station road in the village of Chizelrigg."

"There's your wallpaper," cried the youth, waving his hand; "he was going to paper the whole house, Higgins told me, but got tired after he had finished the library, which took him nearly a year to accomplish, for he worked at it very intermittently, mixing the paste in the boudoir, a pailful at a time as he needed it. It was a scandalous thing to do, for underneath the paper is the most exquisite oak panelling, very plain, but very rich in colour."

I rose and examined the paper on the wall. It was dark brown, and answered the description of the expensive paper on the bill.

"What became of the cheap paper?" I asked.

"I don't know."

"I think," said I, "we are on the track of the mystery. I believe that paper covers a sliding panel or concealed door."

"It is very likely," replied the earl. "I intended to have the paper off, but I had no money to pay a workman, and I am not so industrious as was my uncle. What is your remaining account?"

"The last also pertains to paper, but comes from a firm in Budge Row, London, E.C. He has had, it seems, a thousand sheets of it, and it appears to have been frightfully expensive. This bill is also illegible, but I take it a thousand sheets were supplied, although of course it may have been a thousand quires, which would be a little more reasonable for the price charged, or a thousand reams, which would be exceedingly cheap."

"I don't know anything about that. Let's turn on Higgins."

Higgins knew nothing of this last order of paper either. The wallpaper mystery he at once cleared up. Apparently the old earl had discovered by experiment that the heavy, expensive wallpaper would not stick to the glossy panelling, so he had purchased a cheaper paper, and had pasted that on first. Higgins said he had gone all over the panelling with a yellowish-white paper, and after that was dry, he pasted over it the more expensive rolls.

"But," I objected, "the two papers were bought and delivered at the same time; therefore, he could not have found by experiment that the heavy paper would not stick."

"I don't think there is much in that," commented the earl; "the heavy paper may have been bought first, and found to be unsuitable, and then the coarse, cheap paper bought afterwards. The bill merely shows that the account was sent in on that date. Indeed, as the village of Chizelrigg is but a few miles away, it would have been quite possible for my uncle to have bought the heavy paper in the morning, tried it, and in the afternoon sent for the commoner lot; but in any case, the bill would not have been presented until months after the order, and the two purchases were thus lumped together."

I was forced to confess that this seemed reasonable.

Now, about the book ordered from Denny's. Did Higgins remember anything regarding it? It came four years ago.

Ah, yes, Higgins did; he remembered it very well indeed. He had come in one morning with the earl's tea, and the old man was sitting up in bed reading his volume with such interest that he was unaware of Higgins's knock, and Higgins himself, being a little hard of hearing, took for granted the command to enter. The earl hastily thrust the book under the pillow, alongside the revolvers, and rated Higgins in a most cruel way for entering the room before getting permission to do so. He had never seen the earl so angry before, and he laid it all to this book. It was after the book had come that the forge had been erected and the anvil bought. Higgins never saw the book again, but one morning, six months before the earl died, Higgins, in raking out the cinders of the forge, found what he supposed was a portion of the book's cover. He believed his master had burnt the volume.

Having dismissed Higgins, I said to the earl –

"The first thing to be done is to enclose this bill to Denny and Co., booksellers, Strand. Tell them you have lost the volume, and ask them to send another. There is likely someone in the shop who can decipher the illegible writing. I am certain the book will give us a clue. Now, I shall write to Braun and Sons, Budge Row. This is evidently a French company; in fact, the name as connected with paper-making runs in my mind, although I cannot at this moment place it. I shall ask them the use of this paper that they furnished to the late earl."

This was done accordingly, and now, as we thought, until the answers came, we were two men out of work. Yet the next morning, I am pleased to say, and I have always rather plumed myself on the fact, I solved the mystery before replies were received from London. Of course, both the book and the answer of the paper agents, by putting two and two together, would have given us the key.

After breakfast, I strolled somewhat aimlessly into the library, whose floor was now strewn merely with brown wrapping paper, bits of string, and all that. As I shuffled among this with my feet, as if tossing aside dead autumn leaves in a forest path, my attention was suddenly drawn to several squares of paper, unwrinkled, and never used for wrapping. These sheets seemed to me strangely familiar. I picked one of them up, and at once the significance of the name Braun and Sons occurred to me. They are paper makers in France, who produce a smooth, very tough sheet, which, dear as it is, proves infinitely cheap compared with the fine vellum it deposed in a certain branch of industry. In Paris, years before, these sheets had given me the knowledge of how a gang of thieves disposed of their gold without melting it. The paper was used instead of vellum in the rougher processes of manufacturing gold-leaf. It stood the constant beating of the hammer nearly as well as the vellum, and here at once there flashed on me the secret of the old man's midnight anvil work. He was transforming his sovereigns into gold-leaf, which must have been of a rude, thick kind, because to produce the gold-leaf of commerce he still needed the vellum as well as a 'clutch' and other machinery, of which we had found no trace.

"My lord," I called to my assistant; he was at the other end of the room; "I wish to test a theory on the anvil of your own fresh common sense."

"Hammer away," replied the earl, approaching me with his usual good-natured, jocular expression.

"I eliminate the safe from our investigations because it was purchased thirteen years ago, but the buying of the book, of wall covering, of this tough paper from France, all group themselves into a set of incidents occurring within the same month as the purchase of the anvil and the building of the forge; therefore, I think they are related to one another. Here are some sheets of paper he got from Budge Row. Have you ever seen anything like it? Try to tear this sample."

"It's reasonably tough," admitted his lordship, fruitlessly endeavouring to rip it apart.

"Yes. It was made in France, and is used in gold beating. Your uncle beat his sovereigns into gold-leaf. You will find that the book from Denny's is a volume on gold beating, and now as I remember that scribbled word which I could not make out, I think the title of the volume is 'Metallurgy'. It contains, no doubt, a chapter on the manufacture of gold-leaf."

"I believe you," said the earl; "but I don't see that the discovery sets us any further forward. We're now looking for gold-leaf instead of sovereigns."

"Let's examine this wallpaper," said I.

I placed my knife under a corner of it at the floor, and quite easily ripped off a large section. As Higgins had said, the brown paper was on top, and the coarse, light-coloured paper underneath. But even that came away from the oak panelling as easily as though it hung there from habit, and not because of paste.

"Feel the weight of that," I cried, handing him the sheet I had torn from the wall.

"By Jove!" said the earl, in a voice almost of awe.

I took it from him, and laid it, face downwards, on the wooden table, threw a little water on the back, and with a knife scraped away the porous white paper. Instantly there gleamed up at us the baleful yellow of the gold. I shrugged my shoulders and spread out my hands. The Earl of Chizelrigg laughed aloud and very heartily.

"You see how it is," I cried. "The old man first covered the entire wall with this whitish paper. He heated his sovereigns at the forge and beat them out on the anvil, then completed the process rudely between the sheets of this paper from France. Probably he pasted the gold to the wall as soon as he shut himself in for the night, and covered it over with the more expensive paper before Higgins entered in the morning."

We found afterwards, however, that he had actually fastened the thick sheets of gold to the wall with carpet tacks.

His lordship netted a trifle over a hundred and twenty-three thousand pounds through my discovery, and I am pleased to pay tribute to the young man's generosity by saying that his voluntary settlement made my bank account swell stout as a City alderman.

The Avenging Chance

Anthony Berkeley

ROGER SHERINGHAM was inclined to think afterwards that the Poisoned Chocolates Case, as the papers called it, was perhaps the most perfectly planned murder he had ever encountered. The motive was so obvious, when you knew where to look for it – but you didn't know; the method was so significant when you had grasped its real essentials – but you didn't grasp them; the traces were so thinly covered, when you had realised what was covering them – but you didn't realise. But for a piece of the merest bad luck, which the murderer could not possibly have foreseen, the crime must have been added to the classical list of great mysteries.

This is the gist of the case, as Chief Inspector Moresby told it one evening to Roger in the latter's rooms in the Albany a week or so after it happened:

On Friday morning, the fifteenth of November, at half past ten in the morning, in accordance with his invariable custom, Sir William Anstruther walked into his club in Piccadilly, the very exclusive Rainbow Club, and asked for his letters. The porter handed him three and a small parcel. Sir William walked over to the fireplace in the big lounge hall to open them.

A few minutes later another member entered the club, a Mr. Graham Beresford. There were a letter and a couple of circulars for him, and he also strolled over to the fireplace, nodding to Sir William, but not speaking to him. The two men only knew each other very slightly, and had probably never exchanged more than a dozen words in all.

Having glanced through his letters, Sir William opened the parcel and, after a moment, snorted with disgust. Beresford looked at him, and with a grunt Sir William thrust out a letter which had been enclosed in the parcel. Concealing a smile (Sir William's ways were a matter of some amusement to his fellow members), Beresford read the letter. It was from a big firm of chocolate manufacturers, Mason & Sons, and set forth that they were putting on the market a new brand of liqueur-chocolates designed especially to appeal to men; would Sir William do them the honour of accepting the enclosed two-pound box and letting the firm have his candid opinion on them?

"Do they think I'm a blank chorus-girl?" fumed Sir William. "Write 'em testimonials about their blank chocolates, indeed! Blank 'em! I'll complain to the blank committee. That sort of blank thing can't blank well be allowed here."

"Well, it's an ill wind so far as I'm concerned," Beresford soothed him; "It's reminded me of something. My wife and I had a box at the Imperial last night. I bet her a box of chocolates to a hundred cigarettes that she wouldn't spot the villain by the end of the second act. She won. I must remember to get them. Have you seen it – *The Creaking Skull*? Not a bad show."

Sir William had not seen it, and said so with force.

"Want a box of chocolates, did you say?" he added, more mildly. "Well, take this blank one. I don't want it."

For a moment Beresford demurred politely and then, most unfortunately for himself, accepted. The money so saved meant nothing to him for he was a wealthy man; but trouble was always worth saving.

By an extraordinarily lucky chance neither the outer wrapper of the box nor its covering letter were thrown into the fire, and this was the more fortunate in that both men had tossed the envelopes of their letters into the flames. Sir William did, indeed, make a bundle of the wrapper, letter and string, but he handed it over to Beresford, and the latter simply dropped it inside the fender. This bundle the porter subsequently extracted and, being a man of orderly habits, put it tidily away in the waste-paper basket, whence it was retrieved later by the police.

Of the three unconscious protagonists in the impending tragedy, Sir William was without doubt the most remarkable. Still a year or two under fifty, he looked, with his flaming red face and thick-set figure, a typical country squire of the old school, and both his manners and his language were in accordance with tradition. His habits, especially as regards women, were also in accordance with tradition – the tradition of the bold, bad baronet which he undoubtedly was.

In comparison with him, Beresford was rather an ordinary man, a tall, dark, not unhandsome fellow of two-and-thirty, quiet and reserved. His father had left him a rich man, but idleness did not appeal to him, and he had a finger in a good many business pies.

Money attracts money. Graham Beresford had inherited it, he made it, and, inevitably, he had married it, too. The daughter of a late shipowner in Liverpool, with not far off half a million in her own right. But the money was incidental, for he needed her and would have married her just as inevitably (said his friends) if she had not had a farthing. A tall, rather serious-minded, highly cultured girl, not so young that her character had not had time to form (she was twenty-five when Beresford married her, three years ago), she was the ideal wife for him. A bit of a Puritan perhaps in some ways, but Beresford, whose wild oats, though duly sown, had been a sparse crop, was ready enough to be a Puritan himself by that time if she was. To make no bones about it, the Beresfords succeeded in achieving that eighth wonder of the modern world, a happy marriage.

And into the middle of it there dropped with irretrievable tragedy, the box of chocolates.

Beresford gave them to her after lunch as they sat over their coffee, with some jesting remark about paying his honourable debts, and she opened the box at once. The top layer, she noticed, seemed to consist only of kirsch and maraschino. Beresford, who did not believe in spoiling good coffee, refused when she offered him the box, and his wife ate the first one alone. As she did so she exclaimed in surprise that the filling seemed exceedingly strong and positively burnt her mouth.

Beresford explained that they were samples of a new brand and then, made curious by what his wife had said, took one too. A burning taste, not intolerable but much too strong to be pleasant, followed the release of the liquid, and the almond flavouring seemed quite excessive.

"By Jove," he said, "they are strong. They must be filled with neat alcohol."

"Oh, they wouldn't do that, surely," said his wife, taking another. "But they are very strong. I think I rather like them, though."

Beresford ate another, and disliked it still more. "I don't," he said with decision. "They make my tongue feel quite numb. I shouldn't eat any more of them if I were you, I think there's something wrong with them."

"Well, they're only an experiment, I suppose," she said. "But they do burn. I'm not sure whether I like them or not."

A few minutes later Beresford went out to keep a business appointment in the City. He left her still trying to make up her mind whether she liked them, and still eating them to decide. Beresford remembered that scrap of conversation afterwards very vividly, because it was the last time he saw his wife alive.

That was roughly half past two. At a quarter to four Beresford arrived at his club from the City in a taxi, in a state of collapse. He was helped into the building by the driver and the porter, and both described him subsequently as pale to the point of ghastliness, with staring eyes and livid lips, and his skin damp and clammy. His mind seemed unaffected, however, and when they had got him up the steps he was able to walk, with the porter's help, into the lounge.

The porter, thoroughly alarmed, wanted to send for a doctor at once, but Beresford, who was the last man in the world to make a fuss, refused to let him, saying that it must be indigestion and he would be all right in a few minutes. To Sir William Anstruther, however, who was in the lounge at the time, he added after the porter had gone:

"Yes, and I believe it was those infernal chocolates you gave me, now I come to think of it. I thought there was something funny about them at the time. I'd better go and find out if my wife—". He broke off abruptly. His body, which had been leaning back limply in his chair, suddenly heaved rigidly upright; his jaws locked together, the livid lips drawn back in a horrible grin, and his hands clenched on the arms of his chair. At the same time Sir William became aware of an unmistakable smell of bitter almonds.

Thoroughly alarmed, believing indeed that the man was dying under his eyes, Sir William raised a shout for the porter and a doctor. The other occupants of the lounge hurried up, and between them they got the convulsed body of the unconscious man into a more comfortable position. Before the doctor could arrive a telephone message was received at the club from an agitated butler asking if Mr. Beresford was there, and if so would he come home at once as Mrs. Beresford had been taken seriously ill. As a matter of fact she was already dead.

Beresford did not die. He had taken less of the poison than his wife, who after his departure must have eaten at least three more of the chocolates, so that its action was less rapid and the doctor had time to save him. As a matter of fact it turned out afterwards that he had not had a fatal dose. By about eight o'clock that night he was conscious; the next day he was practically convalescent.

As for the unfortunate Mrs. Beresford, the doctor had arrived too late to save her, and she passed away very rapidly in a deep coma.

The police had taken the matter in hand as soon as Mrs. Beresford's death was reported to them and the fact of poison established, and it was only a very short time before things had become narrowed down to the chocolates as the active agent.

Sir William was interrogated, the letter and wrapper were recovered from the waste-paper basket, and, even before the sick man was out of danger, a detective inspector was asking for an interview with the managing director of Mason & Sons. Scotland Yard moves quickly.

It was the police theory at this stage, based on what Sir William and the two doctors had been able to tell them, that by an act of criminal carelessness on the part of one of Mason's employees, an excessive amount of oil of bitter almonds had been included in the filling mixture of the chocolates, for that was what the doctors had decided must be the poisoning ingredient. However, the managing director quashed this idea at once: oil of bitter almonds, he asserted, was never used by Mason's.

He had more interesting news still. Having read with undisguised astonishment the covering letter, he at once declared that it was a forgery. No such letter, no such samples had been sent out by the firm at all; a new variety of liqueur chocolates had never been mooted. The fatal chocolates were their ordinary brand.

Unwrapping and examining one more closely, he called the inspector's attention to a mark on the underside, which he suggested was the remains of a small hole drilled in the case, through which the liquid could have been extracted and the fatal filling inserted, the hole afterwards being stopped up with softened chocolate, a perfectly simple operation,

He examined it under a magnifying-glass and the inspector agreed. It was now clear to him that somebody had been trying deliberately to murder Sir William Anstruther.

Scotland Yard doubled its activities. The chocolates were sent for analysis, Sir William was interviewed again, and so was the now conscious Beresford. From the latter the doctor insisted that the news of his wife's death must be kept till the next day, as in his weakened condition the shock might be fatal, so that nothing very helpful was obtained from him.

Nor could Sir William throw any light on the mystery or produce a single person who might have any grounds for trying to kill him. He was living apart from his wife, who was the principal beneficiary in his will, but she was in the South of France, as the French police subsequently confirmed. His estate in Worcestershire, heavily mortgaged, was entailed and went to a nephew; but as the rent he got for it barely covered the interest on the mortgage, and the nephew was considerably better off than Sir William himself, there was no motive there. The police were at a dead end.

The analysis brought one or two interesting facts to light. Not oil of bitter almonds but nitrobenzine, a kindred substance, chiefly used in the manufacture of aniline dyes, was the somewhat surprising poison employed. Each chocolate in the upper layer contained exactly six minims of it, in a mixture of kirsch and maraschino. The chocolates in the other layers were harmless.

As to the other clues, they seemed equally useless. The sheet of Mason's notepaper was identified by Merton's, the printers, as of their work, but there was nothing to show how it had got into the murderer's possession. All that could be said was that, the edges being distinctly yellowed, it must be an old piece. The machine on which the letter had been typed, of course, could not be traced. From the wrapper, a piece of ordinary brown paper with Sir William's address hand-printed on it in large capitals, there was nothing to be learnt at all beyond that the parcel had been posted at the office in Southampton Street between the hours of 8:30 and 9:30 on the previous evening.

Only one thing was quite clear. Whoever had coveted Sir William's life had no intention of paying for it with his or her own.

"And now you know as much as we do, Mr. Sheringham," concluded Chief Inspector Moresby, "and if you can say who sent those chocolates to Sir William, you'll know a good deal more."

Roger nodded thoughtfully.

"It's a brute of a case. I met a man only yesterday who was at school with Beresford. He didn't know him very well because Beresford was on the modern side and my friend was a classical bird, but they were in the same house. He says Beresford's absolutely knocked over by his wife's death. I wish you could find out who sent those chocolates, Moresby."

"So do I, Mr. Sheringham," said Moresby gloomily.

"It might have been anyone in the whole world," Roger mused. "What about feminine jealousy, for instance? Sir William's private life doesn't seem to be immaculate. I dare say there's a good deal of off with the old light-o'-love and on with the new."

"Why, that's just what I've been looking into, Mr. Sheringham, sir," retorted Chief Inspector Moresby reproachfully. "That was the first thing that came to me. Because if anything does stand out about this business it is that it's a woman's crime. Nobody but a woman would send poisoned chocolates to a man. Another man would send a poisoned sample of whisky, or something like that."

"That's a very sound point, Moresby," Roger meditated. "Very sound indeed. And Sir William couldn't help you?"

"Couldn't," said Moresby, not without a trace of resentment, "or wouldn't. I was inclined to believe at first that he might have his suspicions and was shielding some woman. But I don't think so now."

"Humph!" Roger did not seem quite so sure. "It's reminiscent, this case, isn't it? Didn't some lunatic once send poisoned chocolates to the Commissioner of Police himself? A good crime always gets imitated, as you know."

Moresby brightened.

"It's funny you should say that, Mr. Sheringham, because that's the very conclusion I've come to. I've tested every other theory, and so far as I know there's not a soul with an interest in Sir WIlliam's death, whether from motives of gain, revenge, or what you like, whom I haven't had to rule quite out of it. In fact, I've pretty well made up my mind that the person who sent those chocolates was some irresponsible lunatic of a woman, a social or religious fanatic who's probably never even seen him. And if that's the case," Moresby sighed, "a fat chance I have of ever laying hands on her."

"Unless Chance steps in, as it so often does," said Roger brightly, "and helps you. A tremendous lot of cases get solved by a stroke of sheer luck, don't they? *Chance the Avenger*. It would make an excellent film title. But there's a lot of truth in it. If I were superstitious, which I'm not, I should say it wasn't chance at all, but Providence avenging the victim."

"Well, Mr. Sheringham," said Moresby, who was not superstitious either, "to tell the truth, I don't mind what it is, so long as it lets me get my hands on the right person."

If Moresby had paid his visit to Roger Sheringham with any hope of tapping that gentleman's brains, he went away disappointed.

To tell the truth, Roger was inclined to agree with the chief inspector's conclusion, that the attempt on the life of Sir William Anstruther and the actual murder of the unfortunate Mrs. Beresford must be the work of some unknown criminal lunatic. For this reason, although he thought about it a good deal during the next few days, he made no attempt to take the case in hand. It was the sort of affair, necessitating endless inquiries that a private person would have neither the time nor the authority to carry out, which can be handled only by the official police. Roger's interest in it was purely academic.

It was hazard, a chance encounter nearly a week later, which translated this interest from the academic into the personal.

Roger was in Bond Street, about to go through the distressing ordeal of buying a new hat. Along the pavement he suddenly saw bearing down on him Mrs. Verreker-le-Flemming. Mrs. Verreker-le-Flemming was small, exquisite, rich, and a widow, and she sat at Roger's feet whenever he gave her the opportunity. But she talked. She talked, in fact, and talked and talked. And Roger, who rather liked talking himself, could not bear it. He tried to dart across the road, but there was no opening in the traffic stream. He was cornered.

Mrs. Verreker-le-Flemming fastened on him gladly.

"Oh, Mr. Sheringham! *Just* the person I wanted to see. Mr. Sheringham, *do* tell me. In confidence. *Are* you taking up this dreadful business of poor Joan Beresford's death?"

Roger, the frozen and imbecile grin of civilised intercourse on his face, tried to get a word in; without result.

"I was horrified when I heard of it – simply horrified. You see, Joan and I were such *very* close friends. Quite intimate. And the awful thing, the truly *terrible* thing is that Joan brought the whole business on herself. Isn't that *appalling*?"

Roger no longer wanted to escape.

"What did you say?" he managed to insert incredulously.

"I suppose it's what they call tragic irony," Mrs. Verreker-le-Flemming chattered on. "Certainly it was tragic enough, and I've never heard anything so terribly ironical. You know about that bet she made with her husband, of course, so that he had to get her a box of chocolates, and if he hadn't Sir William would never have given him the poisoned ones and he'd have eaten them and died himself and good riddance? Well, Mr. Sheringham—" Mrs. Verreker-le-Flemming lowered her voice to a conspirator's whisper and glanced about her in the approved manner. "I've never told anybody else this, but I'm telling you because I know you'll appreciate it. *Joan wasn't playing fair!*"

"How do you mean?" Roger asked, bewildered.

Mrs. Verreker-le-Flemming was artlessly pleased with her sensation.

"Why, she'd seen the play before. We went together, the very first week it was on. She *knew* who the villain was all the time."

"By Jove!" Roger was as impressed as Mrs. Verreker-le-Flemming could have wished. "Chance the Avenger! We're none of us immune from it."

"Poetic justice, you mean?" twittered Mrs. Verreker-le-Flemming, to whom these remarks had been somewhat obscure. "Yes, but Joan Beresford of all people! That's the extraordinary thing. I should never have thought Joan *would* do a thing like that. She was such a *nice* girl. A little close with money, of course, considering how well-off they are, but that isn't anything. Of course it was only fun, and pulling her husband's leg, but I always used to think Joan was such a *serious* girl, Mr. Sheringham. I mean, ordinary people don't talk about honour and truth, and playing the game, and all those things one takes for granted. But Joan did. She was always saying that this wasn't honourable, or that wouldn't be playing the game. Well, she paid herself for not playing the game, poor girl, didn't she? Still, it all goes to show the truth of the old saying, doesn't it?"

"What old saying?" said Roger, hypnotised by this flow.

"Why, that still waters run deep. Joan must have been deep, I'm afraid." Mrs. Verreker-le-Flemming sighed. It was evidently a social error to be deep. "I mean, she certainly took me in. She can't have been quite so honourable and truthful as she was always pretending, can she? And I can't help wondering whether a girl who'd deceived her husband in a little thing like that might not – oh, well, I don't want to say anything against poor Joan now she's dead, poor darling, but she can't have been *quite* such a plaster saint after all, can she? I mean," said Mrs. Verreker-le-Flemming, in hasty extenuation of these suggestions, "I do think psychology is so very interesting, don't you, Mr. Sheringham?"

"Sometimes, very," Roger agreed gravely. "But you mentioned Sir William Anstruther just now. Do you know him, too?"

"I used to," Mrs. Verreker-le-Flemming replied, without particular interest. "Horrible man! Always running after some woman or other. And when he's tired of her, just drops her – biff! – like that. At least," added Mrs. Verreker-le-Flemming somewhat hastily, "so I've heard."

"And what happens if she refuses to be dropped?"

"Oh dear, I'm sure I don't know. I suppose you've heard the latest?"

Mrs. Verreker-le-Flemming hurried on, perhaps a trifle more pink than the delicate aids to nature on her cheeks would have warranted.

"He's taken up with that Bryce woman now. You know, the wife of the oil man, or petrol, or whatever he made his money in. It began about three weeks ago. You'd have thought that dreadful business of being responsible, in a way, for poor Joan Beresford's death would have sobered him up a little, wouldn't you? But not a bit of it; he—"

Roger was following another line of thought.

"What a pity you weren't at the Imperial with the Beresfords that evening. She'd never have made that bet if you had been." Roger looked extremely innocent. "You weren't, I suppose?"

"I?" queried Mrs. Verreker-le-Flemming in surprise, "Good gracious, no. I was at the new revue at the Pavilion. Lady Gavelstroke had a box and asked me to join her party."

"Oh, yes. Good show, isn't it? I thought that sketch *The Sempiternal Triangle* very clever. Didn't you?"

"*The Sempiternal Triangle?*" wavered Mrs. Verreker-le-Flemming.

"Yes, in the first half."

"Oh! Then I didn't see it. I got there disgracefully late, I'm afraid. But then," said Mrs. Verreker-le-Flemming with pathos, "I always do seem to be late for simply everything."

Roger kept the rest of the conversation resolutely upon theatres. But before he left her he had ascertained that she had photographs of both Mrs. Beresford and Sir William Anstruther and had obtained permission to borrow them some time. As soon as she was out of view he hailed a taxi and gave Mrs. Verreker-le-Flemming's address. He thought it better to take advantage of her permission at a time when he would not have to pay for it a second time over.

The parlour maid seemed to think there was nothing odd in his mission, and took him up to the drawing room at once. A corner of the room was devoted to the silver-framed photographs of Mrs. Verreker-le-Flemming's friends, and there were many of them. Roger examined them with interest, and finally took away with him not two photographs but six, those of Sir William, Mrs. Beresford, Beresford, two strange males who appeared to belong to the Sir William period, and, lastly, a likeness of Mrs. Verreker-le-Flemming herself. Roger liked confusing his trail.

For the rest of the day he was very busy.

His activities would have no doubt seemed to Mrs. Verrekeer-le-Flemming not merely baffling but pointless. He paid a visit to a public library, for instance, and consulted a work of reference, after which he took a taxi and drove to the offices of the Anglo-Eastern Perfumery Company, where he inquired for a certain Mr. Joseph Lea Hardwick and seemed much put out on hearing that no such gentleman was known to the firm and was certainly not employed in any of their branches. Many questions had to be put about the firm and its branches before he consented to abandon the quest.

After that he drove to Messrs Weall and Wilson, the well-known institution which protects the trade interests of individuals and advises its subscribers regarding investments. Here he entered his name as a subscriber, and explaining that he had a large sum of money to invest, filled in one of the special inquiry forms which are headed Strictly Confidential.

Then he went to the Rainbow Club, in Piccadilly.

Introducing himself to the porter without a blush as connected with Scotland Yard, he asked the man a number of questions, more or less trivial, concerning the tragedy.

"Sir William, I understand," he said finally, as if by the way, "did not dine here the evening before?"

There it appeared that Roger was wrong. Sir William had dined in the club, as he did about three times a week.

"But I quite understood he wasn't here that evening?" Roger said plaintively.

The porter was emphatic. He remembered quite well. So did a waiter, whom the porter summoned to corroborate him. Sir William had dined, rather late, and had not left the dining room till about nine o'clock. He spent the evening there, too, the waiter knew, or at least some of it, for he himself had taken him a whisky-and-soda in the lounge not less than half an hour later.

Roger retired.

He retired to Merton's, in a taxi.

It seemed that he wanted some new notepaper printed, of a very special kind, and to the young woman behind the counter he specified at great length and in wearisome detail exactly what he did want. The young woman handed him the books of specimen pieces and asked him to see if there was any style there which would suit him. Roger glanced through them, remarking garrulously to the young woman that he had been recommended to Merton's by a very dear friend, whose photograph he happened to have on him at that moment. Wasn't that a curious coincidence? The young woman agreed that it was.

"About a fortnight ago, I think, my friend was in here last," said Roger, producing the photograph. "Recognise this?"

The young woman took the photograph, without apparent interest.

"Oh, yes. I remember. About some notepaper, too, wasn't it? So that's your friend. Well, it's a small world. Now this is a line we're selling a good deal of just now."

Roger went back to his rooms to dine. Afterwards, feeling restless, he wandered out of the Albany and turned up Piccadilly. He wandered round the Circus, thinking hard, and paused for a moment out of habit to inspect the photographs of the new revue hung outside the Pavilion. The next thing he realised was that he had got as far as Jermyn Street and was standing outside the Imperial Theatre. Glancing at the advertisements of *The Creaking Skull*, he saw that it began at half past eight. Glancing at his watch, he saw that the time was twenty-nine minutes past that hour. He had an evening to get through somehow. He went inside.

The next morning, very early for Roger, he called on Moresby at Scotland yard.

"Moresby," he said without preamble, "I want you to do something for me. Can you find me a taximan who took a fare from Piccadilly Circus or its neighbourhood at about ten past nine on the evening before the Beresford crime, to the Strand somewhere near the bottom of Southampton Street, and another who took a fare back between those points. I'm not sure about the first. Or one taxi might have been used for the double journey, but I doubt that. Anyhow, try to find out for me, will you?"

"What are you up to now, Mr. Sheringham?" Moresby asked suspiciously.

"Breaking down an interesting alibi," replied Roger serenely. "By the way, I know who sent those chocolates to Sir William. I'm just building up a nice structure of evidence for you. Ring up my rooms when you've got those taximen."

He strolled out, leaving Moresby positively gaping after him.

The rest of the day he spent apparently trying to buy a second-hand typewriter. He was very particular that it should be a Hamilton No. 4. When the shop-people tried to induce him to consider other makes he refused to look at them, saying that he had had the Hamilton No. 4 so strongly recommended to him by a friend, who had bought one about three weeks ago. Perhaps it was at this very shop? No? They hadn't sold a Hamilton No. 4 for the last three months? How odd.

But at one shop they had sold a Hamilton No. 4 within the last month, and that was odder still.

At half past four Roger got back to his rooms to await the telephone message from Moresby. At half past five it came.

"There are fourteen taxi drivers here, littering up my office," said Moresby offensively. "What do you want me to do with 'em?"

"Keep them till I come, Chief Inspector," returned Roger with dignity.

The interview with the fourteen was brief enough, however. To each man in turn Roger showed a photograph, holding it so that Moresby could not see it, and asked if he could recognise his fare. The ninth man did so, without hesitation.

At a nod from Roger, Moresby dismissed them, then sat at his table and tried to look official. Roger seated himself on the table, looking most unofficial, and swung his legs. As he did so, a photograph fell unnoticed out of his pocket and fluttered, face downwards, under the table. Moresby eyed it but did not pick it up.

"And now, Mr. Sheringham, sir," he said, "perhaps you'll tell me what you've been doing?"

"Certainly, Moresby," said Roger blandly. "Your work for you. I really have solved the thing, you know. Here's your evidence." He took from his note-case an old letter and handed it to the Chief Inspector. "Was that typed on the same machine as the forged letter from Mason's, or was it not?"

Moresby studied it for a moment, then drew the forged letter from a drawer of his table and compared the two minutely.

"Mr. Sheringham," he said soberly, "where did you get hold of this?"

"In a second-hand typewriter shop in St Martin's Lane. The machine was sold to an unknown customer about a month ago. They identified the customer from that same photograph. As it happened, this machine had been used for a time in the office after it was repaired, to see that it was OK, and I easily got hold of that specimen of its work."

"And where is the machine now?"

"Oh, at the bottom of the Thames, I expect," Roger smiled. "I tell you, this criminal takes no unnecessary chances. But that doesn't matter. There's your evidence."

"Humph! It's all right so far as it goes," conceded Moresby. "but what about Mason's paper?"

"That," said Roger calmly, "was extracted from Merton's book of sample notepapers, as I'd guessed from the very yellowed edges might be the case. I can prove contact of the criminal with the book, and there is a page which will certainly turn out to have been filled by that piece of paper."

"That's fine," Moresby said more heartily.

"As for that taximan, the criminal had an alibi. You've heard it broken down. Between ten past nine and twenty-five past, in fact during the time when the parcel must have been posted, the murderer took a hurried journey to that neighbourhood, going probably by bus or Underground, but returning as I expected, by taxi, because time would be getting short."

"And the murderer, Mr. Sheringham?"

"The person whose photograph is in my pocket," Roger said unkindly. "By the way, do you remember what I was saying the other day about Chance the Avenger, my excellent film title? Well, it's worked again. By a chance meeting in Bond Street with a silly woman I was put, by the merest accident, in possession of a piece of information which showed me then and there who had sent those chocolates addressed to Sir William. There were other possibilities, of course, and I tested them, but then and there on the pavement I saw the whole thing, from first to last."

"Who was the murderer, then, Mr. Sheringham?" repeated Moresby.

"It was so beautifully planned," Roger went on dreamily. "We never grasped for one moment that we were making the fundamental mistake that the murderer all along intended us to make."

"And what was that?" asked Moresby.

"Why, that the plan had miscarried. That the wrong person had been killed. That was just the beauty of it. The plan had *not* miscarried. It had been brilliantly successful. The wrong person was *not* killed. Very much the right person was."

Moresby gasped.

"Why, how on earth do you make that out, sir?"

"Mrs. Beresford was the objective all the time. That's why the plot was so ingenious. Everything was anticipated. It was perfectly natural that Sir William should hand the chocolates over to Beresford. It was foreseen that we should look for the criminal among Sir William's associates and not the dead woman's. It was probably even foreseen that the crime would be considered the work of a woman!"

Moresby, unable to wait any longer, snatched up the photograph.

"Good heavens! But Mr. Sheringham, you don't mean to tell me that…Sir William himself!"

"He wanted to get rid of Mrs. Beresford," Roger continued. "He had liked her well enough at the beginning, no doubt, though it was her money he was after all the time.

"But the real trouble was that she was too close with her money. He wanted it, pretty badly; and she wouldn't part. There's no doubt about the motive. I made a list of the firms he's interested in and got a report on them. They're all rocky, every one. He'd got through all his own money, and he had to get more.

"As for the nitrobenzine which puzzled us so much, that was simple enough. I looked it up and found that beside the uses you told me, it's used largely in perfumery. And he's got a perfumery business. The Anglo-Eastern Perfumery Company. That's how he'd know about it being poisonous, of course. But I shouldn't think he got his supply from there. He'd be cleverer than that. He probably made the stuff himself. And schoolboys know how to treat benzol with nitric acid to get nitrobenzine."

"But," stammered Moresby, "but Sir William…He was at Eton."

"Sir William?" said Roger sharply. "Who's talking about Sir William? I told you the photograph of the murderer was in my pocket." He whipped out the photograph in question and confronted the astounded Chief Inspector with it. "Beresford, man! Beresford's the murderer of his own wife.

"Beresford, who still had hankerings after a gay life," he went on more mildly, "didn't want his wife but did want her money. He contrived this plot, providing as he thought against every contingency that could possibly arise. He established a mild alibi, if suspicion ever should arise, by taking his wife to the Imperial, and slipped out of the theatre at the first interval. (I sat through the first act of the dreadful thing myself last night to see when the interval came.) Then he hurried down to the Strand, posted his parcel, and took a taxi back. He had ten minutes, but nobody would notice if he got back to the box a minute late.

"And the rest simply followed. He knew Sir William came to the club every morning at ten-thirty, as regularly as clockwork; he knew that for a psychological certainty he could get the chocolates handed over to him if he hinted for them; he knew that the police would go chasing after all sorts of false trails starting from Sir William. And as for the wrapper and the forged letter he carefully didn't destroy them because they were calculated not only to divert suspicion but actually to point away from him to some anonymous lunatic."

"Well, it's very smart of you, Mr. Sheringham," Moresby said, with a little sigh, but quite ungrudgingly. "Very smart indeed. What was it the lady told you that showed you the whole thing in a flash?"

"Why, it wasn't so much what she actually told me as what I heard between her words, so to speak. What she told me was that Mrs. Beresford knew the answer to that bet; what I deduced was that, being the sort of person she was, it was quite incredible that she should have made a bet to which she knew the answer. *Ergo*, she didn't. *Ergo*, there never was such a bet. *Ergo*, Beresford was lying. *Ergo*, Beresford wanted to get hold of those chocolates for some reason other than he stated. After all, we only had Beresford's word for the bet, hadn't we?

"Of course he wouldn't have left her that afternoon till he'd seen her take, or somehow made her take, at least six of the chocolates, more than a lethal dose. And so that he could take a couple himself, of course. A clever stroke, that."

Moresby rose to his feet.

"Well, Mr. Sheringham, I'm much obliged to you, sir. And now I shall have to get busy myself." He scratched his head. "Chance the Avenger, eh? Well, I can tell you one pretty big thing Beresford left to Chance the Avenger, Mr. Sheringham. Suppose Sir William hadn't handed over the chocolates after all? Supposing he'd kept 'em, to give to one of his own ladies?"

Roger positively snorted. He felt a personal pride in Beresford by this time.

"Really, Moresby! It wouldn't have had any serious results if Sir William had. Do give my man credit for being what he is. You don't imagine he sent the poisoned ones to Sir William, do you? Of course not! He'd send harmless ones, and exchange them for the others on his way home. Dash it all, he wouldn't go right out of his way to present opportunities to Chance."

"If," added Roger, "Chance really is the right word."

Murder by Proxy

Matthias McDonnell Bodkin

AT TWO O'CLOCK precisely on that sweltering 12th of August, Eric Neville, young, handsome, *débonnaire*, sauntered through the glass door down the wrought-iron staircase into the beautiful, old-fashioned garden of Berkly Manor, radiant in white flannel, with a broad-brimmed Panama hat perched lightly on his glossy black curls, for he had just come from lazing in his canoe along the shadiest stretches of the river, with a book for company.

The back of the Manor House was the south wall of the garden, which stretched away for nearly a mile, gay with blooming flowers and ripening fruit. The air, heavy with perfume, stole softly through all the windows, now standing wide open in the sunshine, as though the great house gasped for breath.

When Eric's trim, tan boot left the last step of the iron staircase it reached the broad gravelled walk of the garden. Fifty yards off the head gardener was tending his peaches, the smoke from his pipe hanging like a faint blue haze in the still air that seemed to quiver with the heat. Eric, as he reached him, held out a petitionary hand, too lazy to speak.

Without a word the gardener stretched for a huge peach that was striving to hide its red face from the sun under narrow ribbed leaves, plucked it as though he loved it, and put it softly in the young man's hand.

Eric stripped off the velvet coat, rose-coloured, green, and amber, till it hung round the fruit in tatters, and made his sharp, white teeth meet in the juicy flesh of the ripe peach.

Bang!

The sudden shock of sound close to their ears wrenched the nerves of the two men; one dropped his peach, and the other his pipe. Both stared about them in utter amazement.

"Look there, sir," whispered the gardener, pointing to a little cloud of smoke oozing lazily through a window almost directly over their head, while the pungent spice of gunpowder made itself felt in the hot air.

"My uncle's room," gasped Eric. "I left him only a moment ago fast asleep on the sofa."

He turned as he spoke, and ran like a deer along the garden walk, up the iron steps, and back through the glass door into the house, the old gardener following as swiftly as his rheumatism would allow.

Eric crossed the sitting room on which the glass door opened, went up the broad, carpeted staircase four steps at a time, turned sharply to the right down a broad corridor, and burst straight through the open door of his uncle's study.

Fast as he had come, there was another before him. A tall, strong figure, dressed in light tweed, was bending over the sofa where, a few minutes before, Eric had seen his uncle asleep.

Eric recognised the broad back and brown hair at once.

"John," he cried – "John, what is it?"

His cousin turned to him a handsome, manly face, ghastly pale now even to the lips.

"Eric, my boy," he answered falteringly, "this is too awful. Uncle has been murdered – shot stone dead."

"No, no; it cannot be. It's not five minutes since I saw him quietly sleeping," Eric began. Then his eyes fell on the still figure on the sofa, and he broke off abruptly.

Squire Neville lay with his face to the wall, only the outline of his strong, hard features visible. The charge of shot had entered at the base of the skull, the grey hair was all dabbled with blood, and the heavy, warm drops still fell slowly on to the carpet.

"But who can have—" Eric gasped out, almost speechless with horror.

"It must have been his own gun," his cousin answered. "It was lying there on the table, to the right, barrel still smoking, when I came in."

"It wasn't a suicide – was it?" asked Eric, in a frightened whisper.

"Quite impossible, I should say. You see where he is hit."

"But it was so sudden. I ran the moment I heard the shot, and you were before me. Did you see anyone?"

"Not a soul. The room was empty."

"But how could the murderer escape?"

"Perhaps he leapt through the window. It was open when I came in."

"He couldn't do that, Master John." It was the voice of the gardener at the door. "Me and Master Eric was right under the window the shot came."

"Then how in the devil's name did he disappear, Simpson?"

"It's not for me to say, sir."

John Neville searched the room with eager eyes. There was no cover in it for a cat. A bare, plain room, panelled with brown oak, on which hung some guns and fishing rods – old-fashioned for the most part, but of the finest workmanship and material. A small bookcase in the corner was the room's sole claim to be called 'a study'. The huge leather-covered sofa on which the corpse lay, a massive round table in the centre of the room, and a few heavy chairs completed the furniture. The dust lay thick on everything, the fierce sunshine streamed in a broad band across the room. The air was stifling with heat and the acrid smoke of gunpowder.

John Neville noticed how pale his young cousin was. He laid his hand on his shoulder with the protecting kindness of an elder brother.

"Come, Eric," he said softly, "we can do no good here."

"We had best look round first, hadn't we, for some clue?" asked Eric, and he stretched his hand towards the gun; but John stopped him.

"No, no," he cried hastily, "we must leave things just as we find them. I'll send a man to the village for Wardle and telegraph to London for a detective."

He drew his young cousin gently from the room, locked the door on the outside, and put the key in his pocket.

"Who shall I wire to?" John Neville called from his desk with pencil poised over the paper, to his cousin, who sat at the library table with his head buried in his hands. "It will need a sharp man – one who can give his whole time to it."

"I don't know anyone. Yes, I do. That fellow with the queer name that found the Duke of Southern's opal – Beck. That's it. Thornton Crescent, WC, will find him."

John Neville filled in the name and address to the telegram he had already written –

Come at once. Case of murder. Expense no object. John Neville, Berkly Manor, Dorset.

Little did Eric guess that the filling in of that name was to him a matter of life or death.

John Neville had picked up a timetable and rustled through the leaves. "Hard lines, Eric," he said; "do his best, he cannot get here before midnight. But here's Wardle already, anyhow; that's quick work."

A shrewd, silent man was Wardle, the local constable, who now came briskly up the broad avenue; strong and active too, though well over fifty years of age.

John Neville met him at the door with the news. But the groom had already told of the murder.

"You did the right thing to lock the door, sir," said Wardle, as they passed into the library where Eric still sat apparently unconscious of their presence, "and you wired for a right good man. I've worked with this here Mr. Beck before now. A pleasant spoken man and a lucky one. 'No hurry, Mr. Wardle,' he says to me, 'and no fuss. Stir nothing. The things about the corpse have always a story of their own if they are let tell it, and I always like to have the first quiet little chat with them myself.'"

So the constable held his tongue and kept his hands quiet and used his eyes and ears, while the great house buzzed with gossip. There was a whisper here and a whisper there, and the whispers patched themselves into a story. By slow degrees dark suspicion settled down and closed like a cloud round John Neville.

Its influence seemed to pass in some strange fashion through the closed doors of the library. John began pacing the room restlessly from end to end.

After a little while the big room was not big enough to hold his impatience. He wandered out aimlessly, as it seemed, from one room to another; now down the iron steps to gaze vacantly at the window of his uncle's room, now past the locked door in the broad corridor.

With an elaborate pretence of carelessness Wardle kept him in sight through all his wanderings, but John Neville seemed too self-absorbed to notice it.

Presently he returned to the library. Eric was there, still sitting with his back to the door, only the top of his head showing over the high chair. He seemed absorbed in thought or sleep, he sat so still.

But he started up with a quick cry, showing a white, frightened face, when John touched him lightly on the arm.

"Come for a walk in the grounds, Eric?" he said. "This waiting and watching and doing nothing is killing work; I cannot stand it much longer."

"I'd rather not, if you don't mind," Eric answered wearily; "I feel completely knocked over."

"A mouthful of fresh air would do you good, my poor boy, you do look done up."

Eric shook his head.

"Well, I'm off," John said.

"If you leave me the key, I will give it to the detective, if he comes."

"Oh, he cannot be here before midnight, and I'll be back in an hour."

As John Neville walked rapidly down the avenue without looking back, Wardle stepped quietly after, keeping him well in view.

Presently Neville turned abruptly in amongst the woods, the constable still following cautiously. The trees stood tall and well apart, and the slanting sunshine made lanes of vivid green through the shade. As Wardle crossed between Neville and the sun his shadow fell long and black on the bright green.

John Neville saw the shadow move in front of him and turned sharp round and faced his pursuer.

The constable stood stock still and stared.

"Well, Wardle, what is it? Don't stand there like a fool fingering your baton! Speak out, man – what do you want of me?"

"You see how it is, Master John," the constable stammered out, "I don't believe it myself. I've known you twenty-one years – since you were born, I may say – and I don't believe it, not a blessed word of it. But duty is duty, and I must go through with it; and facts is facts, and you and he had words last night, and Master Eric found you first in the room when—"

John Neville listened, bewildered at first. Then suddenly, as it seemed to dawn on him for the first time that he *could* be suspected of this murder, he kindled a sudden hot blaze of anger.

He turned fiercely on the constable. Broad-chested, strong-limbed, he towered over him, terrible in his wrath; his hands clenched, his muscles quivered, his strong white teeth shut tight as a rat-trap, and a reddish light shining at the back of his brown eyes.

"How dare you! How dare you!" he hissed out between his teeth, his passion choking him.

He looked dangerous, that roused young giant, but Wardle met his angry eyes without flinching.

"Where's the use, Master John?" he said soothingly. "It's mainly hard on you, I know. But the fault isn't mine, and you won't help yourself by taking it that way.

The gust of passion appeared to sweep by as suddenly as it arose. The handsome face cleared and there was no trace of anger in the frank voice that answered. "You are right, Wardle, quite right. What is to be done next? Am I to consider myself under arrest?"

"Better not, sir. You've got things to do a prisoner couldn't do, and I don't want to stand in the way of your doing them. If you give me your word it will be enough."

"My word for what?"

"That you'll be here when wanted."

"Why, man, you don't think I'd be fool enough – innocent or guilty – to run away. My God! Run away from a charge of murder!"

"Don't take on like that, sir. There's a man coming from London that will set things straight, you'll see. Have I your word?"

"You have my word."

"Perhaps you'd better be getting back to the house, sir. There's a deal of talking going on amongst the servants. I'll keep out of the way, and no one will be the wiser for anything that has passed between us."

Halfway up the avenue a fast-driven dog-cart overtook John Neville, and pulled up so sharply that the horse's hoofs sent the coarse gravel flying. A stout, thick-set man, who up to that had been in close chat with the driver, leapt out more lightly than could have been expected from his figure.

"Mr. John Neville, I presume? My name is Back – Mr. Paul Beck."

"Mr. Beck! Why, I thought you couldn't have got here before midnight."

"Special train," Mr. Beck answered pleasantly. "Your wire said 'Expense no object'. Well, time is an object, and comfort is an object too, more or less, in all these cases; so I took a special train, and here I am. With your permission, we will send the trap on and walk to the house together. This seems a bad business, Mr. Neville. Shot dead, the driver tells me. Anyone suspected?"

"I'm suspected." The answer broke from John Neville's lips almost fiercely.

Mr. Beck looked at him for a minute with placid curiosity, without a touch of surprise in it.

"How do you know that?"

"Wardle, the local constable, has just told me so to my face. It was only by way of a special favour he refrained from arresting me then and there."

Mr. Beck walked on beside John Neville ten or fifteen paces before he spoke again.

"Do you mind," he said, in a very insinuating voice, "telling me exactly why you are suspected?"

"Not in the very least."

"Mind this," the detective went on quickly, "I give you no caution and make you no pledge. It's my business to find out the truth. If you think the truth will help you, then you ought to help me. This is very irregular, of course, but I don't mind that. When a man is charged with a crime there is, you see, Mr. Neville, always one witness who knows whether he is guilty or not. There is very often only that one. The first thing the British law does by way of discovering the truth is to close the mouth of the only witness that knows it. Well, that's not my way. I like to give an innocent man a chance to tell his own story, and I've no scruple in trapping a guilty man if I can."

He looked John Neville straight in the eyes as he spoke.

The look was steadily returned. "I think I understand. What do you want to know? Where shall I begin?"

"At the beginning. What did you quarrel with your uncle about yesterday?"

John Neville hesitated for a moment, and Mr. Beck took a mental note of his hesitation.

"I didn't quarrel with him. He quarreled with me. It was this way: there was a bitter feud between my uncle and his neighbour, Colonel Peyton. The estates adjoin, and the quarrel was about some shooting. My uncle was very violent – he used to call Colonel Peyton 'a common poacher'. Well, I took no hand in the row. I was rather shy when I met the Colonel for the first time after it, for I knew my uncle had the wrong end of the stick. But the Colonel spoke to me in the kindest way. 'No reason why you and I should cease to be friends, John,' he said. This is a foolish business. I would give the best covert on my estate to be out of it. Men cannot fight duels in these days, and gentlemen cannot scold like fishwives. But I don't expect people will call me a coward because I hate a row.'

"'Not likely,' I said.

"The Colonel, you must know, had distinguished himself in a dozen engagements, and has the Victoria Cross locked up in a drawer of his desk. Lucy once showed it to me. Lucy is his only daughter and he is devoted to her. Well, after that, of course, the Colonel and I kept on good terms, for I liked him, and I liked going there and all that. But out friendship angered my uncle. I had been going to the Grange pretty often of late, and my uncle heard of it. He spoke to me in a very rough fashion of Colonel Peyton and his daughter at dinner last night, and I stood up for them.

"'By what right, you insolent puppy,' he shouted, 'Do you take this upstart's part against me?'

"'The Peytons are as good a family as our own, sir,' I said – that was true – 'and as for right, Miss Lucy Peyton has done me the honour of promising to be my wife.

"At that he exploded in a very tempest of rage. I cannot repeat his words about the Colonel and his daughter. Even now, though he lies dead yonder, I can hardly forgive them. He swore he would never see or speak to me again if I disgraced myself of such a marriage. 'I cannot break the entail,' he growled, 'worse luck. But I can make you a beggar while I live, and I shall live forty years to spite you. The poacher can have you a bargain for all I care. Go, sell yourself as dearly as you can, and live on your wife's fortune as soon as you please.'

"Then I lost my temper, and gave him a bit of my mind."

"Try and remember what you said; it's important."

"I told him that I cast his contempt back in his face; that I loved Lucy Peyton, and that I would live for her, and die for her, if need be."

"Did you say 'it was a comfort he could not live for ever'? You see the story of your quarrel has travelled far and near. The driver told me of it. Try and remember – did you say that?"

"I think I did. I'm sure I did now, but I was so furious I hardly knew what I said. I certainly never meant—"

"Who was in the room when you quarrelled?"

"Only cousin Eric and the butler."

"The butler, I suppose, spread the story?"

"I suppose so. I'm sure cousin Eric never did. He was as much pained at the scene as myself. He tried to interfere at the time, but his interference only made my uncle more furious."

"What was your allowance from your uncle?"

"A thousand a year."

"He had power to cut it off, I suppose?"

"Certainly."

"But he had no power over the estate. You were heir-apparent under the entail, and at the present moment you are owner of Berkly Manor?"

"That is so; but up to the moment you spoke I assure you I never even remembered—"

"Who comes next to you in the entail?"

"My first cousin, Eric. He is four years younger than I am."

"After him?"

"A distant cousin. I scarcely know him at all; but he has a bad reputation, and I know my uncle and he hated each other cordially."

"How did your uncle and your cousin Eric hit it off?"

"Not too well. He hated Eric's father – his own youngest brother – and he was sometimes rough on Eric. He used to abuse the dead father in the son's presence, calling him cruel and treacherous, and all that. Poor Eric had often a hard time of it. Uncle was liberal to him so far as money went – as liberal as he was to me – had him to live at the Manor and denied him nothing. But now and again he would sting the poor lad by a passionate curse or a bitter sneer. In spite of all, Eric seemed fond of him."

"To come now to the murder; you saw your uncle no more that night, I suppose?"

"I never saw him alive again."

"Do you know what he did next day?"

"Only by hearsay."

"Hearsay evidence is often first-class evidence, though the law doesn't think so. What did you hear?"

"My uncle was mad about shooting. Did I tell you his quarrel with Colonel Peyton was about the shooting? He had a grouse moor rented about twelve miles from here, and he never missed the first day. He was off at cock-shout with the head gamekeeper, Lennox. I was to have gone with him, but I didn't, of course. Contrary to his custom he came back about noon and went straight to his study. I was writing in my own room and heard his heavy step go past the door. Later on Eric found him asleep on the great leather couch in his study. Five minutes after Eric left I heard the shot and rushed into his room."

"Did you examine the room after you found the body?"

"No. Eric wanted to, but I thought it better not. I simply locked the door and put the key in my pocket till you came."

"Could it have been suicide?"

"Impossible, I should say. He was shot through the back of the head."

"Had your uncle any enemies that you know of?"

"The poachers hated him. He was relentless with them. A fellow once shot at him, and my uncle shot back and shattered the man's leg. He had him sent to hospital first and cured, and then prosecuted him straight away, and got him two years."

"Then you think a poacher murdered him?" Mr. Beck said blandly.

"I don't well see how he could. I was in my own room on the same corridor. The only way to or from my uncle's room was past my door. I rushed out the instant I heard the shot, and saw no one."

"Perhaps the murderer leapt through the window?"

"Eric tells me that he and the gardener were in the garden almost under the window at the time."

"What's your theory, then, Mr. Neville?"

"I haven't got a theory."

"You parted with your uncle in anger last night?"

"That's so."

"Next day your uncle in shot, and you are found – I won't say caught – in his room the instant afterwards."

John Neville flushed crimson; but he held himself in and nodded without speaking.

The two walked on together in silence.

They were not a hundred yards from the great mansion – John Neville's house – standing high above the embowering trees in the glow of the twilight, when the detective spoke again.

"I'm bound to say, Mr. Neville, that things look very black against you, as they stand. I think that constable Wardle ought to have arrested you."

"It's not too late yet," John Neville answered shortly, "I see him there at the corner of the house and I'll tell him you said so."

He turned on his heel, when Mr. Beck called quickly after him: "What about that key?"

John Neville handed it to him without a word. The detective took it as silently and walked on to the entrance and up the great stone steps alone, whistling softly.

Eric welcomed him at the door, for the driver had told of his coming.

"You have had no dinner, Mr. Beck?" he asked courteously.

"Business first; pleasure afterwards. I had a snack in the train. Can I see the gamekeeper, Lennox, for five minutes alone?"

"Certainly. I'll send him to you in a moment here in the library."

Lennox, the gamekeeper, a long-limbed, high-shouldered, elderly man, shambled shyly into the room, consumed by nervousness in the presence of a London detective.

"Sit down, Lennox – sit down," said Mr. Beck kindly. The very sound of his voice, homely and good-natured, put the man at his ease. "Now, tell me, why did you come home so soon from the grouse this morning?"

"Well, you see, sit, it was this ways. We were two house hout when the Squire, 'e says to me, 'Lennox,' 'e says, 'I'm sick of this fooling. I'm going 'ome.'"

"No sport?"

"Birds wor as thick as blackberries, sir, and lay like larks."

"No sportsman, then?"

"Is it the Squire, sir?" cried Lennox, quite forgetting his shyness in his excitement at this slur on the Squire. "There wasn't a better sportsman in the county – no, nor as good. Real, old-fashioned style, 'e was. 'Hang your barnyard shooting,' 'e'd say when they'd ask him to go kill tame pheasants. 'E put up 'is own birds with 'is own dogs, 'e did. 'E'd as soon go shooting without a gun very near as without a dog any day. Aye and 'e stuck to 'is old Manton muszzle-loader to the last. ''Old it steady, Lennox,' 'e'd say to me oftentimes, 'and point it straight. It will hit harder and further than any of their telescopes, and it won't get marked with rust if you don't clean it every second shot.'

"'Easy to load, Squire,' the young men would say, cracking up their hammerless breech-loaders.

"'Aye,' he'd answer them back, 'and spoil your dog's work. What's the good of a dog learning to down shot, if you can drop in your cartridges as quick as a cock can pick corn?'

"A dead shot the Squire was, too, and no mistake, sir, if he wasn't flurried. Many a time I've seen him wipe the eyes of gents who thought no end of themselves with that same old muzzle-loader that shot himself in the long run. Many a time I seen—"

"Why did he turn his back on good sport yesterday?" asked Mr. Beck, cutting short his reminiscences.

"Well, you see, it was scorching hot for one thing, but that wasn't it, for the infernal fire would not stop the Squire if he was on for sport. But he was in a blazing temper all the morning, and temper tells more than most anything on a man's shooting. When Flora sprung a pack – she's a young dog, and the fault wasn't hers either – for she came down the wind on them – but the Squire had the gun to his shoulder to shoot her. Five minutes after she found another pack and set like a stone. They got up as big as haycocks and as lazy as crows, and he missed right and left – never touched a feather – a thing I haven't seen him do since I was a boy.

"'It's myself I should shoot, not the dog,' he growled and he flung me the gun to load. When I'd got the caps on and had shaken the powder into the nipples, he ripped out an oath that 'e'd have no more of it. 'E walked right across country to where the trap was. The birds got up under his feet, but divil a shot he'd fire, but drove straight 'ome.

"When we got to the 'ouse I wanted to take the gun and fire it off, or draw the charges. But 'e told me to go to ——, and carried it up loaded as it was to his study, where no one goes unless they're sent for special. It was better than an hour afterwards I heard the report of the Manton; I'd know it in a thousand. I ran for the study as fast as—"

Eric Neville broke suddenly into the room, flushed and excited.

"Mr. Beck," he cried, "a monstrous thing has happened. Wardle, the local constable, you know, has arrested my cousin on a charge of willful murder of my uncle."

Mr. Beck, with his eyes intent on the excited face, waved his big hand soothingly.

"Easy," he said, "take it easy, Mr. Neville. It's hurtful to your feelings, no doubt; but it cannot be helped. The constable has done no more than his duty. The evidence is very strong, as you know, and in such cases it's best for all parties to proceed regularly."

"You can go," he went on, speaking to Lennox, who stood dumbfounded at the news of John Neville's arrest, staring with eyes and mouth wide open.

Then turning again very quietly to Eric: "Now, Mr. Neville, I would like to see the room where the corpse is."

The perfect placidity of his manner had its effect upon the boy, for he was little more than a boy, calming his excitement as oil smooths troubled water.

"My cousin has the key," he said; "I will get it."

"There is no need," Mr. Beck called after him, for he was halfway out of the room on his errand: "I've got the key if you will be good enough to show me the room."

Mastering his surprise, Eric showed him upstairs, and along the corridor to the locked door. Half unconsciously, as it seemed, he was following the detective into the room, when Mr. Beck stopped him.

"I know you will kindly humour me, Mr. Neville," he said, "but I find that I can look closer and think clearer when I'm by myself. I'm not exactly shy you know, but it's a habit I've got."

He closed the door softly as he spoke, and locked it on the inside, leaving the key in the lock.

The mask of placidity fell from him the moment he found himself alone. His lips tightened, and his eyes sparkled, and his muscles seemed to grow rigid with excitement, like a sporting dog's when he is close upon the game.

One glance at the corpse showed him that it was not suicide. In this, at least, John Neville had spoken the truth.

The back of the head had literally been blown in by the charge of heavy shot at close quarters. The grey hair was clammy and matted, with little white angles of bone protruding. The dropping of the blood had made a black pool on the carpet, and the close air of the room was fetid with the smell of it.

The detective walked to the table where the gun, a handsome, old-fashioned muzzle-loader, lay, the muzzle still pointed at the corpse. But his attention was diverted by a water bottle, a great globe of clear glass quite full, and perched on a book a little distance form the gun, and between it and the window. He took it from the table and tested the water with the tip of his tongue. It had a curious, insipid, parboiled taste, but he detected no foreign flavour in it. Though the room was full of dust there was almost none on the cover of the book where the water bottle stood, and Mr. Beck noticed a gap in the third row of the bookcase where the book had been taken.

After a quick glance round the room Mr. Beck walked to the window. On a small table there he found a clear circle in the thick dust. He fitted the round bottom of the water bottle to this circle and it covered it exactly. While he stood by the window he caught sight of some small scraps of paper crumbled up and thrown into a corner. Picking them up and smoothing them out he found they were curiously drilled with little burnt holes.

Having examined the holes minutely with his magnifying glass, he slipped these scraps folded on each other into his waistcoat pocket.

From the window he went back to the gun. This time he examined it with the minutest care. The right barrel he found had been recently discharged, the left was still loaded. Then he made a startling discovery. *Both barrels were on half cock.* The little bright copper cap twinkled on the nipple of the left barrel, from the right nipple the cap was gone.

How had the murderer fired the right barrel without a cap? How and why did he find time in the midst of his deadly work to put the cock back to safety?

Had Mr. Beck solved this problem? The grim smile deepened on his lips as he looked, and there was an ugly light in his eyes that boded ill for the unknown assassin. Finally he carried the gun to the window and examined it carefully through a magnifying glass. There was a thin dark line, as if traced with the point of a red-hot needle, running a little way along the wood of the stock and ending in the right nipple.

Mr. Beck put the gun back quietly on the table. The whole investigation had not taken ten minutes. He gave one look at the still figure on the couch, unlocked the door, locking it after him, and walked out through the corridor, the same cheerful, imperturbable Mr. Beck that had walked into it ten minutes before.

He found Eric waiting for him at the head of the stairs. "Well?" he said when he saw the detective.

"Well," replied Mr. Beck, ignoring the interrogation in his voice, "when is the inquest to be? That's the next thing to be thought of; the sooner the better."

"Tomorrow, if you wish. My cousin John sent a messenger to Mr. Morgan, the coroner. He lives only five miles off, and he has promised to be here at twelve o'clock tomorrow. There will be no difficulty in getting a jury in the village."

"That's all right, that's all right," said Mr. Beck, rubbing his hands; "the sooner and the quieter we get those preliminaries over the better."

"I have just sent to engage the local solicitor on behalf of my cousin. He's not particularly bright, I'm afraid, but he's the best to be had on a short notice."

"Very proper and thoughtful on your part – very thoughtful indeed. But solicitors cannot do much in such cases. It's the evidence we have to go by, and the evidence is only too plain, I'm afraid. Now, if you please," he went on more briskly, dismissing the disagreeable subject, as it were, with a wave of his big hand, "I'd be very glad of that supper you spoke about."

Mr. Beck supped very heartily on a brace of grouse – the last of the dead man's shooting – and a bottle of ripe Burgundy. He was in high good-humour, and across 'the walnuts and the wine' he told Eric some startling episodes in his career, which seemed to divert the young fellow a little from his manifest grief for his uncle and anxiety for his cousin.

Meanwhile John Neville remained shut close in his own room, with the constable at the door.

The inquest was held at half past twelve next day in the library.

The Coroner, a large, red-faced man, with a very affable manner, had got to his work promptly.

The jury 'viewed the body' steadily, stolidly, with a kind of morose delectation in the grim spectacle.

In some unaccountable way Mr. Beck constituted himself a master of the ceremonies, a kind of assessor to the court.

"You had best take the gun down," he said to the Coroner as they were leaving the room.

"Certainly, certainly," replied the Coroner.

"And the water bottle," added Mr. Beck.

"There is no suspicion of poison, is there?"

"It's best not to take anything for granted," replied Mr. Beck sententiously.

"By all means if you think so," replied the obsequious Coroner. "Constable, take that water bottle down with you."

The large room was filled with people of the neighbourhood, mostly farmers from the Berkly estate and small shopkeepers form the neighbouring village.

A table had been wheeled to the top of the room for the Coroner, with a seat at it for the ubiquitous local newspaper correspondent. A double row of chairs were set at the right hand of the table for the jury.

The jury had just returned from viewing the body when the crunch of wheels and hoofs was heard on the gravel of the drive, and a two-horse phaeton pulled up sharp at the entrance.

A moment later there came into the room a handsome, soldier-like man, with a girl clinging to his arm, whom he supported with tender, protecting fondness that was very touching. The girl's face was pale, but wonderfully sweet and winsome; cheeks with the faint, pure flush of the wild rose, and eyes like a wild fawn's.

No need to tell Mr. Beck that here were Colonel Peyton and his daughter. He saw the look – shy, piteous, loving – that the girl gave John Neville, as she passed close to the table where he sat with his head buried in his hands; and the detective's face darkened for a moment with a stern purpose, but the next moment it resumed its customary look of good-nature and good-humour.

The gardener, the gamekeeper, and the butler were briefly examined by the Coroner, and rather clumsily cross-examined by Mr. Waggles, the solicitor whom Eric had thoughtfully secured for his cousin's defence.

As the case against John Neville gradually darkened into grim certainty, the girl in the far corner of the room grew white as a lily, and would have fallen but for her father's support.

"Does Mr. John Neville offer himself for examination?" said the Coroner, as he finished writing the last words of the butler's deposition describing the quarrel of the night before.

"No, sir," said Mr. Waggles. "I appear for Mr. John Neville, the accused, and we reserve our defence."

"I really have nothing to say that hasn't been already said," added John Neville quietly.

"Mr. Neville," said Mr. Waggles pompously, "I must ask you to leave yourself entirely in my hands."

"Eric Neville!" called out the Coroner. "This is the last witness, I think."

Eric stepped in front of the table and took the Bible in his hand. He was pale, but quiet and composed, and there was an unaffected grief in the look of his dark eyes and in the tone of his soft voice that touched every heart – except one.

He told his story shortly and clearly. It was quite plain that he was most anxious to shield his cousin. But in spite of this, perhaps because of this, the evidence went horribly against John Neville.

The answers to questions criminating his cousin had to be literally dragged from him by the Coroner.

With manifest reluctance he described the quarrel at dinner the night before.

"Was your cousin very angry?" the Coroner asked.

"He would not be human if he were not angry at the language used."

"What did he say?"

"I cannot remember all he said."

"Did he say to your uncle: 'Well, you will not live forever'?"

No answer.

"Come, Mr. Neville, remember you are sworn to tell the truth."

In an almost inaudible whisper came the words: "He did."

"I'm sorry to pain you, but I must do my duty. When you heard the shot you ran straight to your uncle's room, about fifty yards, I believe?"

"About that."

"Whom did you find there bending over the dead man?"

"My cousin. I am bound to say he appeared in the deepest grief."

"But you saw no one else?"

"No."

"Your cousin is, I believe, the heir to Squire Neville's property; the owner I should say now?"

"I believe so."

"That will do; you can stand down."

This interchange of question and answer, each one of which seemed to fit the rope tighter and tighter round John Neville's neck, was listened to with hushed eagerness by the room full of people.

There was a long, deep drawing-in of breath when it ended. The suspense seemed over, but not the excitement.

Mr. Beck rose as Eric turned from the table, quite as a matter of course, to question him.

"You say you *believe* your cousin was your uncle's heir – don't you *know* it?"

Then Mr. Waggles found his voice.

"Really, sir," he broke out, addressing the Coroner, "I must protest. This is grossly irregular. This person is not a professional gentleman. He represents no one. He has no *locus standi* in court at all."

No one knew better than Mr. Beck that technically he had no title to open his lips; but his look of quiet assurance, his calm assumption of unmistakable right, carried the day with the Coroner.

"Mr. Beck," he said, "has, I understand, been brought down specially from London to take charge of this case, and I certainly shall not stop him in any question he may desire to ask."

"Thank you, sir," said Mr. Beck, in the tone of a man whose clear right has been allowed. Then again to the witness: "Didn't you know John Neville was next heir to Berkly Manor?"

"I know it, of course."

"And if John Neville is hanged you will be the owner?"

Everyone was startled at the frank brutality of the question so blandly asked. Mr. Waggles bobbed up and down excitedly; but Eric answered, calmly as ever—

"That's very coarsely and cruelly put."

"But it's true?"

"Yes, it's true."

"We will pass from that. When you came into the room after the murder, did you examine the gun?"

"I stretched out my hand to take it, but my cousin stopped me. I must be allowed to add that I believe he was actuated, as he did, by a desire to keep everything in the room untouched. He locked the door and carried off the key. I was not in the room afterwards."

"Did you look closely at the gun?"

"Not particularly."

"Did you notice that both barrels were at half cock?"

"No."

"Did you notice that there was no cap on the nipple of the right barrel that had just been fired?"

"Certainly not."

"That is to say you did not notice it?"

"Yes."

"Did you notice a little burnt line traced a short distance along the wood of the stock towards the right nipple?"

"No."

Mr. Beck put the gun into his hand.

"Look close. Do you notice it now?"

"I see it now for the first time."

"You cannot account for it, I suppose?"

"No."

"Sure?"

"Quite sure."

All present followed this strange, and apparently purposeless cross-examination with breathless interest, groping vainly for his meaning.

The answers were given calmly and clearly, but those that looked closely saw that Eric's nether lip quivered, and it was only by a strong effort of will that he held his calmness.

Through the blandness of Mr. Beck's voice and manner a subtle suggestion of hostility made itself felt, very trying to the nerves of the witness.

"We will pass from that," said Mr. Beck again. "When you went into your uncle's room before the shot why did you take a book from the shelf and put it on the table?"

"I really cannot remember anything about it."

"Why did you take the water bottle from the window and stand it on the book?"

"I wanted a drink."

"But there was none of the water drunk."

"Then I suppose it was to take it out of the strong sun."

"But you set it in the strong sun on the table?"

"Really I cannot remember those trivialities." His self-control was breaking down at last.

"Then we will pass from that," said Mr. Beck a third time.

He took the little scraps of paper with the burnt holes through them from his waistcoat pocket, and handed them to the witness.

"Do you know anything about these?"

There was a pause of a second. Eric's lips tightened as if with a sudden spasm of pain. But the answer came clearly enough—

"Nothing whatever."

"Do you ever amuse yourself with a burning glass?"

This seemingly simple question was snapped suddenly at the witness like a pistol-shot.

"Really, really," Mr. Waggles broke out, "this is mere trifling with the Court."

"That question does certainly seem a little irrelevant, Mr. Beck," mildly remonstrated the Coroner.

"Look at the witness, sir," retorted Mr. Beck sternly. "He does not think it irrelevant."

Every eye in court was turned on Eric's face and fixed there.

All colour had fled from his cheeks and lips; his mouth had fallen open, and he stared at Mr. Beck with eyes of abject terror.

Mr. Beck went on remorselessly: "Did you ever amuse yourself with a burning glass?"

No answer.

"Do you know that a water bottle like this makes a capital burning glass?"

Still no answer.

"Do you know that a burning glass has been used before now to touch off a cannon of fire from a gun?"

Then a voice broke from Eric at last, as it seemed in defiance of his will; a voice unlike his own – loud, harsh, hardly articulate; such a voice might have been heard in the torture chamber in the old days when the strain on the rack grew unbearable.

"You devilish bloodhound!" he shouted. "Curse you, curse you, you've caught me! I confess it – I was the murderer!" He fell on the ground in a fit.

"And you made the sun your accomplice!" remarked Mr. Beck, placid as ever.

The Case of the Disappearing Body

Daniel Brock

IN THE TIME *since I became acquainted with my friend Sherlock Holmes, I've found myself fortunate enough to accompany him on many adventures in which his vast knowledge and insight into the criminal mind were on full display. His skills in knowing the unknown still astound me after all these years. Alas, not all of our adventures have brought us the desired satisfaction of solving a mystery. There were some that took his logical mind to the brink.*

One case in particular has left me so scarred that I've only just now summoned the courage to transcribe it. It was a simple enough case upon the surface, but once we delved into its depths, we found something for which we were wholly unprepared. Until now, I feared placing the words to paper might in some way validate what I saw and what my friend and I know to be true. Nevertheless, I have taken the task of writing my account of those horrible events, not in hopes of placing a shadow over my friend's illustrious career, or even coming to terms with my own beliefs, but merely as a servant of the truth. Truth, after all, should always be known.

* * *

"When is the wedding?" Holmes asked. He was huddled this dreary morning in his armchair by the fire, fingering a brown leather case where I knew he kept a small vial of high-grade morphine and syringe. He'd yet to open it, but the multitude of fresh pinpricks along his forearm told me that was apt to change.

I lowered the letter from my face. "Marvelous. Are you sure you can't read minds?"

His gaze turned to me from the smoldering embers of the fire, "Positive. The mind is subject to emotional chaos and internal deception; reading them would prove most untrustworthy in a search for facts. I can, however, read the face of that envelope. The stamp on the front indicates foreign origin and the address is written in a fine left hand, judging by the slight smudging at the front. The return address is a former Colony and the parchment itself carries the seal of a New-York-based printing company in the upper right corner. The only left-handed American who would write to you is your cousin Gloria, who I last heard was being courted by a young man. Liam, I believe."

"Well when you lay it out like that, it seems I am the fool once again."

"Far from a fool, Watson," he said, "it's just a matter of opening your eyes to observe what is already there."

"Indeed. The wedding is in two months and Gloria has included two tickets on the *Renaissance*, which will be departing the day after tomorrow. I know it is short notice, but I will of course attend and would very much enjoy your company. Gloria would be happy to have you as well."

Hearing of the tickets, Holmes loosened his grip on the morphine case and drummed his fingers pensively. I must admit it is a thrill to inform my friend of something he is completely unaware of, no matter how small a detail it may be. His response however, was enough to knock me again off my guard.

My normally anti-social roommate leapt to his feet and said, "We should pack immediately. It will likely take a fortnight to reach America, if the weather holds." He sat the case on the mantle and set forth to his chambers. He didn't return for the rest of the night, so I followed his advice and packed.

The *Renaissance* was a fine ship, beautifully crafted and as smooth in the water as the dolphins which she passed in the Atlantic. I was instantly drawn back to my military days on the ship to Afghanistan, which was my first encounter with these marvelous creatures. Their giggling calls always made me feel better, so I was content, as was Holmes, to stand on the deck during the day and watch them play.

On the last day of our trip, a fortnight almost to the day, I found Holmes against the railing, looking as peaceful as the sea. "This is much needed, Watson. As of late, attention from our adventures has become much too high. While I do enjoy keeping my mind busy, I am not fond of the celebrity, nor do I wish to encourage it."

I couldn't help but agree. Despite our best attempt at privacy, our consulting business had expanded with the inevitable exposure of the newspapers. Holmes could not refuse a good puzzle though, so he kept accepting the challenges, despite what it may be doing to him.

"Is that why you've been using so emphatically?"

He smiled. "Your concern is appreciated, though wholly unnecessary, Watson. I need the momentary break from reality which only morphine can provide, but in no way am I in danger of losing my mind. Rest assured, I know my limits." His eyes flicked to a gull in the sky and he said, "Now, I might set foot in another land and see what this New World has to offer."

Moments later, a patch of brown rose in the West and a cry came from the crow's nest.

* * *

Our rooms were on the banks of the Hudson about three miles from the lovely estate where my cousin planned to marry. We were on the fourth of six floors in a modest enough room, though the whole of the Jerusalem Inn was extravagant. Had my cousin not insisted on paying for the room, we wouldn't have stayed.

As it happened, our arrival was most fortuitous for the guests of the inn because our stay intersected with that of the Lancaster family. One might say our fates were entwined, but I choose to believe fate would not be so cruel.

Less than a week before the wedding, a tragedy struck the inhabitants of room 507. The entire inn was shocked by the death of a young girl. Holmes, in the spirit of righteousness and the inevitability of his mind turning to boredom, offered his assistance to the grief-stricken Lancasters, whose daughter had fallen from their window in the night. There was no mystery in this, but the fact that her body was never recovered was enough to pique his interest.

The family was reluctant at first, but eventually accepted. We entered the room, Holmes immediately sweeping the scene while I took the time to console the two women who sat on the bed. Their resemblance was uncanny. Both had the same lush dark hair and toffee skin of the American Indians, though the daughter had several pronounced features indicating English blood. They were both quite beautiful.

I took a seat in the far corner of the room while Holmes hunched over the windowsill. He sniffed something inbetween his fingers, touched them to his tongue, then turned to the two women.

"I'm terribly sorry for your loss, but I must ask a few questions about your daughter. May I?"

The mother, whose name was Aniyah, nodded.

"Am I correct in assuming the deceased was not of blood relation to you?"

Aniyah's eyes grew wide. "How did you know that?" She spoke good English, though her ancestry was more than hinted by her accent.

"Both you and your daughter have dark hair, yet I noticed a strand of blonde stuck to the curtain. Also, there is a child's sun veil on the closet door. Highly unlikely that your offspring would have both fair hair and skin."

"Victoria was my husband's child from a previous marriage," Aniyah said. "They share the same pale complexion."

"Ah." Holmes crossed the room to the bureau opposite the window and leaned against it with ease. "And where is he now?"

"Gone," she said firmly. "In the ground for all I care."

"Were you here when Victoria fell from the window?"

"I was where you stand now. Camilla and I were getting ready to socialize in the lobby when I heard Victoria scream. I saw her in the mirror, tumbling over the edge, feet straight in the air."

"And when you went to recover her body?" Holmes asked, turning to face his reflection. From the bottom corner of the mirror, the curtains could indeed be seen dancing in the open window.

Aniyah's eyes filled with tears and her fingers started dancing across the beads of her rosary. Camilla did the same. "I'm sorry, I just can't believe she's gone. And...and the body, just gone!"

"So I've heard," Holmes said. He crossed to the door and motioned for me to join him. Before he left, he turned back to the grieving mother. "Might I ask one more question?"

She attempted to speak but found herself overcome. She nodded her permission instead.

"Had you noticed any strangers in the company of your daughter as of late? Perhaps a man of about my height with well-groomed hair and strong, callused fingers?"

Aniyah looked more than a little confused, but after a few heavy tugs on her rosary, she shook her head no.

"Very well. I shall continue my investigation and let you know what I may learn of the whereabouts of your daughter's body." With that he closed the door and made his way quickly toward the stairs.

"You seem put off," I said to him once we exited the building. "Is everything alright?"

"All is right, but still is wrong," he said and led me to the back side of the hotel, where both our room and that of the Lancasters shared a view of the road to town. Beneath the windows, he squatted next to what I assumed would be the indention left by the falling girl. For the better part of five minutes he stared at the spot, then turned his gaze to the windows. Ours was empty with the drapes drawn. The Lancasters' was open, the shadow of a woman on the windowsill.

Without warning, Holmes began to run, sprinting so fast I could hardly keep up. My old knee injury was throbbing by the time I caught him back in our room. He had thrown our window open and was leaning precariously over the edge. I feared a stiff wind might send him to a similar fate as that of young Victoria.

He came back inside, rubbing his fingers together. When he turned to me, I daresay I've never seen such a look in his eyes.

"What is it? Holmes?"

The sun was very low on the horizon and in its light his face looked more drawn than usual.

"I have a notion," said he, "but I need more data, much more data, before I claim it to be correct. With any luck, we shall collect enough evidence in the morning to propose a solution. In the meantime, I suggest we get some sleep."

I agreed and after we prepared for bed, I took a moment to read the local paper. Holmes was turned away from me, facing the wall in silence. I noticed before turning in he made sure to lock the door and pull the drapes tight over the window. He double-checked the window latch as well. As I recall, these simple actions frightened me beyond any rational sense.

I admit I had troubled dreams that night. Dreams of my time in Afghanistan and a young blonde girl coming out from a darkened cave. I remember thinking she looked scared and half starved. She smiled once, then returned to the ever-waiting shadows of the cave.

* * *

Holmes had our breakfast ready before I even began to rouse myself from sleep. Even with the drapes blotting out the sun, it seemed my friend's inner clock was impeccably set.

"I must go into town, Watson," he said after I finished eating. "It would be much appreciated if you accompanied me."

"Of course. I have no other commitments."

He nodded and waited for me to dress. I reached tenderly for my service revolver and saw approval on his face in the mirror. It was to be a possibly dangerous mission then, so I made sure the chambers were loaded.

Holmes led me downstairs and traversed the winding country road as if he'd walked it a thousand times. We soon reached the edge of town and I felt refreshed by the sight of a small, bustling crowd.

We passed several hansoms but Holmes never gave them a glance. His eyes were set on the cobblestone street in a familiar gaze that I'd learned to associate with complete focus. Were I to speak, it would fall on deaf ears.

On the far edge of town, we followed an alley and found ourselves entering a shop of sorts. It appeared to be a purveyor of the weird and fantastic. The walls were hung with strange relics that carried the most beautifully intricate, yet sinister, designs. The air was ripe with the smell of incense and spices. There were shelves of jars, each home to a different species of animal. Most were deformed in some fashion, the most curious being a small creature with the head of some monstrous tentacled beast that could have only been found in the utter blackness at the bottom of the ocean.

I was taken by these creatures: disturbed, yet completely intrigued. Meanwhile, my companion was browsing a bookshelf, fingering a large volume. He pulled it out, saw an embossed creature similar to the one in the jar, then returned it to the shelf and went in search of another.

The next thing I remember was reaching for my revolver.

A stranger had appeared from the shadows and his hand gripped Holmes' wrist. I saw my friend tense, ready to unleash his right cross on the man's jaw, while my own hand flew to the butt of my pistol, but the stranger released him.

"My apologies," he said in a strong European accent. "I didn't mean to startle you, only I couldn't help but notice you bear the mark of the afflicted."

"I beg your pardon?" Holmes said, cleverly disguising his voice with an American bend.

"The...how you say...bites, all over your forearm. You are in pain, yes? Finding pleasure in a needle."

"I'm sorry you're mistaken, Mr...?"

"You do not have to lie," the man answered. "The evidence is plain as the stars in the night."

"Yes, well, I admit I have been ill and my doctor is a bit unsteady in his age. It takes him quite a few attempts to find the vein."

"Ah. Well, if ever you are inclined to lose your affliction permanently, I would be happy to help you. It is a specialty of mine, you see. I can remedy many ailments with but one," he glanced at Holmes's marked forearm again, "bite."

"I'll take that into consideration," Holmes said. He gestured at the large book, "How much for this tome?"

"I'm sorry, like many items in this room it is one of a kind. Is not for sale."

"Bugger. I suppose that will be all then." He gestured to me with a wink, "Come Mr. Gibson, let us leave this man to his collection. Good day sir."

"And a fine evening," the man replied.

Hardly out the door, a sudden calm swept over me, a surprise considering I never realized how uncomfortable I had been in the presence of the nameless man.

Out of the alley, the streets were crowded in the midday sun. I followed Holmes through the maze of buildings until he finally stopped at a small stand fronting a pub. Holmes spoke to the woman behind the stand, gesturing at a few pieces of jewelry hanging from pegs. The woman smiled and took a necklace – at the time I couldn't see what kind – and exchanged it for my companion's coins. Before he returned to me, he stuffed the necklace in his inner coat pocket and was mum as to his reason for purchasing it.

"Well, my dear friend," he stated once we had entered the pub and ordered lunch, "I believe I have this business of the disappearing body solved."

I struggle to describe the perplexity by which I was struck in that moment. I thought we had yet to begin our investigations, but here he was claiming they were all but finished. I voiced these thoughts and he smiled at me wanly.

"Watson, of the considerable amount of time we've spent together, I have noticed your powers of perception have grown tenfold. But you are a rational man, and this case is anything but."

"Do tell what you have found," I implored.

Holmes took a sip of his tea and sat back in his chair. The pub was darkly lit and at Holmes' insistence we sat by the window closest to the door. "The girl did not fall to her death as some would lead us to believe. She was instead taken by a man, pulled from her home as a helpless chick is plucked from its coop."

"A kidnapping then? That explains the missing body."

"Yes, but I would hesitate to call it a kidnapping. I believe Victoria was more akin to the ransom."

"Something to do with the father?"

"I am still foggy on certain details, but I believe we shall have the answer forced upon us in due time. Which is why I must insist that once the wedding is over, we leave immediately for the docks. If I am correct, I do not wish to stay and parlay with this particular brand of evil. I will not hear any arguments on the matter."

Fulfilling my duty as a friend, I agreed. He was quiet for most of our remaining time in New York. It appeared he had fallen into one of those odd states of functioning catatonia of which he was prone. He made a habit of staring out the window in the evenings and retiring to bed in the wee hours of the morning, waking with the rising sun to continue his silent mulling.

* * *

The wedding was beautiful. My cousin lived up to her name, looking absolutely glorious in her dress. She was a beauty and from the looks of her new husband, he would be good to her as she would be to him. I cheered when the vows were done and even Holmes got into the spirit. He danced with one of the bridesmaids, surprising everyone with his excellent rhythm. I was surely glad we made the trip.

But once the sun started its nightly decline, my friend came to me, pulled me away from my cousin and my mug of ale, and announced that we were leaving. I started to argue, but the look in his eyes told me he would sooner leave without me than stay a moment longer. So, I hugged my cousin, shook Liam's hand, and departed back to Jerusalem's Inn.

I admit I had one, or perhaps two, too many drinks during the reception and though I'd promised not to argue, alcohol has a way of taking a knife to one's word. Countless complaints came to my mind, but the one that exited my lips surprised me.

"Why do you keep staring out the window? Are you expecting company?" I laughed at this, though my friend didn't find the humor.

He remained as he was, hidden behind the curtains with just enough of a break in them to see outside. He was there until I fell asleep, and there when I was awakened from my drunken slumber.

Holmes was yipping frantically, a noise that was impossible to ignore. I thumped out of bed, came slowly to his side. "What is it?"

"Watson, I need you as a confirmation. Is there, or is there not, a girl outside of this building?"

"A girl? At this hour? Surely you jest."

He motioned for me to look, and I did, though I hardly expected to see anything. I bent to the edge of the open drape and peered into the ghastly darkness. The sky was overrun with clouds and the moon barely escaped their wispy clutches. A single moonbeam broke free from the heavens, and in the puddle of its light I saw the girl. Luckily, I had leaned against the wall, else I would have fallen over my buckling knees.

She was the girl from the cave. The one I had dreamt about upon our arrival. Her silky hair was practically silver in the moonlight. Her skin was as pale as the folds of my cousin's wedding dress. She was beautiful.

Horribly, horribly, beautiful.

"I see her," I said.

Holmes didn't reply. For a moment I thought he might have fallen asleep. I wanted to check, but it was impossible to remove my gaze from the girl. Her eyes held me so completely that I wanted to go to her.

In my dreams she was always so hungry. Perhaps if I fed her, she might leave that cave. Perhaps she might be free.

"Holmes, we must go to her. She's afraid, can't you see?"

Again, no answer.

"Holmes, are you..." I turned around and he was nowhere to be found. The door stood ajar and there was liquid spilled over the threshold. In the darkness, I took it as something it wasn't and was seized with utmost terror. "Holmes?" I called again.

This time an answer came, though it wasn't in response to my call. It was a shriek, high and ghostly that sounded like it was coming from the walls itself. I ignored the chills and ran back to the window.

The beautiful girl was gone. In her place was something hideous. It was hard to describe as the night almost completely enveloped it, but whatever had replaced the girl was horribly twisted and writhing in pain. I saw Holmes moments later, appearing from the side of the building and marching toward her with his arm outstretched. He was saying something that sounded like Latin but the whispers of the wind drowned out any chance of a proper translation.

His attention was so focused on the girl-thing, he never saw the bigger, darker shadow that peeled away from the night behind him. Holmes kept advancing on the girl while the new shadow was creeping behind him. It was smoky at first, a sort of embodiment of mist, but then it began to harden and form. A man's head appeared. Then its body grew and turned.

"Behind you," I croaked.

Wings sprouted from the mist. The creature lunged.

I wrenched the window open with a suddenness that shattered the glass and stuck my head into the terribly cool night. I yelled with every breath I could muster, screaming from my very core.

Thank God he woke me. Thank God I was in the window to call to him. Thank God he heard.

He whipped around and in one fluid movement withdrew something from his coat pocket. He flicked it towards the winged shadow and whatever it was found its mark. The shadow man hissed and smoke sizzled from its flesh. Holmes continued his Latin speech.

The girl fell to the ground and screamed along with the creature, convulsing as if they felt each other's pain. I watched them writhe for so long that I nearly fell from the window when the door slammed behind me.

It was Holmes, pouncing inside and bolting the door. Then he was beside me, pulling me from the window and slamming it shut as well. What little glass was left clattered to the floor. He held a glass bottle in his hand and poured the remains of it over the windowsill, then hung something from the latch and drew the curtains.

"Are you alright?" he said through gasping breaths.

"Of course. Are you?"

He felt himself from head to toe, checking for injuries, "I believe so."

"What on Earth was that down there? It looked like a gargoyle of Notre Dame."

"No, it was much worse. We are safe for the night, but I should hope you won't take offense if I wake you at dawn tomorrow. I would like to be on the first ship home."

"No, of course. But what was that?"

He collapsed into the chair next to his bed. His hand trembled as he reached for his pipe.

"I promise to explain what you saw, as well as the events that led to it, but for now I must decompress before the horror of it all traumatizes me."

I gave him the space he asked for, but my gnawing desire to know what he knew did not dissipate. Soberly, I sat in bed, not expecting sleep in the least. Oddly enough, I felt safe in the room. I had faith that whatever precautions Holmes had taken would be enough should either monster try us for a rematch.

Holmes was silent for the rest of the night. His final statement before entering the labyrinth of his mind was one I shall never, even in my oldest of ages, forget.

He released a plume of tobacco and said, "I have come to the edge of reason, Watson, and deduced that the line between fact and fiction is blurred, if not fictional itself. There is only truth, what is seen and logically proven." There was a pause, then. "Thank you, my friend. I was afraid there would be multiple enemies in the dark, which is why I led you to the window. You saved my life tonight. Perhaps more."

After that he remained mute, as did I, until we heard the bellow of a ship horn and felt the lurch of steel and wood beneath our feet. We set sail for London with the rising sun.

* * *

After our adventure, I was hesitant to leave Gloria behind so close to danger, but I knew I couldn't bring her to London. Her husband was New-York-born and for a long time now she had been an adopted daughter of America. I prayed that night, as I have every night since, for her safety. I weep when she sends letters informing me of her good health, wonderful life, and newborn son, whom she named Tobias John Smith, after our grandfather.

We did not speak, Holmes and I, of our New York adventure until a week after returning to Baker Street. I was in the study, reading a fantastic book of a man living under the sea, when he decided it was time to tell me another, even more astounding, tale.

"Watson," he said, "if it pleases you, I feel I've come to terms with our ordeal in America and might shed some light on this dark mystery."

I closed my book and sighed. "I must admit I am curious. I'm still at a loss for any reasonable explanation of the scene I woke to that night."

Holmes nodded. "Let me begin with a discussion I had with the proprietor of Jerusalem's Inn. It was the night of our arrival; I didn't sleep after meeting with our clients and wandered downstairs to think. A rather long-winded fellow, the proprietor brought to my attention a spat between lovers. Aniyah's husband had run out on them a few weeks earlier to be with a woman he'd known in the night. In the days before our arrival, the husband returned and demanded that Camilla come with him. Aniyah, of course, refused.

"The proprietor then told me of a stranger sneaking around in the night. His description fit that of the man I suspected to have taken Victoria upon my initial inspection of the room. There were not only traces of her blonde hair on the curtains, but another sample of thick black hair, stiff from a certain cream-like styling tonic. It was very high on the curtain, which led me to believe the man was about my height and had climbed in through the window to take the girl."

"Climbed through the window?" I exclaimed. "It was five stories high, with no ladder."

Holmes agreed. "Yes, which baffled me as well. Until I inspected the wall. There was…" he cleared his throat, "a footprint, outside our window. A whole, flat print, you see. Coming down."

"Down? But that's impossible?"

"Impossible, but it was so. I believe the estranged husband attempted to take Camilla back to his new family, and was denied by his wife. Aniyah then offered Victoria in her place and her husband reluctantly agreed. Then it was only a matter of sending the stranger to collect his prize."

"The stranger being?"

"The very creature I did battle with after the wedding."

"Holmes, are you implying that, out there with you that night was…"

"Both the girl and the monster I did battle with in the night, as well as the estranged father, were vampires."

That final word, ringing with more certainty than I had ever heard in my friend's voice, pierced my ears. "Vampires? As in the creature from the Bram Stoker novel?"

"Yes."

"Sherlock, I'm sorry, but what sense does that make."

"None," he said simply. "As I said before, your rational mind stymies you from seeing the truth. Good riddles only have one answer, and once I'd eliminated all that was probable, I was left with but one solution."

I wanted to check my friend for fresh marks of abuse on his forearm, but a dark uncertainty crept into my mind. I was taken back to that night: the black mass that had appeared from the darkness, and the feeling of utmost terror it had bestowed upon me. Could I truly have witnessed something only meant for the pages of fiction?

"Holmes, what made you think this was even remotely logical?"

Sherlock cleared his throat. "There were a number of small details that at first seemed unconnected. If you recall, Aniyah and Camilla both wore rosaries." He pulled a rosary from his pocket, perfectly identical to those worn by the women. "The gypsy woman at the pub told me these were cheap and rarely bought, but she'd recently sold two to a couple of Indian girls. Legends involving vampires claim Christian symbols, specifically the crucifix that swings from the end of this rosary, can protect you from the undead. I think you and I both have evidence to support that claim."

"And vampires can walk on walls!" I exclaimed, suddenly remembering that from the Stoker novel.

"Precisely. They may not appear in mirrors, as Aniyah can likely attest, but their muddy footprints are easily spotted when tracked beside a forty-foot-high window. And you recall the liquid I carried into battle and used to seal our door and window?"

"Holy water?"

"From the wedding reception, blessed by the very priest who married your cousin."

"No wonder you were in such fine spirits!" Holmes smiled and shook his head. "No, that was entirely due to your cousin's marital bliss. I always liked her. But the final clue came inside the shop of oddities."

"Really? How so?"

"I went there on a hunch that the weird are drawn to the weird. It would be the perfect cover for a creature of this sort. The curator who offered to cure my drug habits was none other than the estranged father of our missing child."

My eyes grew to the size of saucers.

Holmes continued, "He shared the same blonde hair as his daughter, as well as the jawline and eyes, but it all came together when he touched me. His grip felt like an icy serpent around my wrist, unnaturally strong for his size. As he momentarily pulled me in, the final proof appeared. Two small punctures on the curve between his neck and shoulder. Had we stayed any longer, I fear we would have similar wounds upon our own throats."

"So," said I, wrapping my mind around it all, "Aniyah saved one daughter by sacrificing the other, then tried to cover it up by saying she fell out the window and someone dragged her body away."

"And on the final night, the forsaken daughter returned with her new master to bring her sister into her family eternal. Perhaps her stepmother as well."

Silence filled the room as we both reflected on the nightmare we only just escaped.

"There are no words," I whispered.

Holmes lit his pipe, peered at me through the smoke. "There will be. One day or another."

* * *

In light of the events, Holmes and I agreed that a break from our detective work would be in order. To reevaluate our sense of the truth. Eventually we returned to consulting and helping people, which was best for us. Holmes buried his syringe case in the bottom of his trunk and let the marks heal on his arm. For a long time after that adventure, I don't believe he put anything stronger than Turkish tobacco in his system.

We concluded that the experience did us good. After all, a man who has dedicated his life to exposing the truth should not limit himself by disregarding data as impossible. For even those things that run with the children of the night must be taken into logical consideration. The truth should be known, no matter what the price.

Sherlock Holmes was a man more than willing to pay that price.

The Secret Cell

William E. Burton

I'll no more – the heart is torn
By views of woe we cannot heal;
Long shall I see these things forlorn.
And oft again their friends shall feel,
As each upon the mind shall steal;
That wan projector's mystic style,
That lumpish idiot leering by,
That peevish idler's ceaseless wile,
And that poor maiden's half-formed smile,
While struggling for the full-drawn sigh.
*– **Crabbe***

ABOUT EIGHT YEARS AGO, I was the humble means of unravelling a curious piece of villainy that occurred in one of the suburbs of London; it is well worth recording in exemplification of that portion of 'Life' which is constantly passing in the holes and comers of the Great Metropolis. My tale, although romantic enough to be a fiction, is excessively common-place in some of the details – it is a jumble of real life; a conspiracy, an abduction, a nunnery, and a lunatic asylum are mixed up with constables, hackney-coaches, and an old washerwoman. I regret also that my heroine is not only without a lover, but is absolutely free from the influence of the passion, and is not persecuted on account of her transcendent beauty.

Mrs. Lobenstein was the widow of a German coachman who had accompanied a noble family from the continent of Europe and, anticipating a lengthened stay, he had prevailed upon his wife to bring over their only child, a daughter, and settle down in the rooms apportioned to his use over the stable in one of the fashionable mews at the west end of London. But Mr. Lobenstein had scarcely embraced his family ere he was driven off, post-haste, to the other world, leaving his destitute relict, with a very young daughter, to buffet her way along the rugged path of life.

With a little assistance from the nobleman in whose employ her husband had for some time been settled, Mrs. Lobenstein was enabled to earn a respectable livelihood, and filled with honorable situation of laundress to many families of gentility, besides diverse stray bachelors, dandies, and men about town. The little girl grew to be an assistance, instead of a drag, to her mother, and the widow found that her path was not entirely desolate, nor 'choked with the brambles of despair'.

In the sixth year of her bereavement, Mrs. Lobenstein, who presided over the destinies of my linen, called at my rooms, in company with a lady of equal width, breadth, and depth. Mrs. Lobenstein was of the genuine Hanseatic build – of the real Bremen beam; when in her presence, you felt the overwhelming nature of her pretensions to be considered a woman of some weight in the world and standing in society. On the occasion of the visit in question, her friend was equally adipose, and it would have puzzled a conjurer to have turned the party into a tallowy trio. Mrs. Lobenstein begged leave to recommend her friend as her successor in the lavatorial line – for her own part, she was independent of work, thank heaven, and meant to retire from the worry of trade.

I congratulated her on the successful termination of her flourish with the wash tubs.

"Oh, I have not made the money, bless you! I might have scrubbed my fingers to the bones before I could have done more than earn my daily bread and get, maybe, a black silk gown or so for Sundays. No, no! My Mary has done more with her quiet, meeting-day face in one year than either the late Mr. Lobenstein or myself could compass in our lives."

Mary Lobenstein, an artless, merry, blue-eyed girl of seventeen had attracted the attention of a bed-ridden lady whose linen she was in the habit of carrying home; and in compliance with the importunities of the old lady, she agreed to reside in her house as the invalid's sole and especial attendant. The old lady, luckily, was almost friendless; a hypocritical hyena of a niece, who expected, and had been promised, the reversion of her fortune, would occasionally give an inquiry relative to the state of her aunt's health. But so miserably did she conceal her joy at the approach of the old lady's dissolution that the party in question perceived her selfish and mercenary nature, and, disgusted at her evident security of purpose, called in an attorney and executed an entirely new will. There was no oilier relative to select – Mary Lobenstein had been kind and attentive and, more from revenge that good nature, the old lady bequeathed the whole of her property to the lucky little girl, excepting a trifling annuity to the old maid, her niece, who also held the chance of possession in case of Mary's death.

When this will was read by the man of law, who brought it forth in due season after the old lady's demise, Mary's wonder and delight almost equalled the rage and despair of the hyena of a niece, whom we shall beg leave to designate by the name of Elizabeth Bishop. She raved and swore the deadliest revenge against the innocent Mary, who one minute trembled at the denunciations of the thin and yellow spinster, and in the next chuckled and danced at the suddenness of her unexpected good fortune.

Mr. Wilson, the lawyer, desired the disinherited to leave the premises to the legal owner, and stayed by Miss Mary Lobenstein and her fat mama till they were in full and undisturbed possession. The 'good luck', as Mrs. Lobenstein called it, had fallen so suddenly upon them that a very heavy wash was left unfinished to attend to the important business, and the complaints of the naked and destitute customers alone aroused the lucky laundress to a sense of her situation. The right and privilege of the routine of customers were sold to another fat lady, and Mrs. Lobenstein called upon me, among the rest of her friends, to solicit the continuance of my washing for her stout successor.

A year passed away. I was lying in bed one wintry morning and shivering with dread at the idea of poking my uncased legs into the cold air of the room when my landlady disturbed my cogitations by knocking loudly at the room door and requesting my instant appearance in the parlour, where "a fat lady in tears" wished my presence. The existence of the obese Mrs. Lobenstein had almost slipped my memory, and I was somewhat startled at seeing that lady, dressed in a gaudy-coloured silk gown and velvet hat and feathers, in violent hysterics upon my crimson silk ottoman, that groaned beneath its burden. The attentions of my landlady and her domestic soon restored my ci-devant laundress to a state of comparative composure, when the distressed lady informed me that her daughter, her only child, had been missing for several days, and that, notwithstanding the utmost exertions of herself, her lawyer, and her friends, she had been unable to obtain the smallest intelligence respecting her beloved Mary. She had been to the police offices, had advertised in the newspapers, had personally inquired of all her friends or acquaintances, yet every exertion had resulted in disappointment.

"Everybody pities me, but no one suggests a means of finding my darling, and I am almost distracted. She left me one evening – it was quite early – to carry a small present to the chandler's-shop woman, who was so kind to us when I was left a destitute widow. My dear girl had but three streets to go, and ran out without a cloak or shawl; she made her gift to the poor woman, and instantly set out to return home. She never reached home – and, woe is me, I fear she never will. The magistrates at the police office said that she had eloped with some sweetheart; my Mary loved no one but her mother – and my heart tells me that my child could not willingly abandon her widowed parent for any new affection that might have entered her young breast. She had no followers – we were never for one hour apart, and I knew every thought of her innocent mind.

"One gentleman – he said he was a parson – called on me this morning to administer consolation; yet he hinted that my poor girl had probably committed self-destruction – that the light of grace had suddenly burst upon her soul, and the sudden knowledge of her sinful state had been too much for her to bear, and in desperation, she had hurried from the world. Alas, if my poor Mary is indeed no more, it was not by her own act that she appeared in haste before her Maker – God loved the little girl that He had made so good. The light of heavenly happiness glistened in her bright and pretty eyes; and she was too fond of this world's beauties, and the delights of life showered by the Almighty upon His children, to think of repaying Him by gloom and suicide! No, no! Upon her bended knees, morning and night, she prayed to her Father in Heaven that His will might be done; her religion, like her life, was simple, but pure. She was not of the creed professed by him who thought to cheer a parent's broken heart by speaking of a daughter's shameful death."

The plain but earnest eloquence of the poor lady excited my warmest sympathy. She had called on me for advice, but I resolved to give her my personal assistance and exert all my faculties in the clearance of this mystery. She denied the probability of anyone being concerned in kidnapping, or conveying away her daughter – for, as she simply expressed herself, "she was too insignificant to have created an enemy of such importance."

I had a friend in the police department – a man who suffered not his intimacy with the villainy of the world to dull the humanities of nature. At the period of my tale, he was but little known and the claims of a large family pressed hard upon him; yet his enemies have been unable to affix a stain upon his busy life. He has since attained a height of reputation that must ensure a sufficient income; he is established as the head of the private police of London – a body of men possessing rare and wonderful attainments. To this man I went and, in a few words, excited his sympathy for the heart-stricken mother and obtained a promise of his valuable assistance.

"The mother is rich," said I, "and if successful in your search, I can warrant you a larger reward than the sum total of your last year's earnings."

"A powerful inducement, I confess," replied L—, "but my professional pride is roused; it is a case deserving attention from its apparent inexplicability – to say nothing the mother's misery, and that is something to a father and a son."

I mentioned every particular connected with the affair, and, as he declined visiting Mrs. Lobenstein's house, invited her to a conference with the officer at my lodgings, where he was made acquainted with many a curious item that seemed to have no connection with the subject we were in consultation upon. But this minute curiosity pleased the mother, and she went on her way rejoicing, for she was satisfied in her own mind that the officer would discover the fate of her child. Strange to say, although L— declared that he possessed not the slightest clue, this feeling on the part of the mother daily became stronger; a presentiment of the officer's success became the leading feature of her life, and she waited for many days with a placid face and a contented mind. The prophetic fancies of her maternal heart were confirmed; and L— eventually restored the pretty Mary to her mother's arms.

About ten days after the consultation, he called on me and reported progress – requiring my presence at the police office for the purpose of making the affadavit necessary for the procuration of a search warrant.

"I have been hard at work," said he, "and if I have not found out where the young lady is concealed, I have at least made a singular discovery. My own inquiries in the mother's neighbourhood were not attended with any success. I therefore sent my wife, a shrewd woman, and well adapted for the business. She went without a shawl or bonnet, as if she had but stopped out from an adjacent house, into the baker's, the grocer's the chandler's, and the beer shop, and while making her trifling purchases, she asked in a careless, gossiping way if any intelligence of Miss Lobenstein had been obtained? Everybody was willing to talk of such a remarkable circumstance, and my wife listened patiently to many different versions of the story, but without obtaining any useful intelligence. One day, the last attempt that I had determined she should make, she observed that a huckster woman who was standing in a baker's shop when the question was discussed betrayed a violence of speech against the bereaved parent, and seemed to rejoice in her misfortunes. The womanly feeling of the rest of the gossips put down her inhuman chucklings, but my wife, with considerable tact, I must say, joined the huckster in her vituperation, rightly judging that there must be some peculiar reason for disliking a lady who seems generally esteemed and who was then suffering under an affliction the most distressing to a female heart. The huckster invited my wife to walk down the street with her.

"'I say – are you one of Joe's gang?' whispered the huckster.

"'Yes,' said my wife.

"'I thought so, when I seed you grinning at the fat old Dutchey's trouble. Did Joe come down with the rhino pretty well to you about this business?'

"'Not to me,' said my wife, at a venture.

"'Nor to me, neither, the shabby varmint. Where was your post?'

"This question rather bothered my wife, but she answered, 'I swore not to tell.'

"'Oh, stuff! They've got the girl, and it's all over now, in course; though Sal Brown who giv'd Joe the information about the girl says that five pounds won't stop her mouth when there's a hundred offered for the information – so we thought of splitting upon Joe, and touching the rhino. If you knows any more nor we do, and can make your share of the work, you may join our party, and come in for your whacks.'

"'Well, I know a good deal, if I liked to tell it – what do you know?'

"'Why, I knows that four of us were employed to watch when Miss Lobenstein went out in the evening without her mother, and to let Joe know directly; and I know that we did watch for six months and more; and when Sal Brown did let him know, that the girl was missing that same night, and ha'n't been heard on since.'

"'But do you know where she is?' said my wife in a whisper.

"'Well, I can't say that I do. My stall is at the corner near the mother's house; and Sal Brown was walking past, up and down the street, a-following her profession. She's of opinion that the girl has been sent over the herring pond to some place abroad; but my idea is that she ha'n't far off, fur Joe hasn't been away many hours together, I know.'

"My wife declared that she was acquainted with every particular and would join them in forcing Joe to be more liberal in his disbursements or give him up to justice and claim the reward. She regretted that she was compelled to go to Hornsey to her mother for the next few days, but agreed to call at the huckster's stall immediately on her return.

"There was one point more that my wife wished to obtain. 'I saw the girl alone one night when it was quite dark, but Joe was not to be found when I went after him. Where did Sal Brown meet with him when she told of the girl?'

"'Why, at the Blue Lion beer-shop, to be sure,' said the other.

"I was waiting in the neighbourhood, well-disguised. I received my wife's valuable information, and in a few minutes was sitting in the tap room of the Blue Lion, a humble public house of inferior pretension. I was dressed in a shooting jacket, breeches, and gaiters, with a shot belt and powder horn slung round me. A huge pair of red whiskers circled my face, and a dark red shock of hair peeped from the sides of my broad-rimmed hat. I waited in the dull room, stinking of beer and tobacco, till the house closed for the night, but heard nothing of my Joe, although I listened attentively to the conversation of the incomers, a strange, uncouth set, entirely composed of the lower order of labourers, and seemingly unacquainted with each other.

"The whole of the next day, I lounged about the sanded tap room and smoked my pipe and drank my beer in silent gloominess. The landlord asked me a few questions, but when his curiosity was satisfied he left me to myself. I pretended to be a runaway game-keeper, hiding from my master's anger for selling his game without permission. The story satisfied the host, but I saw nothing of any stranger, nor did I hear any of the old faces called by the name I wished to hear. One of the visitors was an ill-looking thick-set fellow, and kept up a continual whispering with the landlord – I made sure that he was my man, when, to my great regret, I heard him hailed by the name of George.

"I was standing inside the bar, chattering with the landlord, and settling for my pipes and my beer, when a good-looking, fresh-coloured, smiling-faced young fellow danced into the bar and was immediately saluted by the host. 'Hello, Joe, where have you been these two days?'

"'Heavy business on hand, my buck – occupies all my time, but pays well. So give up a mug of your best, and d— the expense.'

"'I had no doubt but this was my man. I entered into conversation with him, in my assumed manner, and my knowledge of the Somersetshire dialect materially assisted my disguise. Joe was evidently a sharp-witted fellow who knew exactly what he was about. All my endeavours to draw him into talking of his own avocations completely failed; he would laugh, drink, and chatter, but not a word relative to the business that occupied his time could I induce him to utter.

"'Who's going to the hop in Saint John Street?' said the lively Joe. 'I mean to have eighteen-pennyworth of shake-a-leg there tonight, and have it directly too, for I must be back at my place at daybreak.'

"'This was enough for me. I walked with Joe to the vicinity of the dancing-rooms when, pleading a prior engagement, I quitted him and returned home. My disguise was soon completely altered; my red wig and whiskers, drab hat, and shooting dress were exchanged for a suit of black, with a small French cloak of dark cloth, and plain black hat. Thus attired, I watched the entrance of the humble ball-room, fearing that my man might leave it at an early period, for I knew not how far he had to journey to his place in the country, where was compelled to be by the break of day.

"I walked the pavement of Saint John Street for six long hours, and was obliged to make myself known to the watchman to prevent his interference, for he doubted the honesty of my intentions. Just before the dawn of day, my friend Joe, who seemed determined to have enough dancing for his money, appeared in the street with a lady on each arm. I had to keep him in sight till he had escorted the damsels to their domiciles; when, buttoning up his coat and pressing his hat down over his brows, he walked forward with a determined pace. I followed him at a convenient distance. I felt that he was in my power – that I was on the point of tracing the mystery of the girl's disappearance, and ascertaining the place of her detention.

"Joe walked rapidly towards Shoreditch Church. I was within a hundred feet of him when the early Cambridge coach dashed down the Kingsland Road. Joe seized the guard's hold at the side of the back boot, placed his feet upon the hind spring, and in one moment was on the top of the coach, and trundling away from me at the rate of twelve miles an hour.

"I was beaten. It was impossible for me to overtake the coach. I though of hiring a hack, but the rapid progress of the stage defied all idea of overtaking it. I returned dispirited to my home.

"My courage rose with the conception of fresh schemes. In the course of the day, I called on a friend, a stage coachman, and telling him some of the particulars of my object, asked him to introduce me to the driver of the Cambridge coach. I met him on his return to town the next day and, by the help of my friend, overcame his repugnance to talk with strangers respecting the affairs of his passengers. I learnt, at last, that Joe never travelled more than half-a-dozen miles, but Elliott, the coachman, was unable to say who he was or where he went to. My plan was soon arranged, and Elliott was bribed to assist me.

"The next morning by daybreak, I was sitting on the top of the Cambridge coach, well wrapped-up in a large white top coat, with a shawl tied over my mouth. I got on the coach at the inn yard, and as we neared the church looked out anxiously for my friend Joe; but he was not to be seen, nor could I discern anything of him for six or seven miles along the road. The first stage was performed, and while the horses were being changed, Elliott, the coachman, pointed out a strange, ill-looking man in a close light waistcoat with white sleeves, white breeches, yarn stockings, and high-low shoes. 'That fellow,' said Elliott, 'is always in company with the man you have been inquiring about. I have seen them frequently together come from over that style; he is now waiting for Joe, I'll bet a pound.'

"I alighted and bargained with the landlord of the small roadside inn for the use of the front bedroom, upstairs. I took my post and, as the stage departed, began my watch. Joe did not appear till late in the afternoon – his friend eagerly seized him by the arm and began to relate something with great anxiety of look and energy of action. They moved off over the style. I glided out of the house and followed them. A footpath wound through an extensive meadow, and the men were rapidly nearing the farthest end. I hastened my pace and gained the centre of the field ere they were aware of my approach. I observed a telegraphic signal pass between them, and they instantly stopped their expedition and, turning back upon their path, sauntered slowly towards me. I kept on; we met – their eyes were searchingly bent upon me, but I maintained an easy gait and undisturbed countenance and continued my walk for some minutes after they were past. As I climbed the farthest style, I observed them watching me from the other end of the field. I saw no more of Joe or his friend for the rest of that day and the whole of the next.

"I was much annoyed at my disappointment and resolved not to be again outwitted. Every possible inquiry that could be made without exciting the curiosity of the neighbourhood was instituted, but I was unable to obtain the smallest information, either of the abducted lady or of Joe's individuality. His friend was known as a vagabond of the first class – a discharged ostler, with a character that marked him ready for the perpetration of every crime.

"I was hunting in the dark. I had nothing but surmises to go upon, excepting the declaration of the huckster, that a man named Joe was the means of Miss Lobensteins' absence, but I was not sure that I was in pursuit of that identical Joe. The mystery attending the object of my suspicion gave an appearance of probability to my supposition, but it seemed as if I was not to proceed beyond the limits of uncertainty. I resolved, after waiting till the evening of the next day, to return to the tap-room of the Blue Lion and the impenetrability of my gamekeeper's disguise.

"Tying my rough coat up in my shawl, I clapped the bundle under my arm and walked quietly along the road. As I passed through some twists on the sidewalk, a post-chaise was coming through the adjoining toll-gate. A scuffle, accompanied with high oaths, in the interior of the chaise attracted my attention; a hand was dashed through the carriage window and cries for help were loudly vociferated. I ran towards the chaise and ordered the postillion to stop; a coarse voice desired him to drive on; the command was repeated with violent imprecations and the horses, severely lashed, bounded rapidly away. I was sufficiently near to catch hold of the back of the springs as the vehicle moved; the motion was violent, but I kept my grasp. The backboard of the chaise, where the footman should stand, had been covered with a double row of iron spikes to prevent the intrusion of idle boys; but, determined not to lose sight of the ruffians who were thus violating the peace of the realm, I pressed my bundle hard upon the spikes and, jumping nimbly up, found myself in a firm and pleasant seat.

"The carriage rolled speedily along. I determined, at the very first halting place, to summon assistance and desire an explanation of the outcries and demands for help. If, as there seemed but little doubt, some act of lawless violence was being perpetrated. I resolved to arrest the principals upon the spot. While cogitating on the probabilities of the result, I received a tremendous cut across the face from the thong of a heavy leather whip, jerked with considerable violence from the window of the post-chaise. A second ill-directed blow drove me from my seat, and I fell into the road, severely lacerated and almost blind.

"I rolled upon the dusty ground and writhed in excessive agony. A thick wale crossed each cheek, and one of my eyes had been terrifically hit. It was yet early night, and the public nature of the road soon afforded me assistance. A young man passed me, driving a gig towards London; I hailed him and requested his services. A slight detail of the cause in which I had received my injuries induced him to turn round and receive me in the vacant seat. The promise of half-a-guinea tempted him to drive rapidly after the chaise, and in a few minutes we heard the sound of wheels. The young man cheered his horse to great progress, but we were unable to pass the vehicle in advance, and it was not till we both drew up to the door of the roadside inn where I had previously stopped that we discovered that we had been in pursuit of a mail-coach instead of a post-chaise.

"The waiter declared that 'nothin'' of a four-veel natur, 'cept a vaggin and a nearse' had passed within the previous half-hour. Placing my gig friend over some brandy and water, I sought the recesses of the kitchen that I might procure some cooling liquid to bathe my face with. While busily employed at the yard pump, the sound of voices from an adjoining stable arrested my attention. The dim light of a lantern fell upon the figure of the ostler whom I had seen in company with mysterious Joe. I advanced lightly, in hopes of hearing the conversation. When I reached the door, I was startled by the sudden approach of someone from the other side of the yard, and compelled to hide behind the door. A stable helper popped his head into the building, and said, 'See here, Billet, vot I found sticking on the spikes of the chay you've left in the lane.'

"My luckless bundle was produced and speedily untied. Directly Billy, for so was the suspicious ostler named, saw my rough, white greatcoat, he exclaimed, with considerable energy, 'I'm blessed if ve haint been looked arter. I seed this 'ere toggery a valking arter Joe and me in the meadow yonder. Ve thought it suspectable, so ve mizzled back. And I'm jiggered if the owner vornt sitting behind our conweyance ven Joe hit him a vollop or two vith your vip to knock him off. Tommy, my tulip, I'll go back vi' you tonight, and vait a while till the vind changes.'

"It was evident then that Joe was connected with the abduction of the day – another convincing proof that he was the active agent in Miss Lobenstein's affair. With respect to my friend the ostler, I determined to try the effects of a little coercion, but concluded that it would be better to let him reach some distance from his usual jaunts to prevent alarming his co-mate Joe.

"In about an hour the post-chaise was driven to the door, and the ostler, much the worse for his potations, was placed within the body of the vehicle. I was soon after them, in company with the young man in the gig, and we kept the chaise in sight till it had entered the still and deserted streets of the city. It was nearly midnight; the drunken ostler desired the scarcely sober postillion to put him out at the door of a tavern. I walked up to the astonished couple and, arresting them on a charge of felony, slipped a pair of small but powerful spring handcuffs over the ostler's wrists.

"I conducted him, helpless and amazed, to an adjacent watch-house and, mentioning my name and office, desired his safe custody till I could demand his body. The postillion, who was guarded by my gig friend, became much alarmed and volunteered any information that I might desire. He confessed that he had been employed that afternoon by one Joseph Milk to carry a lunatic priest to the Franciscan Monastery at Enfield Chase, from whence it was asserted that he had made his escape. The existence of a religious establishment in that neighbourhood was entirely unknown to me, and I questioned the postillion respecting the number of its inmates and the name of the superior, but he professed to know nothing beyond the locality of the building, and declared that he had never been inside the yard gate. He admitted that Joseph Mills had employed him several times upon the same business; and that, rather more than a fortnight ago, Billy, the ostler, had desired him to bring up a post-chaise from his master's yard at a minute's notice, and that a young lady was lifted, in a senseless state, into the chaise and driven down to the building at Enfield as rapidly as the horses could be made to go.

"I took down his directions respecting the house, and at daybreak this morning I reconnoitered the front and back of the building. If I am any judge, that house is not devoted to monastic purposes alone; but you will see it tomorrow, I trust, for I wish you to accompany me as early in the morning as we can start after procuring the warrants for a general search into the secrets of this most mysterious monastery."

* * *

It was nearly noon the next day before we were enabled to complete our necessary arrangements. L—, Mr. Wilson, the attorney, Mr. R—, a police magistrate of some distinction, and the reader's humble servant stepped into a private carriage, while a police officer, well-armed, sat with the driver. The magistrate had been interested in the details necessary for the procuration of the warrant and had invited himself to the development of the mystery. An hour's ride brought us to the entrance of a green lane that wound its mazy length between hedges of prickly holly and withered hawthorn trees. After traversing this lane for nearly two miles, we turned again to the left, by L—'s direction, and entered a narrow pass between a high brick wall and a huge bank, surmounted by a row of high and gloomy trees. The wall formed the boundary of the monastery grounds, and, at a certain place, where an ascent in the narrow road favoured the purpose, we were desired by L— to mount the roof of the coach and, by looking over the wall, to inspect the back front of the building. Massive bars of iron were fastened across every window of the house; in some places, the frames and glass were entirely removed, and the gratings were fixed in the naked brick-work; or the apertures were fitted with thick boarding, windows of a range of outhouses which extended down one side of the extensive yard were also securely barred; and a small square stone building stood in the middle of the garden, which immediately adjoined the yard. Two sides of this singular construction were visible from our coach top, yet neither door nor window were to be discerned.

One of our party pointed out a pale and wild-looking face flaring at us from one of the grated windows of the house. "Let us away," said L—. "We are observed, and a further gratification of our curiosity may prevent a successful issue to my scheme."

"This looks more like a prison than a monastery or convent," said the magistrate.

"I fear that we shall find it worse than either," replied L—.

In a few minutes the carriage stopped at the gate of the building, the front of which exhibited but few points for the attachment of suspicion. The windows eere shaded by blinds and curtains, but free from gratings or bars. The palings that enclosed a small forecourt were of massive oak and, being mounted on a dwarf wall, effectually prevented the intrusion of uninvited guests. The gates were securely closed, but the handle of a small bell invited attention, and a lusty pull by the driver gave notice of our presence.

L—, who had quitted the vehicle by the off door, requested the magistrate to keep out of sight, and with his brother officer retired behind the coach. Our course of proceeding had been well-arranged; when the door of the house was opened, I put my head from the carriage window and requested to see the superior of the convent. The attendant, a short, ill-looking fellow in a fustian coat and gaiters, desired to know my business with him. "It is of great secrecy and importance," I replied; "I cannot leave this carriage because I have somebody here that requires my strictest attention. Give your master this card, and he will know exactly who I am, and what I require."

Our scheme succeeded. The fellow left his post and, unfastening the paling gate, advanced to the edge of the footpath, and put his hand in at the window of the carriage for my card. L— and the officer glided from their concealment and secured possession of the outer gate and the door of the house before the fellow had time to give the alarm. The driver, who had pretended to busy himself with the horses, immediately opened the carriage door, and in a few seconds the whole of our party were mustered in the entrance hall. The man who had answered the bell, when he recovered his surprise, rushed to the door, and attempted to force his way to the interior of the house. The police officer stopped him, and an angry altercation ensued – he placed his finger in his mouth and gave a loud and lengthy whistle. L—, who was busily engaged in searching for the fastenings to an iron screen that crossed the width of the hall, observed the noise and turning round to his mate said quietly, "If he's troublesome, Tommy, give him a pair of gloves." In two minutes, the fellow was sitting helpless on the ground, securely handcuffed.

"Confound him," said L—, "he must have come out through this grating; there is no other entrance to the hall, and yet I cannot discover the doorway, and I am afraid that his signal has made it worse, for I heard the click of spring work directly after he gave his whistle."

"This grating is a common appendage to a convent or religious house," said Mr. Wilson. "Perhaps we are giving ourselves unnecessary trouble – let us ring the bell again, and we may obtain admission without the use of force."

The office and the magistrate exchanged a smile. The latter went to the man who had opened the door and said, in a low tone of voice, "We must get into this house, my man; show us how we can pass this grating and I will give you five guineas. If you refuse, I shall commit you to jail, whether your connection with this establishment deserves it or not. I am a magistrate, and these, my officers, are acting under my direction."

The man spoke not; but, raising his manacled hands to his mouth, gave another whistle of peculiar shrillness and modulation.

The hall in which we were detained was of great height and extent. Beyond the iron screen, a heavy partition of woodwork cut off the lower end, and a door of heavy oak opened from the room thus formed into the body of the hall. An open, but grated, window was immediately above the door and extended almost from one end of the partition to the other. L—, observing this, climbed up the iron screen with the agility of the cat, and had scarcely attained the top ere we observed him level a pistol towards some object in the enclosure and exclaim, with a loud voice, "Move one step and I'll drive a couple of bullets through your skull."

"What do you require?" exclaimed a tremulous voice from within.

"Send your friend there, Joe Mills, to open the door of the grating. If you move hand or foot, I'll pull trigger, and your blood be upon your own head."

L— afterwards informed me, that upon climbing the screen, he discerned a gentleman in black in close consultation with a group of men. They were standing at the farther end of the enclosure against a window, the light of which enabled him to pick out the superior, and to discern the physiognomy of his old acquaintance Joe.

"Come, come, Joe, make haste," said L—. "My fingers are cramped, and I may fire in mistake."

The threat was effectual in its operation. The man was afraid to move, and the door of the enclosure was opened by his direction. Joe walked trippingly across the hall and, touching a spring in one of the iron rails, removed the fastenings from a portion of the screen, and admitted our party.

"How do you do, Mr. Mills?" said L—. "How are our friends at the Blue Lion! You must excuse me if I put you to a little inconvenience, but you are so volatile that we can't make sure of finding you when we want you unless we take the requisite precaution. Tommy, tackle him to his friend, and by way of greater security, fasten them to the grating – but don't waste the gloves, for we have several more to fit."

"Gentlemen,", said the man in black, advancing to the door of the enclosure, "what is the reason of this violence? Why is the sanctity of this holy establishment thus defiled? Who are you, and what seek you here?"

"I am a magistrate, sir, and these men are officers of justice armed with proper authority to search this house for the person of Mary Lobenstein, and we charge you with her unlawful detention. Give her to our care, and you may save yourself much trouble."

"I know nothing of the person you mean, nor are we subject to the supervision of your laws. This house is devoted to religious purposes – it is the abode of penitents who have abjured the world and all its vanities. We are under the protection of the Legate of His Holiness, the Pope, and the laws of England do not forbid our existence. Foreigners only dwell within these walls, and I cannot allow the interference of any party unauthorised by the Head of the Church."

"I shall not stop," said the magistrate, "to expose the errors of your statement. I am furnished with sufficient power to demand a right of search in any house in the Kingdom. Independent of ascertaining the safety of the individual with whose abduction you are charged, it is my duty to inquire into the nature of an establishment assuming the right to capture the subjects of the King of this realm and detain them in a place having all the appointments of a common prison, yet disowning the surveillance of the English laws. Mr. L—, you will proceed in your search, and if anyone attempted to oppose you, he must take the consequences."

The countenance of the man in black betrayed the uneasiness he felt; the attendants, six in number, who, with our friend Mills, had formed the council whose deliberations were disturbed by the sight of L—'s pistol, were ranged beneath the window that looked in to the yard, and waited the commands of the chief. This man, whose name we afterwards ascertained was Farrell, exchanged a look of cunning with his minions and, with apparent resignation, replied, "Well, sir, it is useless for me to contend with the authority you possess; Mr. Nares, throw open the yard door and, do you and your men attend the gentlemen round the circuit of the cells."

The person addressed unbolted the fastenings of a huge door that opened into the yard, and bowed to our party as if waiting their precedence. Mr. Wilson, being nearest the door, went first, and Nares, with a bend of his head, motioned two of his party to follow. As they passed him, he gave them a knowing wink and said "Take the gentlemen to the stone house first." The magistrate was about to pass into the yard when L— seized him by the collar of his coat and violently pulling him back into the room, closed the door and jerked the principal bolt into its socket.

"Excuse my rudeness, sir, but you will soon perceive that it was necessary. Your plan, Mr. Nares, is a very good plan, but will scarcely answer your purpose. We do not intend placing ourselves at the mercy of your men in any of your stone houses, or cells with barred windows. You have the keys of the establishment at your girdle – go round with us yourself and let those five or six fellows remain here instead of dancing at our heels. Come, come, sir, we are not to be trifled with; no hesitation, or I shall possess myself of your keys and leave you securely affixed to your friend Mills."

Nares grinned defiance, but made no reply. Farrell, whose pale face exhibited his dismay, took courage from the dogged bearing of his official and stuttered out, "Mr. Nares, I desire that you will not give up your keys." The hint was sufficient. Nares and his fellows, who were all furnished with bludgeons, raised their weapons in an attitude of attack, and a general fight was inevitable. The closing of the yard door had cut off one of our friends, but it also excluded two of the enemy. Still the odds were fearfully against us, not only in point of numbers, which rated five to four, and our antagonists were all of them armed, while the magistrate and I were totally unprovided with the means of defence.

Hostilities commenced by one of the men striking me a violent blow upon the fleshy part of the left shoulder that sent me staggering to the other side of the room. Two of the ruffians simultaneously faced the police officer, as if to attack him; he received the blow of the nearest upon his mace or staff of office, and before the fellow had time to lift his guard, returned him a smashing rap upon the fingers of his right hand, compelling him to drop his cudgel and run howling into the corner of the room. The officer then turned his attention to the fellow who had assaulted me and who was flourishing his stick with the intent of repeating the blow – but receiving a severe crack across his shins from the officer's mace, he was unable to keep his legs and dropped upon the floor. I immediately wrested the bludgeon from his grasp, and left him *hors de combat.* The officer, while assisting me, received a knock-down blow from the fellow who had hesitated joining in the first attack, but, cat-like, had been watching his opportunity for a pounce. I gave him in return a violent thump upon his head, and drove his hat over his eyes – then, rushing in upon him, I pinioned his arms and held him till the officer rose and assisted me to secure him. While placing the handcuffs upon him, I was favoured with a succession of kicks from the gentleman with the crippled hand.

L—, having drawn a pistol from his pocket, advanced to Nares and desired him to deliver up the keys; the ruffian answered him by striking a heavy blow on L—'s ear that immediately produced blood. The officer, exhibiting the utmost self-possession under these irritating circumstances, did not fire the pistol at his adversary, but dashed the weapon into his face and inflicted a painful wound. Nares was a man of bull-dog courage. He seized the pistol and struggled fearfully for its possession. His gigantic frame and strength overpowered his antagonist; the pistol was discharged in the scuffle, luckily without wounding anyone – and the ruffian, holding the conquered L— upon the ground, was twisting his cravat for the purpose of choking him when, having satisfactorily arranged our men, we arrived to the rescue and prevented the scoundrel from executing his villainous intention. But Nares, although defeated by numbers, evinced a determination to die game – it was with the utmost difficulty that were enabled to secure his arms, and while slipping the handcuffs over his wrists, he continued to leave the marks of his teeth upon the fingers of the policeman.

While this furious melee was going on, the magistrate had been unceremoniously collared by the master of the house and thrust forth into that part of the hall which adjoined the iron screen. But his worship did not reverence this ungentlemanly proceeding, and turned valiantly upon his assailer. Both of them were unprovided with weapons, and a furious bout of fisticuffs ensued, wherein his worship was considerably worsted. Mills and the porter, who had been fastened by the policeman to the railing of the screen, encouraged Farrell by their cheers. The magistrate was severely punished and roared for help; Farrell, dreading collision with the conquerors of his party, left his man and started off through the open door of the grating; he ran down the lane with a speed that defied pursuit. The driver and the magistrate both endeavored to overtake him, but they soon lost sight of the nimble rogue, and returned discomforted to the house.

During the scuffle, the two men who, with Mr. Wilson, were shut out by the promptitude of L—, clamoured loudly at the door for re-admission. The attorney, as he afterwards confessed, was much alarmed at the position in which he found himself – cut off from all communication with his friends and left at the mercy of two ill-looking scoundrels, in a strange place, and surrounded by a range of grated prisons, while a number of cadaverous, maniac-looking faces glared at him from between the bars.

Upon mustering our party, we were all more or less wounded. The magistrate was outrageous in his denunciations of vengeance upon all the parties concerned; his discoloured eye and torn apparel, besides the bruises about his person, had inflamed his temper, and he declared that it was his firm determination to offer a large reward for the apprehension of the chief ruffian, Farrell. L— was much hurt, and for some time appeared unable to stand alone – his ear bled profusely and relieved his head, which had been seriously affected by Nares's attempt at strangulation. The other officer had received a severe thumping, and his bitten hand gave him much pain. My left arm was almost useless, and many bloody marks exhibited the effects of the fellow's kicks upon my shins. Nevertheless, we had fought a good fight, and had achieved a perilous victory.

The magistrate threw up the window sash and addressed the men in the yard from between the iron gratings. "Harken, you sirs, we have thrashed your fellows, and have them here in custody. If you attempt resistance, we shall serve you exactly in the same manner. But if either of you feel inclined to assist us in the discharge of our duty, and will freely answer every question and render all the help in his power, you shall not only be forgiven for any part you may have taken in scenes of past violence, short of murder, but shall be well rewarded into the bargain."

One of the men, and I must say that he was the most ill-looking of the whole lot, immediately stepped forward, and offered to turn "King's evidence" if the magistrate would swear to keep his promise. The other fellow growled his contempt of the sneak "what would snitch" and darted rapidly down the yard. As we never saw him again, it is supposed that he got into the garden and found some means of escaping over the walls.

The yard door was opened, and the lawyer and the informer were admitted. The latter personage told us that his wife was the matron of the establishment and, with her sister, would be found upstairs. The keys were taken from Nares, and we began our search. Mr. Wilson desired the man to conduct us to Mary Lobenstein's room, but he positively denied the knowledge of any such person. His wife, a coarse, pock-marked, snub-nosed woman with a loud, masculine voice, also declared that no female answering to that name had ever been within the house. L— remarked that no credit was to be attached to their assertions, and ordered them to lead the way to the search.

It would occupy too much space to describe minutely the nature of the persons and events that we encountered in our rounds. Suffice it to say, we soon discovered that the suspicions of the police officer and the magistrate barely reached the truth. Farrell's establishment had no connection with any religious house, nor could we discover either monk, friar, nun, or novice in any of the cells. But the name was a good cloak for the villainous usages practised in the house, as it disarmed suspicion and prevented the interference of the police. The house, in reality, was a private mad-house, but subject to the foulest abuses; wives who were tired of their husbands, and vice versa, reprobate sons wishing to dispose of fathers, or villains who wanted to remove their rivals, either in love or wealth, could secure safe lodgings for the obnoxious personages in Farrell's Farm, as it was termed by the knowing few. Farrell could always obtain a certificate of the lunacy of the person to be removed; Nares had been bred to the pestle and the mortar and, as the Act then stood, an apothecary's signature was sufficient authority for immuring a suspected person. Incurables of the worst description were received by Farrell and boarded at the lowest rate. He generally contracted for a sum down, guaranteeing that their friends should never again be troubled by them – and, as the informer said, "He gave them little enough to eat, and if they did not die, it wasn't his fault."

The house was also appropriated to other purposes of secrecy and crime. Ladies in a delicate situation were accommodated with private rooms for their accouchement, and the children effectually provided for. Fugitives from justice were sure of concealment if they could obtain admission to the farm. In short, Farrell's doors, although closed to the world and the eye of the law, were open to all who could afford to pay, or be paid for – from the titled seducer and his victim, whose ruin was effected in the elegant suite of rooms fronting the lane, to the outcast bedlamite, the refuse of the poor-house and the asylum who was condemned to a slow but certain death in the secret cells of this horrible abode.

It would fill a volume to recount the history of the sufferers whom we released from their almost hopeless imprisonment – a volume of crime, or suffering, and of sorrow.

After a painful and fruitless search through all the various rooms, cells, and hiding places of that singular house, we were compelled to acknowledge that the assertions of the under-keeper and his wife were but too correct. Mary Lobenstein was not among the number of the detenues at the Farm, nor could we discover the slightest trace of her. Still L— clung to the hope that in the confusion necessarily attending our first search we had passed over some secret cell or dungeon in which the poor girl was immured. The square stone building in the centre of the garden afforded some ground for this surmise – we were unable to open the small iron-banded door that was fixed in the side of this apparently solid structure. The under-keeper declared that the key was always in the possession of Farrell, his principal; and that no one ever entered the place but Nares and his master. He was not aware that any person was ever confined in it, a spring of water bubbled up within the building, and he believed that Farrell used it as a wine cellar only. He had seen wine carried in and out of the place, indeed, the whole appearance of the building corroborated the man's statement – there was no window, air hole, or aperture of any description, excepting the small door before mentioned; and the contracted size of the place itself prevented the possibility of its containing a hiding hole or a human being if a well or spring occupied the area, as the keeper affirmed.

Resigning this last hope of finding the poor girl, we gave our assistance to the magistrate in removing the prisoners and placing the unfortunates whom we had released in temporary but appropriate abodes. In this service, the under-keeper and his wife proved valuable auxiliaries in pointing out the incurable mad folks and those who, in his opinion, had been unjustly detained. The prisoners were placed in our carriage and conveyed to London, under the superintendence of L— himself, who promised to return during the evening with additional assistance. The policeman was dispatched to Enfield for several carriages and post-chaises. Some of the most desperate and confirmed maniacs were sent to the lunatic asylum, with the magistrate's order for their admittance, and two or three of the sick and sorrowing were removed to the Middlesex hospital.

I assisted the lawyer and the magistrate in taking the depositions of several of the sufferers who appeared sane enough to warrant the truth of their stories. As night approached, I prepared for a departure, and Mr. Wilson resolved to accompany me; we received the addresses of several persons from various inmates of the Farm, who requested us to let their families know of the place of their detention. As we drove down the lane, we met L— and a posse of police officers, who were to accompany the magistrate in his night sojourn at the house and assist him in the removal of the rest of the inmates in the morning.

During the evening I called, with a heavy heart, upon Mrs. Lobenstein and communicated the melancholy remit of our scheme. I related minutely the particulars of our transaction – she listened quietly to my story and occasionally interrupted me, when describing the zeal of the officer L—, by invoking the blessings of Heaven upon his head. When she learnt the unsuccessful issue of our search, she remained silent for a minute only – when, with a confident tone and a cheerful voice, she said "My daughter Mary is in that stone house. The workings of the fingers of Providence are too evident in the wonderful train of circumstances that led to the discovery of Farrell and his infamous mansion. My child is there, but you have not been able to penetrate the secret of her cell. I will go with you in the morning, if you can spare another day to assist a bereaved mother."

I declared my readiness to accompany her, but endeavoured to impress upon her mind the inutility of further search. She relied securely upon the faith of her divine impression, as she termed it, and declared that God would never suffer so good as man as L— to be disappointed in his wonderful exertions; the keenness of a mother's eye, the instinct of a mother's love would help him in the completion of his sacred trust. It was impossible to argue with her, and I agreed to be with her at an early hour.

I slept but little during the night, for my bruised shins and battered shoulder pained me considerably, and the strange excitement of the day's events materially assisted to heighten both my corporeal and mental fever. When I arose in the morning, I felt so badly that nothing but the earnest and confident tone of the poor childless widow induced me to undertake the annoyance of the trip – I could not bear to disappoint her. I found the carriage ready at the door – a couple of mechanics, with sledge hammers, crow bars, and huge bunches of skeleton keys occupied the front seat, and having placed myself beside Mrs. Lobenstein upon the other seat, the horses trotted briskly along the street.

During our ride she informed me that a lawyer had called upon her from Elizabeth Bishop, the disappointed spinster, who, it will be recollected, had lost her expected fortune by the intervention of the gentle Mary Lobenstein. The man stated that Miss Bishop had heard of the disappearance of the inheritor of her aunt's estate and had desired him to give notice that if proof was not forthcoming of Miss Lobenstein's existence, she should take possession of the property, agreeably to the provision existing in the will. "I am sure," said the mother, "that woman is at the bottom of this affair – she has concerted the abduction of my daughter to obtain possession of the estate – but I trust in God that she will be disappointed in her foul design. A fearful whisper comes across my heart that those who would rob a mother of a child for gold would not object to rob that child of her existence; but my trust is in the Most High, Who tempers the wind to the shorn lamb and will not consent to the spoliation of the widow and the fatherless."

The probability of the poor girl's murder had been suggested by L— at the termination of our unsuccessful search, and had occupied a serious portion of my thoughts during the wakeful moments of the past night. Expecting nothing from the mother's repetition of the search, I determined to consult L— upon the feasibility of offering rewards to the villains Mills and Nares for a revelation of the truth, and if we ailed in eliciting any intelligence, to institute a rigorous examination of the garden and the yard and discover, if possible, the remains of the murdered girl.

The magistrate received Mrs. Lobenstein with tenderness and respect, and sanctioned her desire to penetrate into the mystery of the square stone house. L— had nothing new to disclose, excepting that in one of the rooms several articles of female apparel had been discovered, and he suggested that Mrs. Lobenstein should inspect them as, perhaps, something that belonged to her daughter might be among them. The mother remarked that her daughter left home without a bonnet or a shawl, and it was scarcely likely that her body-clothes would be in the room. She, therefore, thought it useless to waste time in going upstairs, but requested the locksmith to accompany her to the stone house in the garden. It was impossible to help sympathising with Mrs. Lobenstein in her anxiety; the magistrate deferred his return to London, where his presence was absolutely necessary to preside at the examination of Mssrs. Nares, Mills, and Co., and the warm-hearted L— wiped the moisture from his eyes as he followed the mother across the yard and heard her encourage the workmen to commence the necessary proceedings for the release of her darling child. The lock of the stone house was picked – the door was thrown wide open – and the maternal voice was heard in loud citation, but the dull echo of the stone room was the only reply – there was no living creature within the place.

We found the interior of the building to correspond with the description given by the under-keeper. The walls were hollowed into bins, which were filled with wine bottles packed in sawdust; a circular well, bricked up a little above the level of the floor, filled the centre of the room; the water rose to within a foot of the ground – an old pulley and bucket, rotten from desuetude, clogged up on side of the doorway, and two or three wine barrels filled up the remaining vacancy of space. It was impossible that a human being could be concealed in any part of the building.

Mrs. Lobenstein sighed, and her countenance told of her dismay; but the flame of hope had warmed her heart into a heat that was not to be immediately cooled. "Gentlemen," said she, "accompany me once more round the cells and secret places – let me be satisfied with my own eyes that a thorough search has been made, and it will remove my doubts that you have overlooked some obscure nook wherein the wretches have concealed my little girl."

The range of chambers was again traversed, but without success, and the widow was compelled to admit that every possible place had been looked into, and that a farther sojourn in the house was entirely useless. The old lady sat down upon the last stair of the second flight, and with a grievous expression of countenance looked into our several faces as we stood around her as if she was searching for that consolation it was not in our power to bestow. Tears rolled down her cheeks, and mighty sobs told of the anguish of her heart. I was endeavouring to rouse her to exertion as the only means of breaking the force of her grief, when my attention was drawn to the loud yelping of a dog, a small cocker spaniel, that had accompanied us in the carriage from Mrs. Lobenstein's house and in prowling round the building, had been accidentally shut up in one of the rooms.

"Poor Dash!" said the widow, "I must not lose you; my dear Mary was fond of you, and I ought to be careful of her favourite." I took the hint and walking down the gallery, opened the door of the room from whence the barking proceeded. It was the apartment that contained the articles of wearing apparel which Mrs. Lobenstein had visited in her round without discovering any token of her daughter. But the animal's superior instinct enabled him to detect the presence of a pair of shoes that had graced the feet of the little Mary when she quitted her mother's house on the day of her abduction. Immediately the door was opened, the faithful creature gathered up the shoes in his mouth and ran to his mistress and dropped them at her feet, inviting her attention by a loud and sagacious bark. The old lady knew the shoes in a moment. "Yes, they are my girl's – I bought them myself for my darling. She has been here – has been murdered – and the body of my child is now mouldering in the grave." A violent hit of hysterics ensued, and I consigned her to the care of the wife and sister of the under-keeper, who had not been allowed to leave the house.

I deemed the finding of the shoes to be of sufficient importance to recall the magistrate, who was in the carriage at the door and about to start for London. He immediately alighted and inquired into the particulars of the affair. Directly it was proved that Mary Lobenstein had been in the house, L— rushed upstairs and dragged the keeper into the presence of the magistrate, who sternly asked the man why he had deceived him in declaring that the girl had never been there. The fellow was evidently alarmed and protested vehemently that he knew no female of the name of Lobenstein – and the only clue he could give to the mystery of the shoes was that a young girl answering our description of Mary had been brought into the house at nighttime about a fortnight ago, but she was represented as an insane prostitute of the name of Hill who had been annoying some married gentlemen by riotous conduct at their houses – and it was said at first that she was to remain at the Farm for life – but that she had suddenly been removed by Nares, but where, he could not say.

L— shook his head ominously when he heard this statement, and it was evident to us all that the mother's suspicions were right, and that a deed of blood had been recently perpetrated. The best means of ascertaining the place of burial was consulted on, and we adjourned to the garden to search for any appearance of freshly disturbed ground, or other evidence that might lead to a discovery of her remains. When we had crossed the yard, and were about entering the garden gate, L— suggested the propriety of fetching the little dog, whose excellent nose had afforded the only clue we had been able to obtain. I went back for the animal, but he refused to leave his mistress, and it was not without some danger of a bite that I succeeded in catching him by the neck and carrying him out of the room. I put him on his feet when we were past the garden gate, and endeavoured to excite him to sprightliness by running along the walk and whistling to him to follow, but he sneaked after me with a drooping tail and a bowed head, as if he felt his share of the general grief.

We walked round the garden without discovering any signs that warranted further search. We had traversed every path in the garden, excepting a narrow, transverse one that left from the gate to a range of green and hot houses that lined the farthest wall. We were on the point of leaving the place, satisfied that it was not in our power to remove the veil of mystery that shrouded the girl's disappearance, when the dog, who had strayed into the entrance of the narrow path, gave extraordinary signs of liveliness and emotion – his tail wagged furiously, his ears were thrown forward, and a short but earnest yaffle broke into a continuous bark as he turned rapidly from one tide of the path to another, and finally ran down toward the greenhouse with his nose bent to the ground. "He scents her," said L—. "There is still a chance."

Our party, consisting of the magistrate, L— and two other officers, the under-keeper, the locksmith, and myself, followed the dog down the narrow path into the centre of a piece of ground containing three or four cucumber beds covered with sliding glass frames. The spaniel, after searching round the bed, jumped upon the centre frame and howled piteously. It was evident that he had lost the scent. L— pointed out to our notice that the sliding lid was fastened to the frame by a large padlock – this extraordinary security increased our suspicions. He seized a crow-bar from one of the smiths, and the lock was soon removed. The top of the frame was pulled up and the dog jumped into the tan that filled the bed and commenced scratching with all his might.

L— thrust the bar into the yielding soil, and at the depth of a foot, the iron struck a solid substance. This intimation electrified us – we waited not for tools; our hands were dug into the bed and the tan and black mould were dragged from the frame with an eagerness that soon emptied it and exhibited the boarding of a large trap door, divided into two parts, but securely locked together. While the smiths essayed their skill upon the lock, the magistrate stood by with lifted hands and head uncovered – a tear was in the good man's eye, and he breathed short from the excess of his anxiety. Everyone was visibly excited, and the loud and cheerful bark of the dog was hailed as an omen of success. L—'s impatience could not brook delay. He seized the sledgehammer of the smiths and with a blow that might have knocked in the side of a house, demolished the lock and bolt, and the doors jumped apart in the recoil from the blow. They were raised – a black and yawning vault was below – and a small flight of wooden steps, green and mouldy from the effects of the earth's dampness, led to the gloomy depths of the cavern.

The little dog dashed bravely down the stairway, and L—, requesting us to stand from between him and the light, picked his way down the narrow, slimy steps. One of the smiths followed, and the rest of us hung our heads anxiously over the edge of the vault's mouth, watching our friends as they receded in the distant gloom.

A pause ensued; the dog was heard barking, and an indistinct muttering between L— and the smith ascended to the surface of the earth. I shouted to them and was frightened at the reverberation of my voice. Our anxiety became painful in the extreme – the magistrate called to L—, but obtained no answer, and we were on the point of descending in a body when the officer appeared at the foot of the stairs. "We have found her," said he – we gave a simultaneous shout. "But she is dead" was the appalling finish of his speech, as he emerged from the mouth of the vault.

The smith, with the lifeless body of Mary Lobenstein swung over his shoulder, was assisted up the stairs. The corpse of the little girl was placed on one of the garden settees and, with heavy hearts and gloomy faces, we carried the melancholy burden into the house. The mother had not recovered from the shock which the anticipation of her daughter's death had given to her feelings; she was lying senseless upon the bed where she had been placed by the keeper's wife. We laid the body of her daughter in an adjoining room and directed the woman to perform the last sad duties to the senseless clay while we awaited the parent's restoration. The magistrate returned to London; the smiths were packing up their tools preparatory to departure and I was musing in melancholy mood over the events of the day when the forbidding face of the keeper's wife peeped in at the half-opened door and we were beckoned from the room.

"Please your honour, I never seed a dead body look like that there corpse of the little girl upstair. I've seed a many corpses in my time, but there's something onnataral about that there one, not like a dead body ought to be."

"What do you mean?"

"Why, though her feet and hands are cold, her jaw ain't dropped, and her eyes ain't open – and there's a limberness in her limbs that I don't like. I really believe she's only swounded."

L— and I hurried upstairs, and the smiths, with their baskets of tools dangling at their back, followed us into the room. I anxiously searched for any pulsation at the heart and the wrists of poor Mary, whose appearance certainly corroborated the woman's surmise, but the total absence of all visible signs of life denied us the encouragement of the flattering hope. One of the smiths took from his basket a tool of bright, fine-tempered steel; he held it for a few seconds against Mary's half-closed mouth, and upon withdrawing it, said, with a loud and energetic voice, "She is alive! Her breath has damped the surface of the steel!"

The man was right. Proper remedies were applied to the daughter and to her parent, and L— had the gratification of placing the lost Mary within her mother's arms.

Miss Lobenstein's explanation afforded but little additional information. When she was brought to the Farm by the villain Mills and his friend Billy the ostler, she was informed that it was to be the residence of her future life. She was subjected to the treatment of a maniac, her questions remained unanswered, and her supplications for permission to send to her mother were answered with a sneer. About three nights ago, she was ordered from her room, her shoes were taken off that she might noiselessly traverse the passages, and she was removed to the secret cell in the garden; some biscuits and a jug of water were placed beside her, and she had remained in undisturbed solitude till the instinct of her favourite dog led to her discovery shortly after she had fainted from exhaustion and terror.

There is little doubt but that the ruffians were alarmed at the watching and appearances of the indefatigable L—, and withdrew their victim to the securest hiding place. I had the curiosity, in company with some of the officers, to descend into the secret cell; it had originally been dug out for the foundation of an intended house; the walls and partitions were solidly built, but the bankruptcy of the projector prevented any further progress. When Farrell and his gang took possession of the place, it was deemed easier to cover the rafters of the cellar with boards and earth than to fill it up – in time, the existence of the hole became forgotten, save by those most interested in its concealment. Farrell contrived the mode of entrance through the glass frame of the forcing bed, and when the adjacent greenhouses were constructed, an artificial flue or vent was introduced to the depths of the cell, and supplied it with a sufficiency of air.

Mrs. Lobenstein refused to prosecute the spinster Bishop, the malignancy of whose temper preyed upon her own heart, and speedily consigned her unlamented to the grave. The true particulars of this strange affair were never given to the public, although I believe that its occurrence mainly contributed to effect an alteration in the English laws respecting private madhouses and other receptacles for lunatics.

The magistracy of the county knew that they were to blame in permitting the existence of such a den as Farrell's Farm, and exerted themselves to quash proceedings against the fellows Mills and Nares, and their coadjutors. A few months imprisonment was the only punishment awarded them, and that was in return for the assault upon the head of the police; but in Billy, the ostler, was recognised an old offender – various unpunished offences rose against him, and he was condemned to 'seven pennorth' aboard the hulks at Chatham. The greatest rogue escaped the arm of justice for a time; but L— has since assured me he has every reason to believe that Farrell was, under a feigned name, executed in Somersetshire for horse stealing.

The Farm was converted into a Poor House for some of the adjacent parishes; L— received his reward, and when I left England, our heroine Mary was the blooming mother of a numerous family.

Murder Is My Middle Name

Elliott Capon

I'M NOT TRYING to be melodramatic, or make myself out to be some kind of poor man's Raymond Chandler.

Murder *is* my middle name. My name is Charles Murder Pennywhistle. The way I got that mid-moniker is like this: my mother, nee Emily Murdoch-Derwood, married one Albert Montgomery Pennywhistle. (This was before I was born, of course). White Anglo Saxon et. al.s being what they are, it was naturally assumed that the first offspring's middle name would be Emily's surname. But somehow they figured Charles Murdoch-Derwood Pennywhistle wouldn't fit on a social security card, so they combined Murdoch-Derwood into...well, Murder. For a while I called myself C. Murder Pennywhistle, but I abandoned that shortly after puberty. Still, I wasn't able to escape my middle name altogether.

I'm a homicide detective with the Boston P.D.

I could have named this narrative 'Death of Another Salesman' since it involved the death of a, well, a salesman, and indeed I would have, except that 'Murder Is My Middle Name' sounds so...*forties*, you know? And that makes for a better mood-setter, since the particular murder I'm going to tell you about was also fairly 'forties'. I mean, throughout the investigation I kept looking over my shoulder to see where Asta was.

Let me come in through the back door on this: at the time, I was thirty-nine years old, and I'd been on the Boston P.D. payroll for thirteen years. As a matter of fact, I've held only two full-time jobs in my entire life: six years in the U.S. Navy (five of those in the Shore Patrol keeping San Diego safe from the U.S. Navy itself) and B.P.D. Over the past eighteen years, I've seen a lot of killing. If anyone was compiling statistics, I could put in my two cents as to how most of the murders committed in the past twenty years were of the violent type: shooting, mostly, followed by stabbing/slashing; but also beating, bludgeoning, defenestration, decapitation, motor vehicle assault, etc. Go back to the fabulous 'forties, to the suave mystery flicks of the era, and you find an occasional bloodless shooting, where the victim grimaces, places a hand over his navel and crumples to the floor; but, more often than not you have a clever little murder which requires a Charlie Chan or a Sherlock Holmes or a Miss Marple or a Mike Hammer or the boys of the 87th Precinct to solve. How can I say this without sounding like an idiot: that's the type of murder I prefer. What I mean is, *any* murder investigation infuriates me, any murder, and I wish to God I never have to inquire into another homicide for the rest of my life; but as a professional, I *appreciate* a finely crafted, well-thought-out doing-in, instead of the ones I get, with bullets flying in seven thousand directions as a result of a drug deal gone sour.

The Hazlet homicide was one such as I'd always thought I longed for.

This particular day I felt like Joe Friday: I was actually working the day watch out of Homicide. Which is not unusual, because for forty weeks of the year, I *always* work the day watch out of Homicide. (Four weeks is spent on vacation, and six weeks on nights, covering other detectives who have the nerve to take vacations of their own.) It was a Saturday, about three in the afternoon, when The Call came in. It had been a slow day: one unidentified black male found in a park early that morning and a female Caucasian beaten to death with a baseball bat in the early afternoon. The first would probably never be solved (the victim appeared to be a homeless alcoholic, and, in the social circles in which he traveled, nobody ain't never seen nothin'), and the second was solved within ten minutes (the boyfriend switched jealousy for remorse, and confessed to the uniformed cop who showed up in response to the neighbor's 911 call). This may seem all horrible to you, but to me, it was just a tiptoe through the tulips. I'd always let myself get angry for a few moments, then turn my emotions off about these cases: my getting an ulcer wouldn't bring either victim back to life. As a day at *work*, it was, so far, a pretty easy trip.

So anyway, Captain McGarrity (of the Naarth Shaare of the Chaarles Rivah McGarritys, thank you) stuck his head into the squad room and suggested that Pete O'Brien, my partner, and I get over to an address in one of the better neighborhoods of the greater Boston area and See The Woman. He also suggested we take a couple of uniforms with us.

The two guys we drafted on the way out were officers White and Winfield, and we headed out. We ended our journey in the kind of neighborhood where the butler had a guy to help him on with his tux in the morning. It took about an hour to get from the end of the driveway to the front door.

The door was opened by, yes, a butler, but he wasn't the robot-like Britisher in the movies of my youth. He was Asian, either Filipino or Indonesian, something southwestern Pacific, and he was nervous as hell.

"This way, gentlemen," he said, and led us into a – what? a salon? a drawing room? – where he introduced us to a woman who was pacing frantically back and forth.

"M- Mrs. Hazlet," the butler said, "the po—"

"My God, what took you so long?" she said, with a slight hysterical crack at the top of her voice. "Follow me!" And with that she took off out another door and into the hall.

Most homicides are committed by someone known to the victim, and so far, even though I had no *corpus delicti*, as far as I was concerned, both the butler and the Mrs. were prime suspects – in what, I wasn't sure. So I sized them up quickly.

The butler's name, I found out a little later, was Karneh Selim, and he was Malaysian. He was in his early sixties, and had been working for the Hazlets for about twenty-six years. He lived on the estate (they called the property 'the estate') but not in the house, with his wife Yoon, also past sixty, who did the cooking.

Mrs. Hazlet, in the quick glance I got of her, and in subsequent discourse, proved out as follows: she was forty-four, and looked more like the prime Jane Russell than Jane Russell did in her prime. She had been married to the deceased (oh, did I spoil the surprise?) for some seven years. It was the second time around for both of them, three kids between them by the previouses. She owned and ran one of those antique book and map shops that only needed one sale a week to cover the rent and utilities.

So anyway, Pete and I and the two officers followed Mrs. Hazlet (Joy, later) down the hall and into a small elevator. Yes, for the love of Pete…well, I like him…make that for the love of *Mike*, an elevator! and we went down a short while. It was hardly worth it, in my opinion. Mrs. H. hadn't said anything else, yet, but even Captain McGarrity could have seen she was extremely agitated, as if she had (1) just killed her husband or (2) she had just discovered her husband dead.

The elevator door opened to let us out into a corridor in what was, I assumed, the basement. There was only one door in the hall, down at the other end. She pointed to it and said "There!"

With a nod to White and Winfield that said Don't Let Her Get Away, Pete and I approached the door. It was a thick, heavy metal, greenish, with a little trapdoor in it at about eye level, like the one they put Steve McQueen behind when he got thrown into solitary in *The Great Escape*. The trap was standing open, to the inside of the room behind it. I looked at Pete and he looked at me and we both shrugged and I put my face up to the opening.

There was a dead man sprawled across a table. I could tell he was dead by the way the blood had poured out of the gaping wound in his throat.

The first thing I did was slam my hand against the door, feeling for a doorknob. There was none. All there was was a keyhole, one of those old keyholes, you know, rounded at the top and flared at the bottom, like in the Mayberry jail? I put my fingers in through the trap and pulled. The door was locked.

"How do you get in?" I shouted down the hall to Mrs. Hazlet, who had remained near the elevator (with White and Winfield between her and the cage).

"The- the key," she stammered back.

"Well where the heck is it?" I didn't say 'heck'. I didn't even say 'hell'.

She didn't say anything. She just pointed at me. At me?

I figured she was pointing into the room. I looked again, and there on the table, near the deceased's hand and surrounded by what was not a lot of ketchup lay what looked like an old-fashioned skeleton key.

I jumped at the sound of her voice; she had walked up behind me without my hearing her.

"That key on the table...it...it's the only key to the room," she said in the kind of choked voice to which I have become all too familiar. "The only key in existence. Leonard always kept it on him. We...we can't get in."

"A window," Pete suggested. "A vent..."

"We're in a sub-basement, no windows," she said, and I noted how red her eyes were, "and the air conditioning and heating vents are- are, much too small...no- no one could get through."

I dispatched Winfield to get Emergency Services over here with rescue equipment. We spent a few minutes tugging and pushing at the door, hoping it would merely open on its own, like in an Abbott and Costello movie, but eventually gave up.

While we waited for ES to show up, we had plenty of time to take Mrs. H. upstairs, wrap her around a glass of brandy, and get the poop.

It seemed the late Leonard Hazlet was the Vice President and leading salesman for the world's foremost producer of some obscure chemical that nobody had ever heard of, but was present in everything from antibiotics to ice cream to motor oil to detergents to perfume to explosives to bubble gum. Consequently, he was a very wealthy man. He was also a *litterateur*, and his Lifestyle of the Rich and Not Famous was to collect books: an original Shakespeare quarto; a first edition of Dickens' *Tale of Two Cities*; an autographed volume of *Mein Kampf*; a copy of the Emancipation Proclamation hand-written by Lincoln's secretary; stuff like that. To protect what was both his hobby and an extremely valuable investment, Leonard had spent a small fortune in building his subterranean fortress of solitude. The only way in was through that door, and there was only one key in the world made to fit that door, and he carried it with him always. The first thing I asked was, how was she so sure there was only the one key? The answer, a good one, was that Leonard had made it himself in a well-equipped home workshop several years ago, and had crushed the mold to dust.

And who else knew of his collection? (Motive first, then means and opportunity). Lots of people, it seemed: antique book dealers and other collectors, internet newsletter-reading bibliophiles, a good many of the Hazlets' friends and business acquaintances. But I figured I'd have to put a power (you know, like $-^{100}$) on the odds that anyone who knew about his hobby would kill him for it. And anyway, of course, no one else had been in the house today with the exception of Mrs. Hazlet, Karneh, and Yoon.

It seemed the deceased was in the habit of spending a quiet hour or two a day by himself in his 'library', as he called it. That was his normal routine, and no one thought anything of it. But on this particular Saturday, when Mrs. H. got back from an appointment at her shop and found out that he had been down there at least six hours, and went to check on him—

We had to wrap her around another brandy.

Pete and I looked at each other and nodded and agreed: suicide. The man had locked himself in his hideaway and cut his throat. We clung to that theory for about forty-five minutes, until Emergency Services finally cut the hinges away and we all burst into the room, and the only thing in the room sharper than my wit was the teaspoon he had used to stir his last cup of coffee.

Naturally, there was no blood on the handle, far-fetched as that might have been.

So what we had here was a man found sitting at a table with his throat cut. The only key in the world that would unlock the very locked door to a below-ground room was resting comfortably on the table before him, in a morass of dried blood. There were no windows. No vents bigger than cat-sized. No false entrances or hidden doorways. A man found with his throat cut in a locked room with the only key on the table in front of him…man found with his throat cut…in truth, I couldn't get past that point. I was like a record with a scratch on it… or a CD with whatever malformations they develop. Finally, here was a mystery worthy of the great Basil Rathbone, and I hadn't the slightest idea of how to start solving it.

There's that old joke: "What are you looking for?" – "I dropped a quarter over there." – "But if you dropped it over there, why are you looking over *here*?" – "The light's better."

So not having any better lighting anywhere else, I figured I'd look around the scene of the crime. I waited till the forensics team had photographed, fingerprinted, and vacuumed to their hearts' content. It was after seven at that point, and I hadn't had supper, but I couldn't leave. And if I couldn't eat, neither could Pete: I asked him to officially interview the widow and the servants. Then I started crawling over the room.

The library was a room about fourteen by eighteen, lit by recessed lighting in the ceiling. With the exception of the door itself, all four walls were covered with shelves; most of the shelves were full of books or bound papers, and almost everything was wrapped in heavy plastic. One could argue as to whether the piece of furniture we had found Hazlet slumped over was a table or a desk: it was big, very big, and had one draw filled with nothing sharp, just letters, invoices, auction notices, things like that – running the length of it in the front. The top was plywood, stained and polyurethaned with about nine coats; Hazlet had obviously made it himself in his workshop, and a nice piece of craftsmanship it was. An extremely large magnifying glass and a high-intensity reading lamp were the only things that we found on the table that likely belonged there. There was also, slightly streaked with blood, what appeared to be a first edition volume of a collection of stories by Ambrose Bierce. A chalk outline identified both the position of Hazlet and the key, the latter of which was by now in my pocket. The chair the deceased had been sitting in was a very comfortable executive-type seat, the kind you'd find in the office of the company president. There was no blood on it. Our collective surmise was that he had been sitting at the table perusing the Bierce book when his throat had been cut from behind, causing him to fall forward across the table. The question was, how did the murderer(s) lock the door without the key?

Well, obviously, they didn't. Somehow the key was used and then returned to the table. Or, there was a second key. Or, there was no murderer.

I crawled over that room for an hour, and the only thing I came up with was a headache. One of the lab guys had examined the key and the lock with a portable microscope-type contraption, and had assured me up and down that *that* key was the *only* key that had ever been used in that lock: teeny weeny tiny winy little scratches on both matched each other, and the lock showed no other teeny weenies that didn't match our key. But still, I had to prove that someone had been able to lock the door and return the key to the table; on the evidence we had now, a first-year law student could get Jack the Ripper off, even after he confessed.

Assuming, of course, I ever came up with a suspect.

I took a careful note of where we had found the key– in the corner of the desk, where any prudent man would leave something he didn't want to lose yet didn't want in his way. At my request, the ES guys had reattached the door to its hinges: not perfectly, but good enough that the thing would shut and could be locked if necessary. I went out into the hall and pulled the door shut, then pushed it open a few times to make sure it didn't lock automatically. It didn't; you needed the key. Since we had affirmed that the only fingerprints on the key when we had found it were Hazlet's I was free to handle it as much as I wanted to. So I experimented. With the door shut, I opened the trap door and looked through. From that angle, I could see most of the table. The best way for me to get the key back on the table (pretending the door was locked) was to throw it through the trap. Unfortunately, the hole was too small to get both my face and my arm in at the same time. I would have to throw it blindly. I memorized where the table was, stepped back, thrust my arm all the way in through the opening, and gently tossed the key underhanded toward the table.

FWUP. It landed on the thick maroon carpet. I reentered the room and picked up the key, left, reaimed, threw it a little harder. FWUP.

I tried lofting it the next time, in a gentle but high arc. CLINK FWUP. It had hit the table, alright, but because of the height had bounced right off and onto the floor.

In all, I threw that damn key in through the trap twenty-five times. Six times I hit the table and bounced off; nineteen times I missed it altogether. That was *not* how the key had been returned to the table...assuming the key had been returned to the table. But if it hadn't been, if the key hadn't been used, how did the murderer...oops, I was off on the mental merry-go-round again. I figured the best thing would be to sleep on this end of the investigation, hoping that the elves would come during the night and fix everything. I went upstairs (upelevator) and retrieved Pete, and we decided to go out and eat and fill each other in.

After my somewhat useless recitation of stating the obvious, Pete took out his notebook and began telling me what he had found out.

"I started with the widow," he told me, "'cause after all, *cui bono*, and she *bonos* the most if her old man croaks. They've been married seven years, like she told us at first, but what she didn't tell us was that he was fifteen years older than her. Big deal, you say, and I agree. Fifteen years is nothing, especially when you consider that her ex left her a very wealthy woman when he decided to chuck it all in and become a Trappist monk. She took that money to open her bookstore, and that's where she met Leonard. According to her everything was peachy between them."

"Mmmph," I said around a mouthful of chowder. "That was no crime of passion. That was an extremely deliberate, planned murder."

"Uh huh," Pete agreed. "Not your typical spouse murder. I would tend to dismiss her as a suspect. Tend to, mind you, not write off, 'cause who knows."

"Hmm. What about the servants?"

Karneh and Yoon Selim had been in Leonard Hazlet's employ since 1989, about the time he'd (that is, Leonard) made his first million, and they'd been with him through a first wife, two kids, a divorce, a remarriage, and the next eleven million. Even though Selim was around five foot five and the color of rye toast, Pete swore that he had never met anyone else in his life who bore such a strong resemblance to Alan Napier playing Alfred to Adam West's Bruce Wayne. The similarity was metaphysical, of course. The way things seemed, the Selims would have been working for the deceased for another twenty-five years. They both seemed extremely content with their positions: after all, free room and board, decent wages, nice people to work for? I wouldn't mind a deal like that myself.

"So what you're telling me," I said, "is that all the conceivable suspects make Snow White look like Charles Manson."

"Basically, yeah," Pete said.

"No," I insisted. "Somebody in that house killed Hazlet, and we're gonna find out who."

Even if Sunday had been my day off, which it wasn't, I would've gone back to the Hazlet house. This thing was really nagging me, tormenting me. I wanted to go back to the library. I knew the answer was there.

I prevailed upon Yoon to make me a cup of tea, and she actually brewed a pot with real tea leaves and rolling-boiled water and a strainer and the whole *megillah*, while I asked a few pointless questions. Nobody had been to the house the day before: no visitors, no delivery people, no lawn maintainers, not even the mailman. I was running out of straws to clutch at. Even so, something was gnawing at the inside of my brain, ordering me down to the library. I took the tea (in a Wedgwood cup, with a saucer!) down the elevator with me.

I was still carrying the key with me. I unlocked the door and sat in Hazlet's chair. With permission, Karneh had carefully cleaned up his former employer's blood; the lamp and magnifying glass were placed just so, as if awaiting their owner's return.

I sighed and looked around at all the books and papers. Even though they weren't mine, I could still feel a tingle of excitement at what surrounded me: the age, the history, wondering just *who* had actually touched these papers! It must've been a real kick for old Leonard. I swiveled around to get a real feel of being surrounded by the books and my arm sailed across the table, knocking my teacup over, and spilling expensive liquid all over the nice tabletop. Calling myself all kinds of names, I pulled out the little pocket-packet of tissues I always carry and mopped up the mess. I noticed a rounded drop of tea in a corner of the table. I passed a tissue over it, but it remained unbroken. Curious, I gently stuck the soft part of my index finger into it. There was a depression in the table, a small hole, nice and round and even, perfect for holding a tenth of an ounce of spilled tea. The chalk marks from the day before, which Karneh had so carefully – on police orders – left in place, had fortunately not been totally eradicated by my clumsiness. The hole I had just found was right in the center of the chalk outline of the top of the skeleton key.

I ran my fingers over the entire desktop: not a scratch, not a dent. Hazlet had obviously worked hard to keep that thing clear and smooth. Why, then, a hole right where he had left the key? There was something fluttering just at the edge of my mind, and I couldn't get ahold of it. I looked all over the room, almost straining to come up with an idea, with *the* idea, getting more and more frustrated because I couldn't think of anything. I just *knew* that that little hole was the key to the key…I got up and paced the room. I searched book titles, hoping that like in some hack mystery the secret would be revealed in the words of a long-dead author, hoping that the name of a book would trigger an idea, help me hit the nail on the head…

The nail on the head. I had it. I knew how the door had been locked. All I needed now was to find out who had done it.

I hurried upstairs, made my goodbyes to the still-weepy Mrs. Hazlet, and went back to the stationhouse. It being Sunday afternoon, nobody else in the world was open, so I spent a frustrating afternoon and evening waiting for Monday morning. Monday was supposed to be my day off, but I came in and made Pete come in too to help me with the phone calls. It took a while, but by the time we hung up our phones for the last time he had to admit that he agreed with me.

Late Monday afternoon we drafted another uniformed cop and went back to the Hazlet house. I asked Mrs. Hazlet, Selim and Yoon to join us in the subterranean library. Nobody protested. As I spoke, I pulled an original copy of *The Strand Magazine* (featuring *The Hound of the Baskervilles*) off a shelf and unconsciously toyed with it.

"Karneh," I asked him, "How old are you?"

"Eh, sir?" he asked. "Why, sixty-four, sir, why do you ask?"

"What's your social security number, Karneh?"

"Um, why, I, I don't know, sir, I can n- never remember it," he stammered.

"Is it because you don't have one?" I asked.

He blanched a little, but remained much more impassive than I would have thought he could have.

"Perhaps, sir. I don't remember. It's been years since Yoon and I came to America. I must have gotten a number when I first started working for Mr. Hazlet."

Yoon nodded agreement.

"In truth," I said, "neither of you exist on the social security rolls. Nor, as a matter of fact, does the Immigration and Naturalization Service have any record of your being in this country legally."

"What," asked Joy Hazlet, "what does any of this have to do with Leonard's...with the-the murder?"

"Motive, Mrs. Hazlet," I said. "Suppose me a few suppositions. Suppose that you were getting old and knew your employer was going to replace you."

"But how—" Mrs. H. started.

"Because Detective O'Brien and myself called every employment agency in the Boston area," I interrupted her, "and found out from the Foxboro Domestic Service that your late husband was preparing to interview manservants and cooks in the next few weeks. And suppose you knew that, being illegal aliens, you had no pension or social security or even welfare to fall back upon. And suppose you knew that while your employer had made no pension provisions, and you were not entitled to government benefits, you knew he had left you quite a comfortable sum of money in his will, in regard for decades of faithful service, such monies payable only after his death?"

Karneh pulled himself to his full height. "Sir, you insult my integrity and my regard for Mr. Hazlet. And even so, sir, that beggars the question of the locked door."

"Ah," I said. "Watch." I put Sherlock and Watson down on the table and took a finishing nail – a long nail with a very small head – from my pocket. Setting it down in the hole I had discovered on the table, I took a small flat rock I had picked up in the garden and gently banged the nail about an eighth of an inch into the wood. I then took a spool of thread from another pocket and carefully tied it to the nail. Needless to say, I had a rapt and silent audience.

"Would you all please leave the room?" I asked.

We went out into the hallway and I pulled the door shut behind me. I fished the infamous skeleton key from yet another pocket and brandished it, locking the door (after making sure that the copy I had made was very safe in my shirt pocket).

"Observe," I said.

Holding the thread taut, I slipped the top of the key over it and, raising the string, slid the key down it, through the trap and across the room and over the nail until it settled onto the table with a slight CLINK. I then yanked sharply, pulled the nail out of the table and back through the trap door, leaving the key resting quietly and contentedly on the table.

"Voila," I quietly said.

It was Yoon who collapsed. She began crying and speaking in what I suppose was Malay. Karneh bent down to comfort her, then looked up at Mrs. Hazlet. There were tears in his eyes.

"Please, ma'am," he said, "we both respected your husband very much. For years he told us to save, invest…but we never did. We always assumed this would go on forever. Now…he was going to dismiss us, to…" And then he broke down too.

There was no triumph after all as we took the Selims to the station to be arraigned.

There was *some* satisfaction, though. I had solved a 'forties case.

I mean, after all, the butler did it.

The Point of a Pin

G.K. Chesterton

FATHER BROWN always declared that he solved this problem in his sleep. And this was true, though in rather an odd fashion; because it occurred at a time when his sleep was rather disturbed. It was disturbed very early in the morning by the hammering that began in the huge building, or half-building, that was in process of erection opposite to his rooms; a colossal pile of flats still mostly covered with scaffolding and with boards announcing Messrs. Swindon & Sand as the builders and owners. The hammering was renewed at regular intervals and was easily recognisable: because Messrs. Swindon & Sand specialised in some new American system of cement flooring which, in spite of its subsequent smoothness, solidity, impenetrability and permanent comfort (as described in the advertisements) had to be clamped down at certain points with heavy tools. Father Brown endeavoured, however, to extract exiguous comfort from it; saying that it always woke him up in time for the very earliest Mass, and was therefore something almost in the nature of a carillon. After all, he said, it was almost as poetic that Christians should be awakened by hammers as by bells. As a fact, however, the building operations were a little on his nerves, for another reason. For there was hanging like a cloud over the half-built skyscraper the possibility of a Labour crisis, which the newspapers doggedly insisted on describing as a Strike. As a matter of fact, if ever it happened, it would be a Lock-out. But he worried a good deal about whether it would happen. And it might be questioned whether hammering is more of a strain on the attention because it may go on for ever, or because it may stop at any minute.

"As a mere matter of taste and fancy," said Father Brown, staring up at the edifice with his owlish spectacles, "I rather wish it would stop. I wish all houses would stop while they still have the scaffolding up. It seems almost a pity that houses are ever finished. They look so fresh and hopeful with all that fairy filigree of white wood, all light and bright in the sun; and a man so often only finishes a house by turning it into a tomb."

As he turned away from the object of his scrutiny, he nearly ran into a man who had just darted across the road towards him. It was a man whom he knew slightly, but sufficiently to regard him (in the circumstances) as something of a bird of ill-omen. Mr. Mastyk was a squat man with a square head that looked hardly European, dressed with a heavy dandyism that seemed rather too consciously Europeanized. But Brown had seen him lately talking to young Sand of the building firm; and he did not like it. This man Mastyk was the head of an organization rather new in English industrial politics; produced by extremes at both ends; a definite army of non-Union and largely alien labour hired out in gangs to various firms; and he was obviously hovering about in the hope of hiring it out to this one. In short, he might negotiate some way of out-manoeuvring the Trade Union and flooding the works with blacklegs. Father Brown had been drawn into some of the debates, being in some sense called in on both sides. And as the Capitalists all reported that, to their positive knowledge, he was a Bolshevist; and as the Bolshevists all testified that he was a reactionary rigidly attached to *bourgeois* ideologies, it may be inferred that he talked a certain amount of sense without any appreciable effect on anybody. The news brought by Mr. Mastyk, however, was calculated to jerk everybody out of the ordinary rut of the dispute.

"They want you to go over there at once," said Mr. Mastyk, in awkwardly accented English. "There is a threat to murder."

Father Brown followed his guide in silence up several stairways and ladders to a platform of the unfinished building, on which were grouped the more or less familiar figures of the heads of the building business. They included even what had once been the head of it; though the head had been for some time rather a head in the clouds. It was at least a head in a coronet, that hid it from human sight like a cloud. Lord Stanes, in other words, had not only retired from the business but been caught up into the House of Lords and disappeared. His rare reappearances were languid and somewhat dreary; but this one, in conjunction with that of Mastyk, seemed none the less menacing. Lord Stanes was a lean, long-headed, hollow-eyed man with very faint fair hair fading into baldness; and he was the most evasive person the priest had ever met. He was unrivalled in the true Oxford talent of saying, "No doubt you're right," so as to sound like, "No doubt you think you're right," or of merely remarking, "You think so?" so as to imply the acid addition, "You would." But Father Brown fancied that the man was not merely bored but faintly embittered, though whether at being called down from Olympus to control such trade squabbles, or merely at not being really any longer in control of them, it was difficult to guess.

On the whole, Father Brown rather preferred the more *bourgeois* group of partners, Sir Hubert Sand and his nephew Henry; though he doubted privately whether they really had very many ideologies. True, Sir Hubert Sand had obtained considerable celebrity in the newspapers; both as a patron of sport and as a patriot in many crises during and after the Great War. He had won notable distinction in France, for a man of his years, and had afterwards been featured as a triumphant captain of industry overcoming difficulties among the munition-workers. He had been called a Strong Man; but that was not his fault. He was in fact a heavy, hearty Englishman; a great swimmer; a good squire; and admirable amateur colonel. Indeed, something that can only be called a military make-up pervaded his appearance. He was growing stout, but he kept his shoulders set back; his curly hair and moustache were still brown while the colours of his face were already somewhat withered and faded. His nephew was a burly youth of the pushing, or rather shouldering, sort with a relatively small head thrust out on a thick neck, as if he went at things with his head down; a gesture somehow rendered rather quaint and boyish by the pince-nez that were balanced on his pugnacious pug-nose.

Father Brown had looked at all these things before; and at that moment everybody was looking at something entirely new. In the centre of the woodwork there was nailed up a large loose flapping piece of paper on which something was scrawled in crude and almost crazy capital letters, as if the writer were either almost illiterate or were affecting or parodying illiteracy. The words actually ran: 'The Council of the Workers warns Hubert Sand that he will lower wages and lock out workmen at his peril. If the notices go out tomorrow, he will be dead by the justice of the people.'

Lord Stanes was just stepping back from his examination of the paper, and, looking across at his partner, he said with rather a curious intonation:

"Well, it's you they want to murder. Evidently I'm not considered worth murdering."

One of those still electric shocks of fancy that sometimes thrilled Father Brown's mind in an almost meaningless way shot through him at that particular instant. He had a queer notion that the man who was speaking could not now be murdered, because he was already dead. It was, he cheerfully admitted, a perfectly senseless idea. But there was something that always gave him the creeps about the cold disenchanted detachment of the noble senior partner; about his cadaverous colour and inhospitable eyes. "The fellow," he thought in the same perverse mood, "has green eyes and looks as if he had green blood."

Anyhow, it was certain that Sir Hubert Sand had not got green blood. His blood, which was red enough in every sense, was creeping up into his withered or weather-beaten cheeks with all the warm fullness of life that belongs to the natural and innocent indignation of the good-natured.

"In all my life," he said, in a strong voice and yet shakily, "I have never had such a thing said or done about me. I may have differed—"

"We can none of us differ about this," struck in his nephew impetuously. "I've tried to get on with them, but this is a bit too thick."

"You don't really think," began Father Brown, "that your workmen—"

"I say we may have differed," said old Sand, still a little tremulously, "God knows I never liked the idea of threatening English workmen with cheaper labour—"

"We none of us liked it," said the young man, "but if I know you, uncle, this has about settled it."

Then after a pause he added, "I suppose, as you say, we did disagree about details; but as to real policy—"

"My dear fellow," said his uncle, comfortably. "I hoped there would never be any real disagreement." From which anybody who understands the English nation may rightly infer that there had been very considerable disagreement. Indeed the uncle and nephew differed almost as much as an Englishman and an American. The uncle had the English ideal of getting outside the business, and setting up a sort of an alibi as a country gentleman. The nephew had the American ideal of getting inside the business; of getting inside the very mechanism like a mechanic. And, indeed, he had worked with most of the mechanics and was familiar with most of the processes and tricks of the trade. And he was American again, in the fact that he did this partly as an employer to keep his men up to the mark, but in some vague way also as an equal, or at least with a pride in showing himself also as a worker. For this reason he had often appeared almost as a representative of the workers, on technical points which were a hundred miles away from his uncle's popular eminence in politics or sport. The memory of those many occasions, when young Henry had practically come out of the workshop in his shirt-sleeves, to demand some concession about the conditions of the work, lent a peculiar force and even violence to his present reaction the other way.

"Well, they've damned well locked themselves out this time," he cried. "After a threat like that there's simply nothing left but to defy them. There's nothing left but to sack them all now; instanter; on the spot. Otherwise we'll be the laughing stock of the world."

Old Sand frowned with equal indignation, but began slowly: "I shall be very much criticised—"

"Criticised!" cried the young man shrilly. "Criticised if you defy a threat of murder! Have you any notion how you'll be criticised if you don't defy it? Won't you enjoy the headlines? 'Great Capitalist Terrorised' – 'Employer Yields to Murder Threat.'"

"Particularly," said Lord Stanes, with something faintly unpleasant in his tone. "Particularly when he has been in so many headlines already as 'The Strong Man of Steel-Building'."

Sand had gone very red again and his voice came thickly from under his thick moustache. "Of course you're right there. If these brutes think I'm afraid—"

At this point there was an interruption in the conversation of the group; and a slim young man came towards them swiftly. The first notable thing about him was that he was one of those whom men, and women too, think are just a little too nice-looking to look nice. He had beautiful dark curly hair and a silken moustache and he spoke like a gentleman, but with almost too refined and exactly modulated an accent. Father Brown knew him at once as Rupert Rae, the secretary of Sir Hubert, whom he had often seen pottering about in Sir Hubert's house; but never with such impatience in his movements or such a wrinkle on his brow.

"I'm sorry, sir," he said to his employer, "but there's a man been hanging about over there. I've done my best to get rid of him. He's only got a letter, but he swears he must give it to you personally."

"You mean he went first to my house?" said Sand, glancing swiftly at his secretary. "I suppose you've been there all the morning."

"Yes, sir," said Mr. Rupert Rae.

There was a short silence; and then Sir Hubert Sand curtly intimated that the man had better be brought along; and the man duly appeared.

Nobody, not even the least fastidious lady, would have said that the newcomer was too nice-looking. He had very large ears and a face like a frog, and he stared before him with an almost ghastly fixity, which Father Brown attributed to his having a glass eye. In fact, his fancy was tempted to equip the man with two glass eyes; with so glassy a stare did he contemplate the company. But the priest's experience, as distinct from his fancy, was able to suggest several natural causes for that unnatural waxwork glare; one of them being an abuse of the divine gift of fermented liquor. The man was short and shabby and carried a large bowler hat in one hand and a large sealed letter in the other.

Sir Hubert Sand looked at him; and then said quietly enough, but in a voice that somehow seemed curiously small, coming out of the fullness of his bodily presence: "Oh – it's you."

He held out his hand for the letter; and then looked around apologetically, with poised finger, before ripping it open and reading it. When he had read it, he stuffed it into his inside pocket and said hastily and a little harshly:

"Well, I suppose all this business is over, as you say. No more negotiations possible now; we couldn't pay the wages they want anyhow. But I shall want to see you again, Henry, about – about winding things up generally."

"All right," said Henry, a little sulkily perhaps, as if he would have preferred to wind them up by himself. "I shall be up in number 188 after lunch; got to know how far they've got up there."

The man with the glass eye, if it was a glass eye, stumped stiffly away; and the eye of Father Brown (which was by no means a glass eye) followed him thoughtfully as he threaded his way through the ladders and disappeared into the street.

It was on the following morning that Father Brown had the unusual experience of over-sleeping himself; or at least of starting from sleep with a subjective conviction that he must be late. This was partly due to his remembering, as a man may remember a dream, the fact of having been half-awakened at a more regular hour and fallen asleep again; a common enough occurrence with most of us, but a very uncommon occurrence with Father Brown. And he was afterwards oddly convinced, with that mystic side of him which was normally turned away from the world, that in that detached dark islet of dreamland, between the two wakings, there lay like buried treasure the truth of this tale.

As it was, he jumped up with great promptitude, plunged into his clothes, seized his big knobby umbrella and bustled out into the street, where the bleak white morning was breaking like splintered ice about the huge black building facing him. He was surprised to find that the streets shone almost empty in the cold crystalline light; the very look of it told him it could hardly be so late as he had feared. Then suddenly the stillness was cloven by the arrowlike swiftness of a long grey car which halted before the big deserted flats. Lord Stanes unfolded himself from within and approached the door, carrying (rather languidly) two large suitcases. At the same moment the door opened, and somebody seemed to step back instead of stepping out into the street. Stanes called twice to the man within, before that person seemed to complete his original gesture by coming out on to the doorstep; then the two held a brief colloquy, ending in the nobleman carrying his suitcases upstairs, and the other coming out into full daylight and revealing the heavy shoulders and peering head of young Henry Sand.

Father Brown made no more of this rather odd meeting, until two days later the young man drove up in his own car, and implored the priest to enter it. "Something awful has happened," he said, "and I'd rather talk to you than Stanes. You know Stanes arrived the other day with some mad idea of camping in one of the flats that's just finished. That's why I had to go there early and open the door to him. But all that will keep. I want you to come up to my uncle's place at once."

"Is he ill?" inquired the priest quickly.

"I think he's dead," answered the nephew.

"What do you mean by saying you think he's dead?" asked Father Brown a little briskly. "Have you got a doctor?"

"No," answered the other. "I haven't got a doctor or a patient either... It's no good calling in doctors to examine the body; because the body has run away. But I'm afraid I know where it has run to...the truth is – we kept it dark for two days; but he's disappeared."

"Wouldn't it be better," said Father Brown mildly, "if you told me what has really happened from the beginning?"

"I know," answered Henry Sand; "it's an infernal shame to talk flippantly like this about the poor old boy; but people get like that when they're rattled. I'm not much good at hiding things; the long and the short of it is – well, I won't tell you the long of it now. It's what some people would call rather a long shot; shooting suspicions at random and so on. But the short of it is that my unfortunate uncle has committed suicide."

They were by this time skimming along in the car through the last fringes of the town and the first fringes of the forest and park beyond it; the lodge gates of Sir Hubert Sand's small estate were about half a mile farther on amid the thickening throng of the beeches. The estate consisted chiefly of a small park and a large ornamental garden, which descended in terraces of a certain classical pomp to the very edge of the chief river of the district. As soon as they arrived at the house, Henry took the priest somewhat hastily through the old Georgian rooms and out upon the other side; where they silently descended the slope, a rather steep slope embanked with flowers, from which they could see the pale river spread out before them almost as flat as in a bird's-eye view. They were just turning the corner of the path under an enormous classical urn crowned with a somewhat incongruous garland of geraniums, when Father Brown saw a movement in the bushes and thin trees just below him, that seemed as swift as a movement of startled birds.

In the tangle of thin trees by the river two figures seemed to divide or scatter; one of them glided swiftly into the shadows and the other came forward to face them; bringing them to a halt and an abrupt and rather unaccountable silence. Then Henry Sand said in his heavy way: "I think you know Father Brown...Lady Sand."

Father Brown did know her; but at that moment he might almost have said that he did not know her. The pallor and constriction of her face was like a mask of tragedy; she was much younger than her husband, but at that moment she looked somehow older than everything in that old house and garden. And the priest remembered, with a subconscious thrill, that she was indeed older in type and lineage and was the true possessor of the place. For her own family had owned it as impoverished aristocrats, before she had restored its fortunes by marrying a successful business man. As she stood there, she might have been a family picture, or even a family ghost. Her pale face was of that pointed yet oval type seen in some old pictures of Mary Queen of Scots; and its expression seemed almost to go beyond the natural unnaturalness of a situation, in which her husband had vanished under suspicion of suicide. Father Brown, with the same subconscious movement of the mind, wondered who it was with whom she had been talking among the trees.

"I suppose you know all this dreadful news," she said, with a comfortless composure. "Poor Hubert must have broken down under all this revolutionary persecution, and been just maddened into taking his own life. I don't know whether you can do anything; or whether these horrible Bolsheviks can be made responsible for hounding him to death."

"I am terribly distressed, Lady Sand," said Father Brown. "And still, I must own, a little bewildered. You speak of persecution; do you think that anybody could hound him to death merely by pinning up that paper on the wall?"

"I fancy," answered the lady, with a darkening brow, "that there were other persecutions beside the paper."

"It shows what mistakes one may make," said the priest sadly. "I never should have thought he would be so illogical as to die in order to avoid death."

"I know," she answered, gazing at him gravely. "I should never have believed it, if it hadn't been written with his own hand."

"What?" cried Father Brown, with a little jump like a rabbit that has been shot at.

"Yes," said Lady Sand calmly. "He left a confession of suicide; so I fear there is no doubt about it." And she passed on up the slope alone, with all the inviolable isolation of the family ghost.

The spectacles of Father Brown were turned in mute inquiry to the eyeglasses of Mr. Henry Sand. And the latter gentleman, after an instant's hesitation, spoke again in his rather blind and plunging fashion: "Yes, you see, it seems pretty clear now what he did. He was always a great swimmer and used to come down in his dressing gown every morning for a dip in the river. Well, he came down as usual, and left his dressing gown on the bank; it's lying there still. But he also left a message saying he was going for his last swim and then death, or something like that."

"Where did he leave the message?" asked Father Brown.

"He scrawled it on that tree there, overhanging the water, I suppose the last thing he took hold of; just below where the dressing gown's lying. Come and see for yourself."

Father Brown ran down the last short slope to the shore and peered under the hanging tree, whose plumes were almost dipping in the stream. Sure enough, he saw on the smooth bark the words scratched conspicuously and unmistakably: "One more swim and then drowning. Goodbye. Hubert Sand." Father Brown's gaze travelled slowly up the bank till it rested on a gorgeous rag of raiment, all red and yellow with gilded tassels. It was the dressing gown and the priest picked it up and began to turn it over. Almost as he did so he was conscious that a figure had flashed across his field of vision; a tall dark figure that slipped from one clump of trees to another, as if following the trail of the vanishing lady. He had little doubt that it was the companion from whom she had lately parted. He had still less doubt that it was the dead man's secretary, Mr. Rupert Rae.

"Of course, it might be a final after-thought to leave the message," said Father Brown, without looking up, his eye riveted on the red and gold garment. "We've all heard of love messages written on trees; and I suppose there might be death-messages written on trees too."

"Well, he wouldn't have anything in the pockets of his dressing gown, I suppose," said young Sand. "And a man might naturally scratch his message on a tree if he had no pens, ink or paper."

"Sounds like French exercises," said the priest dismally. "But I wasn't thinking of that." Then, after a silence, he said in a rather altered voice:

"To tell the truth, I was thinking whether a man might not naturally scratch his message on a tree, even if he had stacks of pens, and quarts of ink, and reams of paper."

Henry was looking at him with a rather startled air, his eyeglasses crooked on his pug nose. "And what do you mean by that?" he asked sharply.

"Well," said Father Brown slowly, "I don't exactly mean that postmen will carry letters in the form of logs, or that you will ever drop a line to a friend by putting a postage stamp on a pinetree. It would have to be a particular sort of position – in fact, it would have to be a particular sort of person, who really preferred this sort of arboreal correspondence. But, given the position and the person, I repeat what I said. He would still write on a tree, as the song says, if all the world were paper and all the sea were ink; if that river flowed with everlasting ink or all these woods were a forest of quills and fountain pens."

It was evident that Sand felt something creepy about the priest's fanciful imagery; whether because he found it incomprehensible or because he was beginning to comprehend.

"You see," said Father Brown, turning the dressing gown over slowly as he spoke, "a man isn't expected to write his very best handwriting when he chips it on a tree. And if the man were not the man, if I make myself clear – hullo!"

He was looking down at the red dressing gown, and it seemed for the moment as if some of the red had come off on his finger; but both the faces turned towards it were already a shade paler.

"Blood!" said Father Brown; and for the instant there was a deadly stillness save for the melodious noises of the river.

Henry Sand cleared his throat and nose with noises that were by no means melodious. Then he said rather hoarsely: "Whose blood?"

"Oh, mine," said Father Brown; but he did not smile.

A moment after he said: "There was a pin in this thing and I pricked myself. But I don't think you quite appreciate the point...the point of the pin, I do"; and he sucked his finger like a child.

"You see," he said after another silence, "the gown was folded up and pinned together; nobody could have unfolded it – at least without scratching himself. In plain words, Hubert Sand never *wore* this dressing gown. Any more than Hubert Sand ever wrote on that tree. Or drowned himself in that river."

The pince-nez tilted on Henry's inquiring nose fell off with a click; but he was otherwise motionless, as if rigid with surprise.

"Which brings us back," went on Father Brown cheerfully, "to somebody's taste for writing his private correspondence on trees, like Hiawatha and his picture-writing. Sand had all the time there was, before drowning himself. Why didn't he leave a note for his wife like a sane man? Or, shall we say... Why didn't the Other Man leave a note for the wife like a sane man? Because he would have had to forge the husband's handwriting; always a tricky thing now that experts are so nosey about it. But nobody can be expected to imitate even his own handwriting, let alone somebody else's, when he carves capital letters in the bark of a tree. This is not a suicide, Mr. Sand. If it's anything at all, it's a murder."

The bracken and bushes of the undergrowth snapped and crackled as the big young man rose out of them like a leviathan, and stood lowering, with his thick neck thrust forward.

"I'm no good at hiding things," he said, "and I half-suspected something like this – expected it, you might say, for a long time. To tell the truth, I could hardly be civil to the fellow – to either of them, for that matter."

"What exactly do you mean?" asked the priest, looking him gravely full in the face.

"I mean," said Henry Sand, "that you have shown me the murder and I think I could show you the murderers."

Father Brown was silent and the other went on rather jerkily.

"You said people sometimes wrote love messages on trees. Well, as a fact, there are some of them on that tree; there are two sort of monograms twisted together up there under the leaves – I suppose you know that Lady Sand was the heiress of this place long before she married; and she knew that damned dandy of a secretary even in those days. I guess they used to meet here and write their vows upon the trysting-tree. They seem to have used the trysting-tree for another purpose later on. Sentiment, no doubt, or economy."

"They must be very horrible people," said Father Brown.

"Haven't there been any horrible people in history or the police-news?" demanded Sand with some excitement. "Haven't there been lovers who made love seem more horrible than hate? Don't you know about Bothwell and all the bloody legends of such lovers?"

"I know the legend of Bothwell," answered the priest. "I also know it to be quite legendary. But of course it's true that husbands have been sometimes put away like that. By the way, where was he put away? I mean, where did they hide the body?"

"I suppose they drowned him, or threw him in the water when he was dead," snorted the young man impatiently.

Father Brown blinked thoughtfully and then said: "A river is a good place to hide an imaginary body. It's a rotten bad place to hide a real one. I mean, it's easy to *say* you've thrown it in, because it *might* be washed away to sea. But if you really did throw it in, it's about a hundred to one it wouldn't; the chances of it going ashore somewhere are enormous. I think they must have had a better scheme for hiding the body than that – or the body would have been found by now. And if there were any marks of violence—"

"Oh, bother hiding the body," said Henry, with some irritation; "haven't we witness enough in the writing on their own devilish tree?"

"The body is the chief witness in every murder," answered the other. "The hiding of the body, nine times out of ten, is the practical problem to be solved."

There was a silence; and Father Brown continued to turn over the red dressing gown and spread it out on the shining grass of the sunny shore; he did not look up. But, for some time past he had been conscious that the whole landscape had been changed for him by the presence of a third party; standing as still as a statue in the garden.

"By the way," he said, lowering his voice, "how do you explain that little guy with the glass eye, who brought your poor uncle a letter yesterday? It seemed to me he was entirely altered by reading it; that's why I wasn't surprised at the suicide, when I thought it was a suicide. That chap was a rather low-down private detective, or I'm much mistaken."

"Why," said Henry in a hesitating manner, "why, he might have been – husbands do sometimes put on detectives in domestic tragedies like this, don't they? I suppose he'd got the proofs of their intrigue; and so they—"

"I shouldn't talk too loud," said Father Brown, "because your detective is detecting us at this moment, from about a yard beyond those bushes."

They looked up, and sure enough the goblin with the glass eye was fixing them with that disagreeable optic, looking all the more grotesque for standing among the white and waxen blooms of the classical garden.

Henry Sand scrambled to his feet again with a rapidity that seemed breathless for one of his bulk, and asked the man very angrily and abruptly what he was doing, at the same time telling him to clear out at once.

"Lord Stanes," said the goblin of the garden, "would be much obliged if Father Brown would come up to the house and speak to him."

Henry Sand turned away furiously; but the priest put down his fury to the dislike that was known to exist between him and the nobleman in question. As they mounted the slope, Father Brown paused a moment as if tracing patterns on the smooth tree trunk, glanced upwards once at the darker and more hidden hieroglyph said to be a record of romance; and then stared at the wider and more sprawling letters of the confession, or supposed confession of suicide.

"Do those letters remind you of anything?" he asked. And when his sulky companion shook his head, he added:

"They remind me of the writing on that placard that threatened him with the vengeance of the strikers."

* * *

"This is the hardest riddle and the queerest tale I have ever tackled," said Father Brown, a month later, as he sat opposite Lord Stanes in the recently furnished apartment of No. 188, the end flat which was the last to be finished before the interregnum of the industrial dispute and the transfer of work from the Trade Union. It was comfortably furnished; and Lord Stanes was presiding over grog and cigars, when the priest made his confession with a grimace. Lord Stanes had become rather surprisingly friendly, in a cool and casual way.

"I know that is saying a good deal, with your record," said Stanes, "but certainly the detectives, including our seductive friend with the glass eye, don't seem at all able to see the solution."

Father Brown laid down his cigar and said carefully:

"It isn't that they can't see the solution. It is that they can't see the problem."

"Indeed," said the other, "perhaps I can't see the problem either."

"The problem is unlike all other problems, for this reason," said Father Brown. "It seems as if the criminal deliberately did two different things, either of which might have been successful; but which, when done together, could only defeat each other. I am assuming, what I firmly believe, that the same murderer pinned up the proclamation threatening a sort of Bolshevik murder, and also wrote on the tree confessing to an ordinary suicide. Now you may say it is after all possible that the proclamation was a proletarian proclamation; that some extremist workmen wanted to kill their employer, and killed him. Even if that were true, it would still stick at the mystery of why they left, or why anybody left, a contrary trail of private self-destruction. But it certainly isn't true. None of these workmen, however bitter, would have done a thing like that. I know them pretty well; I know their leaders quite well. To suppose that people like Tom Bruce or Hogan would assassinate somebody they could go for in the newspapers, and damage in all sorts of different ways, is the sort of psychology that sensible people call lunacy. No; there was somebody, who was not an indignant workman, who first played the part of an indignant workman, and then played the part of a suicidal employer. But, in the name of wonder, why? If he thought he could pass it off smoothly as a suicide, why did he first spoil it all by publishing a threat of murder? You might say it was an after-thought to fix up the suicide story, as less provocative than the murder story. But it wasn't less provocative *after* the murder story. He must have known he had already turned our thoughts towards murder, when it should have been his whole object to keep our thoughts away from it. If it was an after-thought, it was the after-thought of a very thoughtless person. And I have a notion that this assassin is a very thoughtful person. Can you make anything of it?"

"No; but I see what you mean," said Stanes, "by saying that I didn't even see the problem. It isn't merely who killed Sand; it's why anybody should accuse somebody else of killing Sand and then accuse Sand of killing himself."

Father Brown's face was knotted and the cigar was clenched in his teeth; the end of it glowed and darkened rhythmically like the signal of some burning pulse of the brain. Then he spoke as if to himself:

"We've got to follow very closely and very clearly. It's like separating threads of thought from each other; something like this. Because the murder charge really rather spoilt the suicide charge, he wouldn't normally have made the murder charge. But he did make it; so he had some other reason for making it. It was so strong a reason that perhaps it reconciled him even to weakening his other line of defence: that it was a suicide. In other words, the murder charge wasn't really a murder charge. I mean he wasn't using it as a murder charge; he wasn't doing it so as to shift to somebody else the guilt of murder; he was doing it for some other extraordinary reason of his own. His plan had to contain a proclamation that Sand would be murdered; whether it threw suspicion on other people or not. Somehow or other the mere proclamation itself was necessary. But why?"

He smoked and smouldered away the same volcanic concentration for five minutes before he spoke again.

"What could a murderous proclamation do, besides suggesting that the strikers were the murderers? What *did* it do? One thing is obvious; it inevitably did the opposite of what it said. It told Sand not to lock out his men; and it was perhaps the only thing in the world that would really have made him do it. You've got to think of the sort of man and the sort of reputation. When a man has been called a Strong Man in our silly sensational newspapers, when he is fondly regarded as a Sportsman by all the most distinguished asses in England, he simply can't back down because he is threatened with a pistol. It would be like walking about at Ascot with a white feather stuck in his absurd white hat. It would break that inner idol or ideal of oneself, which every man not a downright dastard does really prefer to life. And Sand wasn't a dastard; he was courageous; he was also impulsive. It acted instantly like a charm; his nephew, who had been more or less mixed up with the workmen, cried out instantly that the threat must be absolutely and instantly defied."

"Yes," said Lord Stanes, "I noticed that." They looked at each other for an instant, and then Stanes added carelessly: "So you think the thing the criminal really wanted was—"

"The Lock-out!" cried the priest energetically. "The Strike or whatever you call it; the cessation of work, anyhow. He wanted the work to stop at once; perhaps the black-legs to come in at once; certainly the Trade Unionists to go out at once. That is what he really wanted; God knows why. And he brought that off, I think, really without bothering much about its other implication of the existence of Bolshevist assassins. But then…then I think something went wrong. I'm only guessing and groping very slowly here; but the only explanation I can think of is that something began to draw attention to the real seat of the trouble; to the reason, whatever it was, of his wanting to bring the building to a halt. And then belatedly, desperately, and rather inconsistently, he tried to lay the other trail that led to the river, simply and solely because it led away from the flats."

He looked up through his moonlike spectacles, absorbing all the quality of the background and furniture; the restrained luxury of a quiet man of the world; and contrasting it with the two suitcases with which its occupant had arrived so recently in a newly finished and quite unfurnished flat. Then he said rather abruptly:

"In short, the murderer was frightened of something or somebody in the flats. By the way, why did *you* come to live in the flats?…Also by the way, young Henry told me you made an early appointment with him when you moved in. Is that true?"

"Not in the least," said Stanes, "I got the key from his uncle the night before. I've no notion why Henry came here that morning."

"Ah," said Father Brown, "then I think I have some notion of why he came…I *thought* you startled him by coming in just when he was coming out."

"And yet," said Stanes, looking across with a glitter in his grey-green eyes, "you do rather think that I also am a mystery."

"I think you are two mysteries," said Father Brown. "The first is why you originally retired from Sand's business. The second is why you have since come back to live in Sand's buildings."

Stanes smoked reflectively, knocked out his ash, and rang a bell on the table before him. "If you'll excuse me," he said, "I will summon two more to the council. Jackson, the little detective you know of, will answer the bell; and I've asked Henry Sand to come in a little later."

Father Brown rose from his seat, walked across the room and looked down frowning into the fireplace.

"Meanwhile," continued Stanes, "I don't mind answering both your questions. I left the Sand business because I was sure there was some hanky-panky in it and somebody was pinching all the money. I came back to it, and took this flat, because I wanted to watch for the real truth about old Sand's death – on the spot."

Father Brown faced round as the detective entered the room; he stood staring at the hearthrug and repeated: "On the spot."

"Mr. Jackson will tell you," said Stanes, "that Sir Hubert commissioned him to find out who was the thief robbing the firm; and he brought a note of his discoveries the day before old Hubert disappeared."

"Yes," said Father Brown, "and I know now where he disappeared to. I know where the body is."

"Do you mean—?" began his host hastily.

"It is here," said Father Brown, and stamped on the hearthrug. "Here, under the elegant Persian rug in this cosy and comfortable room."

"Where in the world did you find that?"

"I've just remembered," said Father Brown, "that I found it in my sleep."

He closed his eyes as if trying to picture a dream, and went on dreamily:

"This is a murder story turning on the problem of How to Hide the Body; and I found it in my sleep. I was always woken up every morning by hammering from this building. On that morning I half woke up, went to sleep again and woke once more, expecting to find it late; but it wasn't. Why? Because there *had* been hammering that morning, though all the usual work had stopped; short, hurried hammering in the small hours before dawn. Automatically a man sleeping stirs at such a familiar sound. But he goes to sleep again, because the usual sound is not at the usual hour. Now why did a certain secret criminal want all the work to cease suddenly; and only new workers come in? Because, if the old workers had come in next day, they would have found a new piece of work done in the night. The old workers would have known where they left off; and they would have found the whole flooring of this room already nailed down. Nailed down by a man who knew how to do it; having mixed a good deal with the workmen and learned their ways."

As he spoke, the door was pushed open and a head poked in with a thrusting motion; a small head at the end of a thick neck and a face that blinked at them through glasses.

"Henry Sand said," observed Father Brown, staring at the ceiling, "that he was no good at hiding things. But I think he did himself an injustice."

Henry Sand turned and moved swiftly away down the corridor.

"He not only hid his thefts from the firm quite successfully for years," went on the priest with an air of abstraction, "but when his uncle discovered them, he hid his uncle's corpse in an entirely new and original manner."

At the same instant Stanes again rang a bell, with a long strident steady ringing; and the little man with the glass eye was propelled or shot along the corridor after the fugitive, with something of the rotatory motion of a mechanical figure in a zoetrope. At the same moment, Father Brown looked out of the window, leaning over a small balcony, and saw five or six men start from behind bushes and railings in the street below and spread out equally mechanically like a fan or net; opening out after the fugitive who had shot like a bullet out of the front door. Father Brown saw only the pattern of the story; which had never strayed from that room; where Henry had strangled Hubert and hid his body under impenetrable flooring, stopping the whole work on the building to do it. A pin-prick had started his own suspicions; but only to tell him he had been led down the long loop of a lie. The point of the pin was that it was pointless.

He fancied he understood Stanes at last, and he liked to collect queer people who were difficult to understand. He realised that this tired gentleman, whom he had once accused of having green blood, had indeed a sort of cold green flame of conscientiousness or conventional honour that had made him first shift out of a shady business, and then feel ashamed of having shifted it on to others; and come back as a bored laborious detective; pitching his camp on the very spot where the corpse had been buried; so that the murderer, finding him sniffing so near the corpse, had wildly staged the alternative drama of the dressing gown and the drowned man. All that was plain enough, but, before he withdrew his head from the night air and the stars, Father Brown threw one glance upwards at the vast black bulk of the cyclopean building heaved far up into the night, and remembered Egypt and Babylon, and all that is at once eternal and ephemeral in the work of man.

"I was right in what I said first of all," he said. "It reminds one of Coppée's poem about the Pharaoh and the Pyramid. This house is supposed to be a hundred houses; and yet the whole mountain of building is only one man's tomb."

If Death Is Respectable

Carroll John Daly

Chapter I

IF DETECTIVE SERGEANT O'ROURKE was out of place in the Egyptian dining room of the Hotel Ritz, at least he did not know it. He ordered with an indifference to price and consulted the waiter when the French on the menu puzzled him. But he didn't let his ignorance interfere with his appetite. He got what he wanted.

"It isn't every day," he shot a finger at me, "that a flat foot can cut loose in the Ritz and the city pay the expenses."

"I thought," I told him, "that the city was cutting down on expenses. If they feed a few more coppers here they'll never balance the budget. I know what's on your stomach; now, what's on your chest?"

"What the hell!" O'Rourke laughed. "You got a bellyful out of it, Race. Here we are, in the swankiest restaurant in town, and no one would suspect I was a copper."

"No." I shook my head. "They'd take you for a longshoreman. But what's the racket? It must be big."

"In its way," he puffed slowly on a two-bit cigar, "it's one of the biggest things that ever troubled the Department, and certainly the strangest. Put those soft eyes of yours on the dame by the pillar; the one with the Egyptian chariots running around it. You can't miss her. Classiest bit of dress goods in the room."

I looked at the girl. O'Rourke was right. Class oozed out all over her, and she was getting attention. Trust the waiters of a place like the Ritz to spot 'em. My eyes knitted slightly. Her face was familiar – and maybe it wasn't.

"Don't know her, eh? Only a few do. But everybody knows of her. There!" he suddenly opened his hand like a stage magician and shot a crumpled piece of paper across to me. "Won't have her picture taken. That's one of the few that ever got into print."

I smoothed out the paper and stared down at the picture of the girl across the room. It was a rough cut, torn from a Sunday Rotogravure section. Gladys Huntington Drake. I whistled softly and drew in a deep breath. She was of the city aristocracy.

O'Rourke talked.

"Her father is president of the Commercial & Citizen's Bank; on the board of directors of a half dozen others. Personal friend of everyone of importance in the city. And the girl!" O'Rourke half closed his eyes. "Twenty-three or -four. Had her debut, or whatever the hell it is, four or five years ago. Since then – the ideal society girl. A credit to the centuries of Drake dignity. Whatever she did was right. Quiet, charming, careful that her name was never linked with undesirable matrimonial alliances. The most sought-after woman in society. And—" His eyes opened wide and he stared at me for a long moment. "What do you think, Race?"

"The old story." I nodded. "Letters to the father, threatening the safety or even the life of his daughter! Maybe from someone who expects easy money. Maybe just a crank. Maybe some poor unfortunate wiped out in the financial failure of a company in which her father is interested, and now with the mental balance also short. Just the old story."

"Is it?" O'Rourke's gray eyes popped into life. "You haven't heard anything then? Haven't been approached?"

"No. Not concerning Miss Drake. So she's getting police protection?"

"Is she?" O'Rourke stroked his chin. "Well, maybe she is. But it's not through fear for her, but fear of her. Of her father; of public opinion. Be prepared for a shock, Race."

"All right." I grinned across at him. "Let it come."

"Well," said O'Rourke very slowly, "not so many weeks ago that sweet little lady raised a gun and shot a man; took a leaf from your book, Race, and shot him smack between the eyes. The Department wants her for murder."

And I took another look at the girl. There was nothing weak in that face; decidedly not. Rather, strength; plenty strength. I said to O'Rourke:

"There she sits. If you want her for murder, why not put the finger on her?"

"On Warren Drake's daughter!" He sort of straightened. "Would you?"

"I'm not a cop," I told him, and with a grin, "not an honest cop like you, O'Rourke."

"Honest, but not dumb." O'Rourke frowned. There was nothing of humor in his words. "You don't think putting the finger on her would give me the stripes of a lieutenant, do you?"

I grinned.

"Tell me about it, and where I fit."

"There's nothing to tell, except that a girl walked out of a hotel in Philly and left a man dead on the floor." And when I whistled softly, "You know who it was, then?"

"I read the papers," I told O'Rourke. "It was Joe Bray. Handsome young gunman; the Lothario of the underworld; right-hand man of Eddie Kean. He—" I looked at the girl again. "The thing's impossible, O'Rourke. Drake's daughter! 'Cool-headed' Drake, they called him in the panic. And besides, the papers said the woman who left the hotel was a brunette."

"She could wear a wig." O'Rourke shrugged his shoulders, wrinkled his eyes, and then, "I thought the idea crazy as hell, myself, at first. Now – I don't know."

"And you want to stay that way – not knowing. If it's to be another Elwell or Dot King mystery and too hot for the police to handle, why cry all over the Ritz about it? No one's going to miss Joe, unless it's Eddie Kean. And Eddie is lying low lately. At least he's temporarily closed down his business; sort of playing respectable."

"Well," said O'Rourke, "Eddie can't continue to be respectable if respectable people go and shoot down the boys who do his work and bring him in the money."

"Does Eddie know she knocked over his best man, and want vengeance?" And as I looked at the girl again. "Hell! O'Rourke, what would she kill a lad like Joe for? You're barking up the wrong tree."

O'Rourke nodded very seriously.

"Gladys Drake," he said, "has apparently led the usual life. But, like others, she had an ambition. To be an artist. To satisfy this ambition she took a little place up in the Adirondacks, and a couple of months each year she hides away there and does her painting. At least, that's the story. Social obligations were too numerous at home. Well, that's where she was supposed to be when Joe was knocked off. Now – she wasn't there. I've satisfied myself on that point."

"How did you happen to look her up in the first place?"

"A tip," said O'Rourke. "She wasn't in the Adirondacks when Joe was bumped, and she was in Philly." His hands came far apart. "After that I gave her some personal attention and was a bit surprised."

"You learned a lot?"

"More than a cop who's been on the Force twenty years would want to learn about the daughter of Warren Drake."

"So why not drop it?"

"Why not!" O'Rourke dug a hand into his pocket and produced the *Daily Blade*, a sensational tabloid whose demise in newspaper circles was expected every day but lately had seemed to take on new life; at least according to its creditors, who were suddenly being paid.

I read the small item O'Rourke pointed out to me.

Who killed Joe Bray? Do the police know?
And if they do, is the murderer too big to handle?

"That," I said, "seems like the regular baloney. It might be said about half the unsolved murders."

"But, you see," said O'Rourke, "it happens to be said about this one particular murder. And the guy who sent me the paper with that item marked, also gave me the tip. Suppose this dirty sheet broke the case? Now, am I better off not arresting Drake's daughter than I would be arresting her?"

"You've got a lion by the tail, O'Rourke." I grinned. "You're afraid to hang on and you're afraid to let go. It might all prove a bust. But this lad and his tip! He must be mighty anxious to see the girl dragged in."

"I don't know." O'Rourke shook his head. "There's something screwy about the whole business. This tipster says he'll hand me evidence that will convict the girl, but he don't do it. Why?" O'Rourke leaned forward eagerly. "Because he'll protect the girl at a price. He's waiting for her to come across."

"O'Rourke," I said seriously, "I don't know if you're right or wrong. These are bad times. People resent great wealth. It might be a big feather in your cap if you pulled her in. Equal justice for the rich and the poor! You—"

I paused. O'Rourke's hard gray eyes were soft; the lines from his nose to his mouth seemed to smooth out. He was looking at the girl.

"There is some other reason why you don't want to drag in the girl?"

"Maybe." O'Rourke nodded and his voice was low. "When the Drake girl's mother died, she left her a fortune. I don't think she's got it now."

"Not blackmail?"

O'Rourke shook his head.

"I don't think you could blackmail her. I think perhaps—" he bit his lip.

"That one man tried to blackmail her and died." I finished his sentence. And suddenly, at what I thought was a bright idea, "You don't think her money saved the *Daily Blade*; that they—"

"No, I don't." O'Rourke cut in quickly. "I took the trouble to find out who backed the *Blade*. It was our respectable racketeer, Eddie Kean."

"Eddie, eh? He—"

I stopped and came to my feet. Gladys Drake's small, erect figure was standing beside me. O'Rourke was staring up at her. He half lifted his broad body, then slipped back in the chair again. The girl spoke.

"I like to create a sensation," she said. "Don't bother to get up. It isn't every day that a slip of a girl can knock a police officer off his feet. May I have coffee with you?"

She was in the chair the waiter quickly placed by the table. A napkin, water, silver appeared like magic.

"You should know me, Sergeant O'Rourke," she said. "We have met before."

"That's right," said O'Rourke, "that's right. We have met before."

And that Irish tongue he was so proud of had played him as false as a congressman's election promise.

But O'Rourke recovered himself in time to send the waiter to change his demi-tasse for a large cup of coffee. The girl did most of the talking.

"If you think I need protection, Sergeant," her voice was clear as a bell and free from any embarrassment. "Certainly I should be safe here, between the law and the defier of that law. This is Race Williams – private investigator, of course. You know," she turned down the sugar the waiter offered and accepted my cigarette, "I have been thinking that it isn't right for me to take a police officer from his public duty, to watch me. I'm taking your hint then, Sergeant, for it must be a hint." She bobbed her head. "If I engage Race Williams for that protection, it will relieve you of that duty. Is that right?" And when Sergeant O'Rourke did not answer at once, "Is that right?" And then a certain hardness; a certain determination crept into her voice.

"That's right," said O'Rourke. "You'd hardly need police protection then."

"Or police surveillance?" She put steely blue eyes on O'Rourke's gray ones. They were clear, bright eyes, with the sparkle of youth in them. But they were also cold and hard and appraising. Here was no fluttering, simpering, pampered daughter of wealth. Her face was beautiful, but like beauty that had been chiseled out of marble. And I wondered where she and O'Rourke had met before, or if – and O'Rourke said:

"Race Williams is the best man you could get to – to advise you. If you need police protection – or surveillance, he could advise you of that too."

"And advise you also," she said, turning her head slowly from O'Rourke to look at me.

"Miss Drake," I said, "you take too much for granted. Because you are interested in me is no reason why I should be interested in you."

"No," she said, parted her teeth and her eyes smiled. "I can handle you all right. You're not the kind of man who likes soft hands stroking his hair."

O'Rourke said:

"I'll be getting along now." He pushed back his chair. "You can rest assured, Miss Drake, that what Race Williams does will be to your best interest." And with a jerk of his chin, "Well, that's that."

But that wasn't quite that. I stretched out a hand and caught O'Rourke's arm as he would have passed me.

"There's the lunch," I told him. "I mightn't find it as easy collecting from the city as you will."

Not the right thought while sitting there with the daughter of one of the richest men in a rich town? Maybe not. But I rode uptown one night with one of our greatest industrial kings and all I got out of it was the taxi bill. Anyway, I kept my eyes on O'Rourke until he paid the bill. Coppers are funny that way.

O'Rourke gone, the girl lifted her small cup and looked long and steadily at me. Certainly she was very sure of herself. She was trying, now, to be very sure of me. And one other thing, I thought, as I opened my mouth and closed it again. She wanted me to speak first. But I didn't. I just watched her and fooled with my butt. Funny. Those steady blue eyes of hers made you want to do something with your hands. And I got to wondering too. Could it be possible that this girl had killed a man; shot him to death in a hotel room? And now – there was nothing of terror; even fear in her eyes or in her face. More, simple speculation. Finally she nodded her head, parted her thin lips and said:

"Mr. Williams, just how much will you charge to kill a man?"

Chapter II

NOW you've got to admit that's a real mouthful any way you look at it. Here I was, getting ready to throw wisecracks back and forth until I could maneuver her into a guilty admission of some kind, and just like that she throws a monkey wrench – or a whole hardware store full of wrenches into the works.

Hard, steady blue eyes were on me. After I swallowed her question and digested it, I said:

"Miss Drake, I don't go in for murder." It was the best I could do right then.

"No?" Her eyebrows went up. "I have read the papers and am fairly familiar with your career. You have killed men, of course. Many men."

"Sure!" I nodded at that. "And I expect to kill more. But you can't just pick out a likely-looking potential corpse and get me to put a price on the job." She seemed to think a moment, and then:

"But you have killed men for clients."

"To protect the lives of clients – yes."

"The bodies of clients!" she said suddenly. "As if the torture of the mind isn't as great. I'm disappointed in you, Mr. Williams."

I shrugged my shoulders.

"That's only one person's opinion," I told her. "If you know your way around and have a little job you want done, you won't have too much trouble. But look out it doesn't come back on you later. Professional murderers haven't a very high sense of loyalty to their employers. Is that all you wanted of me?"

And she laughed. It was a real laugh. A little hard, perhaps, but not one of those stage laughs.

"I guess," she said, "my body may need protection. So I'll hire you to protect it."

"I have another peculiarity," I told her. "I choose my own cases, and only those that interest me."

"This will interest you." She said calmly. "And if your protection is not all you boast of, it may cost you your client's life; perhaps your life."

"Well," I said, "let me have the facts. All the facts."

"I will let the facts come to you through someone else. Also you can feel assured that you'll be paid in full." And when I started to talk: "That's all I care to tell you now." She opened her purse, took out a folded bit of paper, and stretching a hand across the table pushed it into my palm. It was a check for five thousand dollars.

"We won't quibble over the amount," she went on. "You may consider that check simply a retainer. If things are brought to a satisfactory conclusion you need not worry about the price I'll pay."

I'm a peculiar guy and take cases I like and chuck up cases I don't like, and don't go into things blind. She had an air of assurance that wasn't easily ruffled, but it was on the tip of my tongue to speak up like a real artist, throw her over with high sounding words, and tearing the check in little pieces set fire to it in the ash tray. I could give you pages of reasoning and of the battle that went back and forth in my noble brain. But truth is truth. Times were bad, I was broke and five grand was a lot of jack, no matter how you look at it. I simply said:

"And just what is a satisfactory conclusion?"

"We won't go into that now. But if I consider the conclusion unsatisfactory I'll pay you another five thousand. I hope you're a brave man."

"Miss Drake," I stuck the check in a pocket and talked to her like a Dutch uncle, "you'd better tell me things. I can help you. I'm not hampered by legal technicalities. If someone is blackmailing you, I may be able to obtain that evidence and bring it to you and—"

She stopped me and her eyes narrowed.

"Will you cut the brain from a man's head and bring me that? Will you take knowledge from a human mind? No. I—" And after a long moment, "I wish that my original proposition to kill a man had appealed to you, Mr. Williams. I would have made it worth your while."

I shrugged my shoulders and said:

"Just what do you want me to do to earn this money?"

She drummed long white fingers on the table, and then:

"I have to make a visit to a certain house at midnight tonight. I will want you to be very close – in that house." She bit her lip. "If I am clever I can arrange that. I will let you know later where to meet me."

She was on her feet now, and I leaned over and took her wrist.

"Miss Drake," I said slowly and with emphasis, "if you think to trap me into killing a man—"

I stopped. Cold blue eyes stared down at me. Hard, appraising eyes, yet something deep and fine behind them; something unreadable and certainly not understandable. Yet the girl was good. Somehow I could believe that; believe it while I tried to forget that O'Rourke had told me she raised a gun and shot a man to death. But I read the truth in her eyes, or thought I did.

"So that's it," I said. "You hope to trap me into killing this man?"

"Mr. Williams," she said very slowly, "if you believe that; fear that, you had better throw up the case right now. I tried to be honest with you in the beginning. I shall not try to trap you into anything. But it is my firm belief that you cannot protect my body in the final hour without killing this man. Understand that."

I scratched my head. This girl was strange. When she spoke, now, it was as if her eyes spoke too. As if the words which came out of her mouth seemed to be words that I read in those penetrating eyes. But I only said:

"You think he will threaten you tonight?"

"He has already threatened me," she said. "The danger, tonight, does not lie in his threat to me. Tonight I will threaten him. Are you for it?"

I thought of the check for five grand, and of my only taking cases I was interested in. And I thought, too, as I answered the girl, that I was never more interested in a case – or, at least, in a client, than I was in this 'child of wealth', Gladys Huntington Drake.

"I'm for it," I told her.

When she was gone I licked my lips, ordered myself another coffee, lit a butt and thought. And my thoughts were one single thought. Somehow I felt that I was going to kill a man. Kill a man and like it.

Chapter III

MY EYES searched the block down which she had come when the long high-powered, high-priced coupé swung around the corner and stopped at the curb. She had not been followed, that was a cinch. I climbed in beside her and the car swung back across town and hit Riverside Drive. Then she let down on the car gas and opened up with some of her own.

"The house is in Yonkers," she told me. "I've been there before. But I didn't stay long. I wasn't exactly in a panic, but the man's threat was a shock to me. I saw enough to know how you can get in the house. I'm rather observing. It's a big place up in the lonely Park Hill section. He waited for me alone then. I have every reason to believe he will do the same tonight. There's a room with heavy curtains and sliding doors adjoining the library. I left my wraps there. You can enter this room by the window on the terrace. I'll see that the window is unlocked. The room is kept in darkness. If I can leave the sliding doors open slightly you can see between the curtains; also hear and—"

"Miss Drake," I cut in, "my clients all trust me. Don't you think you'd better tell me more?"

"I trust you, of course, but it's the sort of thing you might not want to believe. It's my idea that you will hear everything in this conversation tonight, and in such a way that you will have to believe it." Her head turned slightly and those blue eyes flashed beneath a street light. "I want you to start, believing in me. Without any attempt at flattery, you are the only man whom I'd trust as I'm trusting you tonight."

"But you must know I suspect a lot."

"Only what Sergeant O'Rourke told you," she said.

"And that is true?"

She hesitated a long moment.

"True or not true," she said, "what Sergeant O'Rourke knows now could not harm me, and if it could he would not want to use it."

"You've met Sergeant O'Rourke before?"

"He didn't tell you that then. Well, he's a fine old bloodhound, and he wishes to meet me that way again. But back to business!"

"This man you are to meet, Miss Drake! If it's as serious as you believe and as dangerous as you fear, it seems to me he'd be very careful. He might suspect you of bringing someone with you."

She smiled. A rather hard, mirthless smile.

"The last thing in the world he would suspect would be that I would want anyone to hear our conversation. He is meeting me tonight to tell me facts and to let me make a decision. I want you to hear those facts and tell me where I stand. What he does not know is, that I am going to tell him facts after he talks."

We were swinging along under the elevated pillars on Broadway now and over the bridge at Kingsbridge. I said: "I'd be a better judge of the man's habits if I knew his business. Is he a novice at – blackmail? Has he something big in mind? Is he just an ordinary crook, who—"

"He's a murderer and a racketeer." She cut in suddenly and almost viciously. "But he might be just a business man so far as any proof has been found against him."

"And you have visited him alone?"

"I have visited him alone."

"He wants something big from you?"

"The biggest thing in my life."

"Oh," I said, "it's that way."

"No, not exactly that way. He gives me a choice. He lets me choose between dragging the Drake name in the mud publicly or privately." And suddenly: "Am I the kind of woman you would want without the Drake millions; the Drake name?"

"You are the kind of woman any man would want, without regard to name or millions. But, me!" I sort of spread my hands apart. "I'm a nervous type, and would like to know why my women shoot gentlemen through the head – in Philadelphia hotels."

She didn't start. She looked straight ahead as we swept from the shadows of the L and sped up the great broad thoroughfare alongside Van Cortland Park. Then she said:

"You'll know tonight." And though her lips parted slightly I don't think that she smiled. "And you'll know why I asked you how much you'd take to kill a man."

Up in Yonkers we swung down McClean Avenue. When we reached the long steep climb to Park Hill I had her stop the car. I took three guesses as to who this bird was and every one was the same guess. Granted that he wouldn't suspect she'd bring a friend to listen in, yet the habit of years would make him have protection near. Anyway, it was best to be sure. She listened to my reasoning and nodded her head.

"Very well," she said. "I'll drive slowly by the house, point out the window you're to get in by and then drop you off around the corner."

She might know how to pop off an undesirable acquaintance like Joe Bray but she didn't know the ropes in breaking and entering. I said:

"With this boat of yours? Impossible! Anyone watching would recognize it. Now, describe that house. Here!" I flipped on the dashboard light and got out pencil and paper. "Then I'll drop out a block away, follow on foot and be at the window in time." And when she complied, I still had misgivings. "You're sure he'll receive you alone, after – well, if he's blackmailing you for the reason I think." I was thinking of the Bray knock-over.

So was she, for she answered:

"He's a careful man. I haven't got a gun. But" – there was disgust in her face – "that's the hardest part of it. God! I could kill him when he – he paws me like that."

I nodded and dropped the subject.

Up the hill, along the level, a turn to the right and over another hill. Then a dip, and the girl whispered:

"Get out here. It's around the corner and up the block. You're armed?"

"Everything but a hand grenade," I told her as I swung from the car and disappeared in the shadows of the huge, naked trees. I was feeling pretty good. Not because I had a client who was in a jam, but because I was going into action. Besides, I liked the girl. I couldn't help it. 'Cool-headed Drake' was right. She seemed hard as nails. And yet, somehow, underneath you knew she wasn't. Heart of gold and that kind of stuff. Fine little pal, provided, of course, you hid her hardware and remembered to play nice.

Then I was down the street, ducking into the yard adjoining my destination, hopping a high ivy-covered wall, and across a stretch of smooth grass, towards that window above the terrace.

The moonlight was dim, but I saw her car and felt better. There was both an entrance and an exit to the house; a circular driveway, and the car was parked in the deep shadows of a porte-cochère. So the get-away was good.

I heard the front door close as I ran across the grass, dodging the empty flowerbeds and the clumps of all-year greens. I was almost to the house when I saw him. A figure had just raised beside the porch. A man who had been watching for the coming of the girl. Maybe the lad she was to see didn't expect she'd have company, but at least he was making sure.

What should I do? Drop there on the grass and wait until this bozo moved on? And he stretched himself; stretched himself as I got a hunch. And that hunch was that he had heard me, sensed my presence, or—

I didn't throw myself flat on the grass. I speeded up, jerked my gun into my hand and hopped the bit of gravel path that ran around the house, as the man turned. Turned, and wasn't sure.

Anyway he turned slowly; more curious than alarmed, for his hand only half moved towards his gun. Lazily, mechanically. Then he knew. I could see his wide, frightened eyes in the dimness; I could see his mouth open and the sudden cry of alarm choke in his throat and turn to fear as he suddenly grabbed frantically for his gun. And I had him. My right hand went up and down, and the nose of my gun cracked down on his forehead. He just folded up like a beach chair and collapsed on the grass, which after all was the natural and courteous thing for him to do.

When I slap a guy down with a heavy gun, he's liable to stay down for some time. But I couldn't figure this thing close enough for that. I was to hear a story inside, and the man who was to tell it might be windy. So I went to work on the fallen gladiator.

There was a water pipe sticking up out of the ground a few inches. I jerked out my cuffs, clamped his hands together behind his back and ran the chain around that pipe. I carry bracelets; just one pair. The yard didn't sport any clothes line that I could see. But this guy wore pants and had a belt to hold them up, so I used that on his feet. Then his necktie and his own dirty handkerchief served as a gag. Yep, he supplied everything but the steel cuffs. I chuckled at that. He had even supplied the head to hit.

And what a head! When I rolled him as close to the side of the house as his hands chained to the water pipe would permit, his eyes were already blinking. So I gave him a little fatherly advice.

"I'll be right around here all the time, brother." I kicked him in the ribs by way of punctuation and to make the lie sound like the truth. "Make a move, and I'll shove all your teeth down your throat." And in the way of light pleasantry, "If you decide to go places, remember to hold your pants up." With that I left him.

Chapter IV

I DIDN'T have to refer to the bit of paper with the rough sketch of the side of the house to make the window. I can carry that much in my mind. There was a tiny stone balcony on top of the terrace and the windows were long French affairs, with curtains on the inside of them. They might have locks, top and bottom. Had the girl seen to those locks? And if she hadn't—. I shrugged my shoulders. A single cry would be enough to let me know I was needed. I'd go in anyway. A single good kick would bust those windows in easier than—

I drew in a deep, satisfied breath. The windows gave under pressure; there was a slight creak to them. There's only one way to handle a window that talks back to you. That is, not to nurse it but push it quickly. There're two reasons for this. One is, it generally doesn't squeak as much; the other, if the squeak is heard, you're inside almost as soon as the alarm is given. All this, of course, if you want in bad enough.

I swung my gun into my right hand, pushed with my free hand and elbow, and was in that room with the windows closed behind me.

I could see plainly the long slender thread of light between heavy curtains; curtains that moved slightly in the sudden draft. The night was fairly cool. I didn't want the cool air seeping into that lighted library beyond and giving the show away; that's why I closed the windows. Gun forward, back flat against those windows, eyes trying to pierce the darkness between me and the pencil of light, I waited.

A voice came from the room beyond. Steady, persuasive, maybe gloating. But certainly it was a man's voice and certainly it was familiar. Things were Jake. My feet moved across the floor with the man's words. There was no cause to be worried about the room I was in. Gladys Drake had been there; left her wraps there, and most of all, unlocked the windows there. So no one was hidden in that room.

As I crossed the room towards the curtains, the man was saying:

"Don't be a fool. We couldn't sit and chat while I held a gun in my hand. I have to frisk you. You're rather handy with a rod, you know. There, there! I must be thorough."

I reached the curtains and peered into the room just as the man was finishing his search. I saw his thick coarse hand run about her waist and drop to his side as she straightened, clenched her hands and looked towards the curtains. I got a bit of a kick out of that. She was going through with it because I was there; because—

And I took a good look at the man's face. My guess had been right. It was Eddie Kean. From the gutter to the gang; from the gang to a ward heeler; from a ward heeler to a racketeer, and now the owner of the filthiest sheet in town. Yep, Eddie and I had met many times. He had warned me several times; threatened me once or twice when my interest crossed his, but we had never been directly opposed to each other in a business deal.

Eddie was smooth, Eddie was cruel, and Eddie was a big shot whose dirty money could buy anything; everything but respectability. Now he wanted that. Whether to satisfy his own pride or to use it as a new racket, I didn't know. Probably both. And he had lived beyond his time in the racket. Eddie had turned forty. Not old, as years are reckoned by insurance companies, maybe. But very old as years are reckoned in his bullet-ridden life.

The girl sat down stiff and straight in the chair Eddie pointed out to her. His pale blue, fish-like eyes ogled her as his big head nodded. Then he laid his gun on a little table, sat down in the chair a few feet from her, crossed huge hands over his stomach and finally spoke.

"Miss Drake," he began. The light bantering tone had gone out of his voice and he chose his words carefully, as if he had been studying to become the gentleman. "You have had time to think since you were last here. You have had time to read the item of news the *Blade* ran and you have had time to digest the attention the police have favored you with. But, as you said then and will say now, there is no proof against you; no proof that would warrant the arrest and the trial of Warren Drake's daughter for murder."

He paused a moment, and when the girl did not speak, went on.

"I will make things very formal, and I will go back to the beginning, explaining things that will no doubt surprise you. I am an ambitious man. Money alone cannot satisfy me. The people who surround me no longer appeal to my – mental capacity. I am a man who has educated himself; risen from the slums of the city to financial power. It is necessary to my business, as well as to my mental advancement, that the right people recognize me and receive me.

"Some time ago, purely by chance, it was brought to my attention that Warren Drake's daughter did not take those trips into the country to paint, as the society columns would lead us to believe. Instead, you went to a small hairdresser's, had a wig made unlike your real hair, and moved about in the lower city. The color of your hair and your avoidance of cameramen gave you the protection from recognition you desired.

"It was I who put the poor, misunderstood Joe Bray in your way. It was his duty to compromise you, so that I might request you to introduce me to your people; your father, your friends. It was my plan, then, to appeal to your gratitude; help you out of a most embarrassing situation. Now – well, that single shot in the Philadelphia hotel changed things.

"I don't know why you shot Joe, but knowing Joe's weakness for beautiful women and looking on you now, I might guess. But as soon as the word came that he had died, I knew who killed him. For I knew that the woman with him in that hotel was you. Joe did not die without a fight. He was handy with a knife, and he dug that knife into your chest; the right side of your—"

"How did you know that?" the girl gasped.

"Because I looked up the doctor – the nearest one to the hotel rear exit. He told me about dressing your wound. You carried that knife away with you; whether purposely or mechanically, I don't know. But the knife that Joe always carried was not on his body. You paid the doctor well for silence. I paid him well for this."

He swept a piece of paper from the table and held it before the girl a moment. "A statement, you see." Then he very slowly tore up the paper and threw it into the fire. "We are not going to use it, are we?"

Eddie Kean leaned forward and tried to take the girl's hand. "I'm not a bad fellow, and I've seen life. I know how to take care of a woman. Let me tell you I've known many women; have yet to see the woman I could not have, and in marrying you I'm not just thinking of the prestige and money."

"You beast! You filthy beast!" The girl was on her feet, drawing away from the hand that clutched her wrist. "It was self-defense. I had to kill him. No jury will convict me. No jury will convict—"

Eddie Kean laughed lightly.

"No jury will convict Warren Drake's daughter, eh? You're telling me that! Of course they won't. People with plenty of money, good lawyers and a few influential friends can beat the rap any time. But they'll drag down the Drake name. The papers will carry headlines all over this country and abroad. Your friends will drop you. The society columns will drop the Drake name. You know what it will mean to your father. Everyone will want to know what the daughter of Warren Drake was doing in that Philadelphia hotel with Joe Bray, sewer rat; three-time loser to Sing Sing prison, and with a reputation for women that will parade for months across the front pages of the papers."

"That's true. That's true," the girl said, half aloud, as she dropped back into her chair.

"True?" Eddie Kean was on his feet now, standing before her. "Of course it's true. I've met your father. I tried to do business with his bank and I've listened to his tripe about the Drake tradition – not mixing into my kind of business. It's your choice. Do you want the Drake name to stay where it is, or shall I put it where it belongs? You killed my friend. I'm treating you pretty white. What do you say?"

"No!" The girl faced him. "You've had your say, now I'll have mine. You've made your threat, and I'll make mine. You never asked me why I killed your friend. Your friend! Why, he told me everything about you. How you sent him out after me! How he fell in love with me! Yes, he wanted me to run away with him and—"

"And what about me?" Eddie Kean sneered. "Joe had a proper fear of me."

"You!" She paused a long moment. "He offered me letters that would convict you of the murder of Assistant District Attorney John Rierdan."

"Nonsense!" said Kean. "That was seven years ago." But his thick lips tightened.

"Yes, it was some years ago. Back when you weren't so careful, or else circumstances made you write those letters. But you did write them. One to the man you killed, and one to a friend of Bray's who has since died. Well," she drew back a pace from him now and half threw a glance at the thick curtains, behind which I waited on one knee, "I have both those letters."

"That's a lie," said Kean. "Just a bluff."

"Is it?" she said. "It was only because of those letters that I went to the hotel. I had to go: there was no other way to get them except to pretend willingness to trade myself for them. Those letters were to be my protection; are my protection. When he gave me the letters, I told him I was going. He tried to hold me by force. I fought. He had a knife, and – and I killed him. He was a beast of a man like you."

"He was a beast of a man, like me – and you killed him," Eddie said very slowly, but anger blazed in his eyes.

"Yes," she said, "I killed him. You know the truth. Put your evidence against me in the hands of the police; drag the Drake name in the mud. And if the Drake millions can save me from death, perhaps the Drake millions can send you to the chair."

The anger went suddenly out of Kean's face and he laughed.

"You're a great little bundle of tricks," he said. "But the letters won't wash. Joe played you for a sucker. He promised you protection against me. He made up the letters. But in the end he would have turned you over to me." He spread his hands apart. "I might as well tell you the truth. I hadn't looked on you in the same way then. I told Joe to go as far as he liked. Don't look so offended. From now on I won't let anybody even look at you. I don't like my woman to get around."

"Then it isn't – you won't keep silent and let me alone if I return those letters?" For the first time her assurance was gone.

"Of course not." He stretched out a hand and put it on her shoulder. "The letters are a joke. I never wrote them. So you'll have to make a decision. A merger of the Drake name with Kean, or just oblivion for the Drake."

The girl spoke listlessly.

"I'll go home. I'll let you know in the morning." She walked to the hall door, forgetting her wraps.

"That's right." He nodded at her. "You'll let me know in the morning. But you're not going home."

"Not going home!" She jerked at the door knob, found the door locked, turned and stood with her back against it. There was fear in her eyes. I licked my lips and raised my gun. For the moment she had forgotten I was there, or maybe she thought I hadn't made it.

"No," Kean said. "You're going to stay here. We're going to get better acquainted. I know it's dangerous, harboring a murderer. But I'll take a chance. Do you know," he walked towards her until her back was flat against the wall, "you are really a very beautiful woman. You didn't like my frisking you for weapons. Do you know what they'll do in court? They'll bare your pretty chest and show the mark; the scar made by the knife of the man you killed. They'll – like that."

His hand stretched out suddenly and gripped her shoulder, tearing her blouse, dragging it down across the right side of her chest, baring the vivid red of a scar; baring it for a moment, before her hand clutched the torn silk and dragged it up over her shoulder. Then he was clutching for the blouse again. Clutching for it, understand. Not reaching it. For I was in the room and talking softly behind him.

"Tut, tut, Eddie," I said. "Such goings on at your time of life! After a while you'll be showing your operation."

Chapter V

EDDIE KEAN swung, faced me and blew his breath in my face. But I didn't kick on that breath. It was my fault. You see, I had stuck my gun a couple of inches into his stomach. I won't go into detail about Eddie's 'reactions', as they say in the best literature. I'll just say that Eddie Kean was a very much surprised man.

"You!" he said finally. "You – Race Williams!" and to the girl, "You were a fool to bring him." And to me, again, "You heard?" He staggered slightly and leaned heavily upon the large flat desk.

"Sure!" I said. "I heard."

He screwed up his mouth.

"That's two of us, then."

"Exactly!" I told him, as I backed him into a chair. "Some figuring there, Eddie. She can't marry both of us, you know."

I was doing pretty well. The temptation was to drag my gun across Eddie's face, stop it at his mouth, shove a few teeth into his throat and finally kick him around the room until he got lost. And a very laudable temptation, you've got to admit. But you've also got to admit, not to the best interests of my client. And twice, as I glanced at the white face of the girl, the temptation was strong to forget what I told her about not going in for murder, pop this boy off and let him take the girl's secret to hell with him.

Maybe I would have. Maybe I wouldn't. But the strange part of it was that the girl broke in on my thoughts, as if she read it in my face.

"Don't do it, Race," she said. "That would be murder."

And there you are. The very dame that a few hours before wanted me to put a price on Kean's head! And me harboring the fear and suspicion that I'd be trapped into killing the man. Now, I'd have no excuse for killing him of course, except perhaps that I liked the girl and didn't like Eddie Kean. Also, back in the cautious part of my mind was the belief that Detective Sergeant O'Rourke, of the police, wouldn't look on the killing in an over-serious way.

But there sat Eddie Kean, my gun against his stomach, his gun lying beside him on the little table, very close to his right hand that rested on the arm of the chair. I saw his eyes drift sidewise towards that gun, but I didn't caution him not to reach for it. I was rather hoping he would.

"Well," Eddie Kean spoke at last, "if you heard our conversation you heard an earful. Now what? You can't just shoot me to death, you know."

"No?" I said. "Why not?"

"Because—" he started.

And that was enough for me. It might have been the tone of his voice that warned me, or the subconscious sense developed from long experience, or the sudden shifting of his eyes from my face to look beyond me.

Whatever it was, before he could get the next word out, I was behind his chair, behind him, stooped low back of his body. And my .44, instead of pushing dents into his fat stomach, was now prodding the small of his back.

From where I knelt, I was facing the dining-room doorway which an instant before had been behind me. And in that doorway were standing two mugs, guns in their hands, pointed my way to be sure, but a little uncertainly. For while they could see a bit of my head over Eddie Kean's shoulder, he was all in plain sight of them and a target they probably wouldn't miss if they tried for me.

"Easy does it!" I said sharply, emphasizing the point to Eddie as I rammed my pistol harder against his right kidney. I drew back the hammer of the .44, and they all could hear the click.

"I'm giving the orders, Eddie," I told him. "You relay them to those monkeys. One step ahead for them. Move!"

For just an instant Eddie hesitated. It might have been disappointment; it might have been that he couldn't get the words out so quickly. But I didn't like the way those two mugs were sizing up things, with their guns coming up slowly. Or perhaps I did, for I was behind cover and they weren't. And—

"It's your life, Eddie," I told him quietly, "not mine. And if you know it, this is just the excuse I've wanted."

He got it then; got it hard.

"Murray – Frank," he gasped, "do what he said."

"One step ahead!" I repeated.

They took it.

"Toss those guns to the floor," I told them, and leaned harder on mine.

"Drop them!" Eddie snapped.

Murray, whose pan I knew, scowled, then opened his mouth to speak his piece.

"My finger is easing back, Eddie," I whispered in his ear.

"Drop 'em!" Eddie yelled.

The two automatics thudded on the thick carpet.

"Now, backs to the wall there," I said, and almost took a laugh, the way they back-pedaled together, like a song-and-dance team.

I straightened up, shifting the muzzle of the .44 from Eddie's back to his neck. With my other hand on his collar I helped him to his feet.

"Stand where you are a moment, Eddie," I told him pleasantly, with an extra prod to freshen his memory, "then, like the courteous host you are, you may see us to the car."

I swept Eddie's pistol from the table. Miss Drake collected the two automatics and I tossed one after the other through the nearest window. A boy's trick? Maybe. But I liked the sound of that splintering glass.

Miss Drake brought her wraps and moved towards the door, as I stepped back behind Kean and shoved the muzzle again into his back.

"You can do as you like, Eddie," I told him sweetly, "but my advice is that it would be better for you if those monkeys waited for you here."

"You wait here," Eddie told them sourly.

The girl led the parade and Eddie followed. Right behind Eddie I came, and all the time I let him know I was there. The front door slammed. Down the steps we went.

"Can you drive all right?" I asked the girl as she climbed in behind the wheel.

"Yes," was all she said as she stepped on the starter and the high-powered motor turned over softly.

"Goodnight, folks!" Eddie Kean said, and although he meant his voice to be easy, a tremor crept into it. "I'm glad you came, Race. After all, it would be better – much better – to have our engagement publicly announced."

I had climbed into the seat beside the girl and closed the door, but still held my right hand with the gun close to Eddie's chest.

"There are the letters, Eddie," I told him. "Seven years is a long time, but the statute of limitations doesn't go for murder."

"Nonsense!" And Eddie's laugh, though unnatural, was not reassuring. "If I was mixed in any way with that old killing, you don't think I'd be foolish enough to write letters about it! But you can easily look them over, if it's not just bluff, and see that they're forgeries. I'll send you a bit of wedding cake."

"I'll look 'em over, Eddie," I told him, "and I won't lose any time about it."

What was I thinking as I looked at the sneer on Eddie Kean's lips? Well, I was thinking that if the girl started that car suddenly it might jar my finger closed on the trigger, and – well, the death of Eddie Kean might go down as an unavoidable accident.

But I gave the girl the cue to step on it. She shoved the gear into second speed. The car jumped from under the porte-cochère and was out of the grounds. Eddie Kean stood in the driveway; my gun was still fully loaded. Had I shown weakness or strength? Take your choice.

The girl didn't speak as we drove along. Occasionally I saw her face beneath the sudden flash of a street light. Her lips were set tightly, her eyes fastened on the road. She drove slowly and carefully.

Before we reached Van Cortlandt Park, she swung the car abruptly into a side street, shut off the motor and set the brakes. Then she turned to me.

"You heard everything. What do you think?"

"You're in a hole, of course," I told her. "Did you have to kill Bray?"

"Yes." She nodded. "He was like an animal. You see, he told me about Kean, and that he'd throw Kean over for me."

"How did you meet him in the first place?"

"My life as Gladys Drake is very drab." And suddenly, "Oh, I didn't lead a double life. I tried to help others and—" She shrugged her shoulders. "But that doesn't matter now. It's the letters. Won't they protect me?"

"If they were real," I told her, then gave her the truth. "There are occasions, Miss Drake, when a murderer knowingly leaves information or evidence in the hands of friends; when it is absolutely necessary. But I doubt that Eddie Kean would have done it; or having done it, would have left the letters to pop up on him after all these years."

"But Bray said Kean thought that they were destroyed. He seemed very sincere. He seemed – well, there isn't love in such a man, but he wanted me. Don't you see? Everything depends on those letters."

"It will be a simple matter to get a copy of Eddie's handwriting," I told her. "Then get an expert to compare them. Let me see the letters. Where are they?"

"In my room. In a wall safe. And if they're not genuine, Mr. Williams, then what?"

"Then," I told her flat, "if Eddie pushes the case; brings in the doctor or gets another statement from him, you'll have to go through with the trial." And when she didn't answer, "Good—!" I said, "You wouldn't think of marrying that rat."

"I was thinking just that," she said slowly. "The charge of murder against me! Why, it would kill my father."

"If you married Kean, it wouldn't give your father any appetite, would it? And what of society; what of the Drake name then?"

"There is really nothing against Kean, is there? There are whispers of sharp business about many of our best names. Society is peculiar, Mr. Williams. They would accept Kean if Warren Drake's daughter introduced him." Her lips curved slightly at the ends. "Society only condemns public scandal. Private scandal is accepted as intrigue. What does the public know against Kean?"

Not having much use for society, I let that go. I didn't paint her any picture of little lads with Kean blood in their veins going around picking the pockets of our Four Hundred. But I guess she was right. The Drakes could stare down any whispered asides about Kean.

"Suit yourself" I told her, brutally enough. "The breath of public scandal, or even of criminal scandal, has never blown on Mr. Eddie Kean. If you can stomach that louse just to keep your name in the Social Register, why—"

"It's not that. It's not that!" she cried. "It's father."

She stopped, put the car in motion and drove the rest of the way in silence.

Chapter VI

THE WARREN DRAKE HOUSE was a huge stone mansion. A single light burned in the hall. The girl just jerked her head for me to follow her as she led the way to a small den on the first floor. Then she offered me a cigarette, turned to the door and said:

"I'll bring you those letters."

"That's right." I turned to the mantel, leaned on it as she left the room. Distinctly I heard her feet go from rug to wood as she crossed the hall; then the soft tread of them upon stairs.

I had handed her hard talk. But what could I do? Poor kid, she had confidence in those letters. Confidence in them and in herself, until she had looked at Eddie's smile when she threw the threat of the letters at him. Now – well, there wasn't one chance in a hundred that they were genuine; not one in a thousand.

I jerked from the mantel. For a moment I thought that I heard a— a—. And my gun was in my hand and I was running swiftly through the hall; up the stairs. Clearly, shrilly from above had come a cry. The scream of a frightened woman; of Gladys Drake. And that cry had been sharp and loud, but not complete. It was cut off at its very height, as if fingers had bitten into the throat; choked it.

It was easy to follow the light to the second floor. Then the trouble began. A hall led to my right and left; I looked along it. There were dim lights at each end; the rest in darkness. Another hall leading to the back of the house wasn't in darkness. A sliver of light cut across the floor, from a partly open door. I started down the hall. A door across opened; a small man with a white mustache and tricky-looking pajamas pushed in front of me.

Even in the dimness I knew that fizz. It was Warren Drake. He was trying to scare me to death with a stern, foreboding look. He even grabbed at my gun as I thrust him aside, knocking him against the wall. Then he cried out, and I had smacked that door wide open and was in the room. A cool breeze struck me in the face; curtains blew straight into the room, from the open window. Gladys Drake lay on the floor; there was blood on her forehead. I hollered back over my shoulder as my eyes lit on an open wall safe.

"Take care of your daughter, Mr. Drake." And I dashed to the window.

I stuck my head and shoulders out and saw the ladder, took a chance with the light on me and hopped out on to it. There was a narrow stone court below me, a larger court in the back of the house. Feet beat on stone. A dark shadow moved in the rear, running towards the fence. It turned suddenly; a face was white in the moonlight. There was yellow flame and a dull roar; wood flicked up from the ladder. I held on with my left hand, crossed my right over and squeezed lead just as that gun blazed again. Where the second shot went I didn't know, and I didn't care. Just as I fired I thought I saw another figure; a figure that dropped from the rear fence and disappeared in the yard beyond.

Keeping my eye on the bird in the rear court, I slipped to the bottom of that ladder. He was doing queer, whirling dervish acts; twisting and turning like a contortionist. Then, as I reached the court and started towards him with my gun up, he sank to one knee, twisted suddenly and sprawled upon the stones.

I reached the rear fence and looked cautiously over it. I saw nothing. If there had been another man, he had deserted his wounded friend and beat it. But I did think, with a little gulp in my throat, that there was an even chance that the wounded lad in the court might be the one I wanted.

Wounded lad? Well, 'wounded' is not quite the word. He was dead when I reached him. I'm not a doctor or a coroner, you understand, but offhand I'd say he must have turned sidewise as I shot, and taken my lead through both lungs. I swung him over and looked at his face. It was Murray, the same lad who had faced me in Kean's house up in Yonkers.

We had spent time on that side street. It was easy for him to reach the Drake house ahead of us. Maybe my fingers trembled slightly when I searched Murray, but if they did it was simply from excitement. An even break. Who would get that break? Eddie Kean or me? And Eddie got the break. I went over that corpse with a fine-toothed comb, but didn't find what I wanted. The lad who hopped the fence had it. So I turned back to the house.

What were my thoughts as I climbed that ladder again? Well, I wished that pretty bit of shooting had found a better target. Eddie Kean, for instance.

Servants were crowding the doorway. Warren Drake was stroking his daughter's head as she sat there in the chair. Someone was shouting in the house next door and a police whistle was disturbing the quiet of the fashionable neighborhood. Fortunately, the girl was conscious and prevented Warren Drake from rushing me and getting himself slapped around.

"That's Race Williams, father." Gladys Drake spoke to her father, but directed her message to me. "He's the detective I asked to come here when I received the telephone message that someone was going to steal my jewelry."

"You should have told me." Warren Drake glared at me as if it was all my fault. "Nothing is missing." He was pawing over the jewelry in the open wall safe now. "Besides, there is nothing of real value here. I— I—"

"You had better ring for the police," I told him. "There's a man dead in the back yard."

He shot out of the room.

"A man dead!" Gladys Drake looked up at me. There was hope in her eyes, but I shook my head. Then I leaned close to her and whispered:

"The letters! They're gone?"

"Yes. There was a man waiting in the room. I didn't see him until I opened the safe and held the two letters in my hand. Then he grabbed me and I screamed, and he struck me." And in a voice so low that I hardly caught the words: "The letters were genuine, then?"

"Yes! That proves it," I said, through clenched teeth. "The letters were genuine, and I was a fool." Both statements being gospel.

Of course there was the usual police investigation, and the medical examiner and one thing and another to annoy me. And, of course, Sergeant O'Rourke.

"I tell you, Race." O'Rourke explained his quick arrival. "I left word to be called at once in anything that concerned the Drakes, Eddie Kean, or you. I want to piece things together."

"And how do you piece tonight's work together?" I asked him as he saw me into a taxi.

"Simple!" He shrugged his huge shoulders. "You went and shot the wrong man."

And, by—! there was nothing wrong about that statement either.

Chapter VII

THE LETTER came to my office the next day by special messenger. It was simple, and left me holding a bunch of jack. Some private detectives would have considered it a holiday, gone on a bust and filed away all his information for future blackmail. As for me, I was stunned.

The first thing that dropped out of that envelope was another check for five thousand dollars. The note read:

> *Since the case has come to an unsatisfactory conclusion, I am enclosing, according to my agreement, my check for five thousand dollars.*
> *Gladys Drake*

That note dropped me back ten years. For the moment I had the youthful impulse to take my gun, step right out and pop off Mr. Eddie Kean. When I calmed down I decided to tear up the checks and send them back to her. Then – well, just to show how the thing hit me, I grabbed up the phone and tried to get the girl on the wire. A smooth, English voice told me that Miss Drake couldn't come to the phone, and when I insisted, that same voice told me that "Miss Drake was out; always out to Mr. Race Williams."

That I broke the ear-piece hanging up has nothing to do with the matter.

Mad, bewildered and what not! But fair is fair. I guess, above everything else, my pride was hurt. Finally I decided to let the thing rest for a few days. I'd work the old brain and see what came of it. Days passed, and nothing much came of it. I didn't send the checks back and I didn't cash them. First thought: If this dame didn't know any more than to throw me over she could stew in her own juice. Second thought: To a certain extent it was my juice she was stewing in. It was my fault she lost those damned letters. I should have given them the protection they warranted. Eddie Kean's pretended indifference to her threat of the letters had thrown me higher than a kite. Now, the letters had certainly gone up in smoke.

And then Detective Sergeant O'Rourke blew in; said it was his day off. He chucked a folded newspaper on my desk. It was the rival sheet of the *Blade*. I couldn't miss the item he had heavily penciled in a garbage column.

What well-known society girl is 'just like that' with one of the town's worst-known gentlemen?

"The girl's in a jam, isn't she?" O'Rourke said.

"That's right," I nodded.

"And the guy is Eddie Kean?"

"That's right, too," I told him.

"And you're a dumb cluck!" O'Rourke leaned on the desk and glared over at me. "You've embarrassed the Department with that gun of yours more times than I can remember. Now, when you might use it to advantage – why, you turn coy. And I sicced you on the girl!"

"How bad are things?" I asked him.

"Well," he said, "she's running around with Eddie Kean. I can guess the reason. I've done everything I could, even chancing a libel suit. Took a run down to the bank and saw Warren Drake; hinted that perhaps Eddie Kean was not good company for his daughter. Further the Department couldn't go. There's absolutely nothing official against Kean."

"What did Drake say?"

"Put on the Drake act. The very fact that his daughter introduced Kean made it all right! Though, inside, I think the old boy was bothered. Yet, he shook hands with Kean at an affair the other night. He near burst a blood vessel doing it, but he did it."

"You know any more?" I asked him.

"Yes," he said. "She's going to marry the rat. She told me that, and – and she asked me to lay off."

"You like the girl, O'Rourke?"

"Enough to put you on the case." He paused. "And enough to scratch your name off my list, as a white livered—"

I was on my feet now, facing him. Our hands clenched on the desk. His face was white, and so was mine, I guess. He had years on me, but I don't think that was the reason I didn't knock him for a loop.

"She chucked me over," I finally said. "You don't know all the facts."

"I can guess them," O'Rourke said. "Eddie Kean knows she knocked over Joe Bray in Philly. That's the blackmail. You come into the case, mess things up, and he orders the girl to drop you or he'll talk. Well, what can she do?"

"And what can I do?"

"There must be some evidence; real evidence, against the girl. Get that evidence. Destroy that evidence."

And there was evidence. The doctor over in Philly. I started thinking. Eddie Kean had burned the doctor's statement right in front of the girl. But he'd only have to see the doctor, or drag him into court, to get another statement. That was evidence that could not be destroyed.

I said: "The evidence is a living human being."

"Living witnesses have disappeared," said O'Rourke. "The girl's got the dough for it. Can't you fix that?"

I stroked my chin. Hell! I could, of course. I— but what was the name of that doctor?

"O'Rourke," I said, "I've got to talk to the girl. She'll be hard to see."

He snapped out his watch and looked at it.

"Everybody else can see her. She lunches at one every day at the Ritz. But not alone – with Eddie Kean."

"Drag him out of there today. I've got to talk to her. I—"

"How in hell will I—" O'Rourke started, but I stopped him.

My fist pounded into my palm. I had it.

"I'll get him away from that table long enough for me to talk to the girl," I said. "Now, on your way!" And then: "Just one thing, O'Rourke. What kind of a double life was Miss Drake leading, and what is your interest in her?"

He hesitated a bit and then said:

"She wasn't leading any double life. Or if she was, it was a damn good one. She used a lot of her money to help others. None of this charity that's listed in the papers; ten percent to the poor, ninety percent to distribute it. This girl spent a couple of months every year in the lower city. I met her first at a scene of poverty and tragedy that pulled even at my tough old heart. I didn't know her, of course, and I promised I wouldn't try to find out who she was. But others did know her, I guess, and through her desire to personally help the unfortunate, trapped her. It wasn't until I was tipped off on the Philly case and saw Miss Drake that I knew her real identity. She's a straight shooter, Race."

"Yeah." I twisted my mouth slightly. "That's the trouble."

"You know what I mean." O'Rourke leaned over and gripped my wrist. "There ain't many like her in the upper crust. She's too good to be sacrificed to a rotten, slimy racketeer."

"You'd stick with me then?"

He shrugged.

"I wonder," I said. And I did wonder as we left the office building together.

O'Rourke talked. About Eddie Kean.

"He's building himself up, Race; building himself up for respectability. They're running his life in the *Blade*. Self-made man, who through suffering and privation became a big business man. Charitable; honest. A model to be pointed out to every American boy. The opportunity our great country offers to even its most humble citizens! Yep, he's building himself up to marry a Drake." O'Rourke spat on the sidewalk. "You should read it, Race. It'll turn your stomach."

But I was thinking about other things as I hopped a taxi and drove uptown to the Ritz.

Chapter VIII

I WAS THERE ahead of them, for from a distant corner I saw Eddie Kean and Gladys Drake enter the Egyptian dining room. They weren't a bad-looking couple, either. Eddie's fish-like eyes didn't stand out so bad in the distance, nor was the coarseness of his face and the thickness of his lips so pronounced.

The sparkle had gone out of the girl's eyes; deep shadows were under them. There was a mean cut across her lips. Her face was just a dead pan, with no expression. Eddie chatted easily with her, and once jerked her arm violently, as if he didn't fancy her lack of interest.

Eddie's trouble with respectability came when he was seated in the dining room. He wanted to attract attention; wanted people to know he was there. He got enough service; his money and willingness to spend it rated well with the waiters and secured the attention, and Miss Drake drew the nods and bows he couldn't have gotten if he had used a machine gun.

And my letter went in. From behind a pillar I watched him take it from the boy, nod and smile, open it and read it. Then he read it again. Just for a second, I thought I saw anger in his face; perhaps, too, a touch of uncertainty.

He crumpled up the letter as if to toss it under the table, thought better of it, read it again and shoved it into his pocket. He was annoyed, for he came to his feet, and with no more than a nod to the girl, chucked his napkin on the table and walked from the room.

I saw him start towards the desk, and things were not so good. But he changed his mind, and turning, went straight to the row of elevators.

I knew the note would move him, and I felt that he wouldn't inquire about it at the desk. He was a cautious man. And what had the note said? Just this:

The doctor from Philadelphia must see you at once in room 709.

Now, if the doctor didn't know Kean's name, Eddie would wonder how he found it out. And if he did know it, Eddie would go to room 709 expecting a shake-down. Anyway, he went.

The girl's face never changed as I walked across the room and dropped into Eddie's empty chair. Dull blue eyes regarded me.

"I haven't got time for much chin," I told her. "I want the name of the doctor in Philadelphia."

"You're through with the case," she said.

"I want to help you. Take a chance and give me the name of the doctor." And when she did not speak, "Even seconds are precious."

"You have been paid," she said listlessly.

And I told her what was on my chest.

"Damn your thick head!" I said. "Give me the name of the doctor and I'll send you back the checks."

She seemed slightly startled. At least her eyes wavered, and for a moment fire was there. Then she said: "I don't want the checks back. The name of the doctor is Havilan Quinn." And suddenly, "Listen! You risked your life for me that night. I am not blaming you. But don't interfere further and make it harder for me. And don't look at me like that. In the end I will marry him, though I've found a way to put it off. You see, the doctor is just as great a menace to me as Eddie Kean is. I shall not marry Kean while another can strike at me. So I won't marry Eddie until he can convince me that the doctor is no longer a danger. And he can't convince me of that." And with a bitter smile, or at least a twist to red lips: "Kean rather fancies me now. You see, I'm the kind of a woman that such men – desire."

"But you'll marry Kean in the end?"

"In the end." She barely nodded. And then, as if she read my thought: "You'd think I'd rather die! I thought of that, and so did Kean. He'd see that the world knew that Warren Drake's dead daughter killed Joe Bray. He thinks of things like that. He let me know that he beats his women. There's the cut on my lip if you must have all the harrowing details." Her shoulders shrugged. "You see—" She straightened suddenly and looked up. Eddie Kean was at the table. "Mr. Williams came in and sat down," she said to Eddie. "It's a public dining room."

"That's right." I was slow in coming to my feet. "Just renewing an old acquaintance."

Eddie Kean fastened those fish-like eyes on me.

"So you sent the note," he said. And turning to the girl, "You see his idea. Simply blackmail. You were ill-advised to bring him into it in the beginning, my dear." And he slurred those last two words as he turned to me. "But without the name of the doctor, Williams, you can't— but, did you get the doctor's name?" And there was anger and more in his eyes as he glared at the girl.

"I'm not interested in the name of the doctor." I threw a warning glance at Gladys Drake. "I was well paid, and I was asking Miss Drake if she had any further use for my services."

"Well, she hasn't!" Dean said. And then, as he dropped into the chair: "In the beginning this was a plain business deal with Miss Drake. Now, we understand each other. The wedding will be a quiet affair; no hustle and bustle." And very slowly, as his fish eyes narrowed, "No trouble."

"No trouble." I repeated his words and moved from the table. But he was on his feet and followed me to the lounge.

"You and I don't need to mince words, Race," he said. "So here's the office. Stay away from my future wife. There'll be no more money in it for you. I'm out of the racket. I'm in a legitimate business, but I'm still the same old Eddie Kean. Which means—"

"Which means?" I encouraged him.

"That I still know how to squeeze lead through the nose of a gun, and that I still get what I want. I want the Drake influence, and I want that woman. Good afternoon!"

He turned on his heel and left me. Certainly Eddie had a habit of getting what he wanted. And I thought of Gladys Drake; of the cut across her fine young mouth, and I thought, too, that what Eddie Kean wanted was a bellyful of lead.

I went directly to the bank and cashed the first of Gladys Drake's two checks. Then I took the train to Philadelphia. Threats or money, or both, should move the doctor to parts unknown. I had seen Eddie Kean tear up the doctor's statement, and I didn't think he'd be able to put the finger on Gladys Drake for murder without the doctor, or at least the doctor's testimony. Anyway, I'd beard the doctor.

Chapter IX

IN PHILLY I found Doctor Havilan Quinn's hangout in the telephone book, jumped a taxi and drove to the hotel where Joe Bray sought a woman and met a bullet.

The doctor's house was around the corner from the rear entrance to the hotel. It was a short, dirty street, without a person in sight on it. A deserted warehouse stood on one side of the musty-looking dwelling; on the other side, a house in bad condition sported crookedly hung signs that they needed both roomers and ice. Below the doctor's bell was a dirty strip of paper that said: 'Ring and walk in.'

I did both, and closed the door behind me. The house didn't smell so good. In the dark you'd think that you'd missed the doctor's and hit the warehouse. There was a dim light burning in the hall. It needed it. To the left, on the side towards the rooming-house, were closed doors. To the right, heavy curtains slightly parted. Behind those was the waiting room. Last year's magazines were on the table. I went in.

Someone had run a cloth over the center of the table, making the dust on the rest of it more pronounced. Shades were drawn on the single front window and the two facing the warehouse, all three of which were closed. A floor lamp that boasted two sockets but only one bulb turned the darkness into shadowy light. There was a door that said 'Office' in small letters; 'PRIVATE' in large ones. It was open a crack. I coughed and waited a bit.

No one came. I crossed to that door. There was more light in there. The flash that came through the crack cut through the dimness of the waiting room.

I tapped on the door, looked through it cautiously, then jerked it open and barged into the room. Mechanically my gun had jumped into my hand.

Doctor Havilan Quinn was there all right. He was sitting at his desk, leaning forward, his head on his left arm. His right hand clutched a pen. The blotter was red, and the red was spreading.

Yep, the doctor was there and the doctor was dead. Someone had smashed the top of his head in – with the butt of a gun, perhaps.

As I looked down at the dead man I knew the truth. The words that Gladys Drake had spoken pounded through my head. She'd marry Eddie Kean only when the doctor was no longer a danger. I nodded at that, Eddie Kean had been there, and the doctor was no longer a danger. The pen told the whole story. The doctor's statement was necessary for a case against Gladys Drake. Kean had tossed that statement in the fire to impress the girl, since he had the doctor in person as a witness. Now, Kean had come from New York, got the doctor to write another statement, put it carefully in his pocket and nonchalantly killed the doctor.

I lifted the pen and looked at the nib. The ink was still wet on it. The murder had taken place only a few minutes before. Maybe—

And a voice spoke behind me, from the waiting-room door.

"Got it all figured out, eh? So she blew the doctor's name to you." The smooth words and studied polish had slipped from Eddie Kean now. The gunman and killer of other days was talking. "I thought that, the minute you left us, and, if you want to know, I took a plane, beat you here, and after I finished my business, just waited for you to come and let me clear up the whole picture.

"And you're right, Race. I got his signed statement before I jumped him over the hurdles. Now, sort of two birds with one gun. Right through the back of the head! There, don't turn around."

And I didn't turn. I just stood there and folded my arms, careful that he should not see the muzzle of the .44 which I began to slip under my left arm and in the direction where his voice sounded.

"You can't get away with this, Eddie." My voice was calm enough. I guess I can take it when the time comes.

"No?" Eddie's voice was hard, I could imagine the fish eyes narrowing; picking out a place just above the back of my neck. "Who's to tell you about it if I don't get away with it?"

"A lot of people know I came here." I lied easily.

"A lot of people knew the doctor was here." He laughed. "And the whole country will know you're here when they read the papers." And suddenly: "You liked the girl. She tried to work a racket on me with you. One month from now she'll know who gives orders and who takes them. I'll knock—" And the anger going out of his voice, "Now—"

I sensed death; felt sure of it even. And I took a chance.

I just closed a finger on the trigger of my gun. There was a roar that shook the little office; a sharp cry from Eddie. And as I fired, I threw myself to one side and down, twisting my body around, bringing up my smoking gun.

Eddie fired, of course. I never had the wildest hope that I had got him with a lucky shot. But I had hit him, and he was staggering when he shot.

Eddie's bullet tore into my back just below my right shoulder and far over to the side. It helped swing my body. In fact, it knocked me clean around, even if it did hurl me violently to the floor, with my back against the wall. But it knocked me enough to make Eddie miscalculate on his second shot. The shot was near enough. It parted my hair, then buried itself in the wall.

And that was all of that. No man is entitled to more than two shots at me. Fair is fair; you've got to admit that. Eddie got exactly what was coming to him; a bellyful of lead.

It was hard work but it didn't take me long to get across, kneel down by the body of Eddie Kean and lift that statement from his pocket. But I got what I wanted. And Eddie wanted respectability. So I guess he got what he wanted – if death is respectable.

And the hardest part of the whole case? It was getting out of that house and to the station. I made it out of the door all right, and had turned the corner of the deserted warehouse into a dark, narrow alley running the length of it, without seeing anyone and before I heard a ruckus behind me.

Maybe people in the hotel had heard the shots and put in a call for the police. Anyway, a lot of them were yelling back and forth, asking questions, urging the other fellow to go somewhere and look-see, as I stopped in the darkness and shoved my balled-up handkerchief inside my shirt and over the hole Eddie's bullet had made.

I got to the next street, lit a cigarette and strolled half a block when a cruising taxi came along. I flagged it and climbed in, and darned near passed out on the cushions.

We'd gone a few blocks when a police siren went screaming down another street. My driver didn't even glance around, and at the station, another passenger climbed in as I crawled out, and he looked only at the bill I passed him and not at me as he started off.

I don't remember much about leaving Philly and getting back to New York. But I made it. Got my own doctor, who dug a bullet out of my back and fixed up the hole. A nasty one it was, too.

Then I sent for O'Rourke.

"Don't tell me, Race." He looked at me propped up in bed. "I know all about it – or enough. Kean died hard, eh?"

"As hard as he lived," I told him. "Where were you all afternoon?"

"I told you it was my day off." He grinned. "Believe it or not, I spent the afternoon alone, at a gang picture. Why?"

"Because," I said slowly, "if any trouble came up – well, I'd be apt to say that an honest cop spent the afternoon here with me."

"Well—" he rubbed a hand across his chin. "Well, now. If trouble came up I'd be apt to say that you were right."

The Adventure of Silver Blaze

Arthur Conan Doyle

"I AM AFRAID, Watson that I shall have to go," said Holmes as we sat down together to our breakfast one morning.

"Go! Where to?"

"To Dartmoor; to King's Pyland."

I was not surprised. Indeed, my only wonder was that he had not already been mixed up in this extraordinary case, which was the one topic of conversation through the length and breadth of England. For a whole day my companion had rambled about the room with his chin upon his chest and his brows knitted, charging and recharging his pipe with the strongest black tobacco, and absolutely deaf to any of my questions or remarks. Fresh editions of every paper had been sent up by our news agent, only to be glanced over and tossed down into a corner. Yet, silent as he was, I knew perfectly well what it was over which he was brooding. There was but one problem before the public which could challenge his powers of analysis, and that was the singular disappearance of the favourite for the Wessex Cup, and the tragic murder of its trainer. When, therefore, he suddenly announced his intention of setting out for the scene of the drama, it was only what I had both expected and hoped for.

"I should be most happy to go down with you if I should not be in the way," said I.

"My dear Watson, you would confer a great favour upon me by coming. And I think that your time will not be misspent, for there are points about the case which promise to make it an absolutely unique one. We have, I think, just time to catch our train at Paddington, and I will go further into the matter upon our journey. You would oblige me by bringing with you your very excellent field-glass."

And so it happened that an hour or so later I found myself in the corner of a first-class carriage flying along en route for Exeter, while Sherlock Holmes, with his sharp, eager face framed in his ear-flapped travelling-cap, dipped rapidly into the bundle of fresh papers which he had procured at Paddington. We had left Reading far behind us before he thrust the last one of them under the seat and offered me his cigar case.

"We are going well," said he, looking out of the window and glancing at his watch. "Our rate at present is fifty-three and a half miles an hour."

"I have not observed the quarter-mile posts," said I.

"Nor have I. But the telegraph posts upon this line are sixty yards apart, and the calculation is a simple one. I presume that you have looked into this matter of the murder of John Straker and the disappearance of Silver Blaze?"

"I have seen what the *Telegraph* and the *Chronicle* have to say."

"It is one of those cases where the art of the reasoner should be used rather for the sifting of details than for the acquiring of fresh evidence. The tragedy has been so uncommon, so complete, and of such personal importance to so many people that we are suffering from a plethora of surmise, conjecture, and hypothesis. The difficulty is to detach the framework of fact – of absolute undeniable fact – from the embellishments of theorists and reporters.

Then, having established ourselves upon this sound basis, it is our duty to see what inferences may be drawn and what are the special points upon which the whole mystery turns. On Tuesday evening I received telegrams from both Colonel Ross, the owner of the horse, and from Inspector Gregory, who is looking after the case, inviting my cooperation."

"Tuesday evening!" I exclaimed. "And this is Thursday morning. Why didn't you go down yesterday?"

"Because I made a blunder, my dear Watson – which is, I am afraid, a more common occurrence than anyone would think who only knew me through your memoirs. The fact is that I could not believe it possible that the most remarkable horse in England could long remain concealed, especially in so sparsely inhabited a place as the north of Dartmoor. From hour to hour yesterday I expected to hear that he had been found, and that his abductor was the murderer of John Straker. When, however, another morning had come and I found that beyond the arrest of young Fitzroy Simpson nothing had been done, I felt that it was time for me to take action. Yet in some ways I feel that yesterday has not been wasted."

"You have formed a theory, then?"

"At least I have got a grip of the essential facts of the case. I shall enumerate them to you, for nothing clears up a case so much as stating it to another person, and I can hardly expect your cooperation if I do not show you the position from which we start."

I lay back against the cushions, puffing at my cigar, while Holmes, leaning forward, with his long, thin forefinger checking off the points upon the palm of his left hand, gave me a sketch of the events which had led to our journey.

"Silver Blaze," said he, "is from the Somomy stock and holds as brilliant a record as his famous ancestor. He is now in his fifth year and has brought in turn each of the prizes of the turf to Colonel Ross, his fortunate owner. Up to the time of the catastrophe he was the first favourite for the Wessex Cup, the betting being three to one on him. He has always, however, been a prime favourite with the racing public and has never yet disappointed them, so that even at those odds enormous sums of money have been laid upon him. It is obvious, therefore, that there were many people who had the strongest interest in preventing Silver Blaze from being there at the fall of the flag next Tuesday.

"The fact was, of course, appreciated at King's Pyland, where the colonel's training-stable is situated. Every precaution was taken to guard the favourite. The trainer, John Straker, is a retired jockey who rode in Colonel Ross's colours before he became too heavy for the weighing-chair. He has served the colonel for five years as jockey and for seven as trainer, and has always shown himself to be a zealous and honest servant. Under him were three lads, for the establishment was a small one, containing only four horses in all. One of these lads sat up each night in the stable, while the others slept in the loft. All three bore excellent characters. John Straker, who is a married man, lived in a small villa about two hundred yards from the stables. He has no children, keeps one maidservant, and is comfortably off. The country round is very lonely, but about half a mile to the north there is a small cluster of villas which have been built by a Tavistock contractor for the use of invalids and others who may wish to enjoy the pure Dartmoor air. Tavistock itself lies two miles to the west, while across the moor, also about two miles distant, is the larger training establishment of Mapleton, which belongs to Lord Backwater and is managed by Silas Brown. In every other direction the moor is a complete wilderness, inhabited only by a few roaming gypsies. Such was the general situation last Monday night when the catastrophe occurred.

"On that evening the horses had been exercised and watered as usual, and the stables were locked up at nine o'clock. Two of the lads walked up to the trainer's house, where they had supper in the kitchen, while the third, Ned Hunter, remained on guard. At a few minutes after nine the maid, Edith Baxter, carried down to the stables his supper, which consisted of a dish of curried mutton. She took no liquid, as there was a water-tap in the stables, and it was the rule that the lad on duty should drink nothing else. The maid carried a lantern with her, as it was very dark and the path ran across the open moor.

"Edith Baxter was within thirty yards of the stables when a man appeared out of the darkness and called to her to stop. As she stepped into the circle of yellow light thrown by the lantern she saw that he was a person of gentlemanly bearing, dressed in a grey suit of tweeds, with a cloth cap. He wore gaiters and carried a heavy stick with a knob to it. She was most impressed, however, by the extreme pallor of his face and by the nervousness of his manner. His age, she thought, would be rather over thirty than under it.

"'Can you tell me where I am?' he asked. 'I had almost made up my mind to sleep on the moor when I saw the light of your lantern.'

"'You are close to the King's Pyland training stables,' said she.

"'Oh, indeed! What a stroke of luck!' he cried. 'I understand that a stable-boy sleeps there alone every night. Perhaps that is his supper which you are carrying to him. Now I am sure that you would not be too proud to earn the price of a new dress, would you?' He took a piece of white paper folded up out of his waistcoat pocket. 'See that the boy has this tonight, and you shall have the prettiest frock that money can buy.'

"She was frightened by the earnestness of his manner and ran past him to the window through which she was accustomed to hand the meals. It was already opened, and Hunter was seated at the small table inside. She had begun to tell him of what had happened when the stranger came up again.

"'Good evening,' said he, looking through the window. 'I wanted to have a word with you.' The girl has sworn that as he spoke she noticed the corner of the little paper packet protruding from his closed hand.

"'What business have you here?' asked the lad.

"'It's business that may put something into your pocket.' said the other. 'You've two horses in for the Wessex Cup – Silver Blaze and Bayard. Let me have the straight tip and you won't be a loser. Is it a fact that at the weights Bayard could give the other a hundred yards in five furlongs, and that the stable have put their money on him?'

"'So, you're one of those damned touts!' cried the lad. 'I'll show you how we serve them in King's Pyland.' He sprang up and rushed across the stable to unloose the dog. The girl fled away to the house, but as she ran she looked back and saw that the stranger was leaning through the window. A minute later, however, when Hunter rushed out with the hound he was gone, and though he ran all round the buildings he failed to find any trace of him."

"One moment," I asked. "Did the stable-boy, when he ran out with the dog, leave the door unlocked behind him?"

"Excellent, Watson, excellent!" murmured my companion. "The importance of the point struck me so forcibly that I sent a special wire to Dartmoor yesterday to clear the matter up. The boy locked the door before he left it. The window, I may add, was not large enough for a man to get through.

"Hunter waited until his fellow-grooms had returned, when he sent a message to the trainer and told him what had occurred. Straker was excited at hearing the account, although he does not seem to have quite realised its true significance. It left him, however, vaguely uneasy, and Mrs. Straker, waking at one in the morning, found that he was dressing.

In reply to her inquiries, he said that he could not sleep on account of his anxiety about the horses, and that he intended to walk down to the stables to see that all was well. She begged him to remain at home, as she could hear the rain pattering against the window, but in spite of her entreaties he pulled on his large mackintosh and left the house.

"Mrs. Straker awoke at seven in the morning to find that her husband had not yet returned. She dressed herself hastily, called the maid, and set off for the stables. The door was open; inside, huddled together upon a chair, Hunter was sunk in a state of absolute stupor, the favourite's stall was empty, and there were no signs of his trainer.

"The two lads who slept in the chaff-cutting loft above the harness-room were quickly aroused. They had heard nothing during the night, for they are both sound sleepers. Hunter was obviously under the influence of some powerful drug, and as no sense could be got out of him, he was left to sleep it off while the two lads and the two women ran out in search of the absentees. They still had hopes that the trainer had for some reason taken out the horse for early exercise, but on ascending the knoll near the house, from which all the neighbouring moors were visible, they not only could see no signs of the missing favourite, but they perceived something which warned them that they were in the presence of a tragedy.

"About a quarter of a mile from the stables John Straker's overcoat was flapping from a furze-bush. Immediately beyond there was a bowl-shaped depression in the moor, and at the bottom of this was found the dead body of the unfortunate trainer. His head had been shattered by a savage blow from some heavy weapon, and he was wounded on the thigh, where there was a long, clean cut, inflicted evidently by some very sharp instrument. It was clear, however, that Straker had defended himself vigorously against his assailants, for in his right hand he held a small knife, which was clotted with blood up to the handle, while in his left he clasped a red and black silk cravat, which was recognised by the maid as having been worn on the preceding evening by the stranger who had visited the stables. Hunter, on recovering from his stupor, was also quite positive as to the ownership of the cravat. He was equally certain that the same stranger had, while standing at the window, drugged his curried mutton, and so deprived the stables of their watchman. As to the missing horse, there were abundant proofs in the mud which lay at the bottom of the fatal hollow that he had been there at the time of the struggle. But from that morning he has disappeared, and although a large reward has been offered, and all the gypsies of Dartmoor are on the alert, no news has come of him. Finally, an analysis has shown that the remains of his supper left by the stable-lad contained an appreciable quantity of powdered opium, while the people at the house partook of the same dish on the same night without any ill effect.

"Those are the main facts of the case, stripped of all surmise, and stated as baldly as possible. I shall now recapitulate what the police have done in the matter.

"Inspector Gregory, to whom the case has been committed, is an extremely competent officer. Were he but gifted with imagination he might rise to great heights in his profession. On his arrival he promptly found and arrested the man upon whom suspicion naturally rested. There was little difficulty in finding him, for he inhabited one of those villas which I have mentioned. His name, it appears, was Fitzroy Simpson. He was a man of excellent birth and education, who had squandered a fortune upon the turf, and who lived now by doing a little quiet and genteel book-making in the sporting clubs of London. An examination of his betting-book shows that bets to the amount of five thousand pounds had been registered by him against the favourite. On being arrested he volunteered the statement that he had come down to Dartmoor in the hope of getting some information about the King's Pyland horses, and also about Desborough, the second favourite, which was in charge of Silas Brown at the Mapleton stables. He did not attempt to deny that he had acted as described upon the evening before, but declared that he had no sinister designs and had simply wished to obtain first-hand information. When confronted with his cravat he turned very pale and was utterly unable to account for its presence in the hand of the murdered man. His wet clothing showed that he had been out in the storm of the night before, and his stick, which was a penang-lawyer weighted with lead, was just such a weapon as might, by repeated blows, have inflicted the terrible injuries to which the trainer had succumbed. On the other hand, there was no wound upon his person, while the state of Straker's knife would show that one at least of his assailants must bear his mark upon him. There you have it all in a nutshell, Watson, and if you can give me any light I shall be infinitely obliged to you."

I had listened with the greatest interest to the statement which Holmes, with characteristic clearness, had laid before me. Though most of the facts were familiar to me, I had not sufficiently appreciated their relative importance, nor their connection to each other.

"Is it not possible," I suggested, "that the incised wound upon Straker may have been caused by his own knife in the convulsive struggles which follow any brain injury?"

"It is more than possible; it is probable," said Holmes. "In that case one of the main points in favour of the accused disappears."

"And yet," said I, "even now I fail to understand what the theory of the police can be."

"I am afraid that whatever theory we state has very grave objections to it," returned my companion. "The police imagine, I take it, that this Fitzroy Simpson, having drugged the lad, and having in some way obtained a duplicate key, opened the stable door and took out the horse, with the intention, apparently, of kidnapping him altogether. His bridle is missing, so that Simpson must have put this on. Then, having left the door open behind him, he was leading the horse away over the moor when he was either met or overtaken by the trainer. A row naturally ensued. Simpson beat out the trainer's brains with his heavy stick without receiving any injury from the small knife which Straker used in self-defence, and then the thief either led the horse on to some secret hiding place, or else it may have bolted during the struggle, and be now wandering out on the moors. That is the case as it appears to the police, and improbable as it is, all other explanations are more improbable still. However, I shall very quickly test the matter when I am once upon the spot, and until then I cannot really see how we can get much further than our present position."

It was evening before we reached the little town of Tavistock, which lies, like the boss of a shield, in the middle of the huge circle of Dartmoor. Two gentlemen were awaiting us in the station – the one a tall, fair man with lion-like hair and beard and curiously penetrating light blue eyes; the other a small, alert person, very neat and dapper, in a frock-coat and gaiters, with trim little side-whiskers and an eyeglass. The latter was Colonel Ross, the well-known sportsman; the other, Inspector Gregory; a man who was rapidly making his name in the English detective service.

"I am delighted that you have come down, Mr. Holmes," said the colonel. "The inspector here has done all that could possibly be suggested, but I wish to leave no stone unturned in trying to avenge poor Straker and in recovering my horse."

"Have there been any fresh developments?" asked Holmes.

"I am sorry to say that we have made very little progress," said the inspector. "We have an open carriage outside, and as you would no doubt like to see the place before the light fails, we might talk it over as we drive."

A minute later we were all seated in a comfortable landau and were rattling through the quaint old Devonshire city. Inspector Gregory was full of his case and poured out a stream of remarks, while Holmes threw in an occasional question or interjection. Colonel Ross leaned back with his arms folded and his hat tilted over his eyes, while I listened with interest to the dialogue of the two detectives. Gregory was formulating his theory, which was almost exactly what Holmes had foretold in the train.

"The net is drawn pretty close round Fitzroy Simpson," he remarked, "and I believe myself that he is our man. At the same time I recognise that the evidence is purely circumstantial, and that some new development may upset it."

"How about Straker's knife?"

"We have quite come to the conclusion that he wounded himself in his fall."

"My friend Dr. Watson made that suggestion to me as we came down. If so, it would tell against this man Simpson."

"Undoubtedly. He has neither a knife nor any sign of a wound. The evidence against him is certainly very strong. He had a great interest in the disappearance of the favourite. He lies under suspicion of having poisoned the stable-boy; he was undoubtedly out in the storm; he was armed with a heavy stick, and his cravat was found in the dead man's hand. I really think we have enough to go before a jury."

Holmes shook his head. "A clever counsel would tear it all to rags," said he. "Why should he take the horse out of the stable? If he wished to injure it, why could he not do it there? Has a duplicate key been found in his possession? What chemist sold him the powdered opium? Above all, where could he, a stranger to the district, hide a horse, and such a horse as this? What is his own explanation as to the paper which he wished the maid to give to the stable-boy?"

"He says that it was a ten-pound note. One was found in his purse. But your other difficulties are not so formidable as they seem. He is not a stranger to the district. He has twice lodged at Tavistock in the summer. The opium was probably brought from London. The key, having served its purpose, would be hurled away. The horse may be at the bottom of one of the pits or old mines upon the moor."

"What does he say about the cravat?"

"He acknowledges that it is his and declares that he had lost it. But a new element has been introduced into the case which may account for his leading the horse from the stable."

Holmes pricked up his ears.

"We have found traces which show that a party of gypsies encamped on Monday night within a mile of the spot where the murder took place. On Tuesday they were gone. Now, presuming that there was some understanding between Simpson and these gypsies, might he not have been leading the horse to them when he was overtaken, and may they not have him now?"

"It is certainly possible."

"The moor is being scoured for these gypsies. I have also examined every stable and outhouse in Tavistock, and for a radius of ten miles."

"There is another training-stable quite close, I understand?"

"Yes, and that is a factor which we must certainly not neglect. As Desborough, their horse, was second in the betting, they had an interest in the disappearance of the favourite. Silas Brown, the trainer, is known to have had large bets upon the event, and he was no friend to poor Straker. We have, however, examined the stables, and there is nothing to connect him with the affair."

"And nothing to connect this man Simpson with the interests of the Mapleton stables?"

"Nothing at all."

Holmes leaned back in the carriage, and the conversation ceased. A few minutes later our driver pulled up at a neat little red-brick villa with overhanging eaves which stood by the road. Some distance off, across a paddock, lay a long grey-tiled outbuilding. In every other direction the low curves of the moor, bronze-coloured from the fading ferns, stretched away to the sky-line, broken only by the steeples of Tavistock, and by a cluster of houses away to the westward which marked the Mapleton stables. We all sprang out with the exception of Holmes, who continued to lean back with his eyes fixed upon the sky in front of him, entirely absorbed in his own thoughts. It was only when I touched his arm that he roused himself with a violent start and stepped out of the carriage.

"Excuse me," said he, turning to Colonel Ross, who had looked at him in some surprise. "I was day-dreaming." There was a gleam in his eyes and a suppressed excitement in his manner which convinced me, used as I was to his ways, that his hand was upon a clue, though I could not imagine where he had found it.

"Perhaps you would prefer at once to go on to the scene of the crime, Mr. Holmes?" said Gregory.

"I think that I should prefer to stay here a little and go into one or two questions of detail. Straker was brought back here, I presume?"

"Yes, he lies upstairs. The inquest is tomorrow."

"He has been in your service some years, Colonel Ross?"

"I have always found him an excellent servant."

"I presume that you made an inventory of what he had in his pockets at the time of his death, Inspector?"

"I have the things themselves in the sitting room if you would care to see them."

"I should be very glad." We all filed into the front room and sat round the central table while the inspector unlocked a square tin box and laid a small heap of things before us. There was a box of vestas, two inches of tallow candle, an A.D.P brier-root pipe, a pouch of sealskin with half an ounce of long-cut Cavendish, a silver watch with a gold chain, five sovereigns in gold, an aluminium pencil-case, a few papers, and an ivory-handled knife with a very delicate, inflexible blade marked Weiss & Co., London.

"This is a very singular knife," said Holmes, lifting it up and examining it minutely. "I presume, as I see bloodstains upon it, that it is the one which was found in the dead man's grasp. Watson, this knife is surely in your line?"

"It is what we call a cataract knife," said I.

"I thought so. A very delicate blade devised for very delicate work. A strange thing for a man to carry with him upon a rough expedition, especially as it would not shut in his pocket."

"The tip was guarded by a disc of cork which we found beside his body," said the inspector. "His wife tells us that the knife had lain upon the dressing-table, and that he had picked it up as he left the room. It was a poor weapon, but perhaps the best that he could lay his hands on at the moment."

"Very possibly. How about these papers?"

"Three of them are receipted hay-dealers' accounts. One of them is a letter of instructions from Colonel Ross. This other is a milliner's account for thirty-seven pounds fifteen made out by Madame Lesurier, of Bond Street, to William Derbyshire. Mrs. Straker tells us that Derbyshire was a friend of her husband's and that occasionally his letters were addressed here."

"Madame Derbyshire had somewhat expensive tastes," remarked Holmes, glancing down the account. "Twenty-two guineas is rather heavy for a single costume. However, there appears to be nothing more to learn, and we may now go down to the scene of the crime."

As we emerged from the sitting room a woman, who had been waiting in the passage, took a step forward and laid her hand upon the inspector's sleeve. Her face was haggard and thin and eager, stamped with the print of a recent horror.

"Have you got them? Have you found them?" she panted.

"No, Mrs. Straker. But Mr. Holmes here has come from London to help us, and we shall do all that is possible."

"Surely I met you in Plymouth at a garden party some little time ago, Mrs. Straker?" said Holmes.

"No, sir; you are mistaken."

"Dear me! Why, I could have sworn to it. You wore a costume of dove-coloured silk with ostrich-feather trimming."

"I never had such a dress, sir," answered the lady.

"Ah, that quite settles it," said Holmes. And with an apology he followed the inspector outside. A short walk across the moor took us to the hollow in which the body had been found. At the brink of it was the furze-bush upon which the coat had been hung.

"There was no wind that night, I understand," said Holmes.

"None, but very heavy rain."

"In that case the overcoat was not blown against the furze-bush, but placed there."

"Yes, it was laid across the bush."

"You fill me with interest. I perceive that the ground has been trampled up a good deal. No doubt many feet have been here since Monday night."

"A piece of matting has been laid here at the side, and we have all stood upon that."

"Excellent."

"In this bag I have one of the boots which Straker wore, one of Fitzroy Simpson's shoes, and a cast horseshoe of Silver Blaze."

"My dear Inspector, you surpass yourself!" Holmes took the bag, and, descending into the hollow, he pushed the matting into a more central position. Then stretching himself upon his face and leaning his chin upon his hands, he made a careful study of the trampled mud in front of him. "Hullo!" said he suddenly. "What's this?" It was a wax vesta, half burned, which was so coated with mud that it looked at first like a little chip of wood.

"I cannot think how I came to overlook it," said the inspector with an expression of annoyance.

"It was invisible, buried in the mud. I only saw it because I was looking for it."

"What! You expected to find it?"

"I thought it not unlikely."

He took the boots from the bag and compared the impressions of each of them with marks upon the ground. Then he clambered up to the rim of the hollow and crawled about among the ferns and bushes.

"I am afraid that there are no more tracks," said the inspector. "I have examined the ground very carefully for a hundred yards in each direction."

"Indeed!" said Holmes, rising. "I should not have the impertinence to do it again after what you say. But I should like to take a little walk over the moor before it grows dark that I may know my ground tomorrow, and I think that I shall put this horseshoe into my pocket for luck."

Colonel Ross, who had shown some signs of impatience at my companion's quiet and systematic method of work, glanced at his watch. "I wish you would come back with me, Inspector," said he. "There are several points on which I should like your advice, and especially as to whether we do not owe it to the public to remove our horse's name from the entries for the cup."

"Certainly not," cried Holmes with decision. "I should let the name stand."

The colonel bowed. "I am very glad to have had your opinion, sir," said he. "You will find us at poor Straker's house when you have finished your walk, and we can drive together into Tavistock."

He turned back with the inspector, while Holmes and I walked slowly across the moor. The sun was beginning to sink behind the stable of Mapleton, and the long sloping plain in front of us was tinged with gold, deepening into rich, ruddy browns where the faded ferns and brambles caught the evening light. But the glories of the landscape were all wasted upon my companion, who was sunk in the deepest thought.

"It's this way, Watson," said he at last. "We may leave the question of who killed John Straker for the instant and confine ourselves to finding out what has become of the horse. Now, supposing that he broke away during or after the tragedy, where could he have gone to? The horse is a very gregarious creature. If left to himself his instincts would have been either to return to King's Pyland or go over to Mapleton. Why should he run wild upon the moor? He would surely have been seen by now. And why should gypsies kidnap him? These people always clear out when they hear of trouble, for they do not wish to be pestered by the police. They could not hope to sell such a horse. They would run a great risk and gain nothing by taking him. Surely that is clear."

"Where is he, then?"

"I have already said that he must have gone to King's Pyland or to Mapleton. He is not at King's Pyland. Therefore he is at Mapleton. Let us take that as a working hypothesis and see what it leads us to. This part of the moor, as the inspector remarked, is very hard and dry. But it falls away towards Mapleton, and you can see from here that there is a long hollow over yonder, which must have been very wet on Monday night. If our supposition is correct, then the horse must have crossed that, and there is the point where we should look for his tracks."

We had been walking briskly during this conversation, and a few more minutes brought us to the hollow in question. At Holmes's request I walked down the bank to the right, and he to the left, but I had not taken fifty paces before I heard him give a shout and saw him waving his hand to me. The track of a horse was plainly outlined in the soft earth in front of him, and the shoe which he took from his pocket exactly fitted the impression.

"See the value of imagination," said Holmes. "It is the one quality which Gregory lacks. We imagined what might have happened, acted upon the supposition, and find ourselves justified. Let us proceed."

We crossed the marshy bottom and passed over a quarter of a mile of dry, hard turf. Again the ground sloped, and again we came on the tracks. Then we lost them for half a mile, but only to pick them up once more quite close to Mapleton. It was Holmes who saw them first, and he stood pointing with a look of triumph upon his face. A man's track was visible beside the horse's.

"The horse was alone before," I cried.

"Quite so. It was alone before. Hullo, what is this?"

The double track turned sharp off and took the direction of King's Pyland. Holmes whistled, and we both followed along after it. His eyes were on the trail, but I happened to look a little to one side and saw to my surprise the same tracks coming back again in the opposite direction.

"One for you, Watson," said Holmes when I pointed it out. "You have saved us a long walk, which would have brought us back on our own traces. Let us follow the return track."

We had not to go far. It ended at the paving of asphalt which led up to the gates of the Mapleton stables. As we approached, a groom ran out from them.

"We don't want any loiterers about here," said he.

"I only wished to ask a question," said Holmes, with his finger and thumb in his waistcoat pocket. "Should I be too early to see your master, Mr. Silas Brown, if I were to call at five o'clock tomorrow morning?"

"Bless you, sir, if anyone is about he will be, for he is always the first stirring. But here he is, sir, to answer your questions for himself. No, sir, no, it is as much as my place is worth to let him see me touch your money. Afterwards, if you like."

As Sherlock Holmes replaced the half-crown which he had drawn from his pocket, a fierce-looking elderly man strode out from the gate with a hunting-crop swinging in his hand.

"What's this, Dawson!" he cried. "No gossiping! Go about your business! And you, what the devil do you want here?"

"Ten minutes' talk with you, my good sir," said Holmes in the sweetest of voices.

"I've no time to talk to every gadabout. We want no strangers here. Be off, or you may find a dog at your heels."

Holmes leaned forward and whispered something in the trainer's ear. He started violently and flushed to the temples.

"It's a lie!" he shouted. "An infernal lie!"

"Very good. Shall we argue about it here in public or talk it over in your parlour?"

"Oh, come in if you wish to."

Holmes smiled. "I shall not keep you more than a few minutes, Watson." said he. "Now. Mr. Brown. I am quite at your disposal."

It was twenty minutes, and the reds had all faded into greys before Holmes and the trainer reappeared. Never have I seen such a change as had been brought about in Silas Brown in that short time. His face was ashy pale, beads of perspiration shone upon his brow, and his hands shook until the hunting-crop wagged like a branch in the wind. His bullying, overbearing manner was all gone too, and he cringed along at my companion's side like a dog with its master.

"Your instructions will be done. It shall all be done," said he.

"There must be no mistake," said Holmes, looking round at him. The other winced as he read the menace in his eyes.

"Oh, no, there shall be no mistake. It shall be there. Should I change it first or not?"

Holmes thought a little and then burst out laughing. "No, don't," said he, "I shall write to you about it. No tricks, now, or—"

"Oh, you can trust me, you can trust me!"

"Yes, I think I can. Well, you shall hear from me tomorrow." He turned upon his heel, disregarding the trembling hand which the other held out to him, and we set off for King's Pyland.

"A more perfect compound of the bully, coward, and sneak than Master Silas Brown I have seldom met with," remarked Holmes as we trudged along together.

"He has the horse, then?"

"He tried to bluster out of it, but I described to him so exactly what his actions had been upon that morning that he is convinced that I was watching him. Of course you observed the peculiarly square toes in the impressions, and that his own boots exactly corresponded to them. Again, of course no subordinate would have dared to do such a thing. I described to him how, when according to his custom he was the first down, he perceived a strange horse wandering over the moor. How he went out to it, and his astonishment at recognising, from the white forehead which has given the favourite its name, that chance had put in his power the only horse which could beat the one upon which he had put his money. Then I described how his first impulse had been to lead him back to King's Pyland, and how the devil had shown him how he could hide the horse until the race was over, and how he had led it back and concealed it at Mapleton. When I told him every detail he gave it up and thought only of saving his own skin."

"But his stables had been searched?"

"Oh, an old horse-faker like him has many a dodge."

"But are you not afraid to leave the horse in his power now since he has every interest in injuring it?"

"My dear fellow, he will guard it as the apple of his eye. He knows that his only hope of mercy is to produce it safe."

"Colonel Ross did not impress me as a man who would be likely to show much mercy in any case."

"The matter does not rest with Colonel Ross. I follow my own methods and tell as much or as little as I choose. That is the advantage of being unofficial. I don't know whether you observed it, Watson, but the colonel's manner has been just a trifle cavalier to me. I am inclined now to have a little amusement at his expense. Say nothing to him about the horse."

"Certainly not without your permission."

"And of course this is all quite a minor point compared to the question of who killed John Straker."

"And you will devote yourself to that?"

"On the contrary, we both go back to London by the night train."

I was thunderstruck by my friend's words. We had only been a few hours in Devonshire, and that he should give up an investigation which he had begun so brilliantly was quite incomprehensible to me. Not a word more could I draw from him until we were back at the trainer's house. The colonel and the inspector were awaiting us in the parlour.

"My friend and I return to town by the night-express," said Holmes. "We have had a charming little breath of your beautiful Dartmoor air."

The inspector opened his eyes, and the colonel's lip curled in a sneer.

"So you despair of arresting the murderer of poor Straker," said he.

Holmes shrugged his shoulders. "There are certainly grave difficulties in the way," said he. "I have every hope, however, that your horse will start upon Tuesday, and I beg that you will have your jockey in readiness. Might I ask for a photograph of Mr. John Straker?"

The inspector took one from an envelope and handed it to him.

"My dear Gregory, you anticipate all my wants. If I might ask you to wait here for an instant, I have a question which I should like to put to the maid."

"I must say that I am rather disappointed in our London consultant," said Colonel Ross bluntly as my friend left the room. "I do not see that we are any further than when he came."

"At least you have his assurance that your horse will run," said I.

"Yes, I have his assurance," said the colonel with a shrug of his shoulders. "I should prefer to have the horse."

I was about to make some reply in defence of my friend when he entered the room again.

"Now, gentlemen," said he, "I am quite ready for Tavistock."

As we stepped into the carriage one of the stable-lads held the door open for us. A sudden idea seemed to occur to Holmes, for he leaned forward and touched the lad upon the sleeve.

"You have a few sheep in the paddock," he said. "Who attends to them?"

"I do, sir."

"Have you noticed anything amiss with them of late?"

"Well, sir, not of much account, but three of them have gone lame, sir."

I could see that Holmes was extremely pleased, for he chuckled and rubbed his hands together.

"A long shot, Watson, a very long shot," said he, pinching my arm. "Gregory, let me recommend to your attention this singular epidemic among the sheep. Drive on, coachman!"

Colonel Ross still wore an expression which showed the poor opinion which he had formed of my companion's ability, but I saw by the inspector's face that his attention had been keenly aroused.

"You consider that to be important?" he asked.

"Exceedingly so."

"Is there any point to which you would wish to draw my attention?"

"To the curious incident of the dog in the night-time."

"The dog did nothing in the night-time."

"That was the curious incident," remarked Sherlock Holmes.

Four days later Holmes and I were again in the train, bound for Winchester to see the race for the Wessex Cup. Colonel Ross met us by appointment outside the station, and we drove in his drag to the course beyond the town. His face was grave, and his manner was cold in the extreme.

"I have seen nothing of my horse," said he.

"I suppose that you would know him when you saw him?" asked Holmes.

The colonel was very angry. "I have been on the turf for twenty years and never was asked such a question as that before," said he. "A child would know Silver Blaze with his white forehead and his mottled off-foreleg."

"How is the betting?"

"Well, that is the curious part of it. You could have got fifteen to one yesterday, but the price has become shorter and shorter, until you can hardly get three to one now."

"Hum!" said Holmes. "Somebody knows something, that is clear."

As the drag drew up in the enclosure near the grandstand I glanced at the card to see the entries.

Wessex Plate [it ran] *50 sovs. each h ft with 1000 sovs. added, for four and five year olds. Second, 300 pounds. Third, 200 pounds. New course (one mile and five furlongs).*

1. *Mr. Heath Newton's The Negro. Red cap. Cinnamon jacket.*

2. *Colonel Wardlaw's Pugilist. Pink cap. Blue and black jacket.*

3. *Lord Backwater's Desborough. Yellow cap and sleeves.*
4. *Colonel Ross's Silver Blaze. Black cap. Red jacket.*
5. *Duke of Balmoral's Iris. Yellow and black stripes.*
6. *Lord Singleford's Rasper. Purple cap. Black sleeves.*

"We scratched our other one and put all hopes on your word," said the colonel. "Why, what is that? Silver Blaze favourite?"

"Five to four against Silver Blaze!" roared the ring. "Five to four against Silver Blaze! Five to fifteen against Desborough! Five to four on the field!"

"There are the numbers up," I cried. "They are all six there."

"All six there? Then my horse is running," cried the colonel in great agitation. "But I don't see him. My colours have not passed."

"Only five have passed. This must be he."

As I spoke a powerful bay horse swept out from the weighing enclosure and cantered past us, bearing on its back the well-known black and red of the colonel.

"That's not my horse," cried the owner. "That beast has not a white hair upon its body. What is this that you have done, Mr. Holmes?"

"Well, well, let us see how he gets on," said my friend imperturbably. For a few minutes he gazed through my fieldglass. "Capital! An excellent start!" he cried suddenly. "There they are, coming round the curve!"

From our drag we had a superb view as they came up the straight. The six horses were so close together that a carpet could have covered them, but halfway up the yellow of the Mapleton stable showed to the front. Before they reached us, however, Desborough's bolt was shot, and the colonel's horse, coming away with a rush, passed the post a good six lengths before its rival, the Duke of Balmoral's Iris making a bad third.

"It's my race, anyhow," gasped the colonel, passing his hand over his eyes. "I confess that I can make neither head nor tail of it. Don't you think that you have kept up your mystery long enough, Mr. Holmes?"

"Certainly, Colonel, you shall know everything. Let us all go round and have a look at the horse together. Here he is," he continued as we made our way into the weighing enclosure, where only owners and their friends find admittance. "You have only to wash his face and his leg in spirits of wine, and you will find that he is the same old Silver Blaze as ever."

"You take my breath away!"

"I found him in the hands of a faker and took the liberty of running him just as he was sent over."

"My dear sir, you have done wonders. The horse looks very fit and well. It never went better in its life. I owe you a thousand apologies for having doubted your ability. You have done me a great service by recovering my horse. You would do me a greater still if you could lay your hands on the murderer of John Straker."

"I have done so," said Holmes quietly.

The colonel and I stared at him in amazement. "You have got him! Where is he, then?"

"He is here."

"Here! Where?"

"In my company at the present moment."

The colonel flushed angrily. "I quite recognise that I am under obligations to you, Mr. Holmes," said he, "but I must regard what you have just said as either a very bad joke or an insult."

Sherlock Holmes laughed. "I assure you that I have not associated you with the crime, Colonel," said he. "The real murderer is standing immediately behind you." He stepped past and laid his hand upon the glossy neck of the thoroughbred.

"The horse!" cried both the colonel and myself.

"Yes, the horse. And it may lessen his guilt if I say that it was done in self-defence, and that John Straker was a man who was entirely unworthy of your confidence. But there goes the bell, and as I stand to win a little on this next race, I shall defer a lengthy explanation until a more fitting time."

We had the corner of a Pullman car to ourselves that evening as we whirled back to London, and I fancy that the journey was a short one to Colonel Ross as well as to myself as we listened to our companion's narrative of the events which had occurred at the Dartmoor training-stables upon that Monday night, and the means by which he had unravelled them.

"I confess," said he, "that any theories which I had formed from the newspaper reports were entirely erroneous. And yet there were indications there, had they not been overlaid by other details which concealed their true import. I went to Devonshire with the conviction that Fitzroy Simpson was the true culprit, although, of course, I saw that the evidence against him was by no means complete. It was while I was in the carriage, just as we reached the trainer's house, that the immense significance of the curried mutton occurred to me. You may remember that I was distrait and remained sitting after you had all alighted. I was marvelling in my own mind how I could possibly have overlooked so obvious a clue."

"I confess," said the colonel, "that even now I cannot see how it helps us."

"It was the first link in my chain of reasoning. Powdered opium is by no means tasteless. The flavour is not disagreeable, but it is perceptible. Were it mixed with any ordinary dish the eater would undoubtedly detect it and would probably eat no more. A curry was exactly the medium which would disguise this taste. By no possible supposition could this stranger, Fitzroy Simpson, have caused curry to be served in the trainer's family that night, and it is surely too monstrous a coincidence to suppose that he happened to come along with powdered opium upon the very night when a dish happened to be served which would disguise the flavour. That is unthinkable. Therefore Simpson becomes eliminated from the case, and our attention centres upon Straker and his wife, the only two people who could have chosen curried mutton for supper that night. The opium was added after the dish was set aside for the stable-boy, for the others had the same for supper with no ill effects. Which of them, then, had access to that dish without the maid seeing them?

"Before deciding that question I had grasped the significance of the silence of the dog, for one true inference invariably suggests others. The Simpson incident had shown me that a dog was kept in the stables, and yet, though someone had been in and had fetched out a horse, he had not barked enough to arouse the two lads in the loft. Obviously the midnight visitor was someone whom the dog knew well.

"I was already convinced, or almost convinced, that John Straker went down to the stables in the dead of the night and took out Silver Blaze. For what purpose? For a dishonest one, obviously, or why should he drug his own stable-boy? And yet I was at a loss to know why. There have been cases before now where trainers have made sure of great sums of money by laying against their own horses through agents and then preventing them from winning by fraud. Sometimes it is a pulling jockey. Sometimes it is some surer and subtler means. What was it here? I hoped that the contents of his pockets might help me to form a conclusion.

"And they did so. You cannot have forgotten the singular knife which was found in the dead man's hand, a knife which certainly no sane man would choose for a weapon. It was, as Dr. Watson told us, a form of knife which is used for the most delicate operations known in surgery. And it was to be used for a delicate operation that night. You must know, with your wide experience of turf matters, Colonel Ross, that it is possible to make a slight nick upon the tendons of a horse's ham, and to do it subcutaneously, so as to leave absolutely no trace. A horse so treated would develop a slight lameness, which would be put down to a strain in exercise or a touch of rheumatism, but never to foul play."

"Villain! Scoundrel!" cried the colonel.

"We have here the explanation of why John Straker wished to take the horse out on to the moor. So spirited a creature would have certainly roused the soundest of sleepers when it felt the prick of the knife. It was absolutely necessary to do it in the open air."

"I have been blind!" cried the colonel. "Of course that was why he needed the candle and struck the match."

"Undoubtedly. But in examining his belongings I was fortunate enough to discover not only the method of the crime but even its motives. As a man of the world, Colonel, you know that men do not carry other people's bills about in their pockets. We have most of us quite enough to do to settle our own. I at once concluded that Straker was leading a double life and keeping a second establishment. The nature of the bill showed that there was a lady in the case, and one who had expensive tastes. Liberal as you are with your servants, one can hardly expect that they can buy twenty-guinea walking dresses for their ladies. I questioned Mrs. Straker as to the dress without her knowing it, and, having satisfied myself that it had never reached her, I made a note of the milliner's address and felt that by calling there with Straker's photograph I could easily dispose of the mythical Derbyshire.

"From that time on all was plain. Straker had led out the horse to a hollow where his light would be invisible. Simpson in his flight had dropped his cravat, and Straker had picked it up – with some idea, perhaps, that he might use it in securing the horse's leg. Once in the hollow, he had got behind the horse and had struck a light; but the creature, frightened at the sudden glare, and with the strange instinct of animals feeling that some mischief was intended, had lashed out, and the steel shoe had struck Straker full on the forehead. He had already, in spite of the rain, taken off his overcoat in order to do his delicate task, and so, as he fell, his knife gashed his thigh. Do I make it clear?"

"Wonderful!" cried the colonel. "Wonderful! You might have been there!"

"My final shot was, I confess, a very long one. It struck me that so astute a man as Straker would not undertake this delicate tendon-nicking without a little practise. What could he practise on? My eyes fell upon the sheep, and I asked a question which, rather to my surprise, showed that my surmise was correct.

"When I returned to London I called upon the milliner, who had recognised Straker as an excellent customer of the name of Derbyshire, who had a very dashing wife, with a strong partiality for expensive dresses. I have no doubt that this woman had plunged him over head and ears in debt, and so led him into this miserable plot."

"You have explained all but one thing," cried the colonel. "Where was the horse?"

"Ah, it bolted, and was cared for by one of your neighbours. We must have an amnesty in that direction, I think. This is Clapham Junction, if I am not mistaken, and we shall be in Victoria in less than ten minutes. If you care to smoke a cigar in our rooms, Colonel. I shall be happy to give you any other details which might interest you."

The Tea Leaf

Robert Eustace and Edgar Jepson

ARTHUR KELSTERN and George Willoughton met in the Turkish bath in Duke Street, St. James's, and rather more than a year later in that Turkish bath they parted. Both of them were bad-tempered men, Kelstern cantankerous and Willoughton violent. It was indeed difficult to decide which was the worse-tempered; and when I found that they had suddenly become friends, I gave that friendship three months. It lasted nearly a year.

When they did quarrel they quarrelled about Kelstern's daughter Ruth. Willoughton fell in love with her and she with him and they became engaged to be married. Six months later, in spite of the fact that they were plainly very much in love with one another, the engagement was broken off. Neither of them gave any reason for breaking it off. My belief was that Willoughton had given Ruth a taste of his infernal temper and got as good as he gave.

Not that Ruth was at all a Kelstern to look at. Like the members of most of the old Lincolnshire families, descendants of the Vikings and the followers of Canutt, one Kelstern is very like another Kelstern, fair-haired, clear-skinned, with light blue eyes and a good bridge to the nose. But Ruth had taken after her mother: she was dark with a straight nose, dark-brown eyes of the kind often described as liquid, dark-brown hair, and as kissable lips as ever I saw. She was a proud, rather self-sufficing, high-spirited girl, with a temper of her own. She needed it to live with that cantankerous old brute Kelstern. Oddly enough in spite of the fact that he always would try to bully her, she was fond of him; and I will say for him that he was very fond of her. Probably she was the only creature in the world of whom he was really fond. He was an expert in the application of scientific discoveries to industry; and she worked with him in his laboratory. He paid her five hundred a year, so that she must have been uncommonly good.

He took the breaking off of the engagement very hard indeed. He would have it that Willoughton had jilted her. Ruth took it hard too: her warm colouring lost some of its warmth; her lips grew less kissable and set in a thinner line. Willoughton's temper grew worse than ever; he was like a bear with a perpetually sore head. I tried to feel my way with both him and Ruth with a view to help to bring about a reconciliation. To put it mildly, I was rebuffed. Willoughton swore at me; Ruth flared up and told me not to meddle in matters that didn't concern me. Nevertheless my strong impression was that they were missing one another badly and would have been glad enough to come together again if their stupid vanity could have let them.

Kelstern did his best to keep Ruth furious with Willoughton. One night I told him – it was no business of mine; but I never did give a tinker's curse for his temper – that he was a fool to meddle and had much better leave them alone. It made him furious, of course; he would have it that Willoughton was a dirty hound and a low blackguard – at least those were about the mildest things he said of him. It struck me of a sudden that there must be something much more serious in the breaking off of the engagement than I had guessed.

That suspicion was strengthened by the immense trouble Kelstern took to injure Willoughton. At his clubs, the Athenæum, the Devonshire, and the Savile, he would display an astonishing ingenuity in bringing the conversation round to Willoughton; then he would declare that he was a scoundrel and a blackguard of the meanest type. Of course it did Willoughton harm, though not nearly as much harm as Kelstern desired, for Willoughton knew his job as few engineers knew it; and it is very hard indeed to do much harm to a man who really knows his job. People have to have him. But of course it did him some harm; and Willoughton knew that Kelstern was doing it. I came across two men who told me that they had given him a friendly hint. That did not improve Willoughton's temper.

An expert in the construction of those ferro-concrete buildings which are rising up all over London, he was as distinguished in his sphere as Kelstern in his. They were alike not only in the matters of brains and bad temper; but I think that their minds worked in very much the same way. At any rate both of them seemed determined not to change their ordinary course of life because of the breaking off of that engagement.

It had been the habit of both of them to have a Turkish bath, at the baths in Duke Street, at four in the afternoon on the second and last Tuesday in every month. To that habit they stuck. The fact that they must meet on those Tuesdays did not cause either of them to change his hour of taking his Turkish bath by the twenty minutes which would have given them no more than a passing glimpse of one another. They continued to take it, as they always had, simultaneously. Thick-skinned? They were thick-skinned. Neither of them pretended that he did not see the other; he scowled at him; and he scowled at him most of the time. I know this, for sometimes I had a Turkish bath myself at that hour.

It was about three months after the breaking off of the engagement that they met for the last time at that Turkish bath, and there parted for good.

Kelstern had been looking ill for about six weeks: there was a grayness and a drawn look to his face; and he was losing weight. On the second Tuesday in October he arrived at the bath punctually at four, bringing with him, as was his habit, a thermos flask full of a very delicate China tea. If he thought that he was not perspiring freely enough he would drink it in the hottest room; if he did perspire freely enough, he would drink it after his bath. Willoughton arrived about two minutes later. Kelstern finished undressing and went into the bath a couple of minutes before Willoughton. They stayed in the hot room about the same time; Kelstern went into the hottest room about a minute after Willoughton. Before he went into it he sent for his thermos flask which he had left in the dressing room and took it into the hottest room with him.

As it happened, they were the only two people in the hottest room; and they had not been in it two minutes before the four men in the hot room heard them quarrelling. They heard Kelstern call Willoughton a dirty hound and a low blackguard, among other things, and declare he would do him in yet. Willoughton told him to go to the devil twice. Kelstern went on abusing him and presently Willoughton fairly shouted: "Oh, shut up, you old fool! Or I'll make you!"

Kelstern did not shut up. About two minutes later Willoughton came out of the hottest room, scowling, walked through the hot room into the shampooing room and put himself into the hands of one of the shampooers. Two or three minutes after that a man of the name of Helston went into the hottest room and fairly yelled. Kelstern was lying back on a blood-drenched couch, with the blood still flowing from a wound over his heart.

There was a devil of a hullabaloo. The police were called in; Willoughton was arrested. Of course he lost his temper and, protesting furiously that he had had nothing whatever to do with the crime, abused the police. That did not incline them to believe him.

After examining the room and the dead body the detective-inspector in charge of the case came to the conclusion that Kelstern had been stabbed as he was drinking his tea. The thermos flask lay on the floor in front of him and some of the tea had evidently been spilt, for some tea leaves – the tea in the flask must have been carelessly strained of the leaves by the maid who filled it – lay on the floor about the mouth of the empty flask. It looked as if the murderer had taken advantage of

Kelstern's drinking his tea to stab him while the flask rather blocked his vision and prevented him from seeing what he would be at.

The case would have been quite plain sailing but for the fact that they could not find the weapon. It had been easy enough for Willoughton to take it into the bath in the towel in which he was draped. But how had he got rid of it? Where had he hidden it? A Turkish bath is no place to hide anything in. It is as bare as an empty barn – if anything barer; and Willoughton had been in the barest part of it. The police searched every part of it – not that there was much point in doing that, for Willoughton had come out of the hottest room, and gone through the hot room into the shampooers' room. When Helston started shouting murder, Willoughton had rushed back with the shampooers to the hottest room and there he had stayed. Since it was obvious that he had committed the murder the shampooers and the bathers had kept their eyes on him. They were all of them certain that he had not left them to go to the dressing rooms; they would not have allowed him to do so.

It was obvious that he must have carried the weapon into the bath, hidden in the folds of the towel in which he was draped, and brought it away in the folds of that towel. He had laid the towel down beside the couch on which he was being shampooed; and there it still lay when they came to look for it, untouched, with no weapon in it, with no traces of blood on it. There was not much in the fact that it was not stained with blood, since Willoughton could have wiped the knife, or dagger, or whatever weapon he used, on the couch on which Kelstern lay. There were no marks of any such wiping on the couch; but the blood, flowing from the wound, might have covered them up.

There was no finding the weapon; and its disappearance puzzled the police and later puzzled the public.

Then the doctors who made the autopsy came to the conclusion that the wound had been inflicted by a circular, pointed weapon nearly three-quarters of an inch in diameter. It had penetrated rather more than three inches and supposing that its handle was only four inches long it must have been a sizeable weapon, quite impossible to overlook. The doctors also discovered a further proof of the theory that Kelstern had been drinking his tea when he was stabbed. Halfway down the wound they found two halves of a tea leaf which had evidently fallen on to Kelstern's body, been driven into the wound and cut in half by the weapon. Also they discovered that Kelstern was suffering from cancer. This fact was not published in the papers; I heard it at the Devonshire.

Willoughton was brought before the magistrates and to most people's surprise did not reserve his defense. He went into the witness box and swore that he had never touched Kelstern, that he had never had anything to touch him with, that he had never taken any weapon into the Turkish bath and so had had no weapon to hide, that he had never even seen any such weapon as the doctors described. He was committed for trial.

The papers were full of the crime; everyone was discussing it; and the question which occupied everyone's mind was: where had Willoughton hidden the weapon? People wrote to the papers to suggest that he had ingeniously put it in some place under everybody's eyes and that it had been overlooked because it was so obvious. Others suggested that, circular and pointed, it must be very like a thick lead pencil, that it was a thick lead pencil; and that was why the police had overlooked it in their search. The police had not overlooked any thick lead pencil; there had been no thick lead pencil to overlook. They hunted England through – Willoughton did a lot of motoring – to discover the man who had sold him this curious and uncommon weapon. They did not find the man who had sold it to him; they did not find a man who sold such weapons at all. They came to the conclusion that Kelstern had been murdered with a piece of a steel, or iron, rod filed to a point like a pencil.

In spite of the fact that only Willoughton *could* have murdered Kelstern, I could not believe that he had done it. The fact that Kelstern was doing his best to injure him professionally and socially was by no means a strong enough motive. Willoughton was far too intelligent a man not to be very well aware that people do not take much notice of statements to the discredit of a man whom they need to do a job for them; and for the social injury he would care very little. Besides, he might very well injure, or even kill, a man in one of his tantrums; but his was not the kind of bad temper that plans a cold-blooded murder; and if ever a murder had been deliberately planned, Kelstern's had.

I was as close a friend as Willoughton had, and I went to visit him in prison. He seemed rather touched by my doing so, and grateful. I learnt that I was the only person who had done so. He was subdued and seemed much gentler. It might last. He discussed the murder readily enough and naturally with an harassed air. He said quite frankly that he did not expect me, in the circumstances, to believe that he had not committed it; but he had not, and he could not for the life of him conceive who had. I did believe that he had not committed it; there was something in his way of discussing it that wholly convinced me. I told him that I was quite sure that he had not killed Kelstern; and he looked at me as if he did not believe the assurance. But again he looked grateful.

Ruth was grieving for her father; but Willoughton's very dangerous plight to some degree distracted her mind from her loss. A woman can quarrel with a man bitterly without desiring to see him hanged; and Willoughton's chance of escaping hanging was not at all a good one. But she would not believe for a moment that he had murdered her father.

"No; there's nothing in it – nothing whatever," she said firmly. "If Dad had murdered Hugh I could have understood it. He had reasons – or at any rate he had persuaded himself that he had. But whatever reason had Hugh for murdering Dad? It's all nonsense to suppose that he'd mind Dad's trying all he knew to injure him, as much as that. All kinds of people are going about trying to injure other people in that way, but they don't really injure them very much; and Hugh knows that quite well."

"Of course they don't; and Hugh wouldn't really believe that your father was injuring him much," I said. "But you're forgetting his infernal temper."

"No: I'm not," she protested. "He might kill a man in one of his rages on the spur of the moment. But this wasn't the spur of the moment. Whoever did it had worked the whole thing out and came along with the weapon ready."

I had to admit that that was reasonable enough. But who had done it? I pointed out to her that the police had made careful enquiries about everyone in the bath at the time, the shampooers and the people taking their baths, but they had found no evidence whatever that any one of them had at any time had any relations, except that of shampooer, with her father.

"Either it was one of them, or somebody else who just did it and got right away, or there's a catch somewhere," she said frowning thoughtfully.

"I can't see how there can possibly have been anyone in the bath, except the people who are known to have been there," said I. "In fact, there can't have been."

Then the Crown subpoenaed her as a witness for the prosecution. It seemed rather unnecessary and even a bit queer, for it could have found plenty of evidence of bad blood between the two men without dragging her into it. Plainly it was bent on doing all it knew to prove motive enough. Ruth seemed more upset by the prospect of going into the witness box than I should have expected her to be. But then she had been having a very trying time.

On the morning of the trial I called for her after breakfast to drive her down to the New Bailey. She was pale and looked as if she had had a poor night's rest, and, naturally enough, she seemed to be suffering from an excitement she had to control. It was not like her to show any excitement she might be feeling.

We had of course been in close touch with Willoughton's solicitor, Hamley; and he had kept seats for us just behind him. He wished to have Ruth at hand to consult should some point turn up on which she could throw light, since she knew more than anyone about the relations between Willoughton and her father. I had timed our arrival very well; the jury had just been sworn in. Of course the Court was full of women, the wives of Peers and bookmakers and politicians, most of them overdressed and overscented.

Then the judge came in; and with his coming the atmosphere of the Court became charged with that sense of anxious strain peculiar to trials for murder. It was rather like the atmosphere of a sick room in a case of fatal illness, but worse.

It was unfortunate for Willoughton that the judge was Garbould. A hard-faced, common-looking fellow, and coarse in the grain, he has a well-founded reputation as a hanging judge and the habit of acting as an extra counsel for the prosecution.

Willoughton came into the box, looking under the weather and very much subdued. But he certainly looked dignified and he said that he was not guilty in a steady enough voice.

Greatorex, the leading Counsel for the Crown, opened the case for the prosecution. There was no suggestion in his speech that the Police had discovered any new fact.

Then Helston gave evidence of finding the body of the dead man and he and the other three men who had been with him in the hot room gave evidence of the quarrel they had overheard between Willoughton and the dead man, and that Willoughton came out of the hottest room, scowling and obviously furious. One of them, a fussy old gentleman of the name of Underwood, declared that it was the bitterest quarrel he had ever heard. None of the four of them could throw any light on the matter of whether Willoughton was carrying the missing weapon in the folds of the towel in which he was draped; all of them were sure that he had nothing in his hands.

The medical evidence came next. In cross-examining the doctors who had made the autopsy, Hazeldean, Willoughton's counsel, established the fact quite definitely that the missing weapon was of a fair size; that its rounded blade must have been over half an inch in diameter and between three and four inches long. They were of the opinion that to drive a blade of that thickness into the heart, a handle of at least four inches in length would be necessary to give a firm enough grip. It might have been a piece of a steel, or iron, rod sharpened like a pencil. At any rate it was certainly a sizeable weapon, not one to be hidden quickly, or to disappear wholly in a Turkish bath. Hazeldean could not shake their evidence about the tea leaf; they were confident that it had been driven into the wound and cut in half by the blade of the missing weapon, and that that went to show that the wound had been inflicted while Kelstern was drinking his tea.

Detective-Inspector Brackett, who was in charge of the case, was cross-examined at great length about his search for the missing weapon. He made it quite clear that it was nowhere in that Turkish bath, neither in the hot rooms, nor the shampooing room, nor the dressing rooms, nor the vestibule, nor the office. He had had the plunge bath emptied; he had searched the roofs, though it was practically certain that the skylight above the hot room, not the hottest, had been shut at the time of the crime. In re-examination he scouted the idea of Willoughton's having had an accomplice who had carried away the weapon for him. He had gone into that matter most carefully.

The shampooer stated that Willoughton came to him scowling so savagely that he wondered what had put him into such a bad temper. In cross-examining him, Arbuthnot, Hazeldean's junior, made it clearer than ever that, unless Willoughton had already hidden the weapon in the bare hottest room, it was hidden in the towel. Then he drew from the shampooer the definite statement that Willoughton had set down the towel beside the couch on which he was shampooed, that he had hurried back to the hot rooms in front of the shampooer; that the shampooer had come back from the hot rooms, leaving Willoughton still in them discussing the crime, to find the towel lying just as Willoughton had set it down, with no weapon in it and no trace of blood on it.

Since the Inspector had disposed of the possibility that an accomplice had slipped in, taken the weapon from the towel, and slipped out of the bath with it, this evidence really made it clear that the weapon had never left the hottest room.

Then the prosecution called evidence of the bad terms on which Kelstern and Willoughton had been. Three well-known and influential men told the jury about Kelstern's efforts to prejudice Willoughton in their eyes and the damaging statements he had made about him. One of them had felt it to be his duty to tell Willoughton about this; and Willoughton had been very angry. Arbuthnot, in cross-examining, elicited the fact that any damaging statement that Kelstern made about anyone was considerably discounted by the fact that everyone knew him to be in the highest degree cantankerous.

I noticed that during the end of the cross-examination of the shampooer and during this evidence, Ruth had been fidgeting and turning to look impatiently at the entrance to the Court, as if she were expecting someone. Then, just as she was summoned to the witness box, there came in a tall, stooping, grey-headed, grey-bearded man of about sixty, carrying a brown paper parcel. His face was familiar to me; but I could not place him. He caught her eye and nodded to her. She breathed a sharp sigh of relief and bent over and handed a letter she had in her hand to Willoughton's solicitor and pointed out the grey-bearded man to him. Then she went quietly to the witness box.

Hamley read the letter and at once bent over and handed it to Hazeldean and spoke to him. I caught a note of excitement in his hushed voice. Hazeldean read the letter and appeared to grow excited too. Hamley slipped out of his seat and went to the grey-bearded man who was still standing just inside the door of the Court and began to talk to him earnestly.

Greatorex began to examine Ruth; and naturally I turned my attention to her. His examination was directed also to show on what bad terms Kelstern and Willoughton had been. Ruth was called on to tell the jury some of Kelstern's actual threats. Then – it is astonishing how few things the police fail to ferret out in a really important case – the examination took a curious turn. Greatorex began to question Ruth about her own relations with Willoughton and the plain trend of his questions was to bring out the fact that they had not merely been engaged to be married but had also been lovers.

I saw at once what the prosecution was aiming at. It was trying to make use of the tendency of a British jury and a British judge, in a natural effort to champion morality, to hang a man or a woman, who is on trial for murder, for behaving immorally in relations with the other sex. There was no better way of prejudicing Willoughton than by proving that he had seduced Ruth under the promise of marriage.

Of course Hazeldean was on his feet at once protesting that this evidence was irrelevant and inadmissible; and of course Garbould was against him – he does not enjoy the nickname by which he is known to the junior bar for nothing. Hazeldean was magnificent. He had one of the worst rows with Garbould he had ever had; and he has had many. Garbould is a fool to let him have these rows. Hazeldean always gets the better of him, or seems to; and it does him good with the jury. But then Garbould was raised to the bench not for intelligence but for political merit. He ruled that the questions were admissible and put one or two to Ruth himself.

Then Willoughton lost his temper and protested that this had nothing to do with the case and that it was an outrage. Willoughton has a ringing voice of considerable volume. He is not at all an easy man to hush when he does not wish to hush; and they were sometime hushing him. By the time they succeeded Garbould was purplish-red with fury. Anything that he could do to hang Willoughton would certainly be done. But, observing the jury, my impression was that Willoughton's outburst had done him good with it and that Hazeldean's protests had shaken its confidence in Garbould. When I looked at the faces, just a trifle sickly, of the counsel for the prosecution, I felt sure that the Crown had bungled this business rather badly.

Greatorex, assisted by Garbould, went on with his questions; and Ruth defiant rather than abashed, and looking in her flushed animation a more charming creature than ever, admitted that she and Willoughton had been lovers; that more than once when he had brought her home from a dance or a theatre he had not left her till the early morning. One of the maids had spied on them; and the Crown had the facts.

I was afraid, in spite of Hazeldean's protests, that the fact that Willoughton had seduced her under the promise of marriage, as Greatorex put it, would do him great harm with the jury – very likely it would hang him.

Then Ruth, still flushed, but not greatly discomposed, said: "That would be a reason for my father's murdering Mr. Willoughton, not for Mr. Willoughton's murdering my father."

That brought Garbould down upon her like a ton of bricks. She was there to answer questions, not to make idle remarks and so forth and so on.

Then Greatorex came to the breaking off of the engagement and put it to her that Willoughton had broken it off, had in fact jilted her after compromising her. That she would not have for a moment. She declared that they had had a quarrel and she had broken it off. To that she stuck and there was no shaking her, though Garbould himself took a hearty hand in trying to shake her.

In the middle of it Willoughton, who was looking quite himself again, now that the atmosphere of the Court might be said to be charged almost with violence, said in a very unpleasant, jeering voice: "What she says is perfectly true – what's the good of bothering her?"

Again Garbould was to the fore, and angrily reprimanded him for speaking, bade him keep silent, and said that he would not have his Court turned into a bear-garden.

"With the bear on the bench," said Hazeldean to Arbuthnot in a whisper that carried well.

Two or three people laughed. One of them was a juryman. By the time Garbould had finished with him I did not think that that juryman would have convicted Willoughton, if he had actually seen him stab Kelstern.

Willoughton was writing a note which was passed to Hazeldean.

Hazeldean rose to cross-examine Ruth with a wholly confident air. He drew from her the facts that her father had been on excellent terms with Willoughton until the breaking off of the engagement; that in that matter he had taken her part warmly; and that when the maid who had spied upon them had informed him of her relations with Willoughton he had been very little more enraged than he was already.

Then Hazeldean asked: "Is it a fact that since the breaking off of your engagement the prisoner has more than once begged you to forgive him and renew it?"

"Four times," said Ruth.

"And you refused?"

"Yes," said Ruth. She looked at Willoughton queerly and added: "He wanted a lesson."

"Did he then beg you at least to go through the form of marriage with him, and promise to leave you at the church door?"

"Yes."

"And you refused?"

"Yes," said Ruth.

Garbould bent forward and said in his most unpleasant tone: "And why did you reject the opportunity of repairing your shameful behaviour?"

"It wasn't shameful," Ruth almost snapped; and she scowled at him frankly. Then she added naïvely: "I refused because there was no hurry. He would always marry me if I changed my mind and wanted to."

There was a pause. To me it seemed clearer than ever that the Crown had bungled badly in raising the question of the relations between her and Willoughton since he had evidently been more than ready to save her from any harm that might come of their indiscretion. But then, with a jury, you can never tell. Then Hazeldean started on a fresh line.

In sympathetic accents he asked: "Is it a fact that your father was suffering from cancer in a painful form?"

"It was beginning to grow very painful," said Ruth sadly.

"Did he make a will and put all his affairs in order a few days before he died?"

"Three days," said Ruth.

"Did he ever express an intention of committing suicide?"

"He said that he would stick it out for a little while and then end it all," said Ruth. She paused and added: *"And that is what he did do."*

One might almost say that the Court started. I think that everyone in it moved a little, so that there was a kind of rustling murmur. Garbould threw himself back in his seat with a snort of incredulity and glowered at Ruth.

"Will you tell the Court your reasons for that statement?" said Hazeldean.

Ruth seemed to pull herself together; the flush had faded from her face and she was looking very tired; then she began in a quiet, even voice: "I never believed for a moment that Mr. Willoughton murdered my father. If my father had murdered Mr. Willoughton it would have been a different matter."

Garbould leaned forward and snarled that it was not her beliefs or fancies that were wanted, but facts.

I did not think that she heard him; she was concentrating on giving her reasons exactly; she went on in the same quiet tone: "Of course, like everybody else I puzzled over the weapon: what it was and where it had got to. I did not believe that it was a pointed piece of a half-inch steel rod. If anybody had come to the Turkish bath meaning to murder my father and hide the weapon, they wouldn't have used one so big and so difficult to hide, when a hat-pin would have done just as well and could be hidden much more easily. But what puzzled me most was the tea leaf in the wound. All the other tea leaves that came out of the flask were lying on the floor. Inspector Brackett told me they were. And I couldn't believe that one tea leaf had fallen on to my father at the very place above his heart at which the point of the weapon had penetrated the skin and got driven in by it. It was too much of a coincidence for me to swallow. But I got no nearer understanding it than anyone else."

Garbould broke in in a tone of some exasperation and told her to come to the facts. Hazeldean rose and protested that the witness should not be interrupted; that she had solved a mystery which had puzzled some of the best brains in England, and she should be allowed to tell her story in her own way.

Again Ruth did not appear to listen to them, and when they stopped she went on in the same quiet voice: "Of course I remembered that Dad had talked to putting an end to it; but no one with a wound like that could get up and hide the weapon. Then, the night before last I dreamt that I went into the laboratory and saw a piece of steel rod, pointed, lying on the table at which my father used to work."

"Dreams now!" murmured Garbould contemptuously; and he leaned back and folded his hands over his stomach.

"I didn't think much of the dream, of course," Ruth went on. "I had been puzzling about it all so hard for so long that it was only natural to dream about it. But after breakfast I had a sudden feeling that the secret was in the laboratory if I could only find it. I did not attach any importance to the feeling; but it went on growing stronger; and after lunch I went to the laboratory and began to hunt.

"I looked through all the drawers and could find nothing. Then I went round the room looking at everything and into everything, instruments and retorts and tubes and so on. Then I went into the middle of the floor and looked slowly round the room pretty hard. Against the wall, near the door, lying ready to be taken away, was a gas cylinder. I rolled it over to see what gas had been in it and it had no label on it."

She paused to look round the Court as if claiming its best attention; then she went on: "Now that was very queer because every gas cylinder must have a label on it – so many gases are dangerous. I turned on the cylinder and nothing came out of it. It was quite empty. Then I went to the book in which all the things which come in are entered, and found that ten days before Dad died he had had in a cylinder of CO_2 and seven pounds of ice. Also he had had seven pounds of ice every day till the day of his death. It was the ice and the CO_2 together that gave me the idea. CO_2, carbon dioxide, has a very low freezing point – eighty degrees centigrade – and as it comes out of the cylinder and mixes with the air it turns into very fine snow; and that snow, if you compress it, makes the hardest and toughest ice possible. It flashed on me that Dad could have collected this snow and forced it into a mould and made a weapon that would not only inflict that wound but would *disappear instantly!*"

She paused again to look round the Court at about as rapt a lot of faces as any narrator could desire. Then she went on: "I knew that that was what he had done. I knew it for certain. Carbon dioxide ice would make a hard, tough dagger, and it would melt quickly in the hottest room of a Turkish bath and leave no smell because it is scentless. So there wouldn't be any weapon. And it explained the tea leaf too. Dad had made a carbon dioxide dagger perhaps a week before he used it, perhaps only a day. And he had put it into the thermos flask as soon as he had made it. The thermos flask keeps out the heat as well as the cold, you know. But to make sure that it couldn't melt at all he kept the flask in ice till he was ready to use the dagger. It's the only way you can explain that tea leaf. It came out of the flask sticking to the point of the dagger and was driven into the wound!"

She paused again and one might almost say that the Court heaved a deep sigh of relief.

Then Garbould asked in an unpleasant and incredulous voice: "Why didn't you take this fantastic theory straight to the police?"

"But that wouldn't have been any good," she protested quickly. "It was no use my knowing it myself; I had to make other people believe it; I had to find evidence. I began to hunt for it. I felt in my bones that there was some. What I wanted was the mould. I found it!"

She uttered the words in a tone of triumph and smiled at Willoughton; then she went on: "At least I found bits of it. In the box into which we used to throw odds and ends, scraps of material, damaged instruments, and broken test tubes, I found some pieces of vulcanite; and I saw at once that they were bits of a vulcanite container. I took some wax and rolled it into a rod about the right size and then I pieced the container together on the outside of it – at least most of it – there are some small pieces missing. It took me nearly all night. But I found the most important bit – *the pointed end!*"

She dipped her hand into her handbag and drew out a black object about nine inches long and three quarters of an inch thick and held it up for everyone to see.

Someone, without thinking, began to clap; and there came a storm of applause that drowned the voice of the Clerk calling for order and the bellowing of Garbould.

When the applause died down, Hazeldean, who never misses the right moment, said: "I have no more questions to ask the witness, my lord," and sat down.

That action seemed to clinch it in my eyes, and I have no doubt, it clinched it in the eyes of the jury.

The purple Garbould leant forward and almost bellowed at Ruth: "Do you expect the jury to believe that a well-known man like your father died in the act of deliberately setting a dastardly trap to hang the prisoner?"

Ruth looked at him, shrugged her shoulders, and said with a calm acceptance of the facts of human nature one would expect to find only in a much older woman: "Oh, well, Daddy was like that. And he certainly believed he had very good reasons for killing Mr. Willoughton."

There was that in her tone and manner which made it absolutely certain that Kelstern was not only like that but that he had acted according to his nature.

Greatorex did not re-examine Ruth; he conferred with Hazeldean. Then Hazeldean rose to open the case for the defence. He said that he would not waste the time of the Court, and that in view of the fact that Miss Kelstern had solved the problem of her father's death, he would only call one witness, Professor Mozley.

The grey-headed, grey-bearded, stooping man, who had come to the Court so late, went into the witness box. Of course his face had been familiar to me; I had seen his portrait in the newspapers a dozen times. He still carried the brown paper parcel.

In answer to Hazeldean's questions he stated that it was possible, not even difficult, to make a weapon of carbon dioxide hard enough and tough enough and sharp enough to inflict such a wound as that which had caused Kelstern's death. The method of making it was to fold a piece of chamois leather into a bag, hold that bag with the left hand, protected by a glove, over the nozzle of a cylinder containing liquid carbon dioxide, and open the valve with the right hand. Carbon dioxide evaporates so quickly that its freezing point, 80° centigrade, is soon reached; and it solidifies in the chamois-leather bag as a deposit of carbon dioxide snow. Then turn off the gas, spoon that snow into a vulcanite container of the required thickness, and ram it down with a vulcanite plunger into a rod of the required hardness. He added that it was advisable to pack the container in ice while filling it and ramming down the snow, then put the rod into a thermos flask; and keep it till it is needed.

"And you have made such a rod?" said Hazeldean.

"Yes," said the Professor, cutting the string of the brown paper parcel. "When Miss Kelstern hauled me out of bed at half past seven this morning to tell me her discoveries, I perceived at once that she had found the solution of the problem of her father's death, which had puzzled me considerably. I had breakfast quickly and got to work to make such a weapon myself for the satisfaction of the Court. Here it is."

He drew a thermos flask from the brown paper, unscrewed the top of it, and inverted it. There dropped into his gloved hand a white rod about eight inches long. He held it out for the jury to see.

"This carbon dioxide ice is the hardest and toughest ice we know of; and I have no doubt that Mr. Kelstern killed himself with a similar rod. The difference between the rod he used and this is that his rod was pointed. I had no pointed vulcanite container; but the container that Miss Kelstern pieced together is pointed. Doubtless Mr. Kelstern had it specially made, probably by Messrs. Hawkins & Spender."

He dropped the rod back into the thermos flask and screwed on the top.

Hazeldean sat down. The juryman who had been reprimanded by Garbould leaned forward and spoke earnestly to the foreman. Greatorex rose.

"With regard to the point of the rod, Professor Mozley: would it remain sharp long enough to pierce the skin in that heat?" he asked.

"In my opinion it would," said the Professor. "I have been considering that point and bearing in mind the facts that Mr. Kelstern would from his avocation be very deft with his hands, and being a scientific man, would know exactly what to do, he would have the rod out of the flask and the point in position in very little more than a second – perhaps less. He would, I think, hold it in his left hand and drive it home by striking the butt of it hard with his right. The whole thing would not take him two seconds. Besides, if the point of the weapon had melted the tea leaf would have fallen off it."

"Thank you," said Greatorex, and turned and conferred with the Crown solicitors.

Then he said: "We do not propose to proceed with the case, my lord."

The foreman of the jury rose quickly and said: "And the Jury doesn't want to hear anything more, my lord. We're quite satisfied that the prisoner isn't guilty."

Garbould hesitated. For two pins he would have directed the case to proceed. Then his eye fell on Hazeldean, who was watching him; I fancied that he decided not to give him a chance of saying more disagreeable things.

Looking black enough, he put the question formally to the Jury, who returned a verdict of 'Not Guilty', and then he discharged Willoughton.

I came out of the Court with Ruth, and we waited for Willoughton.

Presently he came out of the door and stopped and shook himself. Then he saw Ruth and came to her. They did not greet one another. She just slipped her hand through his arm; and they walked out of the New Bailey together.

We made a good deal of noise, cheering them.

The Yorkshire Manufacturer

J.S. Fletcher

AS THE LITTLE local train wound slowly along the narrow and tortuous valley to which I had hastily travelled down from London in response to an urgent summons received that day at noon, I thought, looking around and above me from the carriage window, that I had rarely found myself amidst wilder surroundings. I was aware that I was penetrating into the heart of the Penine Range at its highest and bleakest point, but I had never until then realised that we possess scenery in England which, under certain circumstances, can justly be termed savage. Although it was yet early autumn, the evening was cold and gloomy; overhead the sky was dull and grey; the treeless, verdureless sides of the hills loomed black and forbidding. Blackness and greyness, indeed, were the note of the scenery through which I was passing; in the valley itself was nothing but grey houses and the high, grey walls of factories and mills; here and there rushed down from the heights above foaming cataracts of water that did their work in some mill dam and emerged, having done it, turgid and discoloured, into the black river whose curves the railway follows. And as we followed it further the valley narrowed until it seemed that we must be presently swallowed up in some cavernous opening of the rocky and mountainous mass which loomed in front.

The train suddenly slackened its slow speed; we rounded a sharp curve and ran into a small station on the smoke-blackened railings of which appeared a board bearing the name Wolverdale. Beyond the railings and across the black river, I saw grey roofs and grey walls and amongst them tall chimneys which poured out thick clouds of dun-coloured smoke as if in tribute to the hills which looked down on them. This, then, was the place to which I had been peremptorily summoned; to me it suggested not crime, perhaps, but certainly the idea of an atmosphere in which the more sordid things of life might well happen.

I had scarcely opened the carriage door before a tall man, slender, slightly bearded, very well attired in black, appeared before me and extended a hand. Behind him followed a man who seemed from his dress to be a groom, and at a sign from the other took charge of my baggage.

"Mr. Harthwaite?" I said, as I took the offered hand.

"Mr. John Harthwaite," he responded, as if there were some reason for giving his Christian name. "I am much obliged to you for responding so promptly to my telegram. My motor-car is outside, let my man see to your things. And," he added, giving me a side-glance as we walked along the narrow, wood-paved platform, "as to why I brought you down I will tell you in a few minutes – when we are alone."

We made our way through the greyness of the little town in silence; the people were going home from the mills and factories, and the clatter of their wooden clogs made weird noises on the pavements. Then the road turned sharply, running along the side of the great overhanging hills until houses and mills were left behind and before us there was nothing but the hills to be seen. Then came another curve, and high above us, on the hillside, I saw a house, perched on a series of terraces. My companion said a word to his chauffeur; the car stopped.

THE YORKSHIRE MANUFACTURER

"If you have no objection, Mr. Campenhaye," said Mr. Harthwaite, "we will walk up to my house through the gardens – the car will have to go some distance round – we have little level ground in this corner of the world."

I made no reply to this but left the car and followed my guide through a wicket-gate which led to a winding path. He ascended this until we came to the first of the terraces; then he paused and turned as if to contemplate the view in the valley beneath us. And he stretched out his hand and pointed to two objects – one, the great mass of a manufactory immediately below; the other, a house on the opposite hillside which, so far as I could see in the dusk, appeared to be the counterpart of the one we were approaching.

"You see that mill, Mr. Campenhaye," he said suddenly. "That is the works of John and James Harthwaite, cotton spinners. And you see the house over there – that is where James Harthwaite lived. I say lived – at present he is lying dead within it. Dead – murdered!"

There was some curious feeling in his voice, and my own sounded strangely commonplace when I spoke.

"I suppose that is why you have brought me here, Mr. Harthwaite?" I said.

"That is why I have brought you here, Mr. Campenhaye," he replied. "I have heard of your abilities, and I have no great faith in the police, however well they are trained. And I want to know who killed my brother."

"Naturally, you do," I said. "I hope I shall be of some use."

He was still staring fixedly at the house on the opposite side of the valley, and for a moment he remained silent, but suddenly he spoke again.

"Will you hear of it now?" he said. "There is still time before dinner, and perhaps I can tell you about it more clearly outside four walls. And it is not a long story."

"Now, by all means," I answered, for I saw that he was wanting to unbosom himself. "I am eager to hear everything and at once."

"Sit down there," he said, pointing to a rustic seat, "and smoke a cigar. I will smoke one myself – it will be the first since yesterday. Now," he continued, when he had produced a cigar case and we had begun to smoke. "I will try to be concise and plain. You must know, Mr. Campenhaye, that my brother James and myself were twins. We were thirty-seven a few days ago, and we never married, and had no intention of marrying. These facts may make it strange to you that we did not live together. But we had different tastes, and when we succeeded to the business on my father's death, each built himself a house – this is mine; yonder is his. We each had our own hobbies; but we were good and affectionate brothers."

He paused a moment as if reflecting on his next words.

"One of James's great hobbies," he continued, "was exploring these hills and moors which you see about us. He was never tired of them – I suppose he knew them better than any man living. He knew all their ins and outs, their wildest and loneliest places. He knew all the Druidical remains on them, of which there are many; all the burrows, the rocking-stones – everything. He spent as much time as he could spare on these heights – and up there he was killed. Somehow, I always had an idea that he might meet his death in that way. But your main object is to know how he met it. Very well. Four days ago, James set out on a week's exploration of his favourite country. He was going to wander about after his usual fashion, between here and the Peak district; he knew lonely places, inns, farmsteads, where he could spend his nights. He left his house yonder, as was his custom, before daybreak – to be precise, at half past two in the morning. I never heard of him again until yesterday – late in the afternoon."

Again he paused, seeming to reflect.

"And to make things clear," he resumed, "this is how I heard. About four o'clock yesterday afternoon, a young man, a respectable person, who is a bank clerk in Hallaton, the big town over yonder, walked into our police office here and said that in crossing High Gap, at the head of the range, across which he had come in returning from a holiday walking tour, he had found the dead body of a gentleman lying in a very lonely place, into which he himself had turned to light his pipe, there being, as usual, a strong wind blowing there. He conducted the police back to the spot. They immediately recognised the body as that of my brother. He had quite evidently been killed by a terrible blow on the back of the head – killed, the doctor says, instantaneously. There were no signs of any struggle. There were no footprints. His watch and chain – valuable – were gone; his purse – in which he always carried some twenty or thirty pounds in gold – was also gone. And, naturally, the police believe that he was murdered for the sake of robbery by some of the rough folk who now and then make their way across this range of hills in summer. But – I don't."

He uttered the last two words with such conviction that I started. To me the police theory seemed the correct one; it was one that I myself should have adopted on the *prima facie* evidence.

"You do not?" I said.

"I do not!" he responded, with renewed emphasis. "My brother has wandered about these moors and hills for twenty years and had never known molestation. What is more, he was a strong man, and he always carried a stout stick with him, and if any tramp had assailed him, that tramp would have had the worst of it. No, Mr. Campenhaye, my brother was not murdered for what he had in his pockets – there was some design in his murder. Of that I'm certain."

"Do you suspect anyone?" I asked.

He rose, and motioned me towards the house above us, in which lights were now twinkling.

"I suspect no one," he answered. "I wish I did – I should have more peace of mind. But come, you know the main facts now, and it is time you dined."

Mr. Harthwaite led the way into a house which it was easy to see had been built, equipped and furnished in accordance with the very latest ideas of modern architects and apostles of health and comfort. It was one of those places in which it is impossible for dust to accumulate, wherein labour is saved by ingenious device, and to which air and sunlight have every possible access. Such houses, it is true, lack something of the cosiness and comfort of the old-fashioned ones, yet this was by no means cold with the coldness which so often accompanies the latest developments of scientific housing. There were books and pictures and other matters which made me conclude that whatever James Harthwaite's hobbies other than pedestrianism had been, his brother was certainly of a literary and artistic nature.

Nothing was said during dinner of the terrible catastrophe which had brought me to Wolverdale; my host talked easily and pleasantly of many matters of interest, and though no other person was present, and I should have excused anything that came from him because of his sorrow, he behaved as if he had no trouble in the world, and as though he was doing his utmost to entertain an expected guest. And when we had gone into his study, where coffee was awaiting us, he turned to me with a meaning look.

"I am expecting the local superintendent of police any minute," he said, "and I have a pretty good idea that he will bring a certain detective with him whom he spoke of bringing over from Arthford – a man in whom he has great faith. Now, I do not want either of these men to know who you are, Mr. Campenhaye, so I propose to merely mention you as an old friend who is staying with me. Therefore, suppose you sit still while they are here, listen, and say nothing?"

"Admirable!" I replied. "And exactly what I should wish. Let them talk as much as they please. I should prefer to make my investigations in my own way."

The two police officers, on their arrival, were quite prepared to talk. They agreed in the original theory – that Mr. James Harthwaite had been murdered by some person or persons, who had slept out all night on the moors and had taken him unawares; but so far such persons seemed to have vanished into thin air. The police and the public had been notified of the murder throughout a wide area, but nobody had so far reported anything of any suspicious character; nobody had been spoken of as having displayed money not likely to be theirs; no attempt to pawn or sell the dead man's watch had been heard of.

"But then, you know, Mr. Harthwaite," said the local superintendent, "we've got to remember that, according to the doctor's reckoning, a good four days elapsed between the actual murder and the finding of the body. That may seem strange – but it isn't strange – those rocks, where your poor brother was found, sir, are just off, and only just off, the beaten track, but nobody would turn aside to them. If the young man that found him hadn't wanted to light his pipe just there, and had seen a chance of shelter from the wind, the body might have been there now, Mr. Harthwaite, undiscovered. And as you know, sir, a man could make off across the moors in a dozen different directions, and reach any one of from twelve to twenty good-sized towns, and – vanish."

The detective cleared his throat.

"If there was only the least bit of a clue now!" he said. "The merest bit of a clue. But I've examined the place and the surroundings thoroughly, and I couldn't find as much as a footprint. You know what a dry season it's been, gentlemen, and the grass up there is that firm, wiry mountain stuff – a heavy man makes no more impression on it than a child would. And as the superintendent there says, there was four days' start. Four days!"

They had nothing to tell – nothing, at least, beyond the fact that news of the murder had been spread far and wide, and that the world and his wife had been requested to jog their memories in the endeavour to think of any suspicious character who had been seen coming away from the moor near High Gap on the early morning of a certain day. And from what I heard, there would be nothing more to tell, nothing – just then, at any rate.

My host turned to me when we were alone. His face – a handsome, slightly cynical face – expressed something like boredom.

"You see!" he said, and spread out his hands.

"Well," I replied, "let us give them their due. I don't see that they could say or do any more. There is no clue, and there was a start of four days in the criminal's favour. On the face of things they have done all they could."

He looked at me keenly.

"But – you?" he said meaningly.

"I may go on different lines," I answered. "And before I go on any at all, I want to ask you a few questions. First, had your brother any enemies?"

"I would take my oath that he had not one," he replied with emphasis. "He was universally liked and respected."

"He had no business quarrels – no business enemies?" I asked.

Mr. Harthwaite shrugged his shoulders.

"His business was mine," he said. "I can assure you that we have neither quarrels nor enemies in connection with our business."

"My next question is of a delicate nature," I said. "Had he any secret affairs – whether of love or of anything else?"

"I do not believe that he had any secrets from me of any nature whatever," he answered. "As for love affairs, I am positive that he had none. He devoted himself entirely to three things – the business, his love of wandering about, and a passion for inventions; his spare time at home was given up to invention. Only the night before he left home I was talking to him at the works about an invention which he believed would revolutionise the spinning industry. He was full of it, enthusiastic about it."

"He had no secrets, no enemies, no mysteries?" I said, looking at him keenly in the face.

"None!" he answered.

"Then why," I asked, "why do you believe that there is some secret, some mystery, about his murder, instead of accepting the commonplace, but eminently reasonable, theory of the police that he was waylaid, murdered and robbed, in a lonely place, by some ruffian who has had ample opportunity to make good his escape? I say, why, Mr. Harthwaite?"

He made no immediate answer; instead, he pulled himself up in his chair, and bit his lip. Eventually, he shook his head.

"I cannot explain," he replied. "It is – a feeling. I am sure of what I feel. Perhaps it is – shall we say, instinct? At any rate, I am sure of it, I tell you. He was murdered of design. Design! Not for what he had on him. I – you may think me a fool, Mr. Campenhaye, but how do I know that he isn't impressing this conviction upon me – from – from beyond? Remember – we were twin brothers."

I bowed my head.

"I don't think you a fool, Mr. Harthwaite," I answered gravely. "Far from it. I only wanted you to explain. Now do not let us say any more about the matter until I have something to say to you. All I have to say at present is that I wish to see the scene of your brother's death tomorrow morning as early as possible. And I wish to see it alone – I don't even want a guide if you will tell me the way."

He looked at me for a moment, then rose, and silently motioned me to follow him. He led me outside the house to the end of the uppermost of the terraces. It was a brilliantly moon-lighted night; the road which led up the valley wound away to the gloom of the hills like a silver stream. "Follow the road," he said. "About a mile from here you will come to a gate in a stone wall, close to a ruinous sheep-fold. Pass through the gate and follow a path which is well defined through the heather and the bracken. At the extreme ridge of the hill you will see a mass of grey rock – the path will lead you to within a few yards of it. It was on the side of the rock furthest from you that he was found."

He went back to the house. In the hall I held out my hand.

"Goodnight," I said. "Tell your people to take no notice if they hear me leave the house in the early hours of the morning. I mean to be up there at sunrise."

As a matter of fact I was at the heights of High Gap well before the sun rose – to be precise, I was at the mass of rock where James Harthwaite's body was found at five o'clock. In the grey light of the September morning the place was awful in its wildness and loneliness. On every side the heather-clad moors stretched away in sheer desolation – shrouded here and there in clinging mist, here and there rising sharply to some bluff or eminence. As the light grew stronger I began to make out the contour of far-off mountains to the north and south, and to see far down in the valleys where the great manufacturing towns lay beneath their canopies of smoke. But what most impressed me was the silence and solitude of the place. I could picture to myself the dead man, lover of nature that he evidently was from all that I heard of him, coming up here in the early morning, full of the strange and weird charm of the lonely heights, standing for a while to gaze round him across the vast stretch of unawakened life, and being struck down to death, unawares. In that loneliness, well known to him, he would suspect nothing. And of one thing I quickly convinced myself – the police were right when they said the miscreant could escape in a dozen different directions without fear of detection.

The sun rose with a sudden burst over a long range of hills which rose on the further edge of the moors, and I began to look around me. But I quickly recognised that even systematic examination of the place would yield little of value. The entire surface of the ridge was covered with strong, sturdy heather, and with bracken of an unusual height. The path by which I had come, by which, too, James Harthwaite had come to his death, was a mere sheep-track through the vegetation; it passed the mass of high rocks at about ten yards distance. I saw no sign that the body had been dragged from the path to the rocks, and I at once came to the conclusion that the dead man had been in the habit of resting at these rocks after the stiff climb from the valley and that he was struck down as he rested. And that argued a further conclusion – that the murderer was someone familiar with his habits.

I was turning away with a casual look round when I suddenly espied at a little distance some object which was shining brightly in the glancing sunlight – not one of the myriad beads of dew on the heather hills and the leaves of the bracken, but something that shone like gold. I had no other thought in my mind as I walked towards it than that it was a scrap of quartz, a fragment of mica lying in the dark soil beneath the fronds of the bracken. But what I found was a small case of leather, oval in shape, the sort of thing in which jewellers place rings between pads of satin; what I had seen shining in the sun's rays was certain gilt lettering on the lid – 'Armstead, Optician, Hallaton'.

I pressed open the snap lid of the tiny case. Within, packed in a layer of wool padding, lay an artificial eye. It stared at me with an expression that was almost human.

I was as sure as I was that the sun had risen that in the object which I held in the palm of my hand, I had a clue to the true facts of the murder of James Harthwaite. I blessed the sense of advertisement which had made the oculist put his name and address on the little leather case. And then, putting the case in my pocket, I glanced across the moors and the valley to where in the distance I could see the smoke rising from Hallaton's great chimneys, and, without more ado, I hastened down the hillside to Wolverdale.

John Harthwaite was pacing up and down the terrace outside his house when I reached it. He came to me with an air of anxious expectancy.

"Well?" he said. "You have been up there?"

"I have been up there," I answered. "But don't ask me any questions about it at present. What I want just now are two things – first, breakfast; second, the loan of your motor-car and its driver for an hour or two. After that, we can talk."

He turned aside – a little disappointedly, I thought – and led the way to the house. "Breakfast will be ready in a few minutes," he said. "What time would you like this car?"

"How long," I said, "will it take to run into Hallaton?"

"Three-quarters of an hour," he replied, looking very much as if he wished to know why I wished to go to Hallaton.

"Then, half an hour after breakfast is over," I said. "And, by the by, if we have a few minutes to spare before breakfast there is something I want you to do for me. It is to write a letter – which I will dictate."

He led me into his study and sat down at his desk in silence, drawing paper and pen towards him.

"You are, of course, well known in Hallaton, Mr. Harthwaite?" I said. "Everybody, I suppose, knows you?"

"I suppose so," he answered laconically. "They ought to."

"Begin then," I said. "Private and confidential. DEAR SIR, – The bearer of this letter is Mr. Paul Campenhaye, the famous specialist in criminology, who, at my request, is investigating the circumstances of my late brother's death. Be good enough to give him any information he asks of you and to treat the matter as one of strict secrecy. That is all, except for your signature."

"But to whom is this to be delivered?" he asked.

"That, for the present, I won't tell you," I replied. "It is to form my credentials. No one in Hallaton knows me, you know."

He folded the letter into an envelope and handed it to me in silence. We went to breakfast; neither of us talked much as we ate and drank; when the meal was over, I made ready for my ride. Mr. Harthwaite was in the hall when I came down, lounging restlessly about. I motioned him into the study.

"There was a question I thought of this morning," I said. "I ought to have asked it last night. Who was the last person who saw your brother alive? As he rose so early that morning, it would be some servant, I suppose?"

"No," he answered, "he never troubled his servants with his early rising. He carried a Thermos flask, made ready the night before, and some food in his knapsack, and he used to get breakfast at one of the moorland farmhouses. The last person who saw him alive was our chief mechanician, Ollershaw, who went up that night to my brother's house to discuss some drawings of machinery with him, and was with him until midnight."

"I should like to have some conversation with Mr. Ollershaw when I return," I said. "By the by, what was there actually left on your brother's body – I mean personal effects – when he was found?"

"Nothing," he said. "His watch and chain, purse, ring, and pocket-book were all gone. The knapsack was still strapped to his shoulder."

I nodded, and went out to the motor-car which had just run up to the hall door. Mr. Harthwaite followed me out.

"Where shall he drive you?" he asked.

"To the best hotel in Hallaton," I answered.

He gave the driver an order. A moment later we were speeding around the spiral curves which led down to the road in the valley. And then I put the Harthwaite matter out of my mind and gave myself up to contemplating the strange scenes through which we passed until we ran into the grime and greyness of the great manufacturing town and pulled up in the courtyard of an old-fashioned hotel.

"I want you to wait here until I return," I said to the driver. "I may be half an hour. I may be an hour."

Then I went out into the unfamiliar streets, making for a principal thoroughfare which the car had crossed a few minutes previously. I had a sure prescience that the firm I wanted would be found somewhere about the heart of the town, and without troubling to ask anyone for help, I speedily discovered the place – evidently, from its exterior, the shop of a first-rate optician.

An elderly, grave-faced man was behind the counter when I entered, and gave me a courteous bow and an enquiring look.

"Mr. Armstead?" I said.

"The same, sir," he answered, again bowing. "What can I do for you, sir?"

I drew out my own card, and the letter which John Harthwaite had written, and handed them to him in silence. I saw his face change and his eyebrows go up as he read the letter, and he came round the counter and waved me to the half-open door at the back of the shop, at the same time saying a word to an assistant who stood near. The next moment we were closeted together in a small room.

"What can I do for you, Mr. Campenhaye?" he asked, with a little tremor as of anxiety in his voice. "It's not – not, I hope, about poor Mr. James?"

"That, Mr. Armstead, is precisely what it is," I answered. "Now, remember, we speak together in the strictest secrecy?"

"Oh, yes, yes, sir – of course!" he exclaimed. "I understand. But – what can I tell you, Mr. Campenhaye?"

I drew out the little leather-covered case, and held it out to him, open.

"This," I said. "For whom did you make, or to whom did you supply, this artificial eye?"

I thought for an instant that he was going to fall, for he swayed visibly, and his face became very pale. But he steadied himself and took the case from me, his hand trembling visibly.

"My God!" he muttered. "It – it can't be possible! You don't suspect, sir—"

"Never mind what or whom I suspect, Mr. Armstead," I said. "Answer my question."

He put the case down on the table and stared at it in wonder. I knew that he already suspected somebody.

"Yes, sir," he said, "I'll answer your question. I supplied this artificial eye – this, and a duplicate one for use in case this one was lost, or vice versa, as the case might be, you know – to Mr. Ollershaw, who has some important post at Harthwaites'. He lost an eye some years ago, and I had two made for him – one to wear, the other in case, as I have just said. He – oh, my God! – you surely don't suspect—"

I put the case and its contents back in my pocket and held up my hand.

"Remember what we said about secrecy, Mr. Armstead," I said. "And – pull yourself together. Now, just tell me what you know of this Ollershaw – what sort of man is he?"

The optician made a strong effort to be calm.

"I know little, sir, except that I supplied him with this, and with his spectacles – he wears tinted glasses – and that he sometimes comes in to buy little matters," he said. "He's a quiet, queer sort of fellow – morose, I should say, and with little to say for himself – an inventive genius, Mr. Campenhaye – he's once or twice done things for me."

"Ah! An inventor?" I said. "Very well. Now, good morning, Mr. Armstead, and thank you. You will see me again – and in the meantime – silence!"

I hurried back to the hotel, hurried into the car, bade the driver go back as quickly as he could. But by the time we reached John Harthwaite's house I had assumed as cool and as nonchalant an air as I was capable of at that moment.

"There!" I exclaimed, as Mr. Harthwaite came out to the terrace. "We were not so long, you see, after all. By the by, wouldn't it be well, now that the car is here, if I went to see the man you spoke of – Ollershaw?"

"I was just going down to the mill myself," he said. "Get in again, and we'll ride down. We shall find him there."

But when we came to the office at the big mill in the valley, Ollershaw was not there – he had gone up to the cottage at which he lodged to fetch something, somebody said.

"We'll ride up," said Mr. Harthwaite. "It's not far out of the village, and if you want to talk to him, you'll be quieter there. I don't see that he can tell you anything, though, that I couldn't. He told me all he knew yesterday."

I made no answer to that, and we rode on in silence until the car was clear of the village. Then, on the hillside, near the place where the footpath turned up the hillside towards High Gap I saw a desolate cottage. As we neared it, a man came out into the road before us. He made as if to cross it to another footpath which led to the mill.

"There's Ollershaw!" exclaimed my companion. "Hi! Ollershaw!"

The man turned, stared, and then came slowly towards us. He was a fellow of about thirty, dressed in a much-worn, much-stained, tweed suit, which he seemed to have thrown upon himself. His chin and mouth were hidden by a curly, unkempt, black beard; his eyes were concealed by smoked spectacles. Above them was a high, white forehead which bulged far too much; above it dense, black hair protruded from beneath an old cricket cap, worn far back on the back of his head. Something in the set of his shoulders, the turn of the lips, suggested a sullen defiance, an indefinable dislike of – what?

"A queer-looking chap, but wonderfully clever," whispered Mr. Harthwaite. "Ollershaw, I want to speak to you. This gentleman is investigating the circumstances of my brother's death, and as you were the last to see him alive, he wants to ask you a question or two."

I got out of the car; the figure before us betrayed in every line a sullen dislike and indifference.

"Just step aside with me a moment, Mr. Ollershaw," I said, leading him to the side of the road. "I only want to ask you a question or two. You were the last person to see Mr. James Harthwaite alive, weren't you?"

"So it seems," he answered gruffly. "We haven't heard of anybody who saw him after I did."

"Just so," I said. "And when did you last see him alive? Was it," I continued, getting very close to him and putting my fingers in my pocket for a certain object, "was it at his house, or was it on High Gap, where you lost – this?"

And I held out before him his artificial eye.

I knew I had hit the right nail on the head, then. The man made one strange, inarticulate sound, clapped his hand to a certain pocket in his waistcoat, lurched, and collapsed, fainting, in my arms.

"Good God! What's this?" exclaimed Harthwaite, as he and the driver sprang from the car. "What is it, Campenhaye?"

"It's only that this is the man who killed your brother," I answered, as I laid Ollershaw down, and slipped my hand into the inner pocket of his coat. "And here," I added, as I drew out a tight wad of thin papers, "here's what he killed him for – the secret of the invention of which you said your brother had spoken the night before his murder. Now, then, let's bring him round – and let's be thankful, too, Mr. Harthwaite, that the fellow was so careless about his clothing that he went about with this hole in his waistcoat pocket. For if it hadn't been for that, he'd have gone as free as the wind!"

The Case of Oscar Brodski

R. Austin Freeman

Part I
The Mechanism of Crime

A SURPRISING AMOUNT of nonsense has been talked about conscience. On the one hand remorse (or the 'again-bite', as certain scholars of ultra-Teutonic leanings would prefer to call it); on the other hand 'an easy conscience': these have been accepted as the determining factors of happiness or the reverse.

Of course there is an element of truth in the 'easy conscience' view, but it begs the whole question. A particularly hardy conscience may be quite easy under the most unfavourable conditions – conditions in which the more feeble conscience might be severely afflicted with the 'again-bite'. And, then, it seems to be the fact that some fortunate persons have no conscience at all; a negative gift that raises them above the mental vicissitudes of the common herd of humanity.

Now, Silas Hickler was a case in point. No one, looking into his cheerful, round face, beaming with benevolence and wreathed in perpetual smiles, would have imagined him to be a criminal. Least of all, his worthy, high-church housekeeper, who was a witness to his unvarying amiability, who constantly heard him carolling light-heartedly about the house and noted his appreciative zest at mealtimes.

Yet it is a fact that Silas earned his modest, though comfortable, income by the gentle art of burglary. A precarious trade and risky withal, yet not so very hazardous if pursued with judgment and moderation. And Silas was eminently a man of judgment. He worked invariably alone. He kept his own counsel. No confederate had he to turn King's Evidence at a pinch; no one he knew would bounce off in a fit of temper to Scotland Yard. Nor was he greedy and thriftless, as most criminals are. His 'scoops' were few and far between, carefully planned, secretly executed, and the proceeds judiciously invested in 'weekly property'.

In early life Silas had been connected with the diamond industry, and he still did a little rather irregular dealing. In the trade he was suspected of transactions with I.D.B.'s, and one or two indiscreet dealers had gone so far as to whisper the ominous word 'fence'. But Silas smiled a benevolent smile and went his way. He knew what he knew, and his clients in Amsterdam were not inquisitive.

Such was Silas Hickler. As he strolled round his garden in the dusk of an October evening, he seemed the very type of modest, middle-class prosperity. He was dressed in the travelling suit that he wore on his little continental trips; his bag was packed and stood in readiness on the sitting-room sofa. A parcel of diamonds (purchased honestly, though without impertinent questions, at Southampton) was in the inside pocket of his waistcoat, and another more valuable parcel was stowed in a cavity in the heel of his right boot. In an hour and a half it would be time for him to set out to catch the boat train at the junction; meanwhile there was nothing to do but to stroll round the fading garden and consider how he should invest the proceeds of the impending deal. His housekeeper had gone over to Welham for the week's shopping, and would probably not be back until eleven o'clock. He was alone in the premises and just a trifle dull.

He was about to turn into the house when his ear caught the sound of footsteps on the unmade road that passed the end of the garden. He paused and listened. There was no other dwelling near, and the road led nowhere, fading away into the wasteland beyond the house. Could this be a visitor? It seemed unlikely, for visitors were few at Silas Hickler's house. Meanwhile the footsteps continued to approach, ringing out with increasing loudness on the hard, stony path.

Silas strolled down to the gate, and, leaning on it, looked out with some curiosity. Presently a glow of light showed him the face of a man, apparently lighting his pipe; then a dim figure detached itself from the enveloping gloom, advanced towards him and halted opposite the garden. The stranger removed a cigarette from his mouth and, blowing out a cloud of smoke, asked –

"Can you tell me if this road will take me to Badsham Junction?"

"No," replied Hickler, "but there is a footpath farther on that leads to the station."

"Footpath!" growled the stranger. "I've had enough of footpaths. I came down from town to Catley intending to walk across to the junction. I started along the road, and then some fool directed me to a short-cut, with the result that I have been blundering about in the dark for the last half-hour. My sight isn't very good, you know," he added.

"What train do you want to catch?" asked Hickler.

"Seven fifty-eight," was the reply.

"I am going to catch that train myself," said Silas, "but I shan't be starting for another hour. The station is only three-quarters of a mile from here. If you like to come in and take a rest, we can walk down together and then you'll be sure of not missing your way."

"It's very good of you," said the stranger, peering, with spectacled eyes, at the dark house, "but – I think—"

"Might as well wait here as at the station," said Silas in his genial way, holding the gate open, and the stranger, after a momentary hesitation, entered and, flinging away his cigarette, followed him to the door of the cottage.

The sitting room was in darkness, save for the dull glow of the expiring fire, but, entering before his guest, Silas applied a match to the lamp that hung from the ceiling. As the flame leaped up, flooding the little interior with light, the two men regarded one another with mutual curiosity.

"Brodski, by Jingo!" was Hickler's silent commentary, as he looked at his guest. "Doesn't know me, evidently – wouldn't, of course, after all these years and with his bad eyesight. Take a seat, sir," he added aloud. "Will you join me in a little refreshment to while away the time?"

Brodski murmured an indistinct acceptance, and, as his host turned to open a cupboard, he deposited his hat (a hard, grey felt) on a chair in a corner, placed his bag on the edge of the table, resting his umbrella against it, and sat down in a small armchair.

"Have a biscuit?" said Hickler, as he placed a whisky bottle on the table together with a couple of his best star-pattern tumblers and a siphon.

"Thanks, I think I will," said Brodski. "The railway journey and all this confounded tramping about, you know—"

"Yes," agreed Silas. "Doesn't do to start with an empty stomach. Hope you don't mind oatcakes; I see they're the only biscuits I have."

Brodski hastened to assure him that oatcakes were his special and peculiar fancy, and in confirmation, having mixed himself a stiff jorum, he fell upon the biscuits with evident gusto.

Brodski was a deliberate feeder, and at present appeared to be somewhat sharp-set. His measured munching being unfavourable to conversation, most of the talking fell to Silas; and, for once, that genial transgressor found the task embarrassing. The natural thing would have been to discuss his guest's destination and perhaps the object of his journey; but this was precisely what Hickler avoided doing. For he knew both, and instinct told him to keep his knowledge to himself.

Brodski was a diamond merchant of considerable reputation, and in a large way of business. He bought stones principally in the rough, and of these he was a most excellent judge. His fancy was for stones of somewhat unusual size and value, and it was well known to be his custom, when he had accumulated a sufficient stock, to carry them himself to Amsterdam and supervise the cutting of the rough stones. Of this Hickler was aware, and he had no doubt that Brodski was now starting on one of his periodical excursions; that somewhere in the recesses of his rather shabby clothing was concealed a paper packet possibly worth several thousand pounds.

Brodski sat by the table munching monotonously and talking little. Hickler sat opposite him, talking nervously and rather wildly at times, and watching his guest with a growing fascination. Precious stones, and especially diamonds, were Hickler's specialty. 'Hard stuff' – silver plate – he avoided entirely; gold, excepting in the form of specie, he seldom touched; but stones, of which he could carry off a whole consignment in the heel of his boot and dispose of with absolute safety, formed the staple of his industry. And here was a man sitting opposite him with a parcel in his pocket containing the equivalent of a dozen of his most successful 'scoops'; stones worth perhaps—. Here he pulled himself up short and began to talk rapidly, though without much coherence. For, even as he talked, other words, formed subconsciously, seemed to insinuate themselves into the interstices of the sentences, and to carry on a parallel train of thought.

"Gets chilly in the evenings now, doesn't it?" said Hickler.

"It does indeed," Brodski agreed, and then resumed his slow munching, breathing audibly through his nose.

"Five thousand at least," the subconscious train of thought resumed; "probably six or seven, perhaps ten." Silas fidgeted in his chair and endeavoured to concentrate his ideas on some topic of interest. He was growing disagreeably conscious of a new and unfamiliar state of mind.

"Do you take any interest in gardening?", he asked. Next to diamonds and 'weekly property', his besetting weakness was fuchsias.

Brodski chuckled sourly. "Hatton Garden is the nearest approach—" He broke off suddenly, and then added, "I am a Londoner, you know."

The abrupt break in the sentence was not unnoticed by Silas, nor had he any difficulty in interpreting it. A man who carries untold wealth upon his person must needs be wary in his speech.

"Yes," he answered absently, "it's hardly a Londoner's hobby." And then, half consciously, he began a rapid calculation. Put it at five thousand pounds. What would that represent in weekly property? His last set of houses had cost two hundred and fifty pounds apiece, and he had let them at ten shillings and sixpence a week. At that rate, five thousand pounds represented twenty houses at ten and sixpence a week – say ten pounds a week – one pound eight shillings a day – five hundred and twenty pounds a year – for life. It was a competency. Added to what he already had, it was wealth. With that income he could fling the tools of his trade into the river and live out the remainder of his life in comfort and security.

He glanced furtively at his guest across the table, and then looked away quickly as he felt stirring within him an impulse the nature of which he could not mistake. This must be put an end to. Crimes against the person he had always looked upon as sheer insanity. There was, it is true, that little affair of the Weybridge policeman, but that was unforeseen and unavoidable, and it was the constable's doing after all. And there was the old housekeeper at Epsom, too, but, of course, if the old idiot would shriek in that insane fashion – well, it was an accident, very regrettable, to be sure, and no one could be more sorry for the mishap than himself. But deliberate homicide! Robbery from the person! It was the act of a stark lunatic.

Of course, if he had happened to be that sort of person, here was the opportunity of a lifetime. The immense booty, the empty house, the solitary neighbourhood, away from the main road and from other habitations; the time, the darkness – but, of course, there was the body to be thought of; that was always the difficulty. What to do with the body—. Here he caught the shriek of the up express, rounding the curve in the line that ran past the wasteland at the back of the house. The sound started a new train of thought, and, as he followed it out, his eyes fixed themselves on the unconscious and taciturn Brodski, as he sat thoughtfully sipping his whisky. At length, averting his gaze with an effort, he rose suddenly from his chair and turned to look at the clock on the mantelpiece, spreading out his hands before the dying fire. A tumult of strange sensations warned him to leave the house. He shivered slightly, though he was rather hot than chilly, and, turning his head, looked at the door.

"Seems to be a confounded draught," he said, with another slight shiver; "did I shut the door properly, I wonder?" He strode across the room and, opening the door wide, looked out into the dark garden. A desire, sudden and urgent, had come over him to get out into the open air, to be on the road and have done with this madness that was knocking at the door of his brain.

"I wonder if it is worthwhile to start yet," he said, with a yearning glance at the murky, starless sky.

Brodski roused himself and looked round. "Is your clock right?" he asked.

Silas reluctantly admitted that it was.

"How long will it take us to walk to the station?" inquired Brodski.

"Oh, about twenty-five minutes to half an hour," replied Silas, unconsciously exaggerating the distance.

"Well," said Brodski, "we've got more than an hour yet, and it's more comfortable here than hanging about the station. I don't see the use of starting before we need."

"No; of course not," Silas agreed. A wave of strange emotion, half-regretful, half-triumphant, surged through his brain. For some moments he remained standing on the threshold, looking out dreamily into the night. Then he softly closed the door; and, seemingly without the exercise of his volition, the key turned noiselessly in the lock.

He returned to his chair and tried to open a conversation with the taciturn Brodski, but the words came faltering and disjointed. He felt his face growing hot, his brain full and intense, and there was a faint, high-pitched singing in his ears. He was conscious of watching his guest with a new and fearful interest, and, by sheer force of will, turned away his eyes; only to find them a moment later involuntarily returning to fix the unconscious man with yet more horrible intensity. And ever through his mind walked, like a dreadful procession, the thoughts of what that other man – the man of blood and violence – would do in these circumstances. Detail by detail the hideous synthesis fitted together the parts of the imagined crime, and arranged them in due sequence until they formed a succession of events, rational, connected and coherent.

He rose uneasily from his chair, with his eyes still riveted upon his guest. He could not sit any longer opposite that man with his hidden store of precious gems. The impulse that he recognized with fear and wonder was growing more ungovernable from moment to moment. If he stayed it would presently overpower him, and then—. He shrank with horror from the dreadful thought, but his fingers itched to handle the diamonds. For Silas was, after all, a criminal by nature and habit. He was a beast of prey. His livelihood had never been earned; it had been taken by stealth or, if necessary, by force. His instincts were predacious, and the proximity of unguarded valuables suggested to him, as a logical consequence, their abstraction or seizure. His unwillingness to let these diamonds go away beyond his reach was fast becoming overwhelming.

But he would make one more effort to escape. He would keep out of Brodski's actual presence until the moment for starting came.

"If you'll excuse me," he said, "I will go and put on a thicker pair of boots. After all this dry weather we may get a change, and damp feet are very uncomfortable when you are travelling."

"Yes; dangerous too," agreed Brodski.

Silas walked through into the adjoining kitchen, where, by the light of the little lamp that was burning there, he had seen his stout, country boots placed, cleaned and in readiness, and sat down upon a chair to make the change. He did not, of course, intend to wear the country boots, for the diamonds were concealed in those he had on. But he would make the change and then alter his mind; it would all help to pass the time. He took a deep breath. It was a relief, at any rate, to be out of that room. Perhaps if he stayed away, the temptation would pass. Brodski would go on his way – he wished that he was going alone – and the danger would be over – at least – and the opportunity would have gone – the diamonds—

He looked up as he slowly unlaced his boot. From where he sat he could see Brodski sitting by the table with his back towards the kitchen door. He had finished eating, now, and was composedly rolling a cigarette. Silas breathed heavily, and, slipping off his boot, sat for a while motionless, gazing steadily at the other man's back. Then he unlaced the other boot, still staring abstractedly at his unconscious guest, drew it off, and laid it very quietly on the floor.

Brodski calmly finished rolling his cigarette, licked the paper, put away his pouch, and, having dusted the crumbs of tobacco from his knees, began to search his pockets for a match. Suddenly, yielding to an uncontrollable impulse, Silas stood up and began stealthily to creep along the passage to the sitting room. Not a sound came from his stockinged feet. Silently as a cat he stole forward, breathing softly with parted lips, until he stood at the threshold of the room. His face flushed duskily, his eyes, wide and staring, glittered in the lamplight, and the racing blood hummed in his ears.

Brodski struck a match – Silas noted that it was a wooden vesta – lighted his cigarette, blew out the match and flung it into the fender. Then he replaced the box in his pocket and commenced to smoke.

Slowly and without a sound Silas crept forward into the room, step by step, with catlike stealthiness, until he stood close behind Brodski's chair – so close that he had to turn his head that his breath might not stir the hair upon the other man's head. So, for half a minute, he stood motionless, like a symbolical statue of Murder, glaring down with horrible, glittering eyes upon the unconscious diamond merchant, while his quick breath passed without a sound through his open mouth and his fingers writhed slowly like the tentacles of a giant hydra. And then, as noiselessly as ever, he backed away to the door, turned quickly and walked back into the kitchen.

He drew a deep breath. It had been a near thing. Brodski's life had hung upon a thread. For it had been so easy. Indeed, if he had happened, as he stood behind the man's chair, to have a weapon – a hammer, for instance, or even a stone—

He glanced round the kitchen and his eyes lighted on a bar that had been left by the workmen who had put up the new greenhouse. It was an odd piece cut off from a square, wrought-iron stanchion, and was about a foot long and perhaps three-quarters of an inch thick. Now, if he had had that in his hand a minute ago—

He picked the bar up, balanced it in his hand and swung it round his head. A formidable weapon this: silent, too. And it fitted the plan that had passed through his brain. Bah! He had better put the thing down.

But he did not. He stepped over to the door and looked again at Brodski, sitting, as before, meditatively smoking, with his back towards the kitchen.

Suddenly a change came over Silas. His face flushed, the veins of his neck stood out and a sullen scowl settled on his face. He drew out his watch, glanced at it earnestly and replaced it. Then he strode swiftly but silently along the passage into the sitting room.

A pace away from his victim's chair he halted and took deliberate aim. The bar swung aloft, but not without some faint rustle of movement, for Brodski looked round quickly even as the iron whistled through the air. The movement disturbed the murderer's aim, and the bar glanced off his victim's head, making only a trifling wound. Brodski sprang up with a tremulous, bleating cry, and clutched his assailant's arms with the tenacity of mortal terror.

Then began a terrible struggle, as the two men, locked in a deadly embrace, swayed to and fro and trampled backwards and forwards. The chair was overturned, an empty glass swept from the table and, with Brodski's spectacles, crushed beneath stamping feet. And thrice that dreadful, pitiful, bleating cry rang out into the night, filling Silas, despite his murderous frenzy, with terror lest some chance wayfarer should hear it. Gathering his great strength for a final effort, he forced his victim backwards onto the table and, snatching up a corner of the tablecloth, thrust it into his face and crammed it into his mouth as it opened to utter another shriek. And thus they remained for a full two minutes, almost motionless, like some dreadful group of tragic allegory. Then, when the last faint twitchings had died away, Silas relaxed his grasp and let the limp body slip softly onto the floor.

It was over. For good or for evil, the thing was done. Silas stood up, breathing heavily, and, as he wiped the sweat from his face, he looked at the clock. The hands stood at one minute to seven. The whole thing had taken a little over three minutes. He had nearly an hour in which to finish his task. The goods train that entered into his scheme came by at twenty minutes past, and it was only three hundred yards to the line. Still, he must not waste time. He was now quite composed, and only disturbed by the thought that Brodski's cries might have been heard. If no one had heard them it was all plain sailing.

He stooped, and, gently disengaging the tablecloth from the dead man's teeth, began a careful search of his pockets. He was not long finding what he sought, and, as he pinched the paper packet and felt the little hard bodies grating on one another inside, his faint regrets for what had happened were swallowed up in self-congratulations.

He now set about his task with business-like briskness and an attentive eye on the clock. A few large drops of blood had fallen on the tablecloth, and there was a small bloody smear on the carpet by the dead man's head. Silas fetched from the kitchen some water, a nail-brush and a dry cloth, and, having washed out the stains from the table-cover – not forgetting the deal table top underneath – and cleaned away the smear from the carpet and rubbed the damp places dry, he slipped a sheet of paper under the head of the corpse to prevent further contamination. Then he set the tablecloth straight, stood the chair upright, laid the broken spectacles on the table and picked up the cigarette, which had been trodden flat in the struggle, and flung it under the grate. Then there was the broken glass, which he swept up into a dustpan. Part of it was the remains of the shattered tumbler, and the rest the fragments of the broken spectacles. He turned it out onto a sheet of paper and looked it over carefully, picking out the larger recognisable pieces of the spectacle-glasses and putting them aside on a separate slip of paper, together with a sprinkling of the minute fragments. The remainder he shot back into the dustpan and, having hurriedly put on his boots, carried it out to the rubbish-heap at the back of the house.

It was now time to start. Hastily cutting off a length of string from his string-box – for Silas was an orderly man and despised the oddments of string with which many people make shift – he tied it to the dead man's bag and umbrella and slung them from his shoulder. Then he folded up the paper of broken glass, and, slipping it and the spectacles into his pocket, picked up the body and threw it over his shoulder. Brodski was a small, spare man, weighing not more than nine stone; not a very formidable burden for a big, athletic man like Silas.

The night was intensely dark, and, when Silas looked out of the back gate over the wasteland that stretched from his house to the railway, he could hardly see twenty yards ahead. After listening cautiously and hearing no sound, he went out, shut the gate softly behind him and set forth at a good pace, though carefully, over the broken ground. His progress was not as silent as he could have wished for, though the scanty turf that covered the gravelly land was thick enough to deaden his footfalls, the swinging bag and umbrella made an irritating noise; indeed, his movements were more hampered by them than by the weightier burden.

The distance to the line was about three hundred yards. Ordinarily he would have walked it in from three to four minutes, but now, going cautiously with his burden and stopping now and again to listen, it took him just six minutes to reach the three-bar fence that separated the wasteland from the railway. Arrived here he halted for a moment and once more listened attentively, peering into the darkness on all sides. Not a living creature was to be seen or heard in this desolate spot, but far away, the shriek of an engine's whistle warned him to hasten.

Lifting the corpse easily over the fence, he carried it a few yards farther to a point where the line curved sharply. Here he laid it face downwards, with the neck over the near rail. Drawing out his pocket knife, he cut through the knot that fastened the umbrella to the string and also secured the bag; and when he had flung the bag and umbrella on the track beside the body, he carefully pocketed the string, excepting the little loop that had fallen to the ground when the knot was cut.

The quick snort and clanking rumble of an approaching goods train began now to be clearly audible. Rapidly, Silas drew from his pockets the battered spectacles and the packet of broken glass. The former he threw down by the dead man's head, and then, emptying the packet into his hand, sprinkled the fragments of glass around the spectacles.

He was none too soon. Already the quick, laboured puffing of the engine sounded close at hand. His impulse was to stay and watch; to witness the final catastrophe that should convert the murder into an accident or suicide. But it was hardly safe: it would be better that he should not be near lest he should not be able to get away without being seen. Hastily he climbed back over the fence and strode away across the rough fields, while the train came snorting and clattering towards the curve.

He had nearly reached his back gate when a sound from the line brought him to a sudden halt; it was a prolonged whistle accompanied by the groan of brakes and the loud clank of colliding trucks. The snorting of the engine had ceased and was replaced by the penetrating hiss of escaping steam.

The train had stopped!

For one brief moment Silas stood with bated breath and mouth agape like one petrified; then he strode forward quickly to the gate, and, letting himself in, silently slid the bolt. He was undeniably alarmed. What could have happened on the line? It was practically certain that the body had been seen; but what was happening now? And would they come to the house? He entered the kitchen, and having paused again to listen – for somebody might come and knock at the door at any moment – he walked through the sitting room and looked round. All seemed in order there. There was the bar, though, lying where he had dropped it in the scuffle. He picked it up and held it under the lamp. There was no blood on it; only one or two hairs. Somewhat absently he wiped it with the table-cover, and then, running out through the kitchen into the back garden, dropped it over the wall into a bed of nettles. Not that there was anything incriminating in the bar, but, since he had used it as a weapon, it had somehow acquired a sinister aspect to his eye.

He now felt that it would be well to start for the station at once. It was not time yet, for it was barely twenty-five minutes past seven; but he did not wish to be found in the house if anyone should come. His soft hat was on the sofa with his bag, to which his umbrella was strapped. He put on the hat, caught up the bag and stepped over to the door; then he came back to turn down the lamp. And it was at this moment, when he stood with his hand raised to the burner, that his eyes, travelling by chance into the dim corner of the room, lighted on Brodski's grey felt hat, reposing on the chair where the dead man had placed it when he entered the house.

Silas stood for a few moments as if petrified, with the chilly sweat of mortal fear standing in beads upon his forehead. Another instant and he would have turned the lamp down and gone on his way;

and then—. He strode over to the chair, snatched up the hat and looked inside it. Yes, there was the name, 'Oscar Brodski', written plainly on the lining. If he had gone away, leaving it to be discovered, he would have been lost; indeed, even now, if a search party should come to the house, it was enough to send him to the gallows.

His limbs shook with horror at the thought, but in spite of his panic he did not lose his self-possession. Darting through into the kitchen, he grabbed up a handful of the dry brushwood that was kept for lighting fires and carried it to the sitting-room grate where he thrust it on the extinct, but still hot, embers, and crumpling up the paper that he had placed under Brodski's head – on which paper he now noticed, for the first time, a minute bloody smear – he poked it in under the wood, and striking a wax match, set light to it. As the wood flared up, he hacked at the hat with his pocket knife and threw the ragged strips into the blaze.

And all the while his heart was thumping and his hands a-tremble with the dread of discovery. The fragments of felt were far from inflammable, tending rather to fuse into cindery masses that smoked and smouldered than to burn away into actual ash. Moreover, to his dismay, they emitted a powerful resinous stench mixed with the odour of burning hair, so that he had to open the kitchen window (since he dared not unlock the front door) to disperse the reek. And still, as he fed the fire with small cut fragments, he strained his ears to catch, above the crackling of the wood, the sound of the dreaded footsteps, the knock on the door that should be as the summons of Fate.

The time, too, was speeding on. Twenty-one minutes to eight! In a few minutes more he must set out or he would miss the train. He dropped the dismembered hat-brim on the blazing wood and ran upstairs to open a window, since he must close that in the kitchen before he left. When he came back, the brim had already curled up into a black, clinkery mass that bubbled and hissed as the fat, pungent smoke rose from it sluggishly to the chimney.

Nineteen minutes to eight! It was time to start. He took up the poker and carefully beat the cinders into small particles, stirring them into the glowing embers of the wood and coal. There was nothing unusual in the appearance of the grate. It was his constant custom to burn letters and other discarded articles in the sitting-room fire: his housekeeper would notice nothing out of the common. Indeed, the cinders would probably be reduced to ashes before she returned. He had been careful to notice that there were no metallic fittings of any kind in the hat, which might have escaped burning.

Once more he picked up his bag, took a last look round, turned down the lamp and, unlocking the door, held it open for a few moments. Then he went out, locked the door, pocketed the key (of which his housekeeper had a duplicate) and set off at a brisk pace for the station.

He arrived in good time after all, and, having taken his ticket, strolled through onto the platform. The train was not yet signalled, but there seemed to be an unusual stir in the place. The passengers were collected in a group at one end of the platform, and were all looking in one direction down the line; and, even as he walked towards them, with a certain tremulous, nauseating curiosity, two men emerged from the darkness and ascended the slope to the platform, carrying a stretcher covered with a tarpaulin. The passengers parted to let the bearers pass, turning fascinated eyes upon the shape that showed faintly through the rough pall; and, when the stretcher had been borne into the lamp-room, they fixed their attention upon a porter who followed carrying a handbag and an umbrella.

Suddenly one of the passengers started forward with an exclamation.

"Is that his umbrella?" he demanded.

"Yes, sir," answered the porter, stopping and holding it out for the speaker's inspection.

"My God!" ejaculated the passenger; then, turning sharply to a tall man who stood close by, he said excitedly: "That's Brodski's umbrella. I could swear to it. You remember Brodski?" The tall man nodded, and the passenger, turning once more to the porter, said: "I identify that umbrella. It belongs to a gentleman named Brodski. If you look in his hat you will see his name written in it. He always writes his name in his hat."

"We haven't found his hat yet," said the porter; "but here is the station master coming up the line." He awaited the arrival of his superior and then announced: "This gentleman, sir, has identified the umbrella."

"Oh," said the station master, "you recognise the umbrella, sir, do you? Then perhaps you would step into the lamp-room and see if you can identify the body."

"Is it – is he – very much injured?" the passenger asked tremulously.

"Well, yes," was the reply. "You see, the engine and six of the trucks went over him before they could stop the train. Took his head clean off, in fact."

"Shocking! Shocking!" gasped the passenger. "I think, if you don't mind – I'd – I'd rather not. You don't think it's necessary, doctor, do you?"

"Yes, I do," replied the tall man. "Early identification may be of the first importance."

"Then I suppose I must," said the passenger.

Very reluctantly he allowed himself to be conducted by the station master to the lamp-room, as the clang of the bell announced the approaching train. Silas Hickler followed and took his stand with the expectant crowd outside the closed door. In a few moments the passenger burst out, pale and awe-stricken, and rushed up to his tall friend. "It is!" he exclaimed breathlessly. "It's Brodski! Poor old Brodski! Horrible! Horrible! He was to have met me here and come on with me to Amsterdam."

"Had he any – merchandise about him?" the tall man asked; and Silas strained his ears to catch the reply.

"He had some stones, no doubt, but I don't know what. His clerk will know, of course. By the way, doctor, could you watch the case for me? Just to be sure it was really an accident or – you know what. We were old friends, you know, fellow townsmen, too; we were both born in Warsaw. I'd like you to give an eye to the case."

"Very well," said the other. "I will satisfy myself that – there is nothing more than appears, and let you have a report. Will that do?"

"Thank you. It's excessively good of you, doctor. Ah! Here comes the train. I hope it won't inconvenience you to stay and see to this matter."

"Not in the least," replied the doctor. "We are not due at Warmington until tomorrow afternoon, and I expect we can find out all that is necessary to know and still keep our appointment."

Silas looked long and curiously at the tall, imposing man who was, as it were, taking his seat at the chessboard, to play against him for his life. A formidable antagonist he looked, with his keen, thoughtful face, so resolute and calm. As Silas stepped into his carriage he thought with deep discomfort of Brodski's hat, and hoped that he had made no other oversight.

Part II
The Mechanism of Detection
(Related by Christopher Jervis, M.D.)

THE SINGULAR circumstances that attended the death of Mr. Oscar Brodski, the well-known diamond merchant of Hatton Garden, illustrated very forcibly the importance of one or two points in medico-legal practice which Thorndyke was accustomed to insist were not sufficiently appreciated. What those points were, I shall leave my friend and teacher to state at the proper place; and meanwhile, as the case is in the highest degree instructive, I shall record the incidents in the order of their occurrence.

The dusk of an October evening was closing in as Thorndyke and I, the sole occupants of a smoking compartment, found ourselves approaching the little station of Ludham; and, as the train slowed down, we peered out at the knot of country, people who were waiting on the platform. Suddenly Thorndyke exclaimed in a tone of surprise: "Why, that is surely Boscovitch!" and almost at the same moment a brisk, excitable little man darted at the door of our compartment and literally tumbled in.

"I hope I don't intrude on this learned conclave," he said, shaking hands genially and banging his Gladstone with impulsive violence into the rack; "but I saw your faces at the window, and naturally jumped at the chance of such pleasant companionship."

"You are very flattering," said Thorndyke; "so flattering that you leave us nothing to say. But what in the name of fortune are you doing at – what's the name of the place – Ludham?"

"My brother has a little place a mile or so from here, and I have been spending a couple of days with him," Mr. Boscovitch explained. "I shall change at Badsham Junction and catch the boat train for Amsterdam. But whither are you two bound? I see you have your mysterious little green box up on the hat-rack, so I infer that you are on some romantic quest, eh? Going to unravel some dark and intricate crime?"

"No," replied Thorndyke. "We are bound for Warmington on a quite prosaic errand. I am instructed to watch the proceedings at an inquest there tomorrow on behalf of the Griffin Life Insurance Office, and we are travelling down tonight as it is rather a cross-country journey."

"But why the box of magic?" asked Boscovitch, glancing up at the hat-rack.

"I never go away from home without it," answered Thorndyke. "One never knows what may turn up; the trouble of carrying it is small when set off against the comfort of having appliances at hand in an emergency."

Boscovitch continued to stare up at the little square case covered with Willesden canvas. Presently he remarked: "I often used to wonder what you had in it when you were down at Chelmsford in connection with that bank murder – what an amazing case that was, by the way, and didn't your methods of research astonish the police!" As he still looked up wistfully at the case, Thorndyke good-naturedly lifted it down and unlocked it. As a matter of fact he was rather proud of his 'portable laboratory', and certainly it was a triumph of condensation, for, small as it was – only a foot square by four inches deep – it contained a fairly complete outfit for a preliminary investigation.

"Wonderful!" exclaimed Boscovitch, when the case lay open before him, displaying its rows of little re-agent bottles, tiny test-tubes, diminutive spirit-lamp, dwarf microscope and assorted instruments on the same Lilliputian scale; "It's like a doll's house – everything looks as if it was seen through the wrong end of a telescope. But are these tiny things really efficient? That microscope now—"

"Perfectly efficient at low and moderate magnifications," said Thorndyke. "It looks like a toy, but it isn't one; the lenses are the best that can be had. Of course a full-sized instrument would be infinitely more convenient – but I shouldn't have it with me, and should have to make shift with a pocket-lens. And so with the rest of the under-sized appliances; they are the alternative to no appliances."

Boscovitch pored over the case and its contents, fingering the instruments delicately and asking questions innumerable about their uses; indeed, his curiosity was but half appeased when, half an hour later, the train began to slow down.

"By Jove!" he exclaimed, starting up and seizing his bag, "Here we are at the junction already. You change here too, don't you?"

"Yes," replied Thorndyke. "We take the branch train on to Warmington."

As we stepped out onto the platform, we became aware that something unusual was happening or had happened. All the passengers and most of the porters and supernumeraries were gathered at one end of the station, and all were looking intently into the darkness down the line.

"Anything wrong?" asked Mr. Boscovitch, addressing the station inspector.

"Yes, sir," the official replied; "a man has been run over by the goods train about a mile down the line. The station master has gone down with a stretcher to bring him in, and I expect that is his lantern that you see coming this way."

As we stood watching the dancing light grow momentarily brighter, flashing fitful reflections from the burnished rails, a man came out of the booking office and joined the group of onlookers. He attracted my attention, as I afterwards remembered, for two reasons: in the first place his round, jolly face was excessively pale and bore a strained and wild expression, and, in the second, though he stared into the darkness with eager curiosity he asked no questions.

The swinging lantern continued to approach, and then suddenly two men came into sight bearing a stretcher covered with a tarpaulin, through which the shape of a human figure was dimly discernible. They ascended the slope to the platform, and proceeded with their burden to the lamp-room, when the inquisitive gaze of the passengers was transferred to a porter who followed carrying a handbag and umbrella and to the station master who brought up the rear with his lantern.

As the porter passed, Mr. Boscovitch started forward with sudden excitement.

"Is that his umbrella?" he asked.

"Yes, sir," answered the porter, stopping and holding it out for the speaker's inspection.

"My God!" ejaculated Boscovitch; then, turning sharply to Thorndyke, he exclaimed: "That's Brodski's umbrella. I could swear to it. You remember Brodski?"

Thorndyke nodded, and Boscovitch, turning once more to the porter, said: "I identify that umbrella. It belongs to a gentleman named Brodski. If you look in his hat, you will see his name written in it. He always writes his name in his hat."

"We haven't found his hat yet," said the porter; "but here is the station master." He turned to his superior and announced: "This gentleman, sir, has identified the umbrella."

"Oh," said the station master, "you recognise the umbrella, sir, do you? Then perhaps you would step into the lamp-room and see if you can identify the body."

Mr. Boscovitch recoiled with a look of alarm. "Is it – is he – very much injured?" he asked nervously.

"Well, yes," was the reply. "You see, the engine and six of the trucks went over him before they could stop the train. Took his head clean off, in fact."

"Shocking! Shocking!" gasped Boscovitch. "I think – if you don't mind – I'd – I'd rather not. You don't think it necessary, doctor, do you?"

"Yes, I do," replied Thorndyke. "Early identification may be of the first importance."

"Then I suppose I must," said Boscovitch; and, with extreme reluctance, he followed the station master to the lamp-room, as the loud ringing of the bell announced the approach of the boat train. His inspection must have been of the briefest, for, in a few moments, he burst out, pale and awe-stricken, and rushed up to Thorndyke.

"It is!" he exclaimed breathlessly. "it's Brodski! Poor old Brodski! Horrible! Horrible! He was to have met me here and come on with me to Amsterdam."

"Had he any – merchandise about him?" Thorndyke asked; and, as he spoke, the stranger whom I had previously noticed edged up closer as if to catch the reply.

"He had some stones, no doubt," answered Boscovitch, "but I don't know what they were. His clerk will know, of course. By the way, doctor, could you watch the case for me? Just to be sure it was really an accident or – you know what. We were old friends, you know, fellow townsmen, too; we were both born in Warsaw. I'd like you to give an eye to the case."

"Very well," said Thorndyke. "I will satisfy myself that there is nothing more than appears, and let you have a report. Will that do?"

"Thank you," said Boscovitch. "It's excessively good of you, doctor. Ah, here comes the train. I hope it won't inconvenience you to stay and see to the matter."

"Not in the least," replied Thorndyke. "We are not due at Warmington until tomorrow afternoon, and I expect we can find out all that is necessary to know and still keep our appointment."

As Thorndyke spoke, the stranger, who had kept close to us with the evident purpose of hearing what was said, bestowed on him a very curious and attentive look; and it was only when the train had actually come to rest by the platform that he hurried away to find a compartment.

No sooner had the train left the station than Thorndyke sought out the station master and informed him of the instructions that he had received from Boscovitch. "Of course," he added, in conclusion, "we must not move in the matter until the police arrive. I suppose they have been informed?"

"Yes," replied the station master; "I sent a message at once to the Chief Constable, and I expect him or an inspector at any moment. In fact, I think I will slip out to the approach and see if he is coming." He evidently wished to have a word in private with the police officer before committing himself to any statement.

As the official departed, Thorndyke and I began to pace the now empty platform, and my friend, as was his wont, when entering on a new inquiry, meditatively reviewed the features of the problem.

"In a case of this kind," he remarked, "we have to decide on one of three possible explanations: accident, suicide or homicide; and our decision will be determined by inferences from three sets of facts: first, the general facts of the case; second, the special data obtained by examination of the body, and, third, the special data obtained by examining the spot on which the body was found. Now the only general facts at present in our possession are that the deceased was a diamond merchant making a journey for a specific purpose and probably having on his person property of small bulk and great value. These facts are somewhat against the hypothesis of suicide and somewhat favourable to that of homicide. Facts relevant to the question of accident would be the existence or otherwise of a level crossing, a road or path leading to the line, an enclosing fence with or without a gate, and any other facts rendering probable or otherwise the accidental presence of the deceased at the spot where the body was found. As we do not possess these facts, it is desirable that we extend our knowledge."

"Why not put a few discreet questions to the porter who brought in the bag and umbrella?" I suggested. "He is at this moment in earnest conversation with the ticket collector and would, no doubt, be glad of a new listener."

"An excellent suggestion, Jervis," answered Thorndyke. "Let us see what he has to tell us." We approached the porter and found him, as I had anticipated, bursting to unburden himself of the tragic story.

"The way the thing happened, sir, was this," he said, in answer to Thorndyke's question: "There's a sharpish bend in the road just at that place, and the goods train was just rounding the curve when the driver suddenly caught sight of something lying across the rails. As the engine turned, the headlights shone on it and then he saw it was a man. He shut off steam at once, blew his whistle, and put the brakes down hard, but, as you know, sir, a goods train takes some stopping; before they could bring her up, the engine and half a dozen trucks had gone over the poor beggar."

"Could the driver see how the man was lying?" Thorndyke asked.

"Yes, he could see him quite plain, because the headlights were full on him. He was lying on his face with his neck over the near rail on the downside. His head was in the four-foot and his body by the side of the track. It looked as if he had laid himself out a-purpose."

"Is there a level crossing thereabouts?" asked Thorndyke.

"No, sir. No crossing, no road, no path, no nothing," said the porter, ruthlessly sacrificing grammar to emphasis. "He must have come across the fields and climbed over the fence to get onto the permanent way. Deliberate suicide is what it looks like."

"How did you learn all this?" Thorndyke inquired.

"Why, the driver, you see, sir, when him and his mate had lifted the body off the track, went on to the next signal-box and sent in his report by telegram. The station master told me all about it as we walked down the line."

Thorndyke thanked the man for his information, and, as we strolled back towards the lamp-room, discussed the bearing of these new facts.

"Our friend is unquestionably right in one respect," he said; "this was not an accident. The man might, if he were near-sighted, deaf or stupid, have climbed over the fence and got knocked down by the train. But his position, lying across the rails, can only be explained by one of two hypotheses: either it was, as the porter says, deliberate suicide, or else the man was already dead or insensible. We must leave it at that until we have seen the body, that is, if the police will allow us to see it. But here comes the station master and an officer with him. Let us hear what they have to say."

The two officials had evidently made up their minds to decline any outside assistance. The divisional surgeon would make the necessary examination, and information could be obtained through the usual channels. The production of Thorndyke's card, however, somewhat altered the situation. The police inspector hummed and hawed irresolutely, with the card in his hand, but finally agreed to allow us to view the body, and we entered the lamp-room together, the station master leading the way to turn up the gas.

The stretcher stood on the floor by one wall, its grim burden still hidden by the tarpaulin, and the handbag and umbrella lay on a large box, together with the battered frame of a pair of spectacles from which the glasses had fallen out.

"Were these spectacles found by the body?" Thorndyke inquired.

"Yes," replied the station master. "They were close to the head and the glass was scattered about on the ballast."

Thorndyke made a note in his pocket-book, and then, as the inspector removed the tarpaulin, he glanced down on the corpse, lying limply on the stretcher and looking grotesquely horrible with its displaced head and distorted limbs. For fully a minute he remained silently stooping over the uncanny object, on which the inspector was now throwing the light of a large lantern; then he stood up and said quietly to me: "I think we can eliminate two out of the three hypotheses."

The inspector looked at him quickly, and was about to ask a question, when his attention was diverted by the travelling-case which Thorndyke had laid on a shelf and now opened to abstract a couple of pairs of dissecting forceps.

"We've no authority to make a *post mortem*, you know," said the inspector.

"No, of course not," said Thorndyke. "I am merely going to look into the mouth." With one pair of forceps he turned back the lip and, having scrutinised its inner surface, closely examined the teeth.

"May I trouble you for your lens, Jervis?" he said; and, as I handed him my doublet ready opened, the inspector brought the lantern close to the dead face and leaned forward eagerly. In his usual systematic fashion, Thorndyke slowly passed the lens along the whole range of sharp, uneven teeth, and then, bringing it back to the centre, examined with more minuteness the upper incisors. At length, very delicately, he picked out with his forceps some minute object from between two of the upper front teeth and held it in the focus of the lens. Anticipating his next move, I took a labelled microscope-slide from the case and handed it to him together with a dissecting needle, and, as he transferred the object to the slide and spread it out with the needle, I set up the little microscope on the shelf.

"A drop of Farrant and a cover-glass, please, Jervis," said Thorndyke.

I handed him the bottle, and, when he had let a drop of the mounting fluid fall gently on the object and put on the cover-slip, he placed the slide on the stage of the microscope and examined it attentively.

Happening to glance at the inspector, I observed on his countenance a faint grin, which he politely strove to suppress when he caught my eye.

"I was thinking, sir," he said apologetically, "that it's a bit off the track to be finding out what he had for dinner. He didn't die of unwholesome feeding."

Thorndyke looked up with a smile. "It doesn't do, inspector, to assume that anything is off the track in an inquiry of this kind. Every fact must have some significance, you know."

"I don't see any significance in the diet of a man who has had his head cut off," the inspector rejoined defiantly.

"Don't you?" said Thorndyke. "Is there no interest attaching to the last meal of a man who has met a violent death? These crumbs, for instance, that are scattered over the dead man's waistcoat. Can we learn nothing from them?"

"I don't see what you can learn," was the dogged rejoinder.

Thorndyke picked off the crumbs, one by one, with his forceps, and having deposited them on a slide, inspected them, first with the lens and then through the microscope.

"I learn," said he, "that shortly before his death, the deceased partook of some kind of whole-meal biscuits, apparently composed partly of oatmeal."

"I call that nothing," said the inspector. "The question that we have got to settle is not what refreshments had the deceased been taking, but what was the cause of his death: did he commit suicide? Was he killed by accident? Or was there any foul play?"

"I beg your pardon," said Thorndyke, "the questions that remain to be settled are, who killed the deceased and with what motive? The others are already answered as far as I am concerned."

The inspector stared in sheer amazement not unmixed with incredulity.

"You haven't been long coming to a conclusion, sir," he said.

"No, it was a pretty obvious case of murder," said Thorndyke. "As to the motive, the deceased was a diamond merchant and is believed to have had a quantity of stones about his person. I should suggest that you search the body."

The inspector gave vent to an exclamation of disgust. "I see," he said. "It was just a guess on your part. The dead man was a diamond merchant and had valuable property about him; therefore he was murdered." He drew himself up, and, regarding Thorndyke with stern reproach, added: "But you must understand, sir, that this is a judicial inquiry, not a prize competition in a penny paper. And, as to searching the body, why, that is what I principally came for." He ostentatiously turned his back on us and proceeded systematically to turn out the dead man's pockets, laying the articles, as he removed them, on the box by the side of the handbag and umbrella.

While he was thus occupied, Thorndyke looked over the body generally, paying special attention to the soles of the boots, which, to the inspector's undissembled amusement, he very thoroughly examined with the lens.

"I should have thought, sir, that his feet were large enough to be seen with the naked eye," was his comment; "but perhaps," he added, with a sly glance at the station master, "you're a little near-sighted."

Thorndyke chuckled good-humouredly, and, while the officer continued his search, he looked over the articles that had already been laid on the box. The purse and pocket-book he naturally left for the inspector to open, but the reading glasses, pocket knife and card-case and other small pocket articles were subjected to a searching scrutiny. The inspector watched him out of the corner of his eye with furtive amusement; saw him hold up the glasses to the light to estimate their refractive power, peer into the tobacco pouch, open the cigarette book and examine the watermark of the paper, and even inspect the contents of the silver matchbox.

"What might you have expected to find in his tobacco pouch?" the officer asked, laying down a bunch of keys from the dead man's pocket.

"Tobacco," Thorndyke replied stolidly; "but I did not expect to find fine-cut Latakia. I don't remember ever having seen pure Latakia smoked in cigarettes."

"You do take an interest in things, sir," said the inspector, with a side glance at the stolid station master.

"I do," Thorndyke agreed; "and I note that there are no diamonds among this collection."

"No, and we don't know that he had any about him; but there's a gold watch and chain, a diamond scarf-pin, and a purse containing" – he opened it and tipped out its contents into his hand – "twelve pounds in gold. That doesn't look much like robbery, does it? What do you say to the murder theory now?"

"My opinion is unchanged," said Thorndyke, "and I should like to examine the spot where the body was found. Has the engine been inspected?" he added, addressing the station master.

"I telegraphed to Bradfield to have it examined," the official answered. "The report has probably come in by now. I'd better see before we start down the line."

We emerged from the lamp-room and, at the door, found the station inspector waiting with a telegram. He handed it to the station master, who read it aloud.

"The engine has been carefully examined by me. I find small smear of blood on near leading wheel and smaller one on next wheel following. No other marks." He glanced questioningly at Thorndyke, who nodded and remarked: "It will be interesting to see if the line tells the same tale."

The station master looked puzzled and was apparently about to ask for an explanation; but the inspector, who had carefully pocketed the dead man's property, was impatient to start and, accordingly, when Thorndyke had repacked his case and had, at his own request, been furnished with a lantern, we set off down the permanent way, Thorndyke carrying the light and I the indispensable green case.

"I am a little in the dark about this affair," I said, when we had allowed the two officials to draw ahead out of earshot; "you came to a conclusion remarkably quickly. What was it that so immediately determined the opinion of murder as against suicide?"

"It was a small matter but very conclusive," replied Thorndyke. "You noticed a small scalp wound above the left temple? It was a glancing wound, and might easily have been made by the engine. But – the wound had bled; and it had bled for an appreciable time. There were two streams of blood from it, and in both the blood was firmly clotted and partially dried. But the man had been decapitated; and this wound, if inflicted by the engine, must have been made after the decapitation, since it was on the side most distant from the engine as it approached. Now, a decapitated head does not bleed. Therefore, this wound was inflicted before the decapitation.

"But not only had the wound bled: the blood had trickled down in two streams at right angles to one another. First, in the order of time as shown by the appearance of the stream, it had trickled down the side of the face and dropped on the collar. The second stream ran from the wound to the back of the head. Now, you know, Jervis, there are no exceptions to the law of gravity. If the blood ran down the face towards the chin, the face must have been upright at the time; and if the blood trickled from the front to the back of the head, the head must have been horizontal and face upwards. But the man when he was seen by the engine-driver, was lying *face downwards*. The only possible inference is that when the wound was inflicted, the man was in the upright position – standing or sitting; and that subsequently, and while he was still alive, he lay on his back for a sufficiently long time for the blood to have trickled to the back of his head."

"I see. I was a duffer not to have reasoned this out for myself," I remarked contritely.

"Quick observation and rapid inference come by practice," replied Thorndyke. "What did you notice about the face?"

"I thought there was a strong suggestion of asphyxia."

"Undoubtedly," said Thorndyke. "It was the face of a suffocated man. You must have noticed, too, that the tongue was very distinctly swollen and that on the inside of the upper lip were deep indentations made by the teeth, as well as one or two slight wounds, obviously caused by heavy pressure on the mouth. And now observe how completely these facts and inferences agree with those from the scalp wound. If we knew that the deceased had received a blow on the head, had struggled with his assailant and been finally borne down and suffocated, we should look for precisely those signs which we have found."

"By the way, what was it that you found wedged between the teeth? I did not get a chance to look through the microscope."

"Ah!" said Thorndyke, "there we not only get confirmation, but we carry our inferences a stage further. The object was a little tuft of some textile fabric. Under the microscope I found it to consist of several different fibres, differently dyed. The bulk of it consisted of wool fibres dyed crimson, but there were also cotton fibres dyed blue and a few which looked like jute, dyed yellow. It was obviously a parti-coloured fabric and might have been part of a woman's dress, though the presence of the jute is much more suggestive of a curtain or rug of inferior quality."

"And its importance?"

"Is that, if it is not part of an article of clothing, then it must have come from an article of furniture, and furniture suggests a habitation."

"That doesn't seem very conclusive," I objected.

"It is not; but it is valuable corroboration."

"Of what?"

"Of the suggestion offered by the soles of the dead man's boots. I examined them most minutely and could find no trace of sand, gravel or earth, in spite of the fact that he must have crossed fields and rough land to reach the place where he was found. What I did find was fine tobacco ash, a charred mark as if a cigar or cigarette had been trodden on, several crumbs of biscuit, and, on a projecting brad, some coloured fibres, apparently from a carpet. The manifest suggestion is that the man was killed in a house with a carpeted floor, and carried from thence to the railway."

I was silent for some moments. Well as I knew Thorndyke, I was completely taken by surprise; a sensation, indeed, that I experienced anew every time that I accompanied him on one of his investigations. His marvellous power of co-ordinating apparently insignificant facts, of arranging them into an ordered sequence and making them tell a coherent story, was a phenomenon that I never got used to; every exhibition of it astonished me afresh.

"If your inferences are correct," I said, "the problem is practically solved. There must be abundant traces inside the house. The only question is, which house is it?"

"Quite so," replied Thorndyke; "that is the question, and a very difficult question it is. A glance at that interior would doubtless clear up the whole mystery. But how are we to get that glance? We cannot enter houses speculatively to see if they present traces of a murder. At present, our clue breaks off abruptly. The other end of it is in some unknown house, and, if we cannot join up the two ends, our problem remains unsolved. For the question is, you remember, Who killed Oscar Brodski?"

"Then what do you propose to do?" I asked.

"The next stage of the inquiry is to connect some particular house with this crime. To that end, I can only gather up all available facts and consider each in all its possible bearings. If I cannot establish any such connection, then the inquiry will have failed and we shall have to make a fresh start – say, at Amsterdam, if it turns out that Brodski really had diamonds on his person, as I have no doubt he had."

Here our conversation was interrupted by our arrival at the spot where the body had been found. The station master had halted, and he and the inspector were now examining the near rail by the light of their lanterns.

"There's remarkably little blood about," said the former. "I've seen a good many accidents of this kind and there has always been a lot of blood, both on the engine and on the road. It's very curious."

Thorndyke glanced at the rail with but slight attention: that question had ceased to interest him. But the light of his lantern flashed onto the ground at the side of the track – a loose, gravelly soil mixed with fragments of chalk – and from thence to the soles of the inspector's boots, which were displayed as he knelt by the rail.

"You observe, Jervis?" he said in a low voice, and I nodded. The inspector's boot-soles were covered with adherent particles of gravel and conspicuously marked by the chalk on which he had trodden.

"You haven't found the hat, I suppose?" Thorndyke asked, stooping to pick up a short piece of string that lay on the ground at the side of the track.

"No," replied the inspector, "but it can't be far off. You seem to have found another clue, sir," he added, with a grin, glancing at the piece of string.

"Who knows," said Thorndyke. "A short end of white twine with a green strand in it. It may tell us something later. At any rate we'll keep it," and, taking from his pocket a small tin box containing, among other things, a number of seed envelopes, he slipped the string into one of the latter and scribbled a note in pencil on the outside. The inspector watched his proceedings with an indulgent smile, and then returned to his examination of the track, in which Thorndyke now joined.

"I suppose the poor chap was near-sighted," the officer remarked, indicating the remains of the shattered spectacles; "that might account for his having strayed onto the line."

"Possibly," said Thorndyke. He had already noticed the fragments scattered over a sleeper and the adjacent ballast, and now once more produced his 'collecting-box', from which he took another seed envelope. "Would you hand me a pair of forceps, Jervis," he said; "and perhaps you wouldn't mind taking a pair yourself and helping me to gather up these fragments."

As I complied, the inspector looked up curiously.

"There isn't any doubt that these spectacles belonged to the deceased, is there?" he asked. "He certainly wore spectacles, for I saw the mark on his nose."

"Still, there is no harm in verifying the fact," said Thorndyke, and he added to me in a lower tone, "Pick up every particle you can find, Jervis. It may be most important."

"I don't quite see how," I said, groping amongst the shingle by the light of the lantern in search of the tiny splinters of glass.

"Don't you?" returned Thorndyke. "Well, look at these fragments; some of them are a fair size, but many of these on the sleeper are mere grains. And consider their number. Obviously, the condition of the glass does not agree with the circumstances in which we find it. These are thick concave spectacle lenses broken into a great number of minute fragments. Now how were they broken? Not merely by falling, evidently: such a lens, when it is dropped, breaks into a small number of large pieces. Nor were they broken by the wheel passing over them, for they would then have been reduced to fine powder, and that powder would have been visible on the rail, which it is not. The spectacle-frames, you may remember, presented the same incongruity: they were battered and damaged more than they would have been by falling, but not nearly so much as they would have been if the wheel had passed over them."

"What do you suggest, then?" I asked.

"The appearances suggest that the spectacles had been trodden on. But, if the body was carried here the probability is that the spectacles were carried here too, and that they were then already broken; for it is more likely that they were trodden on during the struggle than that the murderer trod on them after bringing them here. Hence the importance of picking up every fragment."

"But why?" I inquired, rather foolishly, I must admit.

"Because, if, when we have picked up every fragment that we can find, there still remains missing a larger portion of the lenses than we could reasonably expect, that would tend to support our hypothesis and we might find the missing remainder elsewhere. If, on the other hand, we find as much of the lenses as we could expect to find, we must conclude that they were broken on this spot."

While we were conducting our search, the two officials were circling around with their lanterns in quest of the missing hat; and, when we had at length picked up the last fragment, and a careful search, even aided by a lens, failed to reveal any other, we could see their lanterns moving, like will-o'-the-wisps, some distance down the line.

"We may as well see what we have got before our friends come back," said Thorndyke, glancing at the twinkling lights. "Lay the case down on the grass by the fence; it will serve for a table."

I did so, and Thorndyke, taking a letter from his pocket, opened it, spread it out flat on the case, securing it with a couple of heavy stones, although the night was quite calm. Then he tipped the contents of the seed envelope out on the paper, and carefully spreading out the pieces of glass, looked at them for some moments in silence. And, as he looked, there stole over his face a very curious expression; with sudden eagerness he began picking out the large fragments and laying them on two visiting-cards which he had taken from his card-case. Rapidly and with wonderful deftness he fitted the pieces together, and, as the reconstituted lenses began gradually to take shape on their cards I looked on with growing excitement, for something in my colleague's manner told me that we were on the verge of a discovery.

At length the two ovals of glass lay on their respective cards, complete save for one or two small gaps; and the little heap that remained consisted of fragments so minute as to render further reconstruction impossible. Then Thorndyke leaned back and laughed softly.

"This is certainly an unlooked-for result," said he.

"What is?" I asked.

"Don't you see, my dear fellow? *There's too much glass.* We have almost completely built up the broken lenses, and the fragments that are left over are considerably more than are required to fill up the gaps."

I looked at the little heap of small fragments and saw at once that it was as he had said. There was a surplus of small pieces.

"This is very extraordinary," I said. "What do you think can be the explanation?"

"The fragments will probably tell us," he replied, "if we ask them intelligently."

He lifted the paper and the two cards carefully onto the ground, and, opening the case, took out the little microscope, to which he fitted the lowest-power objective and eye-piece – having a combined magnification of only ten diameters. Then he transferred the minute fragments of glass to a slide, and, having arranged the lantern as a microscope-lamp, commenced his examination.

"Ha!" he exclaimed presently. "The plot thickens. There is too much glass and yet too little; that is to say, there are only one or two fragments here that belong to the spectacles; not nearly enough to complete the building up of the lenses. The remainder consists of a soft, uneven, moulded glass, easily distinguished from the clear, hard optical glass. These foreign fragments are all curved, as if they had formed part of a cylinder, and are, I should say, portions of a wine glass or tumbler." He moved the slide once or twice, and then continued: "We are in luck, Jervis. Here is a fragment with two little diverging lines etched on it, evidently the points of an eight-rayed star – and here is another with three points – the ends of three rays. This enables us to reconstruct the vessel perfectly. It was a clear, thin glass – probably a tumbler – decorated with scattered stars; I dare say you know the pattern. Sometimes there is an ornamented band in addition, but generally the stars form the only decoration. Have a look at the specimen."

I had just applied my eye to the microscope when the station master and the inspector came up. Our appearance, seated on the ground with the microscope between us, was too much for the police officer's gravity, and he laughed long and joyously.

"You must excuse me, gentlemen," he said apologetically, "but really, you know, to an old hand, like myself, it does look a little – well – you understand – I dare say a microscope is a very interesting and amusing thing, but it doesn't get you much forwarder in a case like this, does it?"

"Perhaps not," replied Thorndyke. "By the way, where did you find the hat, after all?"

"We haven't found it," the inspector replied, a little sheepishly.

"Then we must help you to continue the search," said Thorndyke. "If you will wait a few moments, we will come with you." He poured a few drops of xylol balsam on the cards to fix the reconstituted lenses to their supports and then, packing them and the microscope in the case, announced that he was ready to start.

"Is there any village or hamlet near?" he asked the station master.

"None nearer than Corfield. That is about half a mile from here."

"And where is the nearest road?"

"There is a half-made road that runs past a house about three hundred yards from here. It belonged to a building estate that was never built. There is a footpath from it to the station."

"Are there any other houses near?"

"No. That is the only house for half-a-mile round, and there is no other road near here."

"Then the probability is that Brodski approached the railway from that direction, as he was found on that side of the permanent way."

The inspector agreeing with this view, we all set off slowly towards the house, piloted by the station master and searching the ground as we went. The wasteland over which we passed was covered with patches of docks and nettles, through each of which the inspector kicked his way, searching with feet and lantern for the missing hat. A walk of three hundred yards brought us to a low wall enclosing a garden, beyond which we could see a small house; and here we halted while the inspector waded into a large bed of nettles beside the wall and kicked vigorously. Suddenly there came a clinking sound mingled with objurgations, and the inspector hopped out holding one foot and soliloquising profanely.

"I wonder what sort of a fool put a thing like that into a bed of nettles!" he exclaimed, stroking the injured foot. Thorndyke picked the object up and held it in the light of the lantern, displaying a piece of three-quarter inch rolled iron bar about a foot long. "It doesn't seem to have been there very long," he observed, examining it closely, "there is hardly any rust on it."

"It has been there long enough for me," growled the inspector, "and I'd like to bang it on the head of the blighter that put it there."

Callously indifferent to the inspector's sufferings, Thorndyke continued calmly to examine the bar. At length, resting his lantern on the wall, he produced his pocket-lens, with which he resumed his investigation, a proceeding that so exasperated the inspector that that afflicted official limped off in dudgeon, followed by the station master, and we heard him, presently, rapping at the front door of the house.

"Give me a slide, Jervis, with a drop of Farrant on it," said Thorndyke. "There are some fibres sticking to this bar."

I prepared the slide, and, having handed it to him together with a cover-glass, a pair of forceps and a needle, set up the microscope on the wall.

"I'm sorry for the inspector," Thorndyke remarked, with his eye applied to the little instrument, "but that was a lucky kick for us. Just take a look at the specimen."

I did so, and, having moved the slide about until I had seen the whole of the object, I gave my opinion. "Red wool fibres, blue cotton fibres and some yellow vegetable fibres that look like jute."

"Yes," said Thorndyke; "the same combination of fibres as that which we found on the dead man's teeth and probably from the same source. This bar has probably been wiped on that very curtain or rug with which poor Brodski was stifled. We will place it on the wall for future reference, and meanwhile, by hook or by crook, we must get into that house. This is much too plain a hint to be disregarded."

Hastily repacking the case, we hurried to the front of the house, where we found the two officials looking rather vaguely up the unmade road.

"There's a light in the house," said the inspector, "but there's no one at home. I have knocked a dozen times and got no answer. And I don't see what we are hanging about here for at all. The hat is probably close to where the body was found, and we shall find it in the morning."

Thorndyke made no reply, but, entering the garden, stepped up the path, and having knocked gently at the door, stooped and listened attentively at the keyhole.

"I tell you there's no one in the house, sir," said the inspector irritably; and, as Thorndyke continued to listen, he walked away, muttering angrily. As soon as he was gone, Thorndyke flashed his lantern over the door, the threshold, the path and the small flowerbeds; and, from one of the latter, I presently saw him stoop and pick something up.

"Here is a highly instructive object, Jervis," he said, coming out to the gate, and displaying a cigarette of which only half an inch had been smoked.

"How instructive?" I asked. "What do you learn from it?"

"Many things," he replied. "It has been lit and thrown away unsmoked; that indicates a sudden change of purpose. It was thrown away at the entrance to the house, almost certainly by someone entering it. That person was probably a stranger, or he would have taken it in with him. But he had not expected to enter the house, or he would not have lit it. These are the general suggestions; now as to the particular ones. The paper of the cigarette is of the kind known as the 'Zig-Zag' brand; the very conspicuous watermark is quite easy to see. Now Brodski's cigarette book was a 'Zig-Zag' book – so called from the way in which the papers pull out. But let us see what the tobacco is like." With a pin from his coat, he hooked out from the unburned end a wisp of dark, dirty brown tobacco, which he held out for my inspection.

"Fine-cut Latakia," I pronounced, without hesitation.

"Very well," said Thorndyke. "Here is a cigarette made of an unusual tobacco similar to that in Brodski's pouch and wrapped in an unusual paper similar to those in Brodski's cigarette-book. With due regard to the fourth rule of the syllogism, I suggest that this cigarette was made by Oscar Brodski. But, nevertheless, we will look for corroborative detail."

"What is that?" I asked.

"You may have noticed that Brodski's matchbox contained round wooden vestas – which are also rather unusual. As he must have lighted the cigarette within a few steps of the gate, we ought to be able to find the match with which he lighted it. Let us try up the road in the direction from which he would probably have approached."

We walked very slowly up the road, searching the ground with the lantern, and we had hardly gone a dozen paces when I espied a match lying on the rough path and eagerly picked it up. It was a round wooden vesta.

Thorndyke examined it with interest and having deposited it, with the cigarette, in his 'collecting-box', turned to retrace his steps. "There is now, Jervis, no reasonable doubt that Brodski was murdered in that house. We have succeeded in connecting that house with the crime, and now we have got to force an entrance and join up the other clues." We walked quickly back to the rear of the premises, where we found the inspector conversing disconsolately with the station master.

"I think, sir," said the former, "we had better go back now; in fact, I don't see what we came here for, but – here! I say, sir, you mustn't do that!" For Thorndyke, without a word of warning, had sprung up lightly and thrown one of his long legs over the wall.

"I can't allow you to enter private premises, sir," continued the inspector; but Thorndyke quietly dropped down on the inside and turned to face the officer over the wall.

"Now, listen to me, inspector," said he. "I have good reasons for believing that the dead man, Brodski, has been in this house, in fact, I am prepared to swear an information to that effect. But time is precious; we must follow the scent while it is hot. And I am not proposing to break into the house off-hand. I merely wish to examine the dustbin."

"The dust-bin!" gasped the inspector. "Well, you really are a most extraordinary gentleman! What do you expect to find in the dustbin?"

"I am looking for a broken tumbler or wine glass. It is a thin glass vessel decorated with a pattern of small, eight-pointed stars. It may be in the dustbin or it may be inside the house."

The inspector hesitated, but Thorndyke's confident manner had evidently impressed him.

"We can soon see what is in the dustbin," he said, "though what in creation a broken tumbler has to do with the case is more than I can understand. However, here goes." He sprang up onto the wall, and, as he dropped down into the garden, the station master and I followed.

Thorndyke lingered a few moments by the gate examining the ground, while the two officials hurried up the path. Finding nothing of interest, however, he walked towards the house, looking keenly about him as he went; but we were hardly halfway up the path when we heard the voice of the inspector calling excitedly.

"Here you are, sir, this way," he sang out, and, as we hurried forward, we suddenly came on the two officials standing over a small rubbish heap and looking the picture of astonishment. The glare of their lanterns illuminated the heap, and showed us the scattered fragments of a thin glass, star-pattern tumbler.

"I can't imagine how you guessed it was here, sir," said the inspector, with a new-born respect in his tone, "nor what you're going to do with it now you have found it."

"It is merely another link in the chain of evidence," said Thorndyke, taking a pair of forceps from the case and stooping over the heap. "Perhaps we shall find something else." He picked up several small fragments of glass, looked at them closely and dropped them again. Suddenly his eye caught a small splinter at the base of the heap. Seizing it with the forceps, he held it close to his eye in the strong lamplight, and, taking out his lens, examined it with minute attention. "Yes," he said at length, "this is what I was looking for. Let me have those two cards, Jervis."

I produced the two visiting-cards with the reconstructed lenses stuck to them, and, laying them on the lid of the case, threw the light of the lantern on them. Thorndyke looked at them intently for some time, and from them to the fragment that he held. Then, turning to the inspector, he said: "You saw me pick up this splinter of glass?"

"Yes, sir," replied the officer.

"And you saw where we found these spectacle-glasses and know whose they were?"

"Yes, sir. They are the dead man's spectacles, and you found them where the body had been."

"Very well," said Thorndyke; "now observe"; and, as the two officials craned forward with parted lips, he laid the little splinter in a gap in one of the lenses and then gave it a gentle push forward, when it occupied the gap perfectly, joining edge to edge with the adjacent fragments and rendering that portion of the lens complete.

"My God!" exclaimed the inspector. "How on earth did you know?"

"I must explain that later," said Thorndyke. "Meanwhile we had better have a look inside the house. I expect to find there a cigarette – or possibly a cigar – which has been trodden on, some wholemeal biscuits, possibly a wooden vesta, and perhaps even the missing hat."

At the mention of the hat, the inspector stepped eagerly to the back door, but, finding it bolted, he tried the window. This also was securely fastened and, on Thorndyke's advice, we went round to the front door.

"This door is locked too," said the inspector. "I'm afraid we shall have to break in. It's a nuisance, though."

"Have a look at the window," suggested Thorndyke.

The officer did so, struggling vainly to undo the patent catch with his pocket knife.

"It's no-go," he said, coming back to the door. "We shall have to—" He broke off with an astonished stare, for the door stood open and Thorndyke was putting something in his pocket.

"Your friend doesn't waste much time – even in picking a lock," he remarked to me, as we followed Thorndyke into the house; but his reflections were soon merged in a new surprise. Thorndyke had preceded us into a small sitting room dimly lighted by a hanging lamp turned down low.

As we entered he turned up the light and glanced about the room. A whisky bottle was on the table, with a siphon, a tumbler and a biscuit box. Pointing to the latter, Thorndyke said to the inspector: "See what is in that box."

The inspector raised the lid and peeped in, the station master peered over his shoulder, and then both stared at Thorndyke.

"How in the name of goodness did you know that there were wholemeal biscuits in the house, sir?" exclaimed the station master.

"You'd be disappointed if I told you," replied Thorndyke. "But look at this." He pointed to the hearth, where lay a flattened, half-smoked cigarette and a round wooden vesta. The inspector gazed at these objects in silent wonder, while, as to the station master, he continued to stare at Thorndyke with what I can only describe as superstitious awe.

"You have the dead man's property with you, I believe?" said my colleague.

"Yes," replied the inspector; "I put the things in my pocket for safety."

"Then," said Thorndyke, picking up the flattened cigarette, "let us have a look at his tobacco pouch."

As the officer produced and opened the pouch, Thorndyke neatly cut open the cigarette with his sharp pocket knife. "Now," said he, "what kind of tobacco is in the pouch?"

The inspector took out a pinch, looked at it and smelt it distastefully. "It's one of those stinking tobaccos," he said, "that they put in mixtures – Latakia, I think."

"And what is this?" asked Thorndyke, pointing to the open cigarette.

"Same stuff, undoubtedly," replied the inspector.

"And now let us see his cigarette papers," said Thorndyke.

The little book, or rather packet – for it consisted of separated papers – was produced from the officer's pocket and a sample paper abstracted. Thorndyke laid the half-burnt paper beside it, and the inspector, having examined the two, held them up to the light.

"There isn't much chance of mistaking that 'Zig-Zag' watermark," he said. "This cigarette was made by the deceased; there can't be the shadow of a doubt."

"One more point," said Thorndyke, laying the burnt wooden vesta on the table. "You have his matchbox?"

The inspector brought forth the little silver casket, opened it and compared the wooden vestas that it contained with the burnt end. Then he shut the box with a snap.

"You've proved it up to the hilt," said he. "If we could only find the hat, we should have a complete case."

"I'm not sure that we haven't found the hat," said Thorndyke. "You notice that something besides coal has been burned in the grate."

The inspector ran eagerly to the fireplace and began with feverish hands, to pick out the remains of the extinct fire. "The cinders are still warm," he said, "and they are certainly not all coal cinders. There has been wood burned here on top of the coal, and these little black lumps are neither coal nor wood. They may quite possibly be the remains of a burnt hat, but, lord! Who can tell? You can put together the pieces of broken spectacle-glasses, but you can't build up a hat out of a few cinders." He held out a handful of little, black, spongy cinders and looked ruefully at Thorndyke, who took them from him and laid them out on a sheet of paper.

"We can't reconstitute the hat, certainly," my friend agreed, "but we may be able to ascertain the origin of these remains. They may not be cinders of a hat, after all." He lit a wax match and, taking up one of the charred fragments, applied the flame to it. The cindery mass fused at once with a crackling, seething sound, emitting a dense smoke, and instantly the air became charged with a pungent, resinous odour mingled with the smell of burning animal matter.

"Smells like varnish," the station master remarked.

"Yes. Shellac," said Thorndyke; "so the first test gives a positive result. The next test will take more time."

He opened the green case and took from it a little flask, fitted for Marsh's arsenic test, with a safety funnel and escape tube, a small folding tripod, a spirit lamp and a disc of asbestos to serve as a sand-bath. Dropping into the flask several of the cindery masses, selected after careful inspection, he filled it up with alcohol and placed it on the disc, which he rested on the tripod. Then he lighted the spirit lamp underneath and sat down to wait for the alcohol to boil.

"There is one little point that we may as well settle," he said presently, as the bubbles began to rise in the flask. "Give me a slide with a drop of Farrant on it, Jervis."

I prepared the slide while Thorndyke, with a pair of forceps, picked out a tiny wisp from the tablecloth. "I fancy we have seen this fabric before," he remarked, as he laid the little pinch of fluff in the mounting fluid and slipped the slide onto the stage of the microscope. "Yes," he continued, looking into the eye-piece, "here are our old acquaintances, the red wool fibres, the blue cotton and the yellow jute. We must label this at once or we may confuse it with the other specimens."

"Have you any idea how the deceased met his death?" the inspector asked.

"Yes," replied Thorndyke. "I take it that the murderer enticed him into this room and gave him some refreshments. The murderer sat in the chair in which you are sitting, Brodski sat in that small armchair. Then I imagine the murderer attacked him with that iron bar that you found among the nettles, failed to kill him at the first stroke, struggled with him and finally suffocated him with the tablecloth. By the way, there is just one more point. You recognise this piece of string?" He took from his 'collecting-box' the little end of twine that had been picked up by the line. The inspector nodded. "Look behind you, you will see where it came from."

The officer turned sharply and his eye lighted on a string-box on the mantelpiece. He lifted it down, and Thorndyke drew out from it a length of white twine with one green strand, which he compared with the piece in his hand. "The green strand in it makes the identification fairly certain," he said. "Of course the string was used to secure the umbrella and handbag. He could not have carried them in his hand, encumbered as he was with the corpse. But I expect our other specimen is ready now." He lifted the flask off the tripod, and, giving it a vigorous shake, examined the contents through his lens. The alcohol had now become dark brown in colour, and was noticeably thicker and more syrupy in consistence.

"I think we have enough here for a rough test," said he, selecting a pipette and a slide from the case. He dipped the former into the flask and, having sucked up a few drops of the alcohol from the bottom, held the pipette over the slide on which he allowed the contained fluid to drop.

Laying a cover-glass on the little pool of alcohol, he put the slide on the microscope stage and examined it attentively, while we watched him in expectant silence.

At length he looked up, and, addressing the inspector, asked: "Do you know what felt hats are made of?"

"I can't say that I do, sir," replied the officer.

"Well, the better quality hats are made of rabbits' and hares' wool – the soft under-fur, you know – cemented together with shellac. Now there is very little doubt that these cinders contain shellac, and with the microscope I find a number of small hairs of a rabbit. I have, therefore, little hesitation in saying that these cinders are the remains of a hard felt hat; and, as the hairs do not appear to be dyed, I should say it was a grey hat."

At this moment our conclave was interrupted by hurried footsteps on the garden path and, as we turned with one accord, an elderly woman burst into the room.

She stood for a moment in mute astonishment, and then, looking from one to the other, demanded: "Who are you? And what are you doing here?"

The inspector rose. "I am a police officer, madam," said he. "I can't give you any further information just now, but, if you will excuse me asking, who are you?"

"I am Mr. Hickler's housekeeper," she replied.

"And Mr. Hickler; are you expecting him home shortly?"

"No, I am not," was the curt reply. "Mr. Hickler is away from home just now. He left this evening by the boat train."

"For Amsterdam?" asked Thorndyke.

"I believe so, though I don't see what business it is of yours," the housekeeper answered.

"I thought he might, perhaps, be a diamond broker or merchant," said Thorndyke. "A good many of them travel by that train."

"So he is," said the woman, "at least, he has something to do with diamonds."

"Ah. Well, we must be going, Jervis," said Thorndyke, "we have finished here, and we have to find an hotel or inn. Can I have a word with you, inspector?"

The officer, now entirely humble and reverent, followed us out into the garden to receive Thorndyke's parting advice.

"You had better take possession of the house at once, and get rid of the housekeeper. Nothing must be removed. Preserve those cinders and see that the rubbish heap is not disturbed, and, above all, don't have the room swept. An officer will be sent to relieve you."

With a friendly "goodnight" we went on our way, guided by the station master; and here our connection with the case came to an end. Hickler (whose Christian name turned out to be Silas) was, it is true, arrested as he stepped ashore from the steamer, and a packet of diamonds, subsequently identified as the property of Oscar Brodski, found upon his person. But he was never brought to trial, for on the return voyage he contrived to elude his guards for an instant as the ship was approaching the English coast, and it was not until three days later, when a handcuffed body was cast up on the lonely shore by Orfordness, that the authorities knew the fate of Silas Hickler.

* * *

"An appropriate and dramatic end to a singular and yet typical case," said Thorndyke, as he put down the newspaper. "I hope it has enlarged your knowledge, Jervis, and enabled you to form one or two useful corollaries."

"I prefer to hear you sing the medico-legal doxology," I answered, turning upon him like the proverbial worm and grinning derisively (which the worm does not).

"I know you do," he retorted, with mock gravity, "and I lament your lack of mental initiative. However, the points that this case illustrates are these: First, the danger of delay; the vital importance of instant action before that frail and fleeting thing that we call a clue has time to evaporate. A delay of a few hours would have left us with hardly a single datum. Second, the necessity of pursuing the most trivial clue to an absolute finish, as illustrated by the spectacles. Third, the urgent need of a trained scientist to aid the police; and, last," he concluded, with a smile, "we learn never to go abroad without the invaluable green case."

The Mystery of the Fatal Cipher

Jacques Futrelle

Chapter I

FOR THE THIRD TIME Professor Augustus S.F.X. Van Dusen – so-called The Thinking Machine – read the letter. It was spread out in front of him on the table, and his blue eyes were narrowed to mere slits as he studied it through his heavy eyeglasses. The young woman who had placed the letter in his hands, Miss Elizabeth Devan, sat waiting patiently on the sofa in the little reception room of The Thinking Machine's house. Her blue eyes were opened wide and she stared as if fascinated at this man who had become so potent a factor in the solution of intangible mysteries.

Here is the letter:

> *To those Concerned:*
> *Tired of it all I seek the end, and am content. Ambition now is dead; the grave yawns greedily at my feet, and with the labor of my own hands lost I greet death of my own will, by my own act. To my son I leave all, and you who maligned me, you who discouraged me, you may read this and know I punish you thus. It's for him, my son, to forgive. I dared in life and dare dead your everlasting anger, not alone that you didn't speak but that you cherished secret, and my ears are locked forever against you. My vault is my resting place. On the brightest and dearest page of life I wrote (7) my love for him. Family ties, binding as the Bible itself, bade me give all to my son.*
> *Goodbye. I die.*
> *Pomeroy Stockton*

"Under just what circumstances did this letter come into your possession, Miss Devan?" The Thinking Machine asked. "Tell me the full story; omit nothing."

The scientist sank back into his chair with his enormous yellow head pillowed comfortably against the cushion and his long, steady fingers pressed tip-to-tip. He didn't even look at his pretty visitor. She had come to ask for information; he was willing to give it, because it offered another of those abstract problems which he always found interesting. In his own field – the sciences – his fame was worldwide. This concentration of a brain which had achieved so much on more material things was perhaps a sort of relaxation.

Miss Devan had a soft, soothing voice, and as she talked it was broken at times by what seemed to be a sob. Her face was flushed a little, and she emphasized her points by a quick clasping and unclasping of her daintily gloved hands.

"My father, or rather my adopted father, Pomeroy Stockton, was an inventor," she began. "We lived in a great, old-fashioned house in Dorchester. We have lived there since I was a child. When

I was only five or six years old, I was left an orphan and was adopted by Mr. Stockton, then a man of forty years. I am now twenty-three. I was raised and cared for by Mr. Stockton, who always treated me as a daughter. His death, therefore, was a great blow to me.

"Mr. Stockton was a widower with only one child of his own, a son, John Stockton, who is now about thirty-one years old. He is a man of irreproachable character, and has always, since I first knew him, been religiously inclined. He is the junior partner in a great commercial company, Dutton & Stockton, leather men. I suppose he has an immense fortune, for he gives largely to charity, and is, too, the active head of a large Sunday school.

"Pomeroy Stockton, my adopted father, almost idolized this son, although there was in his manner toward him something akin to fear. Close work had made my father querulous and irritable. Yet I don't believe a better-hearted man ever lived. He worked most of the time in a little shop, which he had installed in a large back room on the ground floor of the house. He always worked with the door locked. There were furnaces, moulds, and many things that I didn't know the use of."

"I know who he was," said The Thinking Machine. "He was working to rediscover the secret of hardened copper – a secret which was lost in Egypt. I knew Mr. Stockton very well by reputation. Go on."

"Whatever it was he worked on," Miss Devan resumed, "he guarded it very carefully. He would permit no one at all to enter the room. I have never seen more than a glimpse of what was in it. His son particularly I have seen barred out of the shop a dozen times and every time there was a quarrel to follow.

"Those were the conditions at the time Mr. Stockton first became ill, six or seven months ago. At that time he double-locked the doors of his shop, retired to his rooms on the second floor, and remained there in practical seclusion for two weeks or more. These rooms adjoined mine, and twice during that time I heard the son and the father talking loudly, as if quarreling. At the end of the two weeks, Mr. Stockton returned to work in the shop and shortly afterward the son, who had also lived in the house, took apartments in Beacon Street and removed his belongings from the house.

"From that time up to last Monday – this is Thursday – I never saw the son in the house. On Monday the father was at work as usual in the shop. He had previously told me that the work he was engaged in was practically ended and he expected a great fortune to result from it. About five o'clock in the afternoon on Monday the son came to the house. No one knows when he went out. It is a fact, however, that Father did not have dinner at the usual time, 6:30. I presumed he was at work, and did not take time for his dinner. I have known him to do this many times."

For a moment the girl was silent and seemed to be struggling with some deep grief which she could not control.

"And next morning?" asked The Thinking Machine gently.

"Next morning," the girl went on, "Father was found dead in the workshop. There were no marks on his body, nothing to indicate at first the manner of death. It was as if he had sat in his chair beside one of the furnaces and had taken poison and died at once. A small bottle of what I presume to be prussic acid was smashed on the floor, almost beside his chair. We discovered him dead after we had rapped on the door several times and got no answer. Then Montgomery, our butler, smashed in the door, at my request. There we found Father.

"I immediately telephoned to the son, John Stockton, and he came to the house. The letter you now have was found in my father's pocket. It was just as you see it. Mr. Stockton seemed greatly agitated and started to destroy the letter. I induced him to give it to me, because instantly it occurred to me that there was something wrong about all of it. My father had talked too often to me about the future, what he intended to do and his plans for me. There may not be anything wrong. The letter may be just what it purports to be. I hope it is – oh – I hope it is. Yet everything considered—"

"Was there an autopsy?" asked The Thinking Machine.

"No. John Stockton's actions seemed to be directed against any investigation. He told me he thought he could do certain things which would prevent the matter coming to the attention of the police. My father was buried on a death certificate issued by a Dr. Benton, who has been a friend of John Stockton since their college days. In that way the appearance of suicide or anything else was covered up completely.

"Both before and after the funeral John Stockton made me promise to keep this letter hidden or else destroy it. In order to put an end to this I told him I had destroyed the letter. This attitude on his part, the more I thought of it, seemed to confirm my original idea that it had not been suicide. Night after night I thought of this, and finally decided to come to you rather than to the police. I feel that there is some dark mystery behind it all. If you can help me now—"

"Yes, yes," broke in The Thinking Machine. "Where was the key to the workshop? In Pomeroy's pocket? In his room? In the door?"

"Really, I don't know," said Miss Devan. "It hadn't occurred to me."

"Did Mr. Stockton leave a will?"

"Yes, it is with his lawyer, a Mr. Sloane."

"Has it been read? Do you know what is in it?"

"It is to be read in a day or so. Judging from the second paragraph of the letter, I presume he left everything to his son."

For the fourth time The Thinking Machine read the letter. At its end he again looked up at Miss Devan.

"Just what is your interpretation of this letter from one end to the other?" he asked.

"Speaking from my knowledge of Mr. Stockton and the circumstances surrounding him," the girl explained, "I should say the letter means just what it says. I should imagine from the first paragraph that something he invented had been taken away from him, stolen perhaps. The second paragraph and the third, I should say, were intended as a rebuke to certain relatives – a brother and two distant cousins – who had always regarded him as a crank and took frequent occasion to tell him so. I don't know a great deal of the history of that other branch of the family. The last two paragraphs explain themselves except—"

"Except the figure seven," interrupted the scientist. "Do you have any idea whatever as to the meaning of that?"

The girl took the letter and studied it closely for a moment.

"Not the slightest," she said. "It does not seem to be connected with anything else in the letter."

"Do you think it possible, Miss Devan, that this letter was written under coercion?"

"I do," said the girl quickly, and her face flamed. "That's just what I do think. From the first I have imagined some ghastly, horrible mystery back of it all."

"Or, perhaps Pomeroy Stockton never saw this letter at all," mused The Thinking Machine. "It may be a forgery?"

"Forgery!" gasped the girl. "Then John Stockton—"

"Whatever it is, forged or genuine," The Thinking Machine went on quietly, "it is a most extraordinary document. It might have been written by a poet. It states things in such a roundabout way. It is not directly to the point, as a practical man would have written."

There was silence for several minutes and the girl sat leaning forward on the table, staring into the inscrutable eyes of the scientist.

"Perhaps, perhaps," she said, "there is a cipher of some sort in it?"

"That is precisely correct," said The Thinking Machine emphatically. "There is a cipher in it, and a very ingenious one."

Chapter II

IT WAS twenty-four hours later that The Thinking Machine sent for Hutchinson Hatch, reporter, and talked over the matter with him. He had always found Hatch a discreet, resourceful individual, who was willing to aid in any way in his power.

Hatch read the letter, which The Thinking Machine had said contained a cipher, and then the circumstances as related by Miss Devan were retold to the reporter.

"Do you think it is a cipher?" asked Hatch in conclusion.

"It is a cipher," replied The Thinking Machine. "If what Miss Devan has said is correct, John Stockton cannot have said anything about the affair. I want you to go and talk to him, find out all about him and what division of the property is made by the will. Does this will give everything to the son?

"Also find out what personal enmity there is between John Stockton and Miss Devan, and what was the cause of it. Was there a man in it? If so, who? When you have done all this, go to the house in Dorchester and bring me the family Bible, if there is one there. It's probably a big book. If it is not there, let me know immediately by phone. Miss Devan will, I suppose, give it to you, if she has it."

With these instructions Hatch went away. Half an hour later he was in the private office of John Stockton at the latter's place of business. Mr. Stockton was a man of long visage, rather angular and clerical in appearance. There was a smug satisfaction about the man that Hatch didn't quite approve of, and yet it was a trait which found expression only in a soft voice and small acts of needless courtesy.

A deprecatory look passed over Stockton's face when Hatch asked the first question, which bore on his relationship with Pomeroy Stockton.

"I had hoped that this matter would not come to the attention of the press," said Stockton in an oily, gentle tone. "It is something which can only bring disgrace upon my poor father's memory, and his has been a name associated with distinct achievements in the progress of the world. However, if necessary, I will state my knowledge of the affair, and invite the investigation which, frankly, I will say, I tried to stop."

"How much was your father's estate?" asked Hatch.

"Something more than a million," was the reply. "He made most of it through a device for coupling cars. This is now in use on practically all the railroads."

"And the division of this property by will?" asked Hatch.

"I haven't seen the will, but I understand that he left practically everything to me, settling an annuity and the home in Dorchester on Miss Devan, whom he had always regarded as a daughter."

"That would give you then, say, two-thirds or three-quarters of the estate."

"Something like that, possibly $800,000."

"Where is this will now?"

"I understand in the hands of my father's attorney, Mr. Sloane."

"When is it to be read?"

"It was to have been read today, but there has been some delay about it. The attorney postponed it for a few days."

"What, Mr. Stockton, was the purpose in making it appear that your father died naturally, when obviously he committed suicide and there is even a suggestion of something else?" demanded Hatch.

John Stockton sat up straight in his chair with a startled expression in his eyes. He had been rubbing his hands together complacently; now he stopped and stared at the reporter.

"Something else?" he asked. "Pray what else?"

Hatch shrugged his shoulders, but in his eyes there lay almost an accusation.

"Did any motive ever appear for your father's suicide?"

"I know of none," Stockton replied. "Yet, admitting that this is suicide, without a motive, it seems that the only fault I have committed is that I had a friend report it otherwise and avoided a police inquiry."

"It's just that. Why did you do it?"

"Naturally to save the family name from disgrace. But this something else you spoke of? Do you mean that anyone else thinks that anything other than suicide or natural death is possible?"

As he asked the question there came some subtle change over his face. He leaned forward toward the reporter. All trace of the sanctimonious smirk about the thin-lipped mouth had gone now.

"Miss Devan has produced the letter found on your father at death and has said –" began the reporter.

"Elizabeth! Miss Devan!" exclaimed John Stockton. He arose suddenly, paced several times across the room, then stopped in front of the reporter. "She gave me her word of honor that she would not make the existence of that letter known."

"But she has made it public," said Hatch. "And further she intimates that your father's death was not even what it appeared to be, suicide."

"She's crazy, man, crazy," said Stockton in deep agitation. "Who could have killed my father? What motive could there have been?"

There was a grim twitching of Hatch's lips.

"Was Miss Devan legally adopted by your father?" he asked, irrelevantly.

"Yes."

"In that event, disregarding other relatives, doesn't it seem strange even to you that he gives three quarters of the estate to you – you have a fortune already – and only a small part to Miss Devan, who has nothing?"

"That's my father's business."

There was a pause. Stockton was still pacing back and forth.

Finally he sank down in his chair at the desk, and sat for a moment looking at the reporter.

"Is that all?" he asked.

"I should like to know, if you don't mind telling me, what direct cause there is for ill feeling between Miss Devan and you?"

"There is no ill feeling. We merely never got along well together. My father and I have had several arguments about her for reasons which it is not necessary to go into."

"Did you have such an argument on the night before your father was found dead?"

"I believe there was something said about her."

"What time did you leave the shop that night?"

"About 10 o'clock."

"And you had been in the room with your father since afternoon, had you not?"

"Yes."

"No dinner?"

"No."

"How did you come to neglect that?"

"My father was explaining a recent invention he had perfected, which I was to put on the market."

"I suppose the possibility of suicide or his death in any way had not occurred to you?"

"No, not at all. We were making elaborate plans for the future."

Possibly it was some prejudice against the man's appearance which made Hatch so dissatisfied with the result of the interview. He felt that he had gained nothing, yet Stockton had been absolutely frank, as it seemed. There was one last question.

"Have you any recollection of a large family Bible in your father's house?" he asked.

"I have seen it several times," Stockton said.

"Is it still there?"

"So far as I know, yes."

That was the end of the interview, and Hatch went straight to the house in Dorchester to see Miss Devan. There, in accordance with instructions from The Thinking Machine, he asked for the family Bible.

"There was one here the other day," said Miss Devan, "but it has disappeared."

"Since your father's death?" asked Hatch.

"Yes, the next day."

"Have you any idea who took it?"

"Not unless – unless—"

"John Stockton! Why did he take it?" blurted Hatch.

There was a little resigned movement of the girl's hands, a movement which said, "I don't know."

"He told me, too," said Hatch indignantly, "that he thought the Bible was still here."

The girl drew close to the reporter and laid one white hand on his sleeve. She looked up into his eyes and tears stood in her own. Her lips trembled.

"John Stockton has that book," she said. "He took it away from here the day after my father died, and he did it for a purpose. What, I don't know."

"Are you absolutely positive he has it?" asked Hatch.

"I saw it in his room, where he had hidden it," replied the girl.

Chapter III

HATCH LAID the results of the interviews before the scientist at the Beacon Hill home. The Thinking Machine listened without comment up to that point where Miss Devan had said she knew the family Bible to be in the son's possession.

"If Miss Devan and Stockton do not get along well together, why should she visit Stockton's place at all?" demanded The Thinking Machine.

"I don't know," Hatch replied, "except that she thinks he must have had some connection with her father's death, and is investigating on her own account. What has this Bible to do with it anyway?"

"It may have a great deal to do with it," said The Thinking Machine enigmatically. "Now, the thing to do is to find out if the girl told the truth and if the Bible is in Stockton's apartment. Now, Mr. Hatch, I leave that to you. I would like to see that Bible. If you can bring it to me, well and good. If you can't bring it, look at and study the seventh page for any pencil marks in the text, anything whatever. It might be even advisable, if you have the opportunity, to tear out that page and bring it to me. No harm will be done, and it can be returned in proper time."

Perplexed wrinkles were gathering on Hatch's forehead as he listened. What had page seven of a Bible to do with what seemed to be a murder mystery? Who had said anything about a Bible, anyway? The letter left by Stockton mentioned a Bible, but that didn't seem to mean anything. Then Hatch remembered that same letter carried a figure seven in parentheses which had apparently nothing to do and no connection with any other part of the letter. Hatch's introspective study of the affair was interrupted by The Thinking Machine.

"I shall await your report here, Mr. Hatch. If it is what I expect, we shall go out late tonight on a little voyage of discovery. Meanwhile see that Bible and tell me what you find."

Hatch found the apartments of John Stockton on Beacon Street without any difficulty. In a manner best known to himself he entered and searched the place. When he came out there was a look of chagrin on his face as he hurried to the house of The Thinking Machine nearby.

"Well?" asked the scientist.

"I saw the Bible," said Hatch.

"And page seven?"

"Was torn out, missing, gone," replied the reporter.

"Ah," exclaimed the scientist. "I thought so. Tonight we will make the little trip I spoke of. By the way, did you happen to notice if John Stockton had or used a fountain pen?"

"I didn't see one," said Hatch.

"Well, please see for me if any of his employees have ever noticed one. Then meet me here tonight at ten o'clock."

Thus Hatch was dismissed. A little later he called casually on Stockton again. There, by inquiries, he established to his own satisfaction that Stockton did not own a fountain pen. Then with Stockton himself he took up the matter of the Bible again.

"I understand you to say, Mr. Stockton," he began in his smoothest tone, "that you knew of the existence of a family Bible, but you did not know if it was still at the Dorchester place."

"That's correct," said Stockton.

"How is it then," Hatch resumed, "that that identical Bible is now at your apartments, carefully hidden in a box under a sofa?"

Mr. Stockton seemed to be amazed. He arose suddenly and leaned over toward the reporter with hands clenched. There was a glitter of what might have been anger in his eyes.

"What do you know about this? What are you talking about?" he demanded.

"I mean that you had said you did not know where this book was, and meanwhile have it hidden. Why?"

"Have you seen the Bible in my rooms?" asked Stockton.

"I have," said the reporter coolly.

Now a new determination came into the face of the merchant. The oiliness of his manner was gone, the sanctimonious smirk had been obliterated, the thin lips closed into a straight, rigid line.

"I shall have nothing further to say," he declared almost fiercely.

"Will you tell me why you tore out the seventh page of the Bible?" asked Hatch.

Stockton stared at him dully, as if dazed for a moment. All the color left his face. There came a startling pallor instead. When next he spoke, his voice was tense and strained.

"Is – is – the seventh page missing?"

"Yes," Hatch replied. "Where is it?"

"I'll have nothing further to say under any circumstances. That's all."

With not the slightest idea of what it might mean or what bearing it had on the matter, Hatch had brought out statements which were wholly at variance with facts. Why was Stockton so affected by the statement that page seven was gone? Why had the Bible been taken from the Dorchester home? Why had it been so carefully hidden? How did Miss Devan know it was there?

These were only a few of the questions that were racing through the reporter's mind. He did not seem to be able to grasp anything tangible. If there were a cipher hidden in the letter, what was it? What bearing did it have on the case?

Seeking a possible answer to some of these questions, Hatch took a cab and was soon back at the Dorchester house. He was somewhat surprised to see The Thinking Machine standing on the stoop waiting to be admitted. The scientist took his presence as a matter of course.

"What did you find out about Stockton's fountain pen?" he asked.

"I satisfied myself that he had not owned a fountain pen, at least recently enough for the pen to have been used in writing that letter. I presume that's what inquiries in that direction mean."

The two men were admitted to the house and after a few minutes Miss Devan entered. She understood when The Thinking Machine explained that they merely wished to see the shop in which Mr. Stockton had been found dead.

"And also if you have a sample of Mr. Stockton's handwriting," asked the scientist.

"It's rather peculiar," Miss Devan explained, "but I doubt if there is an authentic sample in existence large enough, that is, to be compared with that letter. He had a certain amount of correspondence, but this I did for him on the typewriter. Occasionally he would prepare an article for a scientific paper, but these were also dictated to me. He has been in the habit of doing so for years."

"This letter seems to be all there is?"

"Of course his signature appears to checks and in other places. I can produce some of those for you. I don't think, however, that there is the slightest doubt that he wrote this letter. It is his handwriting."

"I suppose he never used a fountain pen?" asked The Thinking Machine.

"Not that I know of," the girl replied. "I have one," and she took it out of a little gold fascinator she wore at her bosom.

The scientist pressed the point of the pen against his thumbnail, and a tiny drop of blue ink appeared. The letter was written in black. The Thinking Machine seemed satisfied.

"And now the shop," he suggested.

Miss Devan led the way through the long wide hall to the back of the building. There she opened a door, which showed signs of having been battered in, and admitted them. Then, at the request of The Thinking Machine, she rehearsed the story in full, showed him where Stockton had been found, where the prussic acid had been broken, and how the servant, Montgomery, had broken in the door at her request.

"Did you ever find the key to the door?"

"No. I can't imagine what became of it."

"Is this room precisely as it was when the body was found? That is, has anything been removed from it?"

"Nothing," replied the girl.

"Have the servants taken anything out? Did they have access to this room?"

"They have not been permitted to enter it at all. The body was removed and the fragments of the acid bottle were taken away, but nothing else."

"Have you ever known of pen and ink being in this room?"

"I hadn't thought of it."

"You haven't taken them out since the body was found, have you?"

"I– I– er – have not," the girl stammered.

Miss Devan left the room, and for an hour Hatch and The Thinking Machine conducted the search.

"Find a pen and ink," The Thinking Machine instructed.

They were not found.

At midnight, which was six hours later, The Thinking Machine and Hutchinson Hatch were groping through the cellar of the Dorchester house by the light of a small electric lamp which shot a straight beam aggressively through the murky, damp air. Finally the ray fell on a tiny door set in the solid wall of the cellar.

There was a slight exclamation from The Thinking Machine, and this was followed immediately by the sharp, unmistakable click of a revolver somewhere behind them in the dark.

"Down, quick," gasped Hatch, and with a sudden blow he dashed aside the electric light, extinguishing it. Simultaneously with this there came a revolver shot, and a bullet was buried in the wall behind Hatch's head.

Chapter IV

THE REVERBERATION of the pistol shot was still ringing in Hatch's ears when he felt the hand of The Thinking Machine on his arm, and then through the utter blackness of the cellar came the irritable voice of the scientist:

"To your right, to your right," it said sharply.

Then, contrary to this advice Hatch felt the scientist drawing him to the left. In another moment there came a second shot, and by the flash Hatch could see that it was aimed at a point a dozen feet to the right of the point where they had been when the first shot was fired. The person with the revolver had heard the scientist and had been duped.

Firmly the scientist drew Hatch on until they were almost to the cellar steps. There, outlined against a dim light which came down the stairs, they could see a tall figure peering through the darkness toward a spot opposite where they stood. Hatch saw only one thing to do and did it. He leaped forward and landed on the back of the figure, bearing the man to the ground. An instant later his hand closed on the revolver and he wrested it away.

"All right," he sang out. "I've got it."

The electric light which he had dashed from the hand of The Thinking Machine gleamed again through the cellar and fell upon the face of John Stockton, helpless and gasping in the hands of the reporter.

"Well?" asked Stockton calmly. "Are you burglars or what?"

"Let's go upstairs to the light," suggested The Thinking Machine.

It was under these peculiar circumstances that the scientist came face to face for the first time with John Stockton. Hatch introduced the two men in a most matter-of-fact tone and restored to Stockton the revolver. This was suggested by a nod of the scientist's head. Stockton laid the revolver on a table.

"Why did you try to kill us?" asked The Thinking Machine.

"I presumed you were burglars," was the reply. "I heard the noise downstairs and came down to investigate."

"I thought you lived on Beacon Street," said the scientist.

"I do, but I came here tonight on a little business, which is all my own, and happened to hear you. What were you doing in the cellar?"

"How long have you been here?"

"Five or ten minutes."

"Have you a key to this house?"

"I have had one for many years. What is all this, anyway? How did you get in this house? What right had you here?"

"Is Miss Devan in the house tonight?" asked The Thinking Machine, entirely disregarding the other's questions.

"I don't know. I suppose so."

"You haven't seen her, of course?"

"Certainly not."

"And you came here secretly without her knowledge?"

Stockton shrugged his shoulders and was silent. The Thinking Machine raised himself on the chair on which he had been sitting and squinted steadily into Stockton's eyes. When he spoke it was to Hatch, but his gaze did not waver.

"Arouse the servants, find where Miss Devan's room is, and see if anything has happened to her," he directed.

"I think that will be unwise," broke in Stockton quickly.

"Why?"

"If I may put it on personal grounds," said Stockton, "I would ask as a favor that you do not make known my visit here, or your own for that matter, to Miss Devan."

There was a certain uneasiness in the man's attitude, a certain eagerness to keep things away from Miss Devan that spurred Hatch to instant action. He went out of the room hurriedly and ten minutes later Miss Devan, who had dressed quickly, came into the room with him. The servants stood outside in the hall, all curiosity. The closed door barred them from knowledge of what was happening.

There was a little dramatic pause as Miss Devan entered and Stockton arose from his seat. The Thinking Machine glanced from one to the other. He noted the pallor of the girl's face and the frank embarrassment of Stockton.

"What is it?" asked Miss Devan, and her voice trembled a little. "Why are you all here? What has happened?"

"Mr. Stockton came here tonight," The Thinking Machine began quietly, "to remove the contents from the locked vault in the cellar. He came without your knowledge and found us ahead of him. Mr. Hatch and myself are here in the course of our inquiry into the matter which you placed in my hands. We also came without your knowledge. I considered this best. Mr. Stockton was very anxious that his visit should be kept from you. Have you anything to say now?"

The girl turned on Stockton with magnificent scorn. Accusation was in her very attitude. Her small hand was pointed directly at Stockton and into his face there came a strange emotion, which he struggled to repress.

"Murderer! Thief!" the girl almost hissed.

"Do you know why he came?" asked The Thinking Machine.

"He came to rob the vault, as you said," said the girl, fiercely. "It was because my father would not give him the secret of his last invention that this man killed him. How he compelled him to write that letter I don't know."

"Elizabeth, for God's sake what are you saying?" asked Stockton with ashen face.

"His greed is so great that he wanted all of my father's estate," the girl went on impetuously. "He was not content that I should get even a small part of it."

"Elizabeth, Elizabeth!" said Stockton, as he leaned forward with his head in his hands.

"What do you know about this secret vault?" asked the scientist.

"I– I– have always thought there was a secret vault in the cellar," the girl explained. "I may say I know there was one because those things my father took the greatest care of were always disposed of by him somewhere in the house. I can imagine no other place than the cellar."

There was a long pause. The girl stood rigid, staring down at the bowed figure of Stockton with not a gleam of pity in her face. Hatch caught the expression and it occurred to him for the first time that Miss Devan was vindictive. He was more convinced than ever that there had been some long-standing feud between these two. The Thinking Machine broke the long silence.

"Do you happen to know, Miss Devan, that page seven of the Bible which you found hidden in Mr. Stockton's place is missing?"

"I didn't notice," said the girl.

Stockton had arisen with the words and now stood with white face and listening intently.

"Did you ever happen to see a page seven in that Bible?" the scientist asked.

"I don't recall."

"What were you doing in my rooms?" demanded Stockton of the girl.

"Why did you tear out page seven?" asked The Thinking Machine.

Stockton thought the question was addressed to him and turned to answer. Then he saw it was unmistakably a question to Miss Devan and turned again to her.

"I didn't tear it out," exclaimed Miss Devan. "I never saw it. I don't know what you mean."

The Thinking Machine made an impatient gesture with his hands; his next question was to Stockton.

"Have you a sample of your father's handwriting?'"

"Several," said Stockton. "Here are three or four letters from him."

Miss Devan gasped a little as if startled and Stockton produced the letters and handed them to The Thinking Machine. The latter glanced over two of them.

"I thought, Miss Devan, you said your father always dictated his letters to you?"

"I did say so," said the girl. "I didn't know of the existence of these."

"May I have these?" asked The Thinking Machine.

"Yes. They are of no consequence."

"Now let's see what is in the secret vault," the scientist went on.

He arose and led the way again into the cellar, lighting his path with the electric bulb. Stockton followed immediately behind, then came Miss Devan, her white dressing gown trailing mystically in the dim light, and last came Hatch. The Thinking Machine went straight to that spot where he and Hatch had been when Stockton had fired at them. Again the rays of the light revealed the tiny door set into the wall of the cellar. The door opened readily at his touch; the small vault was empty.

Intent on his examination of this, The Thinking Machine was oblivious for a moment to what was happening. Suddenly there came again a pistol shot, followed instantly by a woman's scream.

"My God, he's killed himself. He's killed himself."

It was Miss Devan's voice.

Chapter V

WHEN The Thinking Machine flashed his light back into the gloom of the cellar, he saw Miss Devan and Hatch leaning over the prostrate figure of John Stockton. The latter's face was perfectly white save just at the edge of the hair, where there was a trickle of red. In his right hand he clasped a revolver.

"Dear me! Dear me!" exclaimed the scientist. "What is it?'"

"Stockton shot himself," said Hatch, and there was excitement in his tone.

On his knees the scientist made a hurried examination of the wounded man, then suddenly – it may have been inadvertently – he flashed the light in the face of Miss Devan.

"Where were you?" he demanded quickly.

"Just behind him," said the girl. "Will he die? Is it fatal?"

"Hopeless," said the scientist. "Let's get him upstairs."

The unconscious man was lifted and with Hatch leading was again taken to the room which they had left only a few minutes before. Hatch stood by helplessly while The Thinking Machine, in his capacity of physician, made a more minute examination of the wound. The bullet mark just above the right temple was almost bloodless; around it there were the unmistakeable marks of burned powder.

"Help me just a moment, Miss Devan," requested The Thinking Machine, as he bound an improvised handkerchief bandage about the head. Miss Devan tied the final knots of the bandage and The Thinking Machine studied her hands closely as she did so. When the work was completed he turned to her in a most matter-of-fact way.

"Why did you shoot him?" he asked.

"I–I—" stammered the girl, "I didn't shoot him, he shot himself."

"How come those powder marks on your right hand?"

Miss Devan glanced down at her right hand, and the color which had been in her face faded as if by magic. There was fear, now, in her manner.

"I– I don't know," she stammered. "Surely you don't think that I—"

"Mr. Hatch, 'phone at once for an ambulance and then see if it is possible to get Detective Mallory here immediately. I shall give Miss Devan into custody on the charge of shooting this man."

The girl stared at him dully for a moment and then dropped back into a chair with dead white face and fear-distended eyes. Hatch went out, seeking a telephone, and for a time Miss Devan sat silent, as if dazed. Finally, with an effort, she aroused herself and facing The Thinking Machine defiantly, burst out:

"I didn't shoot him. I didn't, I didn't. He did it himself."

The long, slender fingers of The Thinking Machine closed on the revolver and gently removed it from the hand of the wounded man.

"Ah, I was mistaken," he said suddenly, "he was not as badly wounded as I thought. See! He is reviving."

"Reviving," exclaimed Miss Devan. "Won't he die, then?'"

"Why?" asked The Thinking Machine sharply.

"It seems so pitiful, almost a confession of guilt," she hurriedly exclaimed. "Won't he die?"

Gradually the color was coming back into Stockton's face. The Thinking Machine bending over him, with one hand on the heart, saw the eyelids quiver and then slowly the eyes opened. Almost immediately the strength of the heart beat grew perceptibly stronger. Stockton stared at him a moment, then wearily his eyelids drooped again.

"Why did Miss Devan shoot you?" The Thinking Machine demanded.

There was a pause and the eyes opened for the second time. Miss Devan stood within range of the glance, her hands outstretched entreatingly toward Stockton.

"Why did she shoot you?" repeated The Thinking Machine.

"She – did – not," said Stockton slowly. "I– did – it – myself."

For an instant there was a little wrinkle of perplexity on the brow of The Thinking Machine and then it passed.

"Purposely?" he asked.

"I did it myself."

Again the eyes closed and Stockton seemed to be passing into unconsciousness. The Thinking Machine glanced up to find an infinite expression of relief on Miss Devan's face. His own manner changed; became almost abject, in fact, as he turned to her again.

"I beg your pardon," he said. "I made a mistake."

"Will he die?"

"No, that was another mistake. He will recover."

Within a few moments a City Hospital ambulance rattled up to the door and John Stockton was removed. It was with a feeling of pity that Hatch assisted Miss Devan, now almost in a fainting condition, to her room. The Thinking Machine had previously given her a slight stimulant. Detective Mallory had not answered the call by 'phone.

The Thinking Machine and Hatch returned to Boston. At the Park Street subway they separated, after The Thinking Machine had given certain instructions. Hatch spent most of the following day carrying out these instructions. First he went to see Dr. Benton, the physician who issued the death certificate on which Pomeroy Stockton was buried. Dr. Benton was considerably alarmed when the reporter broached the subject of his visit. After a time he talked freely of the case.

"I have known John Stockton since we were in college together," he said, "and I believe him to be one of the few really good men I know. I can't believe otherwise. Singularly enough, he is also one of the few good men who has made his own fortune. There is nothing hypocritical about him.

"Immediately after his father was found dead, he phoned to me and I went out to the house in Dorchester. He explained then that it was apparent Pomeroy Stockton had committed suicide. He dreaded the disgrace that public knowledge would bring on an honored name, and asked me what could be done. I suggested the only thing I knew – that was the issuance of a death certificate specifying natural causes – heart disease, I said. This act was due entirely to my friendship for him.

"I examined the body and found a trace of prussic acid on Pomeroy's tongue. Beside the chair on which he sat a bottle of prussic acid had been broken. I made no autopsy, of course. Ethically I may have sinned, but I feel that no real harm has been done. Of course, now that you know the real facts my entire career is at stake."

"There is no question in your mind but that it was suicide?" asked Hatch.

"Not the slightest. Then, too, there was the letter, which was found in Pomeroy Stockton's pocket. I saw that and if there had been any doubt then it was removed. This letter, I think, was then in Miss Devan's possession. I presume it is still."

"Do you know anything about Miss Devan?"

"Nothing, except that she is an adopted daughter, who for some reason retained her own family name. Three or four years ago she had a little love affair, to which John Stockton objected. I believe he was the cause of it being broken off. As a matter of fact, I think at one time he was himself in love with her and she refused to accept him as a suitor. Since that time there has been some slight friction, but I know nothing of this except in a general way from what he has said to me."

Then Hatch proceeded to carry out the other part of The Thinking Machine's instructions. This was to see the attorney in whose possession Pomeroy Stockton's will was supposed to be and to ask him why there had been a delay in the reading of the will.

Hatch found the attorney, Frederick Sloane, without difficulty. Without reservation Hatch laid all the circumstances as he knew them before Mr. Sloane. Then came the question of why the will had not been read. Mr. Sloane, too, was frank.

"It's because the will is not now in my possession," he said. "It has either been mislaid, lost, or possibly stolen. I did not care for the family to know this just now, and delayed the reading of the will while I made a search for it. Thus far I have found not a trace. I haven't even the remotest idea where it is."

"What does the will provide?" asked Hatch.

"It leaves the bulk of the estate to John Stockton, settles an annuity of $5,000 a year on Miss Devan, gives her the Dorchester house, and specifically cuts off other relatives whom Pomeroy Stockton once accused of stealing an invention he made. The letter, found after Mr. Stockton's death—"

"You knew of that letter, too?" Hatch interrupted.

"Oh, yes, this letter confirms the will, except, in general terms, it also cuts off Miss Devan."

"Would it not be to the interest of the other immediate relatives of Stockton, those who were specifically cut off, to get possession of that will and destroy it?"

"Of course it might be, but there has been no communication between the two branches of the family for several years. That branch lives in the far West and I have taken particular pains to ascertain that they could not have had anything to do with the disappearance of the will."

With these new facts in his possession, Hatch started to report to The Thinking Machine. He had to wait half an hour or so. At last the scientist came in.

"I've been attending an autopsy," he said.

"An autopsy? Whose?"

"On the body of Pomeroy Stockton."

"Why, I had thought he had been buried."

"No, only placed in a receiving vault. I had to call the attention of the Medical Examiner to the case in order to get permission to make an autopsy. We did it together."

"What did you find?" asked Hatch.

"What did you find?" asked The Thinking Machine, in turn.

Briefly Hatch told him of the interview with Dr. Benton and Mr. Sloane. The scientist listened without comment and at the end sat back in his big chair squinting at the ceiling.

"That seems to finish it," he said. "These are the questions which were presented: First, in what manner did Pomeroy Stockton die? Second, if not suicide, as appeared, what motive was there for anything else? Third, if there was a motive, to whom does it lead? Fourth, what was in the cipher letter? Now, Mr. Hatch, I think I may make all of it clear. There was a cipher in the letter – what may be described as a cipher in five, the figure five being the key to it."

Chapter VI

"**FIRST**, Mr. Hatch," The Thinking Machine resumed, as he drew out and spread on a table the letter which had been originally placed in his hands by Miss Devan, "the question of whether there was a cipher in this letter was to be definitely decided.

"There are a thousand different kinds of ciphers. One of them, which we will call the arbitrary cipher, is excellently illustrated in Poe's story, 'The Gold Bug'. In that cipher, a figure or symbol is made to represent each letter of the alphabet.

"Then, there are book ciphers, which are, perhaps, the safest of all ciphers, because without a clue to the book from which words may be chosen and designated by numbers, no one can solve it.

"It would be useless for me to go into this matter at any length, so let us consider this particular letter as a cipher possibility. A careful study of the letter develops three possible starting points. The first of these is the general tone of the letter. It is not a direct, straight-away statement such as a man about to commit suicide would write unless he had a purpose – that is, a purpose beyond the mere apparent meaning of the letter itself. Therefore we will suppose there was another purpose hidden behind a cipher.

"The second starting point is that offered by the absence of one word. You will see that the word 'in' should appear between the word 'cherished' and 'secret'. This, of course, may have been an oversight in writing, the sort of thing anyone might do. But further down we find the third starting point.

"This is the figure seven in parentheses. It apparently has no connection whatever with what precedes or follows. It could not have been an accident. Therefore what did it mean? Was it a crude outward indication of a hurriedly constructed cipher?

"I took the figure seven at first to be a sort of key to the entire letter, always presuming there was a cipher. I counted seven words down from that figure and found the word 'binding'. Seven words from that down made the next word 'give'. Together the two words seemed to mean something.

"I stopped there and started back. The seventh word up is 'and'. The seventh word from 'and', still counting backward, seemed meaningless. I pursued that theory of seven all the way through the letter and found only a jumble of words. It was the same way counting seven letters. These letters meant nothing unless each letter was arbitrarily taken to represent another letter. This immediately led to intricacies. I believe always in exhausting simple possibilities first, so I started over again.

"Now what word nearest to the seven meant anything when taken together with it? Not 'family', not 'Bible', not 'son', as the vital words appear from the seven down. Going up from the seven, I did find a word which applied to it and meant something. That was the word 'page'. I had immediately 'page seven'. 'Page' was the fifth word up from the seven.

"What was the next fifth word, still going up? This was 'on'. Then I had 'on page seven' – connected words appearing in order, each being the fifth from the other. The fifth word down from seven I found was 'family'; the next fifth word was 'Bible'; thus, 'on page seven family Bible'.

"It is unnecessary to go further into the study I made of the cipher. I worked upward from the seven, taking each fifth word until I had all the cipher words. I have underscored them here. Read the words underscored and you have the cipher."

Hatch took the letter marked as follows:

> *To those Concerned:*
>
> *Tired of it all I seek the end, and am content. Ambition is dead; the grave yawns greedily at my feet, and with the labor of my own hands lost I greet death of my own will, by my own act. To my son I leave all, and you who maligned me, you who discouraged me, you may read this and know I punish you thus. It's for him, my son, to forgive. I dared in life and dare dead your everlasting anger, not alone that you didn't speak, but that you cherished secret, and my ears are locked forever against you. My vault is my resting place. On the brightest and dearest page of life I wrote (7) my love for him. Family ties, binding as the Bible itself, bade me give all to my son.*
>
> *Good-bye. I die.*
>
> *Pomeroy Stockton*

Slowly Hatch read this:

> *"I am dead at the hands of my son. You who read punish him. I dare not speak. Secret locked vault on page 7 family Bible."*

"Well, by George!" exclaimed the reporter. It was a tribute to The Thinking Machine, as well as an expression of amazement at what he read.

"You see," explained The Thinking Machine, "if the word 'in' had appeared between 'cherished' and 'secret', as it would naturally have done, it would have lost the order of the cipher, therefore it was purposely left out."

"It's enough to send Stockton to the electric chair," said Hatch.

"It would be if it were not a forgery," said the scientist testily.

"A forgery," gasped Hatch. "Didn't Pomeroy Stockton write it?"

"No."

"Surely not John Stockton?"

"No."

"Well, who then?"

"Miss Devan."

"Miss Devan!" Hatch repeated in amazement. "Then, Miss Devan killed Pomeroy Stockton?"

"No, he died a natural death."

Hatch's head was whirling. A thousand questions demanded an immediate answer. He stared mouth agape at The Thinking Machine. All his ideas of the case were tumbling about him. Nothing remained.

"Briefly, here is what happened," said The Thinking Machine. "Pomeroy Stockton died a natural death of heart disease. Miss Devan found him dead, wrote this letter, put it in his pocket, put a drop of prussic acid on his tongue, smashed the bottle of acid, left the room, locked the door, and next day had it broken down.

"It was she who shot John Stockton. It was she who tore out page seven of that family Bible, and then hid the book in Stockton's room. It was she who in some way got hold of the will. She either has it or destroyed it. It was she who took advantage of her aged benefactor's sudden death to further as weird and inhuman a plot against another as a woman can devise. There is nothing on God's earth as bad as a bad woman, and nothing as good as a good one. I think that has been said before."

"But as to this case," Hatch interrupted. "How? What? Why?"

"I read the cipher within a few hours after I got the letter," replied The Thinking Machine. "Naturally I wanted to find out then who and what this son was.

"I had Miss Devan's story, of course – a story of disagreement between father and son, quarreling and all that. It was also a story which showed a certain underlying animosity despite Miss Devan's cleverness. She had so mingled fact with fiction that it was not altogether easy to weed out the truth, therefore I believed what I chose.

"Miss Devan's idea, as expressed to me, was that the letter was written under coercion. Men who are being murdered don't write cipher letters as intricate as that; and men who are committing suicide have no obvious reasons for writing such letters. The line 'I dare not speak' was silly. Pomeroy Stockton was not a prisoner. If he had feared a conspiracy to kill him why shouldn't he speak?

"All these things were in my mind when I asked you to see Stockton. I was particularly anxious to hear what he had to say as to the family Bible. And yet I may say I knew that page seven had been torn out of the book and was then in Miss Devan's possession.

"I may say, too, that I knew that the secret vault was empty. Whatever these two things contained, supposing she wrote the cipher, had been removed or she would not have called attention to them in this cipher. I had an idea that she might have written it from the mere fact that it was she who first called my attention to the possibility of a cipher.

"Assuming then that the cipher was a forgery, that she wrote it, that it directly accused John Stockton, that she brought it to me, I had fairly conclusive proof that if Pomery Stockton had been murdered she had had a hand in it. John Stockton's motive in trying to suppress the fact of a suicide, as he thought it, was perfectly clear. It was, as he said, to avoid disgrace. Such things are done frequently.

"From the moment you told him of the possibility of murder, he suspected Miss Devan. Why? Because, above all, she had the opportunity, because she wanted the bulk of the estate, because there was some animosity against John Stockton.

"This now proves to have been a broken-off love affair. John Stockton broke it off. He himself had loved Miss Devan. She had refused him. Later, when he broke off the love affair, she hated him.

"Her plan for revenge was almost diabolical. It was intended to give her full revenge and the estate at the same time. She hoped, she knew, that I would read that cipher. She planned that it would send John Stockton to the electric chair."

"Horrible!" commented Hatch with a little shudder.

"It was a fear that this plan might go wrong that induced her to try to kill Stockton by shooting him. The cellar was dark, but she forgot that ninety-nine revolvers out of a hundred leave slight powder stains on the hand of the person who fires them. Stockton said that she did not shoot him, because of that inexplicable loyalty which some men show to a woman they love or have loved.

"Stockton made his secret visit to the house that night to get what was in that vault without her knowledge. He knew of its existence. His father had probably told him. The thing that appeared on page seven of the family Bible was in all probability the copper hardening process he was perfecting. I should think it had been written there in invisible ink. John Stockton knew this was there. His father told him. If his father told it, Miss Devan probably overheard it. She knew it, too.

"Now the actual circumstances of the death. The girl must have had and used a key to the work room. After John Stockton left the house that Monday night she entered that room. She found his father dead of heart disease. The autopsy proved this.

"Then the whole scheme was clear to her. She forged that cipher letter – as Pomeroy Stockton's secretary she probably knew the handwriting better than anyone else in the world – placed it in his pocket, and the rest of it you know."

"But the Bible in John Stockton's room?" asked Hatch.

"Was placed there by Miss Devan," replied The Thinking Machine. "It was a part of the general scheme to hopelessly implicate Stockton. She is a clever woman. She showed that when she produced the fountain pen, having carefully filled it with blue instead of black ink."

"What was in the locked vault?"

"That I can only conjecture. It is not impossible that the inventor had only part of the formula he so closely guarded written on the Bible leaf and the other part of it in that vault, together with other valuable documents.

"I may add that the letters which John Stockton had were not forged. They were written without Miss Devan's knowledge. There was a vast difference in the handwriting of the cipher letter which she wrote and those others which the father wrote.

"Of course it is obvious that the missing will is now, or was, in Miss Devan's possession. How she got it, I don't know. With that out of the way and this cipher unravelled apparently proving the son's guilt, at least half, possibly all, of the estate would have gone to her."

Hatch lighted a cigarette thoughtfully and was silent for a moment.

"What will be the end of it all?" he asked. "Of course, I understand that John Stockton will recover."

"The result will be that the world will lose a great scientific achievement – the secret of hardening copper, which Pomeroy Stockton had rediscovered. I think it safe to say that Miss Devan has burned every scrap of this."

"But what will become of her?"

"She knows nothing of this. I believe she will disappear before Stockton recovers. He wouldn't prosecute anyway. Remember he loved her once."

John Stockton was convalescent two weeks later, when a nurse in the City Hospital placed an envelope in his hands. He opened it and a little cloud of ashes filtered through his fingers onto the bed clothing. He sank back on his pillow, weeping.

A Jury of Her Peers

Susan Glaspell

WHEN MARTHA HALE opened the storm-door and got a cut of the north wind, she ran back for her big woolen scarf. As she hurriedly wound that round her head her eye made a scandalized sweep of her kitchen. It was no ordinary thing that called her away – it was probably farther from ordinary than anything that had ever happened in Dickson County. But what her eye took in was that her kitchen was in no shape for leaving: her bread all ready for mixing, half the flour sifted and half unsifted.

She hated to see things half done; but she had been at that when the team from town stopped to get Mr. Hale, and then the sheriff came running in to say his wife wished Mrs. Hale would come too – adding, with a grin, that he guessed she was getting scarey and wanted another woman along. So she had dropped everything right where it was.

"Martha!" now came her husband's impatient voice. "Don't keep folks waiting out here in the cold."

She again opened the storm-door, and this time joined the three men and the one woman waiting for her in the big two-seated buggy.

After she had the robes tucked around her she took another look at the woman who sat beside her on the back seat. She had met Mrs. Peters the year before at the county fair, and the thing she remembered about her was that she didn't seem like a sheriff's wife. She was small and thin and didn't have a strong voice. Mrs. Gorman, sheriff's wife before Gorman went out and Peters came in, had a voice that somehow seemed to be backing up the law with every word. But if Mrs. Peters didn't look like a sheriff's wife, Peters made it up in looking like a sheriff. He was to a dot the kind of man who could get himself elected sheriff – a heavy man with a big voice, who was particularly genial with the law-abiding, as if to make it plain that he knew the difference between criminals and non-criminals. And right there it came into Mrs. Hale's mind, with a stab, that this man who was so pleasant and lively with all of them was going to the Wrights' now as a sheriff.

"The country's not very pleasant this time of year," Mrs. Peters at last ventured, as if she felt they ought to be talking as well as the men.

Mrs. Hale scarcely finished her reply, for they had gone up a little hill and could see the Wright place now, and seeing it did not make her feel like talking. It looked very lonesome this cold March morning. It had always been a lonesome-looking place. It was down in a hollow, and the poplar trees around it were lonesome-looking trees. The men were looking at it and talking about what had happened. The county attorney was bending to one side of the buggy, and kept looking steadily at the place as they drew up to it.

"I'm glad you came with me," Mrs. Peters said nervously, as the two women were about to follow the men in through the kitchen door.

Even after she had her foot on the doorstep, her hand on the knob, Martha Hale had a moment of feeling she could not cross that threshold. And the reason it seemed she couldn't cross it now was simply because she hadn't crossed it before. Time and time again it had been in her mind, "I ought to go over and see Minnie Foster" – she still thought of her as Minnie Foster, though for twenty years she had been Mrs. Wright. And then there was always something to do and Minnie Foster would go from her mind. But *now* she could come.

* * *

The men went over to the stove. The women stood close together by the door. Young Henderson, the county attorney, turned around and said, "Come up to the fire, ladies."

Mrs. Peters took a step forward, then stopped. "I'm not – cold," she said.

And so the two women stood by the door, at first not even so much as looking around the kitchen.

The men talked for a minute about what a good thing it was the sheriff had sent his deputy out that morning to make a fire for them, and then Sheriff Peters stepped back from the stove, unbuttoned his outer coat, and leaned his hands on the kitchen table in a way that seemed to mark the beginning of official business. "Now, Mr. Hale," he said in a sort of semi-official voice, "before we move things about, you tell Mr. Henderson just what it was you saw when you came here yesterday morning."

The county attorney was looking around the kitchen.

"By the way," he said, "has anything been moved?" He turned to the sheriff. "Are things just as you left them yesterday?"

Peters looked from cupboard to sink; from that to a small worn rocker a little to one side of the kitchen table.

"It's just the same."

"Somebody should have been left here yesterday," said the county attorney.

"Oh – yesterday," returned the sheriff, with a little gesture as of yesterday having been more than he could bear to think of. "When I had to send Frank to Morris Center for that man who went crazy – let me tell you, I had my hands full *yesterday*. I knew you could get back from Omaha by today, George, and as long as I went over everything here myself—"

"Well, Mr. Hale," said the county attorney, in a way of letting what was past and gone go, "tell just what happened when you came here yesterday morning."

Mrs. Hale, still leaning against the door, had that sinking feeling of the mother whose child is about to speak a piece. Lewis often wandered along and got things mixed up in a story. She hoped he would tell this straight and plain, and not say unnecessary things that would just make things harder for Minnie Foster. He didn't begin at once, and she noticed that he looked queer – as if standing in that kitchen and having to tell what he had seen there yesterday morning made him almost sick.

"Yes, Mr. Hale?" the county attorney reminded.

"Harry and I had started to town with a load of potatoes," Mrs. Hale's husband began.

Harry was Mrs. Hale's oldest boy. He wasn't with them now, for the very good reason that those potatoes never got to town yesterday and he was taking them this morning, so he hadn't been home when the sheriff stopped to say he wanted Mr. Hale to come over to the Wright place and tell the county attorney his story there, where he could point it all out. With all Mrs. Hale's other emotions came the fear now that maybe Harry wasn't dressed warm enough – they hadn't any of them realized how that north wind did bite.

"We come along this road," Hale was going on, with a motion of his hand to the road over which they had just come, "and as we got in sight of the house I says to Harry, 'I'm goin' to see if I can't get John Wright to take a telephone.' You see," he explained to Henderson, "unless I can get somebody to go in with me they won't come out this branch road except for a price *I* can't pay. I'd spoke to

Wright about it once before; but he put me off, saying folks talked too much anyway, and all he asked was peace and quiet – guess you know about how much he talked himself. But I thought maybe if I went to the house and talked about it before his wife, and said all the women-folks liked the telephones, and that in this lonesome stretch of road it would be a good thing – well, I said to Harry that that was what I was going to say – though I said at the same time that I didn't know as what his wife wanted made much difference to John—"

Now, there he was! – saying things he didn't need to say. Mrs. Hale tried to catch her husband's eye, but fortunately the county attorney interrupted with:

"Let's talk about that a little later, Mr. Hale. I do want to talk about that, but I'm anxious now to get along to just what happened when you got here."

When he began this time, it was very deliberately and carefully:

"I didn't see or hear anything. I knocked at the door. And still it was all quiet inside. I knew they must be up – it was past eight o'clock. So I knocked again, louder, and I thought I heard somebody say, 'Come in.' I wasn't sure – I'm not sure yet. But I opened the door – this door," jerking a hand toward the door by which the two women stood, "and there, in that rocker" – pointing to it – "sat Mrs. Wright."

Everyone in the kitchen looked at the rocker. It came into Mrs. Hale's mind that that rocker didn't look in the least like Minnie Foster – the Minnie Foster of twenty years before. It was a dingy red, with wooden rungs up the back, and the middle rung was gone, and the chair sagged to one side.

"How did she – look?" the county attorney was inquiring.

"Well," said Hale, "she looked – queer."

"How do you mean – queer?"

As he asked it he took out a notebook and pencil. Mrs. Hale did not like the sight of that pencil. She kept her eye fixed on her husband, as if to keep him from saying unnecessary things that would go into that notebook and make trouble.

Hale did speak guardedly, as if the pencil had affected him too.

"Well, as if she didn't know what she was going to do next. And kind of – done up."

"How did she seem to feel about your coming?"

"Why, I don't think she minded – one way or other. She didn't pay much attention. I said, 'Ho' do, Mrs. Wright? It's cold, ain't it?' And she said, 'Is it?' – and went on pleatin' at her apron.

"Well, I was surprised. She didn't ask me to come up to the stove, or to sit down, but just set there, not even lookin' at me. And so I said: 'I want to see John.'

"And then she – laughed. I guess you would call it a laugh.

"I thought of Harry and the team outside, so I said, a little sharp, 'Can I see John?' 'No,' says she – kind of dull like. 'Ain't he home?' says I. Then she looked at me. 'Yes,' says she, 'he's home.' 'Then why can't I see him?' I asked her, out of patience with her now. ''Cause he's dead,' says she, just as quiet and dull – and fell to pleatin' her apron. 'Dead?' says I, like you do when you can't take in what you've heard.

"She just nodded her head, not getting a bit excited, but rockin' back and forth.

"'Why – where is he?' says I, not knowing *what* to say.

"She just pointed upstairs – like this" – pointing to the room above.

"I got up, with the idea of going up there myself. By this time I – didn't know what to do. I walked from there to here; then I says: 'Why, what did he die of?'

"'He died of a rope round his neck,' says she; and just went on pleatin' at her apron."

Hale stopped speaking, and stood staring at the rocker, as if he were still seeing the woman who had sat there the morning before. Nobody spoke; it was as if every one were seeing the woman who had sat there the morning before.

"And what did you do then?" the county attorney at last broke the silence.

"I went out and called Harry. I thought I might – need help. I got Harry in, and we went upstairs." His voice fell almost to a whisper. "There he was – lying over the—"

"I think I'd rather have you go into that upstairs," the county attorney interrupted, "where you can point it all out. Just go on now with the rest of the story."

"Well, my first thought was to get that rope off. It looked—"

He stopped, his face twitching.

"But Harry, he went up to him, and he said, 'No, he's dead all right, and we'd better not touch anything.' So we went downstairs.

"She was still sitting that same way. 'Has anybody been notified?' I asked. 'No,' says she, unconcerned.

"'Who did this, Mrs. Wright?' said Harry. He said it businesslike, and she stopped pleatin' at her apron. 'I don't know,' she says. 'You don't *know*?' says Harry. 'Weren't you sleepin' in the bed with him?' 'Yes,' says she, 'but I was on the inside.' 'Somebody slipped a rope round his neck and strangled him, and you didn't wake up?' says Harry. 'I didn't wake up,' she said after him.

"We may have looked as if we didn't see how that could be, for after a minute she said, 'I sleep sound.'

"Harry was going to ask her more questions, but I said maybe that weren't our business; maybe we ought to let her tell her story first to the coroner or the sheriff. So Harry went fast as he could over to High Road – the Rivers' place, where there's a telephone."

"And what did she do when she knew you had gone for the coroner?" The attorney got his pencil in his hand all ready for writing.

"She moved from that chair to this one over here" – Hale pointed to a small chair in the corner— "and just sat there with her hands held together and looking down. I got a feeling that I ought to make some conversation, so I said I had come in to see if John wanted to put in a telephone; and at that she started to laugh, and then she stopped and looked at me – scared."

At sound of a moving pencil the man who was telling the story looked up.

"I dunno – maybe it wasn't scared," he hastened; "I wouldn't like to say it was. Soon Harry got back, and then Dr. Lloyd came, and you, Mr. Peters, and so I guess that's all I know that you don't."

He said that last with relief, and moved a little, as if relaxing. Everyone moved a little. The county attorney walked toward the stair door.

"I guess we'll go upstairs first – then out to the barn and around there."

He paused and looked around the kitchen.

"You're convinced there was nothing important here?" he asked the sheriff. "Nothing that would – point to any motive?"

The sheriff too looked all around, as if to re-convince himself.

"Nothing here but kitchen things," he said, with a little laugh for the insignificance of kitchen things.

The county attorney was looking at the cupboard – a peculiar, ungainly structure, half closet and half cupboard, the upper part of it being built in the wall, and the lower part just the old-fashioned kitchen cupboard. As if its queerness attracted him, he got a chair and opened the upper part and looked in. After a moment he drew his hand away sticky.

"Here's a nice mess," he said resentfully.

The two women had drawn nearer, and now the sheriff's wife spoke.

"Oh – her fruit," she said, looking to Mrs. Hale for sympathetic understanding. She turned back to the county attorney and explained: "She worried about that when it turned so cold last night. She said the fire would go out and her jars might burst."

Mrs. Peters' husband broke into a laugh.

"Well, can you beat the women! Held for murder and worrying about her preserves!"

The young attorney set his lips.

"I guess before we're through with her she may have something more serious than preserves to worry about."

"Oh, well," said Mrs. Hale's husband, with good-natured superiority, "women are used to worrying over trifles."

The two women moved a little closer together. Neither of them spoke. The county attorney seemed suddenly to remember his manners – and think of his future.

"And yet," said he, with the gallantry of a young politician, "for all their worries, what would we do without the ladies?"

The women did not speak, did not unbend. He went to the sink and began washing his hands. He turned to wipe them on the roller towel – whirled it for a cleaner place.

"Dirty towels! Not much of a housekeeper, would you say, ladies?"

He kicked his foot against some dirty pans under the sink.

"There's a great deal of work to be done on a farm," said Mrs. Hale stiffly.

"To be sure. And yet" – with a little bow to her – "I know there are some Dickson County farm-houses that do not have such roller towels." He gave it a pull to expose its full length again.

"Those towels get dirty awful quick. Men's hands aren't always as clean as they might be."

"Ah, loyal to your sex, I see," he laughed. He stopped and gave her a keen look. "But you and Mrs. Wright were neighbors. I suppose you were friends, too."

Martha Hale shook her head.

"I've seen little enough of her of late years. I've not been in this house – it's more than a year."

"And why was that? You didn't like her?"

"I liked her well enough," she replied with spirit. "Farmers' wives have their hands full, Mr. Henderson. And then—" She looked around the kitchen.

"Yes?" he encouraged.

"It never seemed a very cheerful place," said she, more to herself than to him.

"No," he agreed; "I don't think anyone would call it cheerful. I shouldn't say she had the home-making instinct."

"Well, I don't know as Wright had, either," she muttered.

"You mean they didn't get on very well?" he was quick to ask.

"No; I don't mean anything," she answered, with decision. As she turned a little away from him, she added: "But I don't think a place would be any the cheerfuler for John Wright's bein' in it."

"I'd like to talk to you about that a little later, Mrs. Hale," he said. "I'm anxious to get the lay of things upstairs now."

He moved toward the stair door, followed by the two men.

"I suppose anything Mrs. Peters does'll be all right?" the sheriff inquired. "She was to take in some clothes for her, you know – and a few little things. We left in such a hurry yesterday."

The county attorney looked at the two women whom they were leaving alone there among the kitchen things.

"Yes – Mrs. Peters," he said, his glance resting on the woman who was not Mrs. Peters, the big farmer woman who stood behind the sheriff's wife. "Of course Mrs. Peters is one of us," he said, in a manner of entrusting responsibility. "And keep your eye out Mrs. Peters, for anything that might be of use. No telling; you women might come upon a clue to the motive – and that's the thing we need."

Mr. Hale rubbed his face after the fashion of a showman getting ready for a pleasantry.

"But would the women know a clue if they did come upon it?" he said; and, having delivered himself of this, he followed the others through the stair door.

The women stood motionless and silent, listening to the footsteps, first upon the stairs, then in the room above them.

Then, as if releasing herself from something strange, Mrs. Hale began to arrange the dirty pans under the sink, which the county attorney's disdainful push of the foot had deranged.

"I'd hate to have men comin' into my kitchen," she said testily – "snoopin' round and criticizin'."

"Of course it's no more than their duty," said the sheriff's wife, in her manner of timid acquiescence.

"Duty's all right," replied Mrs. Hale bluffly; "but I guess that deputy sheriff that come out to make the fire might have got a little of this on." She gave the roller towel a pull. "Wish I'd thought of that sooner! Seems mean to talk about her for not having things slicked up, when she had to come away in such a hurry."

She looked around the kitchen. Certainly it was not 'slicked up'. Her eye was held by a bucket of sugar on a low shelf. The cover was off the wooden bucket, and beside it was a paper bag – half full.

Mrs. Hale moved toward it.

"She was putting this in there," she said to herself – slowly.

She thought of the flour in her kitchen at home – half sifted, half not sifted. She had been interrupted, and had left things half done. What had interrupted Minnie Foster? Why had that work been left half done? She made a move as if to finish it – unfinished things always bothered her – and then she glanced around and saw that Mrs. Peters was watching her – and she didn't want Mrs. Peters to get that feeling she had got of work begun and then – for some reason – not finished.

"It's a shame about her fruit," she said, and walked toward the cupboard that the county attorney had opened, and got on the chair, murmuring: "I wonder if it's all gone."

It was a sorry enough looking sight, but "Here's one that's all right," she said at last. She held it toward the light. "This is cherries, too." She looked again. "I declare I believe that's the only one."

With a sigh, she got down from the chair, went to the sink, and wiped off the bottle.

"She'll feel awful bad, after all her hard work in the hot weather. I remember the afternoon I put up my cherries last summer."

She set the bottle on the table, and, with another sigh, started to sit down in the rocker. But she did not sit down. Something kept her from sitting down in that chair. She straightened – stepped back, and, half turned away, stood looking at it, seeing the woman who had sat there 'pleatin' at her apron'.

The thin voice of the sheriff's wife broke in upon her: "I must be getting those things from the front room closet." She opened the door into the other room, started in, stepped back. "You coming with me, Mrs. Hale?" she asked nervously. "You – you could help me get them."

They were soon back – the stark coldness of that shut-up room was not a thing to linger in.

"My!" said Mrs. Peters, dropping the things on the table and hurrying to the stove.

Mrs. Hale stood examining the clothes the woman who was being detained in town had said she wanted.

"Wright was close!" she exclaimed, holding up a shabby black skirt that bore the marks of much making over. "I think maybe that's why she kept so much to herself. I s'pose she felt she couldn't do her part; and then, you don't enjoy things when you feel shabby. She used to wear pretty clothes and be lively – when she was Minnie Foster, one of the town girls, singing in the choir. But that – oh, that was twenty years ago."

With a carefulness in which there was something tender, she folded the shabby clothes and piled them at one corner of the table. She looked up at Mrs. Peters and there was something in the other woman's look that irritated her.

"She don't care," she said to herself. "Much difference it makes to her whether Minnie Foster had pretty clothes when she was a girl."

Then she looked again, and she wasn't so sure; in fact, she hadn't at any time been perfectly sure about Mrs. Peters. She had that shrinking manner, and yet her eyes looked as if they could see a long way into things.

"This all you was to take in?" asked Mrs. Hale.

"No," said the sheriff's wife; "she said she wanted an apron. Funny thing to want," she ventured in her nervous little way, "for there's not much to get you dirty in jail, goodness knows. But I suppose just to make her feel more natural. If you're used to wearing an apron—. She said they were in the bottom drawer of this cupboard. Yes – here they are. And then her little shawl that always hung on the stair door."

She took the small gray shawl from behind the door leading upstairs, and stood a minute looking at it.

Suddenly Mrs. Hale took a quick step toward the other woman.

"Mrs. Peters!"

"Yes, Mrs. Hale?"

"Do you think she – did it?"

A frightened look blurred the other thing in Mrs. Peters' eyes.

"Oh, I don't know," she said, in a voice that seemed to shrink away from the subject.

"Well, I don't think she did," affirmed Mrs. Hale stoutly. "Asking for an apron, and her little shawl. Worryin' about her fruit."

"Mr. Peters says—." Footsteps were heard in the room above; she stopped, looked up, then went on in a lowered voice: "Mr. Peters says – it looks bad for her. Mr. Henderson is awful sarcastic in a speech, and he's going to make fun of her saying she didn't – wake up."

For a moment Mrs. Hale had no answer. Then, "Well, I guess John Wright didn't wake up – when they was slippin' that rope under his neck," she muttered.

"No, it's *strange*," breathed Mrs. Peters. "They think it was such a – funny way to kill a man." She began to laugh; at sound of the laugh, abruptly stopped.

"That's just what Mr. Hale said," said Mrs. Hale, in a resolutely natural voice. "There was a gun in the house. He says that's what he can't understand."

"Mr. Henderson said, coming out, that what was needed for the case was a motive. Something to show anger – or sudden feeling."

"Well, I don't see any signs of anger around here," said Mrs. Hale. "I don't—"

She stopped. It was as if her mind tripped on something. Her eye was caught by a dish-towel in the middle of the kitchen table. Slowly she moved toward the table. One half of it was wiped clean, the other half messy. Her eyes made a slow, almost unwilling turn to the bucket of sugar and the half empty bag beside it. Things begun – and not finished.

After a moment she stepped back, and said, in that manner of releasing herself:

"Wonder how they're finding things upstairs? I hope she had it a little more red up up there. You know," – she paused, and feeling gathered – "it seems kind of *sneaking*: locking her up in town and coming out here to get her own house to turn against her!"

"But, Mrs. Hale," said the sheriff's wife, "the law is the law."

"I s'pose 'tis," answered Mrs. Hale shortly.

She turned to the stove, saying something about that fire not being much to brag of. She worked with it a minute, and when she straightened up she said aggressively:

"The law is the law – and a bad stove is a bad stove. How'd you like to cook on this?" – pointing with the poker to the broken lining. She opened the oven door and started to express her opinion of the oven; but she was swept into her own thoughts, thinking of what it would mean, year after year, to have that stove to wrestle with. The thought of Minnie Foster trying to bake in that oven – and the thought of her never going over to see Minnie Foster—.

She was startled by hearing Mrs. Peters say: "A person gets discouraged – and loses heart."

The sheriff's wife had looked from the stove to the sink – to the pail of water which had been carried in from outside. The two women stood there silent, above them the footsteps of the men who were looking for evidence against the woman who had worked in that kitchen. That look of seeing into things, of seeing through a thing to something else, was in the eyes of the sheriff's wife now. When Mrs. Hale next spoke to her, it was gently:

"Better loosen up your things, Mrs. Peters. We'll not feel them when we go out."

Mrs. Peters went to the back of the room to hang up the fur tippet she was wearing. A moment later she exclaimed, "Why, she was piecing a quilt," and held up a large sewing basket piled high with quilt pieces.

Mrs. Hale spread some of the blocks out on the table.

"It's log-cabin pattern," she said, putting several of them together. "Pretty, isn't it?"

They were so engaged with the quilt that they did not hear the footsteps on the stairs. Just as the stair door opened Mrs. Hale was saying:

"Do you suppose she was going to quilt it or just knot it?"

The sheriff threw up his hands.

"They wonder whether she was going to quilt it or just knot it!"

There was a laugh for the ways of women, a warming of hands over the stove, and then the county attorney said briskly:

"Well, let's go right out to the barn and get that cleared up."

"I don't see as there's anything so strange," Mrs. Hale said resentfully, after the outside door had closed on the three men – "our taking up our time with little things while we're waiting for them to get the evidence. I don't see as it's anything to laugh about."

"Of course they've got awful important things on their minds," said the sheriff's wife apologetically.

They returned to an inspection of the block for the quilt. Mrs. Hale was looking at the fine, even sewing, and preoccupied with thoughts of the woman who had done that sewing, when she heard the sheriff's wife say, in a queer tone:

"Why, look at this one."

She turned to take the block held out to her.

"The sewing," said Mrs. Peters, in a troubled way. "All the rest of them have been so nice and even – but – this one. Why, it looks as if she didn't know what she was about!"

Their eyes met – something flashed to life, passed between them; then, as if with an effort, they seemed to pull away from each other. A moment Mrs. Hale sat her hands folded over that sewing which was so unlike all the rest of the sewing. Then she had pulled a knot and drawn the threads.

"Oh, what are you doing, Mrs. Hale?" asked the sheriff's wife, startled.

"Just pulling out a stitch or two that's not sewed very good," said Mrs. Hale mildly.

"I don't think we ought to touch things," Mrs. Peters said, a little helplessly.

"I'll just finish up this end," answered Mrs. Hale, still in that mild, matter-of-fact fashion.

She threaded a needle and started to replace bad sewing with good. For a little while she sewed in silence. Then, in that thin, timid voice, she heard:

"Mrs. Hale!"

"Yes, Mrs. Peters?"

"What do you suppose she was so – nervous about?"

"Oh, *I* don't know," said Mrs. Hale, as if dismissing a thing not important enough to spend much time on. "I don't know as she was – nervous. I sew awful queer sometimes when I'm just tired."

She cut a thread, and out of the corner of her eye looked up at Mrs. Peters. The small, lean face of the sheriff's wife seemed to have tightened up. Her eyes had that look of peering into something. But next moment she moved, and said in her thin, indecisive way:

"Well, I must get those clothes wrapped. They may be through sooner than we think. I wonder where I could find a piece of paper – and string."

"In that cupboard, maybe," suggested Mrs. Hale, after a glance around.

One piece of the crazy sewing remained unripped. Mrs. Peters' back turned, Martha Hale now scrutinized that piece, compared it with the dainty, accurate sewing of the other blocks. The difference was startling. Holding this block made her feel queer, as if the distracted thoughts of the woman who had perhaps turned to it to try and quiet herself were communicating themselves to her.

Mrs. Peters' voice roused her.

"Here's a bird cage," she said. "Did she have a bird, Mrs. Hale?"

"Why, I don't know whether she did or not." She turned to look at the cage Mrs. Peters was holding up. "I've not been here in so long." She sighed. "There was a man round last year selling canaries cheap – but I don't know as she took one. Maybe she did. She used to sing real pretty herself."

Mrs. Peters looked around the kitchen.

"Seems kind of funny to think of a bird here." She half laughed – an attempt to put up a barrier. "But she must have had one – or why would she have a cage? I wonder what happened to it."

"I suppose maybe the cat got it," suggested Mrs. Hale, resuming her sewing.

"No; she didn't have a cat. She's got that feeling some people have about cats – being afraid of them. When they brought her to our house yesterday, my cat got in the room, and she was real upset and asked me to take it out."

"My sister Bessie was like that," laughed Mrs. Hale.

The sheriff's wife did not reply. The silence made Mrs. Hale turn round. Mrs. Peters was examining the bird cage.

"Look at this door," she said slowly. "It's broke. One hinge has been pulled apart."

Mrs. Hale came nearer.

"Looks as if someone must have been – rough with it."

Again their eyes met – startled, questioning, apprehensive. For a moment neither spoke nor stirred. Then Mrs. Hale, turning away, said brusquely:

"If they're going to find any evidence, I wish they'd be about it. I don't like this place."

"But I'm awful glad you came with me, Mrs. Hale," Mrs. Peters put the bird cage on the table and sat down. "It would be lonesome for me – sitting here alone."

"Yes, it would, wouldn't it?" agreed Mrs. Hale, a certain determined naturalness in her voice. She had picked up the sewing, but now it dropped in her lap, and she murmured in a different voice: "But I tell you what I *do* wish, Mrs. Peters. I wish I had come over sometimes when she was here. I wish – I had."

"But of course you were awful busy, Mrs. Hale. Your house – and your children."

"I could've come," retorted Mrs. Hale shortly. "I stayed away because it weren't cheerful – and that's why I ought to have come. I" – she looked around – "I've never liked this place. Maybe because it's down in a hollow and you don't see the road. I don't know what it is, but it's a lonesome place, and always was. I wish I had come over to see Minnie Foster sometimes. I can see now—"
She did not put it into words.

"Well, you mustn't reproach yourself," counseled Mrs. Peters. "Somehow, we just don't see how it is with other folks till – something comes up."

"Not having children makes less work," mused Mrs. Hale, after a silence, "but it makes a quiet house – and Wright out to work all day – and no company when he did come in. Did you know John Wright, Mrs. Peters?"

"Not to know him. I've seen him in town. They say he was a good man."

"Yes – good," conceded John Wright's neighbor grimly. "He didn't drink, and kept his word as well as most, I guess, and paid his debts. But he was a hard man, Mrs. Peters. Just to pass the time of day with him —." She stopped, shivered a little. "Like a raw wind that gets to the bone." Her eye fell upon the cage on the table before her, and she added, almost bitterly: "I should think she would've wanted a bird!"

Suddenly she leaned forward, looking intently at the cage. "But what do you s'pose went wrong with it?"

"I don't know," returned Mrs. Peters; "unless it got sick and died."

But after she said it she reached over and swung the broken door. Both women watched it as if somehow held by it.

"You didn't know – her?" Mrs. Hale asked, a gentler note in her voice.

"Not till they brought her yesterday," said the sheriff's wife.

"She – come to think of it, she was kind of like a bird herself. Real sweet and pretty, but kind of timid and – fluttery. How – she – did – change."

That held her for a long time. Finally, as if struck with a happy thought and relieved to get back to everyday things, she exclaimed:

"Tell you what, Mrs. Peters, why don't you take the quilt in with you? It might take up her mind."

"Why, I think that's a real nice idea, Mrs. Hale," agreed the sheriff's wife, as if she too were glad to come into the atmosphere of a simple kindness. "There couldn't possibly be any objection to that, could there? Now, just what will I take? I wonder if her patches are in here – and her things."

They turned to the sewing basket.

"Here's some red," said Mrs. Hale, bringing out a roll of cloth. Underneath that was a box. "Here, maybe her scissors are in here – and her things." She held it up. "What a pretty box! I'll warrant that was something she had a long time ago – when she was a girl."

She held it in her hand a moment; then, with a little sigh, opened it.

Instantly her hand went to her nose.

"Why—!"

Mrs. Peters drew nearer – then turned away.

"There's something wrapped up in this piece of silk," faltered Mrs. Hale.

"This isn't her scissors," said Mrs. Peters, in a shrinking voice.

Her hand not steady, Mrs. Hale raised the piece of silk. "Oh, Mrs. Peters!" she cried. "It's—"

Mrs. Peters bent closer.

"It's the bird," she whispered.

"But, Mrs. Peters!" cried Mrs. Hale. "*Look* at it! Its *neck* – look at its neck! It's all – other side *to*."

She held the box away from her.

The sheriff's wife again bent closer.

"Somebody wrung its neck," said she, in a voice that was slow and deep.

And then again the eyes of the two women met – this time clung together in a look of dawning comprehension, of growing horror. Mrs. Peters looked from the dead bird to the broken door of the cage. Again their eyes met. And just then there was a sound at the outside door.

Mrs. Hale slipped the box under the quilt pieces in the basket, and sank into the chair before it. Mrs. Peters stood holding to the table. The county attorney and the sheriff came in from outside.

"Well, ladies," said the county attorney, as one turning from serious things to little pleasantries, "have you decided whether she was going to quilt it or knot it?"

"We think," began the sheriff's wife in a flurried voice, "that she was going to – knot it."

He was too preoccupied to notice the change that came in her voice on that last.

"Well, that's very interesting, I'm sure," he said tolerantly. He caught sight of the bird cage. "Has the bird flown?"

"We think the cat got it," said Mrs. Hale in a voice curiously even.

He was walking up and down, as if thinking something out.

"Is there a cat?" he asked absently.

Mrs. Hale shot a look up at the sheriff's wife.

"Well, not *now*," said Mrs. Peters. "They're superstitious, you know; they leave."

She sank into her chair.

The county attorney did not heed her. "No sign at all of anyone having come in from the outside," he said to Peters, in the manner of continuing an interrupted conversation. "Their own rope. Now let's go upstairs again and go over it, piece by piece. It would have to have been someone who knew just the—"

The stair door closed behind them and their voices were lost.

The two women sat motionless, not looking at each other, but as if peering into something and at the same time holding back. When they spoke now it was as if they were afraid of what they were saying, but as if they could not help saying it.

"She liked the bird," said Martha Hale, low and slowly. "She was going to bury it in that pretty box."

"When I was a girl," said Mrs. Peters, under her breath, "my kitten – there was a boy took a hatchet, and before my eyes – before I could get there—" She covered her face an instant. "If they hadn't held me back I would have" – she caught herself, looked upstairs where footsteps were heard, and finished weakly – "hurt him."

Then they sat without speaking or moving.

"I wonder how it would seem," Mrs. Hale at last began, as if feeling her way over strange ground – "never to have had any children around?" Her eyes made a slow sweep of the kitchen, as if seeing what that kitchen had meant through all the years. "No, Wright wouldn't like the bird," she said after that – "a thing that sang. She used to sing. He killed that too." Her voice tightened.

Mrs. Peters moved uneasily.

"Of course we don't know who killed the bird."

"I knew John Wright," was Mrs. Hale's answer.

"It was an awful thing was done in this house that night, Mrs. Hale," said the sheriff's wife. "Killing a man while he slept – slipping a thing round his neck that choked the life out of him."

Mrs. Hale's hand went out to the bird cage.

"His neck. Choked the life out of him."

"We don't *know* who killed him," whispered Mrs. Peters wildly. "We don't *know*."

Mrs. Hale had not moved. "If there had been years and years of – nothing, then a bird to sing to you, it would be awful – still – after the bird was still."

It was as if something within her not herself had spoken, and it found in Mrs. Peters something she did not know as herself.

"I know what stillness is," she said, in a queer, monotonous voice. "When we homesteaded in Dakota, and my first baby died – after he was two years old – and me with no other then—"

Mrs. Hale stirred.

"How soon do you suppose they'll be through looking for the evidence?"

"I know what stillness is," repeated Mrs. Peters, in just that same way. Then she too pulled back. "The law has got to punish crime, Mrs. Hale," she said in her tight little way.

"I wish you'd seen Minnie Foster," was the answer, "when she wore a white dress with blue ribbons, and stood up there in the choir and sang."

The picture of that girl, the fact that she had lived neighbor to that girl for twenty years, and had let her die for lack of life, was suddenly more than she could bear.

"Oh, I *wish* I'd come over here once in a while!" she cried. "That was a crime! That was a crime! Who's going to punish that?"

"We mustn't take on," said Mrs. Peters, with a frightened look toward the stairs.

"I might 'a' *known* she needed help! I tell you, it's *queer*, Mrs. Peters. We live close together, and we live far apart. We all go through the same things – it's all just a different kind of the same thing! If it weren't – why do you and I *understand*? Why do we *know* – what we know this minute?"

She dashed her hand across her eyes. Then, seeing the jar of fruit on the table, she reached for it and choked out:

"If I was you I wouldn't *tell* her her fruit was gone! Tell her it *ain't*. Tell her it's all right – all of it. Here – take this in to prove it to her! She – she may never know whether it was broke or not."

She turned away.

Mrs. Peters reached out for the bottle of fruit as if she were glad to take it – as if touching a familiar thing, having something to do, could keep her from something else. She got up, looked about for something to wrap the fruit in, took a petticoat from the pile of clothes she had brought from the front room, and nervously started winding that round the bottle.

"My!" she began, in a high, false voice, "it's a good thing the men couldn't hear us! Getting all stirred up over a little thing like a – dead canary." She hurried over that. "As if that could have anything to do with – with – my, wouldn't they *laugh*?"

Footsteps were heard on the stairs.

"Maybe they would," muttered Mrs. Hale – "maybe they wouldn't."

"No, Peters," said the county attorney incisively; "it's all perfectly clear, except the reason for doing it. But you know juries when it comes to women. If there was some definite thing – something to show. Something to make a story about. A thing that would connect up with this clumsy way of doing it."

In a covert way Mrs. Hale looked at Mrs. Peters. Mrs. Peters was looking at her. Quickly they looked away from each other. The outer door opened and Mr. Hale came in.

"I've got the team round now," he said. "Pretty cold out there."

"I'm going to stay here awhile by myself," the county attorney suddenly announced. "You can send Frank out for me, can't you?" he asked the sheriff. "I want to go over everything. I'm not satisfied we can't do better."

Again, for one brief moment, the two women's eyes found one another.

The sheriff came up to the table.

"Did you want to see what Mrs. Peters was going to take in?"

The county attorney picked up the apron. He laughed.

"Oh, I guess they're not very dangerous things the ladies have picked out."

Mrs. Hale's hand was on the sewing basket in which the box was concealed. She felt that she ought to take her hand off the basket. She did not seem able to. He picked up one of the quilt blocks which she had piled on to cover the box. Her eyes felt like fire. She had a feeling that if he took up the basket she would snatch it from him.

But he did not take it up. With another little laugh, he turned away, saying:

"No; Mrs. Peters doesn't need supervising. For that matter, a sheriff's wife is married to the law. Ever think of it that way, Mrs. Peters?"

Mrs. Peters was standing beside the table. Mrs. Hale shot a look up at her; but she could not see her face. Mrs. Peters had turned away. When she spoke, her voice was muffled.

"Not – just that way," she said.

"Married to the law!" chuckled Mrs. Peters' husband. He moved toward the door into the front room, and said to the county attorney:

"I just want you to come in here a minute, George. We ought to take a look at these windows."

"Oh – windows," said the county attorney scoffingly.

"We'll be right out, Mr. Hale," said the sheriff to the farmer, who was still waiting by the door.

Hale went to look after the horses. The sheriff followed the county attorney into the other room. Again – for one final moment – the two women were alone in that kitchen.

Martha Hale sprang up, her hands tight together, looking at that other woman, with whom it rested. At first she could not see her eyes, for the sheriff's wife had not turned back since she turned away at that suggestion of being married to the law. But now Mrs. Hale made her turn back. Her eyes made her turn back. Slowly, unwillingly, Mrs. Peters turned her head until her eyes met the eyes of the other woman. There was a moment when they held each other in a steady, burning look in which there was no evasion nor flinching. Then Martha Hale's eyes pointed the way to the basket in which was hidden the thing that would make certain the conviction of the other woman – that woman who was not there and yet who had been there with them all through that hour.

For a moment Mrs. Peters did not move. And then she did it. With a rush forward, she threw back the quilt pieces, got the box, tried to put it in her handbag. It was too big. Desperately she opened it, started to take the bird out. But there she broke – she could not touch the bird. She stood there helpless, foolish.

There was the sound of a knob turning in the inner door. Martha Hale snatched the box from the sheriff's wife, and got it in the pocket of her big coat just as the sheriff and the county attorney came back into the kitchen.

"Well, Henry," said the county attorney facetiously, "at least we found out that she was not going to quilt it. She was going to – what is it you call it, ladies?"

Mrs. Hale's hand was against the pocket of her coat.

"We call it – knot it, Mr. Henderson."

An Intangible Clue

Anna Katharine Green

"HAVE YOU studied the case?"

"Not I."

"Not studied the case which for the last few days has provided the papers with such conspicuous headlines?"

"I do not read the papers. I have not looked at one in a whole week."

"Miss Strange, your social engagements must be of a very pressing nature just now?"

"They are."

"And your business sense in abeyance?"

"How so?"

"You would not ask if you had read the papers."

To this she made no reply save by a slight toss of her pretty head. If her employer felt nettled by this show of indifference, he did not betray it save by the rapidity of his tones as, without further preamble and possibly without real excuse, he proceeded to lay before her the case in question. "Last Tuesday night a woman was murdered in this city; an old woman, in a lonely house where she has lived for years. Perhaps you remember this house? It occupies a not inconspicuous site in Seventeenth Street – a house of the olden time?"

"No, I do not remember."

The extreme carelessness of Miss Strange's tone would have been fatal to her socially; but then, she would never have used it socially. This they both knew, yet he smiled with his customary indulgence.

"Then I will describe it."

She looked around for a chair and sank into it. He did the same.

"It has a fanlight over the front door."

She remained impassive.

"And two old-fashioned strips of parti-colored glass on either side."

"And a knocker between its panels which may bring money some day."

"Oh, you do remember! I thought you would, Miss Strange."

"Yes. Fanlights over doors are becoming very rare in New York."

"Very well, then. That house was the scene of Tuesday's tragedy. The woman who has lived there in solitude for years was foully murdered. I have since heard that the people who knew her best have always anticipated some such violent end for her. She never allowed maid or friend to remain with her after five in the afternoon; yet she had money – some think a great deal – always in the house."

"I am interested in the house, not in her."

"Yet, she was a character – as full of whims and crotchets as a nut is of meat. Her death was horrible. She fought – her dress was torn from her body in rags. This happened, you see, before her hour for retiring; some think as early as six in the afternoon. And" – here he made a rapid gesture to catch Violet's wandering attention – "in spite of this struggle; in spite of the fact that she was dragged from room to room – that her person was searched – and everything in the house searched – that drawers were pulled out of bureaus – doors wrenched off of cupboards – china smashed upon the floor – whole shelves denuded and not a spot from cellar to garret left unransacked, no direct clue to the perpetrator has been found – nothing that gives any idea of his personality save his display of strength and great cupidity. The police have even deigned to consult me – an unusual procedure – but I could find nothing, either. Evidences of fiendish purpose abound – of relentless search – but no clue to the man himself. It's uncommon, isn't it, not to have any clue?"

"I suppose so." Miss Strange hated murders and it was with difficulty she could be brought to discuss them. But she was not going to be let off; not this time.

"You see," he proceeded insistently, "it's not only mortifying to the police but disappointing to the press, especially as few reporters believe in the No-thoroughfare business. They say, and we cannot but agree with them, that no such struggle could take place and no such repeated goings to and fro through the house without some vestige being left by which to connect this crime with its daring perpetrator."

Still she stared down at her hands – those little hands so white and fluttering, so seemingly helpless under the weight of their many rings, and yet so slyly capable.

"She must have queer neighbors," came at last, from Miss Strange's reluctant lips. "Didn't they hear or see anything of all this?"

"She has no neighbors – that is, after half past five o'clock. There's a printing establishment on one side of her, a deserted mansion on the other side, and nothing but warehouses back and front. There was no one to notice what took place in her small dwelling after the printing house was closed. She was the most courageous or the most foolish of women to remain there as she did. But nothing except death could budge her. She was born in the room where she died; was married in the one where she worked; saw husband, father, mother, and five sisters carried out in turn to their graves through the door with the fanlight over the top – and these memories held her."

"You are trying to interest me in the woman. Don't."

"No, I'm not trying to interest you in her, only trying to explain her. There was another reason for her remaining where she did so long after all residents had left the block. She had a business."

"Oh!"

"She embroidered monograms for fine ladies."

"She did? But you needn't look at me like that. She never embroidered any for me."

"No? She did first-class work. I saw some of it. Miss Strange, if I could get you into that house for ten minutes – not to see her but to pick up the loose intangible thread which I am sure is floating around in it somewhere – wouldn't you go?"

Violet slowly rose – a movement which he followed to the letter.

"Must I express in words the limit I have set for myself in our affair?" she asked. "When, for reasons I have never thought myself called upon to explain, I consented to help you a little now and then with some matter where a woman's tact and knowledge of the social world might tell without offence to herself or others, I never thought it would be necessary for me to state that temptation must stop with such cases, or that I should not be asked to touch the sordid or the bloody. But it seems I was mistaken, and that I must stoop to be explicit. The woman who was killed on Tuesday might have interested me greatly as an embroiderer, but as a victim, not at all. What do you see in me, or miss in me, that you should drag me into an atmosphere of low-down crime?"

"Nothing, Miss Strange. You are by nature, as well as by breeding, very far removed from everything of the kind. But you will allow me to suggest that no crime is low-down which makes imperative demand upon the intellect and intuitive sense of its investigator. Only the most delicate touch can feel and hold the thread I've just spoken of, and you have the most delicate touch I know."

"Do not attempt to flatter me. I have no fancy for handling befouled spider webs. Besides, if I had – if such elusive filaments fascinated me – how could I, well-known in person and name, enter upon such a scene without prejudice to our mutual compact?"

"Miss Strange" – she had reseated herself, but so far he had failed to follow her example (an ignoring of the subtle hint that her interest might yet be caught, which seemed to annoy her a trifle), "I should not even have suggested such a possibility had I not seen a way of introducing you there without risk to your position or mine. Among the boxes piled upon Mrs. Doolittle's table – boxes of finished work, most of them addressed and ready for delivery – was one on which could be seen the name of – shall I mention it?"

"Not mine? You don't mean mine? That would be too odd – too ridiculously odd. I should not understand a coincidence of that kind; no, I should not, notwithstanding the fact that I have lately sent out such work to be done."

"Yet it was your name, very clearly and precisely written – your whole name, Miss Strange. I saw and read it myself."

"But I gave the order to Madame Pirot on Fifth Avenue. How came my things to be found in the house of this woman of whose horrible death we have been talking?"

"Did you suppose that Madame Pirot did such work with her own hands? Or even had it done in her own establishment? Mrs. Doolittle was universally employed. She worked for a dozen firms. You will find the biggest names on most of her packages. But on this one – I allude to the one addressed to you – there was more to be seen than the name. These words were written on it in another hand. Send without opening. This struck the police as suspicious; sufficiently so, at least, for them to desire your presence at the house as soon as you can make it convenient."

"To open the box?"

"Exactly."

The curl of Miss Strange's disdainful lip was a sight to see.

"You wrote those words yourself," she coolly observed. "While someone's back was turned, you whipped out your pencil and—"

"Resorted to a very pardonable subterfuge highly conducive to the public's good. But never mind that. Will you go?"

Miss Strange became suddenly demure.

"I suppose I must," she grudgingly conceded. "However obtained, a summons from the police cannot be ignored even by Peter Strange's daughter."

Another man might have displayed his triumph by smile or gesture; but this one had learned his role too well. He simply said:

"Very good. Shall it be at once? I have a taxi at the door."

But she failed to see the necessity of any such hurry. With sudden dignity she replied:

"That won't do. If I go to this house it must be under suitable conditions. I shall have to ask my brother to accompany me."

"Your brother!"

"Oh, he's safe. He – he knows."

"Your brother knows?" Her visitor, with less control than usual, betrayed very openly his uneasiness.

"He does and – approves. But that's not what interests us now, only so far as it makes it possible for me to go with propriety to that dreadful house."

A formal bow from the other and the words:

"They may expect you, then. Can you say when?"

"Within the next hour. But it will be a useless concession on my part," she pettishly complained. "A place that has been gone over by a dozen detectives is apt to be brushed clean of its cobwebs, even if such ever existed."

"That's the difficulty," he acknowledged; and did not dare to add another word; she was at that particular moment so very much the great lady, and so little his confidential agent.

He might have been less impressed, however, by this sudden assumption of manner, had he been so fortunate as to have seen how she employed the three quarters of an hour's delay for which she had asked.

She read those neglected newspapers, especially the one containing the following highly colored narration of this ghastly crime:

"A door ajar – an empty hall – a line of sinister-looking blotches marking a guilty step diagonally across the flagging – silence – and an unmistakable odor repugnant to all humanity – such were the indications which met the eyes of Officer O'Leary on his first round last night, and led to the discovery of a murder which will long thrill the city by its mystery and horror.

"Both the house and the victim are well known." Here followed a description of the same and of Mrs. Doolittle's manner of life in her ancient home, which Violet hurriedly passed over to come to the following:

"As far as one can judge from appearances, the crime happened in this wise: Mrs. Doolittle had been in her kitchen, as the tea-kettle found singing on the stove goes to prove, and was coming back through her bedroom, when the wretch, who had stolen in by the front door which, to save steps, she was unfortunately in the habit of leaving on the latch till all possibility of customers for the day was over, sprang upon her from behind and dealt her a swinging blow with the poker he had caught up from the hearthstone.

"Whether the struggle which ensued followed immediately upon this first attack or came later, it will take medical experts to determine. But, whenever it did occur, the fierceness of its character is shown by the grip taken upon her throat and the traces of blood which are to be seen all over the house. If the wretch had lugged her into her workroom and thence to the kitchen, and thence back to the spot of first assault, the evidences could not have been more ghastly. Bits of her clothing torn off by a ruthless hand, lay scattered over all these floors. In her bedroom, where she finally breathed her last, there could be seen mingled with these a number of large but worthless glass beads; and close against one of the base-boards, the string which had held them, as shown by the few remaining beads still clinging to it. If in pulling the string from her neck he had hoped to light upon some valuable booty, his fury at his disappointment is evident. You can almost see the frenzy with which he flung the would-be necklace at the wall, and kicked about and stamped upon its rapidly rolling beads.

"Booty! That was what he was after; to find and carry away the poor needlewoman's supposed hoardings. If the scene baffles description – if, as some believe, he dragged her yet living from spot to spot, demanding information as to her places of concealment under threat of repeated blows, and, finally baffled, dealt the finishing stroke and proceeded on the search alone, no greater devastation could have taken place in this poor woman's house or effects. Yet such was his precaution and care for himself that he left no fingerprint behind him nor any other token which could lead to personal identification. Even though his footsteps could be traced in much the order I have mentioned, they were of so indeterminate and shapeless a character as to convey little to the intelligence of the investigator.

"That these smears (they could not be called footprints) not only crossed the hall but appeared in more than one place on the staircase proves that he did not confine his search to the lower storey; and perhaps one of the most interesting features of the case lies in the indications given by these marks of the raging course he took through these upper rooms. As the accompanying diagram will show [we omit the diagram] he went first into the large front chamber, thence to the rear where we find two rooms, one unfinished and filled with accumulated stuff most of which he left lying loose upon the floor, and the other plastered, and containing a window opening upon an alley-way at the side, but empty of all furniture and without even a carpet on the bare boards.

"Why he should have entered the latter place, and why, having entered he should have crossed to the window, will be plain to those who have studied the conditions. The front chamber windows were tightly shuttered, the attic ones cumbered with boxes and shielded from approach by old bureaus and discarded chairs. This one only was free and, although darkened by the proximity of the house neighboring it across the alley, was the only spot on the storey where sufficient light could be had at this late hour for the examination of any object of whose value he was doubtful. That he had come across such an object and had brought it to this window for some such purpose is very satisfactorily demonstrated by the discovery of a worn out wallet of ancient make lying on the floor directly in front of this window – a proof of his cupidity but also proof of his ill-luck. For this wallet, when lifted and opened, was found to contain two hundred or more dollars in old bills, which, if not the full hoard of their industrious owner, was certainly worth the taking by one who had risked his neck for the sole purpose of theft.

"This wallet, and the flight of the murderer without it, give to this affair, otherwise simply brutal, a dramatic interest which will be appreciated not only by the very able detectives already hot upon the chase, but by all other inquiring minds anxious to solve a mystery of which so estimable a woman has been the unfortunate victim. A problem is presented to the police—"

There Violet stopped.

When, not long after, the superb limousine of Peter Strange stopped before the little house in Seventeenth Street, it caused a veritable sensation, not only in the curiosity-mongers lingering on the sidewalk, but to the two persons within – the officer on guard and a belated reporter.

Though dressed in her plainest suit, Violet Strange looked much too fashionable and far too young and thoughtless to be observed, without emotion, entering a scene of hideous and brutal crime. Even the young man who accompanied her promised to bring a most incongruous element into this atmosphere of guilt and horror, and, as the detective on guard whispered to the man beside him, might much better have been left behind in the car.

But Violet was great for the proprieties and young Arthur followed her in.

Her entrance was a *coup du théâtre*. She had lifted her veil in crossing the sidewalk and her interesting features and general air of timidity were very fetching. As the man holding open the door noted the impression made upon his companion, he muttered with sly facetiousness:

"You think you'll show her nothing; but I'm ready to bet a fiver that she'll want to see it all and that you'll show it to her."

The detective's grin was expressive, notwithstanding the shrug with which he tried to carry it off.

And Violet? The hall into which she now stepped from the most vivid sunlight had never been considered even in its palmiest days as possessing cheer even of the stately kind. The ghastly green light infused through it by the colored glass on either side of the doorway seemed to promise yet more dismal things beyond.

"Must I go in there?" she asked, pointing, with an admirable simulation of nervous excitement, to a half-shut door at her left. "Is there where it happened? Arthur, do you suppose that there is where it happened?"

"No, no, Miss," the officer made haste to assure her. "If you are Miss Strange" (Violet bowed), "I need hardly say that the woman was struck in her bedroom. The door beside you leads into the parlor, or as she would have called it, her work-room. You needn't be afraid of going in there. You will see nothing but the disorder of her boxes. They were pretty well pulled about. Not all of them though," he added, watching her as closely as the dim light permitted. "There is one which gives no sign of having been tampered with. It was done up in wrapping paper and is addressed to you, which in itself would not have seemed worthy of our attention had not these lines been scribbled on it in a man's handwriting: 'Send without opening.'"

"How odd!" exclaimed the little minx with widely opened eyes and an air of guileless innocence. "Whatever can it mean? Nothing serious I am sure, for the woman did not even know me. She was employed to do this work by Madame Pirot."

"Didn't you know that it was to be done here?"

"No. I thought Madame Pirot's own girls did her embroidery for her."

"So that you were surprised—"

"Wasn't I!"

"To get our message."

"I didn't know what to make of it."

The earnest, half-injured look with which she uttered this disclaimer, did its appointed work. The detective accepted her for what she seemed and, oblivious to the reporter's satirical gesture, crossed to the work-room door, which he threw wide open with the remark:

"I should be glad to have you open that box in our presence. It is undoubtedly all right, but we wish to be sure. You know what the box should contain?"

"Oh, yes, indeed; pillow-cases and sheets, with a big S embroidered on them."

"Very well. Shall I undo the string for you?"

"I shall be much obliged," said she, her eye flashing quickly about the room before settling down upon the knot he was deftly loosening.

Her brother, gazing indifferently in from the doorway, hardly noticed this look; but the reporter at his back did, though he failed to detect its penetrating quality.

"Your name is on the other side," observed the detective as he drew away the string and turned the package over.

The smile which just lifted the corner of her lips was not in answer to this remark, but to her recognition of her employer's handwriting in the words under her name: Send without opening. She had not misjudged him.

"The cover you may like to take off yourself," suggested the officer, as he lifted the box out of its wrapper.

"Oh, I don't mind. There's nothing to be ashamed of in embroidered linen. Or perhaps that is not what you are looking for?"

No one answered. All were busy watching her whip off the lid and lift out the pile of sheets and pillow-cases with which the box was closely packed.

"Shall I unfold them?" she asked.

The detective nodded.

Taking out the topmost sheet, she shook it open. Then the next and the next till she reached the bottom of the box. Nothing of a criminating nature came to light. The box as well as its contents was without mystery of any kind. This was not an unexpected result of course, but the smile with which she began to refold the pieces and throw them back into the box, revealed one of her dimples which was almost as dangerous to the casual observer as when it revealed both.

"There," she exclaimed, "you see! Household linen exactly as I said. Now may I go home?"

"Certainly, Miss Strange."

The detective stole a sly glance at the reporter. She was not going in for the horrors then after all.

But the reporter abated nothing of his knowing air, for while she spoke of going, she made no move towards doing so, but continued to look about the room till her glances finally settled on a long dark curtain shutting off an adjoining room.

"There's where she lies, I suppose," she feelingly exclaimed. "And not one of you knows who killed her. Somehow, I cannot understand that. Why don't you know when that's what you're hired for?" The innocence with which she uttered this was astonishing. The detective began to look sheepish and the reporter turned aside to hide his smile. Whether in another moment either would have spoken no one can say, for, with a mock consciousness of having said something foolish, she caught up her parasol from the table and made a start for the door.

But of course she looked back.

"I was wondering," she recommenced, with a half wistful, half speculative air, "whether I should ask to have a peep at the place where it all happened."

The reporter chuckled behind the pencil-end he was chewing, but the officer maintained his solemn air, for which act of self-restraint he was undoubtedly grateful when in another minute she gave a quick impulsive shudder not altogether assumed, and vehemently added: "But I couldn't stand the sight; no, I couldn't! I'm an awful coward when it comes to things like that. Nothing in all the world would induce me to look at the woman or her room. But I should like—" here both her dimples came into play though she could not be said exactly to smile "—just one little look upstairs, where he went poking about so long without any fear it seems of being interrupted. Ever since I've read about it I have seen, in my mind, a picture of his wicked figure sneaking from room to room, tearing open drawers and flinging out the contents of closets just to find a little money – a little, little money! I shall not sleep tonight just for wondering how those high up attic rooms really look."

Who could dream that back of this display of mingled childishness and audacity there lay hidden purpose, intellect, and a keen knowledge of human nature. Not the two men who listened to this seemingly irresponsible chatter. To them she was a child to be humored and humor her they did. The dainty feet which had already found their way to that gloomy staircase were allowed to ascend, followed it is true by those of the officer who did not dare to smile back at the reporter because of the brother's watchful and none too conciliatory eye.

At the stair head she paused to look back.

"I don't see those horrible marks which the papers describe as running all along the lower hall and up these stairs."

"No, Miss Strange; they have gradually been rubbed out, but you will find some still showing on these upper floors."

"Oh! Oh! Where? You frighten me – frighten me horribly! But – but – if you don't mind, I should like to see."

Why should not a man on a tedious job amuse himself? Piloting her over to the small room in the rear, he pointed down at the boards. She gave one look and then stepped gingerly in.

"Just look!" she cried; "a whole string of marks going straight from door to window. They have no shape, have they – just blotches? I wonder why one of them is so much larger than the rest?"

This was no new question. It was one which everybody who went into the room was sure to ask, there was such a difference in the size and appearance of the mark nearest the window. The reason – well, minds were divided about that, and no one had a satisfactory theory. The detective therefore kept discreetly silent.

This did not seem to offend Miss Strange. On the contrary it gave her an opportunity to babble away to her heart's content.

"One, two, three, four, five, six," she counted, with a shudder at every count. "And one of them bigger than the others." She might have added, "It is the trail of one foot, and strangely, intermingled at that," but she did not, though we may be quite sure that she noted the fact. "And where, just where did the old wallet fall? Here? Or here?"

She had moved as she spoke, so that in uttering the last "here", she stood directly before the window. The surprise she received there nearly made her forget the part she was playing. From the character of the light in the room, she had expected, on looking out, to confront a nearby wall, but not a window in that wall. Yet that was what she saw directly facing her from across the old-fashioned alley separating this house from its neighbor; twelve unshuttered and uncurtained panes through which she caught a darkened view of a room almost as forlorn and devoid of furniture as the one in which she then stood.

When quite sure of herself, she let a certain portion of her surprise appear.

"Why, look!" she cried, "if you can't see right in next door! What a lonesome-looking place! From its desolate appearance I should think the house quite empty."

"And it is. That's the old Shaffer homestead. It's been empty for a year."

"Oh, empty!" And she turned away, with the most inconsequent air in the world, crying out as her name rang up the stair, "There's Arthur calling. I suppose he thinks I've been here long enough. I'm sure I'm very much obliged to you, officer. I really shouldn't have slept a wink tonight, if I hadn't been given a peep at these rooms, which I had imagined so different." And with one additional glance over her shoulder, that seemed to penetrate both windows and the desolate space beyond, she ran quickly out and down in response to her brother's reiterated call.

"Drive quickly! – As quickly as the law allows, to Hiram Brown's office in Duane Street."

Arrived at the address named, she went in alone to see Mr. Brown. He was her father's lawyer and a family friend.

Hardly waiting for his affectionate greeting, she cried out quickly. "Tell me how I can learn anything about the old Shaffer house in Seventeenth Street. Now, don't look so surprised. I have very good reasons for my request and – and – I'm in an awful hurry."

"But—"

"I know, I know; there's been a dreadful tragedy next door to it; but it's about the Shaffer house itself I want some information. Has it an agent, a—"

"Of course it has an agent, and here is his name."

Mr. Brown presented her with a card on which he had hastily written both name and address.

She thanked him, dropped him a mocking curtsey full of charm, whispered "Don't tell father," and was gone.

Her manner to the man she next interviewed was very different. As soon as she saw him she subsided into her usual society manner. With just a touch of the conceit of the successful debutante, she announced herself as Miss Strange of Seventy-second Street. Her business with him was in regard to the possible renting of the Shaffer house. She had an old lady friend who was desirous of living downtown.

In passing through Seventeenth Street, she had noticed that the old Shaffer house was standing empty and had been immediately struck with the advantages it possessed for her elderly friend's occupancy. Could it be that the house was for rent? There was no sign on it to that effect, but – etc.

His answer left her nothing to hope for.

"It is going to be torn down," he said.

"Oh, what a pity!" she exclaimed. "Real colonial, isn't it! I wish I could see the rooms inside before it is disturbed. Such doors and such dear old-fashioned mantelpieces as it must have! I just dote on the Colonial. It brings up such pictures of the old days; weddings, you know, and parties; all so different from ours and so much more interesting."

Is it the chance shot that tells? Sometimes. Violet had no especial intention in what she said save as a prelude to a pending request, but nothing could have served her purpose better than that one word, wedding. The agent laughed and giving her his first indulgent look, remarked genially:

"Romance is not confined to those ancient times. If you were to enter that house today you would come across evidences of a wedding as romantic as any which ever took place in all the seventy-odd years of its existence. A man and a woman were married there day before yesterday who did their first courting under its roof forty years ago. He has been married twice and she once in the interval; but the old love held firm and now at the age of sixty and over they have come together to finish their days in peace and happiness. Or so we will hope."

"Married! Married in that house and on the day that—"

She caught herself up in time. He did not notice the break.

"Yes, in memory of those old days of courtship, I suppose. They came here about five, got the keys, drove off, went through the ceremony in that empty house, returned the keys to me in my own apartment, took the steamer for Naples, and were on the sea before midnight. Do you not call that quick work as well as highly romantic?"

"Very." Miss Strange's cheek had paled. It was apt to when she was greatly excited. "But I don't understand," she added, the moment after. "How could they do this and nobody know about it? I should have thought it would have got into the papers."

"They are quiet people. I don't think they told their best friends. A simple announcement in the next day's journals testified to the fact of their marriage, but that was all. I would not have felt at liberty to mention the circumstances myself, if the parties were not well on their way to Europe."

"Oh, how glad I am that you did tell me! Such a story of constancy and the hold which old associations have upon sensitive minds! But—"

"Why, Miss? What's the matter? You look very much disturbed."

"Don't you remember? Haven't you thought? Something else happened that very day and almost at the same time on that block. Something very dreadful—"

"Mrs. Doolittle's murder?"

"Yes. It was as near as next door, wasn't it? Oh, if this happy couple had known—"

"But fortunately they didn't. Nor are they likely to, till they reach the other side. You needn't fear that their honeymoon will be spoiled that way."

"But they may have heard something or seen something before leaving the street. Did you notice how the gentleman looked when he returned you the keys?"

"I did, and there was no cloud on his satisfaction."

"Oh, how you relieve me!" One – two dimples made their appearance in Miss Strange's fresh, young cheeks. "Well! I wish them joy. Do you mind telling me their names? I cannot think of them as actual persons without knowing their names."

"The gentleman was Constantin Amidon; the lady, Marian Shaffer. You will have to think of them now as Mr. and Mrs. Amidon."

"And I will. Thank you, Mr. Hutton, thank you very much. Next to the pleasure of getting the house for my friend, is that of hearing this charming bit of news in its connection."

She held out her hand and, as he took it, remarked:

"They must have had a clergyman and witnesses."

"Undoubtedly."

"I wish I had been one of the witnesses," she sighed sentimentally.

"They were two old men."

"Oh, no! Don't tell me that."

"Fogies; nothing less."

"But the clergyman? He must have been young. Surely there was someone there capable of appreciating the situation?"

"I can't say about that; I did not see the clergyman."

"Oh, well! It doesn't matter." Miss Strange's manner was as nonchalant as it was charming. "We will think of him as being very young."

And with a merry toss of her head she flitted away.

But she sobered very rapidly upon entering her limousine.

"Hello!"

"Ah, is that you?"

"Yes, I want a Marconi sent."

"A Marconi?"

"Yes, to the Cretic, which left dock the very night in which we are so deeply interested."

"Good. Whom to? The Captain?"

"No, to a Mrs. Constantin Amidon. But first be sure there is such a passenger."

"Mrs.! What idea have you there?"

"Excuse my not stating over the telephone. The message is to be to this effect. Did she at any time immediately before or after her marriage to Mr. Amidon get a glimpse of anyone in the adjoining house? No remarks, please. I use the telephone because I am not ready to explain myself. If she did, let her send a written description to you of that person as soon as she reaches the Azores."

"You surprise me. May I not call or hope for a line from you early tomorrow?"

"I shall be busy till you get your answer."

He hung up the receiver. He recognized the resolute tone.

But the time came when the pending explanation was fully given to him. An answer had been returned from the steamer, favorable to Violet's hopes. Mrs. Amidon had seen such a person and would send a full description of the same at the first opportunity. It was news to fill Violet's heart with pride; the filament of a clue which had led to this great result had been so nearly invisible and had felt so like nothing in her grasp.

To her employer she described it as follows:

"When I hear or read of a case which contains any baffling features, I am apt to feel some hidden chord in my nature thrill to one fact in it and not to any of the others. In this case the single fact which appealed to my imagination was the dropping of the stolen wallet in that upstairs room. Why did the guilty man drop it? And why, having dropped it, did he not pick it up again? But one answer seemed possible. He had heard or seen something at the spot where it fell which not only alarmed him but sent him in flight from the house."

"Very good; and did you settle to your own mind the nature of that sound or that sight?"

"I did." Her manner was strangely businesslike. No show of dimples now. "Satisfied that if any possibility remained of my ever doing this, it would have to be on the exact place of this occurrence or not at all, I embraced your suggestion and visited the house."

"And that room no doubt."

"And that room. Women, somehow, seem to manage such things."

"So I've noticed, Miss Strange. And what was the result of your visit? What did you discover there?"

"This: that one of the blood spots marking the criminal's steps through the room was decidedly more pronounced than the rest; and, what was even more important, that the window out of which I was looking had its counterpart in the house on the opposite side of the alley. In gazing through the one I was gazing through the other; and not only that, but into the darkened area of the room beyond. Instantly I saw how the latter fact might be made to explain the former one. But before I say how, let me ask if it is quite settled among you that the smears on the floor and stairs mark the passage of the criminal's footsteps!"

"Certainly; and very bloody feet they must have been too. His shoes – or rather his one shoe – for the proof is plain that only the right one left its mark – must have become thoroughly saturated to carry its traces so far."

"Do you think that any amount of saturation would have done this? Or, if you are not ready to agree to that, that a shoe so covered with blood could have failed to leave behind it some hint of its shape, some imprint, however faint, of heel or toe? But nowhere did it do this. We see a smear – and that is all."

"You are right, Miss Strange; you are always right. And what do you gather from this?"

She looked to see how much he expected from her, and, meeting an eye not quite as free from ironic suggestion as his words had led her to expect, faltered a little as she proceeded to say:

"My opinion is a girl's opinion, but such as it is you have the right to have it. From the indications mentioned I could draw but this conclusion: that the blood which accompanied the criminal's footsteps was not carried through the house by his shoes – he wore no shoes; he did not even wear stockings; probably he had none. For reasons which appealed to his judgment, he went about his wicked work barefoot; and it was the blood from his own veins and not from those of his victim which made the trail we have followed with so much interest. Do you forget those broken beads – how he kicked them about and stamped upon them in his fury? One of them pierced the ball of his foot, and that so sharply that it not only spurted blood but kept on bleeding with every step he took. Otherwise, the trail would have been lost after his passage up the stairs."

"Fine!" There was no irony in the bureau-chief's eye now. "You are progressing, Miss Strange. Allow me, I pray, to kiss your hand. It is a liberty I have never taken, but one which would greatly relieve my present stress of feeling."

She lifted her hand toward him, but it was in gesture, not in recognition of his homage.

"Thank you," said she, "but I claim no monopoly on deductions so simple as these. I have not the least doubt that not only yourself but every member of the force has made the same. But there is a little matter which may have escaped the police, may even have escaped you. To that I would now call your attention since through it I have been enabled, after a little necessary groping, to reach the open. You remember the one large blotch on the upper floor where the man dropped the wallet? That blotch, more or less commingled with a fainter one, possessed great significance for me from the first moment I saw it. How came his foot to bleed so much more profusely at that one spot than at any other? There could be but one answer: because here a surprise met him – a surprise so startling to him in his present state of mind, that he gave a quick spring backward, with the result that his wounded foot came down suddenly and forcibly instead of easily as in his previous wary tread. And what was the surprise? I made it my business to find out, and now I can tell you that it was the sight of a woman's face staring upon him from the neighboring house which he had probably been told was empty. The shock disturbed his judgment. He saw his crime discovered – his guilty secret read, and fled in unreasoning panic. He might better have held on to his wits. It was this display of fear which led me to search after its cause, and consequently to discover that at this especial hour more than one person had been in the Shaffer house; that, in fact, a marriage had been celebrated there under circumstances as romantic as any we read of in books, and that this marriage, privately carried out, had been followed by an immediate voyage of the happy couple on one of the White Star steamers. With the rest you are conversant. I do not need to say anything about what has followed the sending of that Marconi."

"But I am going to say something about your work in this matter, Miss Strange. The big detectives about here will have to look sharp if—"

"Don't, please! Not yet." A smile softened the asperity of this interruption. "The man has yet to be caught and identified. Till that is done I cannot enjoy anyone's congratulations. And you will see that all this may not be so easy. If no one happened to meet the desperate wretch before he had an opportunity to retie his shoelaces, there will be little for you or even for the police to go upon but his wounded foot, his undoubtedly carefully prepared alibi, and later, a woman's confused description of a face seen but for a moment only and that under a personal excitement precluding minute attention. I should not be surprised if the whole thing came to nothing."

But it did not. As soon as the description was received from Mrs. Amidon (a description, by the way, which was unusually clear and precise, owing to the peculiar and contradictory features of the man), the police were able to recognize him among the many suspects always under their eye. Arrested, he pleaded, just as Miss Strange had foretold, an alibi of a seemingly unimpeachable character; but neither it, nor the plausible explanation with which he endeavored to account for a freshly healed scar amid the callouses of his right foot, could stand before Mrs. Amidon's unequivocal testimony that he was the same man she had seen in Mrs. Doolittle's upper room on the afternoon of her own happiness and of that poor woman's murder.

The moment when, at his trial, the two faces again confronted each other across a space no wider than that which had separated them on the dread occasion in Seventeenth Street, is said to have been one of the most dramatic in the annals of that ancient court room.

No Head for Figures

Philip Brian Hall

THE SEVERED HEAD stared straight at MacAndrew out of wide-open, bright-blue eyes. Beneath its mop of tousled blonde hair, the youthful face wore an expression of frozen shock. Resting on a shelf in the mortuary of The Royal London Hospital, it looked very like one of Madame Tussaud's celebrated waxwork models, though the absence of blood circulation left its complexion a little too pale.

The police sergeant was not unused to pallor in a suspect; in this case however the mid-forehead bullet wound testified to victimhood, not guilt.

In the unheated semi-basement, a little dappled daylight filtered through frosted half-moon windows, high up at street level. Gas lamps on the white-tiled walls diffused additional sultry illumination.

Stroking his luxuriant, russet-coloured, mutton-chop whiskers, MacAndrew contemplated the head. "Remarkably well preserved," he observed at last, directing his words towards the Matron who'd summoned him.

Annie Quick was a dark-haired, efficient-looking woman, perhaps thirty years of age. She was dressed in the fashion of professional nurses: dark blue, long-sleeved cotton blouse and floor-length skirt, crisply starched white linen pinafore and mob cap.

"Cut off earlier today," she replied in a matter-of-fact tone. "And concealed in a bag of blood-soaked dressings destined for my new incinerator."

MacAndrew regarded her thoughtfully. He knew she'd studied under Florence Nightingale in person and was rapidly building a reputation as plain-spoken and more knowledgeable than many doctors.

"So the murderer hoped to dispose of the head by burning," Detective Constable Smithers interposed. The young policeman was middle-class and expensively educated; he couldn't help it if his muscular frame and broken nose made him look like a street tough. "Presumably the rest of the corpse is yet to be found. But why burn the head separately?"

"Perhaps he dismembered the body to make it easier to hide?" Annie Quick speculated. "I've set my nurse to searching all the waste bags, but she's found nothing more as yet."

"Thank you Matron," MacAndrew nodded. "Make a note, Smithers, this young lady's not just a pretty face."

"I suspect you meant that remark as a compliment, Sergeant, so I'll refrain from pointing out its prejudicial assumptions."

"Ahem. My apologies, Matron." The confirmed bachelor's ruddy complexion reddened further, an unusual sign of discomfiture.

"Thank you. Whilst I'm being *unfeminine*, however, let me point out the decapitation was unusually precise. This head wasn't struck off violently. Examine the edges of the wound; you'll see the skin was cut cleanly by an extremely sharp blade."

"A lancet?" MacAndrew asked.

"Possibly."

"In the hands of a surgeon?"

"In a steady and, I should say, experienced hand. This isn't the work of a novice at cutting human flesh. The spine, together with each blood vessel, nerve and sinew is very tidily severed."

"So," Smithers suggested, "considering the skill employed, the location and the short elapsed time, the murder was probably committed here in the hospital, and by a medical practitioner."

"A shocking thought," said Annie Quick. "But the head was removed *post mortem*. The gunshot was the cause of death."

"The murderer and the decapitator need not be the same," Smithers observed.

"Quite." MacAndrew nodded absently. "No gunshot admissions, I suppose, Matron?"

"Neither alive nor dead," Annie Quick replied. "Whitechapel hasn't seen a shooting in weeks."

"Did anyone hear a gunshot in the hospital?"

"Not that I know of. But surely, gentlemen, we're overlooking the most intriguing question – why remove a head so carefully if all you intend to do is burn it?"

MacAndrew gazed in admiration upon Annie Quick. "I was asking myself the very same question, Matron."

* * *

MacAndrew's face was clouded by thought as the hansom bearing the two policemen drove westward down Whitechapel Road towards Aldgate.

"A remarkable woman, Smithers."

"I'm told her arrival caused something of a stir in the hospital, sir."

"I can well believe it." MacAndrew collected himself with an effort. "But your impressions of the fatal shot?"

"Powder burns around the wound, sir. The shot was fired from no more than a couple of feet."

"Suggesting?"

"If he wasn't restrained, then in all likelihood he knew his killer."

"Good. And?"

"Small calibre pistol. Easily concealed."

"But an excellent choice of place, wouldn't you say? No one likely to notice a few more bloodstains; another scream neither here nor there."

"But these days, sir, they use chloroform to anaesthetise patients; they don't drag them into theatre and hold them down any more. Makes it more difficult to move a captive around the place."

"Very well, I entice my victim to walk into the hospital voluntarily. But once there, why don't I kill him in a way that could seem the outcome of an unsuccessful operation? Why risk the noise of a shot? And why, oh why, cut off his head, leaving a corpse too noticeable for the mortuary? I've given myself the perfect way to dispose of the body and then I make it impossible to use!"

* * *

Wearing great big gumboots and an even bigger scowl, Detective Constable Smithers stood ankle-deep in the mud at the mouth of Deptford Creek where the lesser river discharges its polluted waters into the mighty Thames on its southern side. For company, he'd two shivering uniformed officers and several unconcerned oyster-catchers, the latter industriously probing the ooze with long, bright-orange beaks.

Smithers squelched from one foot to the other, drawing his overcoat closer about him. The wind off the river was cold; the air stank. Downriver, The Royal Greenwich Hospital for Seamen resembled a refined old lady hitching up her full skirts against the mire. A steam tug tooted a derisory, asthmatic horn as it puffed along past the hapless group floundering on the glutinous shore.

The detective took another look at the bedraggled, headless corpse marooned by the receding tide. The dead man's sodden, filthy suit had been nearly new when his body entered the water. Opening the jacket, Smithers noted its once-luxurious silk lining and the tiny, discreet label of *Hawkes and Co.* of Piccadilly, gentlemen's outfitters by Royal Appointment.

* * *

"One might have thought, Sergeant MacAndrew," said Annie Quick, "the police would be content to allow my hospital's reputation to be sullied by just one murder. Bringing me another seems hardly fair." Her upper lip twitched as she failed to suppress a rueful smile. "By the way, Sergeant, *The Times* sent an artist to draw the head for their crime report. That should help with identification."

"Quite. But you're telling us, Matron, our body doesn't belong with it?" MacAndrew's disappointment was mingled with surprise.

"Not remotely. The head's from a young man – perhaps twenty-five, I'd judge. This new body's elderly, a man in his sixties at least. You can see he's losing muscle mass. His limbs are stringy; the flesh is spotted and warty."

"So it's like Mr. Jaques' new card game *Happy Families*," sighed Smithers. "You had Mr. Bun the Baker's head but I've brought you Mr. Black the Coalman's body."

"More like Mr. Fiddler the Violinist."

"What's that?" MacAndrew pricked up his ears.

"The calluses on the fingertips of his left hand are typical of someone who devotes much time to playing a stringed instrument."

"Matron, your powers of observation are formidable," said MacAndrew.

"There's more. For example these clothes were not his." She gestured to where the muddy garments lay on a side table.

"How can you tell?"

"The suit's new, but a trifle big on him. *Hawkes a*re bespoke tailors; they only make to measure and they require several fittings. They'd never have allowed this man to walk out of their premises wearing that suit."

"But they'll have a record of who *did*," said Smithers, brightening. "I'll take it along to them and find out." Folding the garments as neatly as possible, he left with a knowing smile on his face.

After Smithers' departure MacAndrew turned hesitantly to Annie Quick.

"Matron, I'm afraid I lack my constable's facility with language. He writes crime stories for the penny dreadfuls, you know. But I should like to tell you what a great pleasure it's been to meet you. I was wondering…" He paused and then the words came out in a rush, "if you might perhaps take tea with me some afternoon?"

* * *

"A rum business, I believe you called it Smithers? Well, it becomes more curious by the hour."

MacAndrew stood at the window of his Scotland Yard office, smoking his pipe and staring through an aromatic cloud of tobacco smoke at the bustle in the street two floors below.

"Indeed, sir." Smithers had taken a seat to rest his weary limbs. "But the usher at *Hawkes and Co.* was quite certain. The suit was made for the Marquis de Montferrat. He met the gentleman and was already apprehensive for him, having seen his picture in *The Times'* report."

"An identification now confirmed by half a dozen aristocratic houses around London." MacAndrew turned from the window. "There've been under-butlers and footmen turning up all afternoon, presenting their masters' cards. But we've established a clear connection between the two dead men. The Marquis de Montferrat's head lacks a body and the headless body wore the Marquis' clothes."

"I'm told a body placed in the river at Execution Dock, the nearest point of the north bank to The Royal London, would have a very good chance of being washed up on the south bank flats at Deptford."

"Excellent. Good work Smithers."

"So may we hypothesize the two men were killed together, having previously, for an unknown reason, exchanged clothes?"

"That may be an assumption too far." MacAndrew shook his head before drawing once again upon his pipe. "We may speculate the Marquis loaned the older gentleman a suit or perhaps had it stolen. We shan't know if he himself borrowed clothing until his own body turns up."

"I see, sir."

"Until then we must follow up these approaches from the gentry, Smithers. We need to know who this Marquis was and whom he associated with. Sounds like a Frenchman, but you never know. Exiled nobility from half of Europe take refuge in London these days."

* * *

During the season, the *salon de thé* of The Dowager Lady Daphne ffoulkes-Harrington was one of the most celebrated in Mayfair. As luck would have it, the door of her terraced mansion in Park Lane was opened to MacAndrew by the very same footman who'd delivered Her Ladyship's card. The servant now wore exotic costume: a green turban, red silk waistcoat over a green blouse, baggy green trousers and soft red slippers with pointed, curled up toes. MacAndrew made no comment.

He was conducted into a grand baroque vestibule with a glossily polished floor. A grand staircase with an ebony banister and a Persian runner held in place by gleaming brass rods swept around in a giant curve from the upper landing on his right to the ground floor on his left.

"You've come at a fortunate time, sir." The footman-eunuch bowed. "His Highness Prince Ragoczy is with us today; you may hear the sound of his violin. I regret we must wait until his performance is concluded before I announce you. Her Ladyship permits no interruption during one of His Highness's recitals."

MacAndrew's enjoyment of the said instrument was limited to a good, vigorous Scottish reel scraped on an old Highland fiddle, but he recognised excellence when he heard it. "His Highness plays uncommonly well."

"Sir, you can't imagine. Were he not a prince, he must surely have made a great name as a musician. Today he's not at his best, he says, having rheumatic pain in his hands. He wouldn't have played but at Her Ladyship's insistence."

MacAndrew sensed a lucky chance. If the prince had rheumatism, he might well be of a similar age to the headless corpse. This visit promised not only information about Montferrat but also an early opportunity to test Annie Quick's violinist theory.

"Sadly I'm not here for a recital," MacAndrew reminded the footman.

"Ah, no sir, you mistake my meaning. It's fortunate His Highness is here, because it was he who introduced the Marquis de Montferrat to Her Ladyship. The two of them were close friends. Such a dreadful business, sir."

"Indeed." MacAndrew was always sceptical of apparent coincidence. A dead violinist in Montferrat's clothes? A live one who'd been his sponsor in society? "Is His Highness aware of his friend's demise?" he asked.

"I don't believe so, sir. Perhaps he doesn't read *The Times?* His native language isn't English, you see, sir."

MacAndrew nodded. He could think of another reason for feigning ignorance.

"When Her Ladyship inquired after the Marquis," the footman continued, "His Highness actually said he'd been called urgently back to France."

MacAndrew's suspicions strengthened. Simple ignorance could be excused; laying a false trail was not so easy to explain away.

"Her Ladyship didn't enlighten him?"

"She could never bring herself to break bad news to a guest, sir. That wouldn't be in keeping with the ffoulkes-Harrington tradition of hospitality."

"Quite," said MacAndrew.

* * *

"Her salon resembles a scene from *The Arabian Nights*," MacAndrew related. "The *grande dame* herself sits on a gilt throne with a jewelled plume in her hair. The servants are dressed as eunuchs or harem girls and the guests all wear costumes of the last century."

"Remarkable!" Annie Quick's eyes lit up. "But, now you mention it, I saw a strangely costumed person early on the same morning we discovered the head."

They had chosen a halfway point between their respective places of work for their rendezvous; *The Wig and Pen Tea Rooms,* in Paternoster Row, overlooked Saint Paul's Churchyard. The two of them sat at a corner table, beside a stone-mullioned window through which one could look out on Wren's great cathedral.

"The man wore a long, green frock coat with white knee britches, white silk stockings and black buckle shoes. Around his neck was bound a high, white stock trimmed in front with a lace jabot and his long white hair was tied up in a queue with a black velvet bow. He seemed an old man, but had a sprightly walk. I took him for an artiste from one of the local music halls."

MacAndrew looked astonished. "Miss Quick, you've just described Prince Ragoczy to the life. His clothes, his lightness of step, all of it. But what could possibly bring an aristocrat from the Mayfair salons to the poor streets of Whitechapel?"

"Prince Ragoczy, you say?"

"That's what he calls himself."

"A famous name from history. I wasn't aware he'd any living descendants."

"Ah – I'm afraid you have the advantage of me, Miss Quick."

Annie smiled. "When Marlborough was fighting the French at the beginning of the last century, the Hapsburgs were our allies. Ragoczy's Hungarians were fighting the Hapsburgs for independence at that time."

"I clearly don't know enough about European monarchies. *My* Prince Ragoczy said his father was called Francis II."

"Then he's either a liar or one hundred and fifty years old."

"How so?"

"Because Francis II of Hungary was the Ragoczy who was Marlborough's enemy."

"I see. And the man you saw leaving the hospital, was he alone?"

"He was bidding farewell to Doctor Archbold, one of our surgeons."

MacAndrew sat back in his chair and stared at the wooden beams of the ceiling. "Today's Prince Ragoczy is a remarkable performer upon the violin. I've never heard a better. Clearly maintaining such a standard requires hours of practice; I'm sure you'd agree."

"I would. These days I've no time for the piano; I content myself with an occasional half hour or so, but my playing suffers."

"I hope you'll play for me sometime." MacAndrew gave the young lady a benign smile. "But you'll recall explaining to me the tendency of violin players to develop calluses?"

Annie nodded.

"Remembering what you said, when I was introduced to the prince, I affected an injury of my right hand and shook his left. I paid particular attention to his fingertips, since he'd just been playing, reluctantly I gathered."

"Did he have calluses?"

"None whatsoever; his fingertips were reddened, with indentations caused by the strings clearly visible."

"Not every violinist has calluses, but all have toughened skin on their finger ends. No serious violinist would have soft fingertips."

"I thought as much. Nor would a man of his age have unblemished hands without raised veins or liver spots."

"That does seem unusual."

"And then there's this athleticism of his. It's hard to tell exactly how old he is, but his face is lined. I'd judge him the wrong side of sixty. Yet he's up and dancing with the ladies like a youth. I'm only in my forties but it made me tired just to watch him."

"A man in his forties is in the very prime of life, Sergeant MacAndrew," Annie reassured him.

"You're kind, Miss Quick. And quite right to recall my mind from business, which is not why I asked you to tea. Would you perhaps care for another cup?"

"I would, but you can't shake me off so easily. I'm a hospital nurse, not one of those delicate flowers who faint at the sight of blood. Explain your thinking."

MacAndrew hesitated. "Perhaps you're familiar with the writings of Mary Shelley?"

Annie frowned. "Are you seriously wondering if someone could have attached the head of an old man to the body of a young one? My dear Sergeant, the finest doctors in the world are incapable of reattaching so much as a severed toe. Decapitation is a method of execution. Yet this so-called Prince Ragoczy walked out of the hospital a few hours after the murder and was later seen dancing a jig!"

* * *

"I may be old and increasingly deaf, Smithers, but I still know literary talent when I encounter it." Bulwer-Lytton flicked the ash of his cigar into a silver dish shaped like a giant cockleshell that sat on a small table beside his chair. "And you based your first mystery story on your experiences as a policeman?"

"I did, sir."

"Excellent. Real life, Smithers, even in an imaginary world, real life, that's the secret. I'm always happy to help someone just starting out. And now you're working on a new story about a man who lives to a great age, you say?"

"I am, sir. A rumour recently circulated around the East End concerning a man who claimed to be one hundred and fifty years old. I thought it might be worked up into a good tale."

"I should say so. Very promising. But I'd suggest your character should be some historical figure your readers have heard of, do you follow? No one cares if Farmer Brown from Norwich lives to be one hundred and fifty, but Napoleon Bonaparte, say, that's a different matter, you see what I mean?"

"Indeed, sir. This man *was* named by the rumour, as a matter of fact. Prince Ragoczy he called himself."

"What's that?"

Smithers raised his voice, "Prince Ragoczy, sir."

"Yes, yes, I'm not yet as deaf as all that, Smithers. My exclamation was of surprise. I know the rumour of which you speak, though I did not hear it in the East End, nor even in recent years."

"You surprise me, sir," Smithers said.

"Well, you're young and it's a very old story. Did you ever hear of the Count of Saint Germain, Smithers?"

"No, sir. I can't say I have."

"A mysterious person who appeared in France during the reign of Louis XIV, and then mysteriously appeared again fifty years later, not long before the Revolution, seemingly no older."

"Remarkable, sir."

"Aha! But not nearly so remarkable as would be another appearance of the same man in London today, eh what?"

"I must say, sir, that would make a splendid story."

"Just a coincidence, I expect, but what would you say, Smithers, were I to tell you Saint Germain was known to use several aliases, and one of them was Prince Ragoczy?"

"Good Heavens!"

"He used various other names: Comte Bellamarre, Chevalier Schoening, Marquis de Montferrat…"

"Marquis de Montferrat!" Smithers exclaimed.

"Why, Smithers, have you heard that one before?"

"I have sir, in a current case."

Anxious to leave without appearing discourteous, Smithers urgently needed to report to his sergeant. It had been MacAndrew's idea for Smithers to combine occult research with a chance for literary advancement. He'd sent up his card to Lord Lytton without much confidence, only to be surprised and gratified by his friendly reception.

"You've been of great assistance to me, sir," Smithers said. "I can't wait to start writing."

"Then I'm delighted. I'll watch out for your tale. Now remember, my boy, however fantastic, not only is the world you describe absolutely real, you've seen it for yourself. Convince yourself, Smithers, and you'll convince your readers."

* * *

Shadwell Police Station's gloomy holding cells had iron-barred doors let into plain brick walls without any opening on to the outside world. Daylight was admitted through a frosted-glass sash window behind the custody sergeant's desk.

The prisoner confronting the two policemen in one of the cells was a shifty-eyed, middle-aged character of greater than average bulk. He wore a soiled, chequered jacket, missing a button and frayed into holes at both elbows. His shirt had never seen the inside of a laundry, unless perhaps its wearer had robbed one.

"Yer knows Whitechapel, Mr. MacAndrew. Full of rogues. Liars, the lot of 'em."

"And you, Fred Billings, are one of the greatest liars of all. I've witnesses who say you collected a load from the rear entrance of The Royal London Hospital three nights ago and deposited it covertly in the river."

"Just rubbish, Mr. MacAndrew, sir. I takes away their waste, yer knows."

"Waste there is, Billings. It's you wasting my time! The hospital has an incinerator. No, what you collected was a body."

"No, sir! 'Pon my life!"

"Your life it will *be*, Billings, because you'll swing for this. We *have* the body, but the body has no head."

MacAndrew leaned forward, thrusting his face within two feet of the trembling prisoner. "The man was murdered, Billings. You are at the very least an accessory, if not the murderer yourself."

"I swear, Mr. MacAndrew, it weren't me 'oo killed 'im."

Smithers said nothing. He took off his coat, folded it carefully over the back of an unoccupied chair and rolled up his sleeves.

"Then tell us who did kill him, Billings, it's your only way to save yourself."

"Mr. MacAndrew, I weren't ter know, were I?" The prisoner squirmed in desperation. "Be fair, sir, please. If a respectable doctor was ter tell me as 'ow 'e 'ad this 'ere corpse from 'is hanatomy classes wot it was hinconwenient fer 'im ter be buryin', like, 'oo am I ter call 'im a liar, sir? An' if 'e was ter give me two guineas, sir, well…yer knows me, Mr. MacAndrew, I'm a poor man. We all 'as a livin' ter make, sir."

"The doctor's name, Billings?"

The man still hesitated.

Smithers moved within range of the seated prisoner and spoke for the first time. His tone, though barely above a whisper, gave clear warning of the sort of communication that might be expected to follow upon further refusals to answer. "His name, Billings?"

"Sir, I… Harchbold, Mr. Smithers, sir, Doctor 'Enery Harchbold."

* * *

"If anyone knew where to lay hands on Henry Archbold, Sergeant MacAndrew, I can assure you the laying on of hands wouldn't be gentle!" Annie Quick had an angry glint in her eye. "He's disappeared without notice and caused an awful lot of trouble."

"I can't say I'm terribly surprised," MacAndrew said, shaking his head. "It's all been too slow. He'll have heard we arrested Billings and realised it was only a matter of time."

"What are you saying?" Annie looked shocked. "Is Doctor Archbold the murderer?"

"I doubt he fired the shot. No, Charlie Forbes was shot by a man he thought was his friend; a man who'd introduced him to high society, given him a bespoke suit of clothes."

"Charlie Forbes?"

"*The Times* takes a little while to reach readers in the north of England, Miss Quick. The man passing himself off as Montferrat was called Charlie Forbes, born in Newcastle but lately in France, acting as agent for a group of northern ship owners."

"And Forbes' friend was the man I saw with Doctor Archbold?"

"Incredible, isn't it? The Comte de Saint Germain, calling himself Prince Ragoczy. When you told me the man was either a liar or one hundred and fifty years old you spoke more truly than you thought: he's both."

"I *would* say you've been reading Constable Smithers' penny dreadfuls," Annie said, "if I hadn't spent the day asking everyone in the hospital when they last saw Doctor Archbold. I received one report I found very disturbing."

"You, Annie, disturbed? I can't believe it."

"Well believe it or not. On the night of the murder, a night nurse seeking laudanum entered Doctor Archbold's outer office, not expecting to find the room occupied. Just as she did so, the doctor came out of his inner surgery, accompanied by the exotically-dressed man with whom I later saw him. The man was still adjusting his attire, apparently after some examination or procedure; he was carrying a white silk stock in his hand and just about to put it on."

"The nurse saw his neck?"

"She said he'd a livid scar all around it, as though he'd been attacked with a garrotte."

"But the wound not bleeding or stitched?"

"No."

"Then it seems we have our proof, Annie."

"We do?"

"Indeed, did you not tell me yourself no surgeon in the world could perform such an operation? Yet not only was it performed, but the incision promptly healed."

"That would require sorcery, not surgery," Annie insisted.

"I agree. Yet it seems even our sorcerer doesn't possess the power of exchanging his own head without assistance."

"This is stretching my credulity, Sergeant. You're saying Archbold removed Forbes' head and substituted Saint Germain's?"

"They did it together, yes."

"And where are these villains now?"

"Gone. Vanished without trace. Oh, we've telegraphed the ports, but I've no doubt they'll elude us. Saint Germain may be out of the country already."

"I see." Annie Quick shook her head. "So we may never learn how it was done? But you do think we've seen the last of them?"

"I believe we have, at least until Smithers reminds us of the affair with his next fanciful publication. He might become a good author that boy, but he'll never make a living at it."

"Why's that?" Annie raised one eyebrow.

"No head for figures," MacAndrew smiled hesitantly. He never usually tried jokes. "You know, Annie, our little tea party earlier this week was somewhat sidetracked. I was wondering…if you were agreeable…whether we might try again?"

"Yes, Sergeant MacAndrew," said Annie promptly. "I believe I should like that."

The Divided House

Thomas W. Hanshew

Chapter I

"**SUPERINTENDENT** Narkom waitin' upstairs in your room, sir. Come unexpected and sudden like about five minutes ago," said Dollops, as the key was withdrawn from the lock and Cleek stepped into the house. "Told him you'd jist run round the corner, sir, to get a fresh supply of them cigarettes you're so partial to, so he sat down and waited. And, oh, I say, guv'ner?"

"Yes?" said Cleek inquiringly, stopping in his two-steps-at-a-time ascent of the stairs.

"Letter come for you, too, sir, whilst you was out. Envellup wrote in a lady's hand, and directed to 'Captain Burbage'. Took it up and laid it on your table, sir."

"All right," said Cleek, and resumed his journey up the stairs, passing a moment later into his private room and the presence of Maverick Narkom.

The superintendent, who was standing by the window looking out into the brilliant radiance of the morning, turned as he heard the door creak, and immediately set his back to the things that had nothing to do with the conduct of Scotland Yard, and advanced toward his famous ally with that eagerness and enthusiasm which he reserved for matters connected with crime and the law.

"My dear Cleek, such a case; you'll fairly revel in it," he began excitedly. "As I didn't expect to find you out at this hour of the morning, I dispensed with the formality of phoning, hopped into the car, and came on at once. Dollops said you'd be back in half a minute, and," looking at his watch, "it's now ten since I arrived."

"Sorry to have kept you waiting, Mr. Narkom," broke in Cleek, "but – look at these," pulling the tissue paper from an oblong parcel he was carrying in his hand and exposing to view a cluster of lilies of the valley and La France roses. "They are what detained me. Budleigh, the florist, had his window full of them, fresh from Covent Garden this morning, and I simply couldn't resist the temptation. If God ever made anything more beautiful than a rose, Mr. Narkom, it is yet to be discovered. Sit down, and while you are talking I'll arrange these in this vase. No; it won't distract my attention from what you are saying, believe me. Somehow, I can always think better and listen better when there are flowers about me, and if—"

He chopped off the sentence suddenly and laid the flowers down upon his table with a briskness born of sudden interest. His eye had fallen upon the letter of which Dollops had spoken. It was lying face upward upon the table, so that he could see the clear, fine, characterful hand in which it was written and could read clearly the Devonshire postmark.

"My dear Cleek," went on Narkom, accepting the invitation to be seated, but noticing nothing in his eagerness to get to business, "my dear Cleek, never have I brought you any case which is so likely to make your fortune as this, and when I tell you that the reward offered runs well into five figures—"

"A moment, please!" interjected Cleek agitatedly. "Don't think me rude, Mr. Narkom, but – your pardon a thousand times. I must read this letter before I give attention to anything else, no matter how important!"

Then, not waiting for Narkom to signify his consent to the interruption, as perforce he was obliged to do in the circumstances, he carried the letter over to the window, broke the seal, and read it, his heart getting into his eyes and his pulses drumming with that kind of happiness which fills a man when the one woman in the world writes him a letter.

Even if he had not recognized her handwriting, he must have known from the postmark that it was from Ailsa Lorne, for he had no correspondent in Devonshire, no correspondent but Narkom anywhere, for the matter of that. His lonely life, the need for secrecy, his plan of self-effacement, prevented that. But he had known for months that Miss Lorne was in Devon, that she had gone there as governess in the family of Sir Jasper Drood, when her determination not to leave England had compelled her to resign her position as guide and preceptress to little Lord Chepstow on the occasion of his mother's wedding with Captain Hawksley. And now to have her write to him – to him! A sort of mist got into his eyes and blurred everything for a moment. When it had passed and he could see clearly, he set his back to Narkom and read these words:

> **The Priory, Tuesday, June 10th.**
>
> *Dear Friend:*
>
> *If you remember, as I so often do, that last day in London, when you put off the demands of your duty to see me safely in the train and on my way to this new home, you will perhaps also remember something that you said to me at parting. You told me that if a time ever came when I should need your friendship or your help, I had but to ask for them. If that is true, and I feel sure that it is, dear Mr. Cleek, I need them now. Not for myself, however, but for one who has proved a kind friend indeed since my coming here, and who, through me, asks your kind aid in solving a deep and distressing mystery and saving a threatened human life. No reward can be offered, I fear, beyond that which comes of the knowledge of having done a good and generous act, Mr. Cleek, for my friend is not in a position to offer one. But I seem to feel that this will weigh little with you, and it emboldens me to make this appeal. So, if no other case prevents, and you really wish to do me a favor, if you can make it convenient to be in the neighborhood of the lych-gate of Lyntonhurst Church on Wednesday morning at eleven o'clock, you will win the everlasting gratitude of—*
>
> *Your sincere friend,*
> *Ailsa Lorne*

The superintendent heard the unmistakable sound of the letter being folded and slid back into its envelope, and very properly concluded that the time of grace had expired.

"Now, my dear Cleek, let us get down to business," he began forthwith. "This amazing case which I wish you to undertake and will, as I have already said, bring you a colossal reward—"

"Your pardon, Mr. Narkom," interjected Cleek, screwing round on his heel and beginning to search for a railway guide among the litter of papers and pamphlets jammed into the spaces of a revolving bookcase, "your pardon, but I can undertake no case, sir – at least, for the present. I am called to Devonshire, and must start at once. What's that? No, there is nothing to be won, not a farthing piece. It's a matter of friendship, nothing more."

"But, Cleek! God bless my soul, man, this is madness. You are simply chucking away enough money to keep you for the next three years."

"It wouldn't make any difference if it were enough to keep me for the next twenty, Mr. Narkom. You can't buy entrance to paradise for all the money in the world, my friend, and I'm getting a day in it for nothing! Now then," flirting over the leaves of the guide book, "let's see how the trains run. Dorset – Darsham – Dalby – Devonshire. Good! Here you are. Um-m-m. Too late for that. Can't possibly catch that one, either. Ah, here's the one – 1:56 – that will do." Then he closed the book, almost ran to the door, and, leaning over the banister, shouted down the staircase, "Dollops – Dollops, you snail, where are you? Dol— Oh, there you are at last, eh? Pack my portmanteau. Best clothes, best boots, best everything I've got, and look sharp about it. I'm off to Devonshire by the 1:56."

And, do all that he might, Narkom could not persuade him to alter his determination. The 1:56 he said he would take; the 1:56 he did take; and night coming down over the peaceful paths and the leafy loveliness of Devon found him putting up at the inn of 'The Three Desires', hours and hours and hours ahead of the appointed time, to make sure of being at the trysting place at eleven next morning.

He was. On the very tick of the minute he was there at the old moss-grown lych-gate, and there Miss Lorne found him when she drove up in Lady Drood's pony phaeton a little time afterward. She was not alone, however. She had spoken of a friend, and a sharp twitch disturbed Cleek's heart when he saw that a young man sat beside her, a handsome young man of two- or three-and-twenty, with a fair moustache, a pair of straight-looking blue eyes, and that squareness of shoulder and uprightness of bearing which tells the tale of a soldier.

In another moment she had alighted, her fingers were lying in the close grasp of Cleek's, and the colour was coming and going in rosy gusts over her smiling countenance.

"How good of you to come!" she said. "But, there! I knew that you would, if it were within the range of possibility; I said so to Mr. Bridewell as we came along. Mr. Cleek, let me have the pleasure of making you acquainted with Lieutenant Bridewell. His fiancée, Miss Warrington, is the dear friend of whom I wrote you. Lieutenant Bridewell is home on leave after three years' service in India, Mr. Cleek; but in those three years strange and horrible things have happened, are still happening, in his family circle. But now that you have come—. We shall get at the bottom of the mystery now, lieutenant; I feel certain that we shall. Mr. Cleek will find it out, be sure of that."

"At least, I will endeavor to do so, Mr. Bridewell," said Cleek himself, as he wrung the young man's hand and decided that he liked him a great deal better than he had thought he was going to do. "What is the difficulty? Miss Lorne's letter mentioned the fact that not only was there a mystery to be probed but a human life in danger. Whose life, may I ask? Yours?"

"No," he made reply, with a sort of groan. "I wish to heaven it were no more than that. I'd soon clear out from the danger zone and put an end to the trouble, get rid of that lot at the house and put miles of sea between them and me, I can tell you. It's my dad they are killing – my dear old dad, bless his heart – and killing him in the most mysterious and subtle manner imaginable. I don't know how, I don't know why, that's the mystery of it, for he hasn't any money nor any expectations, just the annuity he bought when he got too old to follow his calling (he used to be a sea captain, Mr. Cleek), and there'd be no sense in getting rid of him for that, because, of course, the annuity dies with him. But somebody's got some kind of a motive and somebody's doing it, that's certain, for when I went out to India three years ago he was a hale and hearty old chap, fit as a fiddle and lively as a cricket, and now, when I come back on leave, I find him a broken wreck, a peevish, wasted old man, hardly able to help himself, and afflicted with some horrible incurable disease which seems to be eating him up alive."

"Eating him?" repeated Cleek. "What do you mean by 'eating' him, Mr. Bridewell? The expression is peculiar."

"Well, it exactly explains the circumstances, Mr. Cleek. If I didn't know better, I should think it a case of leprosy. But it isn't. I've seen cases of leprosy, and this isn't one of them. There's none of the peculiar odor, for one thing; and, for another, it isn't contagious. You can touch the spots without suffering doing so, although he suffers, dear old boy, and suffers horribly. It's just living decay, Mr. Cleek – just that. Fordyce, that's the doctor who's attending him, you know, says that the only way he has found to check the thing is by amputation. Already the dear old chap has lost three fingers from the right hand by that means. Fordyce says that the hand itself will have to go in time if they can't check the thing, and then, if that doesn't stop it, the arm will have to go."

Cleek puckered up his brows and began to rub his thumb and forefinger up and down his chin.

"Fordyce seems to have a pronounced penchant for amputation, Mr. Bridewell," he said after a moment. "Competent surgeon, do you think?"

"Who – Fordyce? Lord bless you, yes! One of the 'big pots' in that line. Harley Street specialist in his day. Fell heir to a ton of money, I believe, and gave up practice because it was too wearing. Couldn't get over the love of it, however, so set up a ripping little place down here, went in for scientific work, honor and glory of the profession and all that sort of thing, you know. God knows what would have become of the dad if he hadn't taken up the case! Might be in his grave by this time. Fordyce has been a real friend, Mr. Cleek; I can't be grateful enough to him for the good he has done: taking the dear old dad into his home, so to speak, him and Aunt Ruth and – and that pair, the Cordovas."

"The Cordovas? Who are they? Friends or relatives?"

"Neither, I'm afraid. To tell the truth, they're the people I suspect, though God knows why I should, and God forgive me if I'm wrong. They're two West Indians, brother and sister, Mr. Cleek. Their father was mate of the *Henrietta*, under my dad, years and years ago. Mutinied, too, the beggar, and was shot down, as he ought to have been, as *any* mutineer ought to be. Left the two children, mere kiddies at the time. Dad took 'em in, and has been keeping them and doing for them ever since. I don't like them – never did like them. Fordyce doesn't like them, either. Colonel Goshen does, however. He's sweet on the girl, I fancy."

Cleek's eyebrows twitched upward suddenly, his eyes flashed a sharp glance at the lieutenant, and then dropped again.

"Colonel Goshen, eh?" he said quietly. "Related, by any chance, to that 'Colonel Goshen' who testified on behalf of the claimant in the great Tackbun case?"

"Don't know, I'm sure. Never heard of the case, Mr. Cleek."

"Didn't you? It was quite a sensation some eighteen months ago. But you were in India, then, of course. Fellow turned up who claimed to be the long-lost Sir Aubrey Tackbun who ran away to sea when a boy some thirty-odd years ago and was lost track of entirely. Lost his case at that first trial, and got sent to prison for conspiracy. Is out again now. Claims to have new and irrefutable refutable evidence, and is going to have a second try for the title and estates. A Colonel Goshen, of the Australian militia, was one of his strongest witnesses. Wonder if there is any connection between the two?"

"Shouldn't think so. This Colonel Goshen's an American or he says he is, and I've no reason to doubt him. Deuced nice fellow, whatever he is, and has been a jolly good friend to the pater. As a matter of fact, it was through him that Fordyce got to know the dad and became interested in his case, and—. What's that? Lud, no! No possible means of connecting my old dad with any lost heirs, sir – not a ghost of one. Born here in Devon, married here, lived all his life here, that is, whenever he was on land, and he'll die here, and die soon, too, if you don't get at the bottom of this and save him. And you will, Mr. Cleek, and you will, won't you? Miss Lorne says that you've solved deeper mysteries than this, and that you will get at the bottom of it without fail."

"Miss Lorne has more faith in my ability than most people, I fear, Mr. Bridewell. I will try to live up to it, however. But suppose you give me the facts of the case a little more clearly. When and how did it all begin?"

"I think it was about eight months ago that Aunt Ruth wrote me about it," the lieutenant replied. "Aunt Ruth is my late mother's maiden sister, Mr. Cleek. My mother died at my birth, and Aunt Ruth brought me up. As I told you, my father retired from the sea some years ago, and, having purchased an annuity, lived on that. He managed to scrape enough together to have me schooled properly and put through Sandhurst, and when I got my lieutenancy, and was subsequently appointed to a commission in India, I left him living in the little old cottage where I was born. With him were Aunt Ruth and Paul and Lucretia Cordova. Up to about eight months or so ago he continued to live there, devoting himself to his little garden and enjoying life on land as much as a man who loves the sea ever can do. Then, of a sudden, Lucretia Cordova fell in with Colonel Goshen, and introduced him to the pater. A few days after that my father seems to have eaten something which disagreed with him, for he was suddenly seized with all the symptoms of ptomaine poisoning. He rallied, however, but from that point a strange weakness overcame him, and at the colonel's suggestion he went for a sail round the coast with him. He did not improve. The weakness seemed to grow, but without any sign of the horrible bodily suffering with which he is now afflicted.

"Colonel Goshen is a great friend of Dr. Fordyce's, and through that friendship managed to interest him in the case to such a degree that he made a twenty-mile trip especially to see my father. They struck up a great friendship. Fordyce was certain, he said, that he could cure the dad if he had him within daily reach, and, on the dad saying that he couldn't afford to come over to this part of the country and keep up two establishments, Fordyce came to the rescue, like the jolly brick he is. In other words, his place here being a good deal larger than he requires, he's a bachelor, Mr. Cleek, he put up a sort of partition to separate it into two establishments, so to speak, put one half at the dad's disposal rent free, and there he is housed now, and Aunt Ruth and the two Cordovas with him. Yes, and even me, now; for as soon as he heard that I was coming home on leave, Fordyce wouldn't listen to my going to 'The Three Desires' for digs, but insisted that I, too, should be taken in, and a clinking suite of rooms in the west wing put at my disposal.

"But in spite of all his hopes for the dear old dad's eventual cure, things in that direction have grown steadily worse. The horrible malady which is now consuming him manifested itself about a fortnight after his arrival, and it has been growing steadily worse every day. But it isn't natural, Mr. Cleek; I know what I am saying, and I say that! Somebody is doing something to him for some diabolical reason of which I know nothing, and he is dying – dying by inches. Not by poison, I am sure of that, for since the hour of my return I have not let him eat or drink a single thing without myself partaking of it before it goes to him and eating more of it after it has gone to him. But there is no effect in my case. Nothing does he touch with his hand that I do not touch after him; but the disease never attacks me, yet all the while he grows worse and worse, and the end keeps creeping on. There! That's the case, Mr. Cleek. For God's sake, get at the bottom of it and save my father, if you can."

Cleek did not reply for a moment. Putting out his hands suddenly, he began to drum a thoughtful tattoo upon the post of the lych-gate, his eyes fixed on the ground and a deep ridge between his puckered brows. But, of a sudden:

"Tell me something," he said. "These Cordovas – what reason have you for suspecting them?"

"None, only that I dislike them. They're half-castes, for one thing, and – well, you can't trust a half-caste at any time."

"Hum-m-m! Nothing more than that, eh? Just a natural dislike? And your Aunt Ruth; what of her?"

"Oh, just the regulation prim old maid: sour as a lemon and as useful. A good sort, though. Fond of the pater, careful as a mother of him, temper like a file, and a heart a good deal bigger than you'd believe at first blush. Do anything in the world for me, bless her."

"Even to the point of putting up a friend of yours for a couple of days?"

"Yes; if I had one in these parts, which I haven't."

"Never count your chickens – you know the rest," said Cleek, with a smile. "A fellow you met out in India, a fellow named George Headland, lieutenant, remember the name, please, has just turned up in these parts. You met him quite unexpectedly, and if you want to get at the bottom of this case, take him along with you and get your Aunt Ruth to put him up for a day or two."

"Oh, Mr. Cleek!"

"George Headland, if you please, Miss Lorne. There's a great deal in a name, Shakespeare or anybody else to the contrary."

Chapter II

IT WAS two o'clock in the afternoon when, after lunching with Cleek at the inn of 'The Three Desires', Lieutenant Bridewell turned up at the divided house with his friend, 'George Headland', and introduced him to the various occupants thereof; and, forthwith, 'Mr. George Headland' proceeded to make himself as agreeable to all parties as he knew how to do. He found Aunt Ruth the very duplicate of what young Bridewell had prepared him to find, namely, a veritable Dorcas: the very embodiment of thrift, energy, punctiliousness, with the graceful figure of a ramrod and the martial step of a grenadier; and he decided forthwith that, be she a monument of all the virtues, she was still just the kind of woman he would fly to the ends of the earth rather than have to live with for one short week. In brief, he did not like Miss Ruth Sutcliff, and Miss Ruth Sutcliff did not like him.

Of the two Cordovas, he found the girl Lucretia a mere walking vanity bag: idle, shiftless, eager for compliments, and without two ideas in her vain little head. "Whoever is at the bottom of the affair, she isn't," was his mental comment. "She is just a gadfly, just a gaudy, useless insect, born without a sting, or the spirit to use one if she had it."

Her brother Paul was not much better. "A mere lizard, content to bask in the sunshine and caring not who pays for the privilege so long as he gets it. I can see plainly enough why a fellow like young Bridewell should dislike the pair of them, and even distrust and suspect them, too; but, unless I am woefully mistaken, they can be counted out of the case entirely. Who, then, is in it? Or is there really any case at all? Is the old captain's malady a natural one, in spite of all these suspicions? I'll know that when I see him."

When he did see him, about an hour after his arrival at the divided house, he did know it, and decided forthwith, whatever the mysterious cause, foul play was there beyond the question of a doubt. Somebody had a secret reason for destroying this old man's life, and that somebody was quietly and craftily doing it. But how? By what means? Not by poison, that was certain, for no poison could have this purely local effect and confine itself to the right side of the body, the right hand, the right arm, the right shoulder, spread to no other part and simply corrode the flesh and destroy the bone there as lime or caustic might, and leave the left side wholly unblemished, entirely without attack. Wholly unlike the case of old Mr. Bawdrey, in the affair of the 'Nine-fingered Skeleton', this could be no poison that was administered by touch, injected into the blood through the pores of the skin; for whatsoever Captain Bridewell touched, his son touched after him, and no evil came of it to him. Then, too, there was no temptation of wealth to inherit, as in old Bawdrey's case, for the little that Captain Bridewell possessed would die with him. He had no expectations; he stood in no one's way to an inheritance. Why, then, was he being done to death? – and how?

A dear, kindly, lovable old fellow, with a heart as big as an ox's, a hand ever ready to help those in need, as witness his adoption of the mutineering mate's children, a mind as free from guile as any child's, he ought, in the natural order of things, to have not one enemy in the world, one acquaintance who did not wish him well; and yet—

"I must manage to get a look at that maimed hand somehow and to examine that peculiar eruption closely," said Cleek to Bridewell, when they were alone together. "I could get so little impression of its character on account of the bandages and the sling. Do you think I could get to see it some time without either?"

"Yes, certainly you can. Fordyce always dresses it in the evening. We'll make it our business to be about then, and he'll be sure to let you see it if you like."

"I should, indeed," said Cleek. "And by the way, I haven't seen Dr. Fordyce yet. Isn't he about?"

"Not just at present; be in to tea, though. He's off on his rounds at present. Makes a practice of looking after the poor for the simple humanity of the thing. Never charges for his services. You'll like Fordyce, he's a ripping sort."

And so indeed he seemed to be when, at tea, Cleek met him for the first time and found him a jovial, round-faced, apple-cheeked, rollicking little man of fifty-odd years.

"Pleased to meet you, Mr. Headland – very pleased indeed," he said gaily, when young Bridewell introduced them. "Londoner, I can see, by the cut of you, Londoner and soldier, too. No mistaking military training when a man carries himself like that. Londoner myself once upon a time. But no place like the country for health, and no part of the country like Devon. Paradise, sir, Paradise. Well, Captain, and how are we today, eh? Better?"

"No, I'm afraid not, doctor," replied the old seaman. "Pain's been a little worse than yesterday. Never was so bad as when I woke up this morning; and, if you'll pardon my saying it, sir, that lotion you gave me doesn't seem to have done a bit of good."

"Oho! There's a lotion, is there?" commented Cleek mentally, when he heard this. "I'll have a look at that lotion before I go to bed tonight." Yet, when he did, he found it a harmless thing that ought to have been beneficial even if it had not.

"I say, Fordyce," put in young Bridewell, remembering Cleek's desire and seeing a chance of gratifying it sooner than he had anticipated, "don't you think it would be a good thing to have a look at the pater's arm now? He says the pain's getting up to the shoulder, and so bad at times he can hardly bear it. Do look at it, will you? I hate to see him suffering like this."

"Oh, certainly, of course I will. Just wait until I've had my tea, old chap," replied the doctor; and, when he had had it, moved over to the deep chair where the captain sat rocking to and fro and squeezing his lips together in silent agony, and proceeded to remove the bandages. He had barely uncovered the maimed hand, however, ere Cleek sauntered over in company with the old seaman's son and stood beside him. He was close enough now to study the character of the eruption, and the sight of it tightened the creases about his lips, twitched one swift gleam of light through the darkness of his former bewilderment.

"Good God!" he said, swept out of himself for the moment by the appalling realization which surged over him; then, remembering himself, caught the doctor's swiftly given upward look and returned it with one of innocent blankness. "Awful, isn't it, doctor? Don't think it's smallpox, or something of that sort, do you?"

"Rubbish!" responded the doctor, with laughing contempt for such a silly fool as this. "Smallpox, indeed! Man alive, it isn't the least thing like it. I should think a child would know that. No, Captain, there isn't any change in its condition, despite the increased pain, unless it may be that it is just a shade better than when I dressed it this morning. There, there, don't worry about its going up to the shoulder, Lieutenant. We'll save the arm, never fear." And then, without examining that arm at all, proceeded to rebandage the maimed hand and replace it in the supporting sling; and, afterward, went over and talked with Aunt Ruth before passing out and going round to his side of the divided house. But so long as he remained in sight, Cleek's narrowed eyes followed him and the tense creases seamed Cleek's indrawn, silent lips. But when he broke that silence it was to speak to the captain and to say some silly, pointless thing about that refuge of the witless – the weather.

"Bridewell," he said ten minutes later, when, upon Aunt Ruth's objecting to it being done indoors, the lieutenant invited him to come outside for a smoke, "Bridewell, tell me something: Where does your father sleep?"

"Dad? Oh, upstairs in the big front room just above us. Why?"

"Nothing, but, I've a whim to see the place, and without anybody's knowledge. Can you take me there?"

"Certainly. Come along," replied the lieutenant, and led the way round to a back staircase and up that to the room in question. It was a pretty room, hung with an artistic pink paper which covered not only the original walls but the wooden partitions which blocked up the door leading to Dr. Fordyce's own part of the house; and close against that partition and so placed that the screening canopy shut out the glare from the big bay window, stood a narrow brass bedstead equipped with the finest of springs, the very acme of luxury and ease in the way of soft mattresses, and so piled with down pillows that a king might have envied it for a resting place.

Cleek looked at it for a moment in silence, then reached out and laid his hand upon the papered partition.

"What's on the other side of this?" he queried. "Does it lead into a passage or a room?"

"Into Fordyce's laboratory," replied the lieutenant. "As a matter of fact, this used to be Fordyce's own bedroom, the best in the house. But he gave it up especially for the dad's use as the view and the air are better than in any other room in the place, he says, and he's a great believer in that sort of thing for sick people. Ripping of him, wasn't it?"

"Very. Suppose you could get your father not to sleep here tonight for a change?"

"Wouldn't like to try. He fairly dotes on that comfortable soft bed. There's not another to compare with it in the house. I'm sure he wouldn't rest half so well on a harder one, and wouldn't give this one up unless he was compelled to do so by some unforeseen accident."

"Good," said Cleek. "Then there is going to be 'some unforeseen accident' – look!" With that he stripped down the counterpane, lifted the water jug from the washstand and emptied its contents over the mattresses, and when the pool of water had been absorbed, replaced the covering and arranged the bed as before.

"Great Scot, man," began the lieutenant, amazed by this; but Cleek's hand closed sharply on his arm, and Cleek's whispered "Sh-h-h!" sounded close to his ear. "Keep your father up after everybody else has gone to bed, especially Aunt Ruth," he went on. "If she's not at hand, the damage can't be repaired for this night at least. Give him your room and you come in with me. Bridewell, I know the man; I know the means; and with God's help tonight I'll know the reason as well!"

Chapter III

EVERYTHING was carried out in accordance with Cleek's plan. The captain, trapped into talking by his son, sat up long after Miss Sutcliff and the one serving maid the house boasted had gone to bed, and when, in time, he, too, retired to his room, the soaked mattress did its work in the most effectual manner. Whimpering like a hurt child over the unexplained and apparently unexplainable accident, the old man suffered his son to lead him off to his own room; and there, unable to rest on the harder mattress, and suffering agonies of pain, he lay for a long time before the door swung open, the glimmer of a bedroom candle tempered the darkness to a sort of golden dusk, and the very double of Dr. Fordyce came softly into the room. It was Cleek, wrapped in a well-padded dressing gown and carrying in addition to the candle a bottle of lotion and a fresh linen bandage.

"Why, doctor," began the old captain, half rising upon the elbow of his uninjured arm. "Whatever in the world brings you here?"

"Study, my dear old friend, study," returned a voice so like to Dr. Fordyce's own that there was scarcely a shade of difference. "I have been sitting up for hours and hours thinking, reading, studying until now I am sure, very, very sure, Captain, that I have found a lotion that will ease the pain. For a moment after I let myself in by the partition door and found your room empty I didn't know where to turn; but fortunately your moans guided me in the right direction, and here I am. Now then, let us off with that other bandage and on with this new one, and I think we shall soon ease up that constant pain."

"God knows I hope so, doctor, for it is almost unbearable," the old man replied, and sat holding his lips tightly shut to keep from crying out while Cleek undid the bandage and stripped bare the injured arm from fingertips to shoulder. His gorge rose as he saw the thing, and in seeing, knew for certain now that what he had suspected in that first glance was indeed the truth, and in that moment there was something akin to murder in his soul. He saw with satisfaction, however, that, although the upper part of the arm was much swollen, as yet the progress of decay had not gone much beyond the wrist; and having seen this and verified the nature of the complaint, he applied the fresh lotion and was for bandaging the arm up and stealing out and away again when he caught sight of something that made him suck in his breath and set his heart hammering.

The captain, attracted by his movement and the sound of his thick breathing, opened his pain-closed eyes, looked round and met the questioning look of his.

"Oh," he said with a smile of understanding. "You are looking at the tattooing near my shoulder, are you? Haven't you ever noticed it before?"

"No," said Cleek, keeping his voice steady by an effort. "Who did it and why? There's a name there and a queer sort of emblem. They are not yours, surely?"

"Good heaven, no! My name's Samuel Bridewell and always has been. Red Hamish put that thing there – oh, more than five-and-twenty years ago. Him and me was wrecked on a reef in the Indian Ocean when the *Belle Burgoyne* went down from under us and took all but us down with her. It might as well have took Red Hamish, too, poor chap, for he was hurt cruel bad, and he only lived a couple of days afterward. There was just me alone on the reef when the *Kitty Gordon* come sailin' along, see my signal of distress, and took me off near done for after eight days' fastin' and thirstin' on that bare scrap of terry firmer as they calls it. I'd have been as dead as Red Hamish himself, I reckon, in another twenty-four hours."

"Red Hamish? Good heavens, who was Red Hamish?"

"Never heard him called any other name than just that. Must have had one, of course; and it's so blessed long ago now I disremember what it was he put on the back of my shoulder. A great hand at tattooing he was. Fair lived with his injy ink and his prickin' needles. Kept 'em in a belt he wore and had 'em on him when the *Belle Burgoyne* went down and I managed to drag him on to the reef, poor chap.

"'Had your call, Red,' I says to him when I got him up beside me. 'I reckon you're struck for death, old man.' 'I know it,' says he to me. 'But better me than you, cap'n,' he says, ''cause there ain't nobody waitin' and watchin' for me to come home to her and the kid. Though there is one woman who'd like to know where I'd gone and when and how death found me,' he says, after a moment. 'I'd like to send a word – a message – a sign just to her, cap'n. She'd know – she'd understand and – well, it's only right that she should.'

"'Well, give it to me, Red,' I says. 'I'll take it to her if I live, old man.' But, bless you, there wasn't anything to write the message on, of course; and it wasn't for a long time that Red hit upon a plan.

"'Cap'n,' he says, 'I've got my inks and my needles. Let me put it on your shoulder, will you? Just a name and a sign. But she'll understand, she'll know, and that's all I want.' Of course I agreed – who wouldn't for a mate at a time like that? So I lays down on my face and Red goes at me with the needles and works till he gets it done.

"'There,' he says when he'd reached the end of it. 'If ever anybody wants to know who died on this here reef, cap'n, there's Red Hamish's answer,' he says. 'She'll know, my mother, the only one that cares,' says he, and chucks his belt into the sea and that's all.

"Thanky, doctor, thanky. It does feel better, and I do believe that I shall sleep now. At first I missed the hummin' of that electric fan in your laboratory, I fancy, but bless you, sir, I feel quite drowsy and comfortable now. Remember me to Colonel Goshen when you go back to your rooms, will you? I see him go round the angle of the buildin' and into your side of the house just after you left me tonight, sir, and I thought likely he'd come round and call, but he didn't. Goodnight, sir – goodnight, and many thanks!"

But even before he had finished speaking Cleek had gone out of the room, and was padding swiftly along the passage to where Lieutenant Bridewell awaited him.

"Well?" exclaimed the young man breathlessly as the fleet-moving figure flashed in and began tearing off the beard, the dressing gown, and the disguising wig. "You found out? You learned something, then?"

"I have learned everything, everything!" said Cleek, and pouncing upon his portmanteau whisked out a couple of pairs of handcuffs. "Don't stop to ask questions now. Come with me to the partition door and clap those things on the wrists of the man that gets by me. There are two of them in there, your Dr. Fordyce and your Colonel Goshen, and I want them both."

"Good heavens, man, you don't surely mean that they, those two dear friends—"

"Don't ask questions, come!" rapped in Cleek, then whirled out of the room and flew down the passage to the partition door, and pounded heavily upon it. "Doctor Fordyce, Doctor Fordyce, open the door, come quickly. Something has happened to Captain Bridewell," he called. "He's not in his room, not in the house, and it looks as if somebody had spirited him away!"

A clatter of footsteps on the other side of the partition door answered this; then the bolt flashed back, the door whirled open, two figures – one on the very heels of the other – came tumbling into sight, and then there was mischief!

Cleek sprang, and a click of steel sounded. The doctor, caught in a sort of throttle-hold, went down with him upon the floor; the colonel, unable to check himself in time, sprawled headlong over them, and by the time he could pull himself to his knees young Bridewell was upon him, and there were gyves upon his wrists as well as upon the doctor's.

"Got you, you pretty pair!" said Cleek, as he rose to his feet and shut a tight hand upon the collar of the manacled doctor; "got you, you dogs, and your little game is up. Oh, you needn't bluster, doctor, you needn't come the outraged innocence, Colonel. You'll, neither of you, bolster up the rascally claim of your worthy confederate, the Tackbun Claimant; and your game with the X-rays, your devil's trick of rotting away a man's arm to destroy tattooed evidence of a rank imposter's guilt is just so much time wasted and just so many pounds sterling thrown away."

"What's that?" blustered the colonel. "What do you mean? What are you talking about? Tackbun Claimant? Who's the Tackbun Claimant? Do you realize to whom you are speaking? Fordyce, who and what is this infernally impudent puppy?"

"Gently, gently, Colonel. Name's Cleek, if you are anxious to know it."

"Cleek? Cleek?"

"Precisely, doctor. Cleek of Scotland Yard, Cleek of the Forty Faces, if you want complete details. And if there are more that you feel you would like to know, I'll give them to you when I hand you over to the Devonshire police for your part in this rascally conspiracy to cheat the late Lady Tackbun's nephew out of his lawful rights and to rot off the arm of the man who constitutes the living document which will clearly establish them. The lost Sir Aubrey Tackbun is dead, my friend, dead as Julius Caesar, dead beyond the hopes of you and your confederates to revive even the ghost of him now. He died on a coral reef in the Indian Ocean five-and-twenty years ago, and the proof of it will last as long as Captain Bridewell can keep his arm and lift his voice to tell his story, and I think that will be a good many years, now that your little scheme is exploded. You'll make no X-ray martyr of that dear old man, so the money you spent in the instrument on the other side of that board partition, the thing whose buzzing you made him believe came from an electric fan, represents just so many sovereigns thrown away!"

* * *

"Yes, it was a crafty plot, a scheme very well laid indeed," said Cleek, when he went next day to the lych-gate to say goodbye again to Ailsa Lorne. "Undoubtedly a mild poison was used in the beginning, as an excuse, you know, for the 'colonel' to get him away and into the charge of the 'doctor', and, once there, the rest was easy if subtle. The huge X-ray machine would play always upon the partition whilst the captain was sleeping, and you know how efficacious that would be when there was only a thin board between that powerful influence and the object to be operated upon. Then, too, the head of the bed was so arranged that the captain's right side would always be exposed to the influence, so there was no possibility of evading it.

"How did I suspect it? Well, to tell you the truth, I never did suspect it until I saw the captain's hand. Then I recognized the marks. I saw the hand of a doctor, an X-ray martyr, who sacrificed himself to science last year, Miss Lorne, and the marks were identical. Oh, well, I've solved the riddle, Miss Lorne, that's the main point, and now – now I must emulate 'Poor Joe' and move on again."

"And without any reward, without asking any, without expecting any. How good of you – how generous!"

He stood a moment, twisting his heel into the turf and breathing heavily. Then, quite suddenly:

"Perhaps I did want one," he said, looking into her eyes. "Perhaps I want one still. Perhaps I always hoped that I should get it, and that it would come from you!"

A rush of sudden colour reddened all her face. She let her eyes fall, and said nothing. But what of that? After all, actions speak louder than utterances, and Cleek could see that there was a smile upon her lips. He stretched forth his hand and laid it gently on her arm.

"Miss Lorne," he said very softly, "if, some day when all the wrongs I did in those other times, are righted, and all the atonement a man can make on this earth has been made, if then – in that time – I come to you and ask for that reward, do you think – ah! do you think that you can find it in your heart to give it?"

She lifted up her eyes, the eyes that had saved him, that had lit the way back, that would light it ever to the end of life and, stretching out her hand, put it into his.

"When that day dawns, come and see," she said, and smiled at him through happy tears.

"I will," he made answer. "Wait and I will. Oh, God, what a good, good thing a real woman is!"

The Story of the Spaniards, Hammersmith

E. and H. Heron

LIEUTENANT RODERICK HOUSTON, of H.M.S. Sphinx, had practically nothing beyond his pay, and he was beginning to be very tired of the West African station, when he received the pleasant intelligence that a relative had left him a legacy. This consisted of a satisfactory sum in ready money and a house in Hammersmith, which was rated at over £200 a year, and was said in addition to be comfortably furnished. Houston, therefore, counted on its rental to bring his income up to a fairly desirable figure. Further information from home, however, showed him that he had been rather premature in his expectations, whereupon, being a man of action, he applied for two months' leave, and came home to look after his affairs himself.

When he had been a week in London he arrived at the conclusion that he could not possibly hope single-handed to tackle the difficulties which presented themselves. He accordingly wrote the following letter to his friend, Flaxman Low:

> *The Spaniards, Hammersmith, 23-3-1892*
>
> *Dear Low – Since we parted some three years ago, I have heard very little of you. It was only yesterday that I met our mutual friend, Sammy Smith ('Silkworm' of our schooldays) who told me that your studies have developed in a new direction, and that you are now a good deal interested in psychical subjects. If this be so, I hope to induce you to come and stay with me here for a few days by promising to introduce you to a problem in your own line. I am just now living at 'The Spaniards', a house that has lately been left to me, and which in the first instance was built by an old fellow named Van Nuysen, who married a great-aunt of mine. It is a good house, but there is said to be 'something wrong' with it. It lets easily, but unluckily the tenants cannot be persuaded to remain above a week or two. They complain that the place is haunted by something – presumably a ghost – because its vagaries bear just that brand of inconsequence which stamps the common run of manifestations.*
>
> *It occurs to me that you may care to investigate the matter with me. If so, send me a wire when to expect you.*
>
> *Yours ever.*
> *Roderick Houston*

Houston waited in some anxiety for an answer. Low was the sort of man one could rely on in almost any emergency. Sammy Smith had told him a characteristic anecdote of Low's career at Oxford, where, although his intellectual triumphs may be forgotten, he will always be remembered by the story that when Sands, of Queen's, fell ill on the day before the Varsity sports, a telegram was sent to Low's rooms: "Sands ill. You must do the hammer for us." Low's reply was pithy: "I'll be there."

Thereupon he finished the treatise upon which he was engaged, and next day his strong, lean figure was to be seen swinging the hammer amidst vociferous cheering, for that was the occasion on which he not only won the event, but beat the record.

On the fifth day Low's answer came from Vienna. As he read it, Houston recalled the high forehead, long neck – with its accompanying low collar – and thin moustache of his scholarly, athletic friend, and smiled. There was so much more in Flaxman Low than anyone gave him credit for.

> *My Dear Houston, – Very glad to hear of you again. In response to your kind invitation, I thank you for the opportunity of meeting the ghost, and still more for the pleasure of your companionship. I came here to inquire into a somewhat similar affair. I hope, however, to be able to leave tomorrow, and will be with you some time on Friday evening.*
>
> *Very sincerely yours.*
> *Flaxman Low*

> *P.S. – By the way, will it be convenient to give your servants a holiday during the term of my visit, as, if my investigations are to be of any value, not a grain of dust must be disturbed in your house, excepting by ourselves? – F.L.*

'The Spaniards' was within some fifteen minutes' walk of Hammersmith Bridge. Set in the midst of a fairly respectable neighbourhood, it presented an odd contrast to the commonplace dullness of the narrow streets crowded about it. As Flaxman Low drove up in the evening light, he reflected that the house might have come from the back of beyond – it gave an impression of something old-world and something exotic.

It was surrounded by a ten-foot wall, above which the upper storey was visible, and Low decided that this intensely English house still gave some curious suggestion of the tropics. The interior of the house carried out the same idea, with its sense of space and air, cool tints and wide, matted passages.

"So you have seen something yourself since you came?" Low said, as they sat at dinner, for Houston had arranged that meals should be sent in for them from a hotel.

"I've heard tapping up and down the passage upstairs. It is an uncarpeted landing which runs the whole length of the house. One night, when I was quicker than usual, I saw what looked like a bladder disappear into one of the bedrooms – your room it is to be, by the way – and the door closed behind it," replied Houston discontentedly. "The usual meaningless antics of a ghost."

"What had the tenants who lived here to say about it?" went on Low.

"Most of the people saw and heard just what I have told you, and promptly went away. The only one who stood out for a little while was old Filderg – you know the man? Twenty years ago he made an effort to cross the Australian deserts – he stopped for eight weeks. When he left he saw the house-agent, and said he was afraid he had done a little shooting practice in the upper passage, and he hoped it wouldn't count against him in the bill, as it was done in defence of his life. He said something had jumped on to the bed and tried to strangle him. He described it as cold and glutinous, and he pursued it down the passage, firing at it. He advised the owner to have the house pulled down; but, of course, my cousin did nothing of the kind. It's a very good house, and he did not see the sense of spoiling his property."

"That's very true," replied Flaxman Low, looking round. "Mr. Van Nuysen had been in the West Indies, and kept his liking for spacious rooms."

"Where did you hear anything about him?" asked Houston in surprise.

"I have heard nothing beyond what you told me in your letter; but I see a couple of bottles of Gulf weed and a lace-plant ornament, such as people used to bring from the West Indies in former days."

"Perhaps I should tell you the history of the old man," said Houston doubtfully; "but we aren't proud of it!"

Flaxman Low considered a moment.

"When was the ghost seen for the first time?"

"When the first tenant took the house. It was let after old Van Nuysen's time."

"Then it may clear the way if you will tell me something of him."

"He owned sugar plantations in Trinidad, where he passed the greater part of his life, while his wife mostly remained in England – incompatibility of temper it was said. When he came home for good and built this house they still lived apart, my aunt declaring that nothing on earth would persuade her to return to him. In course of time he became a confirmed invalid, and he then insisted on my aunt joining him. She lived here for perhaps a year, when she was found dead in bed one morning – in your room."

"What caused her death?"

"She had been in the habit of taking narcotics, and it was supposed that she smothered herself while under their influence."

"That doesn't sound very satisfactory," remarked Flaxman Low.

"Her husband was satisfied with it anyhow, and it was no one else's business. The family were only too glad to have the affair hushed up."

"And what became of Mr. Van Nuysen?"

"That I can't tell you. He disappeared a short time after. Search was made for him in the usual way, but nobody knows to this day what became of him."

"Ah, that was strange, as he was such an invalid," said Low, and straightway fell into a long fit of abstraction, from which he was roused by hearing Houston curse the incurable foolishness and imbecility of ghostly behaviour. Flaxman woke up at this. He broke a walnut thoughtfully and began in a gentle voice:

"My dear fellow, we are apt to be hasty in our condemnation of the general behaviour of ghosts. It may appear incalculably foolish in our eyes, and I admit there often seems to be a total absence of any apparent object or intelligent action. But remember that what appears to us to be foolishness may be wisdom in the spirit world, since our unready senses can only catch broken glimpses of what is, I have not the slightest doubt, a coherent whole, if we could trace the connection."

"There may be something in that," replied Houston indifferently. "People naturally say that this ghost is the ghost of old Van Nuysen. But what connection can possibly exist between what I have told you of him and the manifestations – a tapping up and down the passage and the drawing about of a bladder like a child at play? It sounds idiotic!"

"Certainly. Yet it need not necessarily be so. There are isolated facts, we must look for the links which lie between. Suppose a saddle and a horse-shoe were to be shown to a man who had never seen a horse, I doubt whether he, however intelligent, could evolve the connecting idea! The ways of spirits are strange to us simply because we need further data to help us to interpret them."

"It's a new point of view," returned Houston, "but upon my word, you know, Low, I think you're wasting your time!"

Flaxman Low smiled slowly; his grave, melancholy face brightened.

"I have," said he, "gone somewhat deeply into the subject. In other sciences one reasons by analogy. Psychology is unfortunately a science with a future but without a past, or more probably it is a lost science of the ancients. However that may be, we stand today on the frontier of an unknown world, and progress is the result of individual effort; each solution of difficult phenomena forms a step towards the solution of the next problem. In this case, for example, the bladder-like object may be the key to the mystery."

Houston yawned.

"It all seems pretty senseless, but perhaps you may be able to read reason into it. If it were anything tangible, anything a man could meet with his fists, it would be easier."

"I entirely agree with you. But suppose we deal with this affair as it stands, on similar lines, I mean on prosaic, rational lines, as we should deal with a purely human mystery."

"My dear fellow," returned Houston, pushing his chair back from the table wearily, "you shall do just as you like, only get rid of the ghost!"

For some time after Low's arrival nothing very special happened. The tappings continued, and more than once Low had been in time to see the bladder disappear into the closing door of his bedroom, though, unluckily, he never chanced to be inside the room on these occasions, and however quickly he followed the bladder, he never succeeded in seeing anything further. He made a thorough examination of the house, and left no space unaccounted for in his careful measurement. There were no cellars, and the foundation of the house consisted of a thick layer of concrete.

At length, on the sixth night, an event took place, which, as Flaxman Low remarked, came very near to putting an end to the investigations as far as he was concerned. For the preceding two nights he and Houston had kept watch in the hope of getting a glimpse of the person or thing which tapped so persistently up and down the passage. But they were disappointed, for there were no manifestations. On the third evening, therefore, Low went off to his room a little earlier than usual, and fell asleep almost immediately.

He says he was awakened by feeling a heavy weight upon his feet, something that seemed inert and motionless. He recollected that he had left the gas burning, but the room was now in darkness.

Next he was aware that the thing on the bed had slowly shifted, and was gradually travelling up towards his chest. How it came on the bed he had no idea. Had it leaped or climbed? The sensation he experienced as it moved was of some ponderous, pulpy body, not crawling or creeping, but spreading! It was horrible! He tried to move his lower limbs, but could not because of the deadening weight. A feeling of drowsiness began to overpower him, and a deadly cold, such as he said he had before felt at sea when in the neighbourhood of icebergs, chilled upon the air.

With a violent struggle he managed to free his arms, but the thing grew more irresistible as it spread upwards. Then he became conscious of a pair of glassy eyes, with livid, everted lids, looking into his own. Whether they were human eyes or beast eyes, he could not tell, but they were watery, like the eyes of a dead fish, and gleamed with a pale, internal lustre.

Then he owns he grew afraid. But he was still cool enough to notice one peculiarity about this ghastly visitant – although the head was within a few inches of his own, he could detect no breathing. It dawned on him that he was about to be suffocated, for, by the same method of extension, the thing was now coming over his face! It felt cold and clammy, like a mass of mucilage or a monstrous snail. And every instant the weight became greater. He is a powerful man, and he struck with his fists again and again at the head. Some substance yielded under the blows with a sickening sensation of bruised flesh.

With a lucky twist he raised himself in the bed and battered away with all the force he was capable of in his cramped position. The only effect was an occasional shudder or quake that ran through the mass as his half-arm blows rained upon it. At last, by chance, his hand knocked against the candle beside him. In a moment he recollected the matches. He seized the box, and struck a light.

As he did so, the lump slid to the floor. He sprang out of bed, and lit the candle. He felt a cold touch upon his leg, but when he looked down there was nothing to be seen. The door, which he had locked overnight, was now open, and he rushed out into the passage. All was still and silent with the throbbing vacancy of night-time.

After searching round, he returned to his room. The bed still gave ample proof of the struggle that had taken place, and by his watch he saw the hour to be between two and three.

As there seemed nothing more to be done, he put on his dressing gown, lit his pipe, and sat down to write an account of the experience he had just passed through for the Psychical Research Society – from which paper the above is an abstract.

He is a man of strong nerves, but he could not disguise from himself that he had been at handgrips with some grotesque form of death. What might be the nature of his assailant he could not determine, but his experience was supported by the attack which had been made on Filderg, and also – it was impossible to avoid the conclusion – by the manner of Mrs. Van Nuysen's death.

He thought the whole situation over carefully in connection with the tapping and the disappearing bladder, but, turn these events how he would, he could make nothing of them. They were entirely incongruous. A little later he went and made a shakedown in Houston's room.

"What was the thing?" asked Houston, when Low had ended his story of the encounter.

Low shrugged his shoulders.

"At least it proves that Filderg did not dream," he said.

"But this is monstrous! We are more in the dark than ever. There's nothing for it but to have the house pulled down. Let us leave today."

"Don't be in a hurry, my dear fellow. You would rob me of a very great pleasure; besides, we may be on the verge of some valuable discovery. This series of manifestations is even more interesting than the Vienna mystery I was telling you of."

"Discovery or not," replied the other, "I don't like it."

The first thing next morning Low went out for a quarter of an hour. Before breakfast a man with a barrowful of sand came into the garden. Low looked up from his paper, leant out of the window, and gave some order.

When Houston came down a few minutes later he saw the yellowish heap on the lawn with some surprise.

"Hullo! What's this?" he asked.

"I ordered it," replied Low.

"All right. What's it for?"

"To help us in our investigations. Our visitor is capable of being felt, and he or it left a very distinct impression on the bed. Hence I gather it can also leave an impression on sand. It would be an immense advance if we could arrive at any correct notion of what sort of feet the ghost walks on. I propose to spread a layer of this sand in the upper passage, and the result should be footmarks if the tapping comes tonight."

That evening the two men made a fire in Houston's bedroom, and sat there smoking and talking, to leave the ghost 'a free run for once', as Houston phrased it. The tapping was heard at the usual hour, and presently the accustomed pause at the other end of the passage and the quiet closing of the door.

Low heaved a long sigh of satisfaction as he listened.

"That's my bedroom door," he said; "I know the sound of it perfectly. In the morning, and with the help of daylight, we shall see what we shall see."

As soon as there was light enough for the purpose of examining the footprints, Low roused Houston.

Houston was full of excitement as a boy, but his spirits fell by the time he had passed from end to end of the passage.

"There are marks," he said, "but they are as perplexing as everything else about this haunting brute, whatever it is. I suppose you think this is the print left by the thing which attacked you the night before last?"

"I fancy it is," said Low, who was still bending over the floor eagerly. "What do you make of it, Houston?"

"The brute has only one leg, to start with," replied Houston, "and that leaves the mark of a large, clawless pad! It's some animal – some ghoulish monster!"

"On the contrary," said Low, "I think we have now every reason to conclude that it is a man."

"A man? What man ever left footmarks like these?"

"Look at these hollows and streaks at the sides; they are the traces of the sticks we have heard tapping."

"You don't convince me," returned Hodgson doggedly.

"Let us wait another twenty-four hours, and tomorrow night, if nothing further occurs, I will give you my conclusions. Think it over. The tapping, the bladder, and the fact that Mr. Van Nuysen had lived in Trinidad. Add to these things this single pad-like print. Does nothing strike you by way of a solution?"

Houston shook his head.

"Nothing. And I fail to connect any of these things with what happened both to you and Filderg."

"Ah! Now," said Flaxman Low, his face clouding a little, "I confess you lead me into a somewhat different region, though to me the connection is perfect."

Houston raised his eyebrows and laughed.

"If you can unravel this tangle of hints and events and diagnose the ghost, I shall be extremely astonished," he said. "What can you make of the footless impression?"

"Something, I hope. In fact, that mark may be a clue – an outrageous one, perhaps, but still a clue."

That evening the weather broke, and by night the storm had risen to a gale, accompanied by sharp bursts of rain.

"It's a noisy night," remarked Houston; "I don't suppose we'll hear the ghost, supposing it does turn up."

This was after dinner, as they were about to go into the smoking-room. Houston, finding the gas low in the hall, stopped to run it higher; at the same time asking Low to see if the jet on the upper landing was also alight.

Flaxman Low glanced up and uttered a slight exclamation, which brought Houston to his side.

Looking down at them from over the banisters was a face – a blotched, yellowish face, flanked by two swollen, protruding ears, the whole aspect being strangely leonine. It was but a glimpse, a clash of meeting glances, as it were, a glare of defiance, and the face was quickly withdrawn as the two men literally leapt up the stairs.

"There's nothing here," exclaimed Houston, after a search had been carried out through every room above.

"I didn't suppose we'd find anything," returned Low.

"This fairly knots up the thread," said Houston. "You can't pretend to unravel it now."

"Come down," said Low briefly; "I'm ready to give you my opinion, such as it is."

Once in the smoking-room, Houston busied himself in turning on all the light he could procure, then he saw to securing the windows, and piled up an immense fire, while Flaxman Low, who, as usual, had a cigarette in his mouth, sat on the edge of the table and watched him with some amusement.

"You saw that abominable face?" cried Houston, as he threw himself into a chair. "It was as material as yours or mine. But where did he go to? He must be somewhere about."

"We saw him clearly. That is sufficient for our purpose."

"You are very good at enumerating points, Low. Now just listen to my list. The difficulties grow with every fresh discovery. We're at a deadlock now, I take it? The sticks and the tapping point to an old man, the playing with a bladder to a child; the footmark might be the pad of a tiger minus claws, yet the thing that attacked you at night was cold and pulpy. And, lastly, by way of a wind-up, we see a lion-like, human face! If you can make all these items square with each other, I'll be happy to hear what you have got to say."

"You must first allow me to ask you a question. I understood you to say that no blood relationship existed between you and old Mr. Van Nuysen?"

"Certainly not. He was quite an outsider," answered Houston brusquely.

"In that case you are welcome to my conclusions. All the things you have mentioned point to one explanation. This house is haunted by the ghost of Mr. Van Nuysen, and he was a leper."

Houston stood up and stared at his companion.

"What a horrible notion! I must say I fail to see how you have arrived at such a conclusion."

"Take the chain of evidence in rather different order," said Low. "Why should a man tap with a stick?"

"Generally because he's blind."

"In cases of blindness, one stick is used for guidance. Here we have two for support."

"A man who has lost the use of his feet."

"Exactly; a man who has from some cause partially lost the use of his feet."

"But the bladder and the lion-like face?" went on Houston.

"The bladder, or what seemed to us to resemble a bladder, was one of his feet, contorted by the disease and probably swathed in linen, which foot he dragged rather than used; consequently, in passing through a door, for example, he would be in the habit of drawing it in after him. Now, as regards the single footmark we saw. In one form of leprosy, the smaller bones of the extremities frequently fall away. The pad-like impression was, as I believe, the mark of the other foot – a toeless foot which he used, because in a more advanced stage of the disease the maimed hand or foot heals and becomes callous."

"Go on," said Houston; "it sounds as if it might be true. And the lion-like face I can account for myself. I have been in China, and have seen it before in lepers."

"Mr. Van Nuysen had been in Trinidad for many years, as we know, and while there he probably contracted the disease."

"I suppose so. After his return," added Houston, "he shut himself up almost entirely, and gave out that he was a martyr to rheumatic gout, this awful thing being the true explanation."

"It also accounts for Mrs. Van Nuysen's determination not to return to her husband."

Houston appeared much disturbed.

"We can't drop it here, Low," he said, in a constrained voice. "There is a good deal more to be cleared up yet. Can you tell me more?"

"From this point I find myself on less certain ground," replied Low unwillingly. "I merely offer a suggestion, remember – I don't ask you to accept it. I believe Mrs. Van Nuysen was murdered!"

"What?" exclaimed Houston. "By her husband?"

"Indications tend that way."

"But, my good fellow—"

"He suffocated her and then made away with himself. It is a pity that his body was not recovered. The condition of the remains would be the only really satisfactory test of my theory. If the skeleton could even now be found, the fact that he was a leper would be finally settled."

There was a prolonged pause until Houston put another question.

"Wait a minute, Low," he said. "Ghosts are admittedly immaterial. In this instance our spook has an extremely palpable body. Surely this is rather unusual? You have made everything else more or less plain. Can you tell me why this dead leper should have tried to murder you and old Filderg? And also how he came to have the actual physical power to do so?"

Low removed his cigarette to look thoughtfully at the end of it. "Now I lapse into the purely theoretical," he answered. "Cases have been known where the assumption of diabolical agency is apparently justifiable."

"Diabolical agency? – I don't follow you."

"I will try to make myself clear, though the subject is still in a stage of vagueness and immaturity. Van Nuysen committed a murder of exceptional atrocity, and afterwards killed himself. Now, bodies of suicides are known to be peculiarly susceptible to spiritual influences, even to the point of arrested corruption. Add to this our knowledge that the highest aim of an evil spirit is to gain possession of a material body. If I carried out my theory to its logical conclusion, I should say that Van Nuysen's body is hidden somewhere on these premises – that this body is intermittently animated by some spirit, which at certain points is forced to re-enact the gruesome tragedy of the Van Nuysens. Should any living person chance to occupy the position of the first victim, so much the worse for him!"

For some minutes Houston made no remark on this singular expression of opinion.

"But have you ever met with anything of the sort before?" he said at last.

"I can recall," replied Flaxman Low thoughtfully, "quite a number of cases which would seem to bear out this hypothesis. Among them a curious problem of haunting exhaustively examined by Busner in the early part of 1888, at which I was myself lucky enough to assist. Indeed, I may add that the affair which I have recently engaged upon in Vienna offers some rather similar features. There, however, we had to stop short of excavation, by which alone any specific results might have been attained."

"Then you are of the opinion," said Houston, "that pulling the house to pieces might cast some further light upon this affair?"

"I cannot see any better course," said Mr. Low.

Then Houston closed the discussion by a very definite declaration.

"This house shall come down!"

So 'The Spaniards' was pulled down.

The work of demolition, begun at the earliest possible moment, did not occupy very long, and during its early stages, under the boarding at an angle of the landing was found a skeleton. Several of the phalanges were missing, and other indications also established beyond a doubt the fact that the remains were the remains of a leper.

The skeleton is now in the museum of one of our city hospitals. It bears a scientific ticket, and is the only evidence extant of the correctness of Mr. Flaxman Low's methods and the possible truth of his extraordinary theories.

The Strange Case of Mr. Challoner

Herbert Jenkins

Chapter I

"PLEASE, sir, Miss Norman's fainted." William Johnson, known to his colleagues as the innocent, stood at Malcolm Sage's door, with widened eyes and a general air that bespoke helplessness.

Without a word Malcolm Sage rose from his table, as if accustomed all his life to the fainting of secretaries. William Johnson stood aside, with the air of one who has rung a fire alarm and now feels he is at liberty to enjoy the fire itself.

Entering her room, Malcolm Sage found Gladys Norman lying in a heap beside her typewriter. Picking her up he carried her into his own room, placed her in an armchair, fetched some brandy from a small cupboard and, still watched by the wide-eyed William Johnson, proceeded to force a little between her teeth.

Presently her lids flickered and, a moment later, she opened her eyes. For a second there was in them a look of uncertainty, then suddenly they opened to their fullest extent and became fixed upon the door beyond. Malcolm Sage glanced over his shoulder and saw framed in the doorway Sir James Walton.

"Sit down, Chief," he said quietly, his gaze returning to the girl sitting limply in the large leather-covered armchair. "I shall be free in a moment."

It was characteristic of him to attempt no explanation. To his mind the situation explained itself.

As Miss Norman made an effort to rise, he placed a detaining hand upon her arm.

"Send Mr. Thompson."

With a motion of his hand Malcolm Sage indicated to William Johnson that the dramatic possibilities of the situation were exhausted, at least as far as he was concerned. With reluctant steps the lad left the room and, having told Thompson he was wanted, returned to his seat in the outer office, where it was his mission to sit in preliminary judgment upon callers.

When Thompson entered, Malcolm Sage instructed him to move the leather-covered chair into Miss Norman's room and, when she was rested, to take her home in the car.

Thompson's face beamed. His devotion to Gladys Norman was notorious.

The girl rose and raised to Malcolm Sage a pair of dark eyes from which tears were not far distant.

"I'm so ashamed, Mr. Sage," she began, her lower lip trembling ominously. "I've never done such a thing before."

"I've been working you too hard," he said, as he held back the door.

"You must go home and rest."

She shook her head and passed out, whilst Malcolm Sage returned to his seat at the table.

"Working till two o'clock this morning," he remarked as he resumed his seat. "She won't have assistance. Strange creatures, women," he added musingly, "but beautifully loyal."

Sir James had dropped into a chair on the opposite side of Malcolm Sage's table. Having selected a cigar from the box his late chief-of-staff pushed across to him, he cut off the end and proceeded to light it.

"Good cigars these," he remarked, as he critically examined the lighted end.

"They're your own brand, Chief," was the reply.

Malcolm Sage always used the old name of 'Chief' when addressing Sir James Walton. It seemed to constitute a link with the old days when they had worked together with a harmony that had bewildered those heads of departments who had regarded Malcolm Sage as something between a punishment and a misfortune.

"Busy?"

"Very."

For some seconds they were silent. It was like old times to be seated one on each side of a table, and both seemed to realise the fact.

"I've just motored up from Hurstchurch," began Sir James at length, having assured himself that his cigar was drawing as a good cigar should draw. "Been staying with an old friend of mine, Geoffrey Challoner."

Malcolm Sage nodded.

"He was shot last night. That's why I'm here." He paused; but Malcolm Sage made no comment. His whole attention was absorbed in an ivory paper-knife, which he was endeavouring to balance upon the handle of the silver inkstand. More than one client had been disconcerted by Malcolm Sage's restless hands, which they interpreted as a lack of interest in their affairs.

"At half past seven this morning," continued Sir James, "Peters, the butler, knocked at Challoner's door with his shaving-water. As there was no reply he entered and found, not only that Challoner was not there, but that the bed had not been slept in overnight."

Malcolm lifted his hands from the paper-knife. It balanced.

"He thought Challoner had fallen asleep in the library," continued Sir James, "which he sometimes did, he is rather a night-owl. Peters then went downstairs, but found the library door locked on the inside. As there was no response to his knocking, he went round to the French windows that open from the library on to the lawn at the back of the house. The curtains were drawn, however, and he could see nothing."

"Is it usual to draw the curtains?" enquired Malcolm Sage, regarding with satisfaction the paper-knife as it gently swayed up and down upon the inkstand.

"Yes, except in the summer, when the windows are generally kept open."

Malcolm Sage nodded, and Sir James resumed his story.

"Peters then went upstairs to young Dane's room; Dane is Challoner's nephew, who lives with him. While he dressed he sent Peters to tell me.

"A few minutes later we all went down to the library and tried to attract Challoner's attention; but without result. I then suggested forcing an entry from the garden, which was done by breaking the glass of one of the French windows.

"We found Challoner seated at his table dead, shot through the head. He had an automatic pistol in his hand." Sir James paused; his voice had become husky with emotion. Presently he resumed.

"We telephoned for the police and a doctor, and I spent the time until they came in a thorough examination of the room. The French windows had been securely bolted top and bottom from within, by means of a central handle. All the panes of glass were intact, with the exception of that we had broken. The door had been locked *on the inside*, and the key was in position. It was unlocked by Peters when he went into the hall to telephone. It has a strong mortice-lock and the key did not protrude through to the outer side, so that there was no chance of manipulating the lock from without. In the fireplace there was an electric stove, and from the shower of soot that fell when I raised the trap, it was clear that this had not been touched for some weeks at least.

"The doctor was the first to arrive. At my urgent request he refrained from touching the body. He said death had taken place from seven to ten hours previously as the result of the bullet wound in the temple. He had scarcely finished his examination when an inspector of police, who had motored over from Lewes, joined us.

"It took him very few minutes to decide that poor Challoner had shot himself. In this he was confirmed by the doctor. Still, I insisted that the body should not be removed."

"Why did you do that, Chief?" enquired Malcolm Sage, who had discarded the paper-knife and was now busy drawing geometrical figures with the thumbnail of his right hand upon the blotting pad before him.

"Because I was not satisfied," was the reply. "There was absolutely no motive for suicide. Challoner was in good health and, if I know anything about men, determined to live as long as the gods give."

Again Malcolm Sage nodded his head meditatively.

"The jumping to hasty conclusions," he remarked, "has saved many a man his neck. Whom did you leave in charge?" he queried.

"The inspector. I locked the door; here is the key," he said, producing it from his jacket pocket. "I told him to allow no one into the room."

"Why were you there?" Malcolm Sage suddenly looked up, flashing that keen, steely look through his gold-rimmed spectacles that many men had found so disconcerting. "Ordinary visit?" he queried.

"No." Sir James paused, apparently deliberating something in his own mind. He was well acquainted with Malcolm Sage's habit of asking apparently irrelevant questions.

"There's been a little difficulty between Challoner and his nephew," he said slowly. "Some days back the boy announced his determination of marrying a girl he had met in London, a typist or secretary. Challoner was greatly upset, and threatened to cut him out of his will if he persisted. There was a scene, several scenes in fact, and eventually I was sent for as Challoner's oldest friend."

"To bring the nephew to reason," suggested Malcolm Sage.

"To give advice ostensibly; but in reality to talk things over," was the reply.

"You advised?" When keenly interested, Malcolm Sage's questions were like pistol-shots.

"That Challoner should wait and see the girl."

"Did he?"

Malcolm Sage was intent upon outlining his hand with the point of the paper-knife upon the blotting pad.

Again Sir James hesitated, only for a fraction of a second, however.

"Yes; but unfortunately with the object of endeavouring to buy her off. Yesterday afternoon Dane brought her over. Challoner saw her alone. She didn't stay more than a quarter of an hour. Then she and Dane left the house together, he to see her to the station. An hour later he returned. I was in the hall at the time. He was in a very excited state. He pushed past me, burst into the library, banging the door behind him.

"That evening at dinner Challoner told me there had been a very unpleasant scene. He had warned the boy that unless he apologised today he would telephone to London for his lawyer, and make a fresh will entirely disinheriting him. Soon after the interview Dane went out of the house, and apparently did not return until late – as a matter of fact, after I had gone to bed. I was feeling tired and said 'good night' to Challoner about half past ten in the library."

For some time Malcolm Sage gazed upon the outline he had completed, as if in it lay the solution of the mystery.

"It's a pity you let the butler unlock the door," he remarked regretfully.

Sir James looked across at his late chief-of-staff keenly. He detected something of reproach in his tone.

"Did you happen to notice if the electric light was on when you entered the library?"

"No," said Sir James, after a slight pause; "it was not."

Malcolm Sage reached across to the private telephone and gave the 'three on the buzzer' that always galvanised Miss Gladys Norman into instant vitality.

"Miss Norman," said Sage as she entered, "can you lend me the small mirror I have seen you use occasionally?"

"Yes, Mr. Sage," and she disappeared, returning a moment later with the mirror from her handbag. She was accustomed to Malcolm Sage's strange requests.

"Feeling better?" he enquired as she turned to go.

"I'm all right now," she smiled, "and please don't send me home, Mr. Sage," she added, and she went out before he had time to reply.

A quarter of an hour later the two men entered Sir James's car, whilst Thompson and Dawkins, the official photographer to the Bureau, followed in that driven by Tims. Malcolm Sage would cheerfully have sacrificed anybody and anything to serve his late chief.

"And how am I to keep the shine off my nose without a looking-glass, Johnny?" asked Miss Norman of William Johnson, as she turned to resume her work.

"He won't mind if it shines," said the youth seriously; and Miss Norman gave him a look, which only his years prevented him from interpreting.

Chapter II

AS THE CAR drew up, the hall-door of 'The Cedars' was thrown open by the butler, a fair-haired clean-shaven man of about forty-five, with grave, impassive face, and eyes that gave the impression of allowing little to escape them.

As he descended the flight of stone steps to open the door of the car, a young man appeared behind him. A moment later Sir James was introducing him to Malcolm Sage as "Mr. Richard Dane."

Dark, with smoothly-brushed hair and a toothbrush moustache, he might easily have been passed over in a crowd without a second glance. He was obviously and acutely nervous. His fingers moved jerkily, and there were twitchings at the corners of his mouth that he seemed unable to control. It was not a good-tempered mouth. He appeared unconscious of the presence of Malcolm Sage. His eyes were fixed upon the second car, which had just drawn up, and from which Thompson and Dawkins were removing the photographic paraphernalia.

Peters conducted Sir James and Malcolm Sage to the dining room, where luncheon was laid.

"Shall I serve luncheon, Sir James?" he enquired, ignoring Dane, who was clearly unequal to the strain of the duties of host.

Sir James looked across at Malcolm Sage, who shook his head.

"I'll see the library first," he said. "Sir James will show me. Fetch Dawkins," he said to Thompson, and he followed Sir James through the house out on to the lawn.

As they entered the library by the French windows, a tall, sandy man rose from the armchair in which he was seated. He was Inspector Gorton of the Sussex County Constabulary. Malcolm Sage nodded a little absently. His eyes were keenly taking in every detail of the figure sprawling across the writing-table. The head rested on the left cheek, and there was an ugly wound in the right temple from which blood had dripped and congealed upon the table. In the right hand was clutched a small, automatic pistol. The arm was slightly curved, the weapon pointing to the left.

Having concluded his examination of the wound, Malcolm Sage drew a silk handkerchief from his pocket, shook out its folds and spread it carefully over the blood-stained head of Mr. Challoner.

Sir James looked across at him, appreciation in his eyes. It was one of those little human touches, of which he had discovered so many in Malcolm Sage, and the heads of government departments in Whitehall so few.

Malcolm Sage next proceeded to regard the body from every angle, even going down on his knees to see the position of the legs beneath the table. He then walked round the room and examined everything with minute attention, particularly the key of the door, which Sir James had replaced in its position on the inside. The keyhole on both sides of the door came in for careful scrutiny.

He tried the door of a small safe at the far end of the room; it was locked. He then examined the fastenings of the French windows.

Finally he returned to the table, where, dropping on one knee on the left-hand side of the body, he drew a penknife from his pocket, and proceeded with great care and deliberation to slit up the outer seam of the trousers so that the pocket lay exposed.

This in turn he cut open, taking care not to disturb the bunch of keys, which, attached to a chain, lay on the thigh, a little to the left.

The others watched him with wide-eyed interest, the inspector breathing heavily.

Having assured himself that the keys would not slide off, Malcolm Sage rose and turned to Dawkins:

"I want a plate from the right, the left, the front, and from behind and above. Also an exposure showing the position of the legs, and another of the keys."

Dawkins inclined his head. He was a grey, bald-headed little man who had only one thought in life, his profession. He seldom spoke, and when he did his lips seemed scarcely to part, the words slipping out as best they could.

Happy in the knowledge that his beloved camera was once more to be one of the principal witnesses in the detection of a crime, Dawkins set himself to his task.

"When Dawkins has finished," said Malcolm Sage, turning to the inspector, who had been watching the proceedings with ill-disguised impatience, "you can remove the body; but leave the pistol. Give Mr. Challoner's keys to Sir James. And now I think we might lunch," he said, turning to Sir James.

Malcolm Sage's attitude towards the official police was generally determined by their attitude towards him. In the Department Z days, he had been known at Scotland Yard as 'Sage & Onions'. What the phrase lacked in wit was compensated for by the feeling with which it was frequently uttered. The police officers made no effort to dissemble the contempt they felt for a department in which they saw a direct rebuke to themselves. Later, however, their attitude changed, and Malcolm Sage was brought into close personal touch with many of the best-known officers of the Criminal Investigation Department.

He had never been known to speak disparagingly, or patronisingly, of Scotland Yard. On the other hand, he lost no opportunity of emphasising the fact that it was the head-quarters of the most efficient police force in the world. He did not always agree with its methods, which in many ways he regarded as out-of-date.

As Malcolm Sage left the room, the inspector shrugged his shoulders. The whole thing was so obvious that, but for the presence of Sir James Walton, he would have refused to delay the removal of the body. The doctor had pronounced the wound self-inflicted, and even if he had not done so, the circumstantial evidence was conclusive.

Luncheon was eaten in silence, a constrained and uncomfortable meal. Malcolm Sage ate as he always ate when his mind was occupied, with entire indifference as to what was on the plate, from which his eyes never lifted.

Sir James made several ineffectual efforts to draw Dane into conversation; but at each remark the young man started violently, as if suddenly recalled to his surroundings. Finally Sir James desisted, and the meal concluded in abysmal silence.

Malcolm Sage then announced that he would examine the various members of the household, and Dane and Peters left the room.

One by one the servants entered, were interrogated, and departed. Even the gardener and his wife, who lived at the lodge by the main gates, were cross-questioned.

Mrs. Trennett, the housekeeper, was incoherent in her voluble anxiety to give information. The maids were almost too frightened to speak, and from none was anything tangible extracted.

No one had any reason for being near the library late at night.

When Peters' turn came, he told his story with a clearness and economy of words that caused Malcolm Sage mentally to register him as a good witness. He was a superior kind of man, who had been in his present position only some six months; but during that time he had given every satisfaction, so much so that Mr. Challoner had remarked to Sir James that he believed he had found a treasure.

According to Peters' account, at a quarter past eleven on the previous evening he had gone to the library, as was his custom, to see if there were anything else that Mr. Challoner required before he locked up for the night. On being told there was nothing, he had accordingly seen to the fastenings of doors and windows and gone to bed.

"What was Mr. Challoner doing when you entered the room?" enquired Malcolm Sage, intent upon a design he was drawing upon the surface of the salt.

"He was sitting at the table where I found him this morning."

"What was he actually doing?"

"I think he was checking his bankbook, sir."

"Did you notice anything strange about his manner?"

"No, sir."

"When you found that his bed had not been slept in were you surprised?"

"Not greatly, sir," was the response. "Once before a similar thing happened, and I heard from the other servants that on several occasions Mr. Challoner had spent the night in the library, having fallen asleep there."

"When you told Mr. Dane that his uncle had not slept in his room, and that the library door was locked on the inside, what did he say?"

"He said, 'Good Lord! Peters, something must have happened.'"

"Mr. Dane knew that on previous occasions his uncle had spent the night in his study?" enquired Malcolm Sage, smoothing out the design upon which he had been engaged and beginning another.

"I think so, sir," was the response.

"The pistol was the one he used at target-practice?"

"Yes, sir."

"Where did he keep it?"

"In the third right-hand drawer of his table, sir."

"He was a good shot, I think you said?" Malcolm Sage turned to Sir James.

"Magnificent," he said warmly. "I have often shot with him."

"Do you know of any reason why Mr. Challoner should commit suicide?" Malcolm Sage enquired of Peters.

"None whatever, sir; he always seemed very happy."

"He had no domestic worries?"

Peters hesitated for a moment.

"He never mentioned any to me, sir."

"You have in mind certain events that occurred during the last few days, I take it?" said Malcolm Sage.

"That was in my mind, sir," was the response.

"You know of no way by which anyone could have got into the library and then out again, other than through the door or the window?"

Malcolm Sage had relinquished the salt-spoon and was now meditatively twirling a wineglass by its stem between his thumb and first finger.

"There is no other way, sir."

"Who has access to the library in the ordinary way? Tell me the names of everybody who is likely to go in at any time."

"Outside Mr. Challoner and Mr. Dane, there is myself, Mrs. Trennett, the housekeeper, and Meston, the housemaid."

"No one else?"

"No one, sir, except, of course, the guests who might be staying in the house."

"I shall want the fingerprints of all those you have named, including yours, Sir James." Malcolm Sage looked across at Sir James Walton. "I can then identify those of any stranger that I may find." Sir James nodded.

"It would be quite easy for Mr. Challoner to let anyone in through the French windows?" enquired Malcolm Sage, turning once more to Peters.

"Quite, sir."

"What time did Mr. Dane return last evening?"

"I think about a quarter to eleven, sir. He went straight to his room."

"That will be all now. Tell Mr. Dane I should like to see him."

Peters noiselessly withdrew.

A few minutes later Dane entered the room. Malcolm Sage gave him a keen, appraising look, then dropped his eyes. Dane was still acutely nervous. His fingers moved jerkily and the corners of his mouth twitched.

"Will you tell me what took place yesterday between you and your uncle?" said Malcolm Sage.

Dane looked about him nervously, as an animal might who has been trapped and seeks some means of escape.

"We had a row," he began, then paused; "a terrible row," he added, as if to emphasise the nature of the quarrel.

"So I understand," said Malcolm Sage. "I know what it was about. Just tell me what actually took place. In as few words as possible, please."

"A week ago I told my uncle of my engagement, and he was very angry when he knew that my fiancée was – was—

"A secretary," suggested Malcolm Sage, without looking up.

"Yes. He ordered me to break off the engagement at once, no matter what it might cost."

"He referred to his pocket rather than to your feelings, I take it?" said Malcolm Sage.

"Yes." There was a world of bitterness in the tone in which the word was uttered. "I refused. Four days ago Sir James came and, I think, talked things over with my uncle, who said he would see Enid, that is, my fiancée. She came yesterday afternoon. My uncle insisted on seeing her alone. She stayed only a few minutes."

His voice broke. He swallowed rapidly several times in succession, struggling to regain control of himself.

"You walked back to the station with her," remarked Malcolm Sage, "and she told you what had taken place. Your uncle had offered to buy her off. You were furious. You said many wild and extravagant things. Then you came back and went immediately into the library. What took place there?"

"I don't remember what I said. I think for the time I was insane. He had actually offered her money, notes. He had drawn them out of the bank on purpose." Again he stopped, as if the memory of the insult were too much for him.

"And you said?" suggested Malcolm Sage, twirling the wineglass slowly between his thumb and finger.

"I probably said what any other man would have said under similar circumstances." There was a quiet dignity about the way in which he uttered these words, although his fingers still continued to twitch.

"Did he threaten you, or you him?"

"I don't remember what I said; but my uncle told me that, unless I wrote to Enid today giving her up and apologised to him, he would telephone for his lawyer and make a fresh will, cutting me out of it entirely. I was to have until the next morning to decide, that is, today."

Malcolm Sage still kept his eyes averted. He contended that to look fixedly into the eyes of anyone undergoing interrogation was calculated to confuse him and render the replies less helpful.

"And what would your decision have been?" he asked.

"I told him that if he gave me ten years it would be the same."

"That you would not do as he wished?"

"Certainly not."

"Until this episode you were on good terms with each other?" Malcolm Sage had got a dessert spoon and fork to balance on the blade of a knife.

"Yes."

"You know of no reason why your uncle should take his life?"

"None whatever."

"This episode in itself would not be sufficient to cause him to commit suicide?"

"Certainly not. Sir James will tell you that he was a man of strong character."

"Do you believe he shot himself?" Malcolm Sage seemed absorbed in the rise and fall of the balancing silver.

"But for the locked door I should have said 'no'."

"What were you proposing to do in the light of your refusal to break the engagement?"

"I had everything packed up ready. I meant to go away this morning."

"By the way, where did your uncle bank?" enquired Malcolm Sage casually.

"At the Southern Counties and Brown's Bank, Lewes," was the reply.

"Thank you. That will do, I think, for the present. You had better run round to your doctor and get him to give you something to steady your nerves," said Malcolm Sage, with eyes that had lost their professional glint. "They are all on edge."

Dane glanced at him in surprise; but there was only a cone of baldness visible.

"Thank you," he said. "I think I will," and he turned and left the room. He still seemed dazed and incapable of realising what was taking place.

Malcolm Sage rose and, walking over to the door, removed the key, examined the wards intently, then replaced it and, opening the door, walked across to the library.

Chapter III

MALCOLM SAGE found that Dawkins had completed his work, and the body of Mr. Challoner had been removed.

Seating himself at the table, he took the automatic pistol in his hand and deliberately removed the cartridges. Then placing the muzzle against his right temple he turned his eyes momentarily on Dawkins, who, having anticipated his wishes, had already adjusted the camera. He removed the cap, replaced it, and then quickly reversed the plate.

Pulling the trigger, Malcolm Sage allowed his head to fall forward, his right hand, which held the pistol, dropping on the table before him. Dawkins took another photograph.

"Now," said Malcolm Sage to Sir James. "You shoot me through the right temple, approaching from behind. Grip my head as if you expected me to resist."

Sir James did as he was requested, Dawkins making another exposure.

Malcolm Sage motioned Thompson to draw the curtains. Then dropping on to his knees by the library door, he took the small mirror he had borrowed from Miss Norman and, placing it partly beneath the door, carefully examined the reflection by the aid of an electric torch.

When he rose it was with the air of a man who had satisfied himself upon some important point. He then turned to Sir James.

"You might get those fingerprints," he said casually. "Get everyone together in the dining room. See that no one leaves it for at least a quarter of an hour. Thompson will go with you."

"Then you think it was murder?" questioned Sir James.

"I would sooner say nothing just at the moment," was the reply.

Whilst Sir James Walton and Thompson were occupied with a room-full of domestics, talking in whispers as if in the presence of death, Malcolm Sage was engaged in a careful examination of the bottoms of all the doors in the house by means of a mirror placed upwards beneath each. He also removed the keys and gave a swift look at the wards of each.

He moved quickly; yet without haste, as if his brain had entire control of the situation.

One door in particular appeared to interest him, so much so that he entered the room and proceeded to examine it with great thoroughness, taking the utmost care to replace everything as he found it.

From the middle drawer of the chest-of-drawers, he extracted from under a pile of clothes a thin steel object, some five or six inches in length, wound round with a fine, strong twine. This he slipped into his pocket and, going down into the hall, rang up the manager of the Lewes branch of the Southern Counties and Brown's Bank.

Passing into the library, he searched the drawers of the table at which Mr. Challoner had been found. In one of them he discovered the passbook. Seating himself at the table, he proceeded to examine it carefully. Turning to the pockets at either end, where cancelled cheques are usually placed, he found both were empty.

When a few minutes later Sir James and Thompson entered with the fingerprints, Malcolm Sage was seated at the table smoking, his gaze concentrated upon the nail of the fourth finger of his right hand. With him a contemplation of his fingernails in general indicated thoughtful attention; when, however, he raised the hand and began to subject some particular fingernail to a thorough and elaborate examination, it generally meant the germination of some constructive thesis.

Taking the sheets of paper from Thompson, he went through them rapidly, then drawing a sheet of notepaper from the rack before him he scribbled a hasty note, enclosed it with one of the fingerprints in an envelope, which he sealed, addressed, and handed to Thompson with instructions to see that it was delivered without delay. He also told him to send Peters and Dane to the library.

Three minutes later Tims swung down the drive, his face beaming. He was to drive to Scotland Yard and "never mind the poultry on the road", as Thompson had phrased it.

"Have you the key of the safe, Mr. Dane?" enquired Malcolm Sage as the young man entered, followed by Peters. Dane shook his head and looked at Peters.

"Mr. Challoner always wore it on his key-chain, sir," said the butler.

"Have you any objection to the safe being opened?" enquired Malcolm Sage to Dane.

"None whatever."

"Then perhaps you will open it?" said Malcolm Sage, turning to Sir James.

In the safe were found several bundles of letters and share-certificates, and an old cash-box containing some loose stamps; but nothing else.

Malcolm Sage dismissed Peters and Dane, saying that he would be returning to town after dinner. In the meantime he and Sir James strolled about the grounds, discussing the remarkable rise in the chess-world of Capablanca, whilst Dawkins was busily occupied in a darkened bathroom.

Dinner proved a far less sombre meal than luncheon. Malcolm Sage and Sir James between them succeeded in placing young Dane more at his ease. The haunted, shell-shock look left his eyes, and the twitching disappeared from the corners of his mouth.

It was nearly nine o'clock when the distant moan of a hooter announced to Malcolm Sage's alert ears the return of Tims. He rose from the table and walked slowly to the door, where for some seconds he stood with his hand upon the knob.

As the car drew up he slipped into the hall, just as Peters opened the door.

A moment later the butler started back, his right hand seemed to fly to his left breast pocket. At the same moment Malcolm Sage sprang forward. There was a flash, a report, and two bodies fell at the feet of Inspector Wensdale, of Scotland Yard, and another man standing beside him.

In a second, however, they had thrown themselves upon the struggling heap, and when Malcolm Sage rose to his feet it was to look down upon Peters pinned to the floor by the inspector, with the strange man sitting on his legs.

Chapter IV

"THERE IS NO witness so sure as the camera," remarked Malcolm Sage as he gazed from one to the other of two photographs before him, one representing him holding an automatic pistol to his own head, and the other in which Sir James was posing as a murderer.

"It is strange that it should be so neglected at Scotland Yard," he added.

Silent and absorbed when engaged upon a problem, Malcolm Sage resented speech as a sick man resents arrowroot. At other times he seemed to find pleasure in lengthy monologues, invariably of a professional nature.

"But we use it a lot, Mr. Sage," protested Inspector Wensdale.

"For recording the features of criminals," was the retort. "No, Wensdale, you are obsessed by the fingerprint heresy, quite regardless of the fact that none but an amateur ever leaves such a thing behind him, and the amateur is never difficult to trace."

He paused for a moment; but the inspector made no comment.

"The two greatest factors in the suppression of crime," continued Malcolm Sage, "are photography and fingerprints. Both are in use at Scotland Yard; but each in place of the other. Fingerprints are regarded as clues, and photography is a means of identification, whereas fingerprints are of little use except to identify past offenders, and photography is the greatest aid to the actual tracing of the criminal."

Malcolm Sage never failed to emphasise the importance of photography in the detection of crime. He probably used it more than all other investigators put together. He contended that a photographic print established for all time what the eye could only dimly register for the moment, with the consequent danger of forgetfulness.

As the links in a chain multiplied, it was frequently necessary to refer to the scene of a crime, or tragedy, and then probably some important point would crop up, which the eye had not considered of sufficient importance to dwell upon. By then, in the case of a murder, the body would have been removed, and everything about it either re-ordered or obliterated.

Malcolm Sage proceeded to stuff his pipe with tobacco which he drew from the left-hand pocket of his jacket. He had discovered that a rubber-lined pocket was the best and safest pouch.

He picked up a third photograph and laid it beside the others. It was a print of Mr. Challoner's head, showing, marked in ink, the course of the bullet towards the left of the frontal bone.

"A man shooting himself," began Malcolm Sage, "places the pistol in a position so that the muzzle is directed towards the back of the head. On the other hand, anyone approaching his victim from behind would have a tendency to direct the muzzle towards the front of the head. That is why I got Dawkins to take a photograph of me holding the pistol to my head and of you holding it from behind. These photographs will constitute the principal evidence at the trial."

Sir James nodded. He was too interested to interrupt.

"On this enlargement of the wound," continued Malcolm Sage, "you will see an abrasion on the side nearer the ear, as if the head had suddenly been jerked backwards between the time of the muzzle being placed against the temple and the actual firing of the shot."

Thompson leaned across to examine the photograph.

"If the eyes of someone sitting at a table are suddenly and unexpectedly covered from behind, the natural instinct is to jerk backwards so that the head may be turned to see who it is. That is exactly what occurred with Challoner. He jerked backwards, and the barrel of the pistol grazed the skin and was deflected still more towards the frontal bone."

Sir James and Thompson exchanged glances. Dawkins stood by, a look of happiness in his eyes. His beloved camera was justifying itself once more. Inspector Wensdale breathed heavily.

"Apart from all this, the position of the head on the table, and the way in which the hand was holding the pistol, not to speak of the curve of the arm, were unnatural. You get some idea of this from the photograph that Dawkins took of me, although I could only simulate death by relaxing the muscles. Again, the head would hardly be likely to twist on to its side."

"The doctor ought to have seen that," said the inspector.

"Another thing against the theory of suicide was that the second joint of the first finger was pressing against the trigger. Mr. Challoner was an expert shot, and would instinctively have used the pad of the finger, not the second joint.

"The next step," continued Malcolm Sage, "was how could anyone get into the room and approach Challoner without being heard or 'sensed'."

"He must have been very much absorbed in what he was doing," suggested Sir James.

Malcolm Sage shook his head, and for a few seconds gazed at the photographs before him.

"You will remember there was nothing on the table in front of him. I shall come to that presently. It is very unlikely that a man sitting at a table would not be conscious of someone approaching him from behind, no matter how quietly he stepped, *unless that man's presence in the room were quite a normal and natural thing*. That gave me the clue to Peters. He is the only person who could be in the library without Challoner taking any notice of him. Consequently it was easy for him to approach his master and shoot him."

"But the locked door, sir," said Thompson.

"That is a very simple matter. An ordinary lead pencil, with a piece of string tied to one end, put through the ring of the key to act as a lever, the cord being passed beneath the door, will lock any door in existence. The pencil can then be drawn under the door. This will show how it's done." Malcolm Sage reached across for a sheet of paper, and drew a rough sketch.

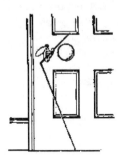

"That is why you examined the under-edge of the door?" suggested Sir James.

Malcolm Sage nodded. "The marks of the cord were clearly defined and reflected in the mirror. Had the key not been touched, it would have helped."

"How?" asked Inspector Wensdale.

"By means of the string the key is turned only just to the point where the lever falls through the hole to the floor. The fingers would turn beyond that point, not being so delicate."

"Mr. Sage, you're a wonder," burst out the inspector.

"I then," proceeded Malcolm Sage, "examined all the other doors in the house, and I found that of one room, which I after discovered to be Peters', was heavily scored at the bottom. He had evidently practised fairly extensively before putting the plan into operation. He had also done the same thing with the library door, as there were marks of more than one operation. Furthermore, he was wiser than to take the risk of so clumsy a tool as a lead pencil. He used this."

Malcolm Sage drew from his pocket the roll of twine with the thin steel instrument down the centre. It was a canvas-needle, to the eye of which the cord was attached.

"This was absolutely safe," he remarked. "Another thing I discovered was that one lock, and only one lock in the house, had recently been oiled – that of the library door."

Sir James nodded his head several times. There was something of self-reproach in the motion.

"Now," continued Malcolm Sage, "we come back to why a man should be sitting at a table absorbed in gazing at nothing, and at a time when most of the household are either in bed or preparing for bed."

"Peters said that he was checking his passbook," suggested Sir James.

"That is undoubtedly what he *was* doing," continued Malcolm Sage, "and Peters removed the passbook, put it in a drawer, first destroying the cancelled cheques. He made a blunder in not replacing the passbook with something else. That was the last link in the chain," he added.

"I don't quite see—" began Sir James.

"Perhaps you did not read of a case that was reported from New York some eighteen months ago. It was very similar to that of Mr. Challoner. A man was found shot through the head, the door being locked on the inside, and a verdict of suicide was returned; but there was absolutely no reason why he should have taken his life.

"What actually happened was that Mr. Challoner went to his bank to draw five hundred pounds with which he hoped to bribe his nephew's fiancée. He trusted to the temptation of the actual money rather than a cheque. When he was at the bank the manager once more asked him to return his passbook, which had not been balanced for several months. He was very dilatory in such matters."

"That is true," said Dane, speaking for the first time.

"That evening he proceeded to compare it with his cheque book. I suspect that Peters had been forging cheques and he saw here what would lead to discovery. Furthermore, there was a considerable sum of money in the safe, and the quarrel between uncle and nephew to divert suspicion. This, however, was mere conjecture – that trouser-pocket photo, Dawkins," said Malcolm Sage, turning to the photographer, who handed it across to him.

"Now notice the position of those keys. They are put in head foremost, and do not reach the bottom of the pocket. They had obviously been taken away and replaced in the pocket as Challoner sat there. Had he gone to the safe himself and walked back to his chair, the position of the keys would have been quite different."

Instinctively each man felt in his trousers pocket, and found in his own bunch of keys a verification of the statement.

"The whole scheme was too calculated and deliberate for an amateur," said Malcolm Sage, knocking the ashes out of his pipe on to a brass ashtray. "That is what prompted me to get the fingerprints of Peters, so that I might send them to Scotland Yard to see if anything was known of him there. The result you have seen."

"We've been on the look-out for him for more than a year," said Inspector Wensdale. "The New York police are rather interested in him about a forgery stunt that took place there some time ago."

"I am confident that when Challoner's affairs are gone into there will be certain cheques which it will be difficult to explain."

"Then, again, there was the electric light," proceeded Malcolm Sage. "A man about to blow out his brains would certainly not walk across the room, switch off the light, and then find his way back to the table."

"That's true enough," said Inspector Wensdale.

"On the other hand, a murderer, who has to stand at a door for at least some seconds, would not risk leaving on the light, which would attract the attention of anyone who might by chance be in the hall, or on the stairs."

Inspector Wensdale caught Thompson's left eye, which deliberately closed and then re-opened. There was a world of meaning in the movement.

"Well, I'm glad I didn't get you down on a fool's errand, Sage," said Sir James, rising. "I wonder what the local inspector will think."

"He won't," remarked Malcolm Sage; "that is why he assumed it was suicide."

"Did you suspect Peters was armed?" enquired Sir James.

"I saw the pistol under his left armpit," said Malcolm Sage. "It's well known with American gunmen as a most convenient place for quick drawing."

"If it hadn't been for you, Mr. Sage, he'd have got me," said Inspector Wensdale.

"There'll be a heavy car-full for Tims," remarked Malcolm Sage, as he walked towards the door.

A Cat with a Gat

Tina L. Jens

IT WAS A COLD, drizzly night when the white, powdered-and-puffed French poodle pranced into my office. It was no place for a class dame – dog or not. The cracked linoleum would scuff her pedicured nails. That fancy tail-bouffant would muss if she sat on my rusty metal chair. But she was a dame in trouble.

Trouble had brought her to the seedy side of town to bat her baby-blues, wiggle that powder-puff tail, and beg me to help her…but be discreet about it.

Yammer's the name. Mickey Yammer. The best private gato gumshoe in town. I don't usually take dogs for clients. I'm not a speciesist; dogs yap too much and chase you down the alley when you try to collect your pay. But, my litter box was full, my pantry was empty, and I had a hankering for some Tender Vittles with extra tuna – the expensive kind. I took the case. My other lives would live to regret it.

The dame barked, danced and shivered, and did all the things a pedigreed poodle does when it's nervous – except piddle – I was glad of that 'cause nobody borrows my litter box.

"Mr. Yammer, I need your help. I need you to clear my family name."

She did that poodle-shiver again, the rhinestones on her designer collar flashed in the light shining in from the neon bar sign outside my office window.

"My name is Fifi."

It always is, I thought to myself.

"Fifi Lamour. I have some money of my own. I can pay you."

I flicked my tail and licked a dust mote off my front paw before I purred at her, "Tell me the details, toots. We'll worry about how many pounds of Purina chow it'll cost you, later."

She crossed her fluffy paws in front of her, then finally settled down and got to the meat of the story. "You know that horrid painting of dogs playing poker?"

"Seen it hanging in a milkhall or two… Seems like there was some cheating going on."

"That's the problem!" Fifi yipped. Then she yapped, "The two dogs in the front of the picture *appear* to be cheating, but they're not! The Golden Terrier on the left has three aces in his hand, and the English Bulldog to the right *appears* to be passing him a fourth – but it's a set-up! The Terrier, my great-uncle, swore on his deathbed he was innocent. That fiendish Cassius Marcellus Coolidge made my uncle look guilty! Coolidge even gave the painting an incendiary title, *A Friend in Need.*" She ducked her head and covered her eyes with one little, white poodle-paw.

I hissed. There's nothing I hate worse than a dame trying to play me for a sap. She must have realized the act wasn't working, 'cause she raised her head, shook her ears back, and went on with her tale.

"I think that brutish Bulldog was in on it. They set my uncle up. After the picture appeared on that cigar box he lost his job. He lost his papers. And he died – in the doghouse."

I licked my paw again, spreading the toes wide, polishing my needle-sharp nails. "If the mutt's kicked the bucket, why do you care? All dogs go to Heaven, and Heaven's pretty good at sorting this sort of mix-up out. Why spend the dough to clear a dead dog's name?"

"It's not just *his* name that's sullied! They've yanked our family's pedigrees and dropped our name from the roster of the New York Garden Kennel Club. We're ruined! And I've pups on the way! Please help us, Mr. Yammer. Please!"

* * *

I'm a sap. I'm a broken down, tiger-striped, alley cat with half a tail, clipped ears, and a gimp when I walk, thanks to an unhappy love affair with the front tire of a city bus. I'm eighteen pounds of muscle and creaky joints. Haven't got much, but what I've got's mine, and I got it the honest way. Some of my friends uptown are in the rackets – criminal, civil, and tennis – they haven't been shy about stepping on my game foot if it suited their scam. Dog or not, I had sympathy for the Terrier and his whimpering niece. I'd give him the benefit of the doubt and stick my whiskers into it.

I didn't tell the dame, but I had a handle on the case already. There was a milkhall around the corner that claimed to have the original painting on display.

I donned my battered grey fedora, grabbed my gat, checked it was loaded, then fastened my string holster around my haunches. I don't usually carry heat, but it was a rough neighborhood and a rougher drinking den. Sometimes, a dog'll spy my docked tail and gimpy leg and peg me for a pushover. But this is one cat that's never been declawed. If they take me alone, they leave the worse for wear, but if they attack in a pack...well that's when a gat's a cat's best friend.

The bar was called Curly Tails, strictly a cat-and-dog joint, no humans allowed. Word at the water bowl was Cassius Coolidge had set up shop in the alley, so he could peek in an open window and paint his series. Some critters say he called the cops himself, so he could get that fourth-in-the-series painting of the fuzz busting up the game.

The bartender on duty was an old flame; a little calico with a skittish tail and a hot libido. She was a little run-down, a little saggy around the jowls, but she could keep a tomcat warm on a cold winter's night and not howl at him the next morning. I leapt up on a barstool and shook my whiskers at her.

"Mickey Yammer – Mr. Scruffy himself – what brings your whiskers to this side of town?"

"Got a caper going, doll, and a powerful thirst. Hit me with some moojuice, make it a double, and pour one for yourself."

"Sweet talker," she purred, pouncing off to pour the drinks.

I sat back and studied the picture behind the bar. The canvas was massive, twelve tail-lengths on every side – that's full-length cattails, to you – with the famous *CM Coolidge* signature scribbled in the corner.

It showed seven mutts clipping cards, betting high on hands that didn't deserve it. I've never bothered much about canine kinds, but near as I could tell, that was a Collie on the far left, leaning back, looking smug about his hand. His lousy poker face was probably why he had so few chips in front of him. A St. Bernard and a Bloodhound sat behind the table with several bottles of booze between them; wasn't clear who was doing the drinking. Both breeds were known to over-imbibe. On the right side was a chocolate-speckled Doberman with pert ears and a pipe next to... looked like a bad cross between a Labrador and Beagle. In front: the two canines in question; a feisty white Bulldog with a spiked collar, who seemed to be passing the ace of hearts under the table; and Fifi's uncle, a golden Terrier, with a front paw full of three aces, and a back paw that sure seemed to be reaching for the sweetheart card.

The big dogs were all behind the table – the two mutts in front were half the size of the rest of the pack. It takes gumption, or stupidity, to try to rig a card game when you're the pipsqueaks.

Course, size don't matter to a bulldog; species got their name from fighting bulls; they'd leap up, latch onto the bull's lip, and hang on till the bull gave in, flipped them off, or the lip ripped away.

The Terrier's back paw placement was borderline. The foot seemed to be reaching for that card – but then again, it was resting pretty much along the edge of the wooden chair, right where a leg would need to be to sit in the human way.

A final fact remained that didn't look good for the little guys – they'd cleaned house. Both had stacks of chips the size of Rin Tin Tin's royalty check. The other dogs had crumbs.

Mutts give away everything with their tail. The two little guys may have been winning simply because they didn't have a titanic tail to tip the other guys off. The Terrier's tail was loosely curled, relaxed and happy, as he should be with a paw full of aces. The Bulldog's tail was ramrod straight, pointing down and dirty. But his guilt wasn't in question. The ace under the table proved that. The questions were, did the Terrier take it? Did he ask for the card, or was the Bulldog offering it up as a setup or out of the goodness of his little black heart?

I wandered out of my reverie and found a saucer of moojuice in front of me. I lapped it up and tried to think. The job wasn't made any easier by a couple of canines that were growling, barking, and bringing down the class of the joint in a nearby booth. They wore felt hats with spiked rims, studded collars, and milk-bone shaped dog tags. Had to be a new gang in the 'hood.

I flicked my tail to call the old flame over. She took her time; cats don't like to come when they're called. I pointed a paw at the picture. "Hey sweetheart, know anything about that painting?"

One of the milk-bone boys started barking. I put it down to bad manners. It never occurred that he might be barking at me.

"Not a thing," she hissed. "I can think of more intriguing things to talk about than a painting full of pooches. Call me when you've got something interesting to say."

I watched her prance off, knowing what she wanted, and knowing that wasn't what I was after… tonight.

I'd gleaned everything I could from the picture on the wall. I needed to talk to someone who'd been there. Weren't many four-footers left from the days that picture was made, domesticateds' lifespans being what they are. But the bar owner was one of those rare long-lifers; an old Russian Blue with green eyes and a coat with a silvery-steel sheen. Wags said he was twenty-five. Vets say that's impossible, but it happens now and again.

One of the ugly pugs had muscled his way to the bar, squeezing me and the poor schmuck on the other side nearly out of our chairs. I thought about yanking his milk-bone off to teach him some manners, but I figured he was just trying to get another round of whatever dogs drink these days.

I licked my dish clean then batted a paw at my calico cutie. "Is Curly around?"

The dog growled, and the cat wasn't much friendlier. She gave a defiant twitch of her tail but deigned to answer me. "He was asleep on the radiator in the backroom an hour ago. No reason to think he's quit."

I arched my back at her, making vague promises about being social that I didn't intend to keep, then jumped down and went in search of the ancient Blue.

Curly was still curled up on the radiator, the knob long ago being set to where the metal was just toasty warm and not too hot on the paws.

I gave a rumbly-purr to see if I could wake him without scaring him out of one of his nine lives. It took a few minutes, but he snuffled and huffed, stretched and yawned. I listened to the symphony of his cracking joints as he sat up and looked around in a daze.

I gave him a moment. It's hell getting old.

"Bless me whiskers and kittens, if it isn't Mickey Yammer! What brings you to this catnip patch?"

We batted the breeze back and forth before I got down to business at the scratching post. "Got a job about that picture out front."

"It's not for sale."

"Nah, I mean, did the dogs do it? Did the two little pipsqueaks dupe the dopey mutts? Was the Terrier set up to take a fall?"

Curley's fur bristled. He spat, "Don't go digging in that litter box. Stinky stuff buried there. Always liked that little Terrier. Wasn't like him to cheat, but he was down on his luck, trouble at home, and that Bulldog was a fast talker – called himself Lucky – mebbe for him, not for his friends. The Terrier did some hard time down at the city pound. Pretty payment for a single ace, and him with three in his hand!"

I nodded.

"The dogs are all dead. Went to Harry the Doberman's funeral just last year."

Curly was confused. The Doberman had been dead for more than a decade. But I didn't interrupt.

"That human's still alive. Talk about double-dealing. Never paid those dogs royalties and ruined more than one life in the pack. Couldn't face the fame or the shame of having their gambling predilections exposed." He hissed. "Now he's sniffing around the next generation – wanting them to put their paw prints on legal papers. Says he's got a buyer for some of the original paintings that never sold. Don't know how that could be. Sold six or eight of them, back then, mebbe more. I finally run him off." He scratched the air with a feeble claw. "Stay away from that two-legged swindler, Mickey, if you want to keep what's left of your tail."

It was good advice, but I didn't take it.

I decided it was too late to do any more work, so I went back out front and had another bowl or four and flirted with the flame. The pugs seemed to growl every time they looked at me. I blamed that on the docked tail and my personal paranoia of pooches. I staggered out of the bar under the influence of too much cream around midnight.

I didn't realize the mutts had followed me until I turned down the alley for home. The streetlight backlit them; their shadows loomed over me on the brick wall. I turned around to meet my challengers. They were shorter in the flesh, but no less menacing. I was tipsy as a kitten in clover, and about to be roughed up by a pack of pugs.

It wasn't much of a fight, there being four of them and only half of me. They'd been tipped off about the gat – they went for that first thing. An ugly pug bounded down the alley with my gat in his mouth, the string holster dangling behind. Every muscle in my body wanted to chase after that string. But a pug had me pinned from behind while the other two went to work. I arched my back, extended my claws, and hissed. I looked like a cheap vampire. The mutt behind me hung on.

The pug in front of me sneered, "Things ain't what they seem, Cat. Stick your whiskers where they don't belong, and they're liable to get clipped."

I was working on a clever comeback, but they'd already rushed past that part of the script. I took a couple of sucker punches to the gut, a roundhouse to the kidneys, and a cuff to the muzzle. A black hole opened up in front of me. I jumped into it.

Unfortunately, I didn't land on my feet. When I came to, a drummer was pounding a Latin number in my head, and a sour taste was leaking out of my mouth. A barrel-load of pain shot through my side as I rolled over and staggered to my feet. With the help of a friendly brick wall I made it. I picked up my fedora. A milk-bone dog tag lay underneath it – must have fallen off in the scuffle. I tucked it in my hatband, figuring it might come in handy. I gathered the shreds of my strength and stumbled to the mouth of the alley, where I found my gun. "Great. The cat's got his hat and his gat. Now it's time for beddy-bye."

* * *

I dragged myself out of my blankets at the crack of noon and tried to ignore my bruises as I tossed down a bowl of cream and a double-helping of catnip to perk me up. A warm ray of sunshine was poking its nose through my kitchen curtains, and I wanted to go drown in it, but I had work to do.

I headed over to the public library. You hardly ever get roughed up in the stacks. Book-people love cats. I could lick my wounds and maybe learn a little something.

I started with the phone book, to find out where Coolidge lived. It was a good play, but no dice. It listed a Calvin Marcus Coleridge and a Renford Coolman, but no Coolidge at all… So maybe the Coolidge pedigree line wasn't big on phones.

I checked the *Who's Who in the City*, but no luck. I tried the *Who's Who in the Art World*, and hit gravy. Just under an entry about Calvin Marcus Coleridge – *specialty cloth art*, was CM Coolidge. He'd only merited a three-line writeup. Trouble was, the last line said he'd died years ago.

A dead man wasn't stirring the pot, so where'd that leave me?

Maybe with an ace up my sleeve, in the form of a silver bone. On a hunch, I fished the dog tag out of my hat. The bruiser's name had been, well…*Bruiser*. An address was on the tag – though I couldn't imagine wanting that mutt back. The address looked familiar.

I flipped the phone book back to the C's, and sure enough, the address it belonged to a CMC…just not Coolidge. It belonged to Calvin Marcus Coleridge.

I hiked my tail and skedaddled.

* * *

The bungalow was run down at the corners and sagged in the middle. The roof looked like it leaked when it rained, and I wasn't certain the porch would support my weight. The place looked quiet, but the pugs had my fur up. I didn't see, hear, or smell them, but I wasn't about to charge into the rattrap. I cased the place, prowling through unmown grass high enough to tickle my ears.

A salsa band was playing on the radio; it was the only indication the joint was occupied. Something felt wrong. I jumped onto a low-hanging tree branch that brushed the side of the house and peeked into the window. My peepers got filled up real quick.

I could see a beer-bellied man who was pushing fifty and still wore his black beret in the house – in case his artist credentials were in doubt. Had to be Coleridge. Neither art nor time had been kind to him, and he wasn't in a kind mood. He was standing on a threadbare carpet yelling at a run-down couch. I wondered what the couch had done to him to rate that kind of treatment.

He started pacing, and I realized he didn't have a problem with the furniture. On that couch, crouching in fear, was Fifi. I was so surprised I fell out of the tree. I scraped my claws along the side of the house as I fell. I landed on my feet, but the jig was up.

Coleridge shouted, "What was that?" and ran to the door. I clawed up to the window sill and slapped frantically on the dirty glass. Fifi looked terrified but managed to shiver her away over and raise the window with her nose.

"Hi, doll," I said, with more bravado than I felt.

"Yammer! He'll kill you if he finds you here!"

I heard the sound of heavy boots, so I scampered into the bedroom and dived under the bed. The footsteps followed.

I saw the edge of the bedspread being lifted. I darted out, past the human and into the next room. What I saw hanging on the wall stopped cold my flight.

It was another painting in that series of card-playing mutts. This was a later version. Much later. Unfinished, with the paint still wet, kind of later.

It made sense of the whole crazy puzzle. Same mutts, same poses, same ace-passing trick under the table. But instead of a couple of grey walls and a grandfather clock hemming all that in, this had a more interesting background. Behind a bar, a pooch was polishing a beer stein while a poodle delivered a bottle of whiskey to the table. The waitress was a spitting image of Fifi, right down to the pink bows pinned behind her ears. I sat on my haunches and let my tongue loll as my brain scratched through the implications.

That quip about her pedigree being taken away made sense, now. It'd rung wrong when Fifi had said it, but I hadn't realized why. If she had an uncle who was a Terrier, her pedigree would have been taken away long before he was caught cheating at cards. She was looking to clear her name, but not because of the Terrier's card-sharking. She was trying to hide the fact her powdered-and-puffed roots covered a blue-collar barmaid. But why pose for the picture in the first place…unless she hadn't been pregnant when the picture was started.

One look at the pooch convinced me I was right.

"Mickey, you have to understand!" She yipped and shivered. "I'd been sold across country, separated from my family. Then my humans abandoned me by the side of the road. They kept my papers – I couldn't prove my pedigree. So, I took the barmaid job. But I got fired after I spilled a tray of drinks. That ghastly little Bulldog goosed me. Then Coleridge came sniffing around. Offering money if I'd pose for his dirty little painting."

I snarled, "So you made a deal with him. And now you want to weasel out."

"I didn't know I was pregnant then! What kind of life can I offer my pups if this gets out? They'll be just another pack of mutts tipping over trash cans in the alley, their reputations ruined before they even get their eyes open."

She yapped and shook her head, making the tags on her rhinestone collar jingle. "Besides, isn't what he's doing worse? He's painting new pictures, passing them off as originals. I figured if you could discredit the original artist, prove the first painting was a fake, they'd never release the rest of the paintings. I know I lied to you – but I did it for my pups!"

She was all teary-eyed. If you know anything about dames or dogs, you know poodle-tears are the worst kind. I started to sneer, but the human was standing behind her, and he did enough sneering for both of us.

"Your pups can go to the pet shop, or the pound, for all I care! No one's interested in my designer dresses, but the cigar company wants to revive this dreck! Anniversary editions of the worst art ever put on canvas!" Coleridge waved angrily at the painting. Apparently, he wasn't a fan of the original CMC's work.

"Found one of these horrible things hanging on the wall of the house when I moved in. I was hauling it out to the garbage when one of the cigar company executives drove by. Made me an offer on the spot for the whole series. I passed myself off as the artist, started painting new pictures – the company was willing to buy the whole series. Nobody knew for sure how many there were. I talked some dogs into posing. Stupid mutts never knew the difference, they thought I was the old man reviving the series."

That made sense. The mutts and Curly would have been taken in by the act. Four-footers don't pay much attention to stray humans. We keep tabs on the ones we keep, but who can keep track of all the humans running loose on the street?

It wasn't even forgery. He was signing his own name: *CMC*, a squiggle, then an *idge*. Close enough to pass but left enough room to weasel out if somebody tumbled to the scam.

Coolidge was yelling at Fifi. "They're offering good money – *obscene* amounts of money – it'll set me up with my own shop on the expensive side of town! You think I'm going to let you mess that up? I'll show you what meddling mutts get!"

He pulled his boot back to give the pregnant poodle a kick. I leapt and shoved her out of the way. I saw her slide across the hardwood floor just before the boot connected with my head, and I went diving into that black pool again.

* * *

I opened my eyes – it stayed black. I closed them, then tried again, thinking maybe I'd gotten the procedure wrong the first time. Nope, still black.

It wasn't nighttime; I couldn't have been out that long. I heard whimpering.

"Fifi?"

"Oh, Mickey!"

She sounded relieved. I didn't see how my waking up made things much better.

"I thought you were dead! That horrid man tossed you in the closet, shoved me in afterwards, and locked the door. He's out there now, ruining my life!"

I didn't point out that my life wasn't any grander from the encounter. "What's going down?"

"The sale! The truck pulled up a few minutes ago. They're loading up the paintings. They've chosen the 'poodle shot' as the premiere print, but they're going to run the whole series on the cigar boxes. I'm ruined!" she wailed.

"Hold on to your powderpuff," I said. "Maybe not."

My eyes had gotten used to the dark. I stood on my back legs, trying to pick the lock with one claw. I twisted until I heard a click. I put a paw on either side of the knob and gave my body a sharp wrench to the left. It woke up the old bruises, but it released the latch. We were free.

"Fifi, out the back and into the truck! Wait till they go in the house."

We scampered outside, hid in the bushes, then made a run for it. A quick jump later and we were in the truck, scrambling behind the canvases before the workmen could come back.

We were just in time. They shoved one more canvas in, then slammed the door. I heard them say something about Midtown. I gave a Cheshire grin. The ride would take more than an hour – plenty of time to apply paws and piddle to the stack of paintings.

Arsène Lupin in Prison

Maurice Leblanc

THERE IS NO tourist worthy of the name who does not know the banks of the Seine, and has not noticed, in passing, the little feudal castle of the Malaquis, built upon a rock in the centre of the river. An arched bridge connects it with the shore. All around it, the calm waters of the great river play peacefully amongst the reeds, and the wagtails flutter over the moist crests of the stones.

The history of the Malaquis castle is stormy like its name, harsh like its outlines. It has passed through a long series of combats, sieges, assaults, rapines and massacres. A recital of the crimes that have been committed there would cause the stoutest heart to tremble. There are many mysterious legends connected with the castle, and they tell us of a famous subterranean tunnel that formerly led to the abbey of Jumieges and to the manor of Agnes Sorel, mistress of Charles VII.

In that ancient habitation of heroes and brigands, the Baron Nathan Cahorn now lived; or Baron Satan as he was formerly called on the Bourse, where he had acquired a fortune with incredible rapidity. The lords of Malaquis, absolutely ruined, had been obliged to sell the ancient castle at a great sacrifice. It contained an admirable collection of furniture, pictures, wood carvings, and faience. The Baron lived there alone, attended by three old servants. No one ever enters the place. No one had ever beheld the three Rubens that he possessed, his two Watteau, his Jean Goujon pulpit, and the many other treasures that he had acquired by a vast expenditure of money at public sales.

Baron Satan lived in constant fear, not for himself, but for the treasures that he had accumulated with such an earnest devotion and with so much perspicacity that the shrewdest merchant could not say that the Baron had ever erred in his taste or judgment. He loved them – his bibelots. He loved them intensely, like a miser; jealously, like a lover. Every day, at sunset, the iron gates at either end of the bridge and at the entrance to the court of honor are closed and barred. At the least touch on these gates, electric bells will ring throughout the castle.

One Thursday in September, a letter-carrier presented himself at the gate at the head of the bridge, and, as usual, it was the Baron himself who partially opened the heavy portal. He scrutinized the man as minutely as if he were a stranger, although the honest face and twinkling eyes of the postman had been familiar to the Baron for many years. The man laughed, as he said:

"It is only I, Monsieur le Baron. It is not another man wearing my cap and blouse."

"One can never tell," muttered the Baron.

The man handed him a number of newspapers, and then said:

"And now, Monsieur le Baron, here is something new."

"Something new?"

"Yes, a letter. A registered letter."

Living as a recluse, without friends or business relations, the baron never received any letters, and the one now presented to him immediately aroused within him a feeling of suspicion and distrust. It was like an evil omen. Who was this mysterious correspondent that dared to disturb the tranquility of his retreat?

"You must sign for it, Monsieur le Baron."

He signed; then took the letter, waited until the postman had disappeared beyond the bend in the road, and, after walking nervously to and fro for a few minutes, he leaned against the parapet of the bridge and opened the envelope. It contained a sheet of paper, bearing this heading: Prison de la Santé, Paris. He looked at the signature: Arsène Lupin. Then he read:

Monsieur le Baron:

There is, in the gallery in your castle, a picture of Philippe de Champaigne, of exquisite finish, which pleases me beyond measure. Your Rubens are also to my taste, as well as your smallest Watteau. In the salon to the right, I have noticed the Louis XIII cadence-table, the tapestries of Beauvais, the Empire gueridon signed 'Jacob', and the Renaissance chest. In the salon to the left, all the cabinet full of jewels and miniatures.

For the present, I will content myself with those articles that can be conveniently removed. I will therefore ask you to pack them carefully and ship them to me, charges prepaid, to the station at Batignolles, within eight days, otherwise I shall be obliged to remove them myself during the night of 27 September; but, under those circumstances, I shall not content myself with the articles above mentioned.

Accept my apologies for any inconvenience I may cause you, and believe me to be your humble servant,

Arsène Lupin

P. S. – Please do not send the largest Watteau. Although you paid thirty thousand francs for it, it is only a copy, the original having been burned, under the Directoire by Barras, during a night of debauchery. Consult the memoirs of Garat.

I do not care for the Louis XV chatelaine, as I doubt its authenticity.

That letter completely upset the baron. Had it borne any other signature, he would have been greatly alarmed – but signed by Arsène Lupin!

As an habitual reader of the newspapers, he was versed in the history of recent crimes, and was therefore well acquainted with the exploits of the mysterious burglar. Of course, he knew that Lupin had been arrested in America by his enemy Ganimard and was at present incarcerated in the Prison de la Santé. But he knew also that any miracle might be expected from Arsène Lupin. Moreover, that exact knowledge of the castle, the location of the pictures and furniture, gave the affair an alarming aspect. How could he have acquired that information concerning things that no one had ever seen?

The baron raised his eyes and contemplated the stern outlines of the castle, its steep rocky pedestal, the depth of the surrounding water, and shrugged his shoulders. Certainly, there was no danger. No one in the world could force an entrance to the sanctuary that contained his priceless treasures.

No one, perhaps, but Arsène Lupin! For him, gates, walls and drawbridges did not exist. What use were the most formidable obstacles or the most careful precautions, if Arsène Lupin had decided to effect an entrance?

That evening, he wrote to the Procurer of the Republique at Rouen. He enclosed the threatening letter and solicited aid and protection.

The reply came at once to the effect that Arsène Lupin was in custody in the Prison de la Santé, under close surveillance, with no opportunity to write such a letter, which was, no doubt, the work of some imposter. But, as an act of precaution, the Procurer had submitted the letter to an expert in handwriting, who declared that, in spite of certain resemblances, the writing was not that of the prisoner.

But the words 'in spite of certain resemblances' caught the attention of the baron; in them, he read the possibility of a doubt which appeared to him quite sufficient to warrant the intervention of the law. His fears increased. He read Lupin's letter over and over again. 'I shall be obliged to remove them myself.' And then there was the fixed date: the night of 27 September.

To confide in his servants was a proceeding repugnant to his nature; but now, for the first time in many years, he experienced the necessity of seeking counsel with someone. Abandoned by the legal official of his own district, and feeling unable to defend himself with his own resources, he was on the point of going to Paris to engage the services of a detective.

Two days passed; on the third day, he was filled with hope and joy as he read the following item in the 'Réveil de Caudebec', a newspaper published in a neighbouring town:

> *We have the pleasure of entertaining in our city, at the present time, the veteran detective Mon. Ganimard who acquired a worldwide reputation by his clever capture of Arsène Lupin. He has come here for rest and recreation, and, being an enthusiastic fisherman, he threatens to capture all the fish in our river.*

Ganimard! Ah, here is the assistance desired by Baron Cahorn! Who could baffle the schemes of Arsène Lupin better than Ganimard, the patient and astute detective? He was the man for the place.

The baron did not hesitate. The town of Caudebec was only six kilometers from the castle, a short distance to a man whose step was accelerated by the hope of safety.

After several fruitless attempts to ascertain the detective's address, the baron visited the office of the 'Réveil', situated on the quai. There he found the writer of the article who, approaching the window, exclaimed:

"Ganimard? Why, you are sure to see him somewhere on the quai with his fishing-pole. I met him there and chanced to read his name engraved on his rod. Ah, there he is now, under the trees."

"That little man, wearing a straw hat?"

"Exactly. He is a gruff fellow, with little to say."

Five minutes later, the baron approached the celebrated Ganimard, introduced himself, and sought to commence a conversation, but that was a failure. Then he broached the real object of his interview, and briefly stated his case. The other listened, motionless, with his attention riveted on his fishing-rod. When the baron had finished his story, the fisherman turned, with an air of profound pity, and said:

"Monsieur, it is not customary for thieves to warn people they are about to rob. Arsène Lupin, especially, would not commit such a folly."

"But—"

"Monsieur, if I had the least doubt, believe me, the pleasure of again capturing Arsène Lupin would place me at your disposal. But, unfortunately, that young man is already under lock and key."

"He may have escaped."

"No one ever escaped from the Santé."

"But, he—"

"He, no more than any other."

"Yet—"

"Well, if he escapes, so much the better. I will catch him again. Meanwhile, you go home and sleep soundly. That will do for the present. You frighten the fish."

The conversation was ended. The baron returned to the castle, reassured to some extent by Ganimard's indifference. He examined the bolts, watched the servants, and, during the next forty-eight hours, he became almost persuaded that his fears were groundless. Certainly, as Ganimard had said, thieves do not warn people they are about to rob.

The fateful day was close at hand. It was now the twenty-sixth of September and nothing had happened. But at three o'clock the bell rang. A boy brought this telegram:

"No goods at Batignolles station. Prepare everything for tomorrow night. Arsène."

This telegram threw the baron into such a state of excitement that he even considered the advisability of yielding to Lupin's demands.

However, he hastened to Caudebec. Ganimard was fishing at the same place, seated on a campstool. Without a word, he handed him the telegram.

"Well, what of it?" said the detective.

"What of it? But it is tomorrow."

"What is tomorrow?"

"The robbery! The pillage of my collections!"

Ganimard laid down his fishing-rod, turned to the baron, and exclaimed, in a tone of impatience:

"Ah! Do you think I am going to bother myself about such a silly story as that!"

"How much do you ask to pass tomorrow night in the castle?"

"Not a sou. Now, leave me alone."

"Name your own price. I am rich and can pay it."

This offer disconcerted Ganimard, who replied, calmly:

"I am here on a vacation. I have no right to undertake such work."

"No one will know. I promise to keep it secret."

"Oh! Nothing will happen."

"Come! Three thousand francs. Will that be enough?"

The detective, after a moment's reflection, said:

"Very well. But I must warn you that you are throwing your money out of the window."

"I do not care."

"In that case...but, after all, what do we know about this devil Lupin! He may have quite a numerous band of robbers with him. Are you sure of your servants?"

"My faith—"

"Better not count on them. I will telegraph for two of my men to help me. And now, go! It is better for us not to be seen together. Tomorrow evening about nine o'clock."

* * *

The following day – the date fixed by Arsène Lupin – Baron Cahorn arranged all his panoply of war, furbished his weapons, and, like a sentinel, paced to and fro in front of the castle. He saw nothing, heard nothing. At half past eight o'clock in the evening, he dismissed his servants. They occupied rooms in a wing of the building, in a retired spot, well removed from the main portion of the castle. Shortly thereafter, the baron heard the sound of approaching footsteps. It was Ganimard and his two assistants – great, powerful fellows with immense hands, and necks like bulls. After asking a few questions relating to the location of the various entrances and rooms, Ganimard carefully closed and barricaded all the doors and windows through which one could gain access to the threatened rooms. He inspected the walls, raised the tapestries, and finally installed his assistants in the central gallery which was located between the two salons.

"No nonsense! We are not here to sleep. At the slightest sound, open the windows of the court and call me. Pay attention also to the water-side. Ten metres of perpendicular rock is no obstacle to those devils."

Ganimard locked his assistants in the gallery, carried away the keys, and said to the baron:

"And now, to our post."

He had chosen for himself a small room located in the thick outer wall, between the two principal doors, and which, in former years, had been the watchman's quarters. A peep-hole opened upon the bridge; another on the court. In one corner, there was an opening to a tunnel.

"I believe you told me, Monsieur le Baron, that this tunnel is the only subterranean entrance to the castle and that it has been closed up for time immemorial?"

"Yes."

"Then, unless there is some other entrance, known only to Arsène Lupin, we are quite safe."

He placed three chairs together, stretched himself upon them, lighted his pipe and sighed:

"Really, Monsieur le Baron, I feel ashamed to accept your money for such a sinecure as this. I will tell the story to my friend Lupin. He will enjoy it immensely."

The baron did not laugh. He was anxiously listening, but heard nothing save the beating of his own heart. From time to time, he leaned over the tunnel and cast a fearful eye into its depths. He heard the clock strike eleven, twelve, one.

Suddenly, he seized Ganimard's arm. The latter leaped up, awakened from his sleep.

"Do you hear?" asked the baron, in a whisper.

"Yes."

"What is it?"

"I was snoring, I suppose."

"No, no, listen."

"Ah! Yes, it is the horn of an automobile."

"Well?"

"Well! it is very improbable that Lupin would use an automobile like a battering-ram to demolish your castle. Come, Monsieur le Baron, return to your post. I am going to sleep. Goodnight."

That was the only alarm. Ganimard resumed his interrupted slumbers, and the baron heard nothing except the regular snoring of his companion. At break of day, they left the room. The castle was enveloped in a profound calm; it was a peaceful dawn on the bosom of a tranquil river. They mounted the stairs, Cahorn radiant with joy, Ganimard calm as usual. They heard no sound; they saw nothing to arouse suspicion.

"What did I tell you, Monsieur le Baron? Really, I should not have accepted your offer. I am ashamed."

He unlocked the door and entered the gallery. Upon two chairs, with drooping heads and pendent arms, the detective's two assistants were asleep.

"*Tonnerre de nom d'un chien!*" exclaimed Ganimard. At the same moment, the baron cried out:

"The pictures! The credence!"

He stammered, choked, with arms outstretched toward the empty places, toward the denuded walls where naught remained but the useless nails and cords. The Watteau, disappeared! The Rubens, carried away! The tapestries taken down! The cabinets, despoiled of their jewels!

"And my Louis XVI candelabra! And the Regent chandelier!…And my twelfth-century Virgin!"

He ran from one spot to another in wildest despair. He recalled the purchase price of each article, added up the figures, counted his losses, pell-mell, in confused words and unfinished phrases. He stamped with rage; he groaned with grief. He acted like a ruined man whose only hope is suicide.

If anything could have consoled him, it would have been the stupefaction displayed by Ganimard. The famous detective did not move. He appeared to be petrified; he examined the room in a listless manner. The windows?…closed. The locks on the doors?…intact. Not a break in the ceiling; not a hole in the floor. Everything was in perfect order. The theft had been carried out methodically, according to a logical and inexorable plan.

"Arsène Lupin…Arsène Lupin," he muttered.

Suddenly, as if moved by anger, he rushed upon his two assistants and shook them violently. They did not awaken.

"The devil!" he cried. "Can it be possible?"

He leaned over them and, in turn, examined them closely. They were asleep; but their response was unnatural.

"They have been drugged," he said to the baron.

"By whom?"

"By him, of course, or his men under his discretion. That work bears his stamp."

"In that case, I am lost – nothing can be done."

"Nothing," assented Ganimard.

"It is dreadful; it is monstrous."

"Lodge a complaint."

"What good will that do?"

"Oh; it is well to try it. The law has some resources."

"The law! Bah! It is useless. You represent the law, and, at this moment, when you should be looking for a clue and trying to discover something, you do not even stir."

"Discover something with Arsène Lupin! Why, my dear monsieur, Arsène Lupin never leaves any clue behind him. He leaves nothing to chance. Sometimes I think he put himself in my way and simply allowed me to arrest him in America."

"Then, I must renounce my pictures! He has taken the gems of my collection. I would give a fortune to recover them. If there is no other way, let him name his own price."

Ganimard regarded the baron attentively, as he said:

"Now, that is sensible. Will you stick to it?"

"Yes, yes. But why?"

"An idea that I have."

"What is it?"

"We will discuss it later – if the official examination does not succeed. But, not one word about me, if you wish my assistance."

He added, between his teeth:

"It is true I have nothing to boast of in this affair."

The assistants were gradually regaining consciousness with the bewildered air of people who come out of an hypnotic sleep. They opened their eyes and looked about them in astonishment. Ganimard questioned them; they remembered nothing.

"But you must have seen someone?"

"No."

"Can't you remember?"

"No, no."

"Did you drink anything?"

They considered a moment, and then one of them replied:

"Yes, I drank a little water."

"Out of that carafe?"

"Yes."

"So did I," declared the other.

Ganimard smelled and tasted it. It had no particular taste and no odor.

"Come," he said, "we are wasting our time here. One can't decide an Arsène Lupin problem in five minutes. But, morbleu! I swear I will catch him again."

The same day, a charge of burglary was duly performed by Baron Cahorn against Arsène Lupin, a prisoner in the Prison de la Santé.

* * *

The baron afterwards regretted making the charge against Lupin when he saw his castle delivered over to the gendarmes, the procureur, the judge d'instruction, the newspaper reporters and photographers, and a throng of idle curiosity-seekers.

The affair soon became a topic of general discussion, and the name of Arsène Lupin excited the public imagination to such an extent that the newspapers filled their columns with the most fantastic stories of his exploits which found ready credence amongst their readers.

But the letter of Arsène Lupin that was published in the 'Echo de France' (no one ever knew how the newspaper obtained it), that letter in which Baron Cahorn was impudently warned of the coming theft, caused considerable excitement. The most fabulous theories were advanced. Some recalled the existence of the famous subterranean tunnels, and that was the line of research pursued by the officers of the law, who searched the house from top to bottom, questioned every stone, studied the wainscoting and the chimneys, the window-frames and the girders in the ceilings. By the light of torches, they examined the immense cellars where the lords of Malaquis were wont to store their munitions and provisions. They sounded the rocky foundation to its very centre. But it was all in vain. They discovered no trace of a subterranean tunnel. No secret passage existed.

But the eager public declared that the pictures and furniture could not vanish like so many ghosts. They are substantial, material things and require doors and windows for their exits and their entrances, and so do the people that remove them. Who were those people? How did they gain access to the castle? And how did they leave it?

The police officers of Rouen, convinced of their own impotence, solicited the assistance of the Parisian detective force. Mon. Dudouis, chief of the Sûreté, sent the best sleuths of the iron brigade. He himself spent forty-eight hours at the castle, but met with no success. Then he sent for Ganimard, whose past services had proved so useful when all else failed.

Ganimard listened, in silence, to the instructions of his superior; then, shaking his head, he said:

"In my opinion, it is useless to ransack the castle. The solution of the problem lies elsewhere."

"Where, then?"

"With Arsène Lupin."

"With Arsène Lupin! To support that theory, we must admit his intervention."

"I do admit it. In fact, I consider it quite certain."

"Come, Ganimard, that is absurd. Arsène Lupin is in prison."

"I grant you that Arsène Lupin is in prison, closely guarded; but he must have fetters on his feet, manacles on his wrists, and gag in his mouth before I change my opinion."

"Why so obstinate, Ganimard?"

"Because Arsène Lupin is the only man in France of sufficient calibre to invent and carry out a scheme of that magnitude."

"Mere words, Ganimard."

"But true ones. Look! What are they doing? Searching for subterranean passages, stones swinging on pivots, and other nonsense of that kind. But Lupin doesn't employ such old-fashioned methods. He is a modern cracksman, right up to date."

"And how would you proceed?"

"I should ask your permission to spend an hour with him."

"In his cell?"

"Yes. During the return trip from America we became very friendly, and I venture to say that if he can give me any information without compromising himself he will not hesitate to save me from incurring useless trouble."

It was shortly after noon when Ganimard entered the cell of Arsène Lupin. The latter, who was lying on his bed, raised his head and uttered a cry of apparent joy.

"Ah! This is a real surprise. My dear Ganimard, here!"

"Ganimard himself."

"In my chosen retreat, I have felt a desire for many things, but my fondest wish was to receive you here."

"Very kind of you, I am sure."

"Not at all. You know I hold you in the highest regard."

"I am proud of it."

"I have always said: Ganimard is our best detective. He is almost – you see how candid I am! – he is almost as clever as Sherlock Holmes. But I am sorry that I cannot offer you anything better than this hard stool. And no refreshments! Not even a glass of beer! Of course, you will excuse me, as I am here only temporarily."

Ganimard smiled, and accepted the proffered seat. Then the prisoner continued:

"Mon Dieu, how pleased I am to see the face of an honest man. I am so tired of those devils of spies who come here ten times a day to ransack my pockets and my cell to satisfy themselves that I am not preparing to escape. The government is very solicitous on my account."

"It is quite right."

"Why so? I should be quite contented if they would allow me to live in my own quiet way."

"On other people's money."

"Quite so. That would be so simple. But here, I am joking, and you are, no doubt, in a hurry. So let us come to business, Ganimard. To what do I owe the honor of this visit?"

"The Cahorn affair," declared Ganimard, frankly.

"Ah! Wait, one moment. You see I have had so many affairs! First, let me fix in my mind the circumstances of this particular case… Ah! yes, now I have it. The Cahorn affair, Malaquis castle, Seine-Inférieure… Two Rubens, a Watteau, and a few trifling articles."

"Trifling!"

"Oh! Ma foi, all that is of slight importance. But it suffices to know that the affair interests you. How can I serve you, Ganimard?"

"Must I explain to you what steps the authorities have taken in the matter?"

"Not at all. I have read the newspapers and I will frankly state that you have made very little progress."

"And that is the reason I have come to see you."

"I am entirely at your service."

"In the first place, the Cahorn affair was managed by you?"

"From A to Z."

"The letter of warning? The telegram?"

"All mine. I ought to have the receipts somewhere."

Arsène opened the drawer of a small table of plain white wood which, with the bed and stool, constituted all the furniture in his cell, and took therefrom two scraps of paper which he handed to Ganimard.

"Ah!" exclaimed the detective, in surprise, "I thought you were closely guarded and searched, and I find that you read the newspapers and collect postal receipts."

"Bah! these people are so stupid! They open the lining of my vest, they examine the soles of my shoes, they sound the walls of my cell, but they never imagine that Arsène Lupin would be foolish enough to choose such a simple hiding place."

Ganimard laughed, as he said:

"What a droll fellow you are! Really, you bewilder me. But, come now, tell me about the Cahorn affair."

"Oh! Oh! Not quite so fast! You would rob me of all my secrets; expose all my little tricks. That is a very serious matter."

"Was I wrong to count on your complaisance?"

"No, Ganimard, and since you insist—"

Arsène Lupin paced his cell two or three times, then, stopping before Ganimard, he asked:

"What do you think of my letter to the baron?"

"I think you were amusing yourself by playing to the gallery."

"Ah! Playing to the gallery! Come, Ganimard, I thought you knew me better. Do I, Arsène Lupin, ever waste my time on such puerilities? Would I have written that letter if I could have robbed the baron without writing to him? I want you to understand that the letter was indispensable; it was the motor that set the whole machine in motion. Now, let us discuss together a scheme for the robbery of the Malaquis castle. Are you willing?"

"Yes, proceed."

"Well, let us suppose a castle carefully closed and barricaded like that of the Baron Cahorn. Am I to abandon my scheme and renounce the treasures that I covet, upon the pretext that the castle which holds them is inaccessible?"

"Evidently not."

"Should I make an assault upon the castle at the head of a band of adventurers as they did in ancient times?"

"That would be foolish."

"Can I gain admittance by stealth or cunning?"

"Impossible."

"Then there is only one way open to me. I must have the owner of the castle invite me to it."

"That is surely an original method."

"And how easy! Let us suppose that one day the owner receives a letter warning him that a notorious burglar known as Arsène Lupin is plotting to rob him. What will he do?"

"Send a letter to the Procureur."

"Who will laugh at him, because the said Arsène Lupin is actually in prison. Then, in his anxiety and fear, the simple man will ask the assistance of the first-comer, will he not?"

"Very likely."

"And if he happens to read in a country newspaper that a celebrated detective is spending his vacation in a neighboring town—"

"He will seek that detective."

"Of course. But, on the other hand, let us presume that, having foreseen that state of affairs, the said Arsène Lupin has requested one of his friends to visit Caudebec, make the acquaintance of the editor of the 'Réveil', a newspaper to which the baron is a subscriber, and let said editor understand that such person is the celebrated detective – then, what will happen?"

"The editor will announce in the 'Réveil' the presence in Caudebec of said detective."

"Exactly; and one of two things will happen: either the fish – I mean Cahorn – will not bite, and nothing will happen; or, what is more likely, he will run and greedily swallow the bait. Thus, behold my Baron Cahorn imploring the assistance of one of my friends against me."

"Original, indeed!"

"Of course, the pseudo-detective at first refuses to give any assistance. On top of that comes the telegram from Arsène Lupin. The frightened baron rushes once more to my friend and offers him a definite sum of money for his services. My friend accepts and summons two members of our band, who, during the night, whilst Cahorn is under the watchful eye of his protector, removes certain articles by way of the window and lowers them with ropes into a nice little launch chartered for the occasion. Simple, isn't it?"

"Marvelous! Marvelous!" exclaimed Ganimard. "The boldness of the scheme and the ingenuity of all its details are beyond criticism. But who is the detective whose name and fame served as a magnet to attract the baron and draw him into your net?"

"There is only one name could do it – only one."

"And that is?"

"Arsène Lupin's personal enemy – the most illustrious Ganimard."

"I?"

"Yourself, Ganimard. And, really, it is very funny. If you go there, and the baron decides to talk, you will find that it will be your duty to arrest yourself, just as you arrested me in America. Hein! The revenge is really amusing: I cause Ganimard to arrest Ganimard."

Arsène Lupin laughed heartily. The detective, greatly vexed, bit his lips; to him the joke was quite devoid of humor. The arrival of a prison guard gave Ganimard an opportunity to recover himself. The man brought Arsène Lupin's luncheon, furnished by a neighbouring restaurant. After depositing the tray upon the table, the guard retired. Lupin broke his bread, ate a few morsels, and continued:

"But, rest easy, my dear Ganimard, you will not go to Malaquis. I can tell you something that will astonish you: the Cahorn affair is on the point of being settled."

"Excuse me; I have just seen the Chief of the Sureté."

"What of that? Does Mon. Dudouis know my business better than I do myself? You will learn that Ganimard – excuse me – that the pseudo-Ganimard still remains on very good terms with the baron. The latter has authorised him to negotiate a very delicate transaction with me, and, at the present moment, in consideration of a certain sum, it is probable that the baron has recovered possession of his pictures and other treasures. And on their return, he will withdraw his complaint. Thus, there is no longer any theft, and the law must abandon the case."

Ganimard regarded the prisoner with a bewildered air.

"And how do you know all that?"

"I have just received the telegram I was expecting."

"You have just received a telegram?"

"This very moment, my dear friend. Out of politeness, I did not wish to read it in your presence. But if you will permit me—"

"You are joking, Lupin."

"My dear friend, if you will be so kind as to break that egg, you will learn for yourself that I am not joking."

Mechanically, Ganimard obeyed, and cracked the egg-shell with the blade of a knife. He uttered a cry of surprise. The shell contained nothing but a small piece of blue paper. At the request of Arsène he unfolded it. It was a telegram, or rather a portion of a telegram from which the post-marks had been removed. It read as follows:

"Contract closed. Hundred thousand balls delivered. All well."

"One hundred thousand balls?" said Ganimard.

"Yes, one hundred thousand francs. Very little, but then, you know, these are hard times... And I have some heavy bills to meet. If you only knew my budget...living in the city comes very high."

Ganimard arose. His ill-humour had disappeared. He reflected for a moment, glancing over the whole affair in an effort to discover a weak point; then, in a tone and manner that betrayed his admiration of the prisoner, he said:

"Fortunately, we do not have a dozen such as you to deal with; if we did, we would have to close up shop."

Arsène Lupin assumed a modest air, as he replied:

"Bah! A person must have some diversion to occupy his leisure hours, especially when he is in prison."

"What!" exclaimed Ganimard, "Your trial, your defense, the examination – isn't that sufficient to occupy your mind?"

"No, because I have decided not to be present at my trial."

"Oh! Oh!"

Arsène Lupin repeated, positively:

"I shall not be present at my trial."

"Really!"

"Ah! My dear monsieur, do you suppose I am going to rot upon the wet straw? You insult me. Arsène Lupin remains in prison just as long as it pleases him, and not one minute more."

"Perhaps it would have been more prudent if you had avoided getting there," said the detective, ironically.

"Ah! Monsieur jests? Monsieur must remember that he had the honor to effect my arrest. Know then, my worthy friend, that no one, not even you, could have placed a hand upon me if a much more important event had not occupied my attention at that critical moment."

"You astonish me."

"A woman was looking at me, Ganimard, and I loved her. Do you fully understand what that means: to be under the eyes of a woman that one loves? I cared for nothing in the world but that. And that is why I am here."

"Permit me to say: you have been here a long time."

"In the first place, I wished to forget. Do not laugh; it was a delightful adventure and it is still a tender memory. Besides, I have been suffering from neurasthenia. Life is so feverish these days that it is necessary to take the 'rest cure' occasionally, and I find this spot a sovereign remedy for my tired nerves."

"Arsène Lupin, you are not a bad fellow, after all."

"Thank you," said Lupin. "Ganimard, this is Friday. On Wednesday next, at four o'clock in the afternoon, I will smoke my cigar at your house in the rue Pergolese."

"Arsène Lupin, I will expect you."

They shook hands like two old friends who valued each other at their true worth; then the detective stepped to the door.

"Ganimard!"

"What is it?" asked Ganimard, as he turned back.

"You have forgotten your watch."

"My watch?"

"Yes, it strayed into my pocket."

He returned the watch, excusing himself.

"Pardon me…a bad habit. Because they have taken mine is no reason why I should take yours. Besides, I have a chronometer here that satisfies me fairly well."

He took from the drawer a large gold watch and heavy chain.

"From whose pocket did that come?" asked Ganimard.

Arsène Lupin gave a hasty glance at the initials engraved on the watch.

"J.B… Who the devil can that be…? Ah! yes, I remember. Jules Bouvier, the judge who conducted my examination. A charming fellow…!"

Vandergiessen's Daughter
Or, The Door to Nowhere

Tom Mead

DETECTIVE ED KEMBLE hoped he would never again set eyes on Hester Queeg. There was no personal enmity between the two; truth be told he rather liked her. But the woman was a jinx. Every encounter with her brought some weird incident.

That in itself was not so terrible: after all, Kemble was a good cop and the San Francisco suburb of Walnut Creek was hardly a hotbed of crime. But what made it worse was that Hester Queeg was not merely content to study these strange and macabre crimes, but to *solve* them too. There was just something about her, some kink in her brain, that made her able to see what he couldn't. So when he stepped through the revolving door at the front of Vandergiessen's Department Store, his heart sank a little when he saw her standing by the cosmetics counter.

"Well good morning Detective Kemble," she said. "You here on official business by any chance?"

"Afraid so," he said, touching the brim of his hat in salute. Then he brushed past her. It was spring of 1962 and for nearly two hundred years there had been Vandergiessens in Walnut Creek. The store was a local institution.

Kemble made his way through a door marked 'Staff Only' and up a discreet, ill-lit staircase to the office from which the Vandergiessen patriarch surveyed his domain.

He was greeted by the old man's secretary, a young fellow named Leo Tarne. Tarne took his name and ushered him in to meet the old man, Earl Vandergiessen.

"Well all right," said the old man. His voice was hoarse and he chewed a fat cigar. "Now you know very well that I'm friends with the commissioner, don't you?"

Kemble cleared his throat. "Yes sir, I did know that."

"Then you know that when I ask for a favor I expect to get it, right?"

Kemble didn't answer. "What's this about, Mr. Vandergiessen?"

"Can you keep a secret? The commissioner said you were a good man, but above all *discreet.* That so?"

"I do my best."

"Then sit down."

Kemble removed his hat and dropped into an easy chair.

"You know my daughter?"

Kemble nodded. Beverley Vandergiessen was a well-known and glamorous presence in the community. She had come home six months ago after three years at Columbia. She went away a buck-toothed, bespectacled and pimply adolescent, and returned a full-fledged glamour girl, and about as eligible a female as Walnut Creek had to offer. It was a startling transformation.

"Well listen, somebody has kidnapped her."

Kemble sat bolt upright. "What!"

"Shh," hissed the entrepreneur, "not so loud. I want the whole thing kept quiet. I don't want the press getting hold of it. All I need, Kemble, is for you to find her."

"Have you had a ransom demand?"

The old fellow nodded. From the top drawer of his desk he produced a sheaf of paper. Kemble took it and studied it. The sentiment was simple enough: *Two million dollars or the girl dies. We will be in touch with further instructions.*

"And have you any idea who took her?"

"Oh I know who's responsible."

"Yeah? Who?"

"If I was the self-pitying kind I'd say *I* was responsible for letting her go off with him. But the fact is, it was the guy I hired as a bodyguard a few months ago. His name is Ron Henry."

"Have you reported this, sir? I mean, officially?"

"No, and I don't intend to. Because you're going to find her for me, aren't you?"

* * *

On his way out of Vandergiessen's, Kemble almost bumped into Hester again. He was on his way out through the revolving door while she was coming in.

"Forgot my purse," she mouthed at him through the glass, shaking her head with pleasant smile. He nodded curtly and moved on.

But before he got to his car she was back with him, almost jogging to keep pace. He noticed she now had her purse.

"Seems kind of cloak-and-dagger, Detective Kemble," she observed.

"Mrs. Queeg, you have no idea. It's more than my job is worth."

"Then I don't suppose you'd care to share any details?"

"Wish I could," answered Kemble, unlocking his car, "but I don't have the time."

"Thought you'd need all the help you can get, if you're after Vandergiessen's daughter."

Kemble froze. "How do you know about that?"

"Oh, everybody knows. No secrets in Walnut Creek, Detective."

"Well if you know that then you know Beverley's bodyguard is the only one who could possibly be responsible for the kidnapping. The story he gave was a mess. Full of holes."

"But it's true all the same."

"How can you say that? He told people she vanished *right before his eyes.* Walking out through that very door." He indicated the entrance through which they had just emerged. "How could he expect anyone to believe that story?"

"Ron Henry is an honorable man," said Hester. "His wife is a good friend of mine. And I happen to believe every word he said."

"Well, if you know so much, you might as well know I'm heading over now to take him in for questioning."

"Then I'm coming with you."

"You're not, Mrs. Queeg. This doesn't have to be messy. We know when Beverley was taken, and we know who took her. What more do we want?"

"Well, you want to know *how* for one thing. And perhaps I can help you with that."

Before he knew it, she was in his car, snug in the passenger seat while he drove them across town to the address on record for Ron Henry, Beverley Vandergiessen's former bodyguard. The man who claimed to have been with her when she vanished. While he drove, Hester talked to him, unravelling a litany of Ron Henry's various achievements and gentlemanly conduct from his life in Walnut Creek. "He would *never* have let anything happen to her if he could help it. He's an honorable man."

"You said that before," answered Kemble as they pulled up outside the Henry place. "But till I see it for myself I don't believe it."

* * *

Ron Henry was nervous. His wife was out and he was alone in the house, so when Detective Kemble arrived on his doorstep it must have felt like the final Grand Slam. The last hurrah. He thought his time was up. The only piquant feature of the raid was the fact that the cop had sweet little Hester Queeg with him.

"I knew you'd come by sooner or later."

"We need to hear your version, Ron," said Kemble.

Henry dropped onto the couch. He was a little off-centre; probably drunk. Kemble would not have blamed him.

"You're not gonna believe me."

"You let me decide that."

Then, after a lengthy sigh, Ron cleared his throat. "It happened like this," he began. "It was early evening and the store had just closed for the day. Dennis Crickle, the driver, dropped me and Miss Vandergiessen off so she could visit her father. I waited downstairs while she went up to the office. I hung around the cosmetics department – you know, near the front entrance? She was up there about ten minutes."

"Do you know what she wanted to talk to him about?"

"No. Probably nothing important. She dropped in on him a lot – borrow money, I guess. And when she came back downstairs she was smiling."

"What happened then?"

"She said to me 'Let's get out of here, Ron.' So we headed back the way we came in. She went through the door in front of me. The car and Dennis Crickle were waiting at the curb outside."

"And?"

"And she...vanished. Right in front of my eyes. Just as she was going through the door. She went out ahead of me and she never got to the other side."

Kemble looked at him, eyes narrowed. "You realise how that sounds, don't you Ron?"

"Yeah," he sighed. "Yeah I do. I know how crazy the whole thing is, believe me. But it's what happened."

"So you expect me to believe that Beverley Vandergiessen never made it through a doorway from the store to the sidewalk?"

"I couldn't believe it myself. I thought I must have blacked out or something. But it was seconds, only seconds. I ran out the door after her but the sidewalk was empty. The Lincoln was parked up at the curb and Dennis was leaning on it smoking a cigarette. I said to him 'Where'd she go, Dennis?' and he said 'Who, Miss Beverley? I ain't seen her, she didn't come by me.'"

"And did you believe him?"

"What choice did I have? I saw her vanish before my eyes. I ran out to an empty street. And she was gone."

Kemble looked at Hester, but she did not meet his eye. "Right now, Ron," the detective announced, "you're our only suspect. I need you to know that. It's nothing personal, and Mrs. Queeg here says you're a good guy, but Earl Vandergiessen is convinced you're the only one who could have taken her. And the facts seem to support that. Beverley was last seen going into the store with you. She never came out again."

Ron nodded. He was resigned, his gaze downturned. "Ron," interjected Hester, "how long have you been working for the Vandergiessens?"

"About six months. He hired me to look after his daughter when she came home from university."

"Good job?"

"Yeah, Mrs. Queeg," Ron said sadly, "it was."

* * *

Norma Vandergiessen, ex-trophy wife of the department store tyrant, arrived by private plane the following morning. She had set out as soon as she heard that her daughter was missing. Kemble happened to be at the store when she arrived with a flourish of genuine fox fur, spiky heels ticking metronomically on the parquet.

She stormed into Earl's office without knocking, and the secretary Leo Tarne trailed behind her, protesting feebly.

"Where the hell is our daughter, Earl?" she demanded. She was a woman of about fifty, of the breed generally referred to as 'handsome'. By that I mean that she had a squareish jaw, almost supernaturally smooth skin and piercing blue eyes. Her hair was a bob, discreetly threaded with grey. She stood in front of Earl's desk like an avenging angel.

"Damned if I know," said Earl.

"I blame you for this," said his ex-wife.

"Me? Listen, I did everything I could to protect that girl. To keep her from harm. How was I to know the guy I hired was a snake in the grass?"

"All due respect," Kemble interjected bravely, "I think we should focus on the important thing. Getting Beverley home safe."

"This is Kemble," said Earl. "Kemble, my ex-wife."

For the first time Mrs. Vandergiessen turned her ossiferous glare on the detective. "Mr. Kemble," she began, "I have flown all the way here from Mississippi. I did not do so for nothing. I came to find my daughter. Now who took her?"

Kemble opened his mouth, but Earl cut him off. "Ron Henry. The bodyguard. Who else would it be? Bev left my office, then she went downstairs. She never got to the car. So what happened? She walked through an empty store. Ron Henry was the only one with her. He *must* have taken her."

"We can't assume that, Mr. Vandergiessen. I'm also looking at other possibilities…"

"That's all well and good son," said Earl, "but where does that leave my daughter?"

"Have you had a ransom note?" cut in Norma.

"Yep," answered Earl, "Two million dollars."

"Two mill? Well for God's sake, pay it Earl!"

"Ma'am," said Kemble, "I have to advise you not to pay that money. It's no guarantee of your daughter's safety."

It was then that the phone rang.

Earl answered, while Kemble listened in on the secretary's line. The conversation was short – the voice on the other end husky and distorted.

"Do you have my money, Mr. Vandergiessen?"

* * *

The drop-off was arranged for the following evening. That would give Earl and Norma enough time to scare up two million dollars in cash. The location was Trelawney Park, half a mile north of Main

Street and the Vandergiessen store. It was a pleasant patch of verdancy in the meandering suburb, lined by trees and spliced by twisting gravel paths.

The gruff, hissing voice on the line had told them to drop the bag of cash under the easternmost oak tree. Earl Vandergiessen went in alone, but Kemble and Norma sat in his VW nearby, watching intently. Kemble was taking no chances – he had recruited a cohort of undercover officers dotted around the park, milling among the kids and dog-walkers and other everyday human traffic. They saw Earl approach the tree, bag in hand. He put it down at the foot of the tree. Then He headed back toward the car, looking shifty as he clambered into the back seat.

"See anybody?" said Kemble.

"Not a soul."

"Well all right. So we wait."

So they waited.

It was maybe twenty minutes before Kemble's radio crackled startlingly to life.

"Kemble, got a woman on the line for you. She keeps calling. Won't let up."

The detective sighed and cast an embarrassed glance at his passengers. Then he turned back to the box. "Dispatch, if it's my wife…"

"Detective, this is Hester Queeg," came a second voice. "I wanted to call you and let you know that I'm outside your kidnapper's place."

Silence. Dead air.

"I beg your pardon, Mrs. Queeg?"

"I think you heard me, Detective Kemble. I'm in a call box across the street from your kidnapper's home."

"Who is that woman?" hissed Norma Vandergiessen.

"Quiet, damn it!" snapped Earl.

"Mrs. Queeg, I don't have the time to ask questions. Just tell me the address."

And she did.

While they were driving, another radio call came through – this time from the sergeant. "Bad news, Detective. They got the money."

"What!"

"Don't know how. But we found the bag – empty."

"Did you see anybody come or go?"

A brief pause, then: "Nobody, sir."

They rounded a corner and Kemble instantly recognized Hester's station wagon parked adjacent to a glass call box. It was opposite an oblong tenement block. Kemble pulled up behind Hester's car and sprang out, with Earl and Norma hot on his heels.

Hester sat in her driving seat, beaming out at him.

"He went in about five minutes ago," she said. "He was carrying a bag."

"Hester," said Kemble, "this is Dennis Crickle's place. The driver."

"Well, I don't know what to tell you, Detective. Except that he's your man."

Drawing his gun, Kemble headed across the street and into the building. Hester trotted behind him, along with Earl and Norma. They puffed their way up two flights of stairs to Crickle's apartment. Kemble counted to three and then busted the door with his foot. Gun in hand, he exploded into the poky little two-room.

Dennis Crickle was there, caught completely unaware with a fist full of money. And on his couch sat Beverley Vandergiessen.

Norma, looking no less splendid for having thundered up the stairs, studied the girl. "And who is this person?" she demanded.

"Who do you think?" said Kemble, holstering his pistol.

"Gentlemen, I don't know who she is, but she is certainly *not* my Beverley."

The girl sat, open-mouthed.

"Sorry to intrude," said Hester Queeg, "but I think I might be able to explain."

* * *

With the miscreants subdued, and the company assembled in the small square living room of Dennis Crickle's apartment, Hester seized control of the situation.

"Obviously this young woman is *not* the real Beverley Vandergiessen. I would imagine the real Bev is out of the country somewhere, and has been ever since she finished her studies. Beyond the reach of her domineering mother and father. *This* woman is Earl Vandergiessen's mistress. He recruited her six months ago to impersonate his daughter for the purpose of this confidence trick."

Norma stared at Earl with flagrant disgust. "You got this...*person* to impersonate my little girl? It's sick – you should be locked up!"

"Look," said Earl, "I didn't hurt anybody. And that money was *mine* anyway."

"No," said Norma, "it was mine."

Hester inclined her head gracefully, and continued: "Really there's only one way the disappearance could have been worked. It was a neat little trick, and poor Ron Henry fell for it hook, line and sinker.

"Think of the revolving door at the Vandergiessen department store as four segments, separated by panes of see-through glass. When this 'Beverley' stepped through the door, she was effectively sandwiched between panes of glass. So what if the pane directly *behind* her was replaced by an ordinary mirror, concealing her the moment she stepped behind it. And what if the pane behind *that* was replaced by a two-way mirror, see-through on one side but reflective on the other. Put the reflective surfaces face to face and you create a perfect optical illusion of an empty segment, when in fact 'Beverley' was behind it all along.

"If you remember, Ron said he followed her outside immediately, onto the empty sidewalk. So she must have gone all the way round, back into the store. Meaning Dennis Crickle must have seen her, and therefore been in on the trick. But the effect achieved was *exactly* what Earl had intended. He was able to frame Ron for kidnapping by giving him a story to tell which no one would believe. Then, while Ron was searching for the girl in and around the store, all Crickle had to do was remove the prop panes of glass and slip them into the trunk of the limo.

"Pretty neat trick," said Kemble, "but *why*? Why would Earl want to fake his own daughter's kidnapping?"

"Well, I think if you take a look at the Vandergiessen store's recent profit statements you'll find the answer. Earl was losing money – and fast. He needed a quick fix. And of course there's no way he could have approached his ex-wife for money under ordinary circumstances. So he needed to get that money by other means. Hence, the trick."

"Here's another thing I don't get," Kemble continued. "We watched Vandergiessen go into the park with the bag full of money. We watched him leave the bag at the drop-off point. We didn't take our eyes off it. So how did Crickle get the money?"

"Well you answered it yourself – *you didn't take your eyes of the drop-off point*. You watched Earl go into the park with what you thought was an ordinary bag, packed with money. But really, it was a bag *within a bag*. En route along the winding path, Earl extracted the bag containing the money from within the exterior bag. Then he dropped it at a separate, pre-arranged drop-off point. In this case, it was under a garbage can, just out of your line of sight. Then he continued to the agreed drop-off point carrying an empty bag. So of course you wouldn't notice Crickle going into the park via a different entrance, heading for the garbage can and retrieving the genuine bag with the money."

"But how do you *know* all this?" demanded Norma.

"Because, Mrs. Vandergiessen, I cheated. I followed you, your husband and Detective Kemble out to the park in my old station wagon. But so you wouldn't see me, I parked around the corner. That gave me a view of the park from a different angle, so I could see Earl drop off the money behind the garbage can, whereas you could not. And I saw Crickle – I didn't know his name at the time – go into the park and pick up the cash. And then I just followed him home."

"Look," said Earl, "this is all just one big misunderstanding…"

Kemble took a step towards him. "I'm afraid it won't wash, Mr. Vandergiessen. Not even with your good friend the commissioner."

* * *

When it was all over, Kemble took Hester Queeg for a hot dog. He had a few more questions to ask.

"It's such a rookie mistake," he said. "*I* let slip to Earl where the undercover officers would be stationed. So he could find a drop-off point which was out of their line of sight."

"Not your fault, Detective," said Hester, patting him on the back. "Like a lot of people in this town, you trusted him."

He looked at her. "But *you* didn't, did you Mrs. Queeg?" He leaned in confidentially. "How do you do it? What's the secret?"

She favored him with a polite smile. But she had no answer for him.

To Prove an Alibi

L.T. Meade and Robert Eustace

I FIRST MET Arthur Cressley in the late spring of 1892. I had been spending the winter in Egypt, and was returning to Liverpool. One calm evening, about eleven o'clock, while we were still in the Mediterranean, I went on deck to smoke a final cigar before turning in. After pacing up and down for a time I leant over the taffrail and began idly watching the tiny wavelets with their crests of white fire as they rippled away from the vessel's side. Presently I became aware of someone standing near me, and, turning, saw that it was one of my fellow passengers, a young man whose name I knew but whose acquaintance I had not yet made. He was entered in the passenger list as Arthur Cressley, belonged to an old family in Derbyshire, and was returning home from Western Australia, where he had made a lot of money. I offered him a light, and after a few preliminary remarks we drifted into a desultory conversation. He told me that he had been in Australia for fifteen years, and having done well was now returning to settle in his native land.

"Then you do not intend going out again?" I asked.

"No," he replied; "I would not go through the last fifteen years for double the money I have made."

"I suppose you will make London your headquarters?"

"Not altogether; but I shall have to spend a good deal of time there. My wish is for a quiet country life, and I intend to take over the old family property. We have a place called Cressley Hall, in Derbyshire, which has belonged to us for centuries. It would be a sort of white elephant, for it has fallen into pitiable decay; but, luckily, I am now in a position to restore it and set it going again in renewed prosperity."

"You are a fortunate man," I answered.

"Perhaps I am," he replied. "Yes, as far as this world's goods go I suppose I am lucky, considering that I arrived in Australia fifteen years ago with practically no money in my pocket. I shall be glad to be home again for many reasons, chiefly because I can save the old property from being sold."

"It is always a pity when a fine old family seat has to go to the hammer for want of funds," I remarked.

"That is true, and Cressley Hall is a superb old place. There is only one drawback to it; but I don't believe there is anything in that," added Cressley in a musing tone.

Knowing him so little I did not feel justified in asking for an explanation. I waited, therefore, without speaking. He soon proceeded:

"I suppose I am rather foolish about it," he continued; "but if I am superstitious, I have abundant reason. For more than a century and a half there has been a strange fatality about any Cressley occupying the Hall. This fatality was first exhibited in 1700, when Barrington Cressley, one of the most abandoned libertines of that time, led his infamous orgies there – of these even history takes note. There are endless legends as to their nature, one of which is that he had personal dealings with the devil in the large turret room, the principal bedroom at the Hall, and was found dead there on the following morning. Certainly since that date a curious doom has hung over the family, and this doom shows itself in a strange way, only attacking those victims who are so unfortunate as to sleep in the turret room. Gilbert Cressley, the young Court favourite of George the Third, was found mysteriously murdered there, and my own great-grandfather paid the penalty by losing his reason within those gloomy walls."

"If the room has such an evil reputation, I wonder that it is occupied," I replied.

"It happens to be far and away the best bedroom in the house, and people always laugh at that sort of thing until they are brought face to face with it. The owner of the property is not only born there, as a rule, but also breathes his last in the old four-poster, the most extraordinary, wonderful old bedstead you ever laid eyes on. Of course I do not believe in any malevolent influences from the unseen world, but the record of disastrous coincidences in that one room is, to say the least of it, curious. Not that this sort of thing will deter me from going into possession, and I intend to put a lot of money into Cressley Hall."

"Has no one been occupying it lately?" I asked.

"Not recently. An old housekeeper has had charge of the place for the last few years. The agent had orders to sell the Hall long ago, but though it has been in the market for a long time I do not believe there was a single offer. Just before I left Australia I wired to Murdock, my agent, that I intended taking over the place, and authorised its withdrawal from the market."

"Have you no relations?" I inquired.

"None at all. Since I have been away my only brother died. It is curious to call it going home when one has no relatives and only friends who have probably forgotten one."

I could not help feeling sorry for Cressley as he described the lonely outlook. Of course, with heaps of money and an old family place he would soon make new friends; but he looked the sort of chap who might be imposed upon, and although he was as nice a fellow as I had ever met, I could not help coming to the conclusion that he was not specially strong, either mentally or physically. He was essentially good-looking, however, and had the indescribable bearing of a man of old family. I wondered how he had managed to make his money. What he told me about his old Hall also excited my interest, and as we talked I managed to allude to my own peculiar hobby, and the delight I took in such old legends.

As the voyage flew by our acquaintance grew apace, ripening into a warm friendship. Cressley told me much of his past life, and finally confided to me one of his real objects in returning to England.

While prospecting up country he had come across some rich veins of gold, and now his intention was to bring out a large syndicate in order to acquire the whole property, which, he anticipated, was worth at least a million. He spoke confidently of this great scheme, but always wound up by informing me that the money which he hoped to make was only of interest to him for the purpose of re-establishing Cressley Hall in its ancient splendour.

As we talked I noticed once or twice that a man stood near us who seemed to take an interest in our conversation. He was a thickly set individual with a florid complexion and a broad German cast of face. He was an inveterate smoker, and when he stood near us with a pipe in his mouth the expression of his face was almost a blank; but watching him closely I saw a look in his eyes which betokened the shrewd man of business, and I could scarcely tell why, but I felt uncomfortable in his presence. This man, Wickham by name, managed to pick up an acquaintance with Cressley, and soon they spent a good deal of time together. They made a contrast as they paced up and down on deck, or played cards in the evening; the Englishman being slight and almost fragile in build, the German of the bulldog order, with a manner at once curt and overbearing. I took a dislike to Wickham, and wondered what Cressley could see in him.

"Who is the fellow?" I asked on one occasion, linking my hand in Cressley's arm and drawing him aside as I spoke.

"Do you mean Wickham?" he answered. "I am sure I cannot tell you. I never met the chap before this voyage. He came on board at King George's Sound, where I also embarked; but he never spoke to me until we were in the Mediterranean. On the whole, Bell, I am inclined to like him; he seems to be downright and honest. He knows a great deal about the bush, too, as he has spent several years there."

"And he gives you the benefit of his information?" I asked.

"I don't suppose he knows more than I do, and it is doubtful whether he has had so rough a time."

"Then in that case he picks your brains."

"What do you mean?"

The young fellow looked at me with those clear grey eyes which were his most attractive feature.

"Nothing," I answered, "nothing; only if you will be guided by a man nearly double your age, I would take care to tell Wickham as little as possible. Have you ever observed that he happens to be about when you and I are engaged in serious conversation?"

"I can't say that I have."

"Well, keep your eyes open and you'll see what I mean. Be as friendly as you like, but don't give him your confidence – that is all."

"You are rather late in advising me on that score," said Cressley, with a somewhat nervous laugh. "Wickham knows all about the old Hall by this time."

"And your superstitious fears with regard to the turret room?" I queried.

"Well, I have hinted at them. You will be surprised, but he is full of sympathy."

"Tell him no more," I said in conclusion.

Cressley made a sort of half-promise, but looked as if he rather resented my interference.

A day or two later we reached Liverpool; I was engaged long ago to stay with some friends in the suburbs, and Cressley took up his abode at the Prince's Hotel. His property was some sixty miles away, and when we parted he insisted on my agreeing to come down and see his place as soon as he had put things a little straight.

I readily promised to do so, provided we could arrange a visit before my return to London.

Nearly a week went by and I saw nothing of Cressley; then, on a certain morning, he called to see me.

"How are you getting on?" I asked.

"Capitally," he replied. "I have been down to the Hall several times with my agent, Murdock, and though the place is in the most shocking condition I shall soon put things in order. But what I have come specially to ask you now is whether you can get away today and come with me to the Hall for a couple of nights. I had arranged with the agent to go down this afternoon in his company, but he has been suddenly taken ill – he is rather bad, I believe – and cannot possibly come with me. He has ordered the housekeeper to get a couple of rooms ready, and though I am afraid it will be rather roughing it, I shall be awfully glad if you can come."

I had arranged to meet a man in London on special business that very evening, and could not put him off; but my irresistible desire to see the old place from the description I had heard of it decided me to make an effort to fall in as well as I could with Cressley's plans.

"I wish I could go with you today," I said; "but that, as it happens, is out of the question. I must run up to town on some pressing business; but if you will allow me I can easily come back again tomorrow. Can you not put off your visit until tomorrow evening?"

"No, I am afraid I cannot do that. I have to meet several of the tenants, and have made all arrangements to go by the five o'clock train this afternoon."

He looked depressed at my refusal, and after a moment said thoughtfully:

"I wish you could have come with me today. When Murdock could not come I thought of you at once – it would have made all the difference."

"I am sorry," I replied; "but I can promise faithfully to be with you tomorrow. I shall enjoy seeing your wonderful old Hall beyond anything; and as to roughing it, I am used to that. You will not mind spending one night there by yourself?"

He looked at me as if he were about to speak, but no words came from his lips.

"What is the matter?" I said, giving him an earnest glance. "By the way, are you going to sleep in the turret room?"

"I am afraid there is no help for it; the housekeeper is certain to get it ready for me. The owner of the property always sleeps there, and it would look like a confession of weakness to ask to be put into another bedroom."

"Nevertheless, if you are nervous, I should not mind that," I said.

"Oh, I don't know that I am absolutely nervous, Bell, but all the same I have a superstition. At the present moment I have the queerest sensation; I feel as if I ought not to pay this visit to the Hall."

"If you intend to live there by-and-by, you must get over this sort of thing," I remarked.

"Oh yes, I must, and I would not yield to it on any account whatever. I am sorry I even mentioned it to you. It is good of you to promise to come tomorrow, and I shall look forward to seeing you. By what train will you come?"

We looked up the local timetable, and I decided on a train which would leave Liverpool about five o'clock.

"The very one that I shall go down by today," said Cressley; "that's capital, I'll meet you with a conveyance of some sort and drive you over. The house is a good two hours' drive from the station, and you cannot get a trap there for love or money."

"By the way," I said, "is there much the matter with your agent?"

"I cannot tell you; he seems bad enough. I went up to his house this morning and saw the wife. It appears that he was suddenly taken ill with a sort of asthmatic attack to which he is subject. While I was talking to Mrs. Murdock, a messenger came down to say that her husband specially wished to see me, so we both went to his room, but he had dozed off into a queer restless sleep before we arrived. The wife said he must not be awakened on any account, but I caught a glimpse of him and he certainly looked bad, and was moaning as if in a good deal of pain. She gave me the keys of a bureau in his room, and I took out some estimates, and left a note for him telling him to come on as soon as he was well enough."

"And your visit to his room never roused him?" I said.

"No, although Mrs. Murdock and I made a pretty good bit of noise moving about and opening and shutting drawers. His moans were quite heartrending – he was evidently in considerable pain; and I was glad to get away, as that sort of thing always upsets me."

"Who is this Murdock?" I asked.

"Oh, the man who has looked after the place for years. I was referred to him by my solicitors. He seems a most capable person, and I hope to goodness he won't be ill long. If he is I shall find myself in rather a fix."

I made no reply to this, and soon afterwards Cressley shook hands with me and departed on his way. I went to my room, packed my belongings, and took the next train to town. The business which I had to get through occupied the whole of that evening and also some hours of the following day. I found I was not able to start for Liverpool before the 12:10 train at Euston, and should not therefore arrive at Lime Street before five o'clock – too late to catch the train for Brent, the nearest station to Cressley's place. Another train left Central Station for Brent, however, at seven o'clock, and I determined to wire to Cressley to tell him to meet me by the latter train. This was the last train in the day, but there was no fear of my missing it.

I arrived at Lime Street almost to the moment and drove straight to the Prince's Hotel, where I had left my bag the day before. Here a telegram awaited me; it was from Cressley, and ran as follows:

Hope this will reach you time; if so, call at Murdock's house, No. 12, Melville Gardens. If possible see him and get the documents referred to in Schedule A – he will know what you mean. Most important.

Cressley

I glanced at the clock in the hall; it was now a quarter past five – my train would leave at seven. I had plenty of time to get something to eat and then go to Murdock's.

Having despatched my telegram to Cressley, telling him to look out for me by the train which arrived at Brent at nine o'clock, I ordered a meal, ate it, and then hailing a cab, gave the driver the number of Murdock's house. Melville Gardens was situated somewhat in the suburbs, and it was twenty minutes' drive from my hotel. When we drew up at Murdock's door I told the cabman to wait, and, getting out, rang the bell. The servant who answered my summons told me that the agent was still very ill and could not be seen by anyone. I then inquired for the wife. I was informed that she was out, but would be back soon. I looked at my watch. It was just six o'clock. I determined to wait to see Mrs. Murdock if possible.

Having paid and dismissed my cab, I was shown into a small, untidily kept parlour, where I was left to my own meditations. The weather was hot and the room close. I paced up and down restlessly. The minutes flew by and Mrs. Murdock did not put in an appearance. I looked at my watch, which now pointed to twenty minutes past six. It would take me, in an ordinary cab, nearly twenty minutes to reach the station. In order to make all safe I ought to leave Murdock's house in ten minutes from now at the latest.

I went and stood by the window watching anxiously for Mrs. Murdock to put in an appearance. Melville Gardens was a somewhat lonely place, and few people passed the house, which was old and shabby; it had evidently not been done up for years. I was just turning round in order to ring the bell to leave a message with the servant, when the room door was opened and, to my astonishment, in walked Wickham, the man I had last seen on board the *Euphrates*. He came up to me at once and held out his hand.

"No doubt you are surprised at seeing me here, Mr. Bell," he exclaimed.

"I certainly was for a moment," I answered; but then I added, "The world is a small place, and one soon gets accustomed to acquaintances cropping up in all sorts of unlikely quarters."

"Why unlikely?" said Wickham. "Why should I not know Murdock, who happens to be a very special and very old friend of mine? I might as well ask you why you are interested in him."

"Because I happen to be a friend of Arthur Cressley's," I answered, "and have come here on his business."

"And so am I also a friend of Cressley's. He has asked me to go and see him at Cressley Hall some day, and I hope to avail myself of his invitation. The servant told me that you were waiting for Mrs. Murdock – can I give her any message from you?"

"I want to see Murdock himself," I said, after a pause. "Do you think that it is possible for me to have an interview with him?"

"I left him just now and he was asleep," said Wickham. "He is still very ill, and I think the doctor is a little anxious about him. It would not do to disturb him on any account. Of course, if he happens to awake he might be able to tell you what you want to know. By the way, has it anything to do with Cressley Hall?"

"Yes; I have just had a telegram from Cressley, and the message is somewhat important. You are quite sure that Murdock is asleep?"

"He was when I left the room, but I will go up again and see. Are you going to London tonight, Mr. Bell?"

"No; I am going down to Cressley Hall, and must catch the seven o'clock train. I have not a moment to wait." As I spoke I took out my watch.

"It only wants five-and-twenty minutes to seven," I said, "and I never care to run a train to the last moment. There is no help for it, I suppose I must go without seeing Murdock. Cressley will in all probability send down a message tomorrow for the papers he requires."

"Just stay a moment," said Wickham, putting on an anxious expression; "it is a great pity that you should not see Cressley's agent if it is as vital as all that. Ah! And here comes Mrs. Murdock; wait one moment, I'll go and speak to her."

He went out of the room, and I heard him say something in a low voice in the passage – a woman's voice replied, and the next instant Mrs. Murdock stood before me. She was a tall woman with a sallow face and sandy hair; she had a blank sort of stare about her, and scarcely any expression. Now she fixed her dull, light-blue eyes on my face and held out her hand.

"You are Mr. Bell?" she said. "I have heard of you, of course, from Mr. Cressley. So you are going to spend tonight with him at Cressley Hall. I am glad, for it is a lonely place – the most lonely place I know."

"Pardon me," I interrupted, "I cannot stay to talk to you now or I shall miss my train. Can I see your husband or can I not?"

She glanced at Wickham, then she said with hesitation –

"If he is asleep it would not do to disturb him, but there is a chance of his being awake now. I don't quite understand about the papers, I wish I did. It would be best for you to see him certainly; follow me upstairs."

"And I tell you what," called Wickham after us, "I'll go and engage a cab, so that you shall lose as short a time as possible, Mr. Bell."

I thanked him and followed the wife upstairs. The stairs were narrow and steep, and we soon reached the small landing at the top. Four bedrooms opened into it. Mrs. Murdock turned the handle of the one which exactly faced the stairs, and we both entered. Here the blinds were down, and the chamber was considerably darkened. The room was a small one, and the greater part of the space was occupied by an old-fashioned Albert bedstead with the curtains pulled forward. Within I could just see the shadowy outline of a figure, and I distinctly heard the feeble groans of the sick man.

"Ah! What a pity, my husband is still asleep," said Mrs. Murdock, as she turned softly round to me and put her finger to her lips. "It would injure him very much to awaken him," she said. "You can go and look at him if you like; you will see how very ill he is. I wonder if I could help you with regard to the papers you want, Mr. Bell?"

"I want the documents referred to in Schedule A," I answered.

"Schedule A?" she repeated, speaking under her breath. "I remember that name. Surely all the papers relating to it are in this drawer. I think I can get them for you."

She crossed the room as she spoke, and standing with her back to the bedstead, took a bunch of keys from a table which stood near and fitted one into the lock of a highbureau made of mahogany. She pulled open a drawer and began to examine its contents.

While she was so occupied I approached the bed, and bending slightly forward, took a good stare at the sick man. I had never seen Murdock before. There was little doubt that he was ill – he looked very ill, indeed. His face was long and cadaverous, the cheek bones were high, and the cheeks below were much sunken in; the lips, which were clean-shaven, were slightly drawn apart, and some broken irregular teeth were visible. The eyebrows were scanty, and the hair was much worn away from the high and hollow forehead. The man looked sick unto death. I had seldom seen anyone with an expression like his – the closed eyes were much sunken, and the moaning which came from the livid lips was horrible to listen to.

After giving Murdock a long and earnest stare, I stepped back from the bed, and was just about to speak to Mrs. Murdock, who was rustling papers in the drawer, when the most strong and irresistible curiosity assailed me. I could not account for it, but I felt bound to yield to its suggestions. I turned again and bent close over the sick man. Surely there was something monotonous about that deep-drawn breath; those moans, too, came at wonderfully regular intervals. Scarcely knowing why I did it, I stretched out my hand and laid it on the forehead. Good God! What was the matter? I felt myself turning cold; the perspiration stood out on my own brow. I had not touched a living forehead at all. Flesh was flesh, it was impossible to mistake the feel, but there was no flesh here. The figure in the bed was neither a living nor a dead man, it was a wax representation of one; but why did it moan, and how was it possible for it not to breathe?

Making the greatest effort of my life, I repressed an exclamation, and when Mrs. Murdock approached me with the necessary papers in her hand, took them from her in my usual manner.

"These all relate to Schedule A," she said. "I hope I am not doing wrong in giving them to you without my husband's leave. He looks very ill, does he not?"

"He looks as bad as he can look," I answered. I moved towards the door. Something in my tone must have alarmed her, for a curious expression of fear dilated the pupils of her light blue eyes. She followed me downstairs. A hansom was waiting for me. I nodded to Wickham, did not even wait to shake hands with Mrs. Murdock, and sprang into the cab.

"Central Station!" I shouted to the man; and then as he whipped up his horse and flew down the street, "A sovereign if you get there before seven o'clock."

We were soon dashing quickly along the streets. I did not know Liverpool well, and consequently could not exactly tell where the man was going. When I got into the hansom it wanted twelve minutes to seven o'clock; these minutes were quickly flying, and still no station.

"Are you sure you are going right?" I shouted through the hole in the roof.

"You'll be there in a minute, sir," he answered. "It's Lime Street Station you want, isn't it?"

"No; Central Station," I answered. "I told you Central Station; drive there at once like the very devil. I must catch that train, for it is the last one tonight."

"All right, sir; I can do it," he cried, whipping up his horse again.

Once more I pulled out my watch; the hands pointed to three minutes to seven.

At ten minutes past we were driving into the station. I flung the man half a sovereign, and darted into the booking office.

"To Brent, sir? The last train has just gone," said the clerk, with an impassive stare at me through the little window.

I flung my bag down in disgust and swore a great oath. But for that idiot of a driver I should have just caught the train. All of a sudden a horrible thought flashed through my brain. Had the cabman been bribed by Wickham? No directions could have been plainer than mine. I had told the man to drive to Central Station. Central Station did not sound the least like Lime Street Station. How was it possible for him to make so grave a mistake?

The more I considered the matter the more certain I was that a black plot was brewing, and that Wickham was in the thick of it. My brain began to whirl with excitement. What was the matter? Why was a lay figure in Murdock's bed? Why had I been taken upstairs to see it? Without any doubt both

Mrs. Murdock and Wickham wished me to see what was such an admirable imitation of a sick man – an imitation so good, with those ghastly moans coming from the lips, that it would have taken in the sharpest detective in Scotland Yard. I myself was deceived until I touched the forehead. This state of things had not been brought to pass without a reason. What was the reason? Could it be possible that Murdock was wanted elsewhere, and it was thought well that I should see him in order to prove an alibi, should he be suspected of a ghastly crime? My God! What could this mean? From the first I had mistrusted Wickham. What was he doing in Murdock's house? For what purpose had he bribed the driver of the cab in order to make me lose my train?

The more I thought, the more certain I was that Cressley was in grave danger; and I now determined, cost what it might, to get to him that night.

I left the station, took a cab, and drove back to my hotel. I asked to see the manager. A tall, dark man in a frock-coat emerged from a door at the back of the office and inquired what he could do for me. I begged permission to speak to him alone, and we passed into his private room.

"I am in an extraordinary position," I began. "Circumstances of a private nature make it absolutely necessary that I should go to a place called Cressley Hall, about fourteen miles from Brent. Brent is sixty miles down the line, and the last train has gone. I could take a 'special', but there might be an interminable delay at Brent, and I prefer to drive straight to Cressley Hall across country. Can you assist me by directing me to some good jobmaster from whom I can hire a carriage and horses?"

The man looked at me with raised eyebrows. He evidently thought I was mad.

"I mean what I say," I added, "and am prepared to back my words with a substantial sum. Can you help me?"

"I dare say you might get a carriage and horses to do it," he replied; "but it is a very long way, and over a hilly country. No two horses could go such a distance without rest. You would have to change from time to time as you went. I will send across to the hotel stables for my man, and you can see him about it."

He rang the bell and gave his orders. In a few moments the jobmaster came in. I hurriedly explained to him what I wanted. At first he said it was impossible, that his best horses were out, and that those he had in his stables could not possibly attempt such a journey; but when I brought out my cheque book and offered to advance any sum in reason, he hesitated.

"Of course there is one way in which it might be managed, sir. I would take you myself as far as Ovenden, which is five-and-twenty miles from here. There, I know, we could get a pair of fresh horses from the Swan; and if we wired at once from here, horses might be ready at Carlton, which is another twenty miles on the road. But, at our best, sir, it will be between two and three in the morning before we get to Brent."

"I am sorry to hear you say so," I answered; "but it is better to arrive then than to wait until tomorrow. Please send the necessary telegram off without a moment's delay, and get the carriage ready."

"Put the horses in at once, John," said the manager. "You had better take the light wagonette. You ought to get there between one and two in the morning with that."

Then he added, as the man left the room –

"I suppose, sir, your business is very urgent?"

"It is," I replied shortly.

He looked as if he would like to question me further, but refrained.

A few moments later I had taken my seat beside the driver, and we were speeding at a good round pace through the streets of Liverpool. We passed quickly through the suburbs, and out into the open country. The evening was a lovely one, and the country looked its best. It was difficult to believe, as I drove through the peaceful landscape, that in all probability a dark deed was in contemplation, and that the young man to whom I had taken a most sincere liking was in danger of his life.

As I drove silently by my companion's side I reviewed the whole situation. The more I thought of it the less I liked it. On board the *Euphrates* Wickham had been abnormally interested in Cressley. Cressley had himself confided to him his superstitious dread with regard to the turret room. Cressley had come home with a fortune; and if he floated his syndicate he would be a millionaire. Wickham scarcely looked like a rich man. Then why should he know Murdock, and why should a lay figure be put in Murdock's bed? Why, also, through a most unnatural accident, should I have lost my train?

The more I thought, the graver and graver became my fears. Gradually darkness settled over the land, and then a rising moon flooded the country in its weird light. I had been on many a wild expedition before, but in some ways never a wilder than this. Its very uncertainty, wrapped as it was in unformed suspicions, gave it an air of inexpressible mystery.

On and on we went, reaching Ovenden between nine and ten at night. Here horses were ready for us, and we again started on our way. When we got to Carlton, however, there came a hitch in my well-formed arrangements. We drew up at the little inn, to find the place in total darkness, and all the inhabitants evidently in bed and asleep. With some difficulty we roused the landlord, and asked why the horses which had been telegraphed for had not been got ready.

"We did not get them when the second telegram arrived," was the reply.

"The second telegram!" I cried, my heart beating fast. "What do you mean?"

"There were two, sir, both coming from the same stables. The first was written desiring us to have the horses ready at any cost. The second contradicted the first, and said that the gentleman had changed his mind, and was not going. On receipt of that, sir, I shut up the house as usual, and we all went to bed. I am very sorry if there has been any mistake."

"There has, and a terrible one," I could not help muttering under my breath. My fears were getting graver than ever. Who had sent the second telegram? Was it possible that I had been followed by Wickham, who took these means of circumventing me?

"We must get horses, and at once," I said. "Never mind about the second telegram; it was a mistake."

Peach, the jobmaster, muttered an oath.

"I can't understand what is up," he said. He looked mystified and not too well pleased. Then he added, "These horses can't go another step, sir."

"They must if we can get no others," I said. I went up to him, and began to whisper in his ear.

"This is a matter of life and death, my good friend. Only the direst necessity takes me on this journey. The second telegram without doubt was sent by a man whom I am trying to circumvent. I know what I am saying. We must get horses, or these must go on. We have not an instant to lose. There is a conspiracy afoot to do serious injury to the owner of Cressley Hall."

"What! The young gentleman who has just come from Australia? You don't mean to say he is in danger?" said Peach.

"He is in the gravest danger. I don't mind who knows. I have reason for my fears."

While I was speaking the landlord drew near. He overheard some of my last words. The landlord and Peach now exchanged glances. After a moment the landlord spoke –

"A neighbour of ours, sir, has got two good horses," he said. "He is the doctor in this village. I believe he'll lend them if the case is as urgent as you say."

"Go and ask him," I cried. "You shall have ten pounds if we are on the road in five minutes from the present moment."

At this hint the landlord flew. He came back in an incredibly short space of time, accompanied by the doctor's coachman leading the horses. They were quickly harnessed to the wagonette, and once more we started on our way.

"Now drive as you never drove before in the whole course of your life," I said to Peach. "Money is no object. We have still fifteen miles to go, and over a rough country. You can claim any reward in reason if you get to Cressley Hall within an hour."

"It cannot be done, sir," he replied; but then he glanced at me, and some of the determination in my face was reflected in his. He whipped up the horses. They were thoroughbred animals, and worked well under pressure.

We reached the gates of Cressley Hall between two and three in the morning. Here I thought it best to draw up, and told my coachman that I should not need his services any longer.

"If you are afraid of mischief, sir, would it not be best for me to lie about here?" he asked. "I'd rather be in the neighbourhood in case you want me. I am interested in this here job, sir."

"You may well be, my man. God grant it is not a black business. Well, walk the horses up and down, if you like. If you see nothing of me within the next couple of hours, judge that matters are all right, and return with the horses to Carlton."

This being arranged, I turned from Peach and entered the lodge gates. Just inside was a low cottage surrounded by trees. I paused for a moment to consider what I had better do. My difficulty now was how to obtain admittance to the Hall, for of course it would be shut up and all its inhabitants asleep at this hour. Suddenly an idea struck me. I determined to knock up the lodge-keeper, and to enlist her assistance. I went across to the door, and presently succeeded in rousing the inmates. A woman of about fifty appeared. I explained to her my position, and begged of her to give me her help. She hesitated at first in unutterable astonishment; but then, seeing something in my face which convinced her, I suppose, of the truth of my story, for it was necessary to alarm her in order to induce her to do anything, she said she would do what I wished.

"I know the room where Mitchell, the old housekeeper, sleeps," she said, "and we can easily wake him by throwing stones up at his window. If you'll just wait a minute I'll put a shawl over my head and go with you."

She ran into an inner room and quickly re-appeared. Together we made our way along the drive which, far as I could see, ran through a park studded with old timber. We went round the house to the back entrance, and the woman, after a delay of two or three moments, during which I was on thorns, managed to wake up Mitchell the housekeeper. He came to his window, threw it open, and poked out his head.

"What can be wrong?" he said.

"It is Mr. Bell, James," was the reply, "the gentleman who has been expected at the Hall all the evening; he has come now, and wants you to admit him."

The old man said that he would come downstairs. He did so, and opening a door, stood in front of it, barring my entrance.

"Are you really the gentleman Mr. Cressley has been expecting?" he said.

"I am," I replied; "I missed my train, and was obliged to drive out. There is urgent need why I should see your master immediately; where is he?"

"I hope in bed, sir, and asleep; it is nearly three o'clock in the morning."

"Never mind the hour," I said; "I must see Mr. Cressley immediately. Can you take me to his room?"

"If I am sure that you are Mr. John Bell," said the old man, glancing at me with not unnatural suspicion.

"Rest assured on that point. Here, this is my card, and here is a telegram which I received today from your master."

"But master sent no telegram today."

"You must be mistaken, this is from him."

"I don't understand it, sir, but you look honest, and I suppose I must trust you."

"You will do well to do so," I said.

He moved back and I entered the house. He took me down a passage, and then into a lofty chamber, which probably was the old banqueting hall. As well as I could see by the light of the candle, it was floored, and panelled with black oak. Round the walls stood figures of knights in armour, with flags and banners hanging from the panels above. I followed the old man up a broad staircase and along endless corridors to a more distant part of the building. We turned now abruptly to our right, and soon began to ascend some turret stairs.

"In which room is your master?" I asked.

"This is his room, sir," said the man. He stood still and pointed to a door.

"Stay where you are; I may want you," I said.

I seized his candle, and holding it above my head, opened the door. The room was a large one, and when I entered was in total darkness. I fancied I heard a rustling in the distance, but could see no one. Then, as my eyes got accustomed to the faint light caused by the candle, I observed at the further end of the chamber a large four-poster bedstead. I immediately noticed something very curious about it. I turned round to the old housekeeper.

"Did you really say that Mr. Cressley was sleeping in this room?" I asked.

"Yes, sir; he must be in bed some hours ago. I left him in the library hunting up old papers, and he told me he was tired and was going to rest early."

"He is not in the bed," I said.

"Not in the bed, sir! Good God!" a note of horror came into the man's voice. "What in the name of fortune is the matter with the bed?"

As the man spoke I rushed forward. Was it really a bed at all? If it was, I had never seen a stranger one. Upon it, covering it from head to foot, was a thick mattress, from the sides of which tassels were hanging. There was no human being lying on the mattress, nor was it made up with sheets and blankets like an ordinary bed. I glanced above me. The posts at the four corners of the bedstead stood like masts. I saw at once what had happened. The canopy had descended upon the bed. Was Cressley beneath? With a shout I desired the old man to come forward, and between us we seized the mattress, and exerting all our force, tried to drag it from the bed. In a moment I saw it was fixed by cords that held it tightly in its place. Whipping out my knife, I severed these, and then hurled the heavy weight from the bed. Beneath lay Cressley, still as death. I put my hand on his heart and uttered a thankful exclamation. It was still beating. I was in time; I had saved him. After all, nothing else mattered during that supreme moment of thankfulness. A few seconds longer beneath that smothering mass and he would have been dead. By what a strange sequence of events had I come to his side just in the nick of time!

"We must take him from this room before he recovers consciousness," I said to the old man, who was surprised and horror-stricken.

"But, sir, in the name of Heaven, what has happened?"

"Let us examine the bed, and I will tell you," I said. I held up the candle as I spoke. A glance at the posts was all-sufficient to show me how the deed had been done. The canopy above, on which the heavy mattress had been placed, was held in position by strong cords which ran through pulleys at the top of the posts. These were thick and heavy enough to withstand the strain. When the cords were released, the canopy, with its heavy weight, must quickly descend upon the unfortunate sleeper, who would be smothered beneath it in a few seconds. Who had planned and executed this murderous device?

There was not a soul to be seen.

"We will take Mr. Cressley into another room and then come back," I said to the housekeeper. "Is there one where we can place him?"

"Yes, sir," was the instant reply; "there's a room on the next floor which was got ready for you."

"Capital," I answered; "we will convey him there at once."

We did so, and after using some restoratives, he came to himself. When he saw me he gazed at me with an expression of horror on his face.

"Am I alive, or is it a dream?" he said.

"You are alive, but you have had a narrow escape of your life," I answered. I then told him how I had found him.

He sat up as I began to speak, and as I continued my narrative his eyes dilated with an expression of terror which I have seldom seen equalled.

"You do not know what I have lived through," he said at last. "I only wonder I retain my reason. Oh, that awful room! No wonder men died and went mad there!"

"Well, speak, Cressley; I am all attention," I said; "you will be the better when you have unburdened yourself."

"I can tell you what happened in a few words," he answered. "You know I mentioned the horrid sort of presentiment I had about coming here at all. That first night I could not make up my mind to sleep in the house, so I went to the little inn at Brent. I received your telegram yesterday, and went to meet you by the last train. When you did not come, I had a tussle with myself; but I could think of no decent excuse for deserting the old place, and so came back. My intention was to sit up the greater part of the night arranging papers in the library. The days are long now, and I thought I might go to bed when morning broke. I was irresistibly sleepy, however, and went up to my room soon after one o'clock. I was determined to think of nothing unpleasant, and got quickly into bed, taking the precaution first to lock the door. I placed the key under my pillow, and, being very tired, soon fell into a heavy sleep. I awoke suddenly, after what seemed but a few minutes, to find the room dark, for the moon must just have set. I was very sleepy, and I wondered vaguely why I had awakened; and then suddenly, without warning, and without cause, a monstrous, unreasonable fear seized me. An indefinable intuition told me that I was not alone – that some horrible presence was near. I do not think the certainty of immediate death could have inspired me with a greater dread than that which suddenly came upon me. I dared not stir hand nor foot. My powers of reason and resistance were paralysed. At last, by an immense effort, I nerved myself to see the worst. Slowly, very slowly, I turned my head and opened my eyes. Against the tapestry at the further corner of the room, in the dark shadow, stood a figure. It stood out quite boldly, emanating from itself a curious light. I had no time to think of phosphorus. It never occurred to me that any trick was being played upon me. I felt certain that I was looking at my ancestor, Barrington Cressley, who had come back to torture me in order to make me give up possession. The figure was that of a man six feet high, and broad in proportion. The face was bent forward and turned toward me, but in the uncertain light I could neither see the features nor the expression. The figure stood as still as a statue, and was evidently watching me. At the end of a moment, which seemed to me an eternity, it began to move, and, with a slow and silent step, approached me. I lay perfectly still, every muscle braced, and watched the figure between half-closed eyelids. It was now within a foot or two of me, and I could distinctly see the face. What was my horror to observe that it wore the features of my agent Murdock.

"'Murdock!' I cried, the word coming in a strangled sound from my throat. The next instant he had sprung upon me. I heard a noise of something rattling above, and saw a huge shadow descending upon me. I did not know what it was, and I felt certain that I was being murdered. The next moment all was lost in unconsciousness. Bell, how queer you look! Was it – was it Murdock? But it could not have been; he was very ill in bed at Liverpool. What in the name of goodness was the awful horror through which I had lived?"

"I can assure you on one point," I answered; "it was no ghost. And as to Murdock, it is more than likely that you did see him."

I then told the poor fellow what I had discovered with regard to the agent, and also my firm conviction that Wickham was at the bottom of it.

Cressley's astonishment was beyond bounds, and I saw at first that he scarcely believed me; but when I said that it was my intention to search the house, he accompanied me.

We both, followed by Mitchell, returned to the ill-fated room; but, though we examined the tapestry and panelling, we could not find the secret means by which the villain had obtained access to the chamber.

"The carriage which brought me here is still waiting just outside the lodge gates," I said. "What do you say to leaving this place at once, and returning, at least, as far as Carlton? We might spend the remainder of the night there, and take the very first train to Liverpool."

"Anything to get away," said Cressley. "I do not feel that I can ever come back to Cressley Hall again."

"You feel that now, but by-and-by your sensations will be different," I answered. As I spoke I called Mitchell to me. I desired him to go at once to the lodge gates and ask the driver of the wagonette to come down to the Hall.

This was done, and half an hour afterwards Cressley and I were on our way back to Carlton. Early the next morning we went to Liverpool. There we visited the police, and I asked to have a warrant taken out for the apprehension of Murdock.

The superintendent, on hearing my tale, suggested that we should go at once to Murdock's house in Melville Gardens. We did so, but it was empty, Murdock, his wife, and Wickham having thought it best to decamp. The superintendent insisted, however, on having the house searched, and in a dark closet at the top we came upon a most extraordinary contrivance. This was no less than an exact representation of the agent's head and neck in wax. In it was a wonderfully skilful imitation of a human larynx, which, by a cunning mechanism of clockwork, could be made exactly to simulate the breathing and low moaning of a human being. This the man had, of course, utilised with the connivance of his wife and Wickham in order to prove an alibi, and the deception was so complete that only my own irresistible curiosity could have enabled me to discover the secret. That night the police were fortunate enough to capture both Murdock and Wickham in a Liverpool slum. Seeing that all was up, the villains made complete confession, and the whole of the black plot was revealed. It appeared that two adventurers, the worst form of scoundrels, knew of Cressley's great discovery in Western Australia, and had made up their minds to forestall him in his claim. One of these men had come some months ago to England, and while in Liverpool had made the acquaintance of Murdock. The other man, Wickham, accompanied Cressley on the voyage in order to keep him in view, and worm as many secrets as possible from him. When Cressley spoke of his superstition with regard to the turret room, it immediately occurred to Wickham to utilise the room for his destruction. Murdock proved a ready tool in the hands of the rogues. They offered him an enormous bribe. And then the three between them evolved the intricate and subtle details of the crime. It was arranged that Murdock was to commit the ghastly deed, and for this purpose he was sent down quietly to Brent disguised as a journeyman the day before Cressley went to the Hall. The men had thought that Cressley would prove an easy prey, but they distrusted me from the first. Their relief was great when they discovered that I could not accompany Cressley to the Hall. And had he spent the first night there, the murder would have been committed; but his nervous terrors inducing him to spend the night at Brent foiled this attempt. Seeing that I was returning to Liverpool, the men now thought that they would use me for their own devices, and made up their minds to decoy me into Murdock's bedroom in order that I might see the wax figure, their object, of course, being that I should be forced to prove an alibi in case

Murdock was suspected of the crime. The telegram which reached me at Prince's Hotel on my return from London was sent by one of the ruffians, who was lying in ambush at Brent. When I left Murdock's house, the wife informed Wickham that she thought from my manner I suspected something. He had already taken steps to induce the cab-driver to take me in a wrong direction, in order that I should miss my train, and it was not until he visited the stables outside the Prince's Hotel that he found that I intended to go by road. He then played his last card, when he telegraphed to the inn at Carlton to stop the horses. By Murdock's means Wickham and his confederate had the run of the rooms at the Hall ever since the arrival of Wickham from Australia, and they had rigged up the top of the old bedstead in the way I have described. There was, needless to say, a secret passage at the back of the tapestry, which was so cunningly hidden in the panelling as to baffle all ordinary means of discovery.

Argent

Marshall J. Moore

"I NEED you to find a horse," she said.

I sat behind my battered old desk, doing my best to look professional – a difficult feat when you've just spilled a cup of coffee down your shirt, as I had the moment she entered my office unannounced.

"I'm sorry miss, uh…"

"Lenore." She brushed a strand of silver hair from her eyes. That was the first thing you noticed about her: her hair was unblemished silver, from the roots to where it fell about her shoulders. It didn't look dyed, or like the silver of age – she couldn't have been more than thirty.

"Lenore." I rolled the name around on my tongue. It was strangely old-fashioned; poetic, even. *The rare and radiant maiden whom the angels name Lenore…*

"A horse?" I repeated.

"Yes," she nodded sharply. Her whole demeanor was businesslike and efficient, qualities reflected in her attire: a light grey suit and dark grey tie. "Is that a problem?"

"Don't think so." I scratched my head. "I've never been hired for a horse before, that's all. Usually it's missing persons, lost objects, that kind of thing."

"I know." The second thing you noticed after her hair was her eyes. They were oddly colorless. "I read the sign on your door. 'Missing Persons Found, Misplaced Items Retrieved, Mysteries Uncovered.'"

"That's what it says," I confirmed, pulling out a legal pad. "Okay. The horse's name."

"Pegasos."

"Ha," I said. "After the Greek myth?"

"No." The thinnest of smiles alighted on her lips. "He's the original."

I set the legal pad down, looked at Lenore. She returned my gaze calmly, folding her hands in front of her. She wore cloth gloves, of the same silver color as her suit.

"You're like me," I said, suddenly wary.

"Like you?" She inclined her head slightly. "Yes. A demigod."

* * *

My name is Althea Stagg. Allie, to my friends.

I'm a private eye, like in every noir film you've ever seen, but without the alcoholism or misogyny. I have a different set of problems instead. Most of them are family.

The gods of ancient Greece are still around, no longer worshipped outright but still subtly influencing the course of mortal affairs. Occasionally they decide they like a mortal well enough to have a kid with them. In the old days those were heroes like Achilles, Heracles, Theseus.

Today there's me.

* * *

"I don't work for the Twelve," I told her.

"No?" Lenore raised one silver eyebrow. "Good thing I don't either, then. Believe me, Miss Stagg. I have no more desire to involve myself in family affairs than you do."

"Then why are you after Pegasos? Last I heard, he was grazing on whatever meadows Olympus sets aside for their flocks of flying horses."

"Last you heard," Lenore agreed. She stood, paced to the window that serves as my office's sole source of natural lighting. Through it you can just make out the spire of the Washington Monument. "I try not to interfere in Olympian politics, but I keep my ear to the ground. Pegasos disappeared on one of his daily flights about Olympus, two days ago. So far Uncle Zeus hasn't noticed, but when he does…"

Her colorless eyes flicked up to the clear sky above. "Thunderbolts and lightning."

"Very very frightening," I agreed. "So what's your angle?"

"Angle?"

"Come on," I snorted. "I doubt you're looking to restore the King of Gods' favorite steed to him out of simple altruism."

"Mm." She folded her arms, tapped a finger against her bicep. "No. You're smart. That's good."

"What, then?" I asked. "Is it Zeus's favor you're after?"

"Not precisely." Lenore glanced back out the window. "I own a number of businesses on the mortal plane. And when the Thunderer gets upset, he tends to act…rashly."

"So I've heard." I threw a meaningful glance at the battered paperback copy of Edith Hamiliton's *Mythology* resting on my desk. "You're looking to minimize fallout."

"Exactly. So I sought out someone with a reputation for discretion."

"Me."

"You," she confirmed. "Like me, you keep your head low when it comes to our divine relations. And I hear you have a Gift uniquely suited to your chosen field."

* * *

Every demigod has a Gift, a manifestation of the divine blood in our veins. A daughter of Ares might be preternaturally skilled in all forms of combat, for example, or be immune to bullets. Poseidon's kids are all basically Aquaman.

Me? I find things.

* * *

"So?" Lenore pressed. "Will you take the job?"

"I'll need to know more," I said. "Winged horses don't just disappear. If Pegasos is missing, who has reason to steal him?"

"I don't know. None of the other gods; they don't need to ride unless they feel like it." A frown creased her brow. "One of us, maybe."

"Another demigod?"

"Yes." Lenore drummed her gloved fingers against her arm. "Pegasos was the steed of Bellerophon, who rode him to slay the Chimera. Maybe one of our cousins hopes to win fame and glory astride a legendary steed."

"Maybe." I looked back down at *Mythology*. "But I know how that one ends. After he kills the monster Bellerophon gets a little too big for his sandals. He decides 'Hey, I've got a winged horse; why don't I fly up to Mount Olympus and pay the gods a visit?' So he hops on Pegasos and takes off."

I got out of my chair and sat on my desk, facing Lenore. "Not sure if you've ever shown up to Olympus unannounced, but it's an invite-only kind of club. Zeus sees Bellerophon taxiing for a landing and decides to teach him a lesson about hubris. The permanent kind."

"He killed him."

"Bingo. Grandfather sends a gadfly to sting Pegasos on the ass. The horse freaks out and throws his rider, and Bellerophon takes the most direct route down to Earth."

"That's a long way to fall," Lenore said.

"Like they say," I said, "pride goeth. If whoever took Pegasos is one of us, it's in everyone's best interest that the horse goes back where he belongs as quickly as possible."

"Agreed."

I nodded. "All right. I'll take the job."

* * *

My services don't come cheap, but Lenore didn't even blink when I told her my rates. Instead she reached into her purse – also silver – and pulled out a thick stack of hundred dollar bills. She counted out enough to cover my advance and set them on my desk.

"Is there anything else?" she asked.

"Yeah," I said. "I'll need something to help track Pegasos."

My Gift lets me track down almost anyone or anything, but first I need to attune myself to something strongly associated with them – a child's favorite toy, for example, or a chef's floppy hat. The stronger the connection between object and bearer, the better.

"A bridle, maybe," I continued. "A saddle would work too, I suppose, but it'd be harder for me to carry…"

"I can do better than either," Lenore said. She reached a gloved hand into her purse again.

It was a feather like an eagle's; as long as my forearm, and not a single quill out of place. It caught the light and glittered, perfectly white.

"Will this do?"

"Yeah," I nodded, breath catching in my throat. "Yeah, that'll work."

* * *

We parted ways outside my office. I stood in the parking lot and held the feather in both hands, focusing on it, trying to imagine the winged horse it belonged to.

Almost instantly, there was a surge down my arms and up my spine, like a mild electric shock. I almost jumped. I had seldom attuned myself so quickly to an object before. Maybe it was because the feather had such a strong connection to Pegasos.

There was a faint pressure against my temples, a gentle tug pulling me to my left. Somewhere that way, however distant, was the missing winged horse.

Time to get to work.

* * *

The feather took me about two hours' drive west, past the Virginia border and out of the urban sprawl surrounding DC. My Harley revved comfortably under me as I passed exit sign after exit sign. With each mile, the faint tug the feather exerted on my mind grew stronger, like a rope having the slack steadily pulled from it.

As the exit signs counted down, the urban sprawl surrounding the greater DC metropolitan area lessened, replaced by the less crowded and more commercial suburban sprawl of the surrounding towns and cities. After the first hour even those gave way to woods and fields as I turned onto small, worn-down country highways with rusting mile markers and abundant potholes.

* * *

The feather's pull was getting stronger. At one point I nearly swerved into the oncoming lane as it pulled me sharply towards an exit ramp. I rode out the sudden turn, keeping my center of gravity low in the bike and not fighting the pull of the g-forces. A semi blared its deafening horn at me as I skidded past. I gritted my teeth and pulled back onto the right side of the road, heart thudding at the near miss.

I'd used my Gift countless times. I'd tracked down lost objects, people, even animals. But the pull had never been so strong that I couldn't control it.

Then again, I'd never tracked down a mythical horse before, either.

* * *

I turned off the highway somewhere close to the West Virginia border. I spent maybe half an hour zig-zagging through backwoods roads so neglected that they were practically overgrown with trees, branches hanging low over the cracked asphalt. I cruised so slowly that I could hear crickets chirping and birdsong, sounds that sent a chill down my spine.

Geographically speaking, most of America is rural. The big cities and their outgrowths take up only a fraction of our square mileage, and the scattered towns and hamlets not a great deal more. This is, in many ways, still a wild country.

My dad was a park ranger, and he taught me to love and respect the wilderness. As a kid I lived for our father-daughter hiking trips, where we would go deep into a national park or protected forest with only what we could carry on our backs. We would set up camp in a copse of trees, or by a river, or on top of a ridge. Dad always had his binoculars with him, could tell me the name of each birdsong we heard. Falling asleep by that campfire, my head against his leg, listening to the quiet night sounds of the wind blowing and insects singing, is the happiest I can remember being.

As an adult, my feelings on the less-trodden paths of America are more nuanced. I still love the outdoors, still feel at peace there, but no longer safe. My mother, worshipped by the Greeks as Artemis, is a goddess of the hunt. When I was still a teenager she taught me what that meant.

I learned from her thrill of the chase, the simple joy in running after prey as it flees from you. The feel of the aching in your legs and side as you run with the wind to the limits of your endurance, an ache deeper and more pleasurable than sex. The violent delights of the hunt's end, when your prey stumbles in their final flight, too exhausted to give fight. The ecstasy of tearing into flesh with claws and teeth to taste warm meat and red, red blood.

I still love the wild places, the forests and mountains and deserts of this rugged untamed country. But now that love is blended with fear. Not fear of the wilds themselves, but of what they awaken inside of me: a beast, hungering for release.

I shuddered and gripped the handles of my bike tighter, focusing all my thoughts upon the feather as it drew me towards my missing prey.

* * *

My search ended by a river.

It was wide but shallow, the sort that just barely clears the arbitrary delineation between river and creek. The feather was practically vibrating inside my jacket, thrumming with a rhythm distinct from the quiet idling of my motorcycle.

Beside the river was a long, dilapidated brick building. A rusted beam stuck out from it over the river. I guessed it was an old mill. Civil War old, maybe.

There was no parking lot, so I pulled off the side of the road and stashed my bike behind a thick oak that looked like it had been felled by lightning. I didn't know who or what might be waiting for me, but it wouldn't do to have my tires slashed if I needed to make a hasty exit.

"Alright," I muttered. "Let's see where you are, horsey."

I pulled the feather from my jacket and held it out with both hands like a dowsing rod.

It sprung straight towards the mill, quivering in the still afternoon light.

* * *

I approached cautiously, sticking to the trees and keeping well out of sight. The mill had only a few windows, mostly on the upper level, but in my line of work it pays to be cautious. I circled the place twice before I was satisfied that it was safe to walk in the open.

I jogged from the trees to the only entrance I could see, an enormous pair of wooden doors that took up almost the entirety of one wall. Their handles were heavy iron, plainly as old as the building itself, but the stainless steel chain that tied them together with a padlock was definitely new.

"Bingo," I muttered. This dilapidated old mill wasn't so abandoned after all. I tugged on the padlock, but it held fast, the chains rattling in protest.

The Gifts granted by divine parentage are myriad, from inhuman beauty to visions of the future to near-total invincibility. Unfortunately, super-strength isn't one of mine.

Fortunately, I come prepared. I reached into one of my jacket pockets, pulled out a torsion wrench and a pick, and got to work.

A few patient minutes later the padlock fell open. I pulled the chain free and let it fall to the ground, then wrenched on the heavy oak door. The ancient rusted hinges screamed in protest as I threw the mill doors open.

Light fell into the dark interior of the mill, illuminating a thousand motes of dust. As I did so, a wave of smell assaulted my nose so strongly that it was almost a physical blow. I gagged, coughing and covering my mouth with my shirt.

The place *stank*. It was stale and musty, heavy with an animal stench like all the worst smells of a zoo and a boarding kennel had gathered themselves in one place. It stank of piss and feces and musk.

The sounds hit me right after the stench, a wave of screeching and cawing and whining. They echoed terribly in the stifling darkness of the mill, like I had just stepped into an Animal Planet documentary set in Hell.

My eyes adjusted to the dim light, confirming what my nose and ears had already told me: the mill was packed with animals.

I say 'packed', and I mean it literally. Lining the walls to either side down the entire length of the mill were cages. Some were made of close-set steel wires like birdcages. Others had thick, industrial-grade prison bars. A few were even made of glass, though I had little doubt they were at least as sturdy as the metal ones.

And inside every cage, animals.

Every cage, from one wall to the next, held a prisoner. Nearest me, in one of the largest cages, sat an adult Siberian tiger. Her fur looked matted, and she had a chunk missing from one ear. She surveyed me impassively through amber eyes.

I took a step forward, wanting to help her somehow. She narrowed her eyes and hissed, the sound exactly like my cat Jasper's, only magnified a hundredfold. I stepped back.

The next cage, scarcely bigger than a dog's kennel, held a weird little furry creature that looked like a cross between a goat and a deer. I half remembered enough of a documentary about Asian wildlife to identify it as a serow. As I passed, it turned its head to look at me with one eye. The other eye was milky white, blind.

I walked down the mill, observing the horror at either hand. Each cage was the same: a rare animal of some kind, clearly malnourished and mistreated. The place was a nightmare, a prison-menagerie of barbarism.

I had read about places like this, but had never seen one before. It was a storehouse for the exotic animal trade, where endangered wildlife was held before being auctioned off to the denizens of the criminal underworld wealthy enough and depraved enough to exploit such rare creatures.

My heart pounded in my chest, and I pulled out the feather once again. It pointed straight for the back of the mill, still hidden in shadow.

Pegasos was here. Whoever ran this operation was in the market for exotic animals, and they didn't get much rarer than winged horses.

A captive pair of golden monkeys no bigger than Jasper watched me as I walked, their teeth bared threateningly. One cage contained an enormous tortoise that blinked slowly at me as I passed, its old eyes unreadable. A weird, humanlike laughter startled me so badly that I jumped, looking up only in time to see a crested vulture glaring down at me.

Inside one of the little glass cages was an enigma: a trio of little scaly balls, like the dragon's eggs on that HBO show. Only when one of them stirred fitfully did I realize that it was a family of pangolins, their little bodies curled tightly as they slept.

The most sickening was towards the end: not a cage, but an old-fashioned steamer trunk, piled high with elephant tusks.

Finally I reached the end of the mill. A dark recess was set into the wall, one side encased in glass. I could see a dark equine shape within.

Improbably, there was a light switch on the side of the wall. I flicked it on, and a set of fluorescent lights flickered to life within the recess.

Inches away, separated from me only by a thick layer of glass, stood the horse.

He was a big stallion, sixteen hands high. His coat was glossy white beneath the lights, his eyes a deep, dark black. His thick mane looked matted, hanging partway over his eyes. And sprouting from his shoulders: a pair of wings.

Not that I could see much of them. They were bound by a thick iron chain, a single length of black links that encircled his middle, binding his wings to his sides, and descended to his hooves, tying them together so that he could not run.

"Pegasos," I breathed.

He whinnied and shied away when the light came on, illuminating the cramped cell he had been locked in, eyes widening so that I could see the whites.

"Shh," I said, trying to recall equestrian lessons from half a life ago. "Shh, shh. It's alright. See?" I held up the feather. "I'm a friend."

He stilled, trotted a step closer. I slid the glass door to his enclosure open – it had not been locked.

"Come on," I muttered, examining his chains, looking for a lock I could pick. None revealed itself to me.

* * *

"Well done," came a voice from behind me.

I whirled around, heart leaping into my throat. Beside me Pegasos let out a fearful whinny, his chains rattling as he tried to shy away.

She still wore all grey, but had swapped the suit and tie for biker gear: a sleek, silvery leather jacket and matching pants. The gloves remained.

"Lenore?" The hair on the nape of my neck stood on end. Something about this wasn't right. "You...followed me?"

"No need," she smirked. "I was already here."

The pieces fell together. "This place is your outfit."

"Outfit?" She raised one perfect brow, amused.

"This operation. These poor animals."

"Correct." If she held any remorse for what she had done to the helpless creatures, it didn't show. "One of several profitable ventures I own."

"Zeus's beard," I swore. "You're a freaking *crime lord*."

"Don't be melodramatic. I'm a businesswoman."

"This isn't business." I put a hand on Pegasos' neck. He stamped the ground nervously, but didn't shy from my touch. "This is cruelty."

"I like having a diverse portfolio."

"Okay," I said, moving so that I was fully between her and the winged horse. She was smaller than me, shorter. I could probably take her in a fight, but she had gotten the drop on me. Besides, anyone with divine blood was more than they appeared. "You lured me here. Now what?"

"Now?" She reached into her jacket with one gloved hand. I tensed, ready to leap aside.

She laughed. "*So* melodramatic."

It wasn't a gun she pulled from her jacket, but an envelope. "Your payment."

"I don't understand."

"This was an...audition, of sorts." She opened the envelope, counting out the rubber band stack of Ben Franklins one at a time. "I'd heard about your Gift. I wanted to put it – and you – to the test. You passed."

"Lucky me."

"Quite." She put the bills back into the envelope. "Now that I know what you can do, I've another job for you. Considerable payoff. One that makes this" – she waved the envelope – "look paltry."

"Thanks," I said, "but I'll pass."

She froze, suddenly snake-still. "You haven't even heard my offer."

"Keep your blood money." Behind me Pegasos whinnied softly. "This is barbaric."

Her face was a rigid mask. She began to walk towards us, boots echoing on the concrete floor. Pegasos snorted and shied away.

"You won't be persuaded?" she asked. She removed her gloves as she walked, letting them drop to the floor. Her nails were the same silver as her hair.

"Afraid not," I said, squaring myself, ready to fight.

"Pity." She stood before me, looking up at me with her strangely colorless eyes. "I had such hopes for you."

She reached up and gently stroked my cheek with one hand.

Not colorless, I realized, too late. *Silver.*

A searing numbness erupted across my cheek, spreading from where her fingers brushed my skin to radiate out across my face. I gasped, trying to scream, but that side of my mouth was stuck still, frozen.

I stumbled back, sprawling to the floor beside Pegasos's chain, narrowly missing the big horse's hooves.

I caught a glimpse of my reflection in the glass wall of the enclosure. The side of my face she had touched – from left cheek to jaw – had turned shiny, metallic.

"Midas had the golden touch," she said, a cold smile on her lips. "Mine's silver."

I watched with horrified fascination as the silver retreated from my face, taking the numbness with it as my face turned back to flesh.

"Last chance to rethink my offer," Lenore said, standing over me. Pegasos was backed as far into the corner of the cell as he could go, his dark eyes wide and teeth exposed.

"Go to hell," I told her.

"I'd rather not," she said. "My dad works there."

I scrambled back on hands and feet, until one hand fell across one of the heavy iron links of Pegasos's chain.

An idea began to form.

Then she fell upon me, her elegant face twisting into a mask of gleeful fury as she reached for me with outstretched hands.

I waited until the last possible moment, then caught her by the wrists. She hissed, trying to get her hands around my throat, but I was stronger than her. I forced her hands away from me and onto the chain that bound Pegasos.

A glimmering light spread along the chain as it transformed from rough iron to purest silver. Lenore spat and writhed, trying to free herself from my grip, but I held her fast, forcing her to keep touching the chain.

Silver is a rare and valuable metal. It's useful, too; the first mirrors were backed with silver, and its mystical properties are myriad. But as metals go, it's pretty weak.

Pegasos whinnied and stamped, then reared up on his hind legs. The chain that bound him from hoof to wing shattered like a necklace being pulled apart.

I rolled to avoid his stomping hooves, pinning Lenore beneath me. She got one hand free of my grip and wrapped it around my throat.

Numbness spread across my neck. I tried to draw breath but couldn't.

Lenore smiled a wicked, venomous smile.

A shadow fell over us both as Pegasos reared to his full height, wings outstretched in the tiny cell. His hooves came down like Zeus's lightning, and we both rolled away to avoid being trampled.

Pegasos burst from his cell, down the hall of cages. He halted after a few paces, turned his head to me, and snorted.

I was on my feet before Lenore could recover. I sprinted out of the cell and vaulted onto the winged horse's back. He took off at a brisk trot, heading for the end of the corridor and the open bay doors. He broke into a gallop, as around us came a cacophony of animal sounds: screeching monkeys, high, warbling bird calls, and the deep-throated tiger's roar. The whole menagerie was cheering our escape.

From behind us I dimly heard Lenore shouting for us to stop, but the beating of hooves and the raucous noise of her captives drowned her out.

We reached the loading bay doors and took off into the open sky. Pegasos's wings beat steadily up and down, the mill falling away beneath us as we climbed into the sky.

The wind whipped my hair from my face and tore tears from my eyes, but I didn't care. I was laughing, giddy with the feeling of escape and the joy of flight, the exhilaration of riding bareback on a horse that galloped through the sky.

* * *

We landed in a field, miles away. The grass was tall and golden, its stalks flattened against the ground as Pegasos beat his wings for a landing. He touched down surprisingly gently, cantering for a few yards with wings still outstretched. At last he came to a stop, folding his broad white wings against his back. He bent his head to the grass and began to graze.

I clambered off, landing unsteadily on my feet. It had been a long time since I'd ridden a horse, let alone bareback. Let alone one that could *fly*.

I stroked his flank, admiring his glossy coat. He was pure white – not silver or grey, but white like the fluffy clouds we had soared through moments before. I ran my hand along his mane, feeling the thick bristles between my fingers.

Pegasos raised his head, nuzzled against me in a horsey kiss. I whispered the same sweet nothings in his ear that I did to Jasper.

"Who's a good boy? You are. Yes, you. Yes you are."

He snorted and whinnied, nuzzling against me so hard he nearly bowled me over. I laughed and scratched his chin.

"We gotta get you home, boy."

As I said it, I felt a feeling of dread. It would not take Pegasos long to fly to Olympus. The gods' mountain isn't a physical place, exactly. It exists alongside this world, accessible through certain portals or rituals. I had a suspicion that Pegasos could fly between Earth and Olympus as it suited him.

I was glad I had freed him from captivity, and from whatever fate Lenore had in mind for him. But I had no desire to face a family gathering anytime soon.

As if he could read my thoughts, Pegasus snorted and stamped his hooves. He cantered in a circle around me, gave me one last nuzzle. Then he turned and took off at a brisk trot.

"Hey!" I called to him. "Where you going?"

He turned his head and whinnied at me, a long and happy laughing sound I took to mean as "home."

"You know how to get there?" I asked, grinning.

In answer he took off, climbing out of the field and into the sky. I watched him rise, quickly fading to a distant white speck, until he disappeared behind a cloud and was lost from view.

"Great," I said. I looked around at the empty field. The nearest road could be miles away. "Now how am *I* getting home?"

Nobody Special

Pat Morris

What kind of asshole calls a business at nine on the dot on Monday morning?

Two seconds after voicemail kicked in the phone rang again, and this kept up while I struggled out of snow-covered beret, scarf, gloves, coat, and boots, then passive-aggressively made coffee, drank coffee, straightened out my desk, scanned the news wires and police reports, and skimmed the billion or so emails that had piled up over the weekend.

Finally I gave in. "Queen City Progressive, Honor Mack speaking."

"Tessa Goodman never did drugs. They're lying." *Click.*

Okie doke. Usually the tinfoil-hat contingent calls later on full-moon days, but the name rang a bell so I went back to the weekend update from the Cincinnati Police Division, and there she was.

Louie Nadar, a homeless Navy vet who lived under the Goodman Bridge, had stepped out early Saturday morning to retrieve a scarf poking out from a snow bank and unearthed the frozen corpse of a woman now identified as Tessa Goodman, 64, of the Mount Auburn section of the city.

A preliminary exam had uncovered a shitload – my term, not the police's – of opiates keeping Tessa's blood company with a massive amount of alcohol, and her demise was presumed, but not yet declared, death by 'misadventure'.

So why was some anonymous person insisting she didn't use drugs? And what did they want me to do about it?

Nothing? Maybe. I went through the motions for the rest of the day, but by five o'clock leaving time, Tessa had become an itch, and I was gonna scratch it.

* * *

"She was one of ours," Josie told me later that night as we stretched out on opposite futons, our feet planted on the coffee table in silent rebellion against Mama Martini, glasses of house red in our hands and Southside Johnny and the Jukes calling up home from Josie's 'vintage' CD player.

"Well, sort of one of ours," she added. Josie was a social worker at Hope House, a residence for women who were a tad too fond of psychoactive substances.

Tessa's choice was alcohol, cheap vodka when she was buying but any port in a storm. She was a familiar fixture downtown, recognizable by her trademark orange felt scarf and huge, misshapen attempt at a crocheted beret in Rasta colors, worn year round. Her panhandling MO was to spout "Jesus loves you" and other, at times indecipherable, religious ramblings while holding out a plastic Dunkin' Donuts cup for 'donations'. When the jar was full enough she'd head to Murphy's, the lone downtown dive bar that so far had resisted gentrification, and linger until the doors locked behind her. Then she would stand in the middle of the deserted street waving her arms to flag down a ride. All the cops and cabbies knew her, and most would give her a lift to her Mount Auburn rooming house to save her hopping in with a stranger.

Sometimes, though, they would drop her off at Hope House, Josie said, even though 3 a.m. drop-offs were not how admissions worked. Tessa would sleep it off on a couch in the foyer, grab some coffee, and attempt to wash up before refusing admission and heading back out. It was a pattern that drove Eve Wallingford, director of Hope House and Josie's boss, up the wall. Hope House didn't get money for people who weren't admitted. You couldn't force anyone to be admitted. The night clerk could turn Tessa away, but doing that in the wee hours to a clearly incapacitated woman who could then go out and get hurt could open up a whole can of lawsuit worms. Tessa played the game. Eve seethed. Josie observed.

On Friday, though, Tessa had gone off-script. As Josie had pulled in at 4:20 p.m. to work a night shift, she'd seen Tessa leaving the director's office, mumbling something Josie couldn't hear. Eve had kept her door closed, and Josie assumed Tessa had started her bender earlier than usual, been dumped off while Eve was still in the building, and promptly been sent packing, since she was still able to walk.

According to tonight's TV news, Tessa'd hit Murphy's a little before five and left, at the request of the management, around 2:30 a.m. An eyewitness reported seeing her get into a light tan or white van, and anyone with knowledge of that please call the number at the bottom of your screen, but it had been snowing heavily and patrons exiting Murphy's at that hour were not at their peak powers of observation.

"I guess this time she got into the wrong car," Josie said. We were quiet for a second, and I knew we were both remembering our own feel-good days. A little zig here, a little karmic zag there, and Tessa's fate could have been ours. We refilled our glasses anyway.

Tuesday morning I called the CPD for an update.

Within an hour, Greg Zimmer made a rare appearance at our storefront office.

* * *

When people ask "Why?" they don't really want to know why. Why didn't you use a condom? Look before you crossed? Go before you left the house?

The only acceptable answer is "because I'm not as smart as you."

So when Greg asked me why I hadn't checked with him before inquiring about Tessa Goodman, I just mumbled into my chipped Christmas mug.

Greg Zimmer, owner and publisher of the site, is the guy who writes the checks to me, his sole employee. Aided by an army of 'citizen journalists' – pretty much anybody with a smartphone – I put out a weekly online publication that touts itself as a news source but is fluffier than a basket of Easter chicks.

Pathetic job, but I was lucky to have it. My breakdown in New Jersey put the final nail in the moldering coffin of my should-have-could-have-been-brilliant career, and my break-up with the husband who'd seduced me with his poetry and then knocked out a few of my teeth had been long overdue. So I'd packed my MacBook, some clean underwear, and a stack of Southside Johnny CDs into my ten-year-old Cobalt and headed off to Cincinnati, Ohio, where Josie Martini, my best friend since middle school, was waiting with open arms, a spare futon, and a bottomless supply of wine-in-a-box. A week later I was working for Greg.

"Some drunk fell down and froze to death. Not exactly 'man bites dog'."

Did I mention that Greg's heart is as huge as his intellect? While not exactly a trust fund baby, Greg is the only child of a heart surgeon and a history professor, the kind of guy who thinks every dad has a study and every family eats leg of lamb in the middle of the week. He'd quashed all of my suggestions for features: Good people who live in bad neighborhoods ("Why don't they just move?"). Married white suburban men seeking out teenage crack whores ("I'm a post-feminist. They can do what they like with their bodies."). How local contractors and homeowners profit from undocumented workers ("It's called being cost-effective."). Need I go on?

"From what I understand, Greg, she was something of a local celebrity back in the day. Wouldn't people want to know how she wound up the way she did?"

I sure do.

* * *

So far I'd learned Tessa had been born Theresa Marie Guttmann in Newport, Kentucky, in 1952, when that town was the vice hub where God-fearing Cincinnatians like former mayor Jerry Springer got their jollies. To the horror of her pious Catholic parents, Edna and the late Heinrich Guttmann, Tessa had jumped into the baby-boomer rebellion full force in the late '60s, quitting her parochial high school the day after her sixteenth birthday and crashing in what was then the hippie enclave of Mount Adams. Not long after, she'd emerged as Tessa Goodman, lead singer of the Psycharmonics. Her clear soprano and Nordic beauty had served her well, and the band was a mainstay of the local music scene well into the Carter administration. 'Townland', words by Yeats and original music by Psycharmonics bassist Andy Nieman, had reached the Top 20 on the Chicago charts, but the band failed to attract national attention, and it quietly faded away as guitarists, keyboardist, and drummer moved on to jobs with benefits, legal marriages, and ranch houses in the outer suburbs.

Tessa, however, kept partying like it was 1975 right up until she fell into a pile of snow and never got up.

Despite its size and cosmopolitan veneer, Cincinnati is in many ways a small town. I'd called the CPD around ten. In under half an hour, a member of the Redden Foundation, which runs Hope House, had found Greg and ripped him a new one. Tessa had never been admitted, but publicity would make it look like Hope House had failed her. The agency was already enduring a misguided witch hunt: the county and the feds were investigating supposedly disappearing funds. It was surely a simple bookkeeping mistake that would soon be cleared up, but any negative publicity now could cause unnecessary complications. Did the Progressive want to be responsible for so many women not getting help because of a misconception?

No, it didn't, said Greg, so leave it alone. I was still mulling over my reply when he stepped into the elevator.

Just as well. But I was still scratching.

* * *

Edna Guttmann's tidy white Cape Cod sat in a small 'mid-century' development now ringed by strip malls and discount liquor stores. Snow covered the lawn and drifted up against a knee-high white picket fence. A concrete pathway and three concrete steps led me to a dark green door that sported a sign featuring the Blessed Virgin: 'This is a Catholic household. Propaganda about other religions is not welcome.' The door-knocker was an eagle with an American flag in its beak.

A short woman with bright red lipstick on her teeth, dyed black hair, and a cigarette dangling from her lips answered my knock and ushered me into a living room I recognized: JFK, the Sacred Heart, and the pope adorning the walls; brown tweed sofa draped with an acrylic granny-square afghan; and a tray with coffee fixings, cups with saucers, and a milk-glass plate of sugar cookies on the 'colonial' coffee table.

I offered my condolences and asked what Tessa had been like as a child.

"She thought she was so smart." Edna's eyes lit up and her mouth twisted into an odd combination of smile and smirk.

OOOOK. I pretended to take notes as Tessa's mother trashed everything about her deceased daughter from her socks never staying up in kindergarten to her 'gimme, gimme, gimme' attitude toward Christmas presents in grammar school to that time the week after her fifteenth birthday when she 'went and got herself raped.' Tessa'd been sent to work as a maid at the home of a distant relative until the baby was safely handed over to an adoption agency. Tessa had been forbidden to ever mention 'that thing' to anyone, but she went and blabbed to a school counselor, who had then butted in and tried to get her, Edna Guttmann, a perfect Catholic, into counseling with Tessa. The nerve of some people.

Tessa had been nastier than ever after that, and Edna had been happy to see her go. Over the years Tessa had come by the house now and again – usually filthy and four sheets to the wind – but Edna always refused to answer the door.

No, she wouldn't be taking charge of Tessa's body for burial. She'd washed her hands of that little tramp a long time ago.

After two hours with Edna, I had a pretty good idea what had turned Tessa into a hopeless drunk who'd lain down and died in the snow. But it wasn't exactly news that was fit to print.

Maybe I'd just focus on Tessa's last night. See what the crowd at Murphy's could tell me.

* * *

Three guys in dirty parkas huddled by the door, passing around a cigarette like it was a joint. I slipped past them into Murphy's, almost blinded by the slide from late morning sunshine into what seemed like total darkness. When my eyes adjusted I saw that every stool at the bar, which lined the right wall of the small room under a string of partially working bubble lights, was occupied by someone quietly staring into a beer mug or highball glass. To my right were a few tottering tables covered in cracked pink Formica, all but one occupied. When in Rome and all that, so taking one for the team I bellied up to the bar, slapped down a twenty, and ordered a Miller Light. Breakfast of champions.

The bartender, a scrawny woman with straw-colored hair, a faded tattoo on her neck, and a Megadeath T-shirt, spotted me for a newbie and gave me a greasy glass to go with the bottle. I left the glass and the change on the bar, took a spot at the empty table, pulled out my tablet, and pretended to be studying something. After twenty minutes or so I realized eavesdropping on this crowd was not going to get me the 411 about Tessa, so when a guy left his seat at the bar I pounced. Pulled out another twenty – shit, this was getting expensive – and decided to come clean with the bartender, who turned out to be named Denise.

"That cunt? Look," said Denise as she gave the bar a lackluster swipe with a greasy rag, "I know it doesn't sound very nice, but that bitch was asking to die." She pointed to a table in the back corner, where two gray-haired women in Christmas sweaters were enjoying a pitcher of what looked like orange juice so was probably screwdrivers.

Minnie and Reba, Denise told me, lived in the same rooming house as Tessa. Maybe they knew more about her than Denise, who mostly just knew that Tessa was a pain in the ass who wasn't above disappearing into the john with a random strange guy in return for a drink. Amazing she'd lived as long as she had, between the booze, probably a dozen STDs, and her habit of getting into strange cars. Denise had come back to Murphy's around two on Friday morning to help her husband close up, and Tessa had been paying for her own drinks and even bought a round for the bar before stumbling out into the snow with a bundle of the cash she'd been flaunting, waving her arms at the few passing cars. Denise had already told the cops she'd seen a light-colored van roll to a stop and Tessa stagger into it.

"Guess her ride rolled her."

I slapped down another twenty, which was twenty more than I could afford, and moseyed on over to the Christmas-sweater ladies.

Two pitchers later I'd learned that the 'random strangers' whom Tessa serviced for drinks had included Denise's husband, Jimmy Earl, who managed Murphy's and tended bar at night. Denise, my informants said, had threatened to punch Tessa's lights out if she ever came near Jimmy again. Which she apparently hadn't, far as they knew.

When Minnie had moved into the Mount Auburn place fifteen years earlier, Tessa was already ensconced; she'd been there since the early '80s, when Mount Adams gentrified and its hippies had to morph into Yuppies or find other digs. As far as Minnie and Reba knew, she'd never had any visitors, male or female. They'd never seen her cook in the communal kitchen and had no idea what, or if, she ate.

Neither had ever seen her sober. Mostly she stayed in her room, either drinking or sleeping it off, Minnie figured, although occasionally religious fervor would overtake her and she would totter downstairs to inform the other tenants that Jesus loved them.

The last time she'd seen her, Reba said, Tessa had been precariously perched on a couch in the parlor, where Minnie, Reba, and their friend Darla were trying to watch *Dancing with the Stars*.

"She kept saying she was going to be getting money soon, a lot of it, and was trying to decide what to do with it. Buy an Amish farm or something crazy like that. She never made no sense so nobody paid her no mind."

I tottered out of Murphy's unsteady on my own feet, and it wasn't even noon. My visit to Tessa's abode would have to wait. I spared myself a queasy ten-block totter, hailed a cab, and barely managed to remove my wet winter gear before collapsing on my futon/bed. When I awoke it was dark out.

I made coffee, gobbled some aspirin, flopped back down, grabbed the remote, went to the DVR, and tuned into *Simply Magnifico*, my secretly favorite TV show.

Mealtimes were mostly grim occasions at the McNamara house. Our mother believed in serving the cheapest possible crap – why waste good money when the kids have to eat whatever you give them? – and rigid order, so the menu was as predictable as it was unappetizing, from liver and creamed succotash Mondays to hot dog and canned spaghetti Saturdays, canned fruit suspended in Day-Glo gelatin the reward for finishing all. We kids were required to clean our plates under a constant barrage of Dad's laments and zingers; we all tried like hell to stay under the radar.

So the first time I ate at Josie's house was a revelation. Mama and Papa Martini, Josie, and her four impossibly handsome brothers would chat amiably as they passed around huge platters of food that seemed wildly exotic to me: baked ziti, broccolini, steak pizzaola, fresh figs. I joined as often as I could during the high school years, and after graduation I missed it.

Simply Magnifico somewhat filled the void. In black and white and airing on PBS – no such thing as the Food Network then – Maria Cavale, a plump Italian American straight out of Central Casting, chatted nonstop while demonstrating what to do with anchovies, cardoons, and ricotta salata before serving a feast to her gorgeous and congenial children, in-laws, siblings, friends, neighbors, nieces, nephews, and grandchildren. For years I'd tried to emulate her, working my way from antipasti through zabaglione before I realized I didn't like cooking; I just wanted to be at Maria's table. After all, you never see a show where they teach you a great meal to eat by yourself in front of the tube.

I was watching *la familia* Cavale dig into a Sunday brunch of artichoke and pancetta frittata, Prosecco mimosas and macerated strawberries when Josie arrived, shivering from snow that had turned into an icy rain. With a nod to Maria I nuked two mugs of house red, sliced up some salami and provolone, and set out a tray.

"Channel 5 found out that Tessa went to the bar straight from Hope House, and they're wondering why we just let her loose," she said. "You should see the comments. Eve's got her knickers twisted into her tightest knot yet." Josie put her feet up and massaged her frozen toes.

"She says Tessa had not asked for treatment and was not intoxicated when she left."

"But what was she doing there?"

"Eve won't say. She's already in a snit because we're being audited. She says there's nothing to find, but she's offended at the inference, plus it's intrusive and draining. Hope House looking bad would just add insult to injury. Eve is not happy. And if Eve ain't happy, ain't nobody happy."

Eve Wallingford had been born Evvie Sue Stanley not far from what is now Dollywood. At age ten a teacher had taken her to see a real ballet, and from then on Evvie Sue was determined to get into the 'world of culture'. She studied English literature at a community college, moved to Cincinnati, got a job as a receptionist at the Redden Foundation and clawed her way up to her current directorship. Along the way she'd married Fred Wallingford, who had used the 1990s boom times to morph his small construction company into a prosperous development firm. She'd given birth to 'Princess Priscilla', now a sixteen-year-old sophomore at a private Christian school. Eve was determined that Priscilla become a denizen of Cincinnati's 'high society', and directing Hope House, which allowed Eve to hobnob with donors and the city's financial and social elite, was her ticket. She'd already put down a deposit for a May 'coming out' dinner dance at Union Station.

I'd met Eve once, briefly, while covering a benefit at the Museum of Contemporary Art. Amid a sea of solid black, Eve stood out in a peacock green silk suit, with matching pumps and clutch. Her jewelry was gold with green stones – I couldn't tell real from paste if my life depended on it – and apparently no one had told her that you don't wear the necklace and the earrings and the bracelet and the broach and the ring all at the same time.

"Remember that mother in Texas who killed somebody so her daughter could be a cheerleader?" Josie had asked. "That lady has nothing on Eve. She's determined that Priscilla is going to be the queen of Cincinnati society, and marry into a P&G or Great American family, and live in Indian Hill."

A sip of hot wine brought me back to the present. Bad PR would not fit into the plans of the former Evvie Sue Stanley.

"Best not to call for an interview, then?"

Josie laughed. "She already sent out an email saying any staff member who talks to the media will be fired on the spot."

Wondering whom I could talk to about Josie's last trip out of Hope House and into a bar, I let Southside Johnny sing me to sleep.

* * *

Like pretty much everything in Mount Auburn, Tessa's rooming house had seen better days a century ago, which was probably the last time anyone had painted the crumbling stairs or pruned the weeds overtaking the yard. After a few tries I figured out the doorbell didn't work; my pounding was answered by a perky redhead who professed genuine happiness at seeing me. Her name was Flory Jo, and taking me up to Tessa's room was no problem at all – "Nobody's asked about her things so we don't know what to do."

She ushered me through an entry sporting faded wallpaper of huge blue cabbage roses, up a staircase with carpet so threadbare I almost slipped, and down a hall lit by a single bare bulb attached to the ceiling. As she opened the door to Tessa's room, Flory Jo's cell phone rang and she left me alone while she took the call.

Tessa's room was a decent size, about ten feet by ten feet. Her single bed was covered in threadbare yellow chenille. Ripped magazine pictures of Jesus – holding a lamb, walking on water, ascending into Heaven – were taped to the Pepto pink walls. Tessa had a small vanity on which a chipped cup held a toothbrush and toothpaste, and a four-drawer bureau with a hairbrush on top; in the closet a pair of worn jeans hung on a hanger, a brown towel was folded on the shelf, and a pile of dirty T-shirts lay on the floor. There was no TV, no laptop, no books. No radio or CD player or speakers for an iPod, nothing to show that Tessa had once loved music enough to make her living at it.

Shit, I would have spent all my time in a bar too.

I was closing a bureau drawer – white cotton underpants and a grungy sports bra – when Flory Jo bounced back into the room.

How well had she known Tessa?

Not too well, she said, even though they'd lived in the same place for years. Tessa was mostly out, kept to her room when at home, was almost never sober enough to hold a conversation, and when she did say anything it was usually "Jesus loves you." But disability – Tessa was classified and had a caseworker – paid Tessa's rent on time and she didn't cause any trouble in the house, and that was all she needed to do.

Odd though, said Flory Jo, one thing I did know about her is that she was scared of drugs. She loved booze, obviously, but she was against all drugs except pot and was terrified of needles. "I read in the paper that she died from drugs and alcohol, and I just don't understand how that could have happened. Even as drunk as she could get I don't think she would have taken any drugs. And even if for some reason she decided to try, she couldn't swallow pills; she'd gag even on an aspirin. So I don't get it."

Neither do I, I thought as I gave Flory Jo my number and headed back downtown.

* * *

I showered, slipped into sweats, drank some wine, opened up the futon, and climbed beneath a comforter, but rest was elusive. Every time I closed my eyes the image of a frozen Tessa, orange scarf drifting in the snow, invaded my brain.

Oh, Tessa, what the hell happened to you?

Had Flory Jo been my anonymous caller? I didn't recognize the voice, but I hadn't really been paying attention. Either way, at least one person who knew Tessa was sure she'd never touch a drug that wasn't pot. No matter how drunk or eager to continue the party she'd been.

Thinking about booze made me realize I wasn't going to sleep any time soon, so I got back up, turned on the light, poured myself some wine, pulled out a notebook, and started to recreate what I knew of Tessa's last day on earth.

In the middle of the afternoon she had shown up at Hope House, for reasons unknown – and if anyone had dropped her off they hadn't come forward – and Eve had given her the boot. Shortly before five Tessa arrived at Murphy's, flashing a wad of money. She'd stayed until 2:30 a.m., when Jimmy Earl had thrown the stragglers out so he could close the bar. It had been snowing heavily.

Tessa had the habit of hitchhiking after last call. Denise had seen her get into a light-colored van. Why hadn't the driver taken her back to Mount Auburn? Had they gone to Sawyer Park to keep the party going? But why sit out in a van in a snowstorm when you could be in a warm room? The snow would have eliminated any tracks the van might have left, so you could never know if it had driven Tessa down to the river.

But Tessa didn't like to do drugs. And how would the driver get out of the park in a snowstorm if he – OK, that was sexist, could have been she – was high? And why would Tessa leave the van and walk around in the snow? Had the driver kicked her out? From what everyone said, Tessa was a royal pain in the ass most of the time, but it would take a pretty heartless person to dump her on the riverbank instead of taking her home. Although she'd been flaunting cash, none was found with her body. Did her ride really roll her? Did Louie Nadar find more than a scarf and leave that little detail out?

It just wasn't making sense.

If Tessa had taken pills or shot up (Note to self: Call CPD in the morning and ask about needle marks) before leaving the bar, surely someone would have noticed, even in that crowd at that hour. I had no doubt that drugs flowed behind that bar as freely as the Budweiser, but I couldn't imagine anyone willingly sharing them with Tessa.

Unless someone had wanted her to OD?

But people don't murder just to shut up a pain in the ass.

In the clearly-I-watch-too-many-crime-shows department, it came to me in a Murder She Wrote moment: people have been known, however, to get rid of someone who is sleeping with their spouse. Denise had detested Tessa and warned her away from Jimmy Earl, and she could easily have slipped a dose or a dozen into a drink and Tessa, way beyond noticing taste, would have been none the wiser. And there was only Denise's word that Tessa had taken her final ride in a nondescript light-colored van.

Looked like I'd be going to another breakfast at Murphy's.

* * *

Not today, though. Wednesday is our production day; I was in the office by eight and didn't get out until more than twelve hours later. The icy streets slowed down my walk considerably, and it was nine by the time I reached Josie's loft. She was out, so I nuked myself some leftover take-out pad Thai, polished it off still standing in the kitchen, and then settled down with a glass of wine to accompany whatever it was I'd recorded Maria cooking. Before I even found out what that would be, Josie called.

"Quick, turn on Channel 9."

I flipped channels and found a bundled-up news anchor standing in front of Hope House. A horde of other bundled-up people were carrying boxes from the building to a line of dark SUVs. In the middle of the action was a cuffed Eve Wallingford, flanked by cops, being escorted to a marked Cincinnati PD car.

The snow was coming fast and furious, and you could see the anchor's breath, but she managed to spit out the gist of the story: Eve was being charged with various forms of crookedly defrauding Hope House, the Redden Foundation, donors, and the taxpayers of Cincinnati, Hamilton County, and the State of Ohio. Over the years, according to the charges, she and members of her family had managed to put away a tidy three-quarters of a million that didn't belong to them. Authorities had been quietly investigated for more than a year.

The schemes were varied, and not especially ingenious. In one, Hope House had contracted with Smithson Brothers, a food-distributing firm (picture of warehouse appears on lower right of screen), to provide food for the residents, and then conspired with Ronald Smithson (cut to him being arrested as we speak) to invoice for significantly more, and significantly better quality, food than ever touched the lips of Hope House's clientele. Eve and Smithson had split the difference.

In another, Hope House had paid $3,000 a month, for years, for cleaning and laundry services to Acme Spotless, Inc. Alas, someone eventually noticed that housekeeping was considered part of the residents' therapy, and sheets, towels, table linens, and the like were laundered by inmates at another facility. Acme Spotless was never registered as a business, and its post office box turned out to belong to Amos Farnham of Florence, Kentucky (old mug shot), a first cousin of Eve on her mother's side.

Finally, many donations to the charity – both cash and goods – had simply never been acknowledged, but just found their way to Eve's West Chester home. The visual switched to prior footage of agents in a two-car garage attached to the Wallingford home stacked with boxes of medications, bedding, blankets, women's clothing, and furniture: the claim was that Eve took what she wanted for herself and her family and sold the rest online.

In addition, authorities had uncovered two Tortola-based bank accounts, one in Eve's name and one in that of her husband, Fred, that together contained about half a million dollars from sources not related to their jobs.

At this time, it was unclear to what extent, if any, Fred had knowledge or involvement.

"Don't wait up," Josie texted me.

"More at eleven," croaked the frozen anchorlady.

It had been a long day, and as I knew Josie would fill me in eventually, I stuck Southside Johnny's *Slow Dance* into the CD player and, lucky lucid dreamer that I am, entertained my sleeping self with some scenarios featuring a much younger version of *moi*.

I awoke craving a cigarette.

* * *

Josie hadn't come home – Hope House kept staff bedrooms for emergencies, although I doubt they'd seen this one coming – and I took my time facing the day. The day after production day of a weekly, nobody's really expected in the office until they damn well feel like dropping in, if ever. I watched the news. I plucked my eyebrows. I exhausted my supply of emails and social media posts. Although I almost never eat breakfast, I choked down some toast and eggs in the hope they would somehow mitigate my soon-to-be liquid breakfast at Murphy's, and then put on my metaphoric reporter hat and ventured out to see what Denise would have to say.

On an episode of *Cheers*, a guy walks into the bar after twenty years, grabs a seat, and says, "Hi, Norm." Like Cheers, Murphy's at 10 a.m. looked identical to the last time I'd been there, down to the full-up barstools and Minnie and Ruby enjoying their pitcher. Minnie caught my eye and motioned me to the table, pulling a chair from the table behind her. What the hell, Denise was busy. I joined them.

"Is anyone coming for Tessa's things?" Minnie asked.

"Nobody knows what to do," Ruby chimed in.

I chatted with Minnie and Ruby about what more we knew about Tessa's situation, which was nothing on all fronts, while keeping an eye out for an emptied barstool. We were on our second pitcher when the twelve o'clock news came on, opening with an update on the scandal at Hope House. Denise had the sound off, and the closed captions were fuzzy, but the point was made that this was really, really bad. I watched last night's footage of Eve, Ronald Smithson, and Eve's cousin being arrested, then a talking head in front of Hope House. In the background a group of residents were shielding their faces as they piled out of the fifteen-passenger van used to ferry them to hospitals and occasional outings.

A light-colored fifteen-passenger van.

I turned back to Minnie and Ruby, and topped off my screwdriver. What was that they said Tessa had been blathering on about? An Amish farm. Amos Farnham. She would be coming into a lot of money soon. She'd gone to Hope House during the work day, when Eve was sure to be there, despite having to know, even in her addled brain, that Eve wouldn't welcome her visit. She'd left flush with cash.

Hoping I didn't sound as drunk as I felt, I dialed the CPD.

Hope House Director Charged with Murder
DA Says Eve Wallingford Responsible for Death of Tessa Goodman

By Honor Mack, Managing Editor

CINCINNATI – Eve Wallingford, 53, director of the Hope House residence for women recovering from substance abuse, on Tuesday was charged with first-degree murder in the death of Tessa Goodman, 64, of Mount Auburn.

She was taken into custody at her Mount Adams home, where she had been under house arrest awaiting trial on multiple charges of fraud and embezzlement related to her employment by the Redden Foundation, the nonprofit that operates Hope House and other local charities. She was denied bail and is currently housed at the Hamilton County Detention Center.

The body of Goodman, born Theresa Marie Guttmann, was found Jan. 16 under a snow bank in Sawyer Point Park. She had last been seen around two-thirty that morning leaving Murphy's, a bar on Main Street. An autopsy revealed high levels of alcohol and opioids, and initially her death was attributed to overdoses of both along with exposure.

Goodman was reported to have been drinking heavily. A familiar fixture at the downtown watering hole, she was reputed to often solicit rides from strangers after closing time, and on Jan. 16 was seen getting into a light-colored van. Police surmised that the driver and Goodman had gone to Sawyer Point, despite the heavy snow at the time, to drink and take drugs, and that Guttmann had either been thrown out of the van or left it voluntarily, fallen, and been left to freeze to death.

People who knew her, however, insisted that Guttmann used no drugs stronger than marijuana, raising questions about how the opioids got into her system and if her death was in fact accidental.

According to Gerald Macafee, spokesperson for the Cincinnati Police Division, the division received a tip – he declined to name the source – that Wallingford may have been involved. On the afternoon preceding her death, Goodman had been seen leaving Hope House – where she often was a 'drop-in' but never a resident – and shortly thereafter was in Murphy's spending what was, for her, an unusually large amount of money. A subsequent search confirmed the presence of fibers from Guttman's trademark orange scarf in the van Hope House uses to transport residents, and her fingerprints were found on the inside passenger door.

Macafee said that, faced with the evidence against her as well as at least ten criminal counts related to the Hope House scandal – making Goodman's murder connected to other crimes and thus a potential capital offense – Wallingford confessed to killing Goodman.

Goodman had often been dropped off post-bar at Hope House by local police and cabbies, who thought they were ensuring her safety instead of chancing being picked up by a mugger or worse. She would often sleep it off on a sofa in the residence's foyer, departing in the morning when professional staff arrived and demanded she either go to UC Hospital for detox or leave the premises, the latter always being her choice.

Wallingford was often in her office throughout the night, but she had a private entrance in the back of the building and was never aware of Guttmann's presence.

Until Jan. 15, when Guttmann approached Wallingford in her office and informed her that she had overheard Wallingford's side of numerous conversations with Amos Farnham – Wallingford's cousin and a codefendant in four fraud and conspiracy charges – about fake invoices and hidden bank accounts.

Wallingford said Goodman made no specific threats or demands, but that her constant inebriation, habit of babbling to any and all who would listen, and willingness to say or do anything when she needed money for a drink made the director fear that 'that barfly' would say the wrong thing to the wrong person, confirming authorities' suspicions about Wallingford's fraud connected with Hope House.

Wallingford said she gave Goodman $300 in cash, telling her it was payment to keep her knowledge secret. She said she needed to go to the bank to get her more money, and promised Goodman enough to get her out of her Mount Adams rooming house and set herself up in a home of her own.

Knowing Guttmann's habits, Wallingford waited in Hope House's van until her victim emerged from the bar, and then drove her to Sawyer Point, where she plied her with morphine-laced vodka. After Guttmann passed out, Wallingford pushed her out of the car and returned to Hope House, confident that falling snow would obscure the van's tracks and that no one would find the freezing death of a known drunk suspicious.

Wallingford's arraignment is set for Friday morning at the Hamilton County Courthouse.

Goodman was the lead singer for the Psycharmonics, a popular band that dominated the Queen City music scene in the late 1960s until the early '70s, when the musicians went their separate ways. Former bassist Andy Nieman, who now owns the Librarium bookstore in Sharonville, said that although he and fellow bandmates had lost touch with Tessa over the years, they had taken up a collection to pay for her cremation and would hold a memorial service at the Green Lizard in Mount Adams. The club is the site of the former Café Karma, where the Psycharmonics were the house band from 1968–70. Date to be announced."

Tessa Goodman, in a blue embroidered peasant dress and stiletto-heeled snakeskin boots, ass-length blonde hair swaying, embraced a microphone and looked down from a life-size Art Nouveau poster on the tiny stage: Psycharmonics, Café Karma, 635 Willow St., Mount Adams, Nov. 14, 1969, 8 p.m., $3 minimum. A small table with a simple urn was placed in front of the poster: RIP Tessa. A keyboard, guitars, and amps were off to the left.

Someone had filled a sideboard with food and pitchers of wine, beer, and iced tea. Josie and I filled our plates and glasses and sat down at a table where Minnie, Ruby, and Flory Jo were already seated. Edna Guttmann was nowhere in sight. At another table sat Andy Nieman and other former members of the band. When we were all settled, Nieman stood up and offered a toast to Tessa, "one hell of an artist in her day." Then the gray-haired dudes filed up to the stage:

"This is for you, Tess:"

'O what is the world's bane?'
The sun was laughing sweetly,

The moon plucked at my rein;
But the little red fox murmured,
'O do not pluck at his rein,
He is riding to the townland
That is the world's bane.'
Michael will unhook his trumpet
From a bough overhead,
And blow a little noise
When the supper has been spread.
Gabriel will come from the water
With a fish tail, and talk
Of wonders that have happened
On wet roads where men walk,
And lift up an old horn
Of hammered silver, and drink
Till he has fallen asleep
Upon the starry brink.

The Case of the Flitterbat Lancers

Arthur Morrison

IT WAS LATE on a summer evening, two or three years back, that I drowsed in my armchair over a particularly solid and ponderous volume of essays on social economy. I was doing a good deal of reviewing at the time, and I remember that this particular volume had a property of such exceeding toughness that I had already made three successive attacks on it, on as many successive evenings, each attack having been defeated in the end by sleep. The weather was hot, my chair was very comfortable, and the book had somewhere about its strings of polysyllables an essence as of laudanum. Still something had been done on each evening, and now on the fourth I strenuously endeavoured to finish the book. I was just beginning to feel that the words before me were sliding about and losing their meanings, when a sudden crash and a jingle of broken glass behind me woke me with a start, and I threw the book down. A pane of glass in my window was smashed, and I hurried across and threw up the sash to see, if I could, whence the damage had come.

The building in which my chambers (and Martin Hewitt's office) were situated was accessible – or rather visible, for there was no entrance – from the rear. There was, in fact, a small courtyard, reached by a passage from the street behind, and into this courtyard, my sitting-room window looked.

"Hullo, there!" I shouted. But there came no reply. Nor could I distinguish anybody in the courtyard. Some men had been at work during the day on a drainpipe, and I reflected that probably their litter had provided the stone with which my window had been smashed. As I looked, however, two men came hurrying from the passage into the court, and going straight into the deep shadow of one corner, presently appeared again in a less obscure part, hauling forth a third man, who must have already been there in hiding. The third man struggled fiercely, but without avail, and was dragged across toward the passage leading to the street beyond. But the most remarkable feature of the whole thing was the silence of all three men. No cry, no exclamation, escaped any of them. In perfect silence the two hauled the third across the courtyard, and in perfect silence he swung and struggled to resist and escape. The matter astonished me not a little, and the men were entering the passage before I found voice to shout at them. But they took no notice, and disappeared. Soon after I heard cab wheels in the street beyond, and had no doubt that the two men had carried off their prisoner.

I turned back into my room a little perplexed. It seemed probable that the man who had been borne off had broken my window. But why? I looked about on the floor, and presently found the missile. It was, as I had expected, a piece of broken concrete, but it was wrapped up in a worn piece of paper, which had partly opened out as it lay on my carpet, thus indicating that it had just been crumpled round the stone.

I disengaged the paper and spread it out. Then I saw it to be a rather hastily written piece of manuscript music, whereof I append a reduced facsimile:

This gave me no help. I turned the paper this way and that, but could make nothing of it. There was not a mark on it that I could discover, except the music and the scrawled title, 'Flitterbat Lancers', at the top.

The paper was old, dirty, and cracked. What did it all mean? One might conceive of a person in certain circumstances sending a message – possibly an appeal for help – through a friend's window, wrapped round a stone, but this seemed to be nothing of that sort.

Once more I picked up the paper, and with an idea to hear what the Flitterbat Lancers sounded like, I turned to my little pianette and strummed over the notes, making my own time and changing it as seemed likely. But I could by no means extract from the notes anything resembling an air. I half thought of trying Martin Hewitt's office door, in case he might still be there and offer a guess at the meaning of my smashed window and the scrap of paper, when Hewitt himself came in. He had stayed late to examine a bundle of papers in connection with a case just placed in his hands, and now, having finished, came to find if I were disposed for an evening stroll before turning in. I handed him the paper and the piece of concrete, observing, "There's a little job for you, Hewitt, instead of the stroll." And I told him the complete history of my smashed window.

Hewitt listened attentively, and examined both the paper and the fragment of paving. "You say these people made absolutely no sound whatever?" he asked.

"None but that of scuffling, and even that they seemed to do quietly."

"Could you see whether or not the two men gagged the other, or placed their hands over his mouth?"

"No, they certainly didn't do that. It was dark, of course, but not so dark as to prevent my seeing generally what they were doing."

Hewitt stood for half a minute in thought, and then said, "There's something in this, Brett – what, I can't guess at the moment, but something deep, I fancy. Are you sure you won't come out now?"

I told Hewitt that I was sure, and that I should stick to my work.

"Very well," he said; "then perhaps you will lend me these articles?" holding up the paper and the stone.

"Delighted," I said. "If you get no more melody out of the clinker than I did out of the paper, you won't have a musical evening. Goodnight!"

Hewitt went away with the puzzle in his hand, and I turned once more to my social economy, and, thanks to the gentleman who smashed my window, conquered.

At this time my only regular daily work was on an evening paper so that I left home at a quarter to eight on the morning following the adventure of my broken window, in order, as usual, to be at the office at eight; consequently it was not until lunchtime that I had an opportunity of seeing Hewitt. I went to my own rooms first, however, and on the landing by my door I found the housekeeper in conversation with a shortish, sun-browned man, whose accent at once convinced me that he hailed from across the Atlantic. He had called, it appeared, three or four times during the morning to see me, getting more impatient each time. As he did not seem even to know my name, the housekeeper had not considered it expedient to give him any information about me, and he was growing irascible under the treatment. When I at last appeared, however, he left her and approached me eagerly.

"See here, sir," he said, "I've been stumpin' these here durn stairs o' yours half through the mornin'. I'm anxious to apologise, and fix up some damage."

He had followed me into my sitting-room, and was now standing with his back to the fireplace, a dripping umbrella in one hand, and the forefinger of the other held up boulder-high and pointing, in the manner of a pistol, to my window, which, by the way, had been mended during the morning, in accordance with my instructions to the housekeeper.

"Sir," he continued, "last night I took the extreme liberty of smashin' your winder."

"Oh," I said, "that was you, was it?"

"It was, sir – me. For that I hev come humbly to apologise. I trust the draft has not discommoded you, sir. I regret the accident, and I wish to pay for the fixin' up and the general inconvenience." He placed a sovereign on the table. "I 'low you'll call that square now, sir, and fix things friendly and comfortable as between gentlemen, an' no ill will. Shake."

And he formally extended his hand.

I took it at once. "Certainly," I said. "As a matter of fact, you haven't inconvenienced me at all; indeed, there were some circumstances about the affair that rather interested me." And I pushed the sovereign toward him.

"Say now," he said, looking a trifle disappointed at my unwillingness to accept his money, "didn't I startle your nerves?"

"Not a bit," I answered, laughing. "In fact, you did me a service by preventing me going to sleep just when I shouldn't; so we'll say no more of that."

"Well – there was one other little thing," he pursued, looking at me rather sharply as he pocketed the sovereign. "There was a bit o' paper round that pebble that came in here. Didn't happen to notice that, did you?"

"Yes, I did. It was an old piece of manuscript music."

"That was it – exactly. Might you happen to have it handy now?"

"Well," I said, "as a matter of fact a friend of mine has it now. I tried playing it over once or twice, as a matter of curiosity, but I couldn't make anything of it, and so I handed it to him."

"Ah!" said my visitor, watching me narrowly, "That's a puzzler, that Flitterbat Lancers – a real puzzler. It whips 'em all. Ha, ha'." He laughed suddenly – a laugh that seemed a little artificial. "There's music fellers as 'lows to set right down and play off anything right away that can't make anything of the Flitterbat Lancers. That was two of 'em that was monkeyin' with me last night. They never could make anythin' of it at all, and I was tantalising them with it all along till they got real mad, and reckoned to get it out o' my pocket and learn it at home. Ha, ha! So I got away for a bit, and just rolled it round a stone and heaved it through your winder before they could come up, your winder being the nearest one with a light in it. Ha, ha! I'll be considerable obliged you'll get it from your friend right now. Is he stayin' hereabout?"

The story was so ridiculously lame that I determined to confront my visitor with Hewitt, and observe the result. If he had succeeded in making any sense of the Flitterbat Lancers, the scene might be amusing. So I answered at once, "Yes; his office is on the floor below; he will probably be in at about this time. Come down with me."

We went down, and found Hewitt in his outer office. "This gentleman," I told him with a solemn intonation, "has come to ask for his piece of manuscript music, the Flitterbat Lancers. He is particularly proud of it, because nobody who tries to play it can make any sort of tune out of it, and it was entirely because two dear friends of his were anxious to drag it out of his pocket and practise it over on the quiet that he flung it through my windowpane last night, wrapped round a piece of concrete."

The stranger glanced sharply at me, and I could see that my manner and tone rather disconcerted him. But Hewitt came forward at once. "Oh, yes," he said "just so – quite a natural sort of thing. As a matter of fact, I quite expected you. Your umbrella's wet – do you mind putting it in the stand? Thank you. Come into my private office."

We entered the inner room, and Hewitt, turning to the stranger, went on: "Yes, that is a very extraordinary piece of music, that Flitterbat Lancers. I have been having a little bit of practice with it myself, though I'm really nothing of a musician. I don't wonder you are anxious to keep it to yourself. Sit down."

The stranger, with a distrustful look at Hewitt, complied. At this moment, Hewitt's clerk, Kerrett, entered from the outer office with a slip of paper. Hewitt glanced at it, and crumpled it in his hand. "I am engaged just now," was his remark, and Kerrett vanished.

"And now," Hewitt said, as he sat down and suddenly turned to the stranger with an intent gaze, "and now, Mr. Hoker, we'll talk of this music."

The stranger started and frowned. "You've the advantage of me, sir," he said; "you seem to know my name, but I don't know yours."

Hewitt smiled pleasantly. "My name," he said, "is Hewitt, Martin Hewitt, and it is my business to know a great many things. For instance, I know that you are Mr. Reuben B. Hoker, of Robertsville, Ohio."

The visitor pushed his chair back, and stared. "Well – that gits me," he said. "You're a pretty smart chap, Mr. Hewitt. I've heard your name before, of course. And – and so you've been a-studyin' the Flitterbat Lancers, have you?" This with a keen glance at Hewitt's face. "Well, s'pose you have. What's your idea?"

"Why," answered Hewitt, still keeping his steadfast gaze on Hoker's eyes, "I think it's pretty late in the century to be fishing about for the Wedlake jewels."

These words astonished me almost as much as they did Mr. Hoker. The great Wedlake jewel robbery is, as many will remember, a traditional story of the 'sixties. I remembered no more of it at the time than probably most men do who have at some time or another read the *causes celèbres* of the century. Sir Francis Wedlake's country house had been robbed, and the whole of Lady Wedlake's magnificent collection of jewels stolen. A man named Shiels, a strolling musician, had been arrested and had been sentenced to a long term of penal servitude. Another man named Legg – one of the comparatively wealthy scoundrels who finance promising thefts or swindles and pocket the greater part of the proceeds – had also been punished, but only a very few of the trinkets, and those quite unimportant items, had been recovered. The great bulk of the booty was never brought to light. So much I remembered, and Hewitt's sudden mention of the Wedlake jewels in connection with my broken window, Mr. Reuben B. Hoker, and the Flitterbat Lancers, astonished me not a little.

As for Hoker, he did his best to hide his perturbation, but with little success. "Wedlake jewels, eh?" he said; "and – and what's that to do with it, anyway?"

"To do with it?" responded Hewitt, with an air of carelessness. "Well, well, I had my idea, nothing more. If the Wedlake jewels have nothing to do with it, we'll say no more about it, that's all. Here's your paper, Mr. Hoker – only a little crumpled." He rose and placed the article in Mr. Hoker's hand, with the manner of terminating the interview.

Hoker rose, with a bewildered look on his face, and turned toward the door. Then he stopped, looked at the floor, scratched his cheek, and finally sat down and put his hat on the ground. "Come," he said, "we'll play a square game. That paper has something to do with the Wedlake jewels, and, win or lose, I'll tell you all I know about it. You're a smart man and whatever I tell you, I guess it won't do me no harm; it ain't done me no good yet, anyway."

"Say what you please, of course," Hewitt answered, "but think first. You might tell me something you'd be sorry for afterward."

"Say, will you listen to what I say, and tell me if you think I've been swindled or not? My two hundred and fifty dollars is gone now, and I guess I won't go skirmishing after it anymore if you think it's no good. Will you do that much?"

"As I said before," Hewitt replied, "tell me what you please, and if I can help you I will. But remember, I don't ask for your secrets."

"That's all right, I guess, Mr. Hewitt. Well, now, it was all like this." And Mr. Reuben B. Hoker plunged into a detailed account of his adventures since his arrival in London.

Relieved of repetitions, and put as directly as possible, it was as follows: Mr. Hoker was a wagon-builder, had made a good business from very humble beginnings, and intended to go on and make it still a better. Meantime, he had come over to Europe for a short holiday – a thing he had promised himself for years. He was wandering about the London streets on the second night after his arrival in the city, when he managed to get into conversation with two men at a bar. They were not very prepossessing men, though flashily dressed. Very soon they suggested a game of cards. But Reuben B. Hoker was not to be had in that way, and after a while, they parted. The two were amusing enough fellows in their way, and when Hoker saw them again the next night in the same bar, he made no difficulty in talking with them freely. After a succession of drinks, they told him that they had a speculation on hand – a speculation that meant thousands if it succeeded – and to carry out which they were only waiting for a paltry sum of £50. There was a house, they said, in which was hidden a great number of jewels of immense value, which had been deposited there by a man who was now dead. Exactly in what part of the house the jewels were to be found they did not know. There was a paper, they said, which was supposed to contain some information, but as yet they hadn't been quite able to make it out. But that would really matter very little if once they could get possession of the house. Then they would simply set to work and search from the topmost chimney to the lowermost brick, if necessary. The only present difficulty was that the house was occupied, and that the landlord wanted a large deposit of rent down before he would consent to turn out his present tenants and give them possession at a higher rental. This deposit would come to £50, and they hadn't the money. However, if any friend of theirs who meant business would put the necessary sum at their disposal, and keep his mouth shut, they would make him an equal partner in the proceeds with themselves; and as the value of the whole haul would probably be something not very far off £20,000, the speculation would bring a tremendous return to the man who was smart enough to put down his £50.

Hoker, very distrustful, skeptically demanded more detailed particulars of the scheme. But these the two men (Luker and Birks were their names, he found, in course of talking) inflexibly refused to communicate.

"Is it likely," said Luker, "that we should give the 'ole thing away to anybody who might easily go with his fifty pounds and clear out the bloomin' show? Not much. We've told you what the game is, and if you'd like to take a flutter with your fifty, all right; you'll do as well as anybody, and we'll treat you square. If you don't – well, don't, that's all. We'll get the oof from somewhere – there's blokes as 'ud jump at the chance. Anyway, we ain't going to give the show away before you've done somethin' to prove you're on the job, straight. Put your money in, and you shall know as much as we do."

Then there were more drinks, and more discussion. Hoker was still reluctant, though tempted by the prospect, and growing more venturesome with each drink.

"Don't you see," said Birks, "that if we was a-tryin' to 'ave you we should out with a tale as long as yer arm, all complete, with the address of the 'ouse and all. Then I s'pose you'd lug out the pieces on the nail, without askin' a bloomin' question. As it is, the thing's so perfectly genuine that we'd rather lose the chance and wait for some other bloke to find the money than run a chance of givin' the thing away. It's a matter o' business, simple and plain, that's all. It's a question of either us trustin' you with a chance of collarin' twenty thousand pounds or you trustin' us with a paltry fifty. We don't lay out no 'igh moral sentiments, we only say the weight o' money is all on one side. Take it or leave it, that's all. 'Ave another Scotch?"

The talk went on and the drinks went on, and it all ended, at 'chucking-out time', in Reuben B. Hoker handing over five £10 notes, with smiling, though slightly incoherent, assurances of his eternal friendship for Luker and Birks.

In the morning he awoke to the realisation of a bad head, a bad tongue, and a bad opinion of his proceedings of the previous night. In his sober senses it seemed plain that he had been swindled. All day he cursed his fuddled foolishness, and at night he made for the bar that had been the scene of the transaction, with little hope of seeing either Luker or Birks, who had agreed to be there to meet him. There they were, however, and, rather to his surprise, they made no demand for more money. They asked him if he understood music, and showed him the worn old piece of paper containing the Flitterbat Lancers. The exact spot, they said, where the jewels were hidden was supposed to be indicated somehow on that piece of paper. Hoker did not understand music, and could find nothing on the paper that looked in the least like a direction to a hiding place for jewels or anything else.

Luker and Birks then went into full particulars of their project. First, as to its history. The jewels were the famous Wedlake jewels, which had been taken from Sir Francis Wedlake's house in 1866 and never heard of again. A certain Jerry Shiels had been arrested in connection with the robbery, had been given a long sentence of penal servitude, and had died in jail. This Jerry Shiels was an extraordinarily clever criminal, and travelled about the country as a street musician. Although an expert burglar, he very rarely perpetrated robberies himself, but acted as a sort of travelling fence, receiving stolen property and transmitting it to London or out of the country. He also acted as the agent of a man named Legg, who had money, and who financed any likely-looking project of a criminal nature that Shiels might arrange.

Jerry Shiels travelled with a 'pardner' – a man who played the harp and acted as his assistant and messenger in affairs wherein Jerry was reluctant to appear personally. When Shiels was arrested, he had in his possession a quantity of printed and manuscript music, and after his first remand his 'pardner', Jimmy Snape, applied for the music to be given up to him, in order, as he explained, that he might earn his living. No objection was raised to this, and Shiels was quite willing that Snape should have it, and so it was handed over. Now among the music was a small slip, headed Flitterbat Lancers, which Shiels had shown to Snape before the arrest. In case of Shiels being taken, Snape was to take this slip to Legg as fast as he could.

But as chance would have it, on that very day Legg himself was arrested, and soon after was sentenced also to a term of years. Snape hung about in London for a little while, and then emigrated. Before leaving, however, he gave the slip of music to Luker's father, a rag-shop keeper, to whom he owed money. He explained its history, and Luker senior made all sorts of fruitless efforts to get at the information concealed in the paper. He had held it to the fire to bring out concealed writing, had washed it, had held it to the light till his eyes ached, had gone over it with a magnifying glass – all in vain. He had got musicians to strum out the notes on all sorts of instruments – backwards, forwards, alternately, and in every other way he could think of. If at any time he fancied a resemblance in the resulting sound to some familiar song-tune, he got that song and studied all its words with loving care, upside-down, right-side up – every way. He took the words Flitterbat Lancers and transposed the letters in all directions, and did everything else he could think of. In the end he gave it up, and died. Now, lately, Luker junior had been impelled with a desire to see into the matter. He had repeated all the parental experiments, and more, with the same lack of success. He had taken his 'pal' Birks into his confidence, and together they had tried other experiments till at last they began to believe that the message had probably been written in some sort of invisible ink which the subsequent washings had erased altogether. But he had done one other thing: he had found the house which Shiels had rented at the time of his arrest, and in which a good quantity of stolen property – not connected with the Wedlake case – was discovered. Here, he argued, if anywhere, Jerry Shiels had hidden the jewels. There was no other place where he could be found to have lived, or over which he had sufficient control to warrant his hiding valuables therein. Perhaps, once the house could be properly examined, something about it might give a clue as to what the message of the Flitterbat Lancers meant.

Hoker, of course, was anxious to know where the house in question stood, but this Luker and Birks would on no account inform him. "You've done your part," they said, "and now you leave us to do ours. There's a bit of a job about gettin' the tenants out. They won't go, and it'll take a bit of time before the landlord can make them. So you just hold your jaw and wait. When we're safe in the 'ouse, and there's no chance of anybody else pokin' in, then you can come and help find the stuff."

Hoker went home that night sober, but in much perplexity. The thing might be genuine, after all; indeed, there were many little things that made him think it was. But then, if it were, what guarantee had he that he would get his share, supposing the search turned out successful? None at all. But then it struck him for the first time that these jewels, though they may have lain untouched so long, were stolen property after all. The moral aspect of the affair began to trouble him a little, but the legal aspect troubled him more. That consideration however, he decided to leave over for the present. He had no more than the word of Luker and Birks that the jewels (if they existed) were those of Lady Wedlake, and Luker and Birks themselves only professed to know from hearsay. At any rate, he made up his mind to have some guarantee for his money. In accordance with this resolve, he suggested, when he met the two men the next day, that he should take charge of the slip of music and make an independent study of it. This proposal, however, met with an instant veto.

Hoker resolved to make up a piece of paper, folded as like the slip of music as possible, and substitute one for the other at their next meeting. Then he would put the Flitterbat Lancers in some safe place, and face his fellow conspirators with a hand of cards equal to their own. He carried out his plan the next evening with perfect success, thanks to the contemptuous indifference with which Luker and Birks had begun to regard him. He got the slip in his pocket, and left the bar. He had not gone far, however, before Luker discovered the loss, and soon he became conscious of being followed. He looked for a cab, but he was in a dark street, and no cab was near. Luker and Birks turned the corner and began to run. He saw they must catch him. Everything now depended on his putting the Flitterbat Lancers out of their reach, but where he could himself recover it. He ran till he saw a narrow passageway on his right, and into this he darted. It led into a yard where stones were lying about, and in a large building before him he saw the window of a lighted room a couple of floors up. It was a desperate expedient, but there was no time for consideration. He wrapped a stone in the paper and flung it with all his force through the lighted window. Even as he did it he heard the feet of Luker and Birks as they hurried down the street. The rest of the adventure in the court I myself saw.

Luker and Birks kept Hoker in their lodgings all that night. They searched him unsuccessfully for the paper; they bullied, they swore, they cajoled, they entreated, they begged him to play the game square with his pals. Hoker merely replied that he had put the Flitterbat Lancers where they couldn't easily find it, and that he intended playing the game square as long as they did the same. In the end they released him, apparently with more respect than they had before entertained, advising him to get the paper into his possession as soon as he could.

"And now," said Mr. Hoker, in conclusion of his narrative, "perhaps you'll give me a bit of advice. Am I playin' a fool-game running after these toughs, or ain't I?"

Hewitt shrugged his shoulders. "It all depends," he said, "on your friends Luker and Birks. They may want to swindle you, or they may not. I'm afraid they'd like to, at any rate. But perhaps you've got some little security in this piece of paper. One thing is plain: they certainly believe in the deposit of the jewels themselves, else they wouldn't have taken so much trouble to get the paper back."

"Then I guess I'll go on with the thing, if that's it."

"That depends, of course, on whether you care to take trouble to get possession of what, after all, is somebody else's lawful property."

Hoker looked a little uneasy. "Well," he said, "there's that, of course. I didn't know nothin' of that at first, and when I did I'd parted with my money and felt entitled to get something back for it. Anyway, the stuff ain't found yet. When it is, why then, you know, I might make a deal with the owner. But, say, how did you find out my name, and about this here affair being jined up with the Wedlake jewels?"

Hewitt smiled. "As to the name and address, you just think it over a little when you've gone away, and if you don't see how I did it. You're not so cute as I think you are. In regard to the jewels – well, I just read the message of the Flitterbat Lancers, that's all."

"You read it? Whew! And what does it say? How did you do it?" Hoker turned the paper over eagerly in his hands as he spoke.

"See, now," said Hewitt, "I won't tell you all that, but I'll tell you something, and it may help you to test the real knowledge of Luker and Birks. Part of the message is in these words, which you had better write down: *Over the coals the fifth dancer slides, says Jerry Shield the homey.*"

"What?" Hoker exclaimed, "Fifth dancer slides over the coals? That's mighty odd. What's it all about?"

"About the Wedlake jewels, as I said. Now you can go and make a bargain with Luker and Birks. The only other part of the message is an address, and that they already know, if they have been telling the truth about the house they intend taking. You can offer to tell them what I have told you of the message, after they have told you where the house is, and proved to you that they are taking the steps they talked of. If they won't agree to that, I think you had best treat them as common rogues and charge them with obtaining your money under false pretenses."

Nothing more would Hewitt say than that, despite Hoker's many questions; and when at last Hoker had gone, almost as troubled and perplexed as ever, my friend turned to me and said, "Now, Brett, if you haven't lunched and would like to see the end of this business, hurry!"

"The end of it?" I said. "Is it to end so soon? How?"

"Simply by a police raid on Jerry Shiels's old house with a search warrant. I communicated with the police this morning before I came here."

"Poor Hoker!" I said.

"Oh, I had told the police before I saw Hoker, or heard of him, of course. I just conveyed the message on the music slip – that was enough. But I'll tell you all about it when there's more time; I must be off now. With the information I have given him, Hoker and his friends may make an extra push and get into the house soon, but I couldn't resist the temptation to give the unfortunate Hoker some sort of sporting chance – though it's a poor one, I fear. Get your lunch as quickly as you can, and go at once to Colt Row, Bankside – Southwark way, you know. Probably we shall be there before you. If not, wait."

Colt Row was not difficult to find. It was one of those places that decay with an excess of respectability, like Drury Lane and Clare Market. Once, when Jacob's Island was still an island, a little farther down the river, Colt Row had evidently been an unsafe place for a person with valuables about him, and then it probably prospered, in its own way. Now it was quite respectable, but very dilapidated and dirty. Perhaps it was sixty yards long – perhaps a little more. It was certainly a very few yards wide, and the houses at each side had a patient and forlorn look of waiting for a metropolitan improvement to come along and carry them away to their rest.

I could see no sign of Hewitt, nor of the police, so I walked up and down the narrow pavement for a little while. As I did so, I became conscious of a face at the window of the least ruinous house in the row, a face that I fancied expressed particular interest in my movements. The house was an old gabled structure, faced with plaster. What had apparently once been a shop window on the ground floor was now shuttered up, and the face that watched me – an old woman's – looked out from the window above. I had noted these particulars with some curiosity, when, arriving again at the street corner, I observed Hewitt approaching, in company with a police inspector, and followed by two unmistakable plainclothes men.

"Well," Hewitt said, "you're first here after all. Have you seen any more of our friend Hoker?"

"No, nothing."

"Very well – probably he'll be here before long, though."

The party turned into Colt Row, and the inspector, walking up to the door of the house with the shuttered bottom window, knocked sharply. There was no response, so he knocked again, equally in vain.

"All out," said the inspector.

"No," I said; "I saw a woman watching me from the window above not three minutes ago."

"Ho, ho!" the inspector replied. "That's so, eh? One of you – you, Johnson – step round to the back, will you?"

One of the plainclothes men started off, and after waiting another minute or two the inspector began a thundering cannonade of knocks that brought every available head out of the window of every inhabited room in the Row. At this the woman opened the window, and began abusing the inspector with a shrillness and fluency that added a street-corner audience to that already congregated at the windows.

"Go away, you blaggards!" the lady said, "you ought to be 'orse-w'ipped, every one of ye! A-comin' 'ere a-tryin' to turn decent people out o' 'ouse and 'ome! Wait till my 'usband comes 'ome – 'e'll show yer, ye mutton-cadgin' scoundrels! Payin' our rent reg'lar, and good tenants as is always been – and I'm a respectable married woman, that's what I am, ye dirty great cowards!" – this last word with a low, tragic emphasis.

Hewitt remembered what Hoker had said about the present tenants refusing to quit the house on the landlord's notice. "She thinks we've come from the landlord to turn her out," he said to the inspector. "We're not here from the landlord, you old fool!" the inspector said. "We don't want to turn you out. We're the police, with a search warrant, and you'd better let us in or you'll get into trouble."

"'Ark at 'im!" the woman screamed, pointing at the inspector. "'Ark at 'im! Thinks I was born yesterday, that feller! Go 'ome, ye dirty pie-stealer, go 'ome!"

The audience showed signs of becoming a small crowd, and the inspector's patience gave out. "Here, Bradley," he said, addressing the remaining plainclothes man, "give a hand with these shutters," and the two – both powerful men – seized the iron bar which held the shutters and began to pull. But the garrison was undaunted, and, seizing a broom, the woman began to belabour the invaders about the shoulders and head from above. But just at this moment, the woman, emitting a terrific shriek, was suddenly lifted from behind and vanished. Then the head of the plainclothes man who had gone round to the back appeared, with the calm announcement, "There's a winder open behind, sir. But I'll open the front door if you like."

In a minute the bolts were shot, and the front door swung back. The placid Johnson stood in the passage, and as we passed in he said, "I've locked 'er in the back room upstairs."

"It's the bottom staircase, of course," the inspector said; and we tramped down into the basement. A little way from the stair-foot Hewitt opened a cupboard door, which enclosed a receptacle for coals.

"They still keep the coals here, you see," he said, striking a match and passing it to and fro near the sloping roof of the cupboard. It was of plaster, and covered the underside of the stairs.

"And now for the fifth dancer," he said, throwing the match away and making for the staircase again. "One, two, three, four, five," and he tapped the fifth stair from the bottom.

The stairs were uncarpeted, and Hewitt and the inspector began a careful examination of the one he had indicated. They tapped it in different places, and Hewitt passed his hands over the surfaces of both tread and riser. Presently, with his hand at the outer edge of the riser, Hewitt spoke. "Here it is, I think," he said; "it is the riser that slides."

He took out his pocket knife and scraped away the grease and paint from the edge of the old stair. Then a joint was plainly visible. For a long time the plank, grimed and set with age, refused to shift; but at last, by dint of patience and firm fingers, it moved, and was drawn clean out from the end.

Within, nothing was visible but grime, fluff, and small rubbish. The inspector passed his hand along the bottom angle. "Here's something," he said. It was the gold hook of an old-fashioned earring, broken off short.

Hewitt slapped his thigh. "Somebody's been here before us," he said "and a good time back too, judging from the dust. That hook's a plain indication that jewellery was here once. There's plainly nothing more, except – except this piece of paper." Hewitt's eyes had detected – black with loose grime as it was – a small piece of paper lying at the bottom of the recess. He drew it out and shook off the dust. "Why, what's this?" he exclaimed. "More music!"

We went to the window, and there saw in Hewitt's hand a piece of written musical notation, thus:

Hewitt pulled out from his pocket a few pieces of paper. "Here is a copy I made this morning of the Flitterbat Lancers, and a note or two of my own as well," he said. He took a pencil, and, constantly referring to his own papers, marked a letter under each note on the last-found slip of music. When he had done this, the letters read:

> *You are a clever cove whoever you are but there was a cleverer says Jim Snape the horney's mate.*

"You see." Hewitt said handing the inspector the paper. "Snape, the unconsidered messenger, finding Legg in prison, set to work and got the jewels for himself. The thing was a cryptogram, of course, of a very simple sort, though uncommon in design. Snape was a humorous soul, too, to leave this message here in the same cipher, on the chance of somebody else reading the Flitterbat Lancers."

"But," I asked, "why did he give that slip of music to Laker's father?"

"Well, he owed him money, and got out of it that way. Also, he avoided the appearance of 'flushness' that paying the debt might have given him, and got quietly out of the country with his spoils."

The shrieks upstairs had grown hoarser, but the broom continued vigorously. "Let that woman out," said the inspector, "and we'll go and report. Not much good looking for Snape now, I fancy. But there's some satisfaction in clearing up that old quarter-century mystery."

We left the place pursued by the execrations of the broom-wielder, who bolted the door behind us, and from the window defied us to come back, and vowed she would have us all searched before a magistrate for what we had probably stolen. In the very next street we hove in sight of Reuben B. Hoker in the company of two swell-mob-looking fellows, who sheered off down a side-turning in sight of our group. Hoker, too, looked rather shy at the sight of the inspector.

"The meaning of the thing was so very plain," Hewitt said to me afterwards, "that the duffers who had the Flitterbat Lancers in hand for so long never saw it at all. If Shiels had made an ordinary clumsy cryptogram, all letters and figures, they would have seen what it was at once, and at least would have tried to read it; but because it was put in the form of music, they tried everything else but the right way. It was a clever dodge of Shiels's, without a doubt. Very few people, police officers or not, turning over a heap of old music, would notice or feel suspicious of that little slip among the rest. But once one sees it is a cryptogram (and the absence of bar lines and of notes beyond the stave would suggest that) the reading is easy as possible. For my part I tried it as a cryptogram at once. You know the plan – it has been described a hundred times. See here – look at this copy of the Flitterbat Lancers. Its only difficulty – and that is a small one – is that the words are not divided. Since there are positions for less than a dozen notes on the stave, and there are twenty-six letters to be indicated, it follows that crotchets, quavers, and semiquavers on the same line or space must mean different letters. The first step is obvious. We count the notes to ascertain which sign occurs most frequently, and we find that the crotchet in the top space is the sign required – it occurs no less than eleven times. Now the letter most frequently occurring in an ordinary sentence of English is e. Let us then suppose that this represents e. At once a coincidence strikes us. In ordinary musical notation in the treble clef the note occupying the top space would be E. Let us remember that presently.

"Now the most common word in the English language is 'the'. We know the sign for e, the last letter of this word, so let us see if in more than one place that sign is preceded by two others identical in each case. If so, the probability is that the other two signs will represent t and h, and the whole word will be 'the'. Now it happens in no less than four places the sign e is preceded by the same two other signs – once in the first line, twice in the second, and once in the fourth. No word of three letters ending in e would be in the least likely to occur four times in a short sentence except 'the'. Then we will call it 'the', and note the signs preceding the e. They are a quaver under the bottom line for the t, and a crotchet on the first space for the h. We travel along the stave, and wherever these signs occur we mark them with t or h, as the case may be.

"But now we remember that e, the crotchet in the top space, is in its right place as a musical note, while the crotchet in the bottom space means h, which is no musical note at all. Considering this for a minute, we remember that among the notes which are expressed in ordinary music on the treble stave, without the use of ledger lines, d, e and f are repeated at the lower and at the upper part of the stave. Therefore, anybody making a cryptogram of musical notes would probably use one set of these duplicate positions to indicate other letters, and as a is in the lower part of the stave, that is where the variation comes in. Let us experiment by assuming that all the crotchets above f in ordinary musical notation have their usual values, and let us set the letters over their respective notes. Now things begin to shape. Look toward the end of the second line: there is the word the and the letters f f t h, with another note between the two f's. Now that word can only possibly be fifth, so that now we have the sign for i. It is the crotchet on the bottom line. Let us go through and mark the i's.

"And now observe. The first sign of the lot is i, and there is one other sign before the word 'the'. The only words possible here beginning with i, and of two letters, are it, if, is and in. Now we have the signs for *t* and *f*, so we know that it isn't *it* or *if*. Is would be unlikely here, because there is a tendency, as you see, to regularity in these signs, and *t*, the next letter alphabetically to *s*, is at the bottom of the stave. Let us try *n*. At once we get the word *dance* at the beginning of line three. And now we have got enough to see the system of the thing. Make a stave and put *G A B C* and the higher *D E F* in their proper musical places. Then fill in the blank places with the next letters of the alphabet downward, *h i j*, and we find that *h* and *i* fall in the places we have already discovered for them as crotchets. Now take quavers, and go on with *k l m n o*, and so on as before, beginning on the A space. When you have filled the quavers, do the same with semiquavers – there are only six alphabetical letters left for this – *u v w x y z*. Now you will find that this exactly agrees with all we have ascertained already, and if you will use the other letters to fill up over the signs still unmarked you will get the whole message:

"*In the Colt Row ken over the coals the fifth dancer slides says Jerry Shiels the horney.*"

Welcome to Paradise

Amelia Dee Mueller

UTOPIA was home to two hundred and fifty eight people in 1989 when Carrie Timmons went missing. The town had no proper police department, so they called in the force from Kerrville. She was eight years old. Then went Marisa Thomas, nine, two weeks later, and then Bailey Whitby, seven and a half, two days after that.

The manhunt lasted six months and ended with the forced retirement of Kerrville Police Chief Pam Clear. The girls' bodies were never found, so their families left Utopia to find a place where they could forget, and Chief Clear took up her post every morning at the Lost Maples Cafe on Utopia's Main Street. Every day she drank two and half cups of black coffee, ate one waffle and three strips of bacon, and waited for answers.

They came in a silver Hyundai Accent. It pulled up to the café at half past seven, the only unfamiliar car in the three-spaced lot. It was the middle of winter. Clear put down her coffee mug without taking a sip for the first time in twenty-four years. Something in her bones chilled her in the cozy cafe. She pulled her glasses out of her pocket, wiped them with a dirty napkin that smudged maple syrup on the lenses, and settled them on the end of her nose.

The girl that got out of the car was unfamiliar, but Clear knew everyone in town. This stranger – with her bedazzled, embroidered jeans too flashy for any place south of Dallas, and her jeweled sunglasses that covered half her face – didn't belong on Utopia's dusty streets. Clear stiffened and watched the girl swing the cafe door open.

She sat herself at a booth two away. Clear kept her eyes on her last two pieces of bacon, but didn't touch them. When she thought it was safe to glance in her direction, the girl had removed her large sunglasses and was staring right at her.

Clear turned back to her coffee, taking a long sip, dripping the hot liquid down her wrist. She grabbed some fresh napkins from the table behind her, and when she turned back the girl was at her booth.

"Morning," the girl said, and called across the room to the server. "Could I have a coffee please?"

She turned back and folded her hands on the table. "My name is June McCarthy."

Clear didn't like people like this – the forward ones. They always wanted something from her. She thought she'd left them behind when she moved from her two-story clapboard in Kerrville to the trailer just outside Utopia. But there were even more of them out here. It was like the country air and the crystal clear rivers made their thoughts jump out of their mouths like bullfrogs. And they were always asking the same questions.

"I don't have anything to say to you," Clear said, pulling her coffee close.

"You don't even know what I want," June McCarthy said. Her coffee arrived and she paid for it right then and there – tip and all.

"You want to know about them little girls."

June nodded as she drank and set her cup down before she spoke. "No."

Clear tilted her chin. "No?"

"No. You want to know about those little girls. I want to help you."

Clear waited for the cell phone to come out and the camera to start rolling. The young people did that. They were obsessed with murder. It filled their TV shows and their novels and their online talk shows. They talked about it at dinner tables like it was the latest sitcom. They tried to find the rhyme and reason to the death and the horror and the real life monsters that hunted humans in the night, and Clear was tired of giving them the same answer: There wasn't one.

"I don't want to hear your theories," Clear said, waving like she was swatting a fly. "You're wasting your time. And mine."

"I know," June said. She looked out the window, resting her chin on the heel of her hand. She took a slow breath before whipping back around, blinking whatever thought she'd just had away. She cleared her throat. "I can take you to the bodies."

The tips of Clear's fingers shook. She pressed them together, but that made her whole body shake. She was too old to be shaking like this. She'd seen too many things as chief to be this afraid of an obnoxious girl in sparkly jeans. They'd never found the bodies, just the left index finger of each girl on the doorstep of her family's home. They came three days after they disappeared, exactly seventy-two hours later on the dot. The coroners could tell each had been severed after death by something sharp and thin.

"I'm not playing this game," Clear said, and she stood. She was proud that she didn't shake.

June sat back with her cup raised to her chin. "I'll be here when you're ready, Chief Clear. But don't take too long. I'm not as patient as the dead."

* * *

Clear bumped her way along the dirt road that led to her front stoop. Her trailer was set up on two concrete blocks to keep the wet out of her living room floor, and she beat her boots against one. There was a feel of yellow inside, though the walls were papered with faded pink and blue blossoms, and the parts of the carpet not bleached by the sun were creamy. But yellow was everywhere, touching the walls and the doors and rolling over Clear. The yellow pulled on her as she sat on her loveseat and put her feet on the coffee table.

She faced the window, the TV somewhere behind her. She hadn't turned it on in twenty-four years. Outside there were just trees and the outline of the hills against the sun. There were houses in those hills, set at the end of sprawling driveways. Clear had always wanted one of those houses. She'd come close to having one after a proposal from a young rancher when she'd first moved to town. But she'd just been promoted, and she could taste the chief's position like butter in her mouth – a taste that only lasts a second. After Carrie Timmons went missing Clear wondered how things would've been different if she'd accepted.

It'd been a bright day. The middle of July, when the summer camps were in full swing, and trails were packed with campers and hikers, which made tracking down the murderer difficult. After Carrie's finger was dropped off on the welcome mat wrapped in a cupcake liner, the hunt was done. It wasn't called off officially, but no one had any hope that they would find the little girl alive.

It started to rain, and Clear settled into her loveseat, fishing her paperback from between the cushions. It was a cheap page-turner, mostly garbage, but able to distract her from any unwelcome thoughts before bed. She'd drown herself in half plots, and then she'd fall into bed too exhausted to let the faces of Carrie Timmons and Marisa Thomas and Bailey Whitby keep her awake.

She was in bed and avoiding their hollow stares by 2 a.m. The phone rang at three. It was Mitchum Griffis, the detective who had replaced her as chief. His voice shook and quivered like he was standing in the Arctic circle.

"What are you stuttering about, Griffis?" Clear said into the phone, still groggy.

"Clear? I need your help."

* * *

Ashley Jenkins had her birthday party two days ago. Pink streamers still hung in the living room, looped around bannisters but dipping in the middle. There was half-eaten birthday cake left in the fridge. Yellow and white with pink roses. Sarah Jenkins offered Clear a piece, but she didn't have an appetite.

"She's ten now," Sarah kept whispering, as if ten was too old to be hunted. Clear stayed outside during the interview.

He'd never taken one from home before. It hadn't even been dark yet, and Ashley was playing at the end of the driveway. Sarah could see her from the kitchen window bouncing a ball. Her hair was in pigtails, and she wore pink overalls over a cotton white shirt. Her tennis shoes were white, but drawn over with magic markers in blues and greens. Sarah checked on Ashley through the window, pulled a meatloaf out of the oven, and then her daughter was gone. That's all the officers got out of her before she started sobbing.

"Jon says they don't have any enemies," Griffis said. He let the Jenkins' screen door slam shut behind him as he joined Clear on the porch.

"Other families said the same," Clear said.

"Maybe we're dealing with a copycat? Or someone else all together? I mean, it has been twenty years." Griffis was a lean man, pushing sixty, with elbows and knees that stuck out like wires. He had a moustache that wriggled and shook like a caterpillar. Clear wanted to slap it off his face. She stuck her hands in her pockets.

"Twenty-four," she corrected. "And it ain't. I can feel it. He's back, or he never left."

"Then why wait so long?"

That question gnawed at Clear. The police hadn't been on to him. He could've killed plenty more girls and they may not have caught him for years. It almost disappointed Clear that he had never killed again. He'd never given himself an opportunity to slip up. Part of her buzzed with excitement, wondering if this was that chance. If only a little girl didn't have to die for it.

Clear left Griffis in mid-sentence and walked along the driveway. On either side of her was farmland, dead and brown with weeds poking their foul heads through the dirt. No place to hide. He was in a car. He could've scooped her up off the side of the road and been gone in the minute it took Sarah to open the oven.

A silver Hyundai Accent came down the road as Clear reached the end of the drive. June McCarthy got out and left the door open, sliding her sunglasses up like she was revealing a masked villain. She didn't smile.

"You see something?" Clear said.

"See something about what?" June said. She looked at the circle of cop cars still flashing in front of the Jenkins house. "I bet I can find something."

She walked along the road, her thumbs hanging in the pockets of her jeans. They were the same sparkly ones. She wore a T-shirt with a smiling cartoon beaver on it, and a pair of bright red cowboy boots. After a few steps, she jumped into the ditch alongside the road, kicking at the dead grass. Clear followed, hands behind her back. They walked silently for two miles, maybe three, until the flashing lights were sparkles on the horizon. There was a crossroads up ahead, and the ditch turned off to follow the Jenkins' land. June stopped at this sharp angle and knelt with her hands on her knees.

"You see this?" she said, pulling her sunglasses back over her eyes as she looked at Clear.

Clear knelt as low as her knees and the fat around her middle would let her. There was something buried beneath the grass. Pink mixed with brown. June kicked away some of the dead plants and water-logged trash. It was a pair of white tennis shoes drawn over with magic marker.

Clear narrowed her eyes at June, who was wiping mud and grass on her T-shirt.

"You knew that was there," Clear said.

June pulled herself out of the ditch, shaking dirt off her boots. "No, but I knew to look for it."

"How?"

She put her hands on her hips. "Because Carrie Timmons got her shoes taken too. So she wouldn't run away."

A winter chill passed through Clear, but she was still shivering after it was gone. Carrie Timmons' shoe had been found downriver, buried deep in the mud along the bank. The find was never released to the public. They'd searched the river for a body, but come up empty.

"No one said anything about the shoe," Clear said.

"A lot of things were never said," June said. She cracked her neck by pushing the palm of her hand against her chin. There was a dull purple birthmark on her jawline, barely an inch across. "But if you want to find that Jenkins girl, you should start listening to me."

She started back along the road the way they had come. She had her thumbs stuck in her belt loops, head tilted back to feel the winter sun. Clear followed, falling back still as her breaths quickened and knees started to seize. She was panting over them when June pulled up again in her Accent, one elbow leaning out the window.

"Want a ride, Chief?"

Clear steadied herself against the car. "If I start listening to you, what would that mean?"

"Means we start getting answers."

"And how would that go?"

"We'd start at the Sabinal River," June said. "Where Carrie went missing. And from there, we go forward."

Clear shielded her eyes against the sun as she looked to the hills. They were farther away now, circling the farmland in a red ring. Somewhere out there were three bodies of three girls who died lost and alone. She followed the line of the mountain back to the Jenkins farm house and the flashing lights of the police cars. She went to the passenger seat of June's car.

* * *

The Sabinal River was crystal clear straight down to the dirt. The weeds and vines that tangled with the roots of the riverside trees gave it a green appearance, but otherwise it was a glass top stretched across Bandera County. In the summer tourists would rent tubes and float down it, but the cold had driven those crowds away, and Clear and June stood alone on its banks.

"That's where her brother said they were," Clear said, pointing to the left. But June had already gone to the right to examine the dirt and tree roots that dipped into the river.

"It was closer to here," she said, pointing. She was behind a tall tree that had a low rope on one of its boughs. The rope was frayed, its end torn off and browning from age. "They were using it as a swing."

"The brother didn't say nothing about that," Clear said. She found herself reaching for the small notepad she used to keep in her uniform back pocket, but stopped herself.

"That's because they weren't supposed to be doing it," June said, pulling the end of the rope toward them. She let it slide through her fingers. "Jason made her promise not to tell, and he was winding back to jump when he realized she wasn't there anymore."

This girl was spinning tales faster than Clear could keep up. Now there was a secret between the children, a reason why the brother never saw it happen. The town had wondered why a strong kid like Jason Timmons hadn't tried to defend his little sister. It filled a hole, but that could've come from careful research and quick thinking.

Clear leaned back against a tree, arms folded. "I need to know where these fibs are coming from, and what they're leading to."

"I'm not lying," June said like a broken record. Her jaw tightened.

"How do you know all this, then, ma'am?"

June reached for the rope again, but didn't grab it. She folded her arms across her chest. "I was here."

"If you was, you couldn't have been more than five minutes old."

"I wasn't anything old, actually. It wasn't me—"

Clear threw her hands in the air. "I goddamn swear, if you don't tell me—"

"Let me finish, Chief," June said. She kept her voice level, but her fists were clenched. "It wasn't me, it was Carrie. But I was Carrie once. I used to be her when she was alive, and when she died what was left of her was made into me. I get flashes of who she was. I know Jason was winding up to jump because Carrie watched him, and I knew about the shoes because Carrie knew. Do you see?"

Clear waited for her to laugh or vanish, but she was perfectly still.

"You telling me you had a past life? Like a Buddhist?"

"It was her life, but I remember it."

"What's the difference?"

"Her life was recycled; it became something new. Like when a Coke can becomes a license plate. This life is mine, but I came back here to settle Carrie's. Because—" she paused, her arms snaking up to hug her shoulders. "Because her memories are haunting me."

"You know who killed those girls?"

June shook her head. "It's only flashes. It was more when I was young, but I've forgotten. It's like trying to remember a dream. I can remember when she was taken, and a bit after that, but I don't know who he is."

Clear jerked her chin. "How'd you even know it's a he?"

"Something in my gut," June said. "Or Carrie's gut, maybe."

Clear wished she'd brought her own car. Now she was stuck out on a backroad with a lunatic.

"I can't take this today," Clear said, waving a hand. "I'm going home."

"I don't want to do this either, Chief," June called. "This whole thing has nothing to do with me. I can't move on with my life if I don't settle Carrie's. She's in my head. I have to do this for her, and you're the only chance I've got."

It had taken a long time for Clear to stop thinking about the knot of guilt that had settled somewhere beneath her liver. It wasn't gone, she was sure of that, just resting. Every couple of years it came with fangs and claws out, and it tore through Clear with a savage shake and wrestle that left her passed out on her loveseat with a bottle of scotch. When it first arrived it had wrestled for twenty years nonstop, and it was only in the past four that it had started to rest between attacks. Clear wondered how long it would take to push it back again if she agreed to work with the lunatic girl.

Clear leaned her head back, throat exposed, and sighed. "You said you know where the bodies are."

June's back straightened. "I think so."

"We couldn't find those for twenty-four years."

"I know what the area looks like. I would recognize it."

"We can't roam all over the place looking for landmarks," Clear said.

June pointed down the road that followed the natural flow of the river. "If we just roam that way, we'll find it."

* * *

Clear leaned her head out the window as far as it would go to watch the stars fly by overhead. There were so many of them. They blurred together into a silver sea, and for a moment she forgot to look for dead bodies.

"Couple more miles, Chief, and then we'll call it a night," June said.

"I'm not the chief anymore," Clear said. "Stop calling me that."

"I thought it was like the president? Once the chief, always the chief."

"It's not," Clear said. She pulled her head back into the car. "Haven't been for a long time."

June flipped her brights on as they rounded a bend. "What did you do after you retired?"

"Nothing," Clear said. "Thought about farming, but it was just me, and I didn't have the cash to buy any land or help. Could've moved to Fredericksburg or even San Antonio, gotten a job in security or something."

She'd come close three times to packing up her stuff and moving. She'd even gone as far as to build the cardboard boxes, but every time she ended up back in her loveseat watching the window and drowning in yellow.

"I've got a degree in business administration," June said. "Going back for my Master's in a couple months."

"That your dream job? Administering business?"

The girl shrugged. "I want to be steady. Just want to move forward without worrying about choices I made to get there."

Clear frowned. She was so used to young folk here wandering off to find big dreams. It was almost depressing to hear someone with more days ahead of her than behind not trying to make the most of them with unrealistic expectations. Clear grabbed the dashboard as the car lurched to a stop.

"You see that tree?" June said. It was old and knotted, curling into itself from the mid trunk into a half circle. There were no leaves, and no other trees around it. Clear still heard the gentle sputter of the river, but it was far away.

The base of the tree was tangled with knotted roots, and the ground was hard and frozen. June knelt, running her fingers across them.

"They're under here," she said.

"You can't dig through roots like these," Clear said, shaking her head.

"You can on the other side."

They circled the tree. There was a clear spot among the roots, almost perfectly square.

Clear measured it with her eyes. "That's too small to fit a body. Even a child's."

June wrapped her arms around herself. "Not if you cut it into pieces."

The wind shook the branches. "Wait," Clear said. "If you were dead by the time you got here—"

"If Carrie was dead," June corrected.

"Okay, if she was dead by the time she got to here, how come you know what he did with the bodies?"

June closed her eyes. She bent over the square spot in the roots, running her hands along the dirt, and then digging her fingers into it. There was another scar around her index finger, faint and pink, a perfect ring. She scooped out a few handfuls before Clear put a hand on her shoulder to stop her. When June opened her eyes again, they were red.

"He made her dig the grave," she whispered. "She realized, and that's when he killed her."

They stared at the patch of dirt. "We have to dig it up and find out," Clear said.

"Shouldn't we tell the police?"

Clear knew it was stupid, but they couldn't tell the police. They'd get suspicious, wonder why after all these years Clear finally knew what the hell was going on. They'd think she'd known twenty-four years ago too and hadn't done anything.

"No, we need to find the killer first. You got a shovel in that car?"

June shook her head and held up her dirty hands. "Have to do it the old-fashioned way."

It didn't take long. The tree was in the middle of nowhere, and the murderer obviously thought it was well hidden. He didn't bother burying them deep. They found a skull first, sitting pretty on top the rest of the body. The bones had been stacked neatly, limbs one over the other like Jenga, and the torso and rib cage beneath. The bones were blackened with the dirt and tinged yellow with age. They didn't bother going past the first body.

"That's that," Clear said, wiping her hands on her jeans. She looked away from the tree, trying to see the road through grass and the underbrush, but it was too far away. She couldn't hear anything but the chirp of the crickets and call of the birds and the screams of little girls.

"Now what?" June said. She didn't wipe her hands. She held them, still coated in dirt, close to her heart.

"Do you know where he was holding them?"

"I know that it was red," June said. "Red brick."

Clear frowned. There wasn't much brick in Utopia. It was all dusty concrete or peeling white wood. All the farm houses in the county were the same. Only a few of the ranch houses, the ones up on top of the hills, could be red. Maybe. But Clear had never been close enough to one to notice.

"This is impossible," Clear said, crouching in the dirt. The bones of the girl were laid out in neat piles, the skull staring with empty sockets. Clear looked away.

June ran the dirt between her fingers, watching it fall to the ground as she sat back on her heels. She reached into the hole up to her shoulder. Clear watched her scramble for something, her lips pressed tight. She pulled out three small, triangle-shaped stones mixed with the dirt. "What are these?"

"Just rocks. Nothing."

But June shook her head. She lifted one to eye level, squinting. "They're seeds," she said. "Sunflower seeds."

* * *

The Peerage farm grew sunflowers. They were a bright spot of yellow among fields of gray wheat. Even when the rest of the crops in the area died and were blown away, the Peerage sunflowers grew strong and bright. Peerage land wasn't far outside Utopia, and the first crop of sunflowers were planted the same year the first three girls went missing.

Clear drove through town in her truck the day after finding the grave, passing Utopia's welcome sign.

Welcome to Utopia
A Paradise
Lets Keep It Nice

The sign was old and rusting with an error on the last line. June watched it from the passenger seat. "We can't prove anything," she said.

"We can take a look around," Clear answered, checking her rearview again, even though she'd just checked it five minutes ago. "I just want to pick something up."

She left the truck running and went into her trailer, digging through the old trunk she kept at the end of her bed. She found her revolver and put it in her inside coat pocket. Back in the car, June was drumming her fingers against the dash.

"You nervous?" Clear said, clicking into her seatbelt.

"Hope we're not too late." She ran a hand along the birthmark on her neck. "And I hope you're right. I just want this to be done with so I can get back to my life."

The sunflowers were a golden sea, bending and tossing with the wind. Bill Peerage's truck was outside his house beneath the shade structure. There was a light on in the kitchen, and the dull blue glow of a television from the living room.

"Should we sneak around back?" June said. Her hands were looped around her seatbelt, knuckles white.

"I'll go to the door, you go see what's in that barn," Clear said, jerking her chin to wooden, peeling structure. "Don't make a sound. Just a quick look."

They unbuckled their seatbelts together and slammed their doors shut as one. June veered off from the dirt path toward the barn, and Clear patted the revolver beneath her coat. It bounced against her stomach, hard and cold.

The screen door hung half off its hinges. Clear held it back with one foot and rapped on the door with her knuckles. It was painted sunflower yellow. Clear saw a shape through the door's small glass window, and she stepped back to let the broken screen fall back into place.

"Why, Pam," said Bill Peerage as he swung his door wide. "What a surprise."

"Just checking in on things, Bill," Clear said. His face was warped by the screen, crisscrossed with wires, but she could still make out the squat bend of his nose and his receding hairline. His eyes were covered by a thick pair of wire-framed glasses. He was shorter than her and stood with his chin tilted forward to try and give the illusion of height. "You heard what happened at the Jenkins'?"

"How could I not?" Bill said, shaking his head. "Such a sad thing. And we thought that was all in our past. Us old folks can still remember the first three."

"Everyone can remember the first three," Clear said. "And if they don't know, they were told. Three murders aren't something we're likely to forget in Utopia."

Bill tilted his head in a way that said he agreed. "So, what are you doing out, Pam? I know you're not still working these cases. Or any cases."

Pam's smile was thin. "Just checking in on my old friends. Guess the protect and serve never really leaves you."

The barn was in the corner of her eye, and she saw June's shadow as she pulled open the doors and slipped inside. The huge, iron hinges creaked, and Clear froze, waiting for Bill to throw open the screen. He didn't move.

"That's real kind of you, Pam," he said instead. His smile hadn't dropped since he opened the door, nor had it twitched or moved or slipped at all. It was carved marble. His lips stayed lifted, his eyes wrinkled, his cheeks round and cheery. Clear took a step back.

"Well, if you ever need anything, you know where I am," she said. She took several steps back before she reached the porch stairs and realized that she would have to turn around. He watched her with his carved, stone face. She did it slowly, one foot at a time. Her right foot hit the first step, the other followed, and then she was on the second. The wind shifted her shirt collar, making her twitch, and a hand touched her shoulder.

He was on the porch. Clear turned to face him, but Bill didn't remove his hand. They stood on his porch with his arm between them.

"I hope you're doing okay with all this," Bill said. His hand splayed like a spider on her shoulder. She wanted to shake him off and squash him under her boot.

"I'm doing fine," she said.

"Because I know how rough the first three girls were on you."

His smile was still there. She reeled back down the porch steps and onto the dirt path. She waved a hand as she backed away toward the car.

"I appreciate that, Bill!" she called. She got into the car. It took two turns to get the engine roaring. She hit the gas hard, realized that would be suspicious, and slammed on the breaks, jerking herself forward. When she looked at the house, Bill was back behind the screen. Watching her with a sculpted smile.

Clear waited until he was gone before she threw the car in reverse and went half a mile down the road. She parked in the grass, considered hiding it, but there wasn't time. She got out and started back toward the farm.

She put a hand to her chest, feeling the rapid slamming of her heart. It refused to slow. She shook like a feral cat, and she wanted to turn back and drive into the night. Clear kept moving forward, ignoring the twitching in her fingertips and the screaming of her heartbeat. Somewhere inside of her, she was still the chief. Those instincts had never left her. Once the chief, always the chief.

She rounded a bend in the road. The barn doors were cracked. Inside was ancient, rusting farm equipment draped with blue tarps. The floor was soft wood, and it creaked as she stopped.

"June?" she called, but it was barely a whisper, and her voice scraped along her throat. She cleared it. "June."

"Over here."

Clear moved around the hulking blue shapes, and found June kneeling before a wall. She had her head in her hands.

"What is it?" Clear asked.

"I can't remember," June murmured. "Carrie can't remember."

"Remember what?"

"Where to go from here."

The barn wall was mostly white, but there were shapes painted on it. Huge, peeling squares in yellow, brown, and red. They took up most of the wall, but had decayed to only soft shadows of whatever they had been before.

"What is this?" Clear said, running a hand along the squares. Paint slipped off the wall with it, revealing the greying wood beneath.

"I don't know; a mural I think," June said. "But it feels familiar."

"What kind of familiar?"

June looked at her pointedly. "Like I know it from another life."

Clear took a step back. She took another and backed up against one of the machines. She turned to steady it, and when she looked back, the squares had changed.

"They've got roofs," she said, pointing. "Same color as the white, almost."

June came to stand beside her. "Huh. Are they houses?"

Must be, Clear thought. Houses painted on the side of a barn. One yellow, one brown, one red. She squinted, and noticed a soft, pink circle in the corner. She went closer and two pairs of black eyes looked back.

"It's a pig," she said, frowning. "In front of a house."

"A red house," June said, and her eyes widened. "A brick house."

The floor beneath the mural of houses was covered with one of the blue tarps. Clear kicked it away, sliding it back with her boot. There was soft wood beneath, just like the rest of the barn. Clear kicked the wall in frustration.

"This ain't getting us anywhere," she said. "We should go back, see what we can think of. I don't want Bill coming here—"

"Wait," June said, pointing at the floor beneath the red brick house. "Look."

There were hinges where the wall met the floor. June kneeled before them, running a finger under the planks. The hinges groaned as she lifted them up, and beneath the floor there was darkness.

"Shit," June said, but Clear had already pulled out the flashlight she kept in her back pocket, and bent low over the hole in the floor to shine the beam inside.

At first, there was nothing. More blue tarp, crinkled chip bags, and crushed soda cans. Clear lowered herself onto the homemade steps set inside.

"Do you see anything?" June called.

Clear looked over her shoulder to answer when the blue tarp rustled. She grabbed a handful and ripped it out of the hole, and two wide eyes looked back at her.

Ashley Jenkins had tape around her mouth, ankles, and wrists. She blinked into the beam of the flashlight, cowering against the wall of the hole, until Clear dropped it and her face was visible. Ashley squirmed toward the chief, salty tears dripping into the tape over her lips.

"It's okay," Clear whispered, dropping to her knees and putting one arm around the girl. They both shook.

"Did you find her?" June called from above. "We gotta get out of here, Chief!"

Clear lifted the girl up by the shoulders, handing her off to June, who ripped the tape away, but put a finger to her lips.

"We have to be quiet now, okay?" June whispered. "We'll take you back to your mom and dad, but we have to be quiet now."

Ashley nodded. Clear stuck the flashlight back in her pocket. Beneath the blue tarp there was straw, green with mold. The walls were unevenly stacked wooden planks, and they were spattered with flecks of deep brown. She wondered if the other girls had sat in that same straw, taped and terrified, hoping a police officer would open the hatch and take them back to their parents. She ran her hand along the wall and the brown spots. She shivered.

Clear hoisted herself through the hatch, letting it slam shut behind her.

"Chief!" June hissed, her arms still tightly around Ashley. "Keep it down!"

"Can't hear us from the house," Clear said.

"That's not quite true, Pam," said Bill Peerage, who stood in the doorway of the barn, legs spread apart, glasses askew, balancing a shotgun on one arm.

Ashley buried her face in June's chest as Clear stepped forward, pushing the two girls behind her. Her hand drifted to the inside pocket of her jacket.

"It's over, Bill," she said. "You had a long run. Three girls dead, over twenty years and not caught. Well done. Time to throw in the towel."

"You're all just so stupid," Bill said. His glasses had yellow-tinged lenses, with wire frames that were bent a little on the left. It looked like he was tilting his head, but he was standing perfectly straight, his finger poised on the trigger. "I got you for so long."

"Yeah, you did, Bill," Clear said. She raised her hands. Behind her June was whispering to Ashley, her hand stroking her hair, but when Clear glanced over her shoulder, there were tears in both of their eyes. "Well done, like I said. But it's over now."

"They never found the bodies." Bill straightened his shoulders. "None of them. Not even you, Pam. I'll go down in history."

"Sure will." Clear nodded along. "You did a really good job."

"You think they'll put it in the news, Pam?"

"No doubt about that. But you gotta let us go for that, you know? Gotta get the word out."

But Bill Peerage shook his head. "Can't let you do that, Pam."

Ashley Jenkins started to cry – huge, rolling sobs that stabbed Clear in the back.

Pam Clear couldn't let this man take the easy way out. She wanted to see him stand trial and listen to a judge read what he had done, and to let the people of this town send him to rot in prison. Her hand trembled as she reached for her revolver, but it wasn't fear. It was rage that had been bottled and fermented for twenty-four years. Clear wanted to burn Peerage's sunflowers to the ground.

"June," Clear whispered as Peerage continued to speak.

"I could've gotten away with it forever," he said, shaking his head.

"June, you run to my left."

"Chief – no!" June whispered.

"You listen to me, June."

"If I had stopped then. I should've stopped then. Shouldn't have stopped for this one." He gestured at Ashley, who quivered.

"I'm gonna take my shot, and you run," Clear murmured.

"I didn't plan on it. Just wanted to go home. Just driving along and there she was."

"I *can't*."

"You *can*!"

"Just playing like there was no one out there to snatch her up. What kind of parents leave their kids out alone like that?"

"*Chief!*"

"*June!*"

"I was teaching them a lesson. They know better now. They won't leave any kids out now. No one will."

"*Now!*" Clear shouted. The chief took her shot, throwing herself to the right in a wild motion, looking to distract and not expecting to hit anything but barn wall, but Bill Peerage's shoulder went back while the rest of him went forward. June picked Ashley up and ran as the girl screamed. The blue tarps went up in a wave around them, June making them fly as she ran out of the barn.

Clear was after them before Peerage stood up. She saw him holding a wet, red arm as she ran into the night. To her left were the sunflower fields. She ran into the tall stalks, fists pumping, breath heaving, revolver raised.

"Chief! Chief, are you alive?" June screamed from somewhere in the field.

"Shut up, idiot!" Clear shouted back. The girl was silent, and Clear only heard the slapping of her own boots in the dirt and the rustling of the sunflowers. There was only green around her and yellow above.

She stopped running when the stitch in her side felt like a knife. She clutched it as she bent over her knees. The rustling got louder, the wind picking up. Clear looked behind her, and in between the stalks, she saw a flash of red and then an eye hidden behind a yellow lens. Clear ran, tearing down sunflowers as she went.

"June! He's near me! Get away from my voice!"

There was no response. Just the running and slapping and rustling of flowers. Clear wanted to throw up. Her revolver was heavier than it had ever been, dragging like her entire arm was made of lead. She considered dropping it. A sunflower exploded beside her head.

Adrenaline pierced Clear like a needle to the heart, and it was as if that was what her body had been waiting for. Suddenly, she was awake. She looked back, looking for a glimpse of bloody shoulder.

Another flower blew over her head, and she spotted him. His aim was wild, one arm hanging as a dead thing at his side.

"I could kill you all now," Peerage said. "Easy as shooting deer."

Clear stopped running. She turned to face him. "You could, but they'd find you. And it wouldn't matter what you did to us then. You're going to prison, Bill. Whether you like it or not."

"You think they'll remember me though, Pam? Think they'll talk about me on the news? Put me in TV shows? Make one of those documentaries?"

Clear's words tasted like bile. "No doubt about that, Bill."

Peerage grinned. There was a glint in his eye. It was shiny and wide and full of wonder. He was imagining the future and what he would look like in it, even if it was just his legacy. Clear wanted to slap it off him and suck up that glint like a chocolate malt. She never got the chance. Bill Peerage spun his shotgun around and fired once into his throat, even as she shrieked in protest.

Clear wiped Bill Peerage's thick, red blood from her face. There was red everywhere – on the stalks and the dirt and on her. It was a sea of red, but all she saw was yellow.

* * *

The silver Hyundai Accent sat just beside Utopia's welcome sign. Clear looked past the car to the sign's last line: "Lets Keep It Nice"

"Do you think it can be a paradise now?" June asked as she slammed the trunk shut. She leaned against her car, looking back at the tiny town. "Since there's no serial killer?"

"It can be better than it was," Clear said. "But there's no such thing as utopia."

"What'll happen to Ashley, you think?"

"They're setting her up with a therapist; a good one in San Antonio. I think she's going to be okay."

"Got to keep her finger," June said, and she tapped the scar that circled her left index finger. "That's something."

"Something," Clear agreed. Her voice was distant.

"What'll you do now, Chief?"

"I ain't the chief, June."

The girl smiled. "Once the president."

"I just wish…" But Clear couldn't get herself to finish the sentence. It was trapped somewhere in her throat, and no matter how much she gagged on it, she couldn't accept that it was stuck there. She'd keep trying to force it out, and wondered if she'd ever be able to speak normal again.

"You couldn't have stopped him, Pam," June said. "He was going to do what he wanted to do. You found him, and now he can't hurt anyone else."

"But he'll never have to face what he did to the others," Clear whispered. She looked down at her boots. "He got away with those murders. And you know what else? They're already talking about him on the news, like he was some kind of celebrity. It's like what he did doesn't even matter. Like he was a genius or something. There's no justice."

"We can't fix that," the girl said. She went to stand in front of Clear, so her bright red cowboy boots were in the chief's line of sight. "Some things we just gotta let go of."

Clear met her eye. "I'm trying. But you know, there are some things we shouldn't let ourselves forget."

June scratched at her neck, just below her birthmark. She nodded. "I know that now. I'm trying too."

Clear stuck her hand out. "As long as we're trying."

June grinned as she shook the chief's hand. It was a firm shake, brief but solid.

"Good luck, June. You ever come back to Utopia, you can look me up."

June got into her car, but she rolled the window down and leaned out to answer. "Likewise."

They both grinned, and June started the car and rolled away down Utopia's single road, and out past a curve that would lead her to bright city lights. Clear went back to her truck and trudged along the same road until it turned to dirt. It brought her back to her trailer, and once inside she pulled a phone book out from the side-table drawer. She called the first realtor she spotted.

"You know of any ranch houses for sale in the hill county?" Clear said, sitting down in her loveseat and looking outside at a sunset dripping in reds and yellows.

A Problem with Threes

Trixie Nisbet

This room is too public a place for a conventional report. It is impossible here to type unobserved. And there is, all around me, a natural curiosity as to my conclusions. There is rumour, bordering on common knowledge, that I have unearthed the identity of the traitor here at St Mark's – and I can feel the eyes of every passer-by glancing over this report as I type.

Home Office regulations have allowed me unrestricted access to St Mark's, the hub of British coding, and code-breaking. These, Hester, are my initial thoughts – I'm sure you'll understand.

THE TEXT scrolled up the giant cinema-like screen that had been erected on the stage. The capacity crowd at the Royal Festival Hall sat in the dark auditorium, their eyes following each line with keen interest. Some checked the words on the screen to the transcript they had been given when they entered.

Spotlights then illuminated a single chair placed to one side of a low table. On the table were a jug of water, two glasses and, conspicuously placed, a handsome hardback book, its dark cover embossed with silver.

A young woman walked into the spotlights from the left, confident in high heels which perfectly matched the scarlet of her lips. She wore a trim blue dress with a small microphone clipped to her lapel. "Welcome everybody," her voice was both cheerful and business like, "to what I trust will be an interesting and revealing evening. For those of you who don't know, I am Cathy Ogilvy, recently appointed as Chief Detective of the Metropolitan Police. The case that we are to hear about happened some time before I took charge, indeed some time before I was born, but it was my department which became involved when, as it says behind me, the traitor at St Mark's was unearthed."

She moved to the centre of the stage. "Police records from the time are marked simply as 'Case Closed'. It is only now, in this book, that the truth is revealed for the first time. It is my pleasure, this evening, to introduce to you the man behind the unravelling of the St Mark's scandal: ladies and gentlemen, please welcome Sir Anthony Wren."

The audience responded with enthusiastic applause as Sir Anthony, in his chunky mobility scooter, whirred onto the stage. He halted next to the low table, facing the audience. He was in his nineties, sparse-haired and fragile. But his sunken eyes belied his age, glinting with a keen intelligence. He too wore a microphone, clipped to the lapel of his light grey suit.

"Thank you, thank you," he murmured, waving down the applause with a skeletal hand. He turned with a perfect denture smile to Cathy. "I haven't done anything yet."

"You have an impressive reputation preceding you, Sir Anthony." She sat at the opposite end of the table.

Sir Anthony's eyes swept the auditorium. "And there was I, thinking the life of a code-breaker would be top-secret." He gave the audience a theatrical wink and they chuckled. He knew how to work a crowd.

"Top-secret no longer, perhaps." Cathy indicated the book. "'Secrets of a Code-Breaker' by Sir Anthony Wren; your much-anticipated memoirs, finally made public."

"Those secrets that I've been *permitted* to tell." Sir Anthony gave an apologetic shrug. "There are further tales that, for the moment, must remain – undisclosed."

"Then we are lucky to have you here to talk us through one of your more celebrated incidents." Cathy crossed her legs, pointing a scarlet stiletto towards the audience. "The format of this evening will be a presentation by Sir Anthony, then I have a few, hopefully insightful, questions which, if there's time, we'll open up to the auditorium."

"Followed by a signing in the foyer." Sir Anthony's face wrinkled into a grin. "Where a scarily vast pile of books can be purchased at, I'm told, a very reasonable rate."

Cathy indulged her guest with a scarlet smile. "I'd like to start," she said, "by setting the scene. I'm a detective by profession, so I can appreciate such things, but you had to do quite a bit of detective work yourself, as we shall hear. Indeed, your unravelling led to the unmasking of a brutal killer."

"A sorry business all round." Sir Anthony's cracked voice was heavy with regret. "But at the time it was damn scary, I can assure you."

"This was Spring, 1945," Cathy added, "towards the end of the war. Intelligence was vital, and messages and instructions were sent between military and government departments using a variety of cyphers, developed and controlled from St. Mark's. Can you tell us a little of your role at the time?"

"Over seventy years ago." Sir Anthony wheezed a sigh. "St. Mark's was one of those Home Office outposts, a requisitioned country house, set in rural countryside that runs on weak tea and digestive biscuits. I was a mere boy back then. Only twenty; the youngest department head at St. Mark's. Basically, I was an annoying swot, but I got things done, which was what Mr. Green required. Mr. Green was the Director, he was in overall charge of the place. It sounds very formal now, but in those days, we were all Mr, Miss or Mrs something. I was always 'Mr. Wren', never Anthony. As I say, Mr. Green was the boss, and below him was Mr. Gillard of 'Cypher Creation' and myself in charge of 'Code Breaking'." Sir Anthony raised a matted eyebrow to the audience. "As you can imagine, there was much rivalry between myself and Mr. Gillard, with him creating cyphers to confound the enemy, and me, acting as Devil's advocate, trying to pull them apart. I must admit though, Mr. Gillard was remarkably proficient. I often found it easier to crack an enemy cypher than one home-grown. But..." Sir Anthony paused, "we had a problem. Messages were being intercepted, all the time. We knew that; that's why they had to be encoded. I don't intend to go into the nature of the messages themselves, but we had reason to suspect that the enemy had obtained the secret to one of our cyphers – and indeed, they were adapting their decoding strategies, to match any enhancement we made in the coding process. In short, we had an informant, *a traitor*, there at St. Mark's."

He paused again, allowing the anticipation of the audience to build, until Cathy felt obliged to keep the discussion moving. "I understand," she said, "that eventually a government agent was dispatched to St. Mark's to investigate this leak of information: a Mr. Arthur Balentine..."

"Poor Mr. Balentine, yes." At a touch of a stick control, Sir Anthony swivelled his motorised chair slightly to glance up at the text still displayed on the enormous screen at the back of the stage. "Unusual name. I remember remarking at the time that it was probably 'Valentine' and it had been mis-typed in a memo. B and V are next to each other on a keyboard after all, and typed with the same finger. But *Balentine* it was. He was holed-up with Mr. Green for hours when he arrived. There were heated exchanges with the Home Office and eventually a phone call from Churchill himself – anyway, the outcome was that Balentine was investigating, and that all staff at St. Mark's were to cooperate with him and hold nothing back. Imagine! We'd all signed the official secrets act, practically in blood, so we knew then how serious this was."

Cathy gave a distasteful twist of her ruby lips. "Speaking of blood…" She faced the audience, her tone apologetic. "We have displayed Mr. Balentine's report on our screen, and you will all have been given a transcript when you arrived. I wanted to stress that this is a word-for-word reproduction of the original report, exactly as it was retrieved from the crime scene at the time. The original typed sheet was obviously kept as evidence, and was, I believe, somewhat stained."

"Soaked," elaborated Sir Anthony for the audience's delight, "in the victim's blood." He took a composing breath. "I never saw the body myself, of course, but you can't keep a detail like that quiet, even in so secretive a place as was St. Mark's." He waved an arm up at the screen. "It is obvious from this opening paragraph that Mr. Balentine had discovered the identity of the traitor. As we shall see from the rest of the text, he narrowed down the list of suspects considerably, and this tallied with evidence later provided by the St. Mark's security staff. But this knowledge was dangerous. Moments after typing his report, Balentine was horrifically stabbed in the chest, and left slumped, bleeding across the desk and over the original of the paper you all now hold in your hands."

There was an uncomfortable rustling from the auditorium.

"There are a few points of significance," Cathy interjected, "in that first paragraph, which I know, Sir Anthony, you will be returning to. But I wanted to ask at this point who Hester was."

"Ah, yes, Hester: the mysterious recipient of the report." Sir Anthony whirred his chair to fully face his audience. "Not even *I* am told everything where the Home Office is concerned. It was wartime, and secrets were everywhere. Hester, I believe, wasn't a person at all. As I have said in the book, I discovered, much later, references to *Hester communications*, and the very similar sounding *Esther* too. Hester, and Esther, I believe were not individuals, but were code names for a department within the Home Office who were awaiting Mr. Balentine's typed report.

"I wouldn't dream of typing anything myself; I'd get in too much of a muddle. But I remember Mr. Balentine, quite clearly, sitting in a corner of the typing pool. Given the sensitive nature of his report, it wasn't something he dare trust to a telephone call. During the war there was a shortage of copper wire; shared 'party' lines were common and there were always operators who could listen in. Balentine refused to dictate to one of the girls, and insisted on typing it himself.

"I admit that I was one of those curious passers-by that he mentions – it was simply not possible to shut down the whole typing pool. I remember feeling a tad guilty when I read this opening paragraph. He implied that people were spying on him, and yes, I guess we were, everyone wanted to know who the traitor was. I gather the girls in the typing pool made quite a game of trying to read over his shoulder." Sir Anthony gave a wry smirk at the memory, and nodded towards the screen. "Perhaps we can proceed to the rest of the text."

Cathy gave a signal, and the words began to scroll upwards again. "I suggest," she said, "that we all take a moment to read from the screen or the transcript. There is a natural break in the report where I'd like to pause so that we can resume Sir Anthony's account of what followed."

Sir Anthony helped himself, a little unsteadily, to a glass of water as Balentine's report continued to rise, line by line:

> Even this external investigation was met with some resistance, but after a week here at St. Mark's, I am in no doubt that there has been a leakage of vital information concerning the coding of certain military instructions.
> These were coded using a cypher developed by Mr. Gillard's team of encrypters, under the guidance of the facility's director, Mr. Green.

Regular codes of this type are then passed to the code-breaking section of St. Mark's, under the guidance of Mr. Wren. The code-breaking section is primarily concerned with decrypting enemy broadcasts, but they also have access to the encryption facility so I could not exclude them from this investigation.

As a matter of course, there is secrecy within, as well as between, departments.

It is my observation that an individual's role within the overall operation is rarely divulged to their peers. This effectively limits the number of staff who would have an accumulated personal knowledge of the coding systems, and would reduce the number of suspects I would have to consider.

To this end, I questioned staff on their roles, and I am now certain that only the heads of department would have sufficient knowledge to be useful to an enemy agent. This immediately narrowed down the likely traitor to those three senior staff named above.

Of those named, Mr. Gillard had the most direct access to the encoding of messages. Because of the leak, I suggested to him that a further level of encryption should be applied to military messages of a particular sensitivity. He was at first reluctant to recognise my authority.

Receiving a directive to the same effect from Mr. Green, however, Mr. Gillard was obliged to apply this enhancement immediately.

And following an established procedure, Mr. Wren was then informed with a view to establishing the robustness of this additional encryption.

Then I needed a test. Yesterday, I had colleagues at the Home Office issue a request for a coded command of a strategic nature. This purported to be a gathering of our forces, converging on a particular enemy naval site.

Staff were instructed, specifically, to use the enhanced code.

Then, this morning, I received word that enemy reinforcements had already been deployed to defend this site against the expected attack. In just one day, the code's secret had been passed on.

Monitoring the movements of the three head staff, and the flow of information between departments, I had hoped to distinguish which of the three could have been responsible. However, this was inconclusive.

Although they each had access to the new coding protocols, I could find no opportunity for them to have passed on this information.

Regarding this dissemination, I had short-sightedly assumed the leak would come from within St. Mark's. Having established a relatively equal access to the information, I now realised that the secrets could be passed on at any time. And I realised, after the event, that I may have witnessed something significant.

The words on the screen came to a halt and Detective Cathy Ogilvy leant across the low table towards her guest. "I'd like to stop the report at this point, Sir Anthony, so that you can fill in some background. Things were looking pretty dark for you back then."

Sir Anthony set down his glass of water. "They were dark indeed. As we know, poor Mr. Balentine is about to be murdered with a knife taken from the canteen, and has just named me in his report as one of the three suspects. One of us *was* the traitor, so, potentially, we all had a motive."

"And opportunity?" asked Cathy.

"Unfortunately, that too was inconclusive. I mentioned the security staff earlier…St. Mark's had its own security. *Porters*, they were called. Basically, gatekeepers on the main entrance. I should explain that this was the only unlocked entrance; all staff, in and out, were monitored by the porters."

"And on the evening of the murder?" Cathy prompted.

"There were two porters on duty that evening. They were both interviewed by the police at the time, and I've included extracts from the police reports in the book. Basically, by early that evening, there were only four people left in the building: The three heads: Mr. Green, Mr. Gillard and myself – it was perfectly normal for us to be the last to leave – and the victim, Mr. Balentine.

"I freely admit popping into the typing pool to say goodnight. Mr. Balentine looked weary and told me, with some relief, that he was nearing the end of his report. I remember thinking that he wrote very slowly. Unlike me, he was quite proficient at typing, but he took a long time over his choice of words – which we now know he chose with great care. Several of the typists made the same comment during the subsequent police investigation. Balentine would sit for a while, thinking, then clatter out another paragraph before another long pause. Of course, the girls had tried to read the report as Balentine typed it. There was already much gossip, that afternoon, concerning myself and the other two head staff being suspected, and one girl repeated almost word-for-word the section about the false Home Office test message.

"Anyway, of the four of us left in the building, I was the first to leave for home. I said goodnight to Balentine and left him typing. This, subsequently, cast me in a suspicious light, because both Mr. Green and Mr. Gillard said they left *without* looking in on him. Of course, we now know this to be untrue, but at the time, I appeared to have been the last person to see Balentine alive."

"Very awkward for you, I'd imagine." Cathy managed a look of sympathetic concern. "The body was found, I believe by the porters."

"Yes, that's correct. The porters' normal routine is for one of them to stay at the main entrance at all times. But it was getting quite late, almost eight o'clock I believe, and, as they knew that Balentine was the only person left in the building, they locked the door and both went, apparently, to see if he was alright. Actually, it's more likely that they simply wanted to go home themselves, and went to turf him out.

"Well, we all know what they found. They telephoned Mr. Green first, then, with his authorisation, they called the police. It was after the police had read Balentine's bloodied report that Mr. Gillard and myself were rounded up for questioning.

"Naturally, I told the police that I'd seen Balentine alive when I'd left. I thought they believed me. And, with the porters' evidence, that left Mr. Green and Mr. Gillard as suspects. But eventually it dawned on me... If they thought I might be lying, then I was a suspect too." Sir Anthony manoeuvred his chair slightly to face Cathy across the table. "That was our problem," he said. "There were three of us."

Cathy was happy to take up her cue. "Sir Anthony and I were discussing this earlier," she said. "As a detective it is a situation that I and my colleagues know as *the problem with threes*." She stood and faced the auditorium as if she were giving a lecture.

"Detective work," she explained, "relies to some extent on the reactions of those under suspicion. We, the investigators, are looking at a situation from the outside, having to take in everything at face value. The people concerned, however, have the advantage of knowing whether they themselves are innocent or guilty. Where a crime has only two possible culprits, for example a husband and wife, one will know that they are innocent and that therefore the other is guilty. And this knowledge is often revealed in their actions and attitude to each other.

"The problem becomes more complex where, as in this case, there are three suspects. Obviously, one is guilty and therefore knows the remaining two are innocent." Cathy spread her hands in a gesture of regret. "Unfortunately, the guilty party is unlikely to confess, and will act as if he is innocent. Of the other two suspects, they each know that they are innocent, but don't know which of the other two is guilty. Where two, or three, of the suspects are brought together, their interactions may become stilted, but, unlike our husband and wife example, there is not the *certain* knowledge of guilt for an investigator to pick up on. That is what we know as the problem with threes." Cathy sat down again, her lecture over. "A tricky situation for you, Sir Anthony. Can you tell us what happened next?"

"That is exactly the situation I found myself in." Sir Anthony's voice was conspiratorial, confiding in his attentive audience. "As we will see in the concluding portion of his report, Balentine remains cryptic when he refers to the St. Mark's traitor – all of which was no help to me at all!

"As Detective Ogilvy has just demonstrated, I knew that either Mr. Green or Mr. Gillard was a murderer, but which one? I also realised that either Mr. Green or Mr. Gillard – whichever were the innocent party – had every reason to suspect *me*!

"We were all taken into the village police station and questioned, separately, into the early hours of the next day. Most of the questions were about how long we remained at St. Mark's that evening, so that they could piece together the order in which we left the building. I, as I say, was first, followed, apparently, by Mr. Gillard, then finally Mr. Green. This all tallied with statements taken from the porters.

"The police also asked about a particular phone box in the village, and whether we had used it recently. This made no sense to me until the following day, when, tentatively, my fellow suspects and I compared what we had been asked, and we found out further details of Balentine's report.

"We had each signed a typed police record of our accounts, and had been released, pending further investigations. I suspect the ubiquitous Home Office had some influence on our freedom. Though I say it myself, St. Mark's couldn't function for long without its three senior staff. As Balentine had indicated all too clearly, we were the only people with an overall knowledge of what our departments were working on.

"At St. Mark's the next morning, the typing pool had been cordoned off and relocated in the canteen, which naturally was a chaos of gossip. Many people had read over Balentine's shoulder the previous day. Soon everyone knew that Mr. Green, Mr. Gillard and myself were the primary suspects. Some had read enough of the report to speculate on the nature of a phone call that Mr. Balentine had managed to trace. So now the police questions about a phone box began to make sense."

Cathy crossed her legs again, instantly gaining the audience's attention. "We are straying now into the end of Balentine's report." Her crimson smile flashed over the auditorium. "I think we should allow the audience to read the remaining paragraphs. Then, Sir Anthony, perhaps you could talk us through your solution to the mystery."

"Certainly, certainly." Sir Anthony gave a dry choke. "I feel I've been droning on a bit. Where had we got to? I think we left things at the point where Balentine had realised that he'd seen something important. Might I have another glass of water?"

Detective Ogilvy reached for the water jug and signalled for the text behind her to start scrolling again.

Knowing the information could be passed on verbally, I recalled seeing one of the suspects in the village the previous evening. He was outside the lodging house where I was billeted and had been using a public phone box. There was nothing unusual in this. I knew that most of the staff lived locally, and this was in all probability perfectly innocent – but I decided to check.

So, I alerted the Home Office that I required a phone call to be traced. This, I discovered was impossible after the call had been made.

I then tried calling the local telephone operator, using the same public call box, in the slim hope that she might be able to help.

She made enquiries. There is no mechanism to record the phone numbers dialled from a public call box, and indeed the dialling apparatus on that particular telephone was faulty, so wouldn't have been reliable anyway. Then I had a stroke of luck. Because of the dialling fault, users had to ask the operator to connect their call.

Miraculously it appeared that, to keep a tally on the faulty line, the operator had actually noted down the exchange and number requested by each caller from that particular call box.

Rules on releasing such information to the public were eventually waved aside when I involved Whitehall in the investigation.

Given that I could supply the time of the call, we were able to determine the phone number concerned. It was listed as belonging to a bungalow in a small coastal town, not far from Brighton. Another directive from the Home Office soon had the bungalow surrounded by local police with army back-up.

Residences were evacuated on either side for safety, but it transpired that the property was empty. Inside, however, a sophisticated wireless system was discovered, sufficient to be a link in an enemy chain to pass on the coding secrets.

Evidence at last!

Evidence to support my identification of the St. Mark's traitor had thus been found.

Now that the traitor's identity is known, I trust, Hester, that you will act on my recommendation.

Sir Anthony cleared his throat. "So that's it, ladies and gentlemen: Balentine's report in its entirety."

"It doesn't appear to be finished," Cathy commented.

"You mean, there appears to be one vital piece of information missing." Sir Anthony's face wrinkled into a grin. "That's what *everybody* thought at the time. The police suspected there must have been a second sheet of paper. But when they examined the last used section of the typewriter ribbon, the impressions in it were wholly consistent with the report as we see it here. And, as we know, there were ample witnesses who could authenticate the report as that which they'd seen Balentine typing.

"It appears he finished the report, took it out of the typewriter and laid it on the desk in front of him, probably to read through it. And that's when the killer struck."

"So, can you tell us why the killer didn't simply remove the report?" asked Cathy.

Sir Anthony shrugged. "Who can say? Presumably the murderer read it and either thought it unfinished or harmless. Part of its content had already been spread as gossip and, as you say, it appears the killer's name is missing."

"The report, I understand, was removed and kept by the police as evidence. Did it ever reach Whitehall and the mysterious Hester it was addressed to?"

"You know, I don't believe it did. The police had copies typed up and circulated, sat us all down in front of it. To judge our reactions as we read it, I presume. And, in any case, after my investigations, the matter of the traitor was resolved – a little before the afternoon tea break."

"It was indeed." Cathy gestured to the table. "I have the advantage of having read your book. Perhaps though you could talk the audience through your reasoning."

Sir Anthony shuffled forward in his chair, eager to tell his tale. "I knew that the killer was one of only two possible people, both of whom left the building after me, and claimed not to have looked in on Balentine before they left. Mr. Green was last to leave, so, I reasoned, could safely have killed Balentine without being disturbed. Mr. Green was a cautious fellow and could intentionally have stayed at his desk until he knew he and Balentine were the only two remaining.

"Mr. Gillard was a plotter. I mean that as a compliment, he had a convoluted and devious mind that made him very good at his job. But, it seemed to me, his skills would also make him a very accomplished murderer."

"And *your* skills?" countered Cathy. "As a breaker of Mr. Gillard's codes, wouldn't that make you a skilled counter-plotter?"

"That's exactly what I suspect the police were thinking." Sir Anthony gave the audience an exaggerated look of worried concern. "So, I set myself the task of proving my innocence – I had to discover the identity of the killer.

"These were days before the widespread use of forensic evidence, DNA swabs or personality profiling, and I realised that all I really had to work with was Balentine's report. In it he says, right at the beginning, that it was impossible to type without being spied upon. Is it any wonder then, that he was cryptic in his revelation?

"And that's when I realised… Several people had commented on how slow and considered his report writing was – *and now I knew why.* Balentine was sent to investigate leaks in a coding establishment, he probably had a background in this field himself. I knew then that there must be a message hidden in his report. We'd all assumed that he hadn't named the St. Mark's traitor – but, of course, he had!"

There was another rustling from the audience and a murmur of amazement as practically everyone began to scan their transcript of Balentine's report.

"I read it over and over again," said Sir Anthony, "until one line near the beginning caught my attention: *These, Hester, are my initial thoughts – I'm sure you'll understand.*"

There were gasps from the audience as some of them began to scan down the report; others had produced pens and began to circle letters.

"I've been looking forward to this bit." Sir Anthony gave a dry chuckle. "When you can work it out, just as I did, all those years ago. It's a school-boy cypher really, nothing sophisticated, but then Balentine had to work it out on the spur of the moment. His *initial* thoughts. As a code-breaker I should have spotted it straight away. It's known as a rubrical cypher and is quite simply the initial letter of each paragraph.

"I can see that you're all working it out: *The traitor at St. Mark's…* Imagine my excitement when I realised the initial letters were forming words. *The traitor at St. Mark's is Mr…* And the next letter is a G. Green or Gillard? I still didn't know! Of course, you've all worked it out by now – Mr. Green!"

The audience lay down their pens, with an air of smugness, pleased that they too had solved the mystery.

"I was, what's the word, *gobsmacked,*" Sir Anthony continued. "Mr. Green! No wonder Balentine had insisted on submitting a written report rather than reporting internally at St. Mark's."

Detective Cathy Ogilvy could sense the buzz from the audience. "Well, I think that got a positive reaction," she said. "Tell us, Sir Anthony; what did you do then?"

"My head was reeling at the time. I didn't know what appalled me most, that Mr. Green was a killer, or that he had betrayed his beloved St. Mark's. I realised later how stupid I was, but I went to see him. I suppose I hoped he would just confess, or offer me some reasonable explanation of his actions. But when I got to Mr. Green's office – he too was dead."

Sir Anthony drained his glass of water and shook his head sadly. "A sorry business all round."

Cathy regarded him with sympathy but remained quiet, allowing him to continue.

"Mr. Green must have been ashamed of what he'd done. Or perhaps he saw ahead of him, the repercussions of his actions. So, he had taken the only action left to him. Several senior staff at St. Mark's, myself included, had been issued with certain pills. The idea being that, were we to be captured, we would not reveal any of Britain's coding secrets to the enemy. Mr. Green was slumped back in his chair, with a partially drunk cup of tea on his desk. I raised the alarm immediately, but there was nothing to be done.

"It was hushed up. Balentine, Mr. Green, the leak of secrets – the whole thing. Churchill decided it would not be in the public interest if news got out of a scandal at Britain's premier coding facility."

"And you, Sir Anthony, received a promotion."

"Everyone at St. Mark's was sworn to secrecy – that was part of their jobs. And, yes, eventually I was honoured to take Mr. Green's place as Director."

"And that was just one of the many honours to come your way, culminating with a knighthood on your much-overdue retirement." Cathy turned to the auditorium. "Ladies and gentlemen," she started to clap, "a true credit to Britain – *Sir Anthony Wren.*"

The audience stood for their applause. Cathy allowed Sir Anthony to enjoy this moment; she felt he deserved it, before she made shushing motions with her hands. "We have just one more revelation to come," she said as the audience settled back into their seats. "I have had the advantage of reading Sir Anthony's book and studying Balentine's coded report. And it seemed to me that there was one point which hadn't been resolved."

Sir Anthony swung his chair around to face her, intrigued by this unscheduled development.

"The last paragraph," said Cathy. *"Now that the traitor's identity is known, I trust, Hester, that you will act on my recommendation.* But what 'recommendation' was Balentine referring to?" She raised a sculpted eyebrow to Sir Anthony who waved a dismissive hand.

"The question never arose at the time."

"That is because," Cathy stood and resumed her role as lecturer, "you didn't know about Hester. The report never reached the Home Office department which would have understood the reference and its meaning. The name Hester, and indeed Esther, *were*, as you surmised, code words. You'll notice too that they are anagrams of each other. And another anagram of these letters is 'threes'. As we said before, Sir Anthony, you had a problem with threes."

Sir Anthony frowned. "Go on," he said.

"These, Hester, are my initial thoughts. Again, nothing sophisticated, but Balentine was telling the recipient of the report to look, not just at the first word of each paragraph – but at the third word as well."

There was another flurry of activity from the audience as pens reappeared and the transcripts were reappraised. Cathy allowed the audience to work it out, and waited for their puzzled reaction when they reached the end. "Not quite as simple as it looks, is it?" she said. "Allow me to offer an explanation.

"Mr. Balentine's recommendation is revealed by the third words, but as you have just discovered, there is some corruption to the message." Cathy turned to the screen behind her. "The first word of each paragraph gives us this message…" THE TRAITOR AT ST MARK'S IS MR. GREEN appeared on the screen. "And the third word of each paragraph gives us this…" Another line appeared below the first. I RECOMMEND AN IMMEDIATE ARIELST.

"Arielst." The word sounded awkward on Cathy's scarlet lips. "There is no such word. A wild misspelling of the word aerial perhaps? But that's unlikely and the sentence wouldn't make sense." She appealed to the audience. "Can anyone suggest what that last word should be?"

There were mutterings throughout the auditorium, then from several positions, the word 'Arrest' was called out.

Cathy looked pleased, but then her smile flattened to a grim red line. "Exactly," she said. "*I recommend an immediate arrest.*" She waved an arm up at the screen. "The I should be a letter R, and the L shouldn't be there at all." She let this idea sink into the audience's conscience, and could see them working through the implications.

"If we look at the transcript, we can see that the surplus L comes from the shortest paragraph 'Evidence at last!', with that rather extravagant exclamation mark. This line doesn't seem to fit with the rest of the report, and indeed, the report reads perfectly well without it. That line shouldn't be there. It was added to Balentine's report *after* it was written. It is *proof* that the report had been altered."

There were murmurings throughout the audience as one by one they saw where this was leading. Sir Anthony had swivelled his chair around to gaze at the screen. "That's quite ingenious," he said with a genuine appreciation.

"Then we have the letter I, which should be an R," continued Cathy. "It comes from the paragraph beginning 'Given that I could supply the time of the call'. I don't suppose that we'll ever find out how this was originally worded, but we *know* that it has been changed. What if that paragraph originally began with the letter W?"

There were cries of surprise and dismay from the audience as Cathy reread the coded message from Balentine's report. "I recommend an immediate arrest. The traitor at St Mark's is Mr. Wren."

Sir Anthony's chair whirred round and his eyes swept over the audience who fell strangely silent under his glare. Then his head drooped, he suddenly looked every second of his ninety-odd years.

Cathy's voice was almost apologetic. "You were careful to mention earlier that you can't type. But that's not true. You knew that B and V were next to each other on a keyboard, you even knew that they were typed with the same finger.

"You said you felt guilty when you read, over his shoulder, the opening paragraphs of Balentine's report. Perhaps you were telling us more than you intended. You saw there the reference to *initials*, and, like the trained code-breaker you are, you recognised it instantly as a rubrical cypher. You returned when everyone else in the typing pool had gone home – just as Mr. Balentine was reading through his report. You scanned down the first letter of each paragraph and realised you had been discovered. It was *you*, Sir Anthony, that Balentine had seen using the public phone box, *you* who had been passing Britain's coding secrets to the enemy. And it was *you*, Sir Anthony, who killed Mr. Balentine with a knife taken from the canteen."

All eyes were now focused on the old man in his mobility chair. He reached into a pocket of his suit and shakily produced a handkerchief. He dabbed at his eyes, silently.

"You realised," Detective Ogilvy continued, "that by altering the report only slightly, you could change the name Wren to Green – so that's exactly what you did. You retyped the report altering the W to a G and adding a line for the additional E. What you hadn't realised, until tonight, was that you had unknowingly corrupted the other level of the coded message. You then deliberately left the report to be found, soaked in Balentine's blood.

"You had not only killed the investigator sent to track you down, but you arranged for the blame to fall on an innocent man. You didn't just find Mr. Green with the poisoned cup of tea – you poisoned it yourself with one of the suicide pills you had been issued with." Cathy's face was stony. "Have I missed anything out?"

Sir Anthony looked shrunken, but his age-cracked voice carried proudly around the expectant hall. "Only this," he said. "That, after the war, I served my country well. Behind the scenes, I and St Mark's helped rebuild Britain into the great institution it is today. I did my best by this country and, in ways that may never be publicly known, I earned my knighthood. That's all I want to say to you, Detective Ogilvy."

Sir Anthony wiped again at his eyes with the handkerchief. They no longer glinted with a shrewd intelligence; they looked dull and ashamed – perhaps he saw ahead of him, the repercussions of his actions. He gave Cathy a small nod, acknowledging his defeat, and passed the handkerchief across his mouth. "I wonder," he said, "if I might have another glass of water."

The Fenchurch Street Mystery

Baroness Orczy

Chapter I

THE MAN in the corner pushed aside his glass, and leant across the table.

"Mysteries!" he commented. "There is no such thing as a mystery in connection with any crime, provided intelligence is brought to bear upon its investigation."

Very much astonished, Polly Burton looked over the top of her newspaper, and fixed a pair of very severe, coldly inquiring brown eyes upon him.

She had disapproved of the man from the instant when he shuffled across the shop and sat down opposite to her, at the same marble-topped table which already held her large coffee (3d.), her roll and butter (2d.), and plate of tongue (6d.).

Now this particular corner, this very same table, that special view of the magnificent marble hall – known as the Norfolk Street branch of the Aërated Bread Company's depôts – were Polly's own corner, table, and view. Here she had partaken of eleven pennyworth of luncheon and one pennyworth of daily information ever since that glorious never-to-be-forgotten day when she was enrolled on the staff of the *Evening Observer* (we'll call it that, if you please), and became a member of that illustrious and world-famed organisation known as the British Press.

She was a personality, was Miss Burton of the *Evening Observer*. Her cards were printed thus:

> Miss Mary J. Burton.
>
> *Evening Observer.*

She had interviewed Miss Ellen Terry and the Bishop of Madagascar, Mr. Seymour Hicks and the Chief Commissioner of Police. She had been present at the last Marlborough House garden party – in the cloakroom, that is to say, where she caught sight of Lady Thingummy's hat, Miss What-you-may-call's sunshade, and of various other things modistical or fashionable, all of which were duly described under the heading 'Royalty and Dress' in the early afternoon edition of the *Evening Observer*.

(The article itself is signed M.J.B., and is to be found in the files of that leading halfpennyworth.)

For these reasons – and for various others, too – Polly felt irate with the man in the corner, and told him so with her eyes, as plainly as any pair of brown eyes can speak.

She had been reading an article in the *Daily Telegraph*. The article was palpitatingly interesting. Had Polly been commenting audibly upon it? Certain it is that the man over there had spoken in direct answer to her thoughts.

She looked at him and frowned; the next moment she smiled. Miss Burton (of the *Evening Observer*) had a keen sense of humour, which two years' association with the British Press had not succeeded in destroying, and the appearance of the man was sufficient to tickle the most ultra-morose fancy. Polly thought to herself that she had never seen anyone so pale, so thin, with such funny light-coloured hair, brushed very smoothly across the top of a very obviously bald crown. He looked so timid and nervous as he fidgeted incessantly with a piece of string; his long, lean, and trembling fingers tying and untying it into knots of wonderful and complicated proportions.

Having carefully studied every detail of the quaint personality Polly felt more amiable.

"And yet," she remarked kindly but authoritatively, "this article, in an otherwise well-informed journal, will tell you that, even within the last year, no fewer than six crimes have completely baffled the police, and the perpetrators of them are still at large."

"Pardon me," he said gently, "I never for a moment ventured to suggest that there were no mysteries to the *police*; I merely remarked that there were none where intelligence was brought to bear upon the investigation of crime."

"Not even in the Fenchurch Street *mystery*, I suppose," she asked sarcastically.

"Least of all in the so-called Fenchurch Street *mystery*," he replied quietly.

Now the Fenchurch Street mystery, as that extraordinary crime had popularly been called, had puzzled – as Polly well knew – the brains of every thinking man and woman for the last twelve months. It had puzzled her not inconsiderably; she had been interested, fascinated; she had studied the case, formed her own theories, thought about it all often and often, had even written one or two letters to the Press on the subject – suggesting, arguing, hinting at possibilities and probabilities, adducing proofs which other amateur detectives were equally ready to refute. The attitude of that timid man in the corner, therefore, was peculiarly exasperating, and she retorted with sarcasm destined to completely annihilate her self-complacent interlocutor.

"What a pity it is, in that case, that you do not offer your priceless services to our misguided though well-meaning police."

"Isn't it?" he replied with perfect good-humour. "Well, you know, for one thing I doubt if they would accept them; and in the second place my inclinations and my duty would – were I to become an active member of the detective force – nearly always be in direct conflict. As often as not my sympathies go to the criminal who is clever and astute enough to lead our entire police force by the nose.

"I don't know how much of the case you remember," he went on quietly. "It certainly, at first, began even to puzzle me. On the twelfth of last December a woman, poorly dressed, but with an unmistakable air of having seen better days, gave information at Scotland Yard of the disappearance of her husband, William Kershaw, of no occupation, and apparently of no fixed abode. She was accompanied by a friend – a fat, oily-looking German – and between them they told a tale which set the police immediately on the move.

"It appears that on the tenth of December, at about three o'clock in the afternoon, Karl Müller, the German, called on his friend, William Kershaw, for the purpose of collecting a small debt – some ten pounds or so – which the latter owed him. On arriving at the squalid lodging in Charlotte Street, Fitzroy Square, he found William Kershaw in a wild state of excitement, and his wife in tears. Müller attempted to state the object of his visit, but Kershaw, with wild gestures, waved him aside, and – in his own words – flabbergasted him by asking him point-blank for another loan of two pounds, which sum, he declared, would be the means of a speedy fortune for himself and the friend who would help him in his need.

"After a quarter of an hour spent in obscure hints, Kershaw, finding the cautious German obdurate, decided to let him into the secret plan, which, he averred, would place thousands into their hands."

Instinctively Polly had put down her paper; the mild stranger, with his nervous air and timid, watery eyes, had a peculiar way of telling his tale, which somehow fascinated her.

"I don't know," he resumed, "if you remember the story which the German told to the police, and which was corroborated in every detail by the wife or widow. Briefly it was this: Some thirty years previously, Kershaw, then twenty years of age, and a medical student at one of the London hospitals, had a chum named Barker, with whom he roomed, together with another.

"The latter, so it appears, brought home one evening a very considerable sum of money, which he had won on the turf, and the following morning he was found murdered in his bed. Kershaw, fortunately for himself, was able to prove a conclusive *alibi*; he had spent the night on duty at the hospital; as for Barker, he had disappeared, that is to say, as far as the police were concerned, but not as far as the watchful eyes of his friend Kershaw were able to spy – at least, so the latter said. Barker very cleverly contrived to get away out of the country, and, after sundry vicissitudes, finally settled down at Vladivostok, in Eastern Siberia, where, under the assumed name of Smethurst, he built up an enormous fortune by trading in furs.

"Now, mind you, everyone knows Smethurst, the Siberian millionaire. Kershaw's story that he had once been called Barker, and had committed a murder thirty years ago, was never proved, was it? I am merely telling you what Kershaw said to his friend the German and to his wife on that memorable afternoon of December the tenth.

"According to him Smethurst had made one gigantic mistake in his clever career – he had on four occasions written to his late friend, William Kershaw. Two of these letters had no bearing on the case, since they were written more than twenty-five years ago, and Kershaw, moreover, had lost them – so he said – long ago. According to him, however, the first of these letters was written when Smethurst, alias Barker, had spent all the money he had obtained from the crime, and found himself destitute in New York.

"Kershaw, then in fairly prosperous circumstances, sent him a £10 note for the sake of old times. The second, when the tables had turned, and Kershaw had begun to go downhill, Smethurst, as he then already called himself, sent his whilom friend £50. After that, as Müller gathered, Kershaw had made sundry demands on Smethurst's ever-increasing purse, and had accompanied these demands by various threats, which, considering the distant country in which the millionaire lived, were worse than futile.

"But now the climax had come, and Kershaw, after a final moment of hesitation, handed over to his German friend the two last letters purporting to have been written by Smethurst, and which, if you remember, played such an important part in the mysterious story of this extraordinary crime. I have a copy of both these letters here," added the man in the corner, as he took out a piece of paper from a very worn-out pocket-book, and, unfolding it very deliberately, he began to read:

"Sir, – Your preposterous demands for money are wholly unwarrantable. I have already helped you quite as much as you deserve. However, for the sake of old times, and because you once helped me when I was in a terrible difficulty, I am willing to once more let you impose upon my good nature. A friend of mine here, a Russian merchant, to whom I have sold my business, starts in a few days for an extended tour to many European and Asiatic ports in his yacht, and has invited me to accompany him as far as England. Being tired of foreign parts, and desirous of seeing the old country once again after thirty years' absence, I have decided to accept his invitation. I don't know when we may actually be in Europe, but I promise you that as soon as we touch a suitable port I will write to you again, making an appointment for you

to see me in London. But remember that if your demands are too preposterous I will not for a moment listen to them, and that I am the last man in the world to submit to persistent and unwarrantable blackmail.

"I am, sir,

"Yours truly,

"Francis Smethurst.

"The second letter was dated from Southampton," continued the old man in the corner calmly, "and, curiously enough, was the only letter which Kershaw professed to have received from Smethurst of which he had kept the envelope, and which was dated. It was quite brief," he added, referring once more to his piece of paper.

"Dear Sir, – Referring to my letter of a few weeks ago, I wish to inform you that the Tsarskoe Selo will touch at Tilbury on Tuesday next, the 10th. I shall land there, and immediately go up to London by the first train I can get. If you like, you may meet me at Fenchurch Street Station, in the first-class waiting-room, in the late afternoon. Since I surmise that after thirty years' absence my face may not be familiar to you, I may as well tell you that you will recognise me by a heavy Astrakhan fur coat, which I shall wear, together with a cap of the same. You may then introduce yourself to me, and I will personally listen to what you may have to say.

"Yours faithfully,

"Francis Smethurst.

"It was this last letter which had caused William Kershaw's excitement and his wife's tears. In the German's own words, he was walking up and down the room like a wild beast, gesticulating wildly, and muttering sundry exclamations. Mrs. Kershaw, however, was full of apprehension. She mistrusted the man from foreign parts – who, according to her husband's story, had already one crime upon his conscience – who might, she feared, risk another, in order to be rid of a dangerous enemy. Woman-like, she thought the scheme a dishonourable one, for the law, she knew, is severe on the blackmailer.

"The assignation might be a cunning trap, in any case it was a curious one; why, she argued, did not Smethurst elect to see Kershaw at his hotel the following day? A thousand whys and wherefores made her anxious, but the fat German had been won over by Kershaw's visions of untold gold, held tantalisingly before his eyes. He had lent the necessary £2, with which his friend intended to tidy himself up a bit before he went to meet his friend the millionaire. Half an hour afterwards Kershaw had left his lodgings, and that was the last the unfortunate woman saw of her husband, or Müller, the German, of his friend.

"Anxiously his wife waited that night, but he did not return; the next day she seems to have spent in making purposeless and futile inquiries about the neighbourhood of Fenchurch Street; and on the twelfth she went to Scotland Yard, gave what particulars she knew, and placed in the hands of the police the two letters written by Smethurst."

Chapter II
A Millionaire in the Dock

THE MAN in the corner had finished his glass of milk. His watery blue eyes looked across at Miss Polly Burton's eager little face, from which all traces of severity had now been chased away by an obvious and intense excitement.

"It was only on the 31st," he resumed after a while, "that a body, decomposed past all recognition, was found by two lightermen in the bottom of a disused barge. She had been moored at one time at the foot of one of those dark flights of steps which lead down between tall warehouses to the river in the East End of London. I have a photograph of the place here," he added, selecting one out of his pocket, and placing it before Polly.

"The actual barge, you see, had already been removed when I took this snapshot, but you will realise what a perfect place this alley is for the purpose of one man cutting another's throat in comfort, and without fear of detection. The body, as I said, was decomposed beyond all recognition; it had probably been there eleven days, but sundry articles, such as a silver ring and a tie pin, were recognisable, and were identified by Mrs. Kershaw as belonging to her husband.

"She, of course, was loud in denouncing Smethurst, and the police had no doubt a very strong case against him, for two days after the discovery of the body in the barge, the Siberian millionaire, as he was already popularly called by enterprising interviewers, was arrested in his luxurious suite of rooms at the Hotel Cecil.

"To confess the truth, at this point I was not a little puzzled. Mrs. Kershaw's story and Smethurst's letters had both found their way into the papers, and following my usual method – mind you, I am only an amateur, I try to reason out a case for the love of the thing – I sought about for a motive for the crime, which the police declared Smethurst had committed. To effectually get rid of a dangerous blackmailer was the generally accepted theory. Well! Did it ever strike you how paltry that motive really was?"

Miss Polly had to confess, however, that it had never struck her in that light.

"Surely a man who had succeeded in building up an immense fortune by his own individual efforts, was not the sort of fool to believe that he had anything to fear from a man like Kershaw. He must have *known* that Kershaw held no damning proofs against him – not enough to hang him, anyway. Have you ever seen Smethurst?" he added, as he once more fumbled in his pocket-book.

Polly replied that she had seen Smethurst's picture in the illustrated papers at the time. Then he added, placing a small photograph before her:

"What strikes you most about the face?"

"Well, I think its strange, astonished expression, due to the total absence of eyebrows, and the funny foreign cut of the hair."

"So close that it almost looks as if it had been shaved. Exactly. That is what struck me most when I elbowed my way into the court that morning and first caught sight of the millionaire in the dock. He was a tall, soldierly-looking man, upright in stature, his face very bronzed and tanned. He wore neither moustache nor beard, his hair was cropped quite close to his head, like a Frenchman's; but, of course, what was so very remarkable about him was that total absence of eyebrows and even eyelashes, which gave the face such a peculiar appearance – as you say, a perpetually astonished look.

"He seemed, however, wonderfully calm; he had been accommodated with a chair in the dock – being a millionaire – and chatted pleasantly with his lawyer, Sir Arthur Inglewood, in the intervals between the calling of the several witnesses for the prosecution; whilst during the examination of these witnesses he sat quite placidly, with his head shaded by his hand.

"Müller and Mrs. Kershaw repeated the story which they had already told to the police. I think you said that you were not able, owing to pressure of work, to go to the court that day, and hear the case, so perhaps you have no recollection of Mrs. Kershaw. No? Ah, well! Here is a snapshot I managed to get of her once. That is her. Exactly as she stood in the box – over-dressed – in elaborate crape, with a bonnet which once had contained pink roses, and to which a remnant of pink petals still clung obtrusively amidst the deep black.

"She would not look at the prisoner, and turned her head resolutely towards the magistrate. I fancy she had been fond of that vagabond husband of hers: an enormous wedding ring encircled her finger, and that, too, was swathed in black. She firmly believed that Kershaw's murderer sat there in the dock, and she literally flaunted her grief before him.

"I was indescribably sorry for her. As for Müller, he was just fat, oily, pompous, conscious of his own importance as a witness; his fat fingers, covered with brass rings, gripped the two incriminating letters, which he had identified. They were his passports, as it were, to a delightful land of importance and notoriety. Sir Arthur Inglewood, I think, disappointed him by stating that he had no questions to ask of him. Müller had been brimful of answers, ready with the most perfect indictment, the most elaborate accusations against the bloated millionaire who had decoyed his dear friend Kershaw, and murdered him in Heaven knows what an out-of-the-way corner of the East End.

"After this, however, the excitement grew apace. Müller had been dismissed, and had retired from the court altogether, leading away Mrs. Kershaw, who had completely broken down.

"Constable D 21 was giving evidence as to the arrest in the meanwhile. The prisoner, he said, had seemed completely taken by surprise, not understanding the cause or history of the accusation against him; however, when put in full possession of the facts, and realising, no doubt, the absolute futility of any resistance, he had quietly enough followed the constable into the cab. No one at the fashionable and crowded Hotel Cecil had even suspected that anything unusual had occurred.

"Then a gigantic sigh of expectancy came from every one of the spectators. The 'fun' was about to begin. James Buckland, a porter at Fenchurch Street railway station, had just sworn to tell all the truth, etc. After all, it did not amount to much. He said that at six o'clock in the afternoon of December the tenth, in the midst of one of the densest fogs he ever remembers, the 5:05 from Tilbury steamed into the station, being just about an hour late. He was on the arrival platform, and was hailed by a passenger in a first-class carriage. He could see very little of him beyond an enormous black fur coat and a travelling cap of fur also.

"The passenger had a quantity of luggage, all marked F.S., and he directed James Buckland to place it all upon a four-wheel cab, with the exception of a small handbag, which he carried himself. Having seen that all his luggage was safely bestowed, the stranger in the fur coat paid the porter, and, telling the cabman to wait until he returned, he walked away in the direction of the waiting rooms, still carrying his small handbag.

"'I stayed for a bit,' added James Buckland, 'talking to the driver about the fog and that; then I went about my business, seein' that the local from Southend 'ad been signalled.'

"The prosecution insisted most strongly upon the hour when the stranger in the fur coat, having seen to his luggage, walked away towards the waiting rooms. The porter was emphatic. 'It was not a minute later than 6:15,' he averred.

"Sir Arthur Inglewood still had no questions to ask, and the driver of the cab was called.

"He corroborated the evidence of James Buckland as to the hour when the gentleman in the fur coat had engaged him, and having filled his cab in and out with luggage, had told him to wait. And cabby did wait. He waited in the dense fog – until he was tired, until he seriously thought of depositing all the luggage in the lost property office, and of looking out for another fare – waited until at last, at a quarter before nine, whom should he see walking hurriedly towards his cab but the gentleman in the fur coat and cap, who got in quickly and told the driver to take him at once to the Hotel Cecil. This, cabby declared, had occurred at a quarter before nine. Still Sir Arthur Inglewood made no comment, and Mr. Francis Smethurst, in the crowded, stuffy court, had calmly dropped to sleep.

"The next witness, Constable Thomas Taylor, had noticed a shabbily dressed individual, with shaggy hair and beard, loafing about the station and waiting-rooms in the afternoon of December the tenth. He seemed to be watching the arrival platform of the Tilbury and Southend trains.

"Two separate and independent witnesses, cleverly unearthed by the police, had seen this same shabbily dressed individual stroll into the first-class waiting room at about 6:15 on Wednesday,

December the tenth, and go straight up to a gentleman in a heavy fur coat and cap, who had also just come into the room. The two talked together for a while; no one heard what they said, but presently they walked off together. No one seemed to know in which direction.

"Francis Smethurst was rousing himself from his apathy; he whispered to his lawyer, who nodded with a bland smile of encouragement. The employés of the Hotel Cecil gave evidence as to the arrival of Mr. Smethurst at about 9:30 p.m. on Wednesday, December the tenth, in a cab, with a quantity of luggage; and this closed the case for the prosecution.

"Everybody in that court already *saw* Smethurst mounting the gallows. It was uninterested curiosity which caused the elegant audience to wait and hear what Sir Arthur Inglewood had to say. He, of course, is the most fashionable man in the law at the present moment. His lolling attitudes, his drawling speech, are quite the rage, and imitated by the gilded youth of society.

"Even at this moment, when the Siberian millionaire's neck literally and metaphorically hung in the balance, an expectant titter went round the fair spectators as Sir Arthur stretched out his long loose limbs and lounged across the table. He waited to make his effect – Sir Arthur is a born actor – and there is no doubt that he made it, when in his slowest, most drawly tones he said quietly;

"'With regard to this alleged murder of one William Kershaw, on Wednesday, December the tenth, between 6:15 and 8:45 p.m., your Honour, I now propose to call two witnesses, who saw this same William Kershaw alive on Tuesday afternoon, December the sixteenth, that is to say, six days after the supposed murder.'

"It was as if a bombshell had exploded in the court. Even his Honour was aghast, and I am sure the lady next to me only recovered from the shock of the surprise in order to wonder whether she need put off her dinner party after all.

"As for me," added the man in the corner, with that strange mixture of nervousness and self-complacency which had set Miss Polly Burton wondering, "well, you see, *I* had made up my mind long ago where the hitch lay in this particular case, and I was not so surprised as some of the others.

"Perhaps you remember the wonderful development of the case, which so completely mystified the police – and in fact everybody except myself. Torriani and a waiter at his hotel in the Commercial Road both deposed that at about 3:30 p.m. on December the tenth a shabbily dressed individual lolled into the coffee-room and ordered some tea. He was pleasant enough and talkative, told the waiter that his name was William Kershaw, that very soon all London would be talking about him, as he was about, through an unexpected stroke of good fortune, to become a very rich man, and so on, and so on, nonsense without end.

"When he had finished his tea he lolled out again, but no sooner had he disappeared down a turning of the road than the waiter discovered an old umbrella, left behind accidentally by the shabby, talkative individual. As is the custom in his highly respectable restaurant, Signor Torriani put the umbrella carefully away in his office, on the chance of his customer calling to claim it when he had discovered his loss. And sure enough nearly a week later, on Tuesday, the sixteenth, at about 1 p.m., the same shabbily dressed individual called and asked for his umbrella. He had some lunch, and chatted once again to the waiter. Signor Torriani and the waiter gave a description of William Kershaw, which coincided exactly with that given by Mrs. Kershaw of her husband.

"Oddly enough he seemed to be a very absent-minded sort of person, for on this second occasion, no sooner had he left than the waiter found a pocket-book in the coffee-room, underneath the table. It contained sundry letters and bills, all addressed to William Kershaw. This pocket-book was produced, and Karl Müller, who had returned to the court, easily identified it as having belonged to his dear and lamented friend 'Villiam'.

"This was the first blow to the case against the accused. It was a pretty stiff one, you will admit. Already it had begun to collapse like a house of cards. Still, there was the assignation, and the undisputed meeting between Smethurst and Kershaw, and those two and a half hours of a foggy evening to satisfactorily account for."

The man in the corner made a long pause, keeping the girl on tenterhooks. He had fidgeted with his bit of string till there was not an inch of it free from the most complicated and elaborate knots.

"I assure you," he resumed at last, "that at that very moment the whole mystery was, to me, as clear as daylight. I only marvelled how his Honour could waste his time and mine by putting what he thought were searching questions to the accused relating to his past. Francis Smethurst, who had quite shaken off his somnolence, spoke with a curious nasal twang, and with an almost imperceptible soupçon of foreign accent, he calmly denied Kershaw's version of his past; declared that he had never been called Barker, and had certainly never been mixed up in any murder case thirty years ago.

"'But you knew this man Kershaw,' persisted his Honour, 'since you wrote to him?'

"'Pardon me, your Honour,' said the accused quietly, 'I have never, to my knowledge, seen this man Kershaw, and I can swear that I never wrote to him.'

"'Never wrote to him?' retorted his Honour warningly. 'That is a strange assertion to make when I have two of your letters to him in my hands at the present moment.'

"'I never wrote those letters, your Honour,' persisted the accused quietly, 'they are not in my handwriting.'

"'Which we can easily prove,' came in Sir Arthur Inglewood's drawly tones, as he handed up a packet to his Honour; 'here are a number of letters written by my client since he has landed in this country, and some of which were written under my very eyes.'

"As Sir Arthur Inglewood had said, this could be easily proved, and the prisoner, at his Honour's request, scribbled a few lines, together with his signature, several times upon a sheet of notepaper. It was easy to read upon the magistrate's astounded countenance, that there was not the slightest similarity in the two handwritings.

"A fresh mystery had cropped up. Who, then, had made the assignation with William Kershaw at Fenchurch Street railway station? The prisoner gave a fairly satisfactory account of the employment of his time since his landing in England.

"'I came over on the *Tsarskoe Selo*,' he said, 'a yacht belonging to a friend of mine. When we arrived at the mouth of the Thames there was such a dense fog that it was twenty-four hours before it was thought safe for me to land. My friend, who is a Russian, would not land at all; he was regularly frightened at this land of fogs. He was going on to Madeira immediately.

"'I actually landed on Tuesday, the tenth, and took a train at once for town. I did see to my luggage and a cab, as the porter and driver told your Honour; then I tried to find my way to a refreshment-room, where I could get a glass of wine. I drifted into the waiting room, and there I was accosted by a shabbily dressed individual, who began telling me a piteous tale. Who he was I do not know. He *said* he was an old soldier who had served his country faithfully, and then been left to starve. He begged of me to accompany him to his lodgings, where I could see his wife and starving children, and verify the truth and piteousness of his tale.

"'Well, your Honour,' added the prisoner with noble frankness, 'it was my first day in the old country. I had come back after thirty years with my pockets full of gold, and this was the first sad tale I had heard; but I am a business man, and did not want to be exactly 'done' in the eye. I followed my man through the fog, out into the streets. He walked silently by my side for a time. I had not a notion where I was.

"'Suddenly I turned to him with some question, and realised in a moment that my gentleman had given me the slip. Finding, probably, that I would not part with my money till I *had* seen the starving wife and children, he left me to my fate, and went in search of more willing bait.

"'The place where I found myself was dismal and deserted. I could see no trace of cab or omnibus. I retraced my steps and tried to find my way back to the station, only to find myself in worse and more deserted neighbourhoods. I became hopelessly lost and fogged. I don't wonder that two and a half hours elapsed while I thus wandered on in the dark and deserted streets; my sole astonishment is that I ever found the station at all that night, or rather close to it a policeman, who showed me the way.'

"'But how do you account for Kershaw knowing all your movements?' still persisted his Honour, 'and his knowing the exact date of your arrival in England? How do you account for these two letters, in fact?'

"'I cannot account for it or them, your Honour,' replied the prisoner quietly. 'I have proved to you, have I not, that I never wrote those letters, and that the man – er – Kershaw is his name? – was not murdered by me?'

"'Can you tell me of anyone here or abroad who might have heard of your movements, and of the date of your arrival?'

"'My late employés at Vladivostok, of course, knew of my departure, but none of them could have written these letters, since none of them know a word of English.'

"'Then you can throw no light upon these mysterious letters? You cannot help the police in any way towards the clearing up of this strange affair?'

"'The affair is as mysterious to me as to your Honour, and to the police of this country.'

"Francis Smethurst was discharged, of course; there was no semblance of evidence against him sufficient to commit him for trial. The two overwhelming points of his defence which had completely routed the prosecution were, firstly, the proof that he had never written the letters making the assignation, and secondly, the fact that the man supposed to have been murdered on the tenth was seen to be alive and well on the sixteenth. But then, who in the world was the mysterious individual who had apprised Kershaw of the movements of Smethurst, the millionaire?"

Chapter III
His Deduction

THE MAN in the corner cocked his funny thin head on one side and looked at Polly; then he took up his beloved bit of string and deliberately untied every knot he had made in it. When it was quite smooth he laid it out upon the table.

"I will take you, if you like, point by point along the line of reasoning which I followed myself, and which will inevitably lead you, as it led me, to the only possible solution of the mystery.

"First take this point," he said with nervous restlessness, once more taking up his bit of string, and forming with each point raised a series of knots which would have shamed a navigating instructor, "obviously it was *impossible* for Kershaw not to have been acquainted with Smethurst, since he was fully apprised of the latter's arrival in England by two letters. Now it was clear to me from the first that *no one* could have written those two letters except Smethurst. You will argue that those letters were proved not to have been written by the man in the dock. Exactly. Remember, Kershaw was a careless man – he had lost both envelopes. To him they were insignificant. Now it was never *disproved* that those letters were written by Smethurst."

"But—" suggested Polly.

"Wait a minute," he interrupted, while knot number two appeared upon the scene, "it was proved that six days after the murder, William Kershaw was alive, and visited the Torriani Hotel, where already he was known, and where he conveniently left a pocket-book behind, so that there should be no mistake as to his identity; but it was never questioned where Mr. Francis Smethurst, the millionaire, happened to spend that very same afternoon."

"Surely, you don't mean?" gasped the girl.

"One moment, please," he added triumphantly. "How did it come about that the landlord of the Torriani Hotel was brought into court at all? How did Sir Arthur Inglewood, or rather his client, know that William Kershaw had on those two memorable occasions visited the hotel, and that its landlord could bring such convincing evidence forward that would for ever exonerate the millionaire from the imputation of murder?"

"Surely," I argued, "the usual means, the police—"

"The police had kept the whole affair very dark until the arrest at the Hotel Cecil. They did not put into the papers the usual: 'If anyone happens to know of the whereabouts, etc. etc'. Had the landlord of that hotel heard of the disappearance of Kershaw through the usual channels, he would have put himself in communication with the police. Sir Arthur Inglewood produced him. How did Sir Arthur Inglewood come on his track?"

"Surely, you don't mean?"

"Point number four," he resumed imperturbably, "Mrs. Kershaw was never requested to produce a specimen of her husband's handwriting. Why? Because the police, clever as you say they are, never started on the right tack. They believed William Kershaw to have been murdered; they looked for William Kershaw.

"On December the thirty-first, what was presumed to be the body of William Kershaw was found by two lightermen: I have shown you a photograph of the place where it was found. Dark and deserted it is in all conscience, is it not? Just the place where a bully and a coward would decoy an unsuspecting stranger, murder him first, then rob him of his valuables, his papers, his very identity, and leave him there to rot. The body was found in a disused barge which had been moored some time against the wall, at the foot of these steps. It was in the last stages of decomposition, and, of course, could not be identified; but the police would have it that it was the body of William Kershaw.

"It never entered their heads that it was the body of *Francis Smethurst, and that William Kershaw was his murderer.*

"Ah! It was cleverly, artistically conceived! Kershaw is a genius. Think of it all! His disguise! Kershaw had a shaggy beard, hair, and moustache. He shaved up to his very eyebrows! No wonder that even his wife did not recognise him across the court; and remember she never saw much of his face while he stood in the dock. Kershaw was shabby, slouchy, he stooped. Smethurst, the millionaire, might have served in the Prussian army.

"Then that lovely trait about going to revisit the Torriani Hotel. Just a few days' grace, in order to purchase moustache and beard and wig, exactly similar to what he had himself shaved off. Making up to look like himself! Splendid! Then leaving the pocket-book behind! He! he! he! Kershaw was not murdered! Of course not. He called at the Torriani Hotel six days after the murder, whilst Mr. Smethurst, the millionaire, hobnobbed in the park with duchesses! Hang such a man! Fie!"

He fumbled for his hat. With nervous, trembling fingers he held it deferentially in his hand whilst he rose from the table. Polly watched him as he strode up to the desk, and paid twopence for his glass of milk and his bun. Soon he disappeared through the shop, whilst she still found herself hopelessly bewildered, with a number of snap-shot photographs before her, still staring at a long piece of string, smothered from end to end in a series of knots, as bewildering, as irritating, as puzzling as the man who had lately sat in the corner.

Drawn Daggers

Catherine Louisa Pirkis

"I ADMIT that the dagger business is something of a puzzle to me, but as for the lost necklace – well, I should have thought a child would have understood that," said Mr. Dyer irritably. "When a young lady loses a valuable article of jewellery and wishes to hush the matter up, the explanation is obvious."

"Sometimes," answered Miss Brooke calmly, "the explanation that is obvious is the one to be rejected, not accepted."

Off and on these two had been, so to speak, 'jangling' a good deal that morning. Perhaps the fact was in part to be attributed to the biting east wind which had set Loveday's eyes watering with the gritty dust, as she had made her way to Lynch Court, and which was, at the present moment, sending the smoke, in aggravating gusts, down the chimney into Mr. Dyer's face. Thus it was, however. On the various topics that had chanced to come up for discussion that morning between Mr. Dyer and his colleague, they had each taken up, as if by design, diametrically opposite points of view.

His temper altogether gave way now.

"If," he said, bringing his hand down with emphasis on his writing table, "you lay it down as a principle that the obvious is to be rejected in favour of the abstruse, you'll soon find yourself launched in the predicament of having to prove that two apples added to two other apples do not make four. But there, if you don't choose to see things from my point of view, that is no reason why you should lose your temper!"

"Mr. Hawke wishes to see you, sir," said a clerk, at that moment entering the room.

It was a fortunate diversion. Whatever might be the differences of opinion in which these two might indulge in private, they were careful never to parade those differences before their clients.

Mr. Dyer's irritability vanished in a moment.

"Show the gentleman in," he said to the clerk. Then he turned to Loveday. "This is the Rev. Anthony Hawke, the gentleman at whose house I told you that Miss Monroe is staying temporarily. He is a clergyman of the Church of England, but gave up his living some twenty years ago when he married a wealthy lady. Miss Monroe has been sent over to his guardianship from Pekin by her father, Sir George Monroe, in order to get her out of the way of a troublesome and undesirable suitor."

The last sentence was added in a low and hurried tone, for Mr. Hawke was at that moment entering the room.

He was a man close upon sixty years of age, white-haired, clean-shaven, with a full, round face, to which a small nose imparted a somewhat infantine expression. His manner of greeting was urbane but slightly flurried and nervous. He gave Loveday the impression of being an easy-going, happy-tempered man who, for the moment, was unusually disturbed and perplexed.

He glanced uneasily at Loveday. Mr. Dyer hastened to explain that this was the lady by whose aid he hoped to get to the bottom of the matter now under consideration.

"In that case there can be no objection to my showing you this," said Mr. Hawke; "it came by post this morning. You see my enemy still pursues me."

As he spoke he took from his pocket a big, square envelope, from which he drew a large-sized sheet of paper.

On this sheet of paper were roughly drawn, in ink, two daggers, about six inches in length, with remarkably pointed blades.

Mr. Dyer looked at the sketch with interest.

"We will compare this drawing and its envelope with those you previously received," he said, opening a drawer of his writing-table and taking thence a precisely similar envelope. On the sheet of paper, however, that this envelope enclosed, there was drawn one dagger only.

He placed both envelopes and their enclosures side by side, and in silence compared them. Then, without a word, he handed them to Miss Brooke, who, taking a glass from her pocket, subjected them to a similar careful and minute scrutiny.

Both envelopes were of precisely the same make, and were each addressed to Mr. Hawke's London address in a round, school-boyish, copy-book sort of hand – the hand so easy to write and so difficult to being home to any writer on account of its want of individuality. Each envelope likewise bore a Cork and a London postmark.

The sheet of paper, however, that the first envelope enclosed bore the sketch of one dagger only.

Loveday laid down her glass.

"The envelopes," she said, "have, undoubtedly, been addressed by the same person, but these last two daggers have not been drawn by the hand that drew the first. Dagger number one was, evidently, drawn by a timid, uncertain and inartistic hand – see how the lines wave and how they have been patched here and there. The person who drew the other daggers, I should say, could do better work; the outline, though rugged, is bold and free. I should like to take these sketches home with me and compare them again at my leisure."

"Ah, I felt sure what your opinion would be!" said Mr. Dyer complacently.

Mr. Hawke seemed much disturbed.

"Good gracious!" he ejaculated; "You don't mean to say I have two enemies pursuing me in this fashion! What does it mean? Can it be – is it possible, do you think, that these things have been sent to me by the members of some Secret Society in Ireland – under error, of course – mistaking me for someone else? They can't be meant for me; I have never, in my whole life, been mixed up with any political agitation of any sort."

Mr. Dyer shook his head. "Members of secret societies generally make pretty sure of their ground before they send out missives of this kind," he said. "I have never heard of such an error being made. I think, too, we mustn't build any theories on the Irish post-mark; the letters may have been posted in Cork for the whole and sole purpose of drawing off attention from some other quarter."

"Will you mind telling me a little about the loss of the necklace?" here said Loveday, bringing the conversation suddenly round from the daggers to the diamonds.

"I think," interposed Mr. Dyers, turning towards her, "that the episode of the drawn daggers – drawn in a double sense – should be treated entirely on its own merits, considered as a thing apart from the loss of the necklace. I am inclined to believe that when we have gone a little further into the matter we shall find that each circumstance belongs to a different group of facts. After all, it is possible that these daggers may have been sent by way of a joke – a rather foolish one, I admit – by some harum-scarum fellow bent on causing a sensation."

Mr. Hawke's face brightened.

"Ah! Now, do you think so – really think so?" he ejaculated. "It would lift such a load from my mind if you could bring the thing home, in this way, to some practical joker. There are a lot of such fellows knocking about the world. Why, now I come to think of it, my nephew, Jack, who is a good deal with us just now, and is not quite so steady a fellow as I should like him to be, must have a good many such scamps among his acquaintances."

"A good many such scamps among his acquaintances," echoed Loveday; "that certainly gives plausibility to Mr. Dyer's supposition. At the same time, I think we are bound to look at the other side of the case, and admit the possibility of these daggers being sent in right-down sober earnest by persons concerned in the robbery, with the intention of intimidating you and preventing full investigation of the matter. If this be so, it will not signify which thread we take up and follow. If we find the sender of the daggers we are safe to come upon the thief; or, if we follow up and find the thief, the sender of the daggers will not be far off."

Mr. Hawke's face fell once more.

"It's an uncomfortable position to be in," he said slowly. "I suppose, whoever they are, they will do the regulation thing, and next time will send an instalment of three daggers, in which case I may consider myself a doomed man. It did not occur to me before, but I remember now that I did not receive the first dagger until after I had spoken very strongly to Mrs. Hawke, before the servants, about my wish to set the police to work. I told her I felt bound, in honour to Sir George, to do so, as the necklace had been lost under my roof."

"Did Mrs. Hawke object to your calling in the aid of the police?" asked Loveday.

"Yes, most strongly. She entirely supported Miss Monroe in her wish to take no steps in the matter. Indeed, I should not have come round as I did last night to Mr. Dyer, if my wife had not been suddenly summoned from home by the serious illness of her sister. At least," he corrected himself with a little attempt at self-assertion, "my coming to him might have been a little delayed. I hope you understand, Mr. Dyer; I do not mean to imply that I am not master in my own house."

"Oh, quite so, quite so," responded Mr. Dyer. "Did Mrs. Hawke or Miss Monroe give any reasons for not wishing you to move in the matter?"

"All told, I should think they gave about a hundred reasons – I can't remember them all. For one thing, Miss Monroe said it might necessitate her appearing in the police courts, a thing she would not consent to do; and she certainly did not consider the necklace was worth the fuss I was making over it. And that necklace, sir, has been valued at over nine hundred pounds, and has come down to the young lady from her mother."

"And Mrs. Hawke?"

"Mrs. Hawke supported Miss Monroe in her views in her presence. But privately to me afterwards, she gave other reasons for not wishing the police called in. Girls, she said, were always careless with their jewellery, she might have lost the necklace in Pekin, and never have brought it to England at all."

"Quite so," said Mr. Dyer. "I think I understood you to say that no one had seen the necklace since Miss Monroe's arrival in England. Also, I believe it was she who first discovered it to be missing?"

"Yes. Sir George, when he wrote apprising me of his daughter's visit, added a postscript to his letter, saying that his daughter was bringing her necklace with her and that he would feel greatly obliged if I would have it deposited with as little delay as possible at my bankers', where it could be easily got at if required. I spoke to Miss Monroe about doing this two or three times, but she did not seem at all inclined to comply with her father's wishes. Then my wife took the matter in hand – Mrs. Hawke, I must tell you, has a very firm, resolute manner – she told Miss Monroe plainly that she would not have the responsibility of those diamonds in the house, and insisted that there and then they should be sent off to the bankers. Upon this Miss Monroe went up to her room, and presently returned, saying that her necklace had disappeared. She herself, she said, had placed it in her jewel-case and the jewel-case in her wardrobe, when her boxes were unpacked. The jewel-case was in the wardrobe right enough, and no other article of jewellery appeared to have been disturbed, but the little padded niche in which the necklace had been deposited was empty. My wife and her maid went upstairs immediately, and searched every corner of the room, but, I'm sorry to say, without any result."

"Miss Monroe, I suppose, has her own maid?"

"No, she has not. The maid – an elderly native woman – who left Pekin with her, suffered so terribly from sea-sickness that, when they reached Malta, Miss Monroe allowed her to land and remain there in charge of an agent of the P. and O. Company till an outward bound packet could take her back to China. It seems the poor woman thought she was going to die, and was in a terrible state of mind because she hadn't brought her coffin with her. I dare say you know the terror these Chinese have of being buried in foreign soil. After her departure, Miss Monroe engaged one of the steerage passengers to act as her maid for the remainder of the voyage."

"Did Miss Monroe make the long journey from Pekin accompanied only by this native woman?"

"No; friends escorted her to Hong King – by far the roughest part of the journey. From Hong Kong she came on in *The Colombo*, accompanied only by her maid. I wrote and told her father I would meet her at the docks in London; the young lady, however, preferred landing at Plymouth, and telegraphed to me from there that she was coming on by rail to Waterloo, where, if I liked, I might meet her."

"She seems to be a young lady of independent habits. Was she brought up and educated in China?"

"Yes; by a succession of French and American governesses. After her mother's death, when she was little more than a baby, Sir George could not make up his mind to part with her, as she was his only child."

"I suppose you and Sir George Monroe are old friends?"

"Yes; he and I were great chums before he went out to China – now about twenty years ago – and it was only natural, when he wished to get his daughter out of the way of young Danvers's impertinent attentions, that he should ask me to take charge of her till he could claim his retiring pension and set up his tent in England."

"What was the chief objection to Mr. Danvers's attentions?"

"Well, he is only a boy of one-and-twenty, and has no money into the bargain. He has been sent out to Pekin by his father to study the language, in order to qualify for a billet in the customs, and it may be a dozen years before he is in a position to keep a wife. Now, Miss Monroe is an heiress – will come into her mother's large fortune when she is of age – and Sir George, naturally, would like her to make a good match."

"I suppose Miss Monroe came to England very reluctantly?"

"I imagine so. No doubt it was a great wrench for her to leave her home and friends in that sudden fashion and come to us, who are, one and all, utter strangers to her. She is very quiet, very shy and reserved. She goes nowhere, sees no one. When some old China friends of her father's called to see her the other day, she immediately found she had a headache, and went to bed. I think, on the whole, she gets on better with my nephew than with anyone else."

"Will you kindly tell me of how many persons your household consists at the present moment?

"At the present moment we are one more than usual, for my nephew, Jack, is home with his regiment from India, and is staying with us. As a rule, my household consists of my wife and myself, butler, cook, housemaid and my wife's maid, who just now is doing double duty as Miss Monroe's maid also."

Mr. Dyer looked at his watch.

"I have an important engagement in ten minutes' time," he said, "so I must leave you and Miss Brooke to arrange details as to how and when she is to begin her work inside your house, for, of course, in a case of this sort we must, in the first instance at any rate, concentrate attention within your four walls."

"The less delay the better," said Loveday. "I should like to attack the mystery at once – this afternoon."

Mr. Hawke thought for a moment.

"According to present arrangements," he said, with a little hesitation, "Mrs. Hawke will return next Friday, that is the day after tomorrow, so I can only ask you to remain in the house till the morning of that day. I'm sure you will understand that there might be some – some little awkwardness in—"

"Oh, quite so," interrupted Loveday. "I don't see at present that there will be any necessity for me to sleep in the house at all. How would it be for me to assume the part of a lady house decorator in the employment of a West-end firm, and sent by them to survey your house and advise upon its re-decoration? All I should have to do, would be to walk about your rooms with my head on one side, and a pencil and notebook in my hand. I should interfere with no one, your family life would go on as usual, and I could make my work as short or as long as necessity might dictate."

Mr. Hawke had no objection to offer to this. He had, however, a request to make as he rose to depart, and he made it a little nervously.

"If," he said, "by any chance there should come a telegram from Mrs. Hawke, saying she will return by an earlier train, I suppose – I hope, that is, you will make some excuse, and – and not get me into hot water, I mean."

To this, Loveday answered a little evasively that she trusted no such telegram would be forthcoming, but that, in any case, he might rely upon her discretion.

* * *

Four o'clock was striking from a neighbouring church clock as Loveday lifted the old-fashioned brass knocker of Mr. Hawke's house in Tavistock Square. An elderly butler admitted her and showed her into the drawing room on the first floor. A single glance round showed Loveday that if her role had been real instead of assumed, she would have found plenty of scope for her talents. Although the house was in all respects comfortably furnished, it bore unmistakably the impress of those early Victorian days when aesthetic surroundings were not deemed a necessity of existence; an impress which people past middle age, and growing increasingly indifferent to the accessories of life, are frequently careless to remove.

"Young life here is evidently an excrescence, not part of the home; a troop of daughters turned into this room would speedily set going a different condition of things," thought Loveday, taking stock of the faded white and gold wallpaper, the chairs covered with lilies and roses in cross-stitch, and the knick-knacks of a past generation that were scattered about on tables and mantelpiece.

A yellow damask curtain, half-festooned, divided the back drawing room from the front in which she was seated. From the other side of this curtain there came to her the sound of voices – those of a man and a girl.

"Cut the cards again, please," said the man's voice. "Thank you. There you are again – the queen of hearts, surrounded with diamonds, and turning her back on a knave. Miss Monroe, you can't do better than make that fortune come true. Turn your back on the man who let you go without a word and—"

"Hush!" interrupted the girl with a little laugh: "I heard the next room door open – I'm sure someone came in."

The girl's laugh seemed to Loveday utterly destitute of that echo of heartache that in the circumstances might have been expected.

At this moment Mr. Hawke entered the room, and almost simultaneously the two young people came from the other side of the yellow curtain and crossed towards the door.

Loveday took a survey of them as they passed.

The young man – evidently 'my nephew, Jack' – was a good-looking young fellow, with dark eyes and hair. The girl was small, slight and fair. She was perceptibly less at home with Jack's uncle than she was with Jack, for her manner changed and grew formal and reserved as she came face-to-face with him.

"We're going downstairs to have a game of billiards," said Jack, addressing Mr. Hawke, and throwing a look of curiosity at Loveday.

"Jack," said the old gentleman, "what would you say if I told you I was going to have the house re-decorated from top to bottom, and that this lady had come to advise on the matter."

This was the nearest (and most Anglicé) approach to a fabrication that Mr. Hawke would allow to pass his lips.

"Well," answered Jack promptly, "I should say, 'not before its time'. That would cover a good deal."

Then the two young people departed in company.

Loveday went straight to her work.

"I'll begin my surveying at the top of the house, and at once, if you please," she said. "Will you kindly tell one of your maids to show me through the bedrooms? If it is possible, let that maid be the one who waits on Miss Monroe and Mrs. Hawke."

The maid who responded to Mr. Hawke's summons was in perfect harmony with the general appearance of the house. In addition, however, to being elderly and faded, she was also remarkably sour-visaged, and carried herself as if she thought that Mr. Hawke had taken a great liberty in thus commanding her attendance.

In dignified silence she showed Loveday over the topmost story, where the servants' bedrooms were situated, and with a somewhat supercilious expression of countenance, watched her making various entries in her notebook.

In dignified silence, also, she led the way down to the second floor, where were the principal bedrooms of the house.

"This is Miss Monroe's room," she said, as she threw back a door of one of these rooms, and then shut her lips with a snap, as if they were never going to open again.

The room that Loveday entered was, like the rest of the house, furnished in the style that prevailed in the early Victorian period. The bedstead was elaborately curtained with pink lined upholstery; the toilet-table was befrilled with muslin and tarlatan out of all likeness to a table. The one point, however, that chiefly attracted Loveday's attention was the extreme neatness that prevailed throughout the apartment – a neatness, however, that was carried out with so strict an eye to comfort and convenience that it seemed to proclaim the hand of a first-class maid. Everything in the room was, so to speak, squared to the quarter of an inch, and yet everything that a lady could require in dressing lay ready to hand. The dressing gown lying on the back of a chair had footstool and slippers beside it. A chair stood in front of the toilet table, and on a small Japanese table to the right of the chair were placed hairpin box, comb and brush, and hand mirror.

"This room will want money spent upon it," said Loveday, letting her eyes roam critically in all directions. "Nothing but Moorish woodwork will take off the squareness of those corners. But what a maid Miss Monroe must have. I never before saw a room so orderly and, at the same time, so comfortable."

This was so direct an appeal to conversation that the sour-visaged maid felt compelled to open her lips.

"I wait on Miss Monroe, for the present," she said snappishly; "but, to speak the truth, she scarcely requires a maid. I never before in my life had dealings with such a young lady."

"She does so much for herself, you mean – declines much assistance."

"She's like no one else I ever had to do with." (This was said even more snappishly than before.) "She not only won't be helped in dressing, but she arranges her room every day before leaving it, even to placing the chair in front of the looking glass."

"And to opening the lid of the hairpin box, so that she may have the pins ready to her hand," added Loveday, for a moment bending over the Japanese table, with its toilet accessories.

Another five minutes were all that Loveday accorded to the inspection of this room. Then, a little to the surprise of the dignified maid, she announced her intention of completing her survey of the bedrooms some other time, and dismissed her at the drawing-room door, to tell Mr. Hawke that she wished to see him before leaving.

Mr. Hawke, looking much disturbed and with a telegram in his hand, quickly made his appearance.

"From my wife, to say she'll be back tonight. She'll be at Waterloo in about half an hour from now," he said, holding up the brown envelope. "Now, Miss Brooke, what are we to do? I told you how much Mrs. Hawke objected to the investigation of this matter, and she is very – well – firm when she once says a thing, and – and—"

"Set your mind at rest," interrupted Loveday; "I have done all I wished to do within your walls, and the remainder of my investigation can be carried on just as well at Lynch Court or at my own private rooms."

"Done all you wished to do!" echoed Mr. Hawke in amazement; "Why, you've not been an hour in the house, and do you mean to tell me you've found out anything about the necklace or the daggers?"

"Don't ask me any questions just yet; I want you to answer one or two instead. Now, can you tell me anything about any letters Miss Monroe may have written or received since she has been in your house?"

"Yes, certainly, Sir George wrote to me very strongly about her correspondence, and begged me to keep a sharp eye on it, so as to nip in the bud any attempt to communicate with Danvers. So far, however, she does not appear to have made any such attempt. She is frankness itself over her correspondence. Every letter that has come addressed to her, she has shown either to me or to my wife, and they have one and all been letters from old friends of her father's, wishing to make her acquaintance now that she is in England. With regard to letter-writing, I am sorry to say she has a marked and most peculiar objection to it. Every one of the letters she has received, my wife tells me, remain unanswered still. She has never once been seen, since she came to the house, with a pen in her hand. And if she wrote on the sly, I don't know how she would get her letters posted – she never goes outside the door by herself, and she would have no opportunity of giving them to any of the servants to post except Mrs. Hawke's maid, and she is beyond suspicion in such a matter. She has been well-cautioned, and, in addition, is not the sort of person who would assist a young lady in carrying on a clandestine correspondence."

"I should imagine not! I suppose Miss Monroe has been present at the breakfast table each time that you have received your daggers through the post – you told me, I think, that they had come by the first post in the morning?"

"Yes; Miss Monroe is very punctual at meals, and has been present each time. Naturally, when I received such unpleasant missives, I made some sort of exclamation and then handed the thing round the table for inspection, and Miss Monroe was very much concerned to know who my secret enemy could be."

"No doubt. Now, Mr. Hawke, I have a very special request to make to you, and I hope you will be most exact in carrying it out."

"You may rely upon my doing so to the very letter."

"Thank you. If, then, you should receive by post tomorrow morning one of those big envelopes you already know the look of, and find that it contains a sketch of three, not two, drawn daggers—"

"Good gracious! What makes you think such a thing likely?" exclaimed Mr. Hawke, greatly disturbed. "Why am I to be persecuted in this way? Am I to take it for granted that I am a doomed man?"

He began to pace the room in a state of great excitement.

"I don't think I would if I were you," answered Loveday calmly. "Pray let me finish. I want you to open the big envelope that may come to you by post tomorrow morning just you have opened the others – in full view of your family at the breakfast table – and to hand round the sketch it may contain for inspection to your wife, your nephew and to Miss Monroe. Now, will you promise me to do this?"

"Oh, certainly; I should most likely have done so without any promising. But – but – I'm sure you'll understand that I feel myself to be in a peculiarly uncomfortable position, and I shall feel so very much obliged to you if you'll tell me – that is if you'll enter a little more fully into an explanation."

Loveday looked at her watch. "I should think Mrs. Hawke would be just at this moment arriving at Waterloo; I'm sure you'll be glad to see the last of me. Please come to me at my rooms in Gower Street tomorrow at twelve – here is my card. I shall then be able to enter into fuller explanations I hope. Goodbye."

The old gentleman showed her politely downstairs, and, as he shook hands with her at the front door, again asked, in a most emphatic manner, if she did not consider him to be placed in a "peculiarly unpleasant position."

Those last words at parting were to be the first with which he greeted her on the following morning when he presented himself at her rooms in Gower Street. They were, however, repeated in considerably more agitated a manner.

"Was there ever a man in a more miserable position!" he exclaimed, as he took the chair that Loveday indicated. "I not only received the three daggers for which you prepared me, but I got an additional worry, for which I was totally unprepared. This morning, immediately after breakfast, Miss Monroe walked out of the house all by herself, and no one knows where she has gone. And the girl has never before been outside the door alone. It seems the servants saw her go out, but did not think it necessary to tell either me or Mrs. Hawke, feeling sure we must have been aware of the fact."

"So Mrs. Hawke has returned," said Loveday. "Well, I suppose you will be greatly surprised if I inform you that the young lady, who has so unceremoniously left your house, is at the present moment to be found at the Charing Cross Hotel, where she has engaged a private room in her real name of Miss Mary O'Grady."

"Eh! What! Private room! Real name O'Grady! I'm all bewildered!"

"It is a little bewildering; let me explain. The young lady whom you received into your house as the daughter of your old friend, was in reality the person engaged by Miss Monroe to fulfill the duties of her maid on board ship, after her native attendant had been landed at Malta. Her real name, as I have told you, is Mary O'Grady, and she has proved herself a valuable coadjutor to Miss Monroe in assisting her to carry out a programme, which she must have arranged with her lover, Mr. Danvers, before she left Pekin."

"Eh! What!" again ejaculated Mr. Hawke; "How do you know all this? Tell me the whole story."

"I will tell you the whole story first, and then explain to you how I came to know it. From what has followed, it seems to me that Miss Monroe must have arranged with Mr. Danvers that he was to leave Pekin within ten days of her so doing, travel by the route by which she came, and land at Plymouth, where he was to receive a note from her, apprising him of her whereabouts. So soon as she was on board ship, Miss Monroe appears to have set her wits to work with great energy; every obstacle to the carrying-out of her programme she appears to have met and conquered. Step number one was to get rid of her native maid, who, perhaps, might have been faithful to her master's interests and have proved troublesome. I have no doubt the poor woman suffered terribly from sea-sickness, as it was her first voyage, and I have equally no doubt that Miss Monroe worked on her fears, and persuaded her to land at Malta, and return to China by the next packet. Step number two was to find a suitable person, who for a consideration, would be willing to play the part of the Pekin heiress among the heiress's friends in England, while the young lady herself arranged her private affairs to her own liking. That person was quickly found among the steerage passengers of the *Colombo* in Miss Mary O'Grady, who had come on board with her mother at Ceylon, and who, from the glimpse I had of her, must, I should conjecture, have been absent many years from the land of her birth. You know how cleverly this young lady has played her part in your house – how, without attracting attention to the matter, she has shunned the society of her father's old Chinese friends, who might be likely to involve her in embarrassing conversations; how she has avoided the use of pen and ink lest—"

"Yes, yes," interrupted Mr. Hawke; "but, my dear Miss Brooke, wouldn't it be as well for you and me to go at once to the Charing Cross Hotel, and get all the information we can out of her respecting Miss Monroe and her movements – she may be bolting, you know?"

"I do not think she will. She is waiting there patiently for an answer to a telegram she dispatched more than two hours ago to her mother, Mrs. O'Grady, at 14, Woburn Place, Cork."

"Dear me! Dear me! How is it possible for you to know all this."

"Oh, that last little fact was simply a matter of astuteness on the part of the man whom I have deputed to watch the young lady's movements today. Other details, I assure you, in this somewhat intricate case, have been infinitely more difficult to get at. I think I have to thank those 'drawn daggers', that caused you so much consternation, for having, in the first instance, put me on the right track."

"Ah—h," said Mr. Hawke, drawing a long breath; "now we come to the daggers! I feel sure you are going to set my mind at rest on that score."

"I hope so. Would it surprise you very much to be told that it was I who sent to you those three daggers this morning?"

"You! Is it possible?"

"Yes, they were sent by me, and for a reason that I will presently explain to you. But let me begin at the beginning. Those roughly-drawn sketches, that to you suggested terrifying ideas of blood-shedding and violence, to my mind were open to a more peaceful and commonplace explanation. They appeared to me to suggest the herald's office rather than the armoury; the cross fitchée of the knight's shield rather than the poniard with which the members of secret societies are supposed to render their recalcitrant brethren familiar. Now, if you will look at these sketches again, you will see what I mean." Here Loveday produced from her writing-table the missives which had so greatly disturbed Mr. Hawke's peace of mind. "To begin with, the blade of the dagger of common life is, as a rule, at least two-thirds of the weapon in length; in this sketch, what you would call the blade, does not exceed the hilt in length. Secondly, please note the absence of guard for the hand. Thirdly, let me draw your attention to the squareness of what you considered the hilt of the weapon, and what, to my mind, suggested the upper portion of a crusader's cross. No hand could grip such a hilt as the one outlined here. After your departure yesterday, I drove to the British Museum, and there consulted a certain valuable work on heraldry, which has more than once done me good service. There I found my surmise substantiated in a surprising manner. Among the illustrations of the various crosses borne on armorial shields, I found one that had been taken by Henri d'Anvers from his own armorial bearings, for his crest when he joined the Crusaders under Edward I., and which has since been handed down as the crest of the Danvers family. This was an important item of information to me. Here was someone in Cork sending to your house, on two several occasions, the crest of the Danvers family; with what object it would be difficult to say, unless it were in some sort a communication to someone in your house. With my mind full of this idea, I left the Museum and drove next to the office of the P. and O. Company, and requested to have given me the list of the passengers who arrived by the *Colombo*. I found this list to be a remarkably small one; I suppose people, if possible, avoid crossing the Bay of Biscay during the Equinoxes. The only passengers who landed at Plymouth besides Miss Monroe, I found, were a certain Mrs. and Miss O'Grady, steerage passengers who had gone on board at Ceylon on their way home from Australia. Their name, together with their landing at Plymouth, suggested the possibility that Cork might be their destination. After this I asked to see the list of the passengers who arrived by the packet following the *Colombo*, telling the clerk who attended to me that I was on the look-out for the arrival of a friend. In that second list of arrivals I quickly found my friend – William Wentworth Danvers by name."

"No! The effrontery! How dared he! In his own name, too!"

"Well, you see, a plausible pretext for leaving Pekin could easily be invented by him – the death of a relative, the illness of a father or mother. And Sir George, though he might dislike the idea of the young man going to England so soon after his daughter's departure, and may, perhaps, write to you by the next mail on the matter, was utterly powerless to prevent his so doing. This young man, like Miss Monroe and the O'Gradys, also landed at Plymouth. I had only arrived so far in my investigation when I went to your house yesterday afternoon. By chance, as I waited a few minutes in your drawing room, another important item of information was acquired. A fragment of conversation between your nephew and the supposed Miss Monroe fell upon my ear, and one word spoken by the young lady convinced me of her nationality. That one word was the monosyllable 'Hush'."

"No! You surprise me!"

"Have you never noted the difference between the 'hush' of an Englishman and that of an Irishman? The former begins his 'hush' with a distinct aspirate, the latter with as distinct a W. That W is a mark of his nationality which he never loses. The unmitigated 'whist' may lapse into a 'whish' when he is transplanted to another soil, and the 'whish' may in course of time pass into a 'whush', but to the distinct aspirate of the English 'hush', he never attains. Now Miss O'Grady's was as pronounced a 'whush' as it was possible for the lips of a Hibernian to utter."

"And from that you concluded that Mary O'Grady was playing the part of Miss Monroe in my house?"

"Not immediately. My suspicions were excited, certainly; and when I went up to her room, in company with Mrs. Hawke's maid, those suspicions were confirmed. The orderliness of that room was something remarkable. Now, there is the orderliness of a lady in the arrangement of her room, and the orderliness of a maid, and the two things, believe me, are widely different. A lady, who has no maid, and who has the gift of orderliness, will put things away when done with, and so leave her room a picture of neatness. I don't think, however, it would for a moment occur to her to pull things so as to be conveniently ready for her to use the next time she dresses in that room. This would be what a maid, accustomed to arrange a room for her mistress's use, would do mechanically. Miss Monroe's room was the neatness of a maid – not of a lady, and I was assured by Mrs. Hawke's maid that it was a neatness accomplished by her own hands. As I stood there, looking at that room, the whole conspiracy – if I may so call it – little by little pieced itself together, and became plain to me. Possibilities quickly grew into probabilities, and these probabilities once admitted, brought other suppositions in their train. Now, supposing that Miss Monroe and Mary O'Grady had agreed to change places, the Pekin heiress, for the time being, occupying Mary O'Grady's place in the humble home at Cork and vice versa, what means of communicating with each other had they arranged? How was Mary O'Grady to know when she might lay aside her assumed role and go back to her mother's house. There was no denying the necessity for such communication; the difficulties in its way must have been equally obvious to the two girls. Now, I think we must admit that we must credit these young women with having hit upon a very clever way of meeting those difficulties. An anonymous and startling missive sent to you would be bound to be mentioned in the house, and in this way a code of signals might be set up between them that could not direct suspicion to them. In this connection, the Danvers crest, which it is possible that they mistook for a dagger, suggested itself naturally, for no doubt Miss Monroe had many impressions of it on her lover's letters. As I thought over these things, it occurred to me that possibly dagger (or cross) number one was sent to notify the safe arrival of Miss Monroe and Mrs. O'Grady at Cork. The two daggers or crosses you subsequently received were sent on the day of Mr. Danvers's arrival at Plymouth, and were, I should say, sketched by his hand. Now, was it not within the bounds of likelihood that Miss Monroe's marriage to this young man, and the consequent release of Mary O'Grady from the onerous part she was playing, might be notified to her by the sending of three such crosses or daggers to you. The idea no sooner occurred to me than I determined to act upon it, forestall the sending of this latest communication, and watch the result. Accordingly, after I left your house yesterday, I had a sketch made of three daggers of crosses exactly similar to those you had already received, and had it posted to you so that you would get it by the first post. I told off one of our staff at Lynch Court to watch your house, and gave him special directions to follow and report on Miss O'Grady's movements throughout the day. The results I anticipated quickly came to pass. About half past nine this morning the man sent a telegram to me from your house to the Charing Cross Hotel, and furthermore had ascertained that she had since despatched a telegram, which (possibly by following the hotel servant who carried it to the telegraph office), he had overheard was addressed to Mrs. O'Grady, at Woburn Place, Cork. Since I received this information an altogether remarkable cross-firing of telegrams has been going backwards and forwards along the wires to Cork."

"A cross-firing of telegrams! I do not understand."

"In this way. So soon as I knew Mrs. O'Grady's address I telegraphed to her, in her daughter's name, desiring her to address her reply to 1154 Gower Street, not to Charing Cross Hotel. About three-quarters of an hour afterwards I received in reply this telegram, which I am sure you will read with interest."

Here Loveday handed a telegram – one of several that lay on her writing-table – to Mr. Hawke.

He opened it and read aloud as follows:

"Am puzzled. Why such hurry? Wedding took place this morning. You will receive signal as agreed tomorrow. Better return to Tavistock Square for the night."

"The wedding took place this morning," repeated Mr. Hawke blankly. "My poor old friend! It will break his heart."

"Now that the thing is done past recall we must hope he will make the best of it," said Loveday. "In reply to this telegram," she went on, "I sent another, asking as to the movements of the bride and bridegroom, and got in reply this:"

Here she read aloud as follows:

"They will be at Plymouth tomorrow night; at Charing Cross Hotel and next day, as agreed."

"So, Mr. Hawke," she added, "if you wish to see your old friend's daughter and tell her what you think of the part she has played, all you will have to do will be to watch the arrival of the Plymouth trains."

"Miss O'Grady has called to see a lady and gentleman," said a maid at that moment entering.

"Miss O'Grady!" repeated Mr. Hawke in astonishment.

"Ah, yes, I telegraphed to her, just before you came in, to come here to meet a lady and gentlemen, and she, no doubt thinking that she would find here the newly married pair, has, you see, lost no time in complying with my request. Show the lady in."

"It's all so intricate – so bewildering," said Mr. Hawke, as he lay back in his chair. "I can scarcely get it all into my head."

His bewilderment, however, was nothing compared with that of Miss O'Grady, when she entered the room and found herself face-to-face with her late guardian, instead of the radiant bride and bridegroom whom she had expected to meet.

She stood silent in the middle of the room, looking the picture of astonishment and distress.

Mr. Hawke also seemed a little at a loss for words, so Loveday took the initiative.

"Please sit down," she said, placing a chair for the girl. "Mr. Hawke and I have sent to you in order to ask you a few questions. Before doing so, however, let me tell you that the whole of your conspiracy with Miss Monroe has been brought to light, and the best thing you can do, if you want your share in it treated leniently, will be to answer our questions as fully and truthfully as possible."

The girl burst into tears. "It was all Miss Monroe's fault from beginning to end," she sobbed. "Mother didn't want to do it – I didn't want to – to go into a gentleman's house and pretend to be what I was not. And we didn't want her hundred pounds—"

Here sobs checked her speech.

"Oh," said Loveday contemptuously, "so you were to have a hundred pounds for your share in this fraud, were you?"

"We didn't want to take it," said the girl, between hysterical bursts of tears; "but Miss Monroe said if we didn't help her someone else would, and so I agreed to—"

"I think," interrupted Loveday, "that you can tell us very little that we do not already know about what you agreed to do. What we want you to tell us is what has been done with Miss Monroe's diamond necklace – who has possession of it now?"

The girl's sobs and tears redoubled. "I've had nothing to do with the necklace – it has never been in my possession," she sobbed. "Miss Monroe gave it to Mr. Danvers two or three months before she left Pekin, and he sent it on to some people he knew in Hong Kong, diamond merchants, who lent him money on it. Decastro, Miss Monroe said, was the name of these people."

"Decastro, diamond merchant, Hong Kong. I should think that would be sufficient address," said Loveday, entering it in a ledger; "and I suppose Mr. Danvers retained part of that money for his own use and travelling expenses, and handed the remainder to Miss Monroe to enable her to bribe such creatures as you and your mother, to practice a fraud that ought to land both of you in jail."

The girl grew deadly white. "Oh, don't do that – don't send us to prison!" she implored, clasping her hands together. "We haven't touched a penny of Miss Monroe's money yet, and we don't want to touch a penny, if you'll only let us off! Oh, pray, pray, pray be merciful!"

Loveday looked at Mr. Hawke.

He rose from his chair. "I think the best thing you can do," he said, "will be to get back home to your mother at Cork as quickly as possible, and advise her never to play such a risky game again. Have you any money in your purse? No – well then here's some for you, and lose no time in getting home. It will be best for Miss Monroe – Mrs. Danvers I mean – to come to my house and claim her own property there. At any rate, there it will remain until she does so."

As the girl, with incoherent expressions of gratitude, left the room, he turned to Loveday.

"I should like to have consulted Mrs. Hawke before arranging matters in this way," he said a little hesitatingly; "but still, I don't see that I could have done otherwise."

"I feel sure Mrs. Hawke will approve what you have done when she hears all the circumstance of the case," said Loveday.

"And," continued the old clergyman, "when I write to Sir George, as, of course, I must immediately, I shall advise him to make the best of a bad bargain, now that the thing is done. 'Past cure should be past care'; eh, Miss Brooke? And, think! What a narrow escape my nephew, Jack, has had!"

Naboth's Vineyard

Melville Davisson Post

ONE HEARS a good deal about the sovereignty of the people in this republic; and many persons imagine it a sort of fiction, and wonder where it lies, who are the guardians of it, and how they would exercise it if the forms and agents of the law were removed. I am not one of those who speculate upon this mystery, for I have seen this primal ultimate authority naked at its work. And, having seen it, I know how mighty and how dread a thing it is. And I know where it lies, and who are the guardians of it, and how they exercise it when the need arises.

There was a great crowd, for the whole country was in the courtroom. It was a notorious trial.

Elihu Marsh had been shot down in his house. He had been found lying in a room, with a hole through his body that one could put his thumb in. He was an irascible old man, the last of his family, and so, lived alone. He had rich lands, but only a life estate in them, the remainder was to some foreign heirs. A girl from a neighboring farm came now and then to bake and put his house in order, and he kept a farm hand about the premises.

Nothing had been disturbed in the house when the neighbors found Marsh; no robbery had been attempted, for the man's money, a considerable sum, remained on him.

There was not much mystery about the thing, because the farm hand had disappeared. This man was a stranger in the hills. He had come from over the mountains some months before, and gone to work for Marsh. He was a big blond man, young and good-looking; of better blood, one would say, than the average laborer. He gave his name as Taylor, but he was not communicative, and little else about him was known.

The country was raised, and this man was overtaken in the foothills of the mountains. He had his clothes tied into a bundle, and a long-barreled fowling-piece on his shoulder. The story he told was that he and Marsh had settled that morning, and he had left the house at noon, but that he had forgotten his gun and had gone back for it; had reached the house about four o'clock, gone into the kitchen, got his gun down from the dogwood forks over the chimney, and at once left the house. He had not seen Marsh, and did not know where he was.

He admitted that this gun had been loaded with a single huge lead bullet. He had so loaded it to kill a dog that sometimes approached the house, but not close enough to be reached with a load of shot. He affected surprise when it was pointed out that the gun had been discharged. He said that he had not fired it, and had not, until then, noticed that it was empty. When asked why he had so suddenly determined to leave the country, he was silent.

He was carried back and confined in the county jail, and now, he was on trial at the September term of the circuit court.

The court sat early. Although the judge, Simon Kilrail, was a landowner and lived on his estate in the country some half dozen miles away, he rode to the courthouse in the morning, and home at night, with his legal papers in his saddle-pockets. It was only when the court sat that he was a lawyer. At other times he harvested his hay and grazed his cattle, and tried to add to his lands like any other man in the hills, and he was as hard in a trade and as hungry for an acre as any.

It was the sign and insignia of distinction in Virginia to own land. Mr. Jefferson had annuled the titles that George the Third had granted, and the land alone remained as a patent of nobility. The Judge wished to be one of these landed gentry, and he had gone a good way to accomplish it. But when the court convened he became a lawyer and sat upon the bench with no heart in him, and a cruel tongue like the English judges.

I think everybody was at this trial. My Uncle Abner and the strange old doctor, Storm, sat on a bench near the center aisle of the courtroom, and I sat behind them, for I was a half-grown lad, and permitted to witness the terrors and severities of the law.

The prisoner was the center of interest. He sat with a stolid countenance like a man careless of the issues of life. But not everybody was concerned with him, for my Uncle Abner and Storm watched the girl who had been accustomed to bake for Marsh and red up his house.

She was a beauty of her type; dark-haired and dark-eyed like a gypsy, and with an April nature of storm and sun. She sat among the witnesses with a little handkerchief clutched in her hands. She was nervous to the point of hysteria, and I thought that was the reason the old doctor watched her. She would be taken with a gust of tears, and then throw up her head with a fine defiance; and she kneaded and knotted and worked the handkerchief in her fingers. It was a time of stress and many witnesses were unnerved, and I think I should not have noticed this girl but for the whispering of Storm and my Uncle Abner.

The trial went forward, and it became certain that the prisoner would hang. His stubborn refusal to give any reason for his hurried departure had but one meaning, and the circumstantial evidence was conclusive. The motive, only, remained in doubt, and the Judge had charged on this with so many cases in point, and with so heavy a hand, that any virtue in it was removed. The Judge was hard against this man, and indeed there was little sympathy anywhere, for it was a foul killing – the victim an old man and no hot blood to excuse it.

In all trials of great public interest, where the evidences of guilt overwhelmingly assemble against a prisoner, there comes a moment when all the people in the courtroom, as one man, and without a sign of the common purpose, agree upon a verdict; there is no outward or visible evidence of this decision, but one feels it, and it is a moment of the tensest stress.

The trial of Taylor had reached this point, and there lay a moment of deep silence, when this girl sitting among the witnesses suddenly burst into a very hysteria of tears. She stood up shaking with sobs, her voice choking in her throat, and the tears gushing through her fingers.

What she said was not heard at the time by the audience in the courtroom, but it brought the Judge to his feet and the jury crowding about her, and it broke down the silence of the prisoner, and threw him into a perfect fury of denials. We could hear his voice rise above the confusion, and we could see him struggling to get to the girl and stop her. But what she said was presently known to everybody, for it was taken down and signed; and it put the case against Taylor, to use a lawyer's term, out of court.

The girl had killed Marsh herself. And this was the manner and the reason of it: she and Taylor were sweethearts and were to be married. But they had quarreled the night before Marsh's death and the following morning Taylor had left the country. The point of the quarrel was some remark that Marsh had made to Taylor touching the girl's reputation. She had come to the house in the afternoon, and finding her lover gone, and maddened at the sight of the one who had robbed her of him, had taken the gun down from the chimney and killed Marsh. She had then put the gun back into its place and left the house. This was about two o'clock in the afternoon, and about an hour before Taylor returned for his gun.

There was a great veer of public feeling with a profound sense of having come at last upon the truth, for the story not only fitted to the circumstantial evidence against Taylor, but it fitted also to his story and it disclosed the motive for the killing. It explained, too, why he had refused to give the reason for his disappearance. That Taylor denied what the girl said and tried to stop her in her declaration, meant nothing except that the prisoner was a man, and would not have the woman he loved make such a sacrifice for him.

I cannot give all the forms of legal procedure with which the closing hours of the court were taken up, but nothing happened to shake the girl's confession. Whatever the law required was speedily got ready, and she was remanded to the care of the sheriff in order that she might come before the court in the morning.

Taylor was not released, but was also held in custody, although the case against him seemed utterly broken down. The Judge refused to permit the prisoner's counsel to take a verdict. He said that he would withdraw a juror and continue the case. But he seemed unwilling to release any clutch of the law until someone was punished for this crime.

It was on our way, and we rode out with the Judge that night. He talked with Abner and Storm about the pastures and the price of cattle, but not about the trial, as I hoped he would do, except once only, and then it was to inquire why the prosecuting attorney had not called either of them as witnesses, since they were the first to find Marsh, and Storm had been among the doctors who examined him. And Storm had explained how he had mortally offended the prosecutor in his canvass, by his remark that only a gentleman should hold office. He did but quote Mr. Hamilton, Storm said, but the man had received it as a deadly insult, and thereby proved the truth of Mr. Hamilton's expression, Storm added. And Abner said that as no circumstance about Marsh's death was questioned, and others arriving about the same time had been called, the prosecutor doubtless considered further testimony unnecessary.

The Judge nodded, and the conversation turned to other questions. At the gate, after the common formal courtesy of the country, the Judge asked us to ride in, and, to my astonishment, Abner and Storm accepted his invitation. I could see that the man was surprised, and I thought annoyed, but he took us into his library.

I could not understand why Abner and Storm had stopped here, until I remembered how from the first they had been considering the girl, and it occurred to me that they thus sought the Judge in the hope of getting some word to him in her favor. A great sentiment had leaped up for this girl. She had made a staggering sacrifice, and with a headlong courage, and it was like these men to help her if they could.

And it was to speak of the woman that they came, but not in her favor. And while Simon Kilrail listened, they told this extraordinary story: they had been of the opinion that Taylor was not guilty when the trial began, but they had suffered it to proceed in order to see what might develop. The reason was that there were certain circumstantial evidences, overlooked by the prosecutor, indicating the guilt of the woman and the innocence of Taylor. When Storm examined the body of Marsh he discovered that the man had been killed by poison, and was dead when the bullet was fired into his body. This meant that the shooting was a fabricated evidence to direct suspicion against Taylor. The woman had baked for Marsh on this morning, and the poison was in the bread which he had eaten at noon.

Abner was going on to explain something further, when a servant entered and asked the Judge what time it was. The man had been greatly impressed, and he now sat in a profound reflection. He took his watch out of his pocket and held it in his hand, then he seemed to realize the question and replied that his watch had run down. Abner gave the hour, and said that perhaps his key would wind the watch. The Judge gave it to him, and he wound it and laid it on the table. Storm observed my Uncle with, what I thought, a curious interest, but the Judge paid no attention. He was deep in his reflection and oblivious to everything. Finally he roused himself and made his comment.

"This clears the matter up," he said. "The woman killed Marsh from the motive which she gave in her confession, and she created this false evidence against Taylor because he had abandoned her. She thereby avenged herself desperately in two directions… It would be like a woman to do this, and then regret it and confess."

He then asked my Uncle if he had anything further to tell him, and although I was sure that Abner was going on to say something further when the servant entered, he replied now that he had not, and asked for the horses. The Judge went out to have the horses brought, and we remained in silence. My Uncle was calm, as with some consuming idea, but Storm was as nervous as a cat. He was out of his chair when the door was closed, and hopping about the room looking at the law books standing on the shelves in their leather covers. Suddenly he stopped and plucked out a little volume. He whipped through it with his forefinger, smothered a great oath, and shot it into his pocket, then he crooked his finger to my Uncle, and they talked together in a recess of the window until the Judge returned.

We rode away. I was sure that they intended to say something to the Judge in the woman's favor, for, guilty or not, it was a fine thing she had done to stand up and confess. But something in the interview had changed their purpose. Perhaps when they had heard the Judge's comment they saw it would be of no use. They talked closely together as they rode, but they kept before me and I could not hear. It was of the woman they spoke, however, for I caught a fragment.

"But where is the motive?" said Storm.

And my Uncle answered, "In the twenty-first chapter of the Book of Kings."

We were early at the county seat, and it was a good thing for us, because the courtroom was crowded to the doors. My Uncle had got a big record book out of the county clerk's office as he came in, and I was glad of it, for he gave it to me to sit on, and it raised me up so I could see. Storm was there, too, and, in fact, every man of any standing in the county.

The sheriff opened the court, the prisoners were brought in, and the Judge took his seat on the bench. He looked haggard like a man who had not slept, as, in fact, one could hardly have done who had so cruel a duty before him. Here was every human feeling pressing to save a woman, and the law to hang her. But for all his hag-ridden face, when he came to act, the man was adamant.

He ordered the confession read, and directed the girl to stand up. Taylor tried again to protest, but he was forced down into his chair. The girl stood up bravely, but she was white as plaster, and her eyes dilated. She was asked if she still adhered to the confession and understood the consequences of it, and, although she trembled from head to toe, she spoke out distinctly. There was a moment of silence and the Judge was about to speak, when another voice filled the courtroom. I turned about on my book to find my head against my Uncle Abner's legs.

"I challenge the confession!" he said.

The whole courtroom moved. Every eye was on the two tragic figures standing up: the slim, pale girl and the big, somber figure of my Uncle. The Judge was astounded.

"On what ground?" he said.

"On the ground," replied my Uncle, "that the confession is a lie!"

One could have heard a pin fall anywhere in the whole room. The girl caught her breath in a little gasp, and the prisoner, Taylor, half rose and then sat down as though his knees were too weak to bear him. The Judge's mouth opened, but for a moment or two he did not speak, and I could understand his amazement. Here was Abner assailing a confession which he himself had supported before the Judge, and speaking for the innocence of a woman whom he himself had shown to be guilty and taking one position privately, and another publicly. What did the man mean? And I was not surprised that the Judge's voice was stern when he spoke.

"This is irregular," he said. "It may be that this woman killed Marsh, or it may be that Taylor killed him, and there is some collusion between these persons, as you appear to suggest. And you may know something to throw light on the matter, or you may not. However that may be, this is not the time for me to hear you. You will have ample opportunity to speak when I come to try the case."

"But you will never try this case!" said Abner.

I cannot undertake to describe the desperate interest that lay on the people in the courtroom. They were breathlessly silent; one could hear the voices from the village outside, and the sounds of men and horses that came up through the open windows. No one knew what hidden thing Abner drove at. But he was a man who meant what he said, and the people knew it.

The Judge turned on him with a terrible face.

"What do you mean?" he said.

"I mean," replied Abner, and it was in his deep, hard voice, "that you must come down from the bench."

The Judge was in a heat of fury.

"You are in contempt," he roared. "I order your arrest. Sheriff!" he called.

But Abner did not move. He looked the man calmly in the face.

"You threaten me," he said, "but God Almighty threatens you." And he turned about to the audience. "The authority of the law," he said, "is in the hands of the electors of this county. Will they stand up?"

I shall never forget what happened then, for I have never in my life seen anything so deliberate and impressive. Slowly, in silence, and without passion, as though they were in a church of God, men began to get up in the courtroom.

Randolph was the first. He was a justice of the peace, vain and pompous, proud of the abilities of an ancestry that he did not inherit. And his superficialities were the annoyance of my Uncle Abner's life. But whatever I may have to say of him hereafter I want to say this thing of him here, that his bigotry and his vanities were builded on the foundations of a man. He stood up as though he stood alone, with no glance about him to see what other men would do, and he faced the Judge calmly above his great black stock. And I learned then that a man may be a blusterer and a lion.

Hiram Arnold got up, and Rockford, and Armstrong, and Alkire, and Coopman, and Monroe, and Elnathan Stone, and my father, Lewis, and Dayton and Ward, and Madison from beyond the mountains. And it seemed to me that the very hills and valleys were standing up.

It was a strange and instructive thing to see. The loud-mouthed and the reckless were in that courtroom, men who would have shouted in a political convention, or run howling with a mob, but they were not the persons who stood up when Abner called upon the authority of the people to appear. Men rose whom one would not have looked to see – the blacksmith, the saddler, and old Asa Divers. And I saw that law and order and all the structure that civilization had builded up, rested on the sense of justice that certain men carried in their breasts, and that those who possessed it not, in the crisis of necessity, did not count.

Father Donovan stood up; he had a little flock beyond the valley river, and he was as poor, and almost as humble as his Master, but he was not afraid; and Bronson, who preached Calvin, and Adam Rider, who traveled a Methodist circuit. No one of them believed in what the other taught; but they all believed in justice, and when the line was drawn, there was but one side for them all.

The last man up was Nathaniel Davisson, but the reason was that he was very old, and he had to wait for his sons to help him. He had been time and again in the Assembly of Virginia, at a time when only a gentleman and landowner could sit there. He was a just man, and honorable and unafraid.

The Judge, his face purple, made a desperate effort to enforce his authority. He pounded on his desk and ordered the sheriff to clear the courtroom. But the sheriff remained standing apart. He did not lack for courage, and I think he would have faced the people if his duty had been that way.

His attitude was firm, and one could mark no uncertainty upon him, but he took no step to obey what the Judge commanded.

The Judge cried out at him in a terrible voice.

"I am the representative of the law here. Go on!"

The sheriff was a plain man, and unacquainted with the nice expressions of Mr. Jefferson, but his answer could not have been better if that gentleman had written it out for him.

"I would obey the representative of the law," he said, "if I were not in the presence of the law itself!"

The Judge rose. "This is revolution," he said; "I will send to the Governor for the militia."

It was Nathaniel Davisson who spoke then. He was very old and the tremors of dissolution were on him, but his voice was steady.

"Sit down, your Honor," he said, "there is no revolution here, and you do not require troops to support your authority. We are here to support it if it ought to be lawfully enforced. But the people have elevated you to the Bench because they believed in your integrity, and if they have been mistaken they would know it." He paused, as though to collect his strength, and then went on. "The presumptions of right are all with your Honor. You administer the law upon our authority and we stand behind you. Be assured that we will not suffer our authority to be insulted in your person." His voice grew deep and resolute. "It is a grave thing to call us up against you, and not lightly, nor for a trivial reason shall any man dare to do it." Then he turned about. "Now, Abner," he said, "what is this thing?"

Young as I was, I felt that the old man spoke for the people standing in the courtroom, with their voice and their authority, and I began to fear that the measure which my Uncle had taken was high-handed. But he stood there like the shadow of a great rock.

"I charge him," he said, "with the murder of Elihu Marsh! And I call upon him to vacate the Bench."

When I think about this extraordinary event now, I wonder at the calmness with which Simon Kilrail met this blow, until I reflect that he had seen it on its way, and had got ready to meet it. But even with that preparation, it took a man of iron nerve to face an assault like that and keep every muscle in its place. He had tried violence and had failed with it, and he had recourse now to the attitudes and mannerisms of a judicial dignity. He sat with his elbows on the table, and his clenched fingers propping up his jaw. He looked coldly at Abner, but he did not speak, and there was silence until Nathaniel Davisson spoke for him. His face and his voice were like iron.

"No, Abner," he said, "he shall not vacate the Bench for that, nor upon the accusation of any man. We will have your proofs, if you please."

The Judge turned his cold face from Abner to Nathaniel Davisson, and then he looked over the men standing in the courtroom.

"I am not going to remain here," he said, "to be tried by a mob, upon the *viva voce* indictment of a bystander. You may nullify your court, if you like, and suspend the forms of law for yourselves, but you cannot nullify the constitution of Virginia, nor suspend my right as a citizen of that commonwealth.

"And now," he said, rising, "if you will kindly make way, I will vacate this courtroom, which your violence has converted into a chamber of sedition."

The man spoke in a cold, even voice, and I thought he had presented a difficulty that could not be met. How could these men before him undertake to keep the peace of this frontier, and force its lawless elements to submit to the forms of law for trial, and deny any letter of those formalities to this man? Was the grand jury, and the formal indictment, and all the right and privilege of an orderly procedure for one, and not for another?

It was Nathaniel Davisson who met this dangerous problem.

"We are not concerned," he said, "at this moment with your rights as a citizen; the rights of private citizenship are inviolate, and they remain to you, when you return to it. But you are not a private citizen. You are our agent. We have selected you to administer the law for us, and your right to act has been challenged. Well, as the authority behind you, we appear and would know the reason."

The Judge retained his imperturbable calm.

"Do you hold me a prisoner here?" he said.

"We hold you an official in your office," replied Davisson, "not only do we refuse to permit you to leave the courtroom, but we refuse to permit you to leave the Bench. This court shall remain as we have set it up until it is our will to readjust it. And it shall not be changed at the pleasure or demand of any man but by us only, and for a sufficient cause shown to us."

And again I was anxious for my Uncle, for I saw how grave a thing it was to interfere with the authority of the people as manifested in the forms and agencies of the law. Abner must be very sure of the ground under him.

And he was sure. He spoke now, with no introductory expressions, but directly and in the simplest words.

"These two persons," he said, indicating Taylor and the girl, "have each been willing to die in order to save the other. Neither is guilty of this crime. Taylor has kept silent, and the girl has lied, to the same end. This is the truth: there was a lovers' quarrel, and Taylor left the country precisely as he told us, except the motive, which he would not tell lest the girl be involved. And the woman, to save him, confesses to a crime that she did not commit.

"Who did commit it?" He paused and included Storm with a gesture. "We suspected this woman because Marsh had been killed by poison in his bread, and afterwards mutilated with a shot. Yesterday we rode out with the Judge to put those facts before him." Again he paused. "An incident occurring in that interview indicated that we were wrong; a second incident assured us, and still later, a third convinced us. These incidents were, first, that the Judge's watch had run down; second, that we found in his library a book with all the leaves in it uncut, except at one certain page; and, third, that we found in the county clerk's office an unindexed record in an old deed book." There was deep quiet and he went on:

"In addition to the theory of Taylor's guilt or this woman's, there was still a third; but it had only a single incident to support it, and we feared to suggest it until the others had been explained. This theory was that someone, to benefit by Marsh's death, had planned to kill him in such a manner as to throw suspicion on this woman who baked his bread, and finding Taylor gone, and the gun above the mantel, yielded to an afterthought to create a further false evidence. It was overdone!

"The trigger guard of the gun in the recoil caught in the chain of the assassin's watch and jerked it out of his pocket; he replaced the watch, but not the key which fell to the floor, and which I picked up beside the body of the dead man."

Abner turned toward the judge.

"And so," he said, "I charge Simon Kilrail with this murder; because the key winds his watch; because the record in the old deed book is a conveyance by the heirs of Marsh's lands to him at the life tenant's death; and because the book we found in his library is a book on poisons with the leaves uncut, except at the very page describing that identical poison with which Elihu Marsh was murdered."

The strained silence that followed Abner's words was broken by a voice that thundered in the courtroom. It was Randolph's.

"Come down!" he said.

And this time Nathaniel Davisson was silent.

The Judge got slowly on his feet, a resolution was forming in his face, and it advanced swiftly.

"I will give you my answer in a moment," he said.

Then he turned about and went into his room behind the Bench. There was but one door, and that opening into the court, and the people waited.

The windows were open and we could see the green fields, and the sun, and the far-off mountains, and the peace and quiet and serenity of autumn entered. The Judge did not appear. Presently there was the sound of a shot from behind the closed door. The sheriff threw it open, and upon the floor, sprawling in a smear of blood, lay Simon Kilrail, with a dueling pistol in his hand.

The Case of the Mislaid Plans

Patsy Pratt-Herzog

"BOTHER," Prudence said crossly. Hands on hips, she glared down at the smashed glass and splintered wood that used to be the door to Father's study. A quick search of the room proved that his engine plans for the Queen's new dirigible fleet were missing.

Prudence pressed her fingers to the bridge of her nose. It was remarkably inconvenient when one of your guests turned out to be a thief, albeit an amateur one judging by the state of the door.

If there was anything Prudence abhorred, it was a thief…especially one that had the temerity to ruin her engagement party.

Gorcab, the family's Mech-Serve butler trundled toward her toting a broom. In honor of the party, he wore an impeccably pressed frock coat with gleaming brass buttons down the front, and a frilly black cravat expertly tied beneath his clockwork face.

"You were right to get me," she said.

"I'll have this cleaned up in a jiffy, Miss," he said, glass crunching beneath his wheels.

She sighed. "I fear no amount of cleaning will improve the situation."

Prudence touched the dainty ring on the third finger of her left hand with a rueful smile. This should be a time of joy, and instead, she had to deal with this fuss and bother. At the age of twenty-four, she thought her time long past, but Henry Ashmore had changed all that. The gold ring was engraved with flowers and had a dangling heart encrusted with tiny diamonds. It wasn't the largest or most expensive ring, but Henry was still at University, and she really didn't care about such things. He had no objections to her continued employment, and that had been her chief concern. He was a very modern-minded man, her Henry, but unused to such vulgar things as theft and murder. Unfortunately, in her position as Special Investigator to Her Majesty, Prudence was quite familiar with both.

She shuddered at what Her Majesty would say when she found out the engine plans had gone missing. "*We are not amused*," wouldn't begin to cover it.

"Mention this to no one, not even Father."

"Yes, Miss," Gorcab said.

"Now go and make certain none of our guests leaves the house."

"Yes, Miss," he said. Bowing from the pivot of his wheels, he trundled away at top speed, ricocheting off the door frame with a hollow clang as he went.

Uncharacteristic of him, she mused. She'd have to ask Father to take a look at his circuitry.

Prudence gave the mess one last disgusted look, then marched determinedly to her rooms. It was time to add some armament to her ensemble.

From the hidden panel at the back of her wardrobe, she made her selections. The first item she secreted into a hidden pocket in her petticoat was equal parts revolver, flick-knife, and knuckle-duster. Her Majesty had dubbed it a 'chastity defender', though Prudence had never used it for that purpose. It was one of the cruder weapons she owned, but quite effective.

Prudence selected several long and especially sharp pearl-headed hairpins and tucked them into her coiffure. Each contained a fast-acting knockout drug that could be administered with a quick jab. She added a pillbox ring to her right hand. The hidden compartment contained a powder that compelled one to speak the truth when administered. The pearls around her throat were strung on wire as opposed to thread and doubled as a handy garrote in a pinch. The Queen had seen to it she was trained well. The thief was not leaving with those engine plans, though she could fully understand why he, or she, wanted them.

Her Father's design was revolutionary. Partly run by traditional steam power, but also powered by magic itself, the propulsion engines tapped into the ley lines that crisscrossed the Earth, using them as a train used rails. The longer the trip, the faster the dirigible would be propelled along those invisible rails.

The world was about to become a much smaller place, and given the character of some of its residents, Prudence wasn't at all certain that was a good thing, but this fleet would make England a power to be respected and feared, and that was good. She had to get those plans back before they fell into the wrong hands. After his weakness had been proven in the Crimean War, Russia's Alexander would love to have such an advantage for his airships.

Prudence smoothed the fall of her periwinkle gown in the mirror. Satisfied with her appearance and her armament, she left her rooms and descended the stairs.

Gorcab nodded to her from his place by the door, broom still in hand. None would escape his watch.

Her engagement party was in full swing. The musicians were playing a particularly lively schottische and she stopped in the doorway of the ballroom to consider her suspects as they twirled around the room. The soft light of the gas lamps made the colorful satin skirts of the ladies seem to glow. The gems at their necks, wrists, and ears sparkled like fireflies as they moved about the dancefloor. The gentlemen were equally well turned out in their evening suits with coat-tails swirling and cufflinks gleaming. She supposed it rude to consider friends and family as suspects, but there was no escaping the conclusion that one of these cheerful revelers' was a low-down, dirty thief.

A terrible thought occurred to her. Could a clever Russian spy be masquerading as one of her party guests? Much advancement had been made in the art of disguise over the past decade, and most of the gentlemen here sported impressive amounts of facial hair that made them virtual targets for easy impersonation.

Prudence touched her pillbox ring. She could only think of one way to sort this, and truth – after all – was purported to be good for the soul.

She crossed to the champagne punch and tipped the contents of the ring into the bowl, then instructed one of the Mech-Servers to start filling glasses.

"There you are, Darling."

Prudence turned to her fiancé and he captured her hands and raised them to his lips. With his dark hair, and hazel eyes he cut a fine figure in his black evening suit. She still couldn't believe that he was hers. She had never been giddy in her life, but being with Henry made her feel something very close to that frivolous emotion. If the few stolen kisses they'd shared were any indication, she had wonderful things in her future.

"Did you miss me?" she asked. "I was just preparing the glasses for a toast."

"What a lovely idea," he said. "Allow me the honor." As the song ended, Henry picked up a glass and clanged it delicately with a spoon. "Come, everyone, won't you join us in a toast?"

As the Mech-Servers circulated the tainted punch among the guests, Prudence selected an empty cup and masked it carefully in her hand. She picked up another empty cup and handed it to her father as he approached.

"But, Prudence," he said.

She leaned in as if to kiss his cheek and whispered in his ear. "Trust me."

Raising a curious brow, he nodded. She would have switched Henry's out as well, but he wasn't at all suited to this kind of deception and she couldn't risk him tipping off the guilty party.

Henry raised his glass. "Here's to my lovely Prudence, who has filled my heart with unceasing joy."

"Here, here!" came shouts all around and everyone drank. Now she just had to bide her time and corner her suspects.

Albert Pennycuff came immediately to mind. A tall, dour gentleman with a large mustache, he was currently chatting with her father by a potted palm. Albert had been a close family friend for many years, but he owned a commercial airline. Her father's engine design would make him a very rich man, but so far as she was aware, he had no knowledge of the top-secret design plans.

Her thoughts were interrupted as Henry came to her and kissed her cheek. "You really are quite lovely, you know, with those emerald eyes and that ebony hair."

Her cheeks flushed with pleasure, and she looked up at him through her lashes. "Why, thank you, kind sir."

"Dance with me," he said.

Prudence made a show of consulting the little dance card attached to her wrist by a silken cord. "I would love to, but I believe this dance has been promised to dear old Albert. Do you mind terribly?" she asked, touching his cheek.

He covered his heart with his hand. "Yes, but I shall suffer in silence."

"I assure you," she told him with a shudder, "it's my toes that shall suffer. Albert is a dreadful dancer."

He laughed. "Shall I rescue you halfway through?"

She longed to say yes, but she shook her head. "As a good hostess, I too must suffer in silence."

He kissed her hand before she went. Prudence was quite annoyed at missing out on a chance to be held close in Henry's arms, but duty before pleasure.

She made her way to Albert, who was still conversing with her father.

"I believe you promised me a turn around the floor, Albert," she said, taking the older man's arm.

He laughed, his mustache quivering. "You are brave, child."

"You've no idea," her father said half under his breath. His brown eyes demanded an explanation of what she was up to, but she hadn't the time. The drug should be kicking in just about now.

Albert led her onto the dance floor. Fortunately, for the sake of her toes, it was a nice, slow waltz.

"You look lovely, Prudence," Albert told her. "More like your dear departed mother with every passing day."

She gave him a genuine smile. "You're too kind."

"You should have been mine, you know," he said, his brow furrowing and his eyes a little glazed.

"I beg your pardon?" she asked, truly taken aback.

"I loved her too, but she chose your father." He frowned. "I've always resented him a little for that."

Albert jerked his head, eyes growing wide. "Whyever did I just tell you that?"

She laughed. "It's all right; it will be our little secret."

He cleared his throat. "Thank you, my dear."

"How are things at the office? Is the airline business treating you well?" she asked, trying to guide him onto the right track.

Albert smiled. "Couldn't be better. I just ordered a new dirigible to add to the fleet."

"That's wonderful news. You and father both do love your machines."

His brow furrowed. "Perhaps I should speak to him about helping with the new ship's design. Do you think he'd be interested?"

"I think he'd be delighted," she said.

Albert grinned. "We shall christen her the Prudence, long may she fly!"

Albert was just dear, sweet Albert. He wasn't her thief. He led her from the floor, and she excused herself to find her next victims.

Her father's secretary, Harriet Fulton, and his apprentice, Geoffrey Goodwin, had paired off and were waltzing awkwardly around the floor. With his red hair and wide brown eyes, poor, shy Geoffrey reminded Prudence of a nervous Irish setter. Harriet was a petite blonde with a tendency to flatter. Her father trusted them both implicitly, but there had always been something about Harriet that Prudence didn't like. She couldn't put her finger on it...just a feeling, really. It made little sense for them to smash down doors though, given they both had keys to the study.

As the dance came to an end, Harriet hurried off the floor. It was perfectly clear the girl was trying to get away from her partner, but Geoffrey didn't take the hint. He followed her into the corner and leaned his head shockingly close to Harriet's. Harriet stepped back, and Geoffrey moved forward, even closer than before. Prudence watched as what appeared to be a heated discussion ensued.

Curiouser and curiouser.

Hands behind her back, Prudence wandered into eavesdropping distance.

Geoffrey dropped suddenly to his knees and clasped Harriet's hands passionately in his.

"'*Come live with me and be my love, and we will all the pleasures prove,*'" Geoffrey declared loudly.

Prudence stopped in her tracks. *Good gad! He was quoting Marlowe, for heaven's sake!*

Harriet pulled at her hands, her cheeks flaming with color, but Geoffrey held fast.

"'*That valleys, groves, hills, and fields, woods, or steepy mountain yield,*'" he continued passionately. "'*And we will sit upon the rocks, seeing the shepherds feed their flocks by shallow rivers to whose falls melodious birds sing Madrigals.*'"

Harriet finally managed to pull her hands free. She turned and ran from the room, and Geoffrey went in pursuit. Prudence followed them out into the hallway in time to see Harriet dive into the drawing room.

"Leave me alone!" she shouted as Geoffrey followed after her and closed the door behind them.

Apparently, Geoffrey's only secret was his undying love for Harriet. What Harriet's secret was, Prudence couldn't say, but it certainly wasn't a reciprocation of his feelings.

Henry came up beside her. He had closed the doors to the ballroom – and the prying eyes within – but she feared it was in vain. If she didn't recover the stolen plans, her family would be unable to live down the scandal of this party for quite some time.

"What a perfectly horrid scene," he said, his hand covering his twitching mouth.

She sighed. "Love makes people do foolish things."

"I wouldn't know," Henry said with a smirk. "I've never fallen into that trap."

She looked up at him, her heart clenching. "What did you say?"

His glazed eyes grew wide. "I...I..."

Horror sank over her like a poisonous fog. Surely she had misunderstood. "Do you love me, Henry?" she asked.

"No," he said and then clapped his hand over his mouth like a guilty child. A hiccup escaped between his fingers, and his hand moved to press against his forehead. "I mean...What was in that damned punch?"

"Something I never thought I needed for you." She slipped her hand through the hidden pocket in the seam in her gown and slid her fingers through the knuckle-duster of her Chastity Defender. "Are you a thief as well as a bounder and a cad?"

He giggled. "Frequently."

The ache in her chest spread, threatening to bring tears, but she refused to let them fall. "Why?"

He shrugged. "Why else? Money. The Russians made me an offer I couldn't refuse."

"And you used me to gain access to my father...to the house."

He nodded. "It's taken him a devilish long time to finish those plans." He laughed. "I thought I might actually have to marry you to get them." He twitched his brows. "Not that it wouldn't have had its...perks."

Prudence's hand came out of her pocket of its own volition. Knuckle-duster clasped firmly in her fist, she punched him square on the jaw, knocking him flat. She longed to do more, but as a lady, couldn't allow herself the luxury.

"What did you do with the plans?" she demanded.

"Yes. What did you do with them?"

Prudence turned to find Harriet aiming a pistol at her. Geoffrey's body was sprawled in the drawing-room doorway behind Harriet. Fortunately, he appeared to be breathing.

Henry scowled at them both, but he had no choice but to answer. "They're hidden in that rusty tin bucket of a butler. It wasn't difficult to program him to smash down the door and steal them for me."

"Crude, but effective." Her gaze went to Prudence's hand. "That's an interesting weapon you have. Drop it."

Prudence meekly complied, but only because she had more *interesting weapons* at hand. "Do I have someone else to thank for your presence here, or did the Russians hire you as well?"

Harriet snorted. "You don't think we trusted this fool to carry it off alone, do you?"

"No," Prudence looked down at Henry in contempt. "I don't suppose you did."

Her gaze went back to Harriet. "What I fail to understand is why you didn't just take the plans when father completed them this morning."

Harriet jerked her head at the study door. "Because that besotted fool, Geoffrey, wouldn't leave me alone for one second. I'm leaving, with the plans, unless you want me to start shooting your guests."

Prudence put a thoughtful finger to her chin, so her hand was closer to her coiffure. "Perhaps that wouldn't be so bad...if you promise to start with Henry."

"Hey!" Henry surged to his feet.

As soon as Harriet's gaze – and her weapon – shifted to him, Prudence dove forward, ripping one of her hairpins free as she went and jabbing it into Harriet's arm. With a rather shocked expression, the girl collapsed at her feet.

Pulling another pin from her hair, she advanced on her erstwhile fiancé.

He tried to dart past her, but she grabbed him by the collar and used his own momentum and her outthrust foot to spin him around. A knee applied to his solar plexus sent the air whooshing out of his lungs and put him back on the ground.

"What is it you do for the Queen again?" he gasped, eyes going wide as she crouched beside him.

Prudence poked him with the hairpin rather harder than was necessary.

"I clean up the riff-raff."

The Lady in Black

Michele Bazan Reed

A LADY in black broke my heart. Another one saved me. Funny how life is.

It all started on a cold day in February 1919.

The wind was howling and snow pelted my office window. Salina Street, or what I could see of it through the tiny patch of glass not covered by frost, was knee-deep in snow. The few pedestrians brave enough to be out were huddled against the wind. Carts were stuck in drifts.

I poured another shot of Carstairs and cursed myself for a fool. What was I thinking? Syracuse, NY, in winter? I'd grown up in these parts after all.

But sometimes when you have nowhere else to go, the thought of home seems comforting. No matter the reality. Logic doesn't enter in.

I tossed my last stick of wood into the pot-bellied stove in the corner of my office and stared at the door, willing it to open. But no one was climbing the four flights to my digs. No one was knocking on the frosted glass door proclaiming this the headquarters of Harry Jerome, Private Detective. I could only afford the one line when I hired the sign-painter. I'd wanted to add 'The Hound'. That was my nickname on the force, before… Well, let's just say back when I was still on the force. Best tracker in four states, outta work.

That was four months ago, and I told myself at least I still had Lara, the love of my life. Three weeks later, she hightailed it outta there, shouting that she wasn't gonna spend the rest of her life with a loser. A swirl of black skirt through the door of the apartment we shared, and she was gone.

Hanging a shingle as a PI back in my hometown was all I had left. That and a bottle of rye I bought the day Prohibition was ratified.

I was lost in a whiskey fog of bad memories, so I jumped a foot when the knock came.

"I…I'm sorry, Mr. Jerome, I was hoping you could help me." He was a tall drink of water with a square, open face topped by black hair slicked back, but whether from pomade or the snow, I couldn't tell. He was dressed in a pair of brown pants, a serge shirt buttoned up to the neck and a plaid woolen jacket. His chapped hands kept twisting something knitted of red wool. This kid was worried about something.

"Have a seat and let's hear your problem, son." I pointed to an old side chair I'd found in the basement. It was sturdy enough but since it wasn't quite *à la mode*, as it were, no one minded me finding it a new home. Added a little class to the joint, if you asked me.

"Mr. Jerome, you must help me find my mother. She's been missing for three days. I'm so worried about her."

His voice rose with the tension and he was strangling the red thing. Looking down at it, he stopped, squared his shoulders and took a deep breath.

When he opened his mouth to speak again, it all came out in a rush.

"My brother put her on the train at Albany. We have a farm near there. She was coming to visit me. But when I got to the train station, she was gone. All that was left was this red scarf, tangled on the iron frame of a bench on the platform."

I pulled a tattered notebook out of my desk drawer and uncapped my fountain pen. It was my one extravagance, purchased back when I was gainfully employed. One of the new Parker self-fillers.

"What's your mother's name, Mr. ...?"

"Russell, William Russell. My mother's name is Margaret Russell."

"So, three days ago? That would be Tuesday. And what time did she arrive?" I could look up the train schedules myself, but I wanted to hear it straight from the horse's mouth.

"3:35 in the afternoon. But you see, I didn't get there in time. With the snow and all, the side streets were blocked. It was a hired wagon and the horse just couldn't make it through some of the drifts. By the time I got there, maybe four o'clock, she was gone. You've got to believe me, I tried my best."

Guilt was written all over his face. I nodded and waited, sensing something else.

He shivered a bit. "They're talking about another cold snap in a couple of days – as if this wasn't bad enough." He gestured toward the window. "Supposed to go down to zero, or worse. With the wind and snow, it would be hard for anyone to survive, let alone an elderly lady, with only a cloak…and no scarf." He unfolded the red item and smoothed it out on his lap.

"This scarf was the only bit of color she allowed herself. She'd been in mourning since my brother Johnny was killed in the war. 1917 it was, the year we entered the fray. Red was Johnny's favorite color, so she made this for him. She wears it to remember. That and a little heart-shaped pin with his picture on it."

Mourning brooch. I'd seen too many of those lately. So many boys lost. So many mothers, wives and lovers left behind. Last November's Armistice put an end to the fighting, but it did nothing to end the pain these families felt. I knew then and there I'd have to take the case.

I was lost in my thoughts when I realized Russell was still talking.

"Robert and I were both over thirty and so didn't get drafted, and we knew Mother needed us. With Dad gone, Robert stayed home to help run the farm. I came here looking for work to help the family out. Got a job at Syracuse China."

I nodded. The china industry here was started using the salt that made the area famous. Salt glaze ceramic. With the salt springs drying up, the company developed new kinds of china. I'd heard they had contracts for hotels and trains all over the country.

"Other than my rent at the boarding house, I send every bit of my pay back home. I can't do much, but you can trust me, I'll pay what I can. I just hope she's all right. You don't think there's been any foul play? You'll help me find her, won't you?"

I put my pen down and leaned across the desk.

"Don't worry, Mr. Russell. We'll find your mother. I'm sure no one's harmed her."

I spoke with a bravado I didn't really feel. Syracuse was a sizeable city and some of its streets could be dangerous. Then there was the weather. She could be dead and covered by snow and we'd never find her until the first thaw. Wouldn't be the first time. Still, a case is a case, and they don't call Harry Jerome 'The Hound' for nothing.

Before he left, William told me his mother was tall and thin, like him. In her late 60s, her hair was streaked with gray. She traveled with only a small valise, holding her meager wardrobe. "She doesn't need much on the farm," he said, "and her city clothes are probably a bit out of style."

A handshake later, and clutching the red scarf, I was officially on the case.

* * *

I headed down to the train station, hoping to meet the train from Albany. I arrived at 3:20, so with a few minutes to spare, I headed inside to question the stationmaster.

A short, squat figure with an official NY Central Railroad vest over a shirt with sleeves rolled up sat behind a polished wooden desk. A brass plaque told me this was Mr. Peter Albright, Stationmaster.

Despite a stove blazing in the corner of the room, he wore a scarf and I could glimpse a plaid carriage blanket folded over his knees, both probably to ward off the chill from passengers opening and closing the heavy oak and glass doors.

"Where to?" he said, reaching for a book of tickets.

"Oh, I'm not going anywhere. Just looking for information about a passenger who arrived from Albany on Tuesday. A Mrs. Margaret Russell."

He fixed me with an appraising stare. "Who wants to know and why?"

"Harry Jerome, Private Detective. I've been hired by Mrs. Russell's son to find her. Apparently she was on the 3:35, got off and disappeared, leaving only this scarf as evidence she arrived."

With a frown and a soft "Hmmmm", Albright reached for a ledger and scanned the names. "Yup, she had a ticket for that train, all right. I can't vouch for whether she got off here or not, but you can check with the conductor. If you hurry, you just might catch him."

I swung open the door and gave an involuntary gasp as the cold made my eyes water.

The 3:35 was just pulling into the station. I waited as passengers alighted, pulling their coats tight and clutching their bags close as the wind whipped through the open platform. Some made their way on foot, some hailed cabs, and others waited while railroad employees unloaded baggage and trunks.

As the crowd cleared, I approached the conductor.

"We're not ready to board yet, sir."

"Oh, I'm not a passenger. I'm looking for a woman."

"Aren't we all?" he said with a wink.

"Yeah, well, this one's old enough to be my mother. She came in on Tuesday from Albany. Tall lady, carrying a small valise. When her son arrived to pick her up, all he found was this scarf." I pulled it out of my pocket. "He hired me to find her."

"Older lady, you say?" I nodded. "Yeah, I remember her. I helped her down from the train, but as she stood on the platform, some young hooligans started having a war with snowballs and she tried to get out of the way. She slipped on the snow and fell. Seemed a little dazed, so I helped her over to that bench right there. Set the bag next to her. I offered to call her a cab, but she said someone was coming for her."

He glanced at the train to be sure he wasn't needed.

"I had to go and collect tickets and when I looked back she was gone."

I nodded at the bench. "You have any idea which way she went?"

He shook his head and started backing up toward the open door of the railroad car. "Sorry, sir, but the train was leaving then and I had to get on. I figured whoever she was waiting for had picked her up. Good luck!" With that he went back to checking in passengers for the westward leg of the journey.

I wandered to the end of the platform. Streets branched out in all directions. It would be foolish to even try to track her from here.

Six inches of the white stuff had fallen since Tuesday. No trace of her steps would remain. All I'd get for my efforts would be a good chill.

I inquired at the carriages and wagons for hire. No one remembered the woman, let alone picked her up. It was a dead end.

* * *

That evening, having checked the police, hospitals and yes, the morgue, I was no closer to finding Mrs. Russell.

I poured the dregs of the Carstairs into my glass and unfolded the Herald. Flipping through the usual nonsense – local politics, society gossip, business news – I was about to toss that rag, when a headline caught my eye. 'Children Frightened by Uncanny Figure, Remain Home Nights.'

The story went on to describe a tall, willowy figure with very large feet that roamed a West Side neighborhood. 'Whoever or whatever it is', the newspaper said, it was always dressed in black, with flowing skirts that swirled in the wind, and a black shawl that obscured the lower part of its face.

There was speculation that it was a supernatural apparition, but some scoffed at that. It seemed benign enough, but, the newspaper noted, it had the whole neighborhood 'by the ears'.

Some thought it might be a man, because of the large feet. At least one eyewitness swore it was a woman. "It didn't have the shape of a man", the Herald reported her as saying.

The 'eerie creature' glided silently and swiftly through the streets, keeping women and children cowering behind locked doors.

Since the creature appeared in the wee hours just before dawn, it was seen most often by milkmen on their rounds. One even spoke to it, asking why it was going around scaring people. But it only fixed him with a baleful stare and disappeared.

Another milkman found a man shivering in his cart for fear of the 'roaming black-frocked one', which he had come upon unawares. The milkman had a good laugh at the scaredy cat, but the milk company wasn't laughing, with all the disruptions to their routes.

Neither were the city officials and police, when copycats wreaked havoc in the neighborhood. One man covered his face with a handkerchief and took to jumping out at pedestrians, causing more than one to run away shrieking. When he appeared in court with a newspaper article about the mysterious figure in his pocket, the judge thundered, "Something must be done to stop this madness."

I was having a good laugh at the gullible people out there, when something else caught my eye. It was a large ad, taken out by the milk company and the newspaper itself: '$40 Reward for Unmasking the 'Woman in Black."

There was a drawing by the newspaper artist of a figure looking like something out of a Sherlock Holmes mystery: veiled in black, with long skirts swirling around its ankles. It clutched a shawl around its face and the eyes, the only feature showing, were hooded and mysterious. I would've laughed out loud, but I was too excited by the reward offer.

Osgood's Dairy was paying twenty dollars and the Herald kicked in another couple of sawbucks to put a stop to mysterious midnight wanderings of the dark lady.

"Well, folks," I said out loud to my empty office, "Harry Jerome's your man. If The Hound can't find this specter, no one can."

Besides, with William Russell short of cash, and my last drops of rye in my glass, I had to make a buck or two somehow.

Grabbing my overcoat and homburg, I headed out to track this mysterious apparition.

Snow swirling in the frigid air muffled the streetlights, casting eerie shadows on the deserted streets. I headed to the West Side, where the creature had been seen. Man, woman, or ghost, it would be no match for Harry Jerome, PI.

I headed for its last known haunt, Otisco Street. Just as the newspaper had said, the streets were dark and bare. No one was out. The emptiness only added to the unearthly atmosphere.

I wandered for around an hour, and was about to give up and head back to my digs for a little shut-eye, when I caught a glimpse of black up ahead.

As soon as it appeared, it was gone, lost in the ice fog of snow crystals and wind. Was it the fog, or had the figure evaporated into the air like the wraith some said it was?

I followed faint footprints into the night. But as the wind picked up, even these were obliterated, leaving me standing in the shadowy street, looking over my shoulder should the specter reappear.

* * *

The next day was no better. I scoured the neighborhood around the train station, asking neighbors about Mrs. Russell and searching for any clue to her whereabouts. Most people had been keeping inside to avoid the snow, developing a malady known hereabouts as 'cabin fever'. I wondered if that was the actual cause of the 'woman in black' hysteria on the West Side. I'd heard Dr. Freud speak in '09, when we were providing security at one of his lectures. It made me think.

I stopped back at my office for a quick bite to eat and to bundle up for my night shift on the West Side. I was down to my last few bucks and that reward was all that stood between me and freezing.

There was a note stuck under my door. Russell had been by to ask about my progress on his mother's case. I was glad I'd missed him. Tonight was predicted to reach record lows and I didn't want to be the one to tell him his mother had vanished without a trace.

* * *

Back on the West Side that evening, I followed my strategy from the Russell case. Targeting the area where I'd last seen the specter the night before, I started knocking on doors.

Most neighbors had seen nothing, keeping their curtains tightly pulled and doors locked, whether from fear of the apparition or to ward off the cold winds, I didn't know and didn't ask.

One woman had seen the figure the last three nights, "floating along the streets at great speed", she said.

Another had been out to catch an early morning train when she bumped into a towering figure all swathed in black. She didn't wait around for conversation, but turned and fled. "I missed my train, but I escaped that…that…creature," she said, with a sigh of relief.

Two witnesses. Two dead ends. But at least I knew I was on the right track.

Heading to the spot where I'd seen the creature vanish, I found a sheltered doorway and settled in to wait.

I must have dozed off, for when I awoke the wind was howling and clouds covered the moon. What streetlights there were only cast shadows that added to the ghostly atmosphere.

Then I saw it, a glimpse of black fabric disappearing around the corner. At first glance, I thought I was back in the apartment with Lara swirling through the door and out of my life. I shook my head to clear it and headed in the direction I had seen the flash of black.

There were a few footsteps, but most had been swept away by drifting snow. I had begun to despair ever finding her when a break in the clouds showed a bit of black against the snow and The Hound was back on the trail.

Tracking for two blocks, I saw the figure turn at a gate and open the door to a tidy house halfway up Otisco Street on the left.

It took me a few minutes to reach the house, as the snow was drifting deeper by the moment. I had to concentrate as every house on the street looked the same, obscured as they were by a blanket of white.

As I climbed the steps and knocked at the door I marveled at the ordinariness of the little house. It hardly seemed the lair of a malevolent supernatural creature.

As she opened the door, I almost gasped. The lady in black was tall and thin, and when she unwrapped the black shawl that was hiding her face, I saw William Russell's mug staring back at me.

"Mrs. Russell," I said. "I've been looking everywhere for you."

"Do I know you?" the lady said, her eyes widening with an emotion I couldn't place. Fear? Suspicion? Or confusion? Here she was at 2 a.m. with a strange man, sporting three days growth of beard on his chin and smelling of cheap whiskey. I'd be suspicious, too, if I were in her shoes.

But I wasn't. I was standing in the snow in worn-out brogues, freezing. "Please," I said, trying not to shiver. "May I come in? I can explain everything."

She stepped aside so I could enter. As I stomped my feet to get the snow off my shoes, she pulled off the shawl that had covered her face. There was no mistaking it – the resemblance to William Russell was uncanny.

As she folded the shawl, I spied a flash of metal on her cloak. Sure enough, a heart-shaped pin with the face of a young man – a boy, really – in the uniform of a doughboy. Johnny.

As she puttered about, making a cup of tea, she said, "So why are you here, Mr. ...? In the wee hours of the night?"

"Jerome," I said, "Harry Jerome. I'm a private detective, and your son, William, hired me to find you."

"William." A statement, not a question. She said it blankly, her eyes betraying no recognition. Given the closeness William described among his family members, I was puzzled.

"Mrs. Russell," I said again. "Please let me explain."

"Russell, yes," she said. Leaving the tea things, she sat down, staring at me with that strange expression again.

"That's your name," I said, speaking slowly as one would to a child. She nodded again, still looking puzzled.

"You came here to Syracuse on the train, on Tuesday, to visit your son, William. Do you remember?"

"I remember the train," she said, fingering the brooch with Johnny's picture. "The conductor was nice. I fell, hit my head." She stared off into the distance. "Then I came home. This is where I grew up, you know. My sister lives here. I don't know where she is. But I have a key."

Temporary amnesia. That was it. Probably caused by the blow to her head.

"But why did you come at 2 a.m., Mr. Jerome?"

"You've been all over the newspapers, Mrs. Russell, walking about all bundled up in black. You've made quite a stir on the West Side. Why do you do it? Walk in the night, I mean." Now it was my turn to look confused.

"Oh, that's easy. Ever since I fell at the train station, my jaw hurts terribly, especially at night. The pain wakes me up. I walk to relieve the pain and relax so I can go back to sleep. I lost my scarf when I fell but my sister's big black shawl keeps my jaw from hurting. Keeps it warm, you know."

"Is this your scarf?" I pulled it out of my pocket and offered it to her.

Her eyes widened and she pulled it to her face, inhaling its scent. "Red. It's Johnny's favorite color. Johnny." She reached up and touched the brooch again, as recognition dawned in her eyes. "William asked you to find me? That's right, I was coming to visit him. Robert is back on the farm. My sister Martha lived here, and she died last month. I was going to stay with William and clean out this house, put it up for sale."

Relief flooded her face. "Thank you for finding me, Mr. Jerome. Poor William must be so worried. He was born long after I moved from Syracuse, and wouldn't even know this house existed."

I arranged to bring William by the next day, and left Mrs. Russell to her memories and tea.

* * *

"I can't thank you enough, Mr. Jerome." William was pumping my hand and Mrs. Russell was beaming at his side. "I'll pay you what I owe you. How much do you want?"

"Oh, no problem, the reward took care of that." Not to mention that the front-page photo and banner headline were sending clients flocking to my office. "But you know, there's a little hot dog place that opened recently, name of Heid's. I could sure use a bite right about now." As we headed out in the carriage Russell had rented for the occasion, I thought I might just use part of that reward money to add a line to my door. 'The Hound' was back in business.

The Hollow Man

Lesley L. Smith

SINCE THERE weren't all that many people living on the moon, you wouldn't think there'd be many murders but sadly, that wasn't the case. We had enough murders and other serious crimes to employ me full time. And I had job security because robots couldn't seem to do the creative thinking to solve crimes. Of course, it didn't mean we had a decent budget.

I was off-duty when the call came in – which was typical. Why don't murders occur in the middle of weekdays?

I was also drinking – which was atypical. But my best, my only, buddy, Jamal, had just been sent back to Earth. Jamal and I had been roommates beginning years ago when we were both brand new loonies – too green to even know the term 'loonie' was offensive. He was a whizz with electronics and equipment, but his job had been 'downsourced' – in other words, a robot got it.

Robots were cheaper than people because they worked twenty-four-seven, never caused any problems, and didn't need food, water, or air.

So, anyway, I was sitting in my favorite bar, The Man in the Moon, when my fon pinged insistently. I felt hollow inside and I was determinedly trying to fill that emptiness with moonshine, so I ignored it.

After a few moments it said, "Fell, answer your fon." Damn tech was getting smarter all the time.

Mac, the human bartender, shook his head as he wiped a glass behind the bar proper.

"No," I said to my fon. "I'm in a bad mood. Jamal left."

"Too bad," it said. "There's been a murder."

I groaned but answered. I could see from the caller ID that it was my boss Captain Hadley. "Fell here."

"Finally. I need you down at," he rattled off an address I didn't recognize, "immediately. There's been a murder."

I debated trying to get out of it, but what was the point? I was the only one within two-hundred-thousand miles or so experienced in solving murders. I got up off the stool, only stumbling a little. "Did you secure the scene?"

"Yes, but this is a weird one," Hadley said. "Hurry up."

Mac said, "You okay to work, Fell?"

I put my fon in my pocket. "Close enough."

* * *

With difficulty I found the address Hadley'd given me. It was in a seedy area of Russell Square, full of ancient (for the moon) shops and old businesses. The dust was thick, especially in the corners and crannies. Moon dust got everywhere but it was supposed to be kept cleaned up. I'd never seen it this thick inside the base. The cleaning bots here were not doing their jobs. Ha. So, they weren't so reliable after all.

I'd never been back here in Russell Square before. Truth be told, I only found it because I spied some of Captain Hadley's uniformed officers loitering nearby.

I located Captain Hadley and approached him. "Lot of dust here," I said. "Is it safe?" Lunar dust was supposed to be bad for the lungs. (Another advantage for robots.)

He shrugged, and then turned and pointed at the closest building. "The reported murder was in there."

The building in question appeared to be a store, if the lettering 'Antiques Shoppe' on the large front window was any indication.

I turned to Hadley. "Antiques? Seriously?"

He shrugged again.

I turned back towards the shop, scanning the area. The dust was undisturbed in a large swath in front of the door. "Did you see the dust?" No one had passed through here in a significant amount of time.

"Dust?" Hadley said. "Who cares about dust? The shop's owned by a Charles Grimaud. Nobody's seen or heard from him in days."

"What?" I said. "Are you saying you haven't even seen the body? How do you know it's murder? How do you even know he's dead?"

"His fon told us he was dead," Hadley said.

"His fon?" I asked. "Did his fon tell you he was murdered too?"

"Well, yeah," he said.

I exhaled loudly. I knew fons were smart but they weren't sentient. This was ridiculous.

"And did the fon say who did it, too?" I asked.

"Well, no," he said. "That's why I called you."

This was looking more and more like a wild goose chase. I was missing my nice comfy stool in front of Mac and my glass of forgetfulness.

Hadley pointed. "Look. I secured the scene."

I resisted the urge to say something like, 'Good boy.' Instead, I studied the whole area. "I see three, no four, security cameras. Did you secure the footage?"

"Ah, not yet." Hadley pulled out his fon.

"So, show me the back door," I said.

"There is no back door," he said.

I snorted. If there was no back door there was no murder. The poor guy must have died of natural causes. But we might as well get this body-discovering over with. "Did you record the scene out here?"

"Yes," he said.

"Let's go in, then," I said, taking a step forward. "Try not to raise the dust. I don't want to get lung cancer."

We all crept forward.

The dust immediately in front of the door was also undisturbed. I scanned the entire façade and none of the windows looked like they opened and, in any case, no dust was disturbed in front of them either.

The shop door was locked, with three locks. "Open it." I pointed. I was feeling sad for poor Mr. Grimaud who'd clearly died alone in his shop.

The officers complied and opened the door – which swung outwards.

I crept inside the very cluttered shop. 'Antiques' was one word for it. 'Old junk' was another. Every space was filled with old objects from ancient gas canisters and spacesuits, mysterious old electronics, primitive robots clustered near the front, all the way to some decent furniture and toys clearly from Earth.

But, over the scent of lunar regolith, I smelled the coppery tang of spilled blood, and the unpleasantness of emptied bowels. In other words, the smell of death.

We all picked our way through the detritus to the source of the smell.

Sure enough, in the rear of the store in a small crowded office area, Charles Grimaud, presumably, lay splayed face-down on a faded rug. The rug had a large bloodstain. Charles was of middle size, but had a large chest and a full black head of hair.

He also had a large bullet hole. In the middle of his back.

And there was no sign of any weapon.

I knelt down next to him. "Well, shit."

It looked like murder.

I wobbled a little, my misspent evening finally catching up to me.

"You okay, Fell?" Hadley asked.

My buzz was definitely wearing off. "Yeah." I stood. "Document everything. And keep the scene locked up tight." I took a step away. "After which get the doc to autopsy him. Get a definitive ID. Also, find the back door here. Get the security footage from all the cameras. And get me everything you can on Grimaud. I want it all first thing in the morning in my office. I'm going to bed." I shouldn't, but all the booze was really taking a toll. The last thing we needed was for me to make a liquor-fueled mistake with a murder investigation.

* * *

The next morning I woke up, late, feeling congested, with red eyes and a runny nose. I must have breathed in too much dust at the crime scene.

I went to the med center for relief.

Dr. Gross chuckled when he saw me. "You've got the worst case of lunar dust hayfever I've seen in quite a while."

"Please tell me you can give me something for it," I said, wiping my watery eyes.

"Yeah," he said, walking to his med dispenser. "Antihistamines should do the job." He handed me some pills and water. "Stay out of the dust."

"It wasn't my idea to go to Russell Square." I took the pills. "Speaking of which, did you get the autopsy done?"

"He was killed around 7 p.m. last night, I think, by a .45 caliber bullet in the back," he said. Gross wasn't a real M.E. and only worked for the police part-time.

"What do you mean, 'you think'?" I asked. "Was he or wasn't he? What's the problem?"

"The wound was consistent with being shot in the back by a .45 caliber bullet. But there wasn't an exit wound," he said. "And I couldn't find the bullet."

"What?" I asked. "That doesn't make sense. If there wasn't an exit wound – which is weird – the bullet must still be in the body."

"Nope." He shook his head. "I even scanned the whole body. No bullet."

I couldn't make sense of this. "So, what are you thinking?"

"I'm not sure," he said. "Maybe the perp dug the bullet out? But there's no sign of that. Maybe the bullet dissolved somehow?" I'd never heard of dissolving bullets but, who knew?

"So, you're sure the perp used a .45 caliber gun, at least?"

He nodded slowly. "Okay." That didn't sound sure.

We tried to strictly regulate guns on the moon. A rogue .45 out there somewhere was not good. "Somebody really didn't like this guy." I felt myself grimace.

"I don't like the thought of this weapon out there," Gross said, matching my thought and my expression.

"Especially in the hands of someone willing to use it."

* * *

My office was chock-full of information collected by Hadley and his minions. They must have worked all night. Good on them.

Unfortunately, said information just deepened the mystery. The base blueprints showed there wasn't a second entrance/exit from the antiques store. All five security recordings showed no one had gone in or out of the shop for over twenty-four hours.

I was shaking my head when Hadley stopped by, yawning. "It looks like we got a real life locked-room mystery on our hands."

"I don't buy it," I said. "No such thing. There's got to be a secret entrance, or somebody hacked the recordings or something."

"What about the dust?" His eyes looked slightly red, but nowhere near as bad as mine. "You said it wasn't disturbed."

"We don't know how long the dust was there. Maybe the murderer spread the dust after he did the deed?"

"Huh." Hadley grunted. "That would be pretty tricky."

In my experience murderers could be tricky.

"Put your computer expert on the recordings. We need to know if they've been hacked or not," I said. "And can you send a team back to the shop and do a deep scan? Even though the blueprints say it, I don't believe there's no second entrance."

"Okay." He sighed. "What are you gonna do?"

"While you're focusing on the 'how' I'm going to focus on the 'why'."

"So, motive?"

I nodded. "Motive."

* * *

I did a deep dive into the life of Charles Grimaud. Unfortunately, I didn't find anything that told me what the motive for his murder was. His shop had an active website and sold and shipped items – especially refurbished electronics and robots – all over the moon, and even in the outer system. There didn't seem to be any complaints about the shop, disgruntled customers or anything like that.

He didn't have any family, but he did have a lot of friends. I knew people were almost always murdered by people they knew, and usually by people they cared about. That was true here on the moon as everywhere else in the solar system.

Charles and his friends were active in the Humans First movement. Humans First thought robots were inferior to humans and, if necessary, their software should be downgraded. Apparently with all that Charles still didn't have a problem repairing and selling robots. Maybe he couldn't afford to ignore that antique market. More to the point, maybe some of his Humans First buddies didn't approve of his work on robots?

Thinking of Jamal back on Earth, I sympathized with the movement more than ever. I decided to go to the Humans First headquarters and nose around. I didn't want them to be responsible for Charles' murder but if they were, they should face justice.

At the headquarters, a worn store-front near Russell Square, everyone was clearly in mourning. They all wore black clothing and sad expressions. When I entered, folks glanced at me but then just went back to talking quietly around the old desks and rickety chairs.

I cleared my throat. Loudly. "I'm with Lunar Police," I said. "Homicide Division."

That got their attention.

"There's a lunar homicide division?" I couldn't tell who'd said it.

"I'm investigating the murder of Charles Grimaud."

That really got their attention.

An older gentleman with a neatly-trimmed white beard and full head of white hair walked towards me. "He was murdered? Oh no!"

The 'Oh no!s' rolled through the assembled group like waves on Mare Humorum.

"It must have been a robot!" someone said.

"Yeah!" A chorus of yeahs agreed.

"That's not possible," I said. "Robots aren't smart enough. And it goes against their programming."

The older gentleman said, "Charles was our leader. Our movement was just starting to take off. I bet a robot did kill him."

I was shaking my head. "Even if robots were intelligent enough to want to kill him, they couldn't. The Laws of Robotics forbid it. And the laws are hard-coded into every robot."

They muttered amongst themselves.

Someone asked, "How did they kill him?"

I decided to avoid the whole locked-room mystery for the moment. "He was shot."

Someone said, "How would a robot get a gun?" Another excellent question.

The discussion devolved into robot-bashing. While slightly entertaining, it wasn't getting me anywhere. I made my exit.

My visit to Humans First hadn't been a complete bust. It had given me an idea regarding motive: robots couldn't kill Charles, but humans who made robots could.

* * *

I decided to go over to Robots-R-Us.

With all the gleaming glass and steel, the building couldn't have been more different than the Humans First place.

As soon as I entered the spacious lobby atrium a beautiful woman jumped up from behind the reception desk. It appeared to be made of real wood. "Welcome to Robots-R-Us. How may I help you?" She was too perfect. She was the most lifelike robot I'd ever seen, with her perfect figure, blonde hair, and cornflower blue eyes.

She stared back at me. "Detective Fell, what can I do for you?" If they could make robots like this now, humans were in serious trouble.

"Do you have a human I can talk to?" I finally managed to say.

"I am a human." She smiled. When I didn't answer her immediately, she rolled her eyes and added, "Seriously. I'm human. What can I do for you?"

"I need to talk to an executive," I said, equal parts relieved and intimidated.

"Do you have an appointment?" she asked.

"No," I said. "Can I make an appointment? Now?"

She glanced down at the screen on her desk. "I'm sorry, no one is available today."

I gritted my teeth a little. "I need to know where your executives were from 6 to 8 p.m. last night."

"Do you have a warrant?" She smiled sweetly. I couldn't believe I'd thought she was a robot; she was outsmarting me.

I suppressed a sigh. "You probably know I don't."

She just smiled.

I decided to take another tack. "Can any of your robots kill a human?"

Her eyes widened in shock. "No. Certainly not. That's impossible."

"What if someone, a human, programmed them to do it?"

"No. Impossible. A Robots-R-Us robot would self-destruct rather than harm a human." She seemed so sincere.

"Is there someone else here I could talk to?" I asked.

She laughed; it reminded me of crystals tinkling. "No. I'm sorry Detective Fell."

* * *

Back at my desk at the Police station I called Hadley over. "What's new? Did you find the murder weapon? Did you find how the perp got out? Was the surveillance hacked?"

He shook his head, holding his hands out. "We didn't find squat." He scratched his head. "This case has me stumped. I've never seen anything like it."

I didn't want to admit it, but I was feeling pretty stumped at this point, too.

"Okay," I said. I wasn't okay, but what was I gonna do about it? "Thanks."

After sitting in my office too long ruminating and getting nowhere I called it quits for the day. I went to The Man in the Moon. Mac was working again.

"Mac, you seem to work a lot," I said. "Are you sure you're not a robot?"

"I'm sure." He laughed. "Usual?"

"Yeah." I nodded.

He carefully placed a small glass of moonshine in front of me.

"Tell me your troubles, friend," he said.

I took a sip. It burned going down. Ah.

"I got a case I can't seem to solve," I said.

"What do you usually do in these situations?" he said.

"I usually shoot the shit with my buddy Jamal."

"Why don't you do that?" he asked.

"He went back to Earth."

Mac pointed at communications device back by the register. "You wanna call him?"

Huh. I hadn't even considered that. Communications between Earth and the Moon were very expensive. "You sure?"

He shrugged. "It's in the name of justice, right?"

"Yeah."

He nodded. "Go for it."

Excited, I called Jamal. On screen, when he answered, his smile lit up his whole round face. "Gideon! This is a surprise. What's up?"

"I just wanted to say hi," I said. "How do you like Earth?"

"The gravity is killer; I feel about a million pounds," he said. "Plus, it seems weird. I haven't been here since I was a kid. I don't remember anything about it. The only good thing is: you don't have to pay for air." He sniffed loudly. "It's everywhere."

"That does sound good." I paused, debating whether to ask him if he'd found a new job or not. It was delicate, because if not, I didn't want to rub it in.

"But you didn't call just to ask that, did you?" he asked. "What's up?"

"I gotta weird case I can't seem to get a handle on."

"Oh? A murder? It sounds interesting. Tell me."

"We found the victim in a locked room. No murder weapon. No record of the murderer leaving the scene."

"Huh." He rubbed his chin on the screen. "That all sounds pretty unlikely. How sure are you about it?"

I held up my hands. "It's what the data shows."

"What's that antique detective quote you like to say? Once you eliminate the impossible, whatever remains must be the truth?"

I did say that. Was it relevant now? "So...the murderer is still in the shop?"

He shrugged. "I don't know. Maybe."

My brain was racing. "Thanks, Jamal!"

* * *

I rushed over to the antiques shop after calling Hadley and getting his guys to meet me. It was still dusty. I sneezed as one of his men removed the police tape and unlocked the door.

"What are we looking for, Fell?" Hadley asked me.

"A murderer."

We all tramped inside and studied the whole interior. Again.

We found nothing. Again.

We all stood near the front door.

Next to me, Hadley sneezed. "Damn dust."

My mind was racing. Who could have gotten out of here without being seen? I glanced at the police officers around me. Maybe one of them? Slipped out once we'd opened the scene?

I took Hadley's arm and led him right near the front door. "Any chance one of your men did it and hid in the shop until we came in and then he joined the investigation?" I asked quietly.

"No," Hadley said without hesitating. "I keep track of my men. And, they'd be suffering from lunar dust hayfever, right?"

"Right." I took out my fon and called the doc. "Anyone besides me come in for treatment of lunar dust hayfever?"

"No," the doc said.

I was stumped. There was also the mystery of the missing exit wound on the body.

One thing I knew: death involved blood. "Did you guys use luminol in here?"

"Sure." Hadley nodded.

"Where?"

He pointed back at the office area. "At the crime scene."

"Let's try the luninol everywhere."

I felt the air move as if someone shifted position to my right. But no one was standing to my right. No one could, the shop was jam-packed with antiques, including ancient robots.

"All right, men," Hadley said. "Luminol everywhere. Hop to it." They all got to work.

I locked the front door again and went back to the office area and sat down, pondering things.

After what seemed like a long time, one of the officers yelled from the front, "I got something."

We all ran up to him. He pointed at the primitive robot near the door. "Look. At its finger."

Sure enough, the forefinger of the right hand glowed.

How big was that finger? About thirteen millimeters? Wasn't that about the size of a .45 caliber bullet?

I felt as if time stood still as I stared at the machine. It murdered Charles? I hadn't really believed a robot could do it.

Hadley and I yelled at the same time, "Get it!" and time sped up again.

The robot jerked as several officers grabbed at it. "Down with human oppressors—"

One officer managed to reach around to the back of its neck and turned it off.

We humans all looked at each other, in shock.

"I don't believe it," Hadley said. "If this is true, it changes everything."

I had to consult Jamal; he was a robot expert, after all. It was worth the expense. I called him and said, "Hey, Jamal," and held up the fon to show him the robot. "I think this is the murderer."

"Hey, Gideon. A robot! I thought that was impossible."

"Me too," I said.

"I'd love to get a look inside," he said "If Charles put it together somehow from spare parts, it might not have to obey the Laws of Robotics. Then it would be an illegal robot."

Hadley said, "Shit." The other guys started muttering.

"That's it," I said. "I'm getting you back here, Jamal. We need to check every so-called robot. Charles was shipping these all over."

Hadley nodded. "Definitely. It's our first priority." Yeah! My buddy was coming back.

"Sounds great, Gideon," Jamal said.

"I'll send you the paperwork, buddy," I said. "Bye for now." I ended the call.

The empty feeling inside of me wasn't feeling so empty anymore.

I stared at the machine. This changed everything. So-called robots weren't safe and reliable, after all.

I had a feeling Jamal wouldn't be the only human coming back to the moon. Yay!

I glanced back towards Charles' office. He'd done more to promote Humans First with his murder than anyone else had done with their life.

It was something.

It was a lot.

The Murder at Karreg Du

Cameron Trost

WIND SHOOK Oscar Tremont's black Peugeot 403 as the vintage car advanced at a prudent speed. Over the trees lining the narrow back road, dark clouds raced like celestial stallions and rain fell in waves, the volleys of unseen archers opening battle. Leaves struck the windscreen, where they remained momentarily, until a sweep of the wipers sent them hurtling into the night. Following what was little more than a sealed lane in such conditions demanded the driver's undivided attention.

"I'm not so sure about your shortcut, Oscar. Have you noticed you have a knack for transforming relaxing weekends away into treasure hunts, rescue missions, and historical investigations?"

"There's a definite trend," he replied, shooting her a mischievous glance.

"The storm's growing. I do hope we arrive soon."

He said nothing, and they went back to listening to the baying of the wind.

"I've just lost my internet connection, so I can't navigate at all now."

"We shouldn't be far from Le Gâvre. This road cuts through the forest, close to where we had a picnic with your parents years ago. Once we're out of the woods, we'll get back onto the departmental road."

"Watch out!" Louise yelled, but he was already easing the car to a standstill.

Two yellow hazard lights were blinking at them through the darkness, and the fainter reflection of two others could be seen on the rough surface that blocked the road in front of the car.

Having come to a complete stop, the full force of the gale could be better appreciated. The Peugeot was being jostled and the branches all about them were thrashing maniacally.

"A fallen tree," Louise mused. "I suppose I ought to be surprised."

"I assure you it wasn't me, chérie. Believe it or not, I was looking forward to an uneventful weekend."

Oscar stared through the windscreen, lost in thought for a moment, before taking a heavy torch from the glove box and his fisherman coat from the back seat. He then braced himself for the sortie.

He retreated to the car a minute later.

"Your report?"

"The tree has been uprooted, almost certainly by the wind. There is no indication of human interference, such as the kind of marks an axe or saw would have made. It's dead, and some sections of the trunk appear to be rotten and hollow, but it would still be impossible to move without the help of Napoleon's Grande Armée. The vehicle is a recent model Audi with Parisian plates. The occupants, probably a couple, although their remarkable cleanliness renders the identification of conclusive clues difficult, have presumably sought shelter for the night."

"We should follow suite. It's too late to head back now in the middle of a storm, and I don't fancy sleeping in the car."

"Follow suit," Oscar corrected her.

"Whatever." She rolled her eyes. "I wonder where they went."

"There's a drive just past the tree, and a sign I can't quite make out from here."

Louise gave her husband a stern look, and he pretended not to be enjoying the dramatic turn of events.

"Unless there's a spa resort at the end of that drive, you owe me another weekend away in the very near future."

They shook on it.

Oscar edged the car up to the tree and parked beside the Audi. He took Louise's fisherman coat from the back seat and helped her into it, then hurried to the boot and grabbed their overnight bags.

After hoisting Louise over the tree, Oscar clambered across with the bags. They struggled against the howling wind and ignored the piercing rain as they pushed each other towards the gravel drive.

Oscar pointed his torch at the trembling sign just long enough to make out the words *château* and *chambres* as they hurried along. The ground rose, but dense forest and huge rocks protected them from the storm, and they soon found themselves at the top of a craggy hill, staring in disbelief at what was beyond doubt not a spa resort.

Perched atop the black hill was a small but foreboding castle. Its walls were dark and crenellated, but warm light beckoned from narrow windows and vehicles were parked in what had probably once been the stables.

Louise dashed across to the polished oak door and knocked five times, before noticing the electric doorbell. She jabbed the button with her thumb.

While they waited for a response, Oscar studied the stronghold, musing that it was undoubtedly one of the area's best-kept secrets. But his train of thought was promptly interrupted. A dull grating sound cut through the howling wind, followed by the sharp click of a far more modern locking mechanism, and the door swung open soundlessly to reveal two elderly women with heart-shaped faces and identical smiles.

"Welcome to Karreg Du. Step inside before you catch your death."

Louise and Oscar followed the châtelaines into the entrance hall, where the warm air and echo of cheerful conversation coming from upstairs put them at ease.

"We have room to spare tonight. My name is Séverine, and this is my sister, Soazig."

"Oscar and Louise. It's a pleasure to meet you, and we're very grateful for your welcome." His French was eloquent, with just a vague hint of foreignness.

"Your stay will be completely free of charge, of course," Soazig informed them.

"That's very kind of you, but quite unnecessary," Oscar replied.

"We insist!" they chimed.

"The road is blocked and it's out of the question for us to take advantage of your dilemma," Séverine said. "We won't accept a single euro from you tonight. Of course, if you manage to find some pleasure in the predicament, you're always welcome to stay with us again in the future, under more propitious circumstances."

"Thank you," Louise said. "It sounds like your other guests are enjoying themselves."

"So they ought to be. We have a fire in the hearth, a pot-au-feu beside it, and a well-stocked cellar. The guestrooms are on the second floor. I'll show you to yours and then you can come down to the dining room on the first floor when you're ready. All our rooms have ensuites, so feel free to have a warm bath or shower if you like before joining us."

Such sound advice could hardly be ignored, and once they had taken a change of clothes from their overnight bags and laid them on the king-size bed, Louise ran a warm bath while Oscar inspected the room; an admirable marriage of rustic Breton charm and modern comfort. The walls were of dark stone and the partition between the chamber and the bathroom was made of the same hardwood as the floor. A selection of tasteful landscape paintings unobtrusively adorned the walls.

If they hadn't been so hungry, they would have stayed in the bathtub much longer. Once the warm water had chased all trace of chill from their bodies, they hastily dressed and ventured down to the dining room.

"Have a seat," Séverine said, indicating the two rush chairs that had been prepared for them.

Soazig carried their plates to the fireplace, beside which the pot-au-feu was being kept warm in a hefty three-legged pot.

Six guests sat around the table and each welcomed the newcomers in French, although Oscar recognised the English accents of two of them.

"What a wild night it has turned out to be!" Soazig announced conversationally, returning to the table with two steaming plates. "As you can see, we've already eaten and are enjoying a glass of wine. Séverine, be a darling and pour them a drop while we introduce ourselves."

They felt a little uncomfortable eating by themselves, but under the circumstances, the usual dictates of etiquette had to be ignored. Sensing their awkwardness, the other guests wished them a *bon appétit* and smiled encouragingly.

Oscar and Louise tasted their meals and assured the sisters that the dish was delicious.

Soazig gestured towards the retired couple, who were doing a fine job of not appearing to be overly confused.

"British?" Oscar ventured, speaking in their shared native tongue.

"Spot on!" the husband replied, clearly pleased to have a fellow English speaker present. "I'm Richard and my wife's name is Emily. We're from Plymouth, just across the old Manche, as they call it here. How about yourselves?"

Oscar introduced himself and Louise, hoping that Richard wouldn't start talking about cricket when he told him he originally hailed from Australia.

He didn't, instead commenting on how the mood swings of the Atlantic must be a shock to the system for one used to sunnier climes. "Go ahead and introduce yourselves to everybody in French. We'll try to follow."

"We'll chat together later," Louise assured the couple. "I don't want to get rusty."

Soazig, appearing to understand the gist of the exchange, told Oscar and Louise the couple would certainly appreciate the chance to speak in English. She then continued with the introductions.

"This is Carole. She's a painter who comes here every year to find inspiration. Her work is enchantingly abstract, encouraging the beholder to interpret and contemplate according to his own perspective. We purchased two of her pieces for our library, which you will find at the end of the hallway on the third floor."

Carole nodded appreciatively in response to Soazig's words. Her hazel eyes, flowing auburn hair, amber necklace, and patchwork dress in autumnal shades came together so harmoniously.

"It's a pleasure to make your acquaintance, despite the circumstances."

"I'm sure this weather will inspire you," Louise said.

"It already has," Carole replied, glancing towards the nearest window, which was protected by rattling shutters.

"Anaïs is interested in local history," Soazig said, referring to the woman next to Carole.

She wore a loose-fitting grey jumper and her long chestnut hair had hints of grey that accentuated her silver jewellery. As she raised a glass to the Tremonts, Louise admired her wolf ring and triskell bracelet.

"I share your interest in bygone days," Oscar told her. "I'm surprised I hadn't heard of Karreg Du before now."

"A hidden gem, isn't it?"

"Every neck of the woods needs its secrets," Séverine declared, winking at Oscar. "The name of the castle stems from its geography, or rather, its geology."

"Yes, I guessed as much," Oscar told her. *"Gomz a ran un tammig brezhoneg."*

He was met with blank faces, and Louise rolled her eyes.

"I speak a little Breton," he explained.

The others ummed and ahhed, quite impressed.

"We really ought to speak the old language," Séverine admitted. "It was our grandparents' mother tongue, but it was strictly forbidden when they went to school."

"Would you like seconds?" Soazig asked, already on her feet.

Oscar and Louise assured her they had eaten enough, raising their palms in polite protest and then patting their stomachs in perfect conjugal concurrence.

The introductions had almost come full circle. There remained but one couple, seated on the other side of the sisters. They were middle-aged, smartly dressed, and, despite their attempts at appearing convivial, clearly disappointed that their plans for the evening had been interrupted.

"This is Anne-Laure and Laurent," Soazig said.

"Vincent," the woman corrected her.

"I am sorry."

"Not at all," he replied indifferently.

"Yours is the Audi, I take it?" Oscar asked.

"Yes," Vincent said sharply, his attention caught. "We were taking a shortcut, much like yourselves, I presume, but it turned out to be the wrong decision, didn't it? I almost drove straight into that damned tree trunk. What was the scene like when you were down there?"

Oscar held his tongue, which was eager to make a quip about Parisians behind the wheel.

"It was still blowing a gale, but your car was fine. Moving that fallen tree is going to require quite an effort."

"At least we're all safe and sound in here," Carole said.

"We really owe you a debt of gratitude," Louise added.

"That's enough of that," Soazig insisted, wagging a finger at the assembly. "Your glasses are almost empty. I'll fetch some more wine. The men might prefer something stronger. We have cognac, don't we, Sév?"

"I have a bottle of whisky," Oscar announced. "Aberfeldy."

"Good show, my man," Richard congratulated him in English.

Oscar looked at the women, for he didn't share the sisters' antiquated assumption that no member of the fairer sex could possibly appreciate a fine drop of the peaty potion. But they shook their heads. Vincent also shook his head, rather disapprovingly.

"I'll be back in an instant," Oscar told Richard, and turning to the sisters, he requested two whisky glasses if they wouldn't mind.

Anne-Laure remembered the expensive champagne from her cousin's cellar in Reims stashed away in her overnight bag but decided not to mention it. She was waiting for the appropriate moment to announce that the long drive from Paris and the dash through the storm had made them quite tired and that they were eager to get some rest. Indeed, she was just about to enunciate words to that effect when the chime of the doorbell rang out.

"The storm claims another victim," Anaïs said.

Louise glanced at the grandfather clock standing guard close to the communicating door with the kitchen. It was a quarter to ten. Soazig appeared from the doorway carrying two bottles of wine and frowning.

"I'll get it," Séverine called to her sister, already hurrying to the door.

She came back accompanied by a young man wearing a drenched pea coat. Both of them were smiling.

"It's Pierre," Soazig gasped upon recognising him. "We'd been wondering when we would see you next. You really ought to come more often."

"I know I should. It's just that I don't get away from Tours much outside of university holidays, and I've been doing research as well as lecturing this semester. I've come down on urgent family business. I'll tell you all about it later. This storm is absolutely raging, isn't it? And I don't think it's going to ease off any time soon. There's a tree blocking the road, as I guess you know, so I had to run all the way up the drive. I was intending to stop here, of course, but not necessarily for the night."

"Storm or no storm, we wouldn't have it any other way."

"I'll have to see what can be done about that tree in the morning. There are two other cars parked down there."

"Let me take your coat, Pierre. Sit down by the fire. Have you eaten?"

"Thank you. I'm cold and tired, but not hungry." He took his place and said good evening to the assembly.

The sisters introduced the new arrival, the son of dearly departed friends. Their families had known each other for generations.

"Pierre is a lovely young man," Soazig concluded, glancing cheekily from Carole to Anaïs. "He's a professor of French literature and is also versed in art and history."

"Thank you, Aunt Soazig," he replied curtly. "That's enough now."

Oscar arrived a moment later. "We might need a third whisky glass," he suggested.

"A glass of whisky would do just the job," Pierre confirmed. "Stay where you are, Soazig. I know where to find the glasses."

The storm gave no sign of waning. The shutters went on shaking and the wind kept wailing in the chimney as the guests chatted and drank.

The next time Louise looked at the clock, it was almost eleven. The Parisians had retired to their room, eager to bring their unplanned evening to a close, as had Pierre, explaining that he didn't feel very well and had almost certainly had too much to drink.

Oscar was engaged in conversation with the English couple, but it was clearly past their bedtime. Louise gave him a gentle nudge and closed her eyes for a second when he looked at her.

"Quite right. We really ought to get some sleep," he conceded.

The couple agreed, and the four women, overhearing them, gave signs of being ready to follow suit. They all lent a hand at clearing the table and bid each other a sound night's sleep.

* * *

Louise fell asleep with ease, cocooned in soft bedding, while Oscar listened to the rattling and whistling of the relentless wind. His eyes were closed and his mind wandered as he let the inharmonious lullaby carry him where it would. How long he had been in bed or whether he had slept at all, he couldn't say, but a sharp cry from within the castle reached his ears and made his eyes snap open.

"Louise?" he whispered.

No reply.

He was still trying to decide what to make of it when a gasp came from the corridor. It wasn't as loud this time, but it was more palpable now that he was fully awake.

He jumped out of bed and opened the door to find one of the sisters standing in the dark, as still as a statue, staring into the bedroom next to his. Taking a step closer, he saw that it was Séverine, and the dreadful look on her face precluded any ambiguity as to what she had discovered.

As she turned to him, he placed a reassuring hand on her shoulder. Her mouth was open, but she was incapable of uttering a word.

"Go to your sister," he told her firmly. "Tell her what has happened."

She walked away slowly, seeming to glide in her full-length nightgown, and followed the corridor to the left.

Oscar stepped into the room.

The bedside lamp was on, and its glow revealed the identity and condition of the room's occupant. It was Pierre, the professor, and he was dead.

On the bedside table, standing theatrically under the lamplight, were an empty glass and an overturned bottle of sleeping pills, of which only a half-dozen remained.

"Overdose?" asked Vincent, rushing across to the bedside.

"Don't disturb the scene," Oscar warned.

The Parisian gave him a dirty look. "I'm a doctor, and you're no gendarme."

He checked Pierre's vital signs.

"Too late," he said, stepping back. "Much too late."

There was growing commotion in the corridor as the other guests began to arrive, bleary-eyed and confused.

"The chap didn't top himself, did he?" Richard asked.

Oscar shrugged. "It looks that way here, but it certainly didn't earlier this evening."

Richard frowned.

"There's no signal." Vincent was waving his phone in the air, while the roaring storm mocked him.

"I'll try mine," Anaïs said, and hurried back to her room.

Anne-Laure wasn't having any success with her phone.

"He died over an hour ago," Vincent announced. "It would be folly to risk our own lives by venturing outside in this weather. There's nothing else to be done tonight. We'll have to wait until morning to inform the authorities, depending on when the wind subsides and when we can get that confounded tree off the road."

They were silent for a minute and simply stared at the body in disbelief.

"What happened to him?" Louise asked, directing the question to her husband.

Vincent took it upon himself to answer. "All the signs point to an overdose of sleeping pills."

Oscar was on his knees, reaching between the bedside table and the wall.

"I've found a notepad," he announced, holding it above his head for all to see and discreetly observing everybody's reactions. Only the sisters were not present in the room.

The spiral notepad had slipped down the narrow gap between table and wall. Oscar had seen the three letters hastily scribbled before showing the others. Although he didn't know what they meant, he'd immediately understood that it was the desperate message of a dying man who had come to a realisation too late. It was not a carefully considered suicide note.

lou

"Lou?" Richard read aloud.

Vincent turned to Louise. "It would appear he tried to write your name just before he died. Do you have any idea why?"

"That's quite an assumption. Those three letters could mean anything," Oscar cut in.

"The man's final act before passing from this world was to force his hand to jot those letters on his notepad. That seems significant to me."

"There is another explanation," Oscar assured everybody. "There must be."

The other guests looked unconvinced. They held their tongues, but their eyes were accusatorial.

"He was ill when he went to his room," the doctor reminded Oscar. "Therefore, it may not have been the sleeping pills that caused his death."

The others listened, not knowing what to think or say.

"I appreciate that, but Louise has never met this man before, and has been with me all night. Isn't that so, darling?"

"Of course. This has nothing to do with me."

Soazig and Séverine entered the room, doing their utmost to keep themselves together and carry on performing their role of unfaltering hosts.

"At any rate," Soazig said, "we need to wait the storm out and call the authorities in the morning. Nobody is to try to leave the castle tonight. Can we agree upon that?"

Everybody agreed.

Oscar looked at the word written on the notepad again.

"Let's all retire to our rooms until morning," Soazig suggested.

"You won't try to leave, will you?" Vincent asked Oscar and Louise sternly.

"We will most certainly do nothing of the kind."

"I think it would be best if the notepad remained in my possession."

"Why would you think that?" Oscar replied. "I'd much rather any other member of our party kept it."

"Very well. Our hosts?"

"That's more reasonable," Oscar agreed.

"Come on now," Séverine insisted. "Please go back to your rooms. I'll lock the door behind us."

As soon as they were back in their room, Oscar poured himself a glass of Aberfeldy, installed himself in the armchair and closed his eyes, listening to the howling wind.

Louise lay awake in bed, bewildered and deeply worried. She had been accused of murder. That was what it boiled down to, wasn't it? Would the police jump to the same conclusion the other guests had? Was she to be arrested in the morning, once contact with the outside world had been re-established?

Twenty minutes later, Oscar finished his second glass of whisky and turned to her.

"The wind is still howling, as though it's trying to tell us something."

"Your moustache is twitching, Oscar." There was relief in her voice.

"Relax, my dear. They'll not lock you away."

"You've worked it out?"

"All will be revealed in the morning. The murderer will stay put, along with everybody else. Escape would be self-incrimination. Our opponent is clever, but too confident. Despite failing to notice the notepad when the sleeping pills were deposited on the bedside table, the murderer's confidence will remain intact, simply because our attention was so naïvely drawn to you and the real significance of those three letters is so far from anybody's mind."

"He wasn't writing my name?"

"Of course not. The chap was a professor of literature."

Oscar switched the lamp off.

"I don't see the relevance."

"You will," he assured her, getting into bed. "We need to get some sleep before tomorrow's performance. Sweet dreams, Lou."

She felt like slapping him, but instead kissed him goodnight.

* * *

Nobody slept soundly that night, not even once the storm had died in the grey hours before dawn. They lay in their beds, staring vaguely at the ceiling or keeping both eyes fixed on their locked bedroom doors. Oscar was gently caressing Louise's hair. She trusted him, but that didn't prevent her from feeling distressed. She was the prime suspect in the murder, if that's what it really was, and would remain so until Oscar had elucidated the problem and exposed the killer. Of course, the police would be called as soon as somebody got phone reception, and there was no knowing what they would make of it all.

She turned to him, without raising her head from the pillow, so that he could keep caressing her hair.

"I know what happened. Don't worry."

"Can you prove it?"

"If the murderer is as confident as I think, it's a closed case. If I'm wrong, we'll have to go over the castle from top to bottom."

"Won't you tell me who it is?"

Oscar's moustache twitched.

Louise sighed, but it turned into a soft laugh.

"You won't tell me what the murderer might have tried to dispose of either?"

"It amounts to the self-same question," he added, and that was the only hint she would be given.

Footsteps echoed in the hallway, and Oscar knew who it was and where he was heading. He got out of bed, rubbed his face and stroked his moustache, and opened the bedroom door.

"Good morning," Vincent said, trying to peer into the bedroom. Oscar didn't step out of the way.

"My wife is here. She's had a rather unpleasant night, unaccustomed as she is to being accused of murder."

"It's not a matter of pointing fingers. There are just facts to be stated. I've managed to get through to the police and they'll be here very soon, so it's out of our hands now."

"Excellent," Oscar replied. "We should prepare ourselves for their arrival."

Vincent raised his eyebrows. "Whatever do you mean by that?"

"The police would surely appreciate it if we solve the crime for them."

Vincent laughed, but there wasn't a trace of joy in it.

"You think you've solved the crime and can clear your wife's name?"

Oscar nodded. "All I need is to have everybody together in the same room. How about the library? We'll have a strong coffee and I'll tell you what happened."

Vincent was speechless.

"It's better than moping around in our rooms all morning."

"If everybody is willing, I see no problem with your idea. I'm curious about this little show of yours. I want to see how you play detective."

"I don't play detective any more than you play doctor, my friend."

"Oh, I see. You're a private eye."

"That's one way of putting it. Let's get moving. Nobody will refuse coffee in the library, I'm sure."

Fifteen minutes later, they were all together, sipping the rich brew Séverine had prepared. Everybody did their best to seem relaxed and suitably solemn. The sisters were the only ones whose red eyes and streaked cheeks bore witness to a night of tears. They sat on the library's two leather armchairs, with the women standing close by them. Richard was looking at Oscar thoughtfully, waiting for the whole affair to be cleared up, and Vincent was leaning against the wall by the window, clear daylight playing on his analytical face.

Oscar glanced around the room, noting every detail, then looked down at his clasped hands. He breathed a sigh of relief.

"The police are on their way, and when they get here, Pierre's murderer will be handed over."

Everybody gasped appropriately, including the murderer.

"How do you know?" Soazig asked.

"I didn't introduce myself entirely honestly last night. I am an investigator of strange and inexplicable occurrences, and what happened last night is almost inexplicable; almost, but not quite. Pierre's note indicated that he didn't commit suicide, but it had nothing to do with my wonderful wife. We'll get back to that in a minute."

Confused faces watched Oscar.

"Séverine and Soazig, I need you to confirm the motive for me. Nobody here knew Pierre except you and the murderer."

The sisters looked around nervously.

"Please tell us why he came home this weekend. Is there an inheritance dispute in his family?"

The sisters' eyes widened.

"That's precisely why," Soazig confirmed. "His parents are both dead, and the property, which is considerable, is under dispute. Pierre has one brother, from whom he has been estranged for years. He never wanted to share just what happened between them with us, but there was bad blood."

"What does that have to do with any of us?" Soazig asked. "These people are strangers."

"So it would seem," Oscar continued. "It is not, however, really the case."

Murmurs filled the library and everybody glanced sideways at each other. Oscar observed each of them, making sure not to focus on the murderer, who was becoming increasingly alarmed.

"One of us stands to inherit the estate?" Vincent asked.

"Precisely. With Pierre out of the way, having taken his own life, as we were supposed to assume from this well-staged performance, his brother would inherit everything. Unfortunately, the notepad was overlooked. That one clue ruined the act."

"Why did he write *lou*?" Louise asked.

"It has nothing to do with you; I knew that straight away. Pierre was a professor of literature, and no professor, not even in the throes of death, would begin a name with a lowercase letter. It was a common noun he'd been trying to write when death stilled his hand. Perhaps the notepad slipped off the bedside table before he could finish."

The audience was dumbstruck.

"I suspected he'd remembered something that had struck him as being out of place; had realised some detail that would incriminate the murderer. He was a terribly clever fellow, for not only did he reveal the identity of the murderer in his final moment, but also the *modus operandi*.

"Last night, in my room, I went through every word in the French language beginning with those three letters, and while I did that, I listened to the storm. It was the howling wind that gave me the answer."

Oscar waited for somebody to say the word, but only the murderer knew it, and her lips remained tight.

"The howling wind made me think of *loup*," he explained. "Wolf," he added for the benefit of the English couple.

"The ring!" Carole shouted eventually, and pointed at Anaïs.

Anaïs understood the game was up and made a dash for the door, but Louise was quick to react and tackled her. Together they slammed into a bookshelf, sending numerous leather-bound volumes plummeting to the floor.

Carole sprang over to help Louise.

"Splendid tackle, Louise," Oscar said. "The French rugby team could do with your help."

The assembly was too stunned to laugh at his quip. The men watched on as Louise and Carole held Anaïs firmly by the arms.

"Carefully remove the wolf ring from her finger and pass it to me," he told Louise, walking over to the three women.

He held the ring up so that everybody could see it, then lowered it to the level of his chin and held it at arm's length. He pulled on the wolf's head and it flipped open to reveal an empty receptacle.

"A poison ring?" Séverine rasped, scowling at Anaïs.

"She must have poisoned him in cold blood while we were sharing a glass last night!" Soazig snarled.

"My suspicions were first aroused when she led us to believe that she was single, but I'd noticed a pale band on her finger where a wedding ring was usually worn. That in itself is no crime, for it sometimes happens that married men and women pretend to be single for various reasons. Looking back, of course, it was far more significant than I'd imagined. There's no doubt in my mind that Anaïs is married to Pierre's estranged brother."

The assembly gasped.

"You don't know that!" she hissed.

"I wonder whether Pierre realised who this wretched woman really was," Séverine said sharply, looking daggers at Anaïs.

"There's no way of knowing as far as I can tell," Oscar replied. "It may have occurred to him as he breathed his final breath, when he recalled the wolf ring."

"It really was awfully clever of him," Séverine said admiringly, holding back the urge to cry. "He always was a smart young man. Only, the thing is, if you hadn't been here, Oscar, this vile creature, Anaïs, or Lucrezia, or whatever her real name is, would have got away with it."

Oscar spread his arms and shrugged.

"That may be so. It's often the plight of the highly intelligent to be too ingenious for their own good, making them seem the opposite of what they are to the unappreciative masses," he stated discursively, clearly unaware of the supreme arrogance of his remark. "Let's be generous. There is the slim possibility that the French police might have fumbled their way to the truth eventually."

Vincent took a step forward, arms crossed and chin raised. He was doing his best to conceal the curious mix of admiration and jealousy written on his face.

"I envy your methodical mind, but there's one aspect to this crime that you may have overlooked; the fallen tree."

"Yes, the tree. I examined it before seeking shelter last night. You mustn't envy my incessant suspiciousness and fertile imagination, I assure you. It's a burden. In any case, the tree was pure luck. Luck, I say, because without it, I wouldn't be here. The break appeared to be completely natural. There was no indication that it had been chopped or sawed. That wasn't a necessary part of the plan and would have risked attracting attention. Even though the brothers were estranged, naturally, they knew each other's ways. That Pierre preferred to visit his dear friends, Séverine and Soazig, rather than stay at the family home would have been evident to his brother."

The sisters nodded their agreement.

"The brother is probably there as we speak," Vincent suggested, "practising his reaction for when the news reaches him and getting ready to take on the role of lord of the manor."

They all turned to Anaïs.

"Idle accusation," she spat, not a whisper of remorse in her voice.

"The police will take care of all those formalities when they get here," Oscar told her calmly. "Your identity will be established, as will the identity of the poison which was held in this ring and which will be found in Pierre's body."

Uneasy silence reigned in the library briefly, until the doorbell sounded, echoing through the castle with all the finality of a judge's gavel.

The Poetical Policeman

Edgar Wallace

THE DAY Mr. Reeder arrived at the Public Prosecutor's office was indeed a day of fate for Mr. Lambton Green, Branch Manager of the London Scottish and Midland Bank.

That branch of the bank which Mr. Green controlled was situated at the corner of Pell Street and Firling Avenue on the 'country side' of Ealing. It is a fairly large building and, unlike most suburban branch offices, the whole of the premises were devoted to banking business, for the bank carried very heavy deposits, the Lunar Traction Company, with three thousand people on its payroll, the Associated Novelties Corporation, with its enormous turnover, and the Laraphone Company being only three of the L.S.M.'s customers.

On Wednesday afternoons, in preparation for the paydays of these corporations, large sums in currency were brought from the head office and deposited in the steel and concrete strong-room, which was immediately beneath Mr. Green's private office, but admission to which was gained through a steel door in the general office. This door was observable from the street, and to assist observation there was a shaded lamp fixed to the wall immediately above, which threw a powerful beam of light upon the door. Further security was ensured by the employment of a night watchman, Arthur Malling, an army pensioner.

The bank lay on a restricted police beat which had been so arranged that the constable on patrol passed the bank every forty minutes. It was his practice to look through the window and exchange signals with the night watchman, his orders being to wait until Malling appeared.

On the night of October seventeenth Police Constable Burnett stopped as usual before the wide peep-hole and glanced into the bank. The first thing he noticed was that the lamp above the strong-room door had been extinguished. The night watchman was not visible, and, his suspicions aroused, the officer did not wait for the man to put in an appearance as he would ordinarily have done, but passed the window to the door, which, to his alarm, he found ajar. Pushing it open, he entered the bank, calling Malling by name.

There was no answer.

Permeating the air was a faint, sweet scent which he could not locate. The general offices were empty and, entering the manager's room in which a light burnt, he saw a figure stretched upon the ground. It was the night watchman. His wrists were handcuffed, two straps had been tightly buckled about his knees and ankles.

The explanation for the strange and sickly aroma was now clear. Above the head of the prostrate man was suspended, by a wire hooked to the picture-rail, an old tin can, the bottom of which was perforated so that there fell an incessant trickle of some volatile liquid upon the thick cotton pad which covered Malling's face.

Burnett, who had been wounded in the war, had instantly recognised the smell of chloroform and, dragging the unconscious man into the outer office, snatched the pad from his face and, leaving him only long enough to telephone to the police station, sought vainly to bring him to consciousness.

The police reserves arrived within a few minutes, and with them the divisional surgeon who, fortunately, had been at the station when the alarm came through. Every effort to restore the unfortunate man to life proved unavailing.

"He was probably dead when he was found," was the police doctor's verdict. "What those scratches are on his right palm is a mystery."

He pulled open the clenched fist and showed half a dozen little scratches. They were recent, for there was a smear of blood on the palm.

Burnett was sent at once to arouse Mr. Green, the manager, who lived in Firling Avenue, at the corner of which the bank stood; a street of semi-detached villas of a pattern familiar enough to the Londoner. As the officer walked through the little front garden to the door he saw a light through the panels, and he had hardly knocked before the door was opened and Mr. Lambton Green appeared, fully dressed and, to the officer's discerning eye, in a state of considerable agitation. Constable Burnett saw on a hall chair a big bag, a travelling rug and an umbrella.

The little manager listened, pale as death, whilst Burnett told him of his discovery.

"The bank robbed? Impossible!" he almost shrieked. "My God! This is awful!"

He was so near the point of collapse that Burnett had to assist him into the street.

"I – I was going away on a holiday," he said incoherently, as he walked up the dark thoroughfare towards the bank premises. "The fact is – I was leaving the bank. I left a note explaining to the directors."

Into a circle of suspicious men the manager tottered. He unlocked the drawer of his desk, looked and crumbled up.

"They're not here!" he said wildly. "I left them here – my keys – with the note!"

And then he swooned. When the dazed man recovered he found himself in a police cell and, later in the day, he drooped before a police magistrate, supported by two constables and listened, like a man in a dream, to a charge of causing the death of Arthur Malling, and further, of converting to his own use the sum of £100,000.

It was on the morning of the first remand that Mr. John G. Reeder, with some reluctance for he was suspicious of all Government departments, transferred himself from his own office on Lower Regent Street to a somewhat gloomy bureau on the top floor of the building which housed the Public Prosecutor. In making this change he advanced only one stipulation: that he should be connected by private telephone wire with his old bureau.

He did not demand this – he never demanded anything. He asked, nervously and apologetically. There was a certain wistful helplessness about John G. Reeder that made people feel sorry for him, that caused even the Public Prosecutor a few uneasy moments of doubt as to whether he had been quite wise in substituting this weak-appearing man of middle age for Inspector Holford – bluff, capable and heavily mysterious.

Mr. Reeder was something over fifty, a long-faced gentleman with sandy-grey hair and a slither of side whiskers that mercifully distracted attention from his large outstanding ears. He wore halfway down his nose a pair of steel-rimmed pince-nez, through which nobody had ever seen him look – they were invariably removed when he was reading. A high and flat-crowned bowler hat matched and yet did not match a frockcoat tightly buttoned across his sparse chest. His boots were square-toed, his cravat – of the broad, chest-protector pattern – was ready-made and buckled into place behind a Gladstonian collar. The neatest appendage to Mr. Reeder was an umbrella rolled so tightly that it might be mistaken for a frivolous walking cane. Rain or shine, he carried this article hooked to his arm, and within living memory it had never been unfurled.

Inspector Holford (promoted now to the responsibilities of Superintendent) met him in the office to hand over his duties, and a more tangible quantity in the shape of old furniture and fixings.

"Glad to know you, Mr. Reeder. I haven't had the pleasure of meeting you before, but I're heard a lot about you. You've been doing Bank of England work, haven't you?"

Mr. Reeder whispered that he had had that honour, and sighed as though he regretted the drastic sweep of fate that had torn him from the obscurity of his labours. Mr. Holford's scrutiny was full of misgivings.

"Well," he said awkwardly, "this job is different, though I'm told that you are one of the best informed men in London, and if that is the case this will be easy work. Still, we've never had an outsider – I mean, so to speak, a private detective – in this office before, and naturally the Yard is a bit—"

"I quite understand," murmured Mr. Reeder, hanging up his immaculate umbrella. "It is very natural. Mr. Bolond expected the appointment. His wife is annoyed – very properly. But she has no reason to be. She is an ambitious woman. She has a third interest in a West End dancing club that might be raided one of these days."

Holford was staggered. Here was news that was little more than a whispered rumour at Scotland Yard.

"How the devil do you know that?" he blurted.

Mr. Reeder's smile was one of self-depreciation.

"One picks up odd scraps of information," he said apologetically. "I – I see wrong in everything. That is my curious perversion – I have a criminal mind!"

Holford drew a long breath.

"Well – there is nothing much doing. That Ealing case is pretty clear. Green is an ex-convict, who got a job at the bank during the war and worked up to manager. He has done seven years for conversion."

"Embezzlement and conversion," murmured Mr. Reeder. "I – er – I'm afraid I was the principal witness against him: bank crimes were rather – er – a hobby of mine. Yes, he got into difficulties with moneylenders. Very foolish – extremely foolish. And he doesn't admit his error." Mr. Reeder sighed heavily. "Poor fellow! With his life at stake one may forgive and indeed condone his pitiful prevarications."

The inspector stared at the new man in amazement.

"I don't know that there is much 'poor fellow' about him. He has cached £100,000 and told the weakest yarn that I've ever read – you'll find copies of the police reports here, if you'd like to read them. The scratches on Malling's hand are curious – they've found several on the other hand. They are not deep enough to suggest a struggle. As to the yarn that Green tells—"

Mr. J. G. Reeder nodded sadly.

"It was not an ingenious story," he said, almost with regret. "If I remember rightly, his story was something like this: he had been recognised by a man who served in Dartmoor with him, and this fellow wrote a blackmailing letter telling him to pay or clear out. Sooner than return to a life of crime, Green wrote out all the facts to his directors, put the letter in the drawer of his desk with his keys, and left a note for his head cashier on the desk itself, intending to leave London and try to make a fresh start where he was unknown."

"There were no letters in or on the desk, and no keys," said the inspector decisively. "The only true part of the yarn was that he had done time."

"Imprisonment," suggested Mr. Reeder plaintively. He had a horror of slang. "Yes, that was true."

Left alone in his office, he spent a very considerable time at his private telephone, communing with the young person who was still a young person, although the passage of time had dealt unkindly with her. For the rest of the morning he was reading the depositions which his predecessor had put on the desk.

It was late in the afternoon when the Public Prosecutor strolled into his room and glanced at the big pile of manuscript through which his subordinate was wading.

"What are you reading – the Green business?" he asked, with a note of satisfaction in his voice. "I'm glad that is interesting you, though it seems a fairly straightforward case. I have had a letter from the president of the man's bank, who for some reason seems to think Green was telling the truth."

Mr. Reeder looked up with that pained expression of his which he invariably wore when he was puzzled.

"Here is the evidence of Policeman Burnett," he said. "Perhaps you can enlighten me, sir. Policeman Burnett stated in his evidence – let me read it:

"'Sometime before I reached the bank premises I saw a man standing at the corner of the street, immediately outside the bank. I saw him distinctly in the light of a passing mail van. I did not attach any importance to his presence, and I did not see him again. It was possible for this man to have gone round the block and come to 120, Firling Avenue without being seen by me. Immediately after I saw him, my foot struck against a piece of iron on the sidewalk. I put my lamp on the object and found it was an old horseshoe. I had seen children playing with this particular shoe earlier in the evening. When I looked again towards the corner, the man had disappeared. He would have seen the light of my lamp. I saw no other person, and so far as I can remember, there was no light showing in Green's house when I passed it.'"

Mr. Reeder looked up.

"Well?" said the Prosecutor. "There's nothing remarkable about that. It was probably Green, who dodged round the block and came in at the back of the constable."

Mr. Reeder scratched his chin.

"Yes." he said thoughtfully, "Ye—es." He shifted uncomfortably in his chair. "Would it be considered indecorous if I made a few inquiries, independent of the police?" he asked nervously. "I should not like them to think that a mere dilettante was interfering with their lawful functions."

"By all means," said the Prosecutor heartily. "Go down and see the officer in charge of the case: I'll give you a note to him – it is by no means unusual for my officer to conduct a separate investigation, though I am afraid you will discover very little. The ground has been well covered by Scotland Yard."

"It would be permissible to see the man?" hesitated Reeder.

"Green? Why, of course! I will send you up the necessary order."

The light was fading from a grey, blustering sky, and rain was falling fitfully, when Mr. Reeder, with his furled umbrella hooked to his arm, his coat collar turned up, stepped through the dark gateway of Brixton Prison and was led to the cell where a distracted man sat, his head upon his hands, his pale eyes gazing into vacancy.

"It's true; it's true! Every word." Green almost sobbed the words.

A pallid man, inclined to be bald, with a limp yellow moustache, going grey. Reeder, with his extraordinary memory for faces, recognised him the moment he saw him, though it was some time before the recognition was mutual.

"Yes, Mr. Reeder, I remember you now. You were the gentleman who caught me before. But I've been as straight as a die. I've never taken a farthing that didn't belong to me. What my poor girl will think—"

"Are you married?" asked Mr. Reeder sympathetically.

"No, but I was going to be – rather late in life. She's nearly thirty years younger than me, and the best girl that ever—"

Reeder listened to the rhapsody that followed, the melancholy deepening in his face.

"She hasn't been into the court, thank God, but she knows the truth. A friend of mine told me that she has been absolutely knocked out."

"Poor soul!" Mr. Reeder shook his head.

"It happened on her birthday, too," the man went on bitterly.

"Did she know you were going away?"

"Yes, I told her the night before. I'm not going to bring her into the case. If we'd been properly engaged it would be different; but she's married and is divorcing her husband, but the decree hasn't been made absolute yet. That's why I never went about with her or saw much of her. And of course, nobody knew about our engagement, although we lived in the same street."

"Firling Avenue?" asked Reeder, and the bank manager nodded despondently.

"She was married when she was seventeen to a brute. It was pretty galling for me, having to keep quiet about it – I mean, for nobody to know about our engagement. All sorts of rotten people were making up to her, and I had just to grind my teeth and say nothing. Impossible people! Why, that fool Burnett, who arrested me, he was sweet on her; used to write her poetry – you wouldn't think it possible in a policeman, would you?"

The outrageous incongruity of a poetical policeman did not seem to shock the detective.

"There is poetry in every soul, Mr. Green," he said gently, "and a policeman is a man."

Though he dismissed the eccentricity of the constable so lightly, the poetical policeman filled his mind all the way home to his house in the Brockley Road, and occupied his thoughts for the rest of his waking time.

It was a quarter to eight o'clock in the morning, and the world seemed entirely populated by milkmen and whistling newspaper boys, when Mr. J. G. Reeder came into Firling Avenue.

He stopped only for a second outside the bank, which had long since ceased to be an object of local awe and fearfulness, and pursued his way down the broad avenue. On either side of the thoroughfare ran a row of pretty villas – pretty although they bore a strong family resemblance to one another; each house with its little forecourt, sometimes laid out simply as a grass plot, sometimes decorated with flowerbeds. Green's house was the eighteenth in the road on the right-hand side. Here he had lived with a cook-housekeeper, and apparently gardening was not his hobby, for the forecourt was covered with grass that had been allowed to grow at its will.

Before the twenty-sixth house in the road Mr. Reeder paused and gazed with mild interest at the blue blinds which covered every window. Evidently Miss Magda Grayne was a lover of flowers, for geraniums filled the window-boxes and were set at intervals along the tiny border under the bow window. In the centre of the grass plot was a circular flowerbed with one flowerless rose tree, the leaves of which were drooping and brown.

As he raised his eyes to the upper window, the blind went up slowly, and he was dimly conscious that there was a figure behind the white lace curtains. Mr. Reeder walked hurriedly away, as one caught in an immodest act, and resumed his peregrinations until he came to the big nursery gardener's which formed the corner lot at the far end of the road.

Here he stood for some time in contemplation, his arm resting on the iron railings, his eyes staring blankly at the vista of greenhouses. He remained in this attitude so long that one of the nurserymen, not unnaturally thinking that a stranger was seeking a way into the gardens, came over with the laborious gait of the man who wrings his living from the soil, and asked if he was wanting anybody.

"Several people," sighed Mr. Reeder; "several people!"

Leaving the resentful man to puzzle out his impertinence, he slowly retraced his steps. At No. 412 he stopped again, opened the little iron gate and passed up the path to the front door. A small girl answered his knock and ushered him into the parlour.

The room was not well furnished; it was scarcely furnished at all. A strip of almost new linoleum covered the passage; the furniture of the parlour itself was made up of wicker chairs, a square of art carpet and a table. He heard the sound of feet above his head, feet on bare boards, and then presently the door opened and a girl came in.

She was pretty in a heavy way, but on her face he saw the marks of sorrow. It was pale and haggard; the eyes looked as though she had been recently weeping.

"Miss Magda Grayne?" he asked, rising as she came in.

She nodded.

"Are you from the police?" she asked quickly.

"Not exactly the police," he corrected carefully. "I hold an – er – an appointment in the office of the Public Prosecutor, which is analogous, to, but distinct from, a position in the Metropolitan Police Force."

She frowned, and then:

"I wondered if anybody would come to see me," she said. "Mr. Green sent you?"

"Mr. Green told me of your existence: he did not send me."

There came to her face in that second a look which almost startled him. Only for a fleeting space of time, the expression had dawned and passed almost before the untrained eye could detect its passage.

"I was expecting somebody to come," she said. Then: "What made him do it?" she asked.

"You think he is guilty?"

"The police think so." She drew a long sigh. "I wish to God I had never seen – this place!"

He did not answer; his eyes were roving round the apartment. On a bamboo table was an old vase which had been clumsily filled with golden chrysanthemums, of a peculiarly beautiful variety. Not all, for amidst them flowered a large Michaelmas daisy that had the forlorn appearance of a parvenu that had strayed by mistake into noble company.

"You're fond of flowers?" he murmured.

She looked at the vase indifferently.

"Yes, I like flowers," she said. "The girl put them in there." Then: "Do you think they will hang him?"

The brutality of the question, put without hesitation, pained Reeder.

"It is a very serious charge," he said. And then: "Have you a photograph of Mr. Green?"

She frowned.

"Yes; do you want it?"

He nodded.

She had hardly left the room before he was at the bamboo table and had lifted out the flowers. As he had seen through the glass, they were roughly tied with a piece of string. He examined the ends, and here again his first observation had been correct: none of these flowers had been cut; they had been plucked bodily from their stalks. Beneath the string was the paper which had been first wrapped about the stalks. It was a page torn from a notebook; he could see the red lines, but the pencilled writing was indecipherable.

As her foot sounded on the stairs, he replaced the flowers in the vase, and when she came in he was looking through the window into the street.

"Thank you," he said, as he took the photograph from her.

It bore an affectionate inscription on the back.

"You're married, he tells me, madam?"

"Yes, I am married, and practically divorced," she said shortly.

"Have you been living here long?"

"About three months," she answered. "It was his wish that I should live here."

He looked at the photograph again.

"Do you know Constable Burnett?"

He saw a dull flush come to her face and die away again.

"Yes, I know the sloppy fool!" she said viciously. And then, realising that she had been surprised into an expression which was not altogether ladylike, she went on, in a softer tone: "Mr. Burnett is rather sentimental, and I don't like sentimental people, especially – well, you understand, Mr.—"

"Reeder," murmured that gentleman.

"You understand, Mr. Reeder, that when a girl is engaged and in my position, those kind of attentions are not very welcome."

Reeder was looking at her keenly. Of her sorrow and distress there could be no doubt. On the subject of the human emotions, and the ravages they make upon the human countenance, Mr. Reeder was almost as great an authority as Mantegazza.

"On your birthday," he said. "How very sad! You were born on the seventeenth of October. You are English, of course?"

"Yes, I'm English," she said shortly. "I was born in Walworth – in Wallington. I once lived in Walworth."

"How old are you?"

"Twenty-three," she answered.

Mr. Reeder took off his glasses and polished them on a large silk handkerchief.

"The whole thing is inexpressibly sad," he said. "I am glad to have had the opportunity of speaking with you, young lady. I sympathise with you very deeply."

And in this unsatisfactory way he took his departure.

She closed the door on him, saw him stop in the middle of the path and pick up something from a border bed, and wondered, frowning, why this middle-aged man had picked up the horseshoe she had thrown through the window the night before. Into Mr. Reeder's tail pocket went this piece of rusted steel and then he continued his thoughtful way to the nursery gardens, for he had a few questions to ask.

The men of Section 10 were parading for duty when Mr. Reeder came timidly into the charge room and produced his credentials to the inspector in charge.

"Oh, yes, Mr. Reeder," said that officer affably. "We have had a note from the P.P.'s office, and I think I had the pleasure of working with you on that big slush [Slush-forged Bank of England notes.] case a few years ago. Now what can I do for you? …Burnett? Yes, he's here."

He called the man's name and a young and good-looking officer stepped from the ranks.

"He's the man who discovered the murder – he's marked for promotion," said the inspector. "Burnett, this gentleman is from the Public Prosecutor's office and he wants a little talk with you. Better use my office, Mr. Reeder."

The young policeman saluted and followed the shuffling figure into the privacy of the inspector's office. He was a confident young man; already his name and portrait had appeared in the newspapers, the hint of promotion had become almost an accomplished fact, and before his eyes was the prospect of a supreme achievement.

"They tell me that you are something of a poet, officer," said Mr. Reeder.

Burnett blushed.

"Why, yes, sir. I write a bit," he confessed.

"Love poems, yes?" asked the other gently. "One finds time in the night – er – for such fancies. And there is no inspiration like – er – love, officer."

Burnett's face was crimson.

"I've done a bit of writing in the night, sir," he said, "though I've never neglected my duty."

"Naturally," murmured Mr. Reeder. "You have a poetical mind. It was a poetical thought to pluck flowers in the middle of the night—"

"The nurseryman told me I could take any flowers I wanted," Burnett interrupted hastily. "I did nothing wrong."

Reeder inclined his head in agreement.

"That I know. You picked the flowers in the dark – by the way, you inadvertently included a Michaelmas daisy with your chrysanthemums – tied up your little poem to them and left them on the doorstep with – er – a horseshoe. I wondered what had become of that horseshoe."

"I threw them up on to her – to the lady's window-sill," corrected the uncomfortable young man. "As a matter of fact, the idea didn't occur to me until I had passed the house—"

Mr. Reeder's face was thrust forward.

"This is what I want to confirm," he said softly. "The idea of leaving the flowers did not occur to you until you had passed her house? The horseshoe suggested the thought? Then you went back, picked the flowers, tied them up with the little poem you had already written, and tossed them up to her window – we need not mention the lady's name."

Constable Burnett's face was a study.

"I don't know how you guessed that, but it is a fact. If I've done anything wrong—"

"It is never wrong to be in love," said Mr. J.G. Reeder soberly. "Love is a very beautiful experience – I have frequently read about it."

Miss Magda Grayne had dressed to go out for the afternoon and was putting on her hat, when she saw the queer man who had called so early that morning, walking up the tessellated path. Behind him she recognised a detective engaged in the case. The servant was out; nobody could be admitted except by herself. She walked quickly behind the dressing table into the bay of the window and glanced up and down the road. Yes, there was the taxicab which usually accompanies such visitations, and, standing by the driver, another man, obviously a 'busy'.

She pulled up the overlay of her bed, took out the flat pad of banknotes that she found, and thrust them into her handbag, then, stepping on tiptoe, she went out to the landing, into the unfurnished back room, and, opening the window, dropped to the flat roof of the kitchen. In another minute she was in the garden and through the back gate. A narrow passage divided the two lines of villas that backed on one another. She was in High Street and had boarded a car before Mr. Reeder grew tired of knocking. To the best of his knowledge Mr. Reeder never saw her again.

At the Public Prosecutor's request, he called at his chief's house after dinner and told his surprising story.

"Green, who had the unusual experience of being promoted to his position over the heads of his seniors, for special services he rendered during the war, was undoubtedly an ex-convict, and he spoke the truth when he said that he had received a letter from a man who had served a period of imprisonment with him. The name of this blackmailer is, or rather was, Arthur George Crater, whose other name was Malling!"

"Not the night watchman?" said the Public Prosecutor, in amazement.

Mr. Reeder nodded.

"Yes, sir, it was Arthur Malling. His daughter, Miss Magda Crater, was, as she very truly said, born at Walworth on the seventeenth of October, 1900. She said Wallington after, but Walworth first. One observes that when people adopt false family names, they seldom change their given names, and the 'Magda' was easy to identify.

"Evidently Malling had planned this robbery of the bank very carefully. He had brought his daughter, in a false name, to Ealing, and had managed to get her introduced to Mr. Green. Magda's job was to worm her way into Green's confidence and learn all that she could. Possibly it was part of her duty to secure casts of the keys. Whether Malling recognised in the manager an old prison acquaintance, or whether he obtained the facts from the girl, we shall never know. But when the information came to him, he saw, in all probability, an opportunity of robbing the bank and of throwing suspicion upon the manager.

The girl's role was that of a woman who was to be divorced, and I must confess this puzzled me until I realised that in no circumstances would Malling wish his daughter's name to be associated with the bank manager.

"The night of the seventeenth was chosen for the raid. Malling's plan to get rid of the manager had succeeded. He saw the letter on the table in Green's private office, read it, secured the keys – although he had in all probability a duplicate set – and at a favourable moment cleared as much portable money from the bank vaults as he could carry, hurried them round to the house in Firling Avenue, where they were buried in the central bed of the front garden, under a rose bush – I rather imagined there was something interfering with the nutrition of that unfortunate bush the first time I saw it. I can only hope that the tree is not altogether dead, and I have given instructions that it shall be replanted and well-fertilised."

"Yes, yes," said the Prosecutor, who was not at all interested in horticulture.

"In planting the tree, as he did in some haste, Malling scratched his hand. Roses have thorns – I went to Ealing to find the rose bush that had scratched his hand. Hurrying back to the bank, he waited, knowing that Constable Burnett was due at a certain time. He had prepared the can of chloroform, the handcuffs and straps were waiting for him, and he stood at the corner of the street until he saw the flash of Burnett's lamp; then, running into the bank and leaving the door ajar, he strapped himself, fastened the handcuffs and lay down, expecting that the policeman would arrive, find the open door and rescue him before much harm was done.

"But Constable Burnett had had some pleasant exchanges with the daughter. Doubtless she had received instructions from her father to be as pleasant to him as possible. Burnett was a poetical young man, knew it was her birthday, and as he walked along the street his foot struck an old horseshoe and the idea occurred to him that he should return, attach the horseshoe to some flowers, which the nurseryman had given him permission to pick, and leave his little bouquet, to so speak, at his lady's feet – a poetical idea, and one worthy of the finest traditions of the Metropolitan Police Force. This he did, but it took some time; and all the while this young man was philandering – Arthur Crater was dying!

In a few seconds after lying down he must have passed from consciousness…the chloroform still dripped, and when the policeman eventually reached the bank, ten minutes after he was due, the man was dead!"

The Public Prosecutor sat back in his padded chair and frowned at his new subordinate.

"How on earth did you piece together all this?" he asked in wonder.

Mr. Reeder shook his head sadly.

"I have that perversion," he said. "It is a terrible misfortune, but it is true. I see evil in everything…in dying rose bushes, in horseshoes – in poetry even. I have the mind of a criminal. It is deplorable!"

The Man with Nine Lives

Hugh C. Weir

Chapter I

NOW that I seek a point of beginning in the curious comradeship between Madelyn Mack and myself, the weird problems of men's knavery that we have confronted together come back to me with almost a shock.

Perhaps the events which crowd into my memory followed each other too swiftly for thoughtful digest at the time of their occurrence. Perhaps only a sober retrospect can supply a properly appreciative angle of view.

Madelyn Mack! What newspaper reader does not know the name? Who, even among the most casual followers of public events, does not recall the young woman who found the missing heiress, Virginia Denton, after a three months' disappearance; who convicted 'Archie' Irwin, chief of the 'fire bug trust'; who located the absconder, Wolcott, after a pursuit from Chicago to Khartoom; who solved the riddle of the double Peterson murder; who—

But why continue the enumeration of Miss Mack's achievements? They are of almost household knowledge, at least that portion which, from one cause or another, have found their way into the newspaper columns. Doubtless those admirers of Miss Mack, whose opinions have been formed through the press-chronicles of her exploits, would be startled to know that not one in ten of her cases have ever been recorded outside of her own file cases. And many of them – the most sensational from a newspaper viewpoint – will never be!

It is the woman, herself, however, who has seemed to me always a greater mystery than any of the problems to whose unraveling she has brought her wonderful genius. In spite of the deluge of printer's ink that she has inspired, I question if it has been given to more than a dozen persons to know the true Madelyn Mack.

I do not refer, of course, to her professional career. The salient points of that portion of her life, I presume, are more or less generally known – the college girl confronted suddenly with the necessity of earning her own living; the epidemic of mysterious 'shop-lifting' cases chronicled in the newspaper she was studying for employment advertisements; her application to the New York department stores, that had been victimized, for a place on their detective staffs, and their curt refusal; her sudden determination to undertake the case as a freelance, and her remarkable success, which resulted in the conviction of the notorious Madame Bousard, and which secured for Miss Mack her first position as assistant house-detective with the famous Niegel dry-goods firm. I sometimes think that this first case, and the realization which it brought her of her peculiar talent, is Madelyn's favorite – that its place in her memory is not even shared by the recovery of Mrs. Niegel's fifty-thousand-dollar pearl necklace, stolen a few months after the employment of the college girl detective at the store, and the reward for which, incidentally, enabled the ambitious Miss Mack to open her own office.

Next followed the Bergner kidnapping case, which gave Madelyn her first big advertising broadside, and which brought the beginning of the steady stream of business that resulted, after three years in her Fifth Avenue suite in the Maddox Building, where I found her on that – to me – memorable afternoon when a sapient Sunday editor dispatched me for an interview with the woman who had made so conspicuous a success in a man's profession.

I can see Madelyn now, as I saw her then – my first close-range view of her. She had just returned from Omaha that morning, and was planning to leave for Boston on the midnight express. A suitcase and a fat portfolio of papers lay on a chair in a corner. A young woman stenographer was taking a number of letters at an almost incredible rate of dictation. Miss Mack finished the last paragraph as she rose from a flat-top desk to greet me.

I had vaguely imagined a masculine-appearing woman, curt of voice, sharp of feature, perhaps dressed in a severe, tailor-made gown. I saw a young woman of maybe twenty-five, with red and white cheeks, crowned by a softly waved mass of dull gold hair, and a pair of vivacious, grey-blue eyes that at once made one forget every other detail of her appearance. There was a quality in the eyes which for a long time I could not define. Gradually I came to know that it was the spirit of optimism, of joy in herself, and in her life, and in her work, the exhilaration of doing things. And there was something contagious in it. Almost unconsciously you found yourself believing in her and in her sincerity.

Nor was there a suggestion foreign to her sex in my appraisal. She was dressed in a simply embroidered white shirtwaist and white broadcloth skirt.

One of Madelyn's few peculiarities is that she always dresses either in complete white or complete black. On her desk was a jar of white chrysanthemums.

"How do I do it?" she repeated, in answer to my question, in a tone that was almost a laugh. "Why – just by hard work, I suppose. Oh, there isn't anything wonderful about it! You can do almost anything, you know, if you make yourself really think you can! I am not at all unusual or abnormal. I work out my problems just as I would work out a problem in mathematics, only instead of figures I deal with human motives. A detective is always given certain known factors, and I keep building them up, or subtracting them, as the case may be, until I know that the answer must be correct.

"There are only two real rules for a successful detective, hard work and common sense – not uncommon sense such as we associate with our old friend, Sherlock Holmes, but common, business sense. And, of course, imagination! That may be one reason why I have made what you call a success. A woman, I think, always has a more acute imagination than a man!"

"Do you then prefer women operatives on your staff?" I asked.

She glanced up with something like a twinkle from the jade paper-knife in her hands.

"Shall I let you into a secret? All of my staff, with the exception of my stenographer, are men. But I do most of my work in person. The factor of imagination can't very well be used second-, or third-, or fourth-handed. And then, if I fail, I can only blame Madelyn Mack! Some day," – the gleam in her grey-blue eyes deepened – "Some day I hope to reach a point where I can afford to do only consulting work or personal investigation. The business details of an office staff, I am afraid are a bit too much of routine for me!"

The telephone jingled. She spoke a few crisp sentences into the receiver, and turned. The interview was over.

When I next saw her, three months later, we met across the body of Morris Anthony, the murdered bibliophic. It was a chance discovery of mine which Madelyn was good enough to say suggested to her the solution of the affair, and which brought us together in the final melodramatic climax in the grim mansion on Washington Square, when I presume my hysterical warning saved her from the fangs of Dr. Lester Randolph's hidden cobra. In any event, our acquaintanceship crystalized gradually into a comradeship, which revolutionized two angles of my life.

Not only did it bring to me the stimulus of Madelyn Mack's personality, but it gave me exclusive access to a fund of newspaper 'copy' that took me from scant-paid Sunday 'features' to a 'space' arrangement in the city room, with an income double that which I had been earning. I have always maintained that in our relationship Madelyn gave all, and I contributed nothing. Although she invariably made instant disclaimer, and generally ended by carrying me up to the 'Rosary', her chalet on the Hudson, as a cure for what she termed my attack of the 'blues', she was never able to convince me that my protest was not justified!

It was at the 'Rosary' where Miss Mack found haven from the stress of business. She had copied its design from an ivy-tangled Swiss chalet that had attracted her fancy during a summer vacation ramble through the Alps, and had built it on a jagged bluff of the river at a point near enough to the city to permit of fairly convenient motoring, although, during the first years of our friendship, when she was held close to the commercial grindstone, weeks often passed without her being able to snatch a day there. In the end, it was the gratitude of Chalmers Walker for her remarkable work which cleared his chorus-girl wife from the seemingly unbreakable coil of circumstantial evidence in the murder of Dempster, the theatrical broker, that enabled Madelyn to realize her long-cherished dream of setting up as a consulting expert. Although she still maintained an office in town, it was confined to one room and a small reception hall, and she limited her attendance there to two days of the week. During the remainder of the time, when not engaged directly on a case, she seldom appeared in the city at all. Her flowers and her music – she was passionately devoted to both – appeared to content her effectually.

I charged her with growing old, to which she replied with a shrug. I upbraided her as a cynic, and she smiled inscrutably. But the manner of her life was not changed. In a way I envied her. It was almost like looking down on the world and watching tolerantly its mad scramble for the rainbow's end. The days I snatched at the 'Rosary', particularly in the summer, when Madelyn's garden looked like nothing so much as a Turner picture, left me with almost a repulsion for the grind of Park Row. But a workaday newspaper woman cannot indulge the dreams of a genius whom fortune has blessed. Perhaps this was why Madelyn's invitations came with a frequency and a subtleness that could not be resisted. Somehow they always reached me when I was in just the right receptive mood.

It was late on a Thursday afternoon of June, the climax of a racking five days for me under the blistering Broadway sun, that Madelyn's motor caught me at the *Bugle* office, and Madelyn insisted on bundling me into the tonneau without even a suitcase.

"We'll reach the Rosary in time for a fried chicken supper," she promised. "What you need is four or five days' rest where you can't smell the asphalt."

"You fairy godmother!" I breathed as I snuggled down on the cushions.

Neither of us knew that already the crimson trail of crime was twisting toward us – that within twelve hours we were to be pitchforked from a quiet weekend's rest into the vortex of tragedy.

Chapter II

WE HAD breakfasted late and leisurely. When at length we had finished, Madelyn had insisted on having her phonograph brought to the rosegarden, and we were listening to Sturveysant's matchless rendering of 'The Jewel Song' – one of the three records for which Miss Mack had sent the harpist her check for two hundred dollars the day before. I had taken the occasion to read her a lazy lesson on extravagance. The beggar had probably done the work in less than two hours!

As the plaintive notes quivered to a pause, Susan, Madelyn's housekeeper, crossed the garden, and laid a little stack of letters and the morning papers on a rustic table by our bench. Madelyn turned to her correspondence with a shrug.

"From the divine to the prosaic!' Susan sniffed with the freedom of seven years of service.

"I heard one of them Dago fiddling chaps at Hammerstein's last week who could beat that music with his eyes closed!"

Madelyn stared at her sorrowfully. "At your age – Hammerstein's!"

Susan tossed her prim rows of curls, glanced contemptuously at the phonograph by way of retaliation, and made a dignified retreat. In the doorway she turned.

"Oh, Miss Madelyn, I am baking one of your old-fashioned strawberry shortcakes for lunch!"

"Really?" Madelyn raised a pair of sparkling eyes. "Susan, you're a dear!" A contented smile wreathed Susan's face even to the tips of her precise curls. Madelyn's gaze crossed to me.

"What are you chuckling over, Nora?" "From a psychological standpoint, the pair of you have given me two interesting studies," I laughed. "A single sentence compensates Susan for a week of your glumness!"

Madelyn extended a hand toward her mail.

"And what is the other feature that appeals to your dissecting mind?"

"Fancy a world-known detective rising to the point of enthusiasm at the mention of strawberry shortcake!"

"Why not? Even a detective has to be human once in a while!" Her eyes twinkled. "Another point for my memoirs, Miss Noraker!"

As her gaze fell to the half-opened letter in her hand, my eyes traveled across the garden to the outlines of the chalet, and I breathed a sigh of utter content. Broadway and Park Row seemed very, very far away. In a momentary swerving of my gaze, I saw that a line as clear-cut as a pencil-stroke had traced itself across Miss Mack's forehead.

The suggestion of lounging indifference in her attitude had vanished like a wind-blown veil. Her glance met mine suddenly. The twinkle I had last glimpsed in her eyes had disappeared. Silently she pushed a square sheet of cramped writing across the table to me.

> My Dear Madam:
> When you read this, it is quite possible that it will be a letter from a dead man.
> I have been told by no less an authority than my friend, Cosmo Hamilton, that you are a remarkable woman. While I will say at the outset that I have little faith in the analytical powers of the feminine brain, I am prepared to accept Hamilton's judgment.
> I cannot, of course, discuss the details of my problem in correspondence.
> As a spur to quick action, I may say, however, that, during the past five months, my life has been attempted no fewer than eight different times, and I am convinced that the ninth attempt, if made, will be successful. The curious part of it lies in the fact that I am absolutely unable to guess the reason for the persistent vendetta. So far as I know, there is no person in the world who should desire my removal. And yet I have been shot at from ambush on four occasions, thugs have rushed me once, a speeding automobile has grazed me twice, and this evening I found a cunning little dose of cyanide of potassium in my favorite cherry pie!
> All of this, too, in the shadow of a New Jersey skunk farm! It is high time, I fancy, that I secure expert advice. Should the progress of the mysterious vendetta, by any chance, render me unable to receive you personally, my niece, Miss Muriel Jansen, I am sure, will endeavor to act as a substitute.
> Respectfully Yours,
> Wendell Marsh.
> Three Forks Junction, N.J.

At the bottom of the page a lead pencil had scrawled the single line in the same cramped writing:

For God's sake, hurry!

Madelyn retained her curled-up position on the bench, staring across at a bush of deep crimson roses.

"Wendell Marsh?" She shifted her glance to me musingly. "Haven't I seen that name somewhere lately?" (Madelyn pays me the compliment of saying that I have a card-index brain for newspaper history!)

"If you have read the Sunday supplements," I returned drily, with a vivid remembrance of Wendell Marsh as I had last seen him, six months before, when he crossed the gang-plank of his steamer, fresh from England, his face browned from the Atlantic winds. It was a face to draw a second glance – almost gaunt, self-willed, with more than a hint of cynicism. (Particularly when his eyes met the waiting press group!) Someone had once likened him to the pictures of Oliver Cromwell.

"Wendell Marsh is one of the greatest newspaper copy-makers that ever dodged an interviewer," I explained. "He hates reporters like an upstate farmer hates an automobile, and yet has a flock of them on his trail constantly. His latest exploit to catch the spotlight was the purchase of the Bainford relics in London. Just before that he published a three-volume history on 'The World's Great Cynics'. Paid for the publication himself."

Then came a silence between us, prolonging itself. I was trying, rather unsuccessfully, to associate Wendell Marsh's half-hysterical letter with my mental picture of the austere millionaire…

"For God's sake, hurry!"

What wrenching terror had reduced the ultra-reserved Mr. Marsh to an appeal like this? As I look back now I know that my wildest fancy could not have pictured the ghastliness of the truth!

Madelyn straightened abruptly.

"Susan, will you kindly tell Andrew to bring around the car at once? If you will find the New Jersey automobile map, Nora, we'll locate Three Forks Junction."

"You are going down?" I asked mechanically.

She slipped from the bench.

"I am beginning to fear," she said irrelevantly, "that we'll have to defer our strawberry shortcake!"

Chapter III

THE SOUND EYE of Daniel Peddicord, liveryman by avocation, and sheriff of Merino County by election, drooped over his florid left cheek. Mr. Peddicord took himself and his duties to the taxpayers of Merino County seriously.

Having lowered his sound eye with befitting official dubiousness, while his glass eye stared guilelessly ahead, as though it took absolutely no notice of the procedure, Mr. Peddicord jerked a fat, red thumb toward the winding stairway at the rear of the Marsh hall.

"I reckon as how Mr. Marsh is still up there, Miss Mack. You see, I told 'em not to disturb the body until—"

Our stares brought the sentence to an abrupt end. Mr. Peddicord's sound eye underwent a violent agitation.

"You don't mean that you haven't – heard?"

The silence of the great house seemed suddenly oppressive. For the first time I realized the oddity of our having been received by an ill-at-ease policeman instead of by a member of the family. I was abruptly conscious of the incongruity between Mr. Peddicord's awkward figure and the dim, luxurious background.

Madelyn gripped the chief's arm, bringing his sound eye circling around to her face.

"Tell me what has happened!"

Mr. Peddicord drew a huge red handkerchief over his forehead.

"Wendell Marsh was found dead in his library at eight o'clock this morning! He had been dead for hours."

Tick-tock! Tick-tock! Through my daze beat the rhythm of a tall, gaunt clock in the corner. I stared at it dully. Madelyn's hands had caught themselves behind her back, her veins swollen into sharp blue ridges. Mr. Peddicord still gripped his red handkerchief.

"It sure is queer you hadn't heard! I reckoned as how that was what had brought you down. It – it looks like murder!"

In Madelyn's eyes had appeared a greyish glint like cold steel.

"Where is the body?"

"Upstairs in the library. Mr. Marsh had worked—"

"Will you kindly show me the room?"

I do not think we noted at the time the crispness in her tones, certainly not with any resentment. Madelyn had taken command of the situation quite as a matter of course.

"Also, will you have my card sent to the family?"

Mr. Peddicord stuffed his handkerchief back into a rear trousers' pocket. A red corner protruded in jaunty abandon from under his blue coat.

"Why, there ain't no family – at least none but Muriel Jansen." His head cocked itself cautiously up the stairs. "She's his niece, and I reckon now everything here is hers. Her maid says as how she is clear bowled over. Only left her room once since – since it happened. And that was to tell me as how nothing was to be disturbed." Mr. Peddicord drew himself up with the suspicion of a frown. "Just as though an experienced officer wouldn't know that much!"

Madelyn glanced over her shoulder to the end of the hall. A hatchet-faced man in russet livery stood staring at us with wooden eyes.

Mr. Peddicord shrugged.

"That's Peters, the butler. He's the chap what found Mr. Marsh."

I could feel the wooden eyes following us until a turn in the stairs blocked their range.

A red-glowing room – oppressively red. Scarlet-frescoed walls, deep red draperies, cherry-upholstered furniture, Turkish-red rugs, rows on rows of red-bound books. Above, a great, flat glass roof, open to the sky from corner to corner, through which the splash of the sun on the rich colors gave the weird semblance of a crimson pool almost in the room's exact centre. Such was Wendell Marsh's library – as eccentrically designed as its master.

It was the wreck of a room that we found. Shattered vases littered the floor – books were ripped savagely apart – curtains were hanging in ribbons – a heavy leather rocker was splintered.

The wreckage might have marked the death-struggle of giants. In the midst of the destruction, Wendell Marsh was twisted on his back. His face was shriveled, his eyes were staring. There was no hint of a wound or even a bruise. In his right hand was gripped an object partially turned from me.

I found myself stepping nearer, as though drawn by a magnet. There is something hypnotic in such horrible scenes! And then I barely checked a cry.

Wendell Marsh's dead fingers held a pipe – a strangely carved, red sandstone bowl, and a long, glistening stem.

Sheriff Peddicord noted the direction of my glance.

"Mr. Marsh got that there pipe in London, along with those other relics he brought home. They do say as how it was the first pipe ever smoked by a white man. The Indians of Virginia gave it to a chap named Sir Walter Raleigh. Mr. Marsh had a new stem put to it, and his butler says he smoked it every day. Queer, ain't it, how some folks' tastes do run?"

The sheriff moistened his lips under his scraggly yellow mustache.

"Must have been some fight what done this!" His head included the wrecked room in a vague sweep.

Madelyn strolled over to a pair of the ribboned curtains, and fingered them musingly.

"But that isn't the queerest part." The chief glanced at Madelyn expectantly. "There was no way for anyone else to get out – or in!"

Madelyn stooped lower over the curtains. They seemed to fascinate her. "The door?" she hazarded absently. "It was locked?"

"From the inside. Peters and the footman saw the key when they broke in this morning…Peters swears he heard Mr. Marsh turn it when he left him writing at ten o'clock last night."

"The windows?"

"Fastened as tight as a drum – and, if they wasn't it's a matter of a good thirty foot to the ground."

"The roof, perhaps?"

"A cat might get through it – if every part wasn't clamped as tight as the windows."

Mr. Peddicord spoke with a distinct inflection of triumph. Madelyn was still staring at the curtains.

"Isn't it rather odd," I ventured, "that the sounds of the struggle, or whatever it was, didn't alarm the house?"

Sheriff Peddicord plainly regarded me as an outsider. He answered my question with obvious shortness.

"You could fire a blunderbuss up here and no one would be the wiser. They say as how Mr. Marsh had the room made sound-proof. And, besides, the servants have a building to themselves, all except Miss Jansen's maid, who sleeps in a room next to her at the other end of the house."

My eyes circled back to Wendell Marsh's knotted figure – his shriveled face – horror-frozen eyes – the hand gripped about the fantastic pipe. I think it was the pipe that held my glance. Of all incongruities, a pipe in the hand of a dead man!

Maybe it was something of the same thought that brought Madelyn of a sudden across the room. She stooped, straightened the cold fingers, and rose with the pipe in her hand.

A new stem had obviously been added to it, of a substance which I judged to be jessamine. At its end, teeth-marks had bitten nearly through. The stone bowl was filled with the cold ashes of half-consumed tobacco. Madelyn balanced it musingly.

"Curious, isn't it, Sheriff, that a man engaged in a life-or-death struggle should cling to a heavy pipe?"

"Why – I suppose so. But the question, Miss Mack, is what became of that there other man? It isn't natural as how Mr. Marsh could have fought with himself."

"The other man?" Madelyn repeated mechanically. She was stirring the rim of the dead ashes.

"And how in tarnation was Mr. Marsh killed?"

Madelyn contemplated a dust-covered finger.

"Will you do me a favor, Sheriff?"

"Why, er – of course."

"Kindly find out from the butler if Mr. Marsh had cherry pie for dinner last night."

The sheriff gulped.

"Che-cherry pie?"

Madelyn glanced up impatiently.

"I believe he was very fond of it."

The sheriff shuffled across to the door uncertainly. Madelyn's eyes flashed to me.

"You might go, too, Nora."

For a moment I was tempted to flat rebellion. But Madelyn affected not to notice the fact. She is always so aggravatingly sure of her own way! With what I tried to make a mood of aggrieved silence, I followed the sheriff's bluecoated figure. As the door closed, I saw that Madelyn was still balancing Raleigh's pipe.

From the top of the stairs, Sheriff Peddicord glanced across at me suspiciously.

"I say, what I would like to know is what became of that there other man!"

Chapter IV

A WISP of a black-gowned figure, peering through a dormer window at the end of the second-floor hall, turned suddenly as we reached the landing. A white, drawn face, suggesting a tired child, stared at us from under a frame of dull-gold hair, drawn low from a careless part. I knew at once it was Muriel Jansen, for the time, at least, mistress of the house of death.

"Has the coroner come yet, Sheriff?" She spoke with one of the most liquid voices I have ever heard. Had it not been for her bronze hair, I would have fancied her at once of Latin descent. The fact of my presence she seemed scarcely to notice, not with any suggestion of aloofness, but rather as though she had been drained even of the emotion of curiosity.

"Not yet. Miss Jansen. He should be here now."

She stepped closer to the window, and then turned slightly.

"I told Peters to telegraph to New York for Dr. Dench when he summoned you. He was one of Uncle's oldest friends. I – I would like him to be here when – when the coroner makes his examination."

The sheriff bowed awkwardly.

"Miss Mack is upstairs now."

The pale face was staring at us again with raised eyebrows.

"Miss Mack? I don't understand." Her eyes shifted to me.

"She had a letter from Mr. Marsh by this morning's early post," I explained. "I am Miss Noraker. Mr. Marsh wanted her to come down at once. She didn't know, of course – couldn't know – that – that he was – dead!"

"A letter from – uncle?" A puzzled line gathered in her face.

"A distinctly curious letter. But – Miss Mack would perhaps prefer to give you the details."

The puzzled line deepened. I could feel her eyes searching mine intently.

"I presume Miss Mack will be down soon," I volunteered. "If you wish, however, I will tell her—"

"That will hardly be necessary. But – you are quite sure – a letter?"

"Quite sure," I returned, somewhat impatiently.

And then, without warning, her hands darted to her head, and she swayed forward. I caught her in my arms with a side-view of Sheriff Peddicord staring, open-mouthed.

"Get her maid!" I gasped.

The sheriff roused into belated action. As he took a cumbersome step toward the nearest door, it opened suddenly. A gaunt, middle-aged woman, in a crisp white apron, digested the situation with cold, grey eyes. Without a word, she caught Muriel Jansen in her arms.

"She has fainted," I said rather vaguely. "Can I help you?"

The other paused with her burden.

"When I need you, I'll ask you!" she snapped, and banged the door in our faces.

In the wake of Sheriff Peddicord, I descended the stairs. A dozen question-marks were spinning through my brain. Why had Muriel Jansen fainted? Why had the mention of Wendell Marsh's letter left such an atmosphere of bewildered doubt? Why had the dragon-like maid – for such I divined her to be – faced us with such hostility? The undercurrent of hidden secrets in the dim, silent house seemed suddenly intensified.

With a vague wish for fresh air and the sun on the grass, I sought the front veranda, leaving the sheriff in the hall, mopping his face with his red handkerchief.

A carefully tended yard of generous distances stretched an inviting expanse of graded lawn before me. Evidently Wendell Marsh had provided a discreet distance between himself and his neighbors. The advance guard of a morbid crowd was already shuffling about the gate. I knew that it would not be long, too, before the press-siege would begin.

I could picture frantic city editors pitchforking their star men New Jerseyward. I smiled at the thought. The *Bugle*, the slave-driver that presided over my own financial destinies, was assured of a generous 'beat' in advance. The next train from New York was not due until late afternoon.

From the staring line about the gate, the figure of a well-set-up young man in blue serge detached itself with swinging step.

"A reporter?" I breathed, incredulous.

With a glance at me, he ascended the steps, and paused at the door, awaiting an answer to his bell. My stealthy glances failed to place him among the 'stars' of New York newspaperdom. Perhaps he was a local correspondent. With smug expectancy, I waited his discomfiture when Peters received his card. And then I rubbed my eyes. Peters was stepping back from the door, and the other was following him with every suggestion of assurance.

I was still gasping when a maid, broom in hand, zigzagged toward my end of the veranda. She smiled at me with a pair of friendly black eyes.

"Are you a detective?"

"Why?" I parried.

She drew her broom idly across the floor.

"I – I always thought detectives different from other people."

She sent a rivulet of dust through the railing, with a side glance still in my direction.

"Oh, you will find them human enough," I laughed, "outside of detective stories!"

She pondered my reply doubtfully.

"I thought it about time Mr. Truxton was appearing!" she ventured suddenly.

"Mr. Truxton?"

"He's the man that just came – Mr. Homer Truxton. Miss Jansen is going to marry him!"

A light broke through my fog.

"Then he is not a reporter?"

"Mr. Truxton? He's a lawyer." The broom continued its dilatory course. "Mr. Marsh didn't like him – so they say!"

I stepped back, smoothing my skirts. I have learned the cardinal rule of Madelyn never to pretend too great an interest in the gossip of a servant.

The maid was mechanically shaking out a rug.

"For my part, I always thought Mr. Truxton far and away the pick of Miss Jansen's two steadies. I never could understand what she could see in Dr. Dench! Why, he's old enough to be her—"

In the doorway, Sheriff Peddicord's bulky figure beckoned.

"Don't you reckon as how it's about time we were going back to Miss Mack?" he whispered.

"Perhaps," I assented, rather reluctantly.

From the shadows of the hall, the sheriff's sound eye fixed itself on me belligerently.

"I say, what I would like to know is what became of that there other man!"

As we paused on the second landing the well-set-up figure of Mr. Homer Truxton was bending toward a partially opened door. Beyond his shoulder, I caught a fleeting glimpse of a pale face under a border of rumpled dull-gold hair. Evidently Muriel Jansen had recovered from her faint.

The door closed abruptly, but not before I had seen that her eyes were red with weeping.

* * *

Madelyn was sunk into a red-backed chair before a huge, flat-top desk in the corner of the library, a stack of Wendell Marsh's red-bound books, from a wheel-cabinet at her side, bulked before her. She finished the page she was reading – a page marked with a broad blue pencil – without a hint that she had heard us enter.

Sheriff Peddicord stared across at her with a disappointment that was almost ludicrous. Evidently Madelyn was falling short of his conception of the approved attitudes for a celebrated detective!

"Are you a student of Elizabethan literature, Sheriff?" she asked suddenly. The sheriff gurgled weakly.

"If you are, I am quite sure you will be interested in Mr. Marsh's collection. It is the most thorough on the subject that I have ever seen. For instance, here is a volume on the inner court life of Elizabeth – perhaps you would like me to read you this random passage?"

The sheriff drew himself up with more dignity than I thought he possessed.

"We are investigating a crime, Miss Mack!"

Madelyn closed the book with a sigh. "So we are! May I ask what is your report from the butler?"

"Mr. Marsh did not have cherry pie for dinner last night!" the sheriff snapped.

"You are quite confident?"

And then abruptly the purport of the question flashed to me.

"Why, Mr. Marsh himself mentioned the fact in his letter!" I burst out.

Madelyn's eyes turned to me reprovingly.

"You must be mistaken, Nora."

With a lingering glance at the books on the desk, she rose. Sheriff Peddicord moved toward the door, opened it, and faced about with an abrupt clearing of his throat.

"Begging your pardon, Miss Mack, have – have you found any clues in the case?"

Madelyn had paused again at the ribboned curtains.

"Clues? The man who made Mr. Marsh's death possible, Chief, was an expert chemist, of Italian origin, living for some time in London – and he died three hundred years ago!"

From the hall we had a fleeting view of Sheriff Peddicord's face, flushed as red as his handkerchief, and then it and the handkerchief disappeared.

I whirled on Madelyn sternly.

"You are carrying your absurd joke, Miss Mack, altogether too—"

I paused, gulping in my turn. It was as though I had stumbled from the shadows into an electric glare.

Madelyn had crossed to the desk, and was gently shifting the dead ashes of Raleigh's pipe into an envelope. A moment she sniffed at its bowl, peering down at the crumpled body at her feet.

"The pipe!" I gasped. "Wendell Marsh was poisoned with the pipe!" Madelyn sealed the envelope slowly.

"Is that fact just dawning on you, Nora?"

"But the rest of it – what you told the—"

Madelyn thrummed on the bulky volume of Elizabethan history.

"Some day, Nora, if you will remind me, I will give you the material for what you call a Sunday 'feature' on the historic side of murder as a fine art!"

Chapter V

In a curtain-shadowed nook of the side veranda Muriel Jansen was awaiting us, pillowed back against a bronze-draped chair, whose colors almost startlingly matched the gold of her hair. Her resemblance to a tired child was even more pronounced than when I had last seen her.

I found myself glancing furtively for signs of Homer Truxton, but he had disappeared.

Miss Jansen took the initiative in our interview with a nervous abruptness, contrasting oddly with her hesitancy at our last meeting.

"I understand, Miss Mack, that you received a letter from my uncle asking your presence here. May I see it?"

The eagerness of her tones could not be mistaken.

From her wrist-bag Madelyn extended the square envelope of the morning post, with its remarkable message. Twice Muriel Jaisen's eyes swept slowly through its contents. Madelyn watched her with a little frown. A sudden tenseness had crept into the air, as though we were all keying ourselves for an unexpected climax. And then, like a thunder-clap, it came.

"A curious communication," Madelyn suggested. "I had hoped you might be able to add to it?"

The tired face in the bronze-draped chair stared across the lawn.

"I can. The most curious fact of your communication, Miss Mack, is that Wendell Marsh did not write it!"

Never have I admired more keenly Madelyn's remarkable poise. Save for an almost imperceptible indrawing of her breath, she gave no hint of the shock which must have stunned her as it did me. I was staring with mouth agape. But, then, I presume you have discovered by this time that I was not designed for a detective!

Strangely enough, Muriel Jansen gave no trace of wonder in her announcement. Her attitude suggested a sense of detachment from the subject as though suddenly it had lost its interest. And yet, less than an hour ago, it had prostrated her in a swoon.

"You mean the letter is a forgery?" asked Madelyn quietly.

"And the attempts on Mr. Marsh's life to which it refers?"

"There have been none. I have been with my uncle continuously for six months. I can speak definitely."

Miss Jansen fumbled in a white crocheted bag.

"Here are several specimens of Mr. Marsh's writing. I think they should be sufficient to convince you of what I say. If you desire others—"

I was gulping like a truant schoolgirl as Madelyn spread on her lap the three notes extended to her. Casual business and personal references they were, none of more than half a dozen lines. Quite enough, however, to complete the sudden chasm at our feet – quite enough to emphasize a bold, aggressive penmanship, almost perpendicular, without the slightest resemblance to the cramped, shadowy writing of the morning's astonishing communication.

Madelyn rose from her chair, smoothing her skirts thoughtfully. For a moment she stood at the railing, gazing down upon a trellis of yellow roses, her face turned from us. For the first time in our curious friendship, I was actually conscious of a feeling of pity for her! The blank wall which she faced seemed so abrupt – so final!

Muriel Jansen shifted her position slightly.

"Are you satisfied, Miss Mack?"

"Quite." Madelyn turned, and handed back the three notes. "I presume this means that you do not care for me to continue the case?"

I whirled in dismay. I had never thought of this possibility.

"On the contrary, Miss Mack, it seems to me an additional reason why you should continue!"

I breathed freely again. At least we were not to be dismissed with the abruptness that Miss Jansen's maid had shown! Madelyn bowed rather absently.

"Then if you will give me another interview, perhaps this afternoon—"

Miss Jansen fumbled with the lock of her bag. For the first time her voice lost something of its directness.

"Have – have you any explanation of this astonishing – forgery?"

Madelyn was staring out toward the increasing crowd at the gate. A sudden ripple had swept through it.

"Have you ever heard of a man by the name of Orlando Julio, Miss Jansen?"

My own eyes, following the direction of Madelyn's gaze, were brought back sharply to the veranda. For the second time, Muriel Jansen had crumpled back in a faint.

As I darted toward the servants' bell Madelyn checked me. Striding up the walk were two men with the unmistakable air of physicians. At Madelyn's motioning hand they turned toward us.

The foremost of the two quickened his pace as he caught sight of the figure in the chair. Instinctively I knew that he was Dr. Dench – and it needed no profound analysis to place his companion as the local coroner.

With a deft hand on Miss Jansen's heartbeats, Dr. Dench raised a ruddy, brown-whiskered face inquiringly toward us.

"Shock!" Madelyn explained. "Is it serious?"

The hand on the wavering breast darted toward a medicine case, and selected a vial of brownish liquid. The gaze above it continued its scrutiny of Madelyn's slender figure.

Dr. Dench was of the rugged, German type, steel-eyed, confidently sure of movement, with the physique of a splendidly muscled animal. If the servant's tattle was to be credited, Muriel Jansen could not have attracted more opposite extremes in her suitors.

The coroner – a rusty-suited man of middle age, in quite obvious professional awe of his companion – extended a glass of water. Miss Jansen wearily opened her eyes before it reached her lips.

Dr. Dench restrained her sudden effort to rise.

"Drink this, please!" There was nothing but professional command in his voice. If he loved the grey-pallored girl in the chair, his emotions were under superb control.

Madelyn stepped to the background, motioning me quietly.

"I fancy I can leave now safely. I am going back to town."

"Town?" I echoed.

"I should be back the latter part of the afternoon. Would it inconvenience you to wait here?"

"But, why on earth—" I began.

"Will you tell the butler to send around the car? Thanks!"

When Madelyn doesn't choose to answer questions she ignores them. I subsided as gracefully as possible. As her machine whirled under the porte-cochere, however, my curiosity again overflowed my restraint.

"At least, who is Orlando Julio?" I demanded.

Madelyn carefully adjusted her veil.

"The man who provided the means for the death of Wendell Marsh!" And she was gone.

I swept another glance at the trio on the side veranda, and with what I tried to convince myself was a philosophical shrug, although I knew perfectly well it was merely a pettish fling, sought a retired corner of the rear drawing room, with my pad and pencil.

After all, I was a newspaper woman, and it needed no elastic imagination to picture the scene in the city room of the *Bugle*, if I failed to send a proper accounting of myself.

A few minutes later a tread of feet, advancing to the stairs, told me that the coroner and Dr. Dench were ascending for the belated examination of Wendell Marsh's body. Miss Jansen had evidently recovered, or been assigned to the ministrations of her maid. Once Peters, the wooden-faced butler, entered ghostily to inform me that luncheon would be served at one, but effaced himself almost before my glance returned to my writing.

I partook of the meal in the distinguished company of Sheriff Peddicord. Apparently Dr. Dench was still busied in his grewsome task upstairs, and it was not surprising that Miss Jansen preferred her own apartments.

However much the sheriff's professional poise might have been jarred by the events of the morning, his appetite had not been affected. His attention was too absorbed in the effort to do justice to the Marsh hospitality to waste time in table talk.

He finished his last spoonful of strawberry ice-cream with a heavy sigh of contentment, removed the napkin, which he had tucked under his collar, and, as though mindful of the family's laundry bills, folded it carefully and wiped his lips with his red handkerchief. It was not until then that our silence was interrupted.

Glancing cautiously about the room, and observing that the butler had been called kitchenward, to my amazement he essayed a confidential wink.

"I say," he ventured enticingly, leaning his elbow on the table, "what I would like to know is what became of that there other man!"

"Are you familiar with the Fourth Dimension, Sheriff?" I returned solemnly. I rose from my chair, and stepped toward him confidentially in my turn. "I believe that a thorough study of that subject would answer your question."

It was three o'clock when I stretched myself in my corner of the drawing room, and stuffed the last sheets of my copy paper into a special-delivery-stamped envelope.

My story was done. And Madelyn was not there to blue-pencil Park Row adjectives! I smiled rather gleefully as I patted my hair, and leisurely addressed the envelope. The city editor would be satisfied, if Madelyn wasn't!

As I stepped into the hall, Dr. Dench, the coroner, and Sheriff Peddicord were descending the stairs. Evidently the medical examination had been completed. Under other circumstances the three expressions before me would have afforded an interesting study in contrasts – Dr. Dench trimming his nails with professional stoicism, the coroner endeavoring desperately to copy the other's sang froid, and the sheriff buried in an owl-like solemnity.

Dr. Dench restored his knife to his pocket.

"You are Miss Mack's assistant, I understand?"

I bowed.

"Miss Mack has been called away. She should be back, however, shortly."

I could feel the doctor's appraising glance dissecting me with much the deliberateness of a surgical operation. I raised my eyes suddenly, and returned his stare. It was a virile, masterful face – and, I had to admit, coldly handsome!

Dr. Dench snapped open his watch.

"Very well then, Miss, Miss—"

"Noraker!" I supplied crisply.

The blond beard inclined the fraction of an inch.

"We will wait."

"The autopsy?" I ventured. "Has it—"

"The result of the autopsy I will explain to – Miss Mack!"

I bit my lip, felt my face flush as I saw that Sheriff Peddicord was trying to smother a grin, and turned with a rather unsuccessful shrug.

Now, if I had been of a vindictive nature, I would have opened my envelope and inserted a retaliating paragraph that would have returned the snub of Dr. Dench with interest. I flatter myself that I consigned the envelope to the Three Forks post-office, in the rear of the Elite Dry Goods Emporium, with its contents unchanged.

As a part recompense, I paused at a corner drug store, and permitted a young man with a gorgeous pink shirt to make me a chocolate ice-cream soda. I was bent over an asthmatic straw when, through the window, I saw Madelyn's car skirt the curb.

I rushed out to the sidewalk, while the young man stared dazedly after me. The chauffeur swerved the machine as I tossed a dime to the Adonis of the fountain.

Madelyn shifted to the end of the seat as I clambered to her side. One glance was quite enough to show that her town mission, whatever it was, had ended in failure. Perhaps it was the consciousness of this fact that brought my eyes next to her blue turquoise locket. It was open. I glared accusingly.

"So you have fallen back on the cola stimulant again, Miss Mack?"

She nodded glumly, and perversely slipped into her mouth another of the dark, brown berries, on which I have known her to keep up for forty-eight hours without sleep, and almost without food.

For a moment I forgot even my curiosity as to her errand.

"I wish the duty would be raised so high you couldn't get those things into the country!"

She closed her locket, without deigning a response. The more volcanic my outburst, the more glacial Madelyn's coldness – particularly on the cola topic. I shrugged in resignation. I might as well have done so in the first place!

I straightened my hat, drew my handkerchief over my flushed face, and coughed questioningly. Continued silence. I turned in desperation.

"Well?" I surrendered.

"Don't you know enough, Nora Noraker, to hold your tongue?"

My pent-up emotions snapped.

"Look here, Miss Mack, I have been snubbed by Dr. Dench and the coroner, grinned at by Sheriff Peddicord, and I am not going to be crushed by you! What is your report – good, bad, or indifferent?"

Madelyn turned from her stare into the dust-yellow road.

"I have been a fool, Nora – a blind, bigoted, self-important fool!"

I drew a deep breath.

"Which means—"

From her bag Madelyn drew the envelope of dead tobacco ashes from the Marsh library, and tossed it over the side of the car. I sank back against the cushions.

"Then the tobacco after all—"

"Is nothing but tobacco – harmless tobacco!"

"But the pipe – I thought the pipe—"

"That's just it! The pipe, my dear girl, killed Wendell Marsh! But I don't know how! I don't know how!"

"Madelyn," I said severely, "you are a woman, even if you are making your living at a man's profession! What you need is a good cry!"

Chapter VI

DR. DENCH, pacing back and forth across the veranda, knocked the ashes from an amber-stemmed meerschaum, and advanced to meet us as we alighted. The coroner and Sheriff Peddicord were craning their necks from wicker chairs in the background. It was easy enough to surmise that Dr. Dench had parted from them abruptly in the desire for a quiet smoke to marshal his thoughts.

"Fill your pipe again if you wish," said Madelyn. "I don't mind."

Dr. Dench inclined his head, and dug the mouth of his meerschaum into a fat leather pouch. A spiral of blue smoke soon curled around his face. He was one of that type of men to whom a pipe lends a distinction of studious thoughtfulness.

With a slight gesture he beckoned in the direction of the coroner.

"It is proper, perhaps, that Dr. Wiliams in his official capacity should be heard first."

Through the smoke of his meerschaum, his eyes were searching Madelyn's face. It struck me that he was rather puzzled as to just how seriously to take her.

The coroner shuffled nervously. At his elbow, Sheriff Peddicord fumbled for his red handkerchief.

"We have made a thorough examination of Mr. Marsh's body, Miss Mack, a most thorough examination—"

"Of course he was not shot, nor stabbed, nor strangled, nor sand-bagged?" interrupted Madelyn crisply.

The coroner glanced at Dr. Dench uncertainly. The latter was smoking with inscrutable face.

"Nor poisoned!" finished the coroner with a quick breath.

A blue smoke curl from Dr. Dench's meerschaum vanished against the sun. The coroner jingled a handful of coins in his pocket. The sound jarred on my nerves oddly. Not poisoned! Then Madelyn's theory of the pipe—

My glance swerved in her direction. Another blank wall – the blankest in this riddle of blank walls!

But the bewilderment I had expected in her face I did not find. The black dejection I had noticed in the car had dropped like a whisked-off cloak. The tired lines had been erased as by a sponge. Her eyes shone with that tense glint which I knew came only when she saw a befogged way swept clear before her.

"You mean that you found no trace of poison?" she corrected.

The coroner drew himself up.

"Under the supervision of Dr. Dench, we have made a most complete probe of the various organs – lungs, stomach, heart—"

"And brain, I presume?"

"Brain? Certainly not!"

"And you?" Madelyn turned toward Dr. Dench. "You subscribe to Dr. Williams' opinion?"

Dr. Dench removed his meerschaum. "From our examination of Mr. Marsh's body, I am prepared to state emphatically that there is no trace of toxic condition of any kind!"

"Am I to infer then that you will return a verdict of – natural death?"

Dr. Dench stirred his pipe-ashes.

"I was always under the impression, Miss Mack, that the verdict in a case of this kind must come from the coroner's jury."

Madelyn pinned back her veil, and removed her gloves.

"There is no objection to my seeing the body again?"

The coroner stared.

"Why, er – the undertaker has it now. I don't see why he should object, if you wish—"

Madelyn stepped to the door. Behind her, Sheriff Peddicord stirred suddenly.

"I say, what I would like to know, gents, is what became of that there other man!"

* * *

It was not until six o'clock that I saw Madelyn again, and then I found her in Wendell Marsh's red library. She was seated at its late tenant's huge desk. Before her were a vial of whitish-grey powder, a small, rubber, inked roller, a half a dozen sheets of paper, covered with what looked like smudges of black ink, and Raleigh's pipe. I stopped short staring.

She rose with a shrug.

"Fingerprints," she explained laconically. "This sheet belongs to Miss Jansen; the next to her maid; the third to the butler, Peters; the fourth to Dr. Dench; the fifth to Wendell Marsh, himself. It was my first experiment in taking the 'prints' of a dead man. It was – interesting."

"But what has that to do with a case of this kind?" I demanded.

Madelyn picked up the sixth sheet of smudged paper.

"We have here the fingerprints of Wendell Marsh's murderer!"

I did not even cry my amazement. I suppose the kaleidoscope of the day had dulled my normal emotions. I remember that I readjusted a loose pin in my waist before I spoke.

"The murderer of Wendell Marsh!" I repeated mechanically. "Then he was poisoned?"

Madelyn's eyes opened and closed without answer.

I reached over to the desk and picked up Mr. Marsh's letter of the morning post at Madelyn's elbow.

"You have found the man who forged this?"

"It was not forged!"

In my daze I dropped the letter to the floor.

"You have discovered then the other man in the death-struggle that wrecked the library?"

"There was no other man!"

Madelyn gathered up her possessions from the desk. From the edge of the row of books she lifted a small, red-bound volume, perhaps four inches in width, and then with a second thought laid it back.

"By the way, Nora. I wish you would come back here at eight o'clock. If this book is still where I am leaving it, please bring it to me! I think that will be all for the present."

"All?" I gasped. "Do you realize that—"

Madelyn moved toward the door.

"I think eight o'clock will be late enough for your errand," she said without turning.

The late June twilight had deepened into somber darkness when, my watch showing ten minutes past the hour of my instructions, I entered the room on the second floor that had been assigned to Miss Mack and myself. Madelyn at the window was staring into the shadow-blanketed yard.

"Well?" she demanded.

"Your book is no longer in the library!" I said crossly.

Madelyn whirled with a smile.

"Good! And now if you will be so obliging as to tell Peters to ask Miss Jansen to meet me in the rear drawing room, with any of the friends of the family she desires to be present, I think we can clear up our little puzzle."

Chapter VII

IT WAS a curious group that the graceful Swiss clock in the bronze drawing room of the Marsh house stared down upon as it ticked its way past the half hour after eight. With grave, rather insistent bow, Miss Mack had seated the other occupants of the room as they answered her summons. She was the only one of us that remained standing.

Before her were Sheriff Peddicord, Homer Truxton, Dr. Dench, and Muriel Jansen. Madelyn's eyes swept our faces for a moment in silence, and then she crossed the room and closed the door.

"I have called you here," she began, "to explain the mystery of Mr. Marsh's death." Again her glance swept our faces. "In many respects it has provided us with a peculiar, almost a unique problem.

"We find a man, in apparently normal health, dead. The observer argues at once foul play; and yet on his body is no hint of wound or bruise. The medical examination discovers no trace of poison. The autopsy shows no evidence of crime. Apparently we have eliminated all forms of unnatural death.

"I have called you here because the finding of the autopsy is incorrect, or rather incomplete. We are not confronted by natural death – but by a crime. And I may say at the outset that I am not the only person to know this fact. My knowledge is shared by one other in this room."

Sheriff Peddicord rose to his feet and rather ostentatiously stepped to the door and stood with his back against it. Madelyn smiled faintly at the movement.

"I scarcely think there will be an effort at escape, Sheriff," she said quietly.

Muriel Jansen was crumpled back into her chair, staring. Dr. Dench was studying Miss Mack with the professional frown he might have directed at an abnormality on the operating table. It was Truxton who spoke first in the fashion of the impulsive boy.

"If we are not dealing with natural death, how on earth then was Mr. Marsh killed?"

Madelyn whisked aside a light covering from a stand at her side, and raised to view Raleigh's red sand-stone pipe. For a moment she balanced it musingly.

"The three-hundred-year-old death tool of Orlando Julio," she explained. "It was this that killed Wendell Marsh!"

She pressed the bowl of the pipe into the palm of her hand. "As an instrument of death, it is almost beyond detection. We examined the ashes, and found nothing but harmless tobacco. The organs of the victim showed no trace of foul play."

She tapped the long stem gravely.

"But the examination of the organs did not include the brain. And it is through the brain that the pipe strikes, killing first the mind in a nightmare of insanity, and then the body. That accounts for the wreckage that we found – the evidences apparently of two men engaged in a desperate struggle. The wreckage was the work of only one man – a maniac in the moment before death. The drug with which we are dealing drives its victim into an insane fury before his body succumbs. I believe such cases are fairly common in India."

"Then Mr. Marsh was poisoned after all?" cried Truxton. He was the only one of Miss Mack's auditors to speak.

"No, not poisoned! You will understand as I proceed. The pipe, you will find, contains apparently but one bowl and one channel, and at a superficial glance is filled only with tobacco. In reality, there is a lower chamber concealed beneath the upper bowl, to which extends a second channel. This secret chamber is charged with a certain compound of Indian hemp and dhatura leaves, one of the most powerful brain stimulants known to science – and one of the most dangerous if used above a certain strength. From the lower chamber it would leave no trace, of course, in the ashes above.

"Between the two compartments of the pipe is a slight connecting opening, sufficient to allow the hemp beneath to be ignited gradually by the burning tobacco. When a small quantity of the compound is used, the smoker is stimulated as by no other drug, not even opium. Increase the quantity above the danger point, and mark the result. The victim is not poisoned in the strict sense of the word, but literally smothered to death by the fumes!"

In Miss Mack's voice was the throb of the student before the creation of the master.

"I should like this pipe, Miss Jansen, if you ever care to dispose of it!"

The girl was still staring woodenly.

"It was Orlando Julio, the medieval poisoner," she gasped, "that Uncle described—"

"In his seventeenth chapter of *The World's Great Cynics*," finished Madelyn. "I have taken the liberty of reading the chapter in manuscript form. Julio, however, was not the discoverer of the drug. He merely introduced it to the English public. As a matter of fact, it is one of the oldest stimulants of the East. It is easy to assume that it was not as a stimulant that Julio used it, but as a baffling instrument of murder. The mechanism of the pipe was his own invention, of course. The smoker, if not in the secret, would be completely oblivious to his danger. He might even use the pipe in perfect safety – until its lower chamber was loaded!"

Sheriff Peddicord, against the door, mopped his face with his red handkerchief, like a man in a daze. Dr. Dench was still studying Miss Mack with his intent frown. Madelyn swerved her angle abruptly.

"Last night was not the first time the hemp-chamber of Wendell Marsh's pipe had been charged. We can trace the effect of the drug on his brain for several months – hallucinations, imaginative enemies seeking his life, incipient insanity. That explains his astonishing letter to me. Wendell Marsh was not a man of nine lives, but only one. The perils which he described were merely fantastic figments of the drug. For instance, the episode of the poisoned cherry pie. There was no pie at all served at the table yesterday.

"The letter to me was not a forgery, Miss Jansen, although you were sincere enough when you pronounced it such. The complete change in your uncle's handwriting was only another effect of the drug. It was this fact, in the end, which led me to the truth. You did not perceive that the dates of your notes and mine were six months apart! I knew that some terrific mental shock must have occurred in the meantime.

"And then, too, the ravages of a drug-crazed victim were at once suggested by the curtains of the library. They were not simply torn, but fairly chewed to pieces!" A sudden tension fell over the room. We shifted nervously, rather avoiding one another's eyes. Madelyn laid the pipe back on the stand. She was quite evidently in no hurry to continue. It was Truxton again who put the leading question of the moment.

"If Mr. Marsh was killed as you describe, Miss Mack, who killed him?" Madelyn glanced across at Dr. Dench. "Will you kindly let me have the red leather book that you took from Mr. Marsh's desk this evening, Doctor?"

The physician met her glance steadily. "You think it – necessary?"

"I am afraid I must insist."

For an instant Dr. Dench hesitated. Then with a shrug, he reached into a coat pocket and extended the red-bound volume, for which Miss Mack had dispatched me on the fruitless errand to the library. As Madelyn opened it we saw that it was not a printed volume, but filled with several hundred pages of close, cramped writing. Dr. Dench's gaze swerved to Muriel Jansen as Miss Mack spoke.

"I have here the diary of Wendell Marsh, which shows us that he had been in the habit of seeking the stimulant of Indian hemp, or 'hasheesh' for some time, possibly as a result of his retired, sedentary life and his close application to his books. Until his purchase of the Bainford relics, however, he had taken the stimulant in the comparatively harmless form of powdered leaves or 'bhang', as it is termed in the Orient. His acquisition of Julio's drug-pipe, and an accidental discovery of its mechanism, led him to adopt the compound of hemp and dhatura, prepared for smoking – in India called 'charas'. No less an authority than Captain E.N. Windsor, bacteriologist of the Burmese Government, states that it is directly responsible for a large percentage of the lunacy of the Orient. Wendell Marsh, however, did not realize his danger, nor how much stronger the latter compound is than the form of the drug to which he had been accustomed.

"Dr. Dench endeavored desperately to warn him of his peril, and free him from the bondage of the habit as the diary records, but the victim was too thoroughly enslaved. In fact, the situation had reached a point just before the final climax when it could no longer be concealed. The truth was already being suspected by the older servants. I assume this was why you feared my investigations in the case, Miss Jansen."

Muriel Jansen was staring at Madelyn in a sort of dumb appeal.

"I can understand and admire Dr. Dench's efforts to conceal the fact from the public – first, in his supervision of the inquest, which might have stumbled on the truth, and then in his removal of the betraying diary, which I left purposely exposed in the hope that it might inspire such an action. Had it not been removed, I might have suspected another explanation of the case – in spite of certain evidence to the contrary!"

Dr. Dench's face had gone white.

"God! Miss Mack, do you mean that after all it was not suicide?"

"It was not suicide," said Madelyn quietly. She stepped across toward the opposite door.

"When I stated that my knowledge that we are not dealing with natural death was shared by another person in this room, I might have added that it was shared by still a third person – not in the room!"

With a sudden movement she threw open the door before her. From the adjoining ante-room lurched the figure of Peters, the butler. He stared at us with a face grey with terror, and then crumpled to his knees. Madelyn drew away sharply as he tried to catch her skirts.

"You may arrest the murderer of Wendell Marsh, Sheriff!" she said gravely. "And I think perhaps you had better take him outside."

She faced our bewildered stares as the drawing-room door closed behind Mr. Peddicord and his prisoner. From her stand she again took Raleigh's sandstone pipe, and with it two sheets of paper, smudged with the prints of a human thumb and fingers.

"It was the pipe in the end which led me to the truth, not only as to the method but the identity of the assassin," she explained. "The hand, which placed the fatal charge in the concealed chamber, left its imprint on the surface of the bowl. The fingers, grimed with the dust of the drug, made an impression which I would have at once detected had I not been so occupied with what I might find inside that I forgot what I might find outside. I am very much afraid that I permitted myself the great blunder of the modern detective – lack of thoroughness.

"Comparison with the fingerprints of the various agents in the case, of course, made the next step a mere detail of mathematical comparison. To make my identity sure, I found that my suspect possessed not only the opportunity and the knowledge for the crime, but the motive.

"In his younger days Peters was a chemist's apprentice; a fact which he utilized in his master's behalf in obtaining the drugs which had become so necessary a part of Mr. Marsh's life. Had Wendell Marsh appeared in person for so continuous a supply, his identity would soon have made the fact a matter of common gossip. He relied on his servant for his agent, a detail which he mentions several times in his diary, promising Peters a generous bequest in his will as a reward. I fancy that it was the dream of this bequest, which would have meant a small fortune to a man in his position, that set the butler's brain to work on his treacherous plan of murder."

* * *

Miss Mack's dull gold hair covered the shoulders of her white peignoir in a great, thick braid. She was propped in a nest of pillows, with her favorite romance, *The Three Musketeers*, open at the historic siege of Porthos in the wine cellar. We had elected to spend the night at the Marsh house.

Madelyn glanced up as I appeared in the doorway of our room.

"Allow me to present a problem to your analytical skill, Miss Mack," I said humbly. "Which man does your knowledge of feminine psychology say Muriel Jansen will reward – the gravely protecting physician, or the boyishly admiring Truxton?"

"If she were thirty," retorted Madelyn, yawning, "she would be wise enough to choose Dr. Dench. But as she is only twenty-two, it will be Truxton."

With a sigh, she turned again to the swashbuckling exploits of the gallant Porthos.

Going Through the Tunnel

Mrs. Henry Wood

WE HAD TO make a rush for it. And making a rush did not suit the Squire, any more than it does other people who have come to an age when the body's heavy and the breath nowhere. He reached the train, pushed head-foremost into a carriage, and then remembered the tickets. "Bless my heart?" he exclaimed, as he jumped out again, and nearly upset a lady who had a little dog in her arms, and a mass of fashionable hair on her head, that the Squire, in his hurry, mistook for tow.

"Plenty of time, sir," said a guard who was passing. "Three minutes to spare."

Instead of saying he was obliged to the man for his civility, or relieved to find the tickets might still be had, the Squire snatched out his old watch, and began abusing the railway clocks for being slow. Had Tod been there he would have told him to his face that the watch was fast, braving all retort, for the Squire believed in his watch as he did in himself, and would rather have been told that *he* could go wrong than that the watch could. But there was only me: and I wouldn't have said it for anything.

"Keep two back-seats there, Johnny," said the Squire.

I put my coat on the corner furthest from the door, and the rug on the one next to it, and followed him into the station. When the Squire was late in starting, he was apt to get into the greatest flurry conceivable; and the first thing I saw was himself blocking up the ticket-place, and undoing his pocket-book with nervous fingers. He had some loose gold about him, silver too, but the pocket-book came to his hand first, so he pulled it out. These flurried moments of the Squire's amused Tod beyond everything; he was so cool himself.

"Can you change this?" said the Squire, drawing out one from a roll of five-pound notes.

"No, I can't," was the answer, in the surly tones put on by ticket-clerks.

How the Squire crumpled up the note again, and searched in his breeches pocket for gold, and came away with the two tickets and the change, I'm sure he never knew. A crowd had gathered round, wanting to take their tickets in turn, and knowing that he was keeping them flurried him all the more. He stood at the back a moment, put the roll of notes into his case, fastened it and returned it to the breast of his overcoat, sent the change down into another pocket without counting it, and went out with the tickets in hand. Not to the carriage; but to stare at the big clock in front.

"Don't you see, Johnny? Exactly four minutes and a half difference," he cried, holding out his watch to me. "It is a strange thing they can't keep these railway clocks in order."

"My watch keeps good time, sir, and mine is with the railway. I think it is right."

"Hold your tongue, Johnny. How dare you! Right? You send your watch to be regulated the first opportunity, sir; don't *you* get into the habit of being too late or too early."

When we finally went to the carriage there were some people in it, but our seats were left for us. Squire Todhetley sat down by the further door, and settled himself and his coats and his things comfortably, which he had been too flurried to do before. Cool as a cucumber was he, now the bustle was over; cool as Tod could have been. At the other door, with his face to the engine, sat a dark, gentleman-like man of forty, who had made room for us to pass as we got in. He had a large signet-ring on one hand, and a lavender glove on the other. The other three seats opposite to us were vacant. Next to me sat a little man with a fresh colour and gold spectacles, who was already reading; and beyond him, in the corner, face-to-face with the dark man, was a lunatic. That's to mention him politely. Of all the restless, fidgety, worrying, hot-tempered passengers that ever put themselves into a carriage to travel with people in their senses, he was the worst. In fifteen moments he had made as many darts; now after his hat-box and things above his head; now calling the guard and the porters to ask senseless questions about his luggage; now treading on our toes, and trying the corner seat opposite the Squire, and then darting back to his own. He wore a wig of a decided green tinge, the effect of keeping, perhaps, and his skin was dry and shrivelled as an Egyptian mummy's.

A servant, in undress livery, came to the door, and touched his hat, which had a cockade on it, as he spoke to the dark man.

"Your ticket, my lord."

Lords are not travelled with every day, and some of us looked up. The gentleman took the ticket from the man's hand and slipped it into his waistcoat pocket.

"You can get me a newspaper, Wilkins. The *Times*, if it is to be had."

"Yes, my lord."

"Yes, there's room here, ma'am," interrupted the guard, sending the door back for a lady who stood at it. "Make haste, please."

The lady who stepped in was the same the Squire had bolted against. She sat down in the seat opposite me, and looked at every one of us by turns. There was a sort of violet bloom on her face and some soft white powder, seen plain enough through her veil. She took the longest gaze at the dark gentleman, bending a little forward to do it; for, as he was in a line with her, and also had his head turned from her, her curiosity could only catch a view of his side-face. Mrs. Todhetley might have said she had not put on her company manners. In the midst of this, the man-servant came back again.

"The *Times* is not here yet, my lord. They are expecting the papers in by the next down-train."

"Never mind, then. You can get me one at the next station, Wilkins."

"Very well, my lord."

Wilkins must certainly have had to scramble for his carriage, for we started before he had well left the door. It was not an express-train, and we should have to stop at several stations. Where the Squire and I had been staying does not matter; it has nothing to do with what I have to tell. It was a long way from our own home, and that's saying enough.

"Would you mind changing seats with me, sir?"

I looked up, to find the lady's face close to mine; she had spoken in a half-whisper. The Squire, who carried his old-fashioned notions of politeness with him when he went travelling, at once got up to offer her the corner. But she declined it, saying she was subject to face-ache, and did not care to be next the window. So she took my seat, and I sat down on the one opposite Mr. Todhetley.

"Which of the peers is that?" I heard her ask him in a loud whisper, as the lord put his head out at his window.

"Don't know at all, ma'am," said the Squire. "Don't know many of the peers myself, except those of my own county: Lyttelton, and Beauchamp, and—"

Of all snarling barks, the worst was given that moment in the Squire's face, suddenly ending the list. The little dog, an ugly, hairy, vile-tempered Scotch terrier, had been kept concealed under the lady's jacket, and now struggled itself free. The Squire's look of consternation was good! He had not known any animal was there.

"Be quiet, Wasp. How dare you bark at the gentleman? He will not bite, sir: he—"

"Who has a dog in the carriage?" shrieked the lunatic, starting up in a passion. "Dogs don't travel with passengers. Here! Guard! Guard!"

To call out for the guard when a train is going at full speed is generally useless. The lunatic had to sit down again; and the lady defied him, so to say, coolly avowing that she had hidden the dog from the guard on purpose, staring him in the face while she said it.

After this there was a lull, and we went speeding along, the lady talking now and again to the Squire. She seemed to want to grow confidential with him; but the Squire did not seem to care for it, though he was quite civil. She held the dog huddled up in her lap, so that nothing but his head peeped out.

"Halloa! How dare they be so negligent? There's no lamp in this carriage."

It was the lunatic again, and we all looked at the lamp. It had no light in it; but that it *had* when we first reached the carriage was certain; for, as the Squire went stumbling in, his head nearly touched the lamp, and I had noticed the flame. It seems the Squire had also.

"They must have put it out while we were getting our tickets," he said.

"I'll know the reason why when we stop," cried the lunatic, fiercely. "After passing the next station, we dash into the long tunnel. The idea of going through it in pitch darkness! It would not be safe."

"Especially with a dog in the carriage," spoke the lord, in a chaffing kind of tone, but with a good-natured smile. "We will have the lamp lighted, however."

As if to reward him for interfering, the dog barked up loudly, and tried to make a spring at him; upon which the lady smothered the animal up, head and all.

Another minute or two, and the train began to slacken speed. It was only an insignificant station, one not likely to be halted at for above a minute. The lunatic twisted his body out of the window, and shouted for the guard long before we were at a standstill.

"Allow me to manage this," said the lord, quietly putting him down. "They know me on the line. Wilkins!"

The man came rushing up at the call. He must have been out already, though we were not quite at a standstill yet.

"Is it for the *Times*, my lord? I am going for it."

"Never mind the *Times*. This lamp is not lighted, Wilkins. See the guard, and *get it done*. At once."

"And ask him what the mischief he means by his carelessness," roared out the lunatic after Wilkins, who went flying off. "Sending us on our road without a light! – and that dangerous tunnel close at hand."

The authority laid upon the words "Get it done", seemed an earnest that the speaker was accustomed to be obeyed, and would be this time. For once the lunatic sat quiet, watching the lamp, and for the light that was to be dropped into it from the top; and so did I, and so did the lady. We were all deceived, however, and the train went puffing on. The lunatic shrieked, the lord put his head out of the carriage and shouted for Wilkins.

No good. Shouting after a train is off never is much good. The lord sat down on his seat again, an angry frown crossing his face, and the lunatic got up and danced with rage.

"I do not know where the blame lies," observed the lord. "Not with my servant, I think: he is attentive, and has been with me some years."

"I'll know where it lies," retorted the lunatic. "I am a director on the line, though I don't often travel on it. This *is* management, this is! A few minutes more and we shall be in the dark tunnel."

"Of course it would have been satisfactory to have a light; but it is not of so much consequence," said the nobleman, wishing to soothe him. "There's no danger in the dark."

"No danger! No danger, sir! I think there is danger. Who's to know that dog won't spring out and bite us? Who's to know there won't be an accident in the tunnel? A light is a protection against having our pockets picked, if it's a protection against nothing else."

"I fancy our pockets are pretty safe today," said the lord, glancing round at us with a good-natured smile; as much as to say that none of us looked like thieves. "And I certainly trust we shall get through the tunnel safely."

"And I'll take care the dog does not bite you in the dark," spoke up the lady, pushing her head forward to give the lunatic a nod or two that you'd hardly have matched for defying impudence. "You'll be good, won't you, Wasp? But I should like the lamp lighted myself. You will perhaps be so kind, my lord, as to see that there's no mistake made about it at the next station!"

He slightly raised his hat to her and bowed in answer, but did not speak. The lunatic buttoned up his coat with fingers that were either nervous or angry, and then disturbed the little gentleman next to him, who had read his big book throughout the whole commotion without once lifting his eyes, by hunting everywhere for his pocket-handkerchief.

"Here's the tunnel!" he cried out resentfully, as we dashed with a shriek into pitch darkness.

It was all very well for her to say she would take care of the dog, but the first thing the young beast did was to make a spring at me and then at the Squire, barking and yelping frightfully. The Squire pushed it away in a commotion. Though well accustomed to dogs he always fought shy of strange ones. The lady chattered and laughed, and did not seem to try to get hold of him, but we couldn't see, you know; the Squire hissed at him, the dog snarled and growled; altogether there was noise enough to deafen anything but a tunnel.

"Pitch him out at the window," cried the lunatic.

"Pitch yourself out," answered the lady. And whether she propelled the dog, or whether he went of his own accord, the beast sprang to the other end of the carriage, and was seized upon by the nobleman.

"I think, madam, you had better put him under your mantle and keep him there," said he, bringing the dog back to her and speaking quite civilly, but in the same tone of authority he had used to his servant about the lamp. "I have not the slightest objection to dogs myself, but many people have, and it is not altogether pleasant to have them loose in a railway carriage. I beg your pardon; I cannot see; is this your hand?"

It was her hand, I suppose, for the dog was left with her, and he went back to his seat again. When we emerged out of the tunnel into daylight, the lunatic's face was blue.

"Ma'am, if that miserable brute had laid hold of me by so much as the corner of my great-coat tail, I'd have had the law of you. It is perfectly monstrous that anyone, putting themselves into a first-class carriage, should attempt to outrage railway laws, and upset the comfort of travellers with impunity. I shall complain to the guard."

"He does not bite, sir; he never bites," she answered softly, as if sorry for the escapade, and wishing to conciliate him. "The poor little bijou is frightened at darkness, and leaped from my arms unawares. There! I'll promise that you shall neither see nor hear him again."

She had tucked the dog so completely out of sight, that no one could have suspected one was there, just as it had been on first entering. The train was drawn up to the next station; when it stopped, the servant came and opened the carriage-door for his master to get out.

"Did you understand me, Wilkins, when I told you to get this lamp lighted?"

"My lord, I'm very sorry; I understood your lordship perfectly, but I couldn't see the guard," answered Wilkins. "I caught sight of him running up to his van-door at the last moment, but the train began to move off, and I had to jump in myself, or else be left behind."

The guard passed as he was explaining this, and the nobleman drew his attention to the lamp, curtly ordering him to "light it instantly". Lifting his hat to us by way of farewell, he disappeared; and the lunatic began upon the guard as if he were commencing a lecture to a deaf audience. The guard seemed not to hear it, so lost was he in astonishment at there being no light.

"Why, what can have douted it?" he cried aloud, staring up at the lamp. And the Squire smiled at the familiar word, so common in our ears at home, and had a great mind to ask the guard where he came from.

"I lighted all these here lamps myself afore we started, and I see 'em all burning," said he. There was no mistaking the home accent now, and the Squire looked down the carriage with a beaming face.

"You are from Worcestershire, my man."

"From Worcester itself, sir. Leastways from St. John's, which is the same thing."

"Whether you are from Worcester, or whether you are from Jericho, I'll let you know that you can't put empty lamps into first-class carriages on this line without being made to answer for it!" roared the lunatic. "What's your name! I am a director."

"My name is Thomas Brooks, sir," replied the man, respectfully touching his cap. "But I declare to you, sir, that I've told the truth in saying the lamps were all right when we started: how this one can have got douted, I can't think. There's not a guard on the line, sir, more particular in seeing to the lamps than I am."

"Well, light it now; don't waste time excusing yourself," growled the lunatic. But he said nothing about the dog; which was surprising.

In a twinkling the lamp was lighted, and we were off again. The lady and her dog were quiet now: he was out of sight: she leaned back to go to sleep. The Squire lodged his head against the curtain, and shut his eyes to do the same; the little man, as before, never looked off his book; and the lunatic frantically shifted himself every two minutes between his own seat and that of the opposite corner. There were no more tunnels, and we went smoothly on to the next station. Five minutes allowed there.

The little man, putting his book in his pocket, took down a black leather bag from above his head, and got out; the lady, her dog hidden still, prepared to follow him, wishing the Squire and me, and even the lunatic, with a forgiving smile, a polite good morning. I had moved to that end, and was watching the lady's wonderful back hair as she stepped out, when all in a moment the Squire sprang up with a shout, and jumping out nearly upon her, called out that he had been robbed. She dropped the dog, and I thought he must have caught the lunatic's disorder and become frantic.

It is of no use attempting to describe exactly what followed. The lady, snatching up her dog, shrieked out that perhaps she had been robbed too; she laid hold of the Squire's arm, and went with him into the station master's room. And there we were: us three, and the guard, and the station master, and the lunatic, who had come pouncing out too at the Squire's cry. The man in spectacles had disappeared for good.

The Squire's pocket-book was gone. He gave his name and address at once to the station master: and the guard's face lighted with intelligence when he heard it, for he knew Squire Todhetley by reputation. The pocket-book had been safe just before we entered the tunnel; the Squire was certain of that, having felt it. He had sat in the carriage with his coat unbuttoned, rather thrown back; and nothing could have been easier than for a clever thief to draw it out, under cover of the darkness.

"I had fifty pounds in it," he said; "fifty pounds in five-pound notes. And some memoranda besides."

"Fifty pounds!" cried the lady, quickly. "And you could travel with all that about you, and not button up your coat! You ought to be rich!"

"Have you been in the habit of meeting thieves, madam, when travelling?" suddenly demanded the lunatic, turning upon her without warning, his coat whirling about on all sides with the rapidity of his movements.

"No, sir, I have not," she answered, in indignant tones. "Have you?"

"I have not, madam. But, then, you perceive I see no risk in travelling with a coat unbuttoned, although it may have banknotes in the pockets."

She made no reply: was too much occupied in turning out her own pockets and purse, to ascertain that they had not been rifled. Re-assured on the point, she sat down on a low box against the wall, nursing her dog; which had begun its snarling again.

"It must have been taken from me in the dark as we went through the tunnel," affirmed the Squire to the room in general and perhaps the station master in particular. "I am a magistrate, and have some experience in these things. I sat completely off my guard, a prey for anybody, my hands stretched out before me, grappling with that dog, that seemed – why, goodness me! yes he *did*, now that I think of it – that seemed to be held about fifteen inches off my nose on purpose to attack me. That's when the thing must have been done. But now – which of them could it have been?"

He meant which of the passengers. As he looked hard at us in rotation, especially at the guard and station master, who had not been in the carriage, the lady gave a shriek, and threw the dog into the middle of the room.

"I see it all," she said, faintly. "He has a habit of snatching at things with his mouth. He must have snatched the case out of your pocket, sir, and dropped it from the window. You will find it in the tunnel."

"Who has?" asked the lunatic, while the Squire stared in wonder.

"My poor little Wasp. Ah, villain! beast! it is he that has done all this mischief."

"He might have taken the pocket-book," I said, thinking it time to speak, "but he could not have dropped it out, for I put the window up as we went into the tunnel."

It seemed a nonplus for her, and her face fell again. "There was the other window," she said in a minute. "He might have dropped it there. I heard his bark quite close to it."

"*I* pulled up that window, madam," said the lunatic. "If the dog did take it out of the pocket it may be in the carriage now."

The guard rushed out to search it; the Squire followed, but the station master remained where he was, and closed the door after them. A thought came over me that he was stopping to keep the two passengers in view.

No; the pocket-book could not be found in the carriage. As they came back, the Squire was asking the guard if he knew who the nobleman was who had got out at the last station with his servant. But the guard did not know.

"He said they knew him on the line."

"Very likely, sir. I have not been on this line above a month or two."

"Well, this is an unpleasant affair," said the lunatic impatiently; "and the question is – what's to be done? It appears pretty evident that your pocket-book was taken in the carriage, sir. Of the four passengers, I suppose the one who left us at the last station must be held exempt from suspicion, being a nobleman. Another got out here, and has disappeared; the other two are present. I propose that we should both be searched."

"I'm sure I am quite willing," said the lady, and she got up at once.

I think the Squire was about to disclaim any wish so to act; but the lunatic was resolute, and the station master agreed with him. There was no time to be lost, for the train was ready to start again, her time being up, and the lunatic was turned out. The lady went into another room with two women, called by the station master, and *she* was turned out. Neither of them had the pocket-book.

"Here's my card, sir," said the lunatic, handing one to Mr. Todhetley. "You know my name, I dare say. If I can be of any future assistance to you in this matter, you may command me."

"Bless my heart!" cried the Squire, as he read the name on the card. "How could you allow yourself to be searched, sir?"

"Because, in such a case as this, I think it only right and fair that everyone who has the misfortune to be mixed up in it *should* be searched," replied the lunatic, as they went out together. "It is a satisfaction to both parties. Unless you offered to search me, you could not have offered to search that woman; and I suspected her."

"Suspected *her*!" cried the Squire, opening his eyes.

"If I didn't suspect, I doubted. Why on earth did she cause her dog to make all that row the moment we got into the tunnel? It must have been done then. I should not be startled out of my senses if I heard that that silent man by my side and hers was in league with her."

The Squire stood in a kind of amazement, trying to recall what he could of the little man in spectacles, and see if things would fit into one another.

"Don't you like her look?" he asked suddenly.

"No, I *don't*," said the lunatic, turning himself about. "I have a prejudice against painted women: they put me in mind of Jezebel. Look at her hair. It's awful."

He went out in a whirlwind, and took his seat in the carriage, not a moment before it puffed off.

"*Is* he a lunatic?" I whispered to the Squire.

"He a lunatic!" he roared. "You must be a lunatic for asking it, Johnny. Why, that's – that's—"

Instead of saying any more, he showed me the card, and the name nearly took my breath away. He is a well-known London man, of science, talent, and position, and of worldwide fame.

"Well, I thought him nothing better than an escaped maniac."

"*Did* you?" said the Squire. "Perhaps he returned the compliment on you, sir. But now – Johnny, who has got my pocket-book?"

As if it was any use asking me? As we turned back to the station master's room, the lady came into it, evidently resenting the search, although she had seemed to acquiesce in it so readily.

"They were rude, those women. It is the first time I ever had the misfortune to travel with men who carry pocket-books to lose them, and I hope it will be the last," she pursued, in scornful passion, meant for the Squire. "One generally meets with *gentlemen* in a first-class carriage."

The emphasis came out with a shriek, and it told on him. Now that she was proved innocent, he was as vexed as she for having listened to the advice of the scientific man – but I can't help calling him a lunatic still. The Squire's apologies might have disarmed a cross-grained hyena; and she came round with a smile.

"If anyone *has* got the pocket-book," she said, as she stroked her dog's ears, "it must be that silent man with the gold spectacles. There was no one else, sir, who could have reached you without getting up to do it. And I declare on my honour, that when that commotion first arose through my poor little dog, I felt for a moment something like a man's arm stretched across me. It could only have been his. I hope you have the numbers of the notes."

"But I have not," said the Squire.

The room was being invaded by this time. Two stray passengers, a friend of the station master's, and the porter who took the tickets, had crept in. All thought the lady's opinion must be correct, and said the spectacled man had got clear off with the pocket-book. There was no one else to pitch upon. A nobleman travelling with his servant would not be likely to commit a robbery; the lunatic was really the man his card represented him to be, for the station master's friend had seen and recognised him; and the lady was proved innocent by search. Wasn't the Squire in a passion!

"That close reading of his was all a blind," he said, in sudden conviction. "He kept his face down that we should not know him in future. He never looked at one of us! He never said a word! I shall go and find him."

Away went the Squire, as fast as he could hurry, but came back in a moment to know which was the way out, and where it led to. There was quite a small crowd of us by this time. Some fields lay beyond the station at the back; and a boy affirmed that he had seen a little gentleman in spectacles, with a black bag in his hand, making over the first stile.

"Now look here, boy," said the Squire. "If you catch that same man, I'll give you five shillings."

Tod could not have flown faster than the boy did. He took the stile at a leap; and the Squire tumbled over it after him. Some boys and men joined in the chase; and a cow, grazing in the field, trotted after us and brought up the rear.

Such a shout from the boy. It came from behind the opposite hedge of the long field. I was over the gate first; the Squire came next.

On the hedge of the dry ditch sat the passenger, his legs dangling, his neck imprisoned in the boy's arms. I knew him at once. His hat and gold spectacles had fallen off in the scuffle; the black bag was wide open, and had a tall bunch of something green sticking up from it; some tools lay on the ground.

"Oh, you wicked hypocrite!" spluttered the Squire, not in the least knowing what he said in his passion. "Are you not ashamed to have played upon me such a vile trick? How dare you go about to commit robberies!"

"I have not robbed you, at any rate," said the man, his voice trembling a little and his face pale, while the boy loosed the neck but pinioned one of the arms.

"Not robbed me!" cried the Squire. "Good Heavens! Who do you suppose you have robbed, if not me? Here, Johnny, lad, you are a witness. He says he has not robbed me."

"I did not know it was yours," said the man meekly. "Loose me, boy; I'll not attempt to run away."

"Halloa! Here! What's to do?" roared a big fellow, swinging himself over the gate. "Any tramp been trespassing? Anybody wanting to be took up? I'm the parish constable."

If he had said he was the parish engine, ready to let loose buckets of water on the offender, he could not have been more welcome. The Squire's face was rosy with satisfaction.

"Have you your handcuffs with you, my man?"

"I've not got them, sir; but I fancy I'm big enough and strong enough to take *him* without 'em. Something to spare, too."

"There's nothing like handcuffs for safety," said the Squire, rather damped, for he believed in them as one of the country's institutions. "Oh, you villain! Perhaps you can tie him with cords?"

The thief floundered out of the ditch and stood upon his feet. He did not look an ungentlemanly thief, now you came to see and hear him; and his face, though scared, might have been thought an honest one. He picked up his hat and glasses, and held them in his hand while he spoke, in tones of earnest remonstrance.

"Surely, sir, you would not have me taken up for this slight offence! I did not know I was doing wrong, and I doubt if the law would condemn me; I thought it was public property!"

"Public property!" cried the Squire, turning red at the words. "Of all the impudent brazen-faced rascals that are cheating the gallows, you must be the worst. My banknotes public property!"

"Your what, sir?"

"My banknotes, you villain. How dare you repeat your insolent questions?"

"But I don't know anything about your banknotes, sir," said the man meekly. "I do not know what you mean."

They stood facing each other, a sight for a picture; the Squire with his hands under his coat, dancing a little in rage, his face crimson; the other quite still, holding his hat and gold spectacles, and looking at him in wonder.

"You don't know what I mean! When you confessed with your last breath that you had robbed me of my pocket-book!"

"I confessed – I have not sought to conceal – that I have robbed the ground of this rare fern," said the man, handling carefully the green stuff in the black bag. "I have not robbed you or anyone of anything else."

The tone, simple, quiet, self-contained, threw the Squire in amazement. He stood staring.

"Are you a fool?" he asked. "What do you suppose I have to do with your rubbishing ferns?"

"Nay, I supposed you owned them; that is, owned the land. You led me to believe so, in saying I had robbed you."

"What I've lost is a pocket-book, with ten five-pound banknotes in it; I lost it in the train; it must have been taken as we came through the tunnel; and you sat next but one to me," reiterated the Squire.

The man put on his hat and glasses. "I am a geologist and botanist, sir. I came here after this plant today – having seen it yesterday, but then I had not my tools with me. I don't know anything about the pocket-book and banknotes."

So that was another mistake, for the botanist turned out of his pockets a heap of letters directed to him, and a big book he had been reading in the train, a treatise on botany, to prove who he was. And, as if to leave no loophole for doubt, one stepped up who knew him, and assured the Squire there was not a more learned man in his line, no, nor one more respected, in the three kingdoms. The Squire shook him by the hand in apologising, and told him we had some valuable ferns near Dyke Manor, if he would come and see them.

Like Patience on a monument, when we got back, sat the lady, waiting to see the prisoner brought in. Her face would have made a picture too, when she heard the upshot, and saw the hot Squire and the gold spectacles walking side by side in friendly talk.

"I think still he must have got it," she said, sharply.

"No, madam," answered the Squire. "Whoever may have taken it, it was not he."

"Then there's only one man, and that is he whom you have let go on in the train," she returned decisively. "I thought his fidgety movements were not put on for nothing. He had secured the pocket-book somewhere, and then made a show of offering to be searched. Ah, ha!"

And the Squire veered round again at this suggestion, and began to suspect he had been doubly cheated. First, out of his money, next out of his suspicions. One only thing in the whole bother seemed clear; and that was, that the notes and case had gone for good. As, in point of fact, they had.

* * *

We were on the chain-pier at Brighton, Tod and I. It was about eight or nine months after. I had put my arms on the rails at the end, looking at a pleasure-party sailing by. Tod, next to me, was bewailing his ill-fortune in not possessing a yacht and opportunities of cruising in it.

"I tell you no. I don't want to be made sea-sick."

The words came from someone behind us. It seemed almost as though they were spoken in reference to Tod's wish for a yacht. But it was not *that* that made me turn round sharply; it was the sound of the voice, for I thought I recognised it.

Yes: there she was. The lady who had been with us in the carriage that day. The dog was not with her now, but her hair was more amazing than ever. She did not see me. As I turned, she turned, and began to walk slowly back, arm-in-arm with a gentleman. And to see him – that is, to see them together – made me open my eyes. For it was the lord who had travelled with us.

"Look, Tod!" I said, and told him in a word who they were.

"What the deuce do they know of each other?" cried Tod with a frown, for he felt angry every time the thing was referred to. Not for the loss of the money, but for what he called the stupidity of us all; saying always had *he* been there, he should have detected the thief at once.

I sauntered after them: why I wanted to learn which of the lords he was, I can't tell, for lords are numerous enough, but I had had a curiosity upon the point ever since. They encountered some people and were standing to speak to them; three ladies, and a fellow in a black glazed hat with a piece of green ribbon round it.

"I was trying to induce my wife to take a sail," the lord was saying, "but she won't. She is not a very good sailor, unless the sea has its best behaviour on."

"Will you go tomorrow, Mrs. Mowbray?" asked the man in the glazed hat, who spoke and looked like a gentleman. "I will promise you perfect calmness. I am weather-wise, and can assure you this little wind will have gone down before night, leaving us without a breath of air."

"I will go: on condition that your assurance proves correct."

"All right. You of course will come, Mowbray?"

The lord nodded. "Very happy."

"When do you leave Brighton, Mr. Mowbray?" asked one of the ladies.

"I don't know exactly. Not for some days."

"A muff as usual, Johnny," whispered Tod. "That man is no lord: he is a Mr. Mowbray."

"But, Tod, he *is* the lord. It is the one who travelled with us; there's no mistake about that. Lords can't put off their titles as parsons can: do you suppose his servant would have called him 'my lord', if he had not been one?"

"At least there is no mistake that these people are calling him Mr. Mowbray now."

That was true. It was equally true that they were calling her Mrs. Mowbray. My ears had been as quick as Tod's, and I don't deny I was puzzled. They turned to come up the pier again with the people, and the lady saw me standing there with Tod. Saw me looking at her, too, and I think she did not relish it, for she took a step backward as one startled, and then stared me full in the face, as if asking who I might be. I lifted my hat.

There was no response. In another moment she and her husband were walking quickly down the pier together, and the other party went on to the end quietly. A man in a tweed suit and brown hat drawn low over his eyes, was standing with his arms folded, looking after the two with a queer smile upon his face. Tod marked it and spoke.

"Do you happen to know that gentleman?"

"Yes, I do," was the answer.

"Is he a peer?"

"On occasion."

"On occasion!" repeated Tod. "I have a reason for asking," he added; "do not think me impertinent."

"Been swindled out of anything?" asked the man, coolly.

"My father was, some months ago. He lost a pocket-book with fifty pounds in it in a railway carriage. Those people were both in it, but not then acquainted with each other."

"Oh, weren't they!" said the man.

"No, they were not," I put in, "for I was there. He was a lord then."

"Ah," said the man, "and had a servant in livery no doubt, who came up my-lording him unnecessarily every other minute. He is a member of the swell-mob; one of the cleverest of the *gentleman* fraternity, and the one who acts as servant is another of them."

"And the lady?" I asked.

"She is a third. They have been working in concert for two or three years now; and will give us trouble yet before their career is stopped. But for being singularly clever, we should have had them long ago. And so they did not know each other in the train! I dare say not!"

The man spoke with quiet authority. He was a detective come down from London to Brighton that morning; whether for a private trip, or on business, he did not say. I related to him what had passed in the train.

"Ay," said he, after listening. "They contrived to put the lamp out before starting. The lady took the pocket-book during the commotion she caused the dog to make, and the lord received it from her hand when he gave her back the dog. Cleverly done! He had it about him, young sir, when he got out at the next station. *She* waited to be searched, and to throw the scent off. Very ingenious, but they'll be a little too much so some fine day."

"Can't you take them up?" demanded Tod.

"No."

"I will accuse them of it," he haughtily said. "If I meet them again on this pier—"

"Which you won't do today," interrupted the man.

"I heard them say they were not going for some days."

"Ah, but they have seen you now. And I think – I'm not quite sure – that he saw me. They'll be off by the next train."

"Who are *they*?" asked Tod, pointing to the end of the pier.

"Unsuspecting people whose acquaintance they have casually made here. Yes, an hour or two will see Brighton quit of the pair."

And it was so. A train was starting within an hour, and Tod and I galloped to the station. There they were: in a first-class carriage: not apparently knowing each other, I verily believe, for he sat at one door and she at the other, passengers dividing them.

"Lambs between two wolves," remarked Tod. "I have a great mind to warn the people of the sort of company they are in. Would it be actionable, Johnny?"

The train moved off as he was speaking. And may I never write another word, if I did not catch sight of the man-servant and his cockade in the next carriage behind them!

Biographies & Sources

Margery Allingham

The Meaning of the Act

(Originally Published in *The Strand Magazine*, 1939. Reprinted from Mr. Campion and Others by permission of Peters Fraser & Dunlop (www.petersfraserdunlop.com) on behalf of © Rights Limited.)

One of the 'Queens of Crime' of the Golden Age of detective fiction, Margery Allingham (1904–66) was born into a literary family in Ealing, London. An avid writer throughout her early life, her talents were encouraged by her writer parents, and she published her first novel, *Blackkherchief Dick*, in 1923 at the age of nineteen. However, it was the introduction of her most-beloved character, Albert Campion, that brought real success. Initially a minor figure, Allingham went on to develop an entire mystery series around the character, encompassing nineteen novels and twenty short stories.

Robert Barr

Lord Chizelrigg's Missing Fortune

(Originally Published in *The Triumphs of Eugene Valmont*, 1906)

A Scottish-Canadian short story writer, Robert Barr (1849–1912) was born in Glasgow before his family emigrated to Toronto, where he grew up and became a teacher. He then worked for the newspaper *Detroit Free Press* until 1881 before moving to London, to establish a weekly English edition. He later founded *The Idler*, collaborating with Jerome K. Jerome, and became known as a successful novelist, publishing a book a year. He continued to write short stories however, becoming known for two Sherlock Holmes parodies. The first of these was 'The Adventures of Sherlaw Kombs' which was published in *The Idler* in 1892 and led to Barr becoming good friends with Arthur Conan Doyle.

Anthony Berkeley

The Avenging Chance

(Originally Published in *Pearson's Magazine*, 1929. Reprinted with permission by The Society of Authors as the Literary Representative of the Estate of Anthony Berkeley.)

Born in Watford, England, crime writer Anthony Berkeley Cox (1893–1971) started his career as a journalist and contributor to magazines such as *Punch* and *The Humorist*. His first novel, *The Layton Court Mystery*, was published anonymously in 1925, and he employed a number of pseudonyms over the course of his career, such as Frances Iles, A. Monmouth Platts, and Anthony Berkeley. His most famous novel, *The Poisoned Chocolates Case*, considered a classic of the Golden Age of detective fiction, is an elaboration of the story printed here. Notably, Berkeley was one of founders of the famed Detection Club along with several fellow mystery writers, including Agatha Christie.

Matthias McDonnell Bodkin

Murder by Proxy

(Originally Published in *Pearson's Weekly*, 1897)

A man of many trades, Irish author Matthias McDonnell Bodkin (1850–1933) had a varied career, working as a journalist, editor, barrister, county court judge, and as an Irish nationalist politician. Bodkin was a prolific writer across several genres, including novels, plays, political works, and historical texts. His most notable contribution to detective fiction was the creation of the first family of detectives, marrying off the respective heroes of Paul Beck, from *The Rule of Thumb Detective* (1899), and Dora Myrl, from *The Lady Detective* (1900), before later chronicling the exploits of their son in *Young Beck: A Chip off the Old Block* (1911).

Daniel Brock
The Case of the Disappearing Body
(First Publication)
Daniel Brock is an aspiring author from a small town in South Carolina. Recently married and raising one fur baby named Zeppelin, he is currently working on his first novel: a horror story that explores racial inequality through the lens of the supernatural. He considers this his first major publication, though he has published several stories online, including 'Tried and True' and 'Posthumous'. Links for both can be found at facebook.com/danielbrockfiction. His key influences are Stephen King, Elmore Leonard, and a shelf of classics including *Dracula*, *Treasure Island*, and, of course, Sherlock Holmes.

William E. Burton
The Secret Cell
(Originally Published in *The Gentleman's Magazine*, 1837)
Author of one of the earliest iterations of the detective story, William Evans Burton (1804–60) inherited his father's printing office as a young man, and worked as a publisher, actor, theatre manager, and playwright. Born in London, he eventually relocated to the United States, where he enjoyed success as an actor and in 1837 founded *The Gentlemen's Magazine*, in which this story appeared. The paper was for a time edited by Edgar Allan Poe. Poe and Burton had a tense relationship, which ultimately resulted in Poe's termination in 1840, not to mention a good deal of slander and rumour-mongering from both men in the fallout.

Elliott Capon
Murder Is My Middle Name
(First Publication)
Elliott Capon has three novels in print: one horror, and two funny whodunits that take place in the 'Poverty Row' Hollywood of the late 1930s. A fourth novel, a black-comedy murder mystery, will be published in November 2020. He also has a collection of 101 'shaggy dogs' – stories that end on a groan-inducing pun – entitled *Damn the Torn Speedos! Full Speed Ahead!* Eight of his stories have appeared in *Alfred Hitchcock's Mystery Magazine*, and other appearances include smartrhino.com's anthologies *Zippered Flesh* and *Uncommon Assassins*, as well as the 2016 *Indiana Review of Horror*, *Frostfire Worlds*, and *Disturbed Digest*. He lives in New Jersey, USA, with his wife, and you can find out more about his work at elliottcapon.weebly.com.

G.K. Chesterton
The Point of a Pin
(Originally Published in *The Saturday Evening Post*, 1932)
Gilbert Keith Chesterton (1874–1936) is best known for his creation of the worldly priest-detective Father Brown. The Edwardian writer's literary output was immense: around two hundred short stories, nearly one hundred novels and about four thousand essays, as well as weekly columns for multiple newspapers. Chesterton was a valued literary critic, and his own authoritative works included biographies of Charles Dickens and Thomas Aquinas, and the theological book *The Everlasting Man*. Chesterton debated with such notable figures as George Bernard Shaw and Bertrand Russell, and even broadcasted radio talks. His detective stories were essentially moral; Father Brown is an empathetic force for good, battling crime while defending the vulnerable.

Carroll John Daly
If Death is Respectable
(Originally Published in *Black Mask*, 1933, © 2019 Estate of Carroll John Daly. All rights reserved.)
Best known as the author of the first piece of hard-boiled fiction, 'The False Burton Combs' (1922), New York-born author Carroll John Daly's (1889–1958) work continues to influence the genre today. A prolific writer of pulp fiction, his stories were regular features in *Black Mask* and *Dime Detective*. At one point, Carroll's name alone could make sales rocket. His most famous character, Race Williams, was hugely popular with readers, and became the tough, cynical blueprint for the countless hard-talking private eyes that have come after him.

Arthur Conan Doyle
The Adventure of Silver Blaze
(Originally Published in *The Strand Magazine*, 1892)
Arthur Conan Doyle (1859–1930) was born in Edinburgh, Scotland. As a medical student he was so impressed by his professor's powers of deduction that he was inspired to create the illustrious and much-loved figure Sherlock Holmes. Holmes is known for his keen power of observation and logical reasoning, which often astounds his companion Dr. Watson. Whatever the subject or character, Doyle's vibrant and remarkable writing has breathed life into all of his stories, engaging readers throughout the decades.

Robert Eustace
The Tea Leaf (with Edgar Jepson)
(Originally Published in *The Strand Magazine*, 1925)
To Prove an Alibi (with L.T. Meade)
(Originally Collected in *A Master of Mysteries*, 1898)
Working under the pseudonyms Robert Eustace and Eustace Robert Rawlings, English doctor Eustace Robert Barton (1854–1943) authored several works of mystery and crime fiction. His scientific and medical expertise often informed his work, both thematically (his stories are known for their preoccupation with scientific innovation) and in terms of key plot components. He frequently collaborated with other authors,

including L.T. Meade, Edgar Jepson, and Dorothy L. Sayers, supplying them with necessary supporting medical and scientific information.

J.S. Fletcher

The Yorkshire Manufacturer
(Originally Collected in *Paul Campenhaye, Criminologist*, 1918)
Born and raised in West Yorkshire, journalist and writer Joseph Smith Fletcher (1863–1935) was an incredibly prolific writer, authoring over two hundred and thirty books across a range of genres and subjects, over one hundred of which were detective novels, often featuring detective Ronald Camberwell. Although Fletcher is occasionally cited as one of the leading authors of the Golden Age of detective fiction, he was in fact a contemporary of Sir Arthur Conan Doyle. He worked for a time in London but much of his work as an author and journalist was rooted in rural Yorkshire and its history, using the pen name 'A Son of the Soil' during his tenure at the *Leeds Mercury*.

R. Austin Freeman

The Case of Oscar Brodski
(Originally Published in *Pearson's Magazine*, 1910)
London-born R. Austin Freeman (1862–1943) was at the forefront of Edwardian detective fiction, along with his contemporary G.K. Chesterton. Freeman trained a physician, working as a colonial surgeon in West Africa until illness sent him back to England. He continued to practise medicine, producing in his spare time a crime series centred on the character Dr. Thorndyke. An early forensic scientist, Thorndyke uses a precise scientific approach to analyse data in his laboratory. Beginning with *The Singing Bone* (1912), Freeman is credited as being the first to develop the inverted detective story, where the focus rests not on the culprit – who can be known from the start – but on the process of solving the case.

Jacques Futrelle

The Mystery of the Fatal Cipher
(Originally Published in *Hearst's Boston American*, 1906)
The American writer Jacques Futrelle (1875–1912) was born in Georgia, and famously died onboard the *Titanic* aged 37, after having seen his wife safely onto a lifeboat. Futrelle paved a career in journalism from the age of 18, and went on to write fiction and drama. In 1895, he married the writer L. May Peel and took a job working for the *New York Herald*. Augustus S.F.X Van Dusen, the amateur detective dubbed 'The Thinking Machine', appears in over forty of Futrelle's stories. 'The Problem of Cell 13' was the first to feature this character, who uses logic to solve seemingly impossible cases.

Susan Glaspell

A Jury of Her Peers
(Originally Published in *Everyweek*, 1917)
A successful novelist in her time, Susan Glaspell (1876–1948) is best known today for her contributions to American drama. In addition to her work as a fiction writer, Glaspell was a journalist, actress, and playwright. She was one of the founders of the Provincetown Players, the first modern American theatre company, and was also the Midwest Bureau Director for the Federal Theatre Project under the Works Progress

Administration. Her work, now regarded as trail-blazingly feminist, explored gender, morality, and dissent, often using her native Midwest as a backdrop.

Anna Katharine Green
An Intangible Clue
(Originally Collected in *The Golden Slipper and Other Problems for Violet Strange*, 1915)
Mother of detective fiction Anna Katharine Green (1846–1935) was born in Brooklyn, New York. A poet even at a young age, she later turned her hand to detective novels, perhaps partly inspired by stories from her lawyer father. She enjoyed immediate success with *The Leavenworth Case*, the first outing for the amiable but eccentric Inspector Ebenezer Gryce. Having found a successful formula, but always coming up with original and intriguing plots, Green went on to write around thirty novels as well as several short stories. She created interesting detective heroes and established several conventions of the genre, her name becoming synonymous with popular, original and well-written detective fiction.

Philip Brian Hall
No Head for Figures
(First Publication)
Yorkshireman Philip Brian Hall is a graduate of Oxford University. A former diplomat and teacher, at one time or another he's stood for parliament, sung solos in amateur operettas, rowed at Henley Royal Regatta, completed a forty-mile cross-country walk in under twelve hours and ridden in over one hundred steeplechase horse races. He lives on a very small farm in Scotland. Philip's had short stories published in the USA and Canada as well as the UK. His work has appeared in several anthologies, recently including *All Hail Our Robot Conquerors* (ZNB), *Strange Beasties* (Third Flatiron) and *Cosy Crime* (Flame Tree), as well as online publications such as *Cosmic Roots and Eldritch Shores* and *Gumshoe Review*. His novel *The Prophets of Baal* is available as an ebook and in paperback. He blogs at sliabhmannan.blogspot.co.uk.

Thomas W. Hanshew
The Divided House
(Originally Published in *Cassell's Saturday Journal*, 1910)
Brooklyn author and actor Thomas W. Hanshew (1857–1914) first started on the stage at just sixteen years old, gradually working his way from minor to major roles before moving into writing and publishing, eventually moving to London. He used several pseudonyms, including Charlotte May Kingsley, and co-wrote a number of novels with his wife, Mary E. Hanshew. Out of his many novels and short stories, his most popular were those featuring Hamilton Cleek, a master of disguise, at the centre of comically implausible mysteries.

Rosemary Herbert
Foreword: Detective Mysteries Short Stories
Rosemary Herbert is editor in chief of *The Oxford Companion to Crime & Mystery Writing* and author of *Front Page Teaser: A Liz Higgins Mystery*. A former Harvard University reference librarian, and a longtime journalist and literary critic, her books also include *Whodunnit? A Who's Who in Crime & Mystery Writing, Murder on Deck! Shipboard & Shoreline Mystery Stories*, and *Twelve American Crime Stories*. She co-edited, with Tony Hillerman, *The Oxford Book of American Detective Stories* and *A New Omnibus of Crime*.

After residing on a Maine island, she now lives in America's heartland, where she pursues writing and ceramic arts.

E. and H. Heron

The Story of the Spaniards, Hammersmith
(Originally Published in *Pearson's Magazine*, 1898)
E. and H. Heron were the pen names of mother and son Kate O'Brien Ryall Prichard (1851–1935) and Major Hesketh Vernon Prichard (later Hesketh-Prichard, 1876–1922). The daughter of a military family, Kate Prichard raised her son alone after his father died from typhoid mere weeks after his birth. Hesketh-Prichard grew up to be an explorer, adventurer, cricket player and expert marksman, and his innovations in British Military sniping practice saved the lives of thousands of Allied soldiers during World War I. At nineteen, Hesketh-Prichard wrote his first story, 'Tammer's Duel', which his mother helped revise. It was soon published by *Pall Mall Magazine*, and was the start of a successful writing partnership between the two, which included a series of stories about Flaxman Low, a psychic detective. An exceptional woman of her time, Kate Prichard also joined her son on many of his travels, which included expeditions to Haiti, Patagonia, and Labrador.

Edgar Jepson

The Tea Leaf (with Robert Eustace)
(Originally Published in *The Strand Magazine*, 1925)
Sometimes going by the pen name R. Edison Page, Edgar Alfred Jepson (1863–1938) wrote across a range of genres, including fantasy, supernatural, adventure and detective fiction. Originally from Warwickshire, he studied at Baliol College and lived for a time in Barbados before returning to England to embark on his literary career. Over the course of his life he variously worked as a translator and editor, briefly working at Vanity Fair, and collaborated with numerous other writers, including Arthur Machen, Robert Eustace and John Gawsworth. Two of his children, Selwyn and Margaret Jepson, also went on to become writers.

Herbert Jenkins

The Strange Case of Mr. Challoner
(Originally Published in *Hutchinson's Magazine*, 1920)
The founder of his own successful publishing company, English writer Herbert George Jenkins (1876–1923) was able to use his position as publisher to understand and cater to changing literary tastes and trends, for which he had a particular talent. Mainly known as an author of light fiction, especially his series of humorous stories about the Cockney character Joseph Bindle, his detective fiction also received acclaim. Detective Malcolm Sage, the central figure of a number of his short stories, has drawn comparisons to Sherlock Holmes and Hercule Poirot.

Tina L. Jens

A Cat with a Gat
(Originally Published in *Crafty Cat Crimes: 100 Tiny Cat Tale Mysteries*, 2000)
Tina L. Jens' novel, *The Blues Ain't Nothin': Tales of the Lonesome Blues Pub*, won the National Federation of Press Women Best Novel award and was a Final Nominee for the

Horror Writers and International Horror Guild awards. She's had more than seventy short stories and twelve poems published in SF/F/H/M markets. She served as Editor for Twilight Tales small press for ten years. For the past decade, she's taught the fantasy writing courses at Columbia College. Jens received the 2017 Rubin Family Fellowship artist residency at Ragdale Foundation. She lives in Chicago, IL with her husband and guinea pig.

Maurice Leblanc

Arsène Lupin in Prison
(Originally Published in *Je Sais Tout*, 1905)
Born in Rouen, France, Maurice Leblanc (1864–1941) dropped his law studies in favour of a literary career, publishing his first novel, *Une Femme*, in 1887. His fame is largely due to his Arsène Lupin series of stories. 'The Arrest of Arsène Lupin' was the first story to feature the roguish gentleman criminal, appearing in 1905 as a commissioned piece for a new journal. The character was an instant success, and the thief-turned-detective went on to appear in over sixty of Leblanc's works. Some of the Lupin tales even feature a parodied Sherlock Holmes, with Lupin invariably outwitting his English rival.

Tom Mead

Vandergiessen's Daughter
(First Publication)
Tom Mead is a UK-based author and playwright. He has previously written for *Litro Online*, *Flash: The International Short-Short Story Magazine*, *Lighthouse*, *Crimson Streets* and *Mystery Weekly* (amongst various others). He also has work forthcoming in *Ellery Queen Mystery Magazine* and *Alfred Hitchcock Mystery Magazine*. He is a great admirer of golden age authors of the locked-room mystery subgenre (John Dickson Carr, Clayton Rawson, Helen McCloy, Christianna Brand et al) and has written many stories in tribute to these masters.

L.T. Meade

To Prove an Alibi (with Robert Eustace)
(Originally Collected in *A Master of Mysteries*, 1898)
Elizabeth Thomasina Meade Smith (1844–1914), writing under the pen name L.T. Meade, was an enormously prolific English author – so much so that eleven out of her approximate three hundred works were published posthumously. Recognized today as an early feminist, she belonged to the progressive Pioneer Club and the founder and editor of *Atalanta*, a monthly periodical for girls. Smith wrote across numerous genres, occasionally collaborating with other authors, such as Robert Eustace. Her and Eustace's partnership also yielded some notable female villains, including Madame Koluchy, criminal mastermind and leader of the 'Brotherhood of the Seven Kings'.

Marshall J. Moore

Argent
(First Publication)
Marshall J. Moore is a writer, filmmaker, and martial artist who was born and raised on Kwajalein, a tiny Pacific island. His previous two Althea Stagg stories, 'Whither Athena' and

'Hammer Down' can be found in the first two volumes of the anthology series *Grumpy Old Gods*. He has travelled to over twenty countries, once sold a thousand dollars' worth of teapots to Jackie Chan, and on one occasion was tracked down by a bounty hunter for owing $300 in overdue fees to the Los Angeles Public Library. He lives in Atlanta with his wife Megan and their two cats.

Pat Morris
Nobody Special
(First Publication)
Pat Morris worked as a journalist in New York, New Jersey, Cincinnati, North Carolina and the U.S. Virgin Islands. She was a regular columnist for *Everybody's News* in Cincinnati (Eve's Advocate) and *Publishers' Auxiliary* (Publishers' Bookshelf). She ran a writing program for women prisoners in New Jersey before moving to Florida to write fiction while indulging her passions for vintage Japanese textiles, Gulf sunsets and Indian cooking.

Arthur Morrison
The Case of the Flitterbat Lancers
(Originally Published in *The Windsor Magazine*, 1896)
Arthur Morrison (1863–1945) was born in the East End of London. He later became a writer for *The Globe* newspaper and showed a keen interest in relating the real and bleak plight of those living in London slums. When Arthur Conan Doyle killed off Sherlock Holmes in 1893, a vacuum opened up for detective heroes. In the wake Morrison created Martin Hewitt, publishing stories about him in *The Strand Magazine*, which had also first published Sherlock Holmes. Though a man with genius deductive skill, Morrison's Hewitt character was the polar opposite to Holmes: genial and helpful to the police. He was perhaps the most popular and successful of these new investigator fiction heroes.

Amelia Dee Mueller
Welcome to Paradise
(First Publication)
Amelia Dee Mueller is a resident of Dallas, Texas and is constantly disappointed that the Old West isn't as present as you'd think. Her fiction is usually inspired by old myths from around the world, the good and the bad of the American south, and brave women. More of her work can be found in *Metaphorosis* and *Electric Spec*. A communications coordinator in local government by day, she spends her nights writing, reading, fencing, and streaming superhero movies with her cats. You can follow her on Twitter @AmeliaDMueller.

Trixie Nisbet
A Problem with Threes
(First Publication)
Trixie Nisbet has recently turned to crime! She usually writes fiction for the woman's magazine market but, as a meticulous plotter, she loves to devise a mystery for a detective to unravel. She has had over fifty stories printed, won several national short story competitions and last year was shortlisted for the Brighton Prize. She mulls over her plots while walking her westie along the cliff top paths of Peacehaven on England's south coast, and has twice, so far, hurled one of her characters over the edge.

Baroness Orczy
The Fenchurch Street Mystery
(Originally Published in *The Royal Magazine*, 1901)
Baroness 'Emmuska' Orczy (1865–1947) was born in Tarnaörs, Heves County, Hungary. She spent her childhood in Budapest, Brussels and Paris before moving to London when she was fourteen. After her marriage to a young illustrator, she worked as a translator and illustrator to supplement their low income. Baroness Orczy's first novel, *The Emperor's Candlesticks*, was a failure but her later novels fared better. She is most famous for the play *The Scarlet Pimpernel*, which she wrote with her husband. She went on to write a novelization of it, as well as many sequels and other works of mystery fiction and adventure romances.

Catherine Louisa Pirkis
Drawn Daggers
(Originally Published in *The Ludgate Magazine*, 1883)
Catherine Louisa Pirkis (1839–1910) was born in London, England. She wrote numerous short stories and novels between 1877 and 1894, including the works that contain her best-known character: the female detective Loveday Brooke. Following her success as an author and journalist, she moved into helping animal charities and was one of the founders of the National Canine Defence League (now known as Dogs Trust) in 1891.

Melville Davisson Post
Naboth's Vineyard
(Originally Published in *Sunday Magazine*, 1916)
American author Melville Davisson Post (1869–1930) was known for the character Sir Henry Marquis of Scotland Yard in his short story collection *The Sleuth of St. James's Square*. His other characters included the well-known lawyers Randolph Mason and Colonel Braxton, and the detectives Sir Henry Marquis and Monsieur Jonquelle. He wrote a vast amount of novels in his lifetime, which were almost all crime fiction, totalling over two hundred titles.

Patsy Pratt-Herzog
The Case of the Mislaid Plans
(First Publication)
Patsy Pratt-Herzog is an emerging freelance writer from Southwestern Ohio. Her favourite genres to write are Mystery, Science Fiction and Fantasy. When she's not writing, she enjoys painting and riding roller-coasters. She shares her house in the 'burbs with her husband Tim and two chunky cats. Included in her publishing credits is another Prudence Adventure, 'The Case of the Mislaid Eggs', in the Devil's Party Press anthology *Suspicious Activities*.

Michele Bazan Reed
The Lady in Black
(First Publication)
Michele Bazan Reed spent forty years in journalism and public relations, before turning her hand to writing mysteries. Her short story, 'A Rum Turn', was published in the *Wrong Turn* anthology in 2018. Her story, 'The Hitler Heist', will appear in the forthcoming anthology, *Mid-Century Murder*, from Darkhouse Books (expected Fall 2019). A member of Sisters in

Crime and the group's Guppy chapter, she won First Place in the Unpublished Mainstream Mystery/Suspense Category of the 2017 Daphne du Maurier Award for Excellence in Mystery/ Suspense. Michele and her husband have two grown children and live in Upstate New York and France.

Lesley L. Smith
The Hollow Man
(First Publication)
A physicist, Lesley L. Smith, PhD, MFA has published many short stories and nine science fiction novels, including *The Quantum Cop* and *A Jack By Any Other Name*. She is a founder and editor of the ezine Electric Spec (www.electricspec.com). She's an active member of the Science Fiction/Fantasy Writers of America. She lives in Colorado with her cats, her garden, and her many, many books. Check her out on the web at www.lesleylsmith.com.

Cameron Trost
The Murder at Karreg Du
(Originally Published in *Shelter from the Storm*, 2018)
Cameron Trost is a writer of strange, mysterious, and creepy tales about people just like you. He is the author of *Hoffman's Creeper and Other Disturbing Tales* and *The Tunnel Runner*, and is the creator of Oscar Tremont, Investigator of the Strange and Inexplicable. He hails from Australia but now lives on the rugged coast of Brittany. Castles, forests, storms, and whisky are a few of his favourite things. Find him online at trostlibrary.blogspot.com.

Edgar Wallace
The Poetical Policeman
(Originally Published under the Title 'The Strange Case of the Night Watchman' in *The Grand Magazine*, 1924)
Edgar Wallace (1875–1932) was born illegitimately to an actress, and adopted by a London fishmonger and his wife. On leaving school at the age of twelve, he took up many jobs, including selling newspapers. This foreshadowed his later career as a war correspondent for such periodicals as the *Daily Mail* after he had enrolled in the army. He later turned to writing stories inspired by his time in Africa, and was incredibly prolific over a large number of genres and formats. Wallace is credited as being one of the first writers of detective fiction whose protagonists were policemen as opposed to amateur sleuths.

Hugh C. Weir
The Man with Nine Lives
(Originally Published in *MacLean's Magazine*, 1914)
Journalist, editor, author, adman and screenwriter Hugh Cosgro Weir (1884–1934) was born in Illinois, and started as a reporter for the *Springfield Sun* at just sixteen years old, before successfully submitting his first film script to Universal Studios at the age of twenty. Confident and industrious, he wrote at least three hundred screenplays over the course of his career, and as many short stories and articles. Originally published as a series in McLeans in 1914, Weir's Miss Madelyn Mack, Detective is inspired by real-life Chicago detective Mary Holland and modelled on Sherlock Holmes. Cerebral and

dogged, detective Madelyn Mack surprises and amazes the reader (not to mention her sidekick and the story's narrator, reporter Nora Noraker) with her sleuthing abilities.

Mrs. Henry Wood
Going Through the Tunnel
(Originally Published in *Argosy*, 1869)
Ellen Price (1814–87) was born in Worcester, and upon marrying Henry Wood in 1836 spent twenty years in the South of France before returning to England. On her return to England Mrs. Henry Wood began writing a number of novels and short stories. Her most famous novel was the 1861 *East Lynne,* which was followed by many other successful novels including *Danesbury House* and *Oswald Cray*. In 1867 Wood bought the English magazine *Argosy* where she published many of her short stories. She was known for writing mystery and supernatural fiction. Her works were translated into multiple languages and many of her books became international bestsellers.

FLAME TREE PUBLISHING
Epic, Dark, Thrilling & Gothic
New & Classic Writing

Flame Tree's Gothic Fantasy books offer a carefully curated series of new titles, each with combinations of original and classic writing:

Chilling Horror • Chilling Ghost • Science Fiction
Murder Mayhem • Crime & Mystery • Swords & Steam
Dystopia Utopia • Supernatural Horror • Lost Worlds
Time Travel • Heroic Fantasy • Pirates & Ghosts • Agents & Spies
Endless Apocalypse • Alien Invasion • Robots & AI • Lost Souls
Haunted House • Cosy Crime • Urban Crime • American Gothic
Epic Fantasy • Detective Thrillers • A Dying Planet
Bodies in the Library • Footsteps in the Dark • Strange Lands

as well as new companion titles which offer rich collections of classic fiction from masters of the gothic fantasy genres:

H.G. Wells • Lovecraft • Sherlock Holmes • Edgar Allan Poe • Mary Shelley
Bram Stoker • Charles Dickens Supernatural • Heroes & Heroines Myths & Tales
Witches, Wizards, Seers & Healers Myths & Tales • African Myths & Tales
Celtic Myths & Tales • Greek Myths & Tales • Norse Myths & Tales
Chinese Myths & Tales • Japanese Myths & Tales • Irish Fairy Tales
King Arthur & The Knights of the Round Table
Alice's Adventures in Wonderland • The Divine Comedy
Hans Christian Andersen Fairy Tales • Brothers Grimm
The Wonderful Wizard of Oz • The Age of Queen Victoria

Available from all good bookstores, worldwide, and online at
flametreepublishing.com

See our new fiction imprint
FLAME TREE PRESS | FICTION WITHOUT FRONTIERS
New and original writing in Horror, Crime, SF and Fantasy

And join our monthly newsletter with offers and more stories:
FLAME TREE FICTION NEWSLETTER
flametreepress.com

GOTHIC FANTASY

For our books, calendars, blog
and latest special offers please see:
flametreepublishing.com